MAN'S BOOK

FLIGHT INTO DANGER
John Castle and Arthur Hailey

★

A PRAYER FOR
THE SHIP
Douglas Reeman

★

THE TASTE OF ASHES
Howard Browne

★

also a short story
THE LION CALL
R. A. J. Maguire

ODHAMS PRESS LIMITED
LONG ACRE, LONDON

CONTENTS

FLIGHT INTO DANGER

John Castle and Arthur Hailey

*"Flight Into Danger" is published by
Souvenir Press Ltd.*

The Authors

John Castle achieved the rare distinction of becoming a writer of international status with his very first book, *The Password is Courage.* A Londoner of 36, his main interests (apart from writing, which, he says, "I get down to only under pressure, and then really to avoid gardening") are "finding out how the other half lives," typography and design; listening to music and exploring out-of-the-way villages with interesting histories and comfortable pubs. A lover of Dickens and the Mediterranean ("I need sunshine to make me feel human"), Mr. Castle prefers a quiet, unobtrusive life with his family.

Always keenly concerned with aeroplanes, he admits to a good deal of sympathy with George Spencer in *Flight Into Danger,* for he was shot down into the North Sea while returning from the first thousand-bomber raid on Hamburg.

★

Arthur Hailey is a post-war immigrant from Luton to Canada who discovered a flair for television playwriting and with phenomenal speed established himself as one of that medium's most brilliant exponents. Mr. Hailey's love of aeroplanes dates from the war, his own part in which, as a pilot in the R.A.F., he describes with characteristic modesty as "unspectacular". Now 38, he lives with his wife Sheila and three small children in Scarborough, a suburb of Toronto.

CHAPTER ONE: 2205-0045

STEADY rain slanting through the harsh glare of its headlights, the taxicab swung into the approach to Winnipeg Airport, screeched protestingly round the asphalt curve and, braking hard, came to a spring-shuddering stop outside the bright neons of the reception building. Its one passenger almost leaped out, tossed a couple of bills to the driver, seized an overnight bag and hurried to the swing doors.

Inside, the warmth and lights of the big hall halted him for a moment. With one hand he turned down the collar of his damp topcoat, glanced at the wall clock above him, then half strode, half ran to where the departure desk of Cross-Canada Airlines stood bar-like in a corner, deserted now except for the passenger agent checking through a manifest. As the man reached him the agent picked up a small stand microphone on the desk, summoned the man to silence with a lift of his eyebrows, and with measured precision began to speak.

"Flight 98. Flight 98. Direct fleetliner service to Vancouver, with connections for Victoria, Seattle and Honolulu, leaving immediately through gate four. All passengers for Flight 98 to gate four, please. No smoking till you are in the air."

A group of people rose from the lounge seats, or detached themselves from a bored perusal of the news-stand, and made their way thankfully across the hall. The man in the topcoat opened his mouth to speak but was practically elbowed aside by an elderly woman stuttering in her anxiety.

"Young man," she demanded, "is Flight 63 from Montreal in yet?"

"No, madam," said the passenger agent smoothly. "It's running," he consulted his list, "approximately thirty-seven minutes late."

"Oh, dear. I've arranged for my niece to be in—"

"Look," said the man in the topcoat urgently, "have you got a seat on Flight 98 for Vancouver?"

The passenger agent shook his head. "Sorry, sir. Not one. Have you checked with Reservations?"

7

"Didn't have time. Came straight to the Airport on the chance of a cancellation." The man slapped the desk in frustration. "You sometimes have one, I know."

"Quite right, sir. But with the big game on in Vancouver tomorrow things are chock full. All our flights are completely booked—I doubt if you'll be able to get out of here before tomorrow afternoon."

The man swore softly, dropped his bag to the floor, and tipped his dripping felt hat to the back of his head. "Of all the lousy deals. I've got to be in Vancouver by tomorrow noon at the latest."

"Don't be so rude," snapped the old lady testily. "I was talking. Now, young man, listen carefully. My niece is bringing with her—"

"Just a moment, madam," cut in the passenger agent. He leaned across the desk and tapped the sleeve of the man with his pencil. "Look, I'm not supposed to tell you this . . ."

"Yes, what?"

"Well, really!" exploded the old lady.

"There's a charter flight in from Toronto. They're going out to the coast for this game. I believe they were a few seats light when they came in. Perhaps you could grab one of those."

"That's great," exclaimed the man in the topcoat, picking up his bag again. "Do you think there's a chance?"

"No harm in trying."

"Where do I ask then? Who's the guy to see?"

The agent grinned and waved across the hall. "Right over there. The Maple Leaf Air Charter. But mind, I didn't say a thing."

"This is scandalous!" stormed the old lady. "I'll have you know that my niece—"

"Thanks a lot," said the man. He walked briskly over to a smaller desk displaying the fascia board of the air charter company, behind which another agent, this time in a dark lounge suit instead of the smart uniform of the Cross-Canada Airlines, sat busily writing. He looked up as the man arrived, pencil poised, all attention. "Sir?"

"I wonder, can you help me? Have you by any chance a seat left on a flight to Vancouver?"

"Vancouver. I'll see." The pencil checked rapidly down a passenger list. Then: "Uh-huh, just one. Flight's leaving straight away, though; it's overdue as it is."

"That's fine, fine. Can I have that seat, please?"

The agent reached for a ticket stub. "Name, sir?"

"George Spencer." It was entered quickly, with the flight details.

"That's sixty-five dollars for the one-way trip, sir. Thank you; glad to be of service. Any bags, sir?"

"Only one. I'll keep it with me."

In a moment the bag was weighed and labelled.

"Here you are then, sir. The ticket is your boarding pass. Go to gate three and ask for Flight 714. Please hurry, sir: the plane's about to leave."

Spencer nodded, turned away to give a thumbs-up to the Cross-Canada desk, where the passenger agent grimaced in acknowledgment over the old lady's shoulder, and hurried to the departure gate. Outside, the chill night air pulsated with the whine of aero engines; as with any busy airport after dark, all seemed to be in confusion but was in fact part of a strictly regulated, unvarying pattern. A commissionaire directed him across the floodlit apron, gleaming in the rain, to a waiting aircraft whose four propellers were shining silver discs in the light of the overhead arc lamps. Already men were preparing to disengage the passenger ramp. Bounding across the intervening puddles, Spencer reached them, handed over the detachable half of his ticket, and ran lightly up the steps, the backlash from the propellers plucking at his hat. He ducked into the aircraft and stood there fighting to regain his breath. He was joined shortly by a stewardess, a mackintosh draped round her, who smiled at him and made fast the door.

"Out of condition, I guess," he said apologetically.

"Good evening, sir. Pleased to have you aboard."

"I was lucky to make it."

"There's a seat for-ard," said the girl.

Spencer slipped out of his coat, took off his hat, and walked along the aisle till he came to the vacant seat. He bundled his coat with some difficulty into an empty spot on the luggage rack, remarking, "They never seem to make these things big enough," to the neighbouring passenger who sat looking up at him, disposed of his bag under the seat, and then sank gratefully down on to the soft cushions.

"Good evening," came the stewardess's sprightly voice over the public address system. "The Maple Leaf Air Charter Company welcomes aboard its new passengers to Flight 714. We hope you will enjoy your flight. Please fasten your safety belts. We shall be taking off in a few moments."

As Spencer fumbled with his catch, the man next to him

grunted, "That's a pretty sobering sentence. Don't often see it," and nodded down to a small notice on the back of the seat in front reading *Your lifebelt is under the seat.*

Spencer laughed. "*I'd* certainly have been sunk if I hadn't caught this bus," he said.

"Oh? Pretty keen fan, eh?"

"Fan?" Spencer remembered that this was a charter flight for a ball game. "Er—no," he said hastily. "I hadn't given the game a thought. I hate to admit it but I'm rushing off to Vancouver to keep a business appointment. I'd sure like to see that match but it's out of the question, I'm afraid."

His companion lowered his voice as conspiratorially as was possible against the rising note of the engines. "I shouldn't say that too loudly, if I were you. This plane is crammed with square-heads who are going to Vancouver with one purpose only—and that's to root like hell for their boys and to roar damnation and defiance at the enemy. They're quite likely to do you harm if you use such a light tone about it."

Spencer chuckled again and leaned out from his seat to look round the crowded cabin. There was evidence in plenty of a typical, noisy, roistering but good-natured party of sports fans travelling with the one objective of vanquishing the opposing team and triumphing with their own. To Spencer's immediate right sat a man and his wife, their noses buried in the lurid pages of sports magazines. Behind them, four supporters were pouring rye into paper tumblers and preparing to make a night of it by arguing the respective merits of various players; a snatch of their conversation came over to him like a breath of the field itself. "Haggerty? *Haggerty?* Don't give me that stuff. He's not in the same league as the Thunderbolt. Now *there's* a man for you, if you like. . . ." Behind the slightly alcoholic foursome were other obvious team supporters wearing favours with the colours of their team; mostly big, red-faced men intent on playing the game that lay ahead in Vancouver before it took place.

Spencer turned to the man beside him. Trained to observe detail, he noted the quiet suit, of good cut originally but now well crumpled, the tie that didn't match, the lined face and greying hair, the indefinable impression of confidence and authority. A face of character, Spencer decided. Behind it the red lights of the perimeter track had begun to slide past as the aircraft rolled forward.

"I sound like a heretic," said Spencer conversationally, "but I must confess that I'm on my way to the coast on a sales trip, and a mighty important one at that."

His companion showed a polite interest. "What do you sell?" he inquired.

"Trucks. Lots of trucks."

"Trucks, eh? I thought they were sold by dealers."

"So they are. I get called for when a deal is cooking that involves maybe thirty to a hundred trucks. The local salesmen don't like me too well because they say I'm the sharpshooter from head office who turns up with the special prices and clinches a deal that perhaps they've spent weeks nursing. Still, it's a reasonable living." Spencer rummaged for his cigarettes, then stopped himself. "Heck, we're not in the air yet, are we?"

"If we are, we're flying pretty low. And at nil knots."

"Just as well, then." Spencer stretched his legs in front of him. "Man, I'm tired. It's been one of those goofy days that send you up the wall. Know what I mean?"

"I think so."

"First this bird decides he likes a competitor's trucks better after all. Then, when I've sold him the prop and figure I can close the order over supper tonight and be back with my wife and kids by tomorrow night, I get a wire telling me to drop everything and be in Vancouver by lunchtime tomorrow. A big contract is going off the rails there and fast. So Buster must go in and save the day." Spencer sighed, then sat upright in mock earnestness. "Hey, if you want forty or fifty trucks today I can give you a good discount. Feel like running a fleet?"

The man beside him laughed. "Sorry, no. I couldn't use that many, I'm afraid. A bit outside my usual line of country."

"What country is that?" asked Spencer.

"Medicine."

"A doctor, eh?"

"Yes, a doctor. And therefore of no use to you in the disposal of trucks, I'm afraid. I couldn't afford to buy one, let alone forty. Football is the only extravagance I can allow myself, and for that I'd travel anywhere, provided I could find the time. Hence my trip tonight."

Leaning back on the headrest of his seat, Spencer said, "Glad to have you around, doctor. If I can't sleep you can prescribe me a sedative."

As he spoke the engines thundered to full power, the whole aircraft vibrating as it strained against the wheel brakes.

The doctor put his mouth to Spencer's ear and bellowed, "A sedative would be no good in this racket. I never could understand why they have to make all this noise before take-off."

Spencer nodded; then, when after a few seconds the roar had subsided sufficiently for him to make himself heard without much trouble, he said, "It's the usual run-up of the engines. It's always done before the plane actually starts its take-off. Each engine has two magnetos, in case one packs in during flight, and in the run-up each engine in turn is opened to full throttle and each of the mags tested separately. When the pilot has satisfied himself that they are running okay he takes off, but not before. Airlines have to be fussy that way, thank goodness."

"You sound as though you knew a lot about it."

"Not really. I used to fly fighters in the war but I'm pretty rusty now after ten years. Reckon I've forgotten most of it."

"Here we go," commented the doctor as the engine roar took on a deeper note. A powerful thrust in the backs of their seats told them the aircraft was gathering speed on the runway; almost immediately a slight lurch indicated that they were airborne and the engines settled back to a steady hum. Still climbing, the aircraft banked steeply and Spencer watched the receding airport lights as they rose steadily over the wingtip.

"You may unfasten your safety belts," announced the public address. "Smoke if you wish."

"Never sorry when that bit's over," grunted the doctor, releasing his catch and accepting a cigarette. "Thanks. By the way, I'm Baird, Bruno Baird."

"Glad to know you, doc. I'm Spencer, plain George Spencer, of the Fulbright Motor Company."

For some time the two men lapsed into silence, absently watching their cigarette smoke rise slowly in the cabin until it was caught by the air-conditioning stream and sucked away. Spencer's thoughts were sombre. There would have to be some kind of a show-down when he got back to head office, he decided. Although he had explained the position on the telephone to the local Winnipeg man before calling a taxi for the airport, that order would take some holding on to now. It would have to be a big show in Vancouver to justify this snafu. It might be a good idea to use the whole thing as a lever for a pay raise when he got back. Or better yet, promotion. As a manager in the dealer sales division, which the old man had often mentioned but never got around to, Mary and he, Bobsie and little Kit, could get out of that frame house and move up to Parkway Heights. Or pay off the bills—the new water tank, school fees, instalments on the Chev and the deep freeze, hospital charges for Mary's last confinement. Not both, Spencer reflected broodingly; not both, even on manager's pay.

Doctor Baird, trying to decide whether to go to sleep or to take this excellent opportunity to catch up on the airmail edition of the *B.M.J.*, in fact did neither and found himself instead thinking about the small-town surgery he had abandoned for a couple of days. Wonder how Evans will cope, he thought. Promising fellow, but absurdly young. Hope to goodness he remembers that Mrs. Lowrie has ordinary mist. expect. and not the patent medicine fiddle-me-rees she's always agitating for. Still Doris would keep young Evans on the right track; doctors' wives were wonderful like that. Had to be, by jiminy. That was a thing Lewis would have to learn in due time: to find the right woman. The doctor dozed a little and his cigarette burnt his fingers, promptly waking him up.

The couple in the seats across the aisle were still engrossed in their sports papers. To describe Joe Greer was to describe Hazel Greer: a pair more alike would be hard to imagine. Both had the rosy skin and the keen, clear eyes of the open air, both bent over the closely printed sheets as if the secrets of the universe were there displayed. "Barley sugar?" asked Joe when the airline tray came round. "Uh-huh," replied Hazel. Then, munching steadily, down again went the two brown heads of hair.

The four in the seats behind were starting their third paper-enclosed round of rye. Three were of the familiar type: beefy, argumentative, aggressive, out to enjoy themselves with all the customary restraints cast aside for two memorable days. The fourth was a short, thin, lean-featured man of lugubrious expression and indeterminate age who spoke with a full, round Lancashire accent. "'Ere's t'Lions t'morrer," he called, raising his paper cup in yet another toast to their heroes. His friends acknowledged the rubric solemnly. One of them, his coat lapel displaying a badge which appeared to depict a mangy alley cat in rampant mood but presumably represented the king of beasts himself, passed round his cigarette case and remarked, not for the first time, "Never thought we'd make it, though. When we had to wait at Toronto with that fog around, I said to myself, 'Andy,' I said, 'this is one bit of hell-raising you're going to have to miss.' Still, we're only a few hours late for all that and we can always sleep on the plane."

"Not before we eat, though, I hope," said one of the others. "I'm starving. When do they bring round the grub?"

"Should be along soon, I reckon. They usually serve dinner about eight, but everything's been put behind with that hold-up."

"Never mind. 'Ave a drink while you wait," suggested the Lancashire man, who rejoiced in the nickname of 'Ot-pot, holding out the bottle of rye.

"Go easy, boy. We haven't got too much."

"Ah, there's plenty more where this came from. Come on now. It'll help you sleep."

The rest of the fifty-six passengers, who included three or four women, were reading or talking, all looking forward to the big game and excited to be on the last leg of their trans-continental journey. From the port windows could be seen the twinkling blue and yellow lights of the last suburbs of Winnipeg, before they were swallowed in cloud as the aircraft climbed.

In the tiny but well-appointed galley Stewardess Janet Benson prepared for dinner, a belated meal that she should have served over two hours earlier. The mirror over the glassware cabinet reflected the exhilaration she always felt at the beginning of a flight, an exuberance which she was thankful to hide in the privacy of her own quarters. Taking from built-in cupboards the necessary napkins and cutlery, Janet hummed contentedly to herself. Waitressing was the least attractive part of a stewardess's duties, and Janet knew that she was in for a very exhausting hour catering for the stomachs of a plane-load of hungry people, but nevertheless she felt confident and happy. Many of her flying colleagues, if they could have watched the swing of her blonde hair from beneath her airline cap and the movements of her trim body as she busied herself efficiently about the galley, would have given an appreciative sucking-in of breath and echoed her confidence. At twenty-one, Janet was just tasting life and finding it good.

Forward on the flight deck, the only sound was the steady drone and throb of the engines. Both pilots sat perfectly still except for an occasional leg or arm movement, their faces faintly illumined in the glow of light from the myriad dials on the instrument panels. From the earphones half covering their ears came the sudden crackle of conversation between another aircraft and the ground. Round their necks hung small boom microphones.

Captain Dunning stretched himself in his seat, flexing his muscles, and blew out through the luxuriant growth of his moustache in an unconscious mannerism that his crew knew well. He looked older than his thirty-one years.

"How are the cylinder head temperatures on No. 3 engine, Pete?" he asked, his eyes flickering momentarily to the first officer.

Pete stirred and glanced at the panel. "Okay now, skip. I had it checked at Winnipeg but they couldn't find anything wrong. Seems to have righted itself. It's not heating up now."

"Good." Dun peered ahead at the night sky. A thin moon shone bleakly down on the banks of cloud. Shredded wisps of cotton wool lazily approached, to suddenly whisk by; or occasionally the ship would plunge into a tumble of grey-white cloud, to break free in a second or two like a spaniel leaving the water and shaking itself free of the clinging drops. "With a bit of luck it'll be a clear run through," he commented. "The met report was reasonable for a change. Not often you keep to the original flight plan on this joyride."

"You said it," agreed the first officer. "In a month or so's time it'll be a very different story."

The aircraft began to bump and yaw a little as she hit a succession of thermal currents and for a few minutes the captain concentrated on correcting her trim. Then he remarked, "Are you planning to take in this ball game in Vancouver, if there's time to rest up first?"

The first officer hesitated before answering. "I don't know yet," he answered. "I'll see how it works out."

The captain looked sharply at him. "What d'you mean? See how what works out? If you've got your eyes on Janet, you can take them off again. She's too young to come under the corrupting influence of a young Casanova like you."

Few people looked less deserving of this description than the fresh-faced, thoughtful-eyed first officer, still in his twenties. "Go easy, skipper," he protested, colouring. "I never corrupted anyone in my life."

"Jeepers, that's a likely story. Well, don't aim to start with Janet." The captain grinned. "Half the airlines personnel of Canada regard it as a permanent assignment to try to date her. Don't make life hard for yourself, you chump."

Twelve feet away from them, on the other side of a sliding door, the subject of their conversation was collecting orders for the evening meal.

"Would you like dinner now, sir?" she asked quietly, bending forward with a smile.

"Eh? What's that? Oh, yes please." Baird slipped back into the present and nudged Spencer who was practically asleep. "Wake up, there. Want some dinner?"

Spencer yawned and gathered himself together. "Dinner? I sure do. You're late, miss, aren't you? I thought I'd missed it long ago."

"We were held up in Toronto, sir, and haven't served dinner yet," said Janet Benson. "What would you like? We've lamb chop or grilled salmon."

"Er—yes, please."

Janet's smile tightened a little. "Which, sir?" she asked patiently.

Spencer came fully awake. "Oh, yes—I'm sorry, miss. I'll have lamb."

"Me too," said Baird.

Back in the galley, Janet was fully occupied for the next half hour in preparing and serving meals. Eventually everyone who felt like eating had been served with a main course and she was free to pick up the telephone in the galley and press the intercom buzzer.

"Flight deck," came the voice of Pete.

"I'm finally serving dinner," said Janet. "Better late than never. What'll it be—lamb chop or grilled salmon?"

"Hold it." She could hear him putting the question to the captain. "Janet, skipper says he'll have the lamb—no, just a sec, he's changed his mind. Is the fish good?"

"Looks okay to me," said Janet chirpily. "Had no complaints."

"Skipper will take salmon, then. Better make it two. Big help-ings, mind. We're growing boys."

"All right—double portions as usual. Two fish coming up."

She quickly arranged two trays and took them forward, balanc-ing them with practised ease against the almost imperceptible movements of the aircraft. Pete had come back to open the sliding door for her and relieved her of one tray. The captain had com-pleted his switch-over to automatic pilot and was now halfway through his routine radio check with Control at Winnipeg.

"Height 16,000," he continued, speaking into the tiny micro-phone held before his mouth on a slender plastic arm. "Course 285 true. Airspeed 210 knots. Ground speed 174 knots. ETA Vancouver 0505 Pacific standard. Over."

He switched from transmit to receive and there was a clearly audible crackle from his earpiece as the acknowledgment came on the air. "Flight 714. This is Winnipeg Control. Roger Out."

Dun reached for his log sheet, made an entry, then slid his seat back so that he was well clear of the controls but still within easy reach of them if it were necessary for him to take them over again quickly. Pete was starting to eat, a tray resting on a pillow laid across his knees.

"Shan't be long, skip," he said.

"There's no hurry," replied Dun, stretching his arms above his head as far as they could go in the confined cockpit. "I can wait. Enjoy it. How is the fish, anyway?"

"Not bad," mumbled the first officer, his mouth full. "If there were about three or four times as much it might be a square meal."

The captain chuckled. "You'd better watch that waistline, Pete." He turned to the stewardess, who was waiting in the shadow behind the seat. "Everything okay at the back, Janet? How are the football fans?"

Janet shrugged. "Very quiet now. That long wait at Toronto must have tired them out. Four of them have been knocking back the rye pretty steadily, but there's been no need to speak to them about it. It'll help to keep them quiet. It looks like being a peaceful, easy night—fingers crossed."

Pete raised a quizzical eyebrow. "Uh-huh, young woman. That's the kind of night to watch, when trouble starts to brew. I'll bet someone's getting ready to be sick right now."

"Not yet," said Janet lightly. "But you warn me when *you're* going to fly the ship and I'll get the bags ready."

"Good for you," said the captain. "I'm glad you found out about him."

"How's the weather?" asked Janet.

"Oh—now let's see. General fog east of the mountains, extending nearly as far as Manitoba. There's nothing to bother us up there, though. It should be a smooth ride all the way to the coast."

"Good. Well, keep Junior here off the controls while I serve coffee, won't you?"

She slipped away before Pete could retort, made her way through the passenger deck taking orders for coffee, and within a short while brought a tray up forward to the pilots. Dun had by that time eaten his dinner, and he now drained his coffee with satisfaction. Pete had taken the controls and was intent on the instrument dials as the captain got to his feet.

"Keep her steaming, Pete. I'll just tuck the customers up for the night."

Pete nodded without turning round. "Right, skipper."

The captain followed Janet out into the brightly lit passenger section, blinking, and stopped first at the seats occupied by Spencer and Baird, who handed their trays to the stewardess.

"Good evening," said Dun. "Everything all right?"

Baird looked up. "Why sure, thanks. Very nice meal. We were ready for it, too."

"Yes, I'm sorry it was so late. '

The doctor waved aside his apology. "Nonsense. You can hardly be blamed if Toronto decides to have a bit of fog. Well," he added, settling himself back in his seat, "I'm going to get my head down for a doze."

"That goes for me as well," said Spencer with a yawn.

"I hope you have a comfortable night," said Dun, switching off their reading lights. "The stewardess will bring you some rugs." He passed on down the aisle, having a few words with each of the passengers in a subdued tone, explaining to some how the seats could be reclined, and describing to others the flight's progress and expected weather conditions.

"Well, it's me for dreamland," said Spencer. "One thing, doctor —at least you won't be getting any calls tonight."

"How long is it?" murmured Baird drowsily, his eyes closed. "A good seven hours anyways. Better make the most of it. 'Night."

"Goodnight, doc," grunted Spencer, wriggling the padded head-rest into the small of his neck. "Boy, I can sure use some shut-eye."

Blanketed off by thick cloud into a cold, remote world of her own, the aircraft droned steadily on her course. Sixteen thousand feet beneath her lay the prairies of Saskatchewan, silent and sleeping.

Dun had reached the whisky-drinking quartet and politely forbade any further consumption of liquor that night.

"You know," he told them with a reproving grin, "this sort of thing isn't permitted anyway. Just don't let me see any more bottles or you'll have to get out and walk."

"Any objection to cards?" inquired one of the party, holding a flask to the nearest light and turning down the corners of his mouth at the small amount of nectar that remained.

"Not in the least," said Dun. "So long as you don't disturb the other passengers."

"Pity the poor captain," said the man from Lancashire. "What's it like—taking a massive job like this through t'night?"

"Routine," said Dun. "Just plain, dull routine."

"Comes to that, every flight is just routine, I s'pose?"

"Well, yes. I guess that's so."

"Until summat happens—eh?"

There was an outburst of chuckles in which Dunning joined before moving on. Only the Lancastrian, through the haze of his evening's drinking, looked temporarily thoughtful at his own words.

CHAPTER TWO: 0045-0145

THE captain had almost completed his rounds and was enjoying a few moments' relaxed chaffing with one of the passengers, a little man who appeared to have travelled with him before.

"I know it looks a bit like RCAF," Dun was saying, fingering his great bush of a moustache apologetically, "but I've had it so long I couldn't part with it now—it's an old friend, you know."

"I'll bet it's a wow with the girls," said the little man. "What do they call you—Beaver?"

"Well, no," replied Dun, a suspicion of a grin under his foliage. "We're a pretty highbrow lot on this airline. It's either 'Have yer Dun, then?' or, most often, just Dunsinane."

"Just what?" asked the little man.

"Dunsinane," said the captain very deliberately. "Surely you know? Where's your Macbeth?"

The little man stared up at him. "Where's my Macbeth?" he repeated vacantly. "Hey, what are you giving me?"

The captain had moved on. While he had been speaking his eyes had been fixed on the stewardess, further along the aisle, who was bending over a woman, the palm of her hand on the passenger's forehead. As he approached, the woman, who lay rather than sat in her seat, slumped back against the headrest, suddenly grimaced. Her eyes contracted as if with pain. The captain touched the stewardess lightly on the arm.

"Anything wrong, Miss Benson?" he asked.

Janet straightened. "The lady is feeling a little under the weather, captain," she said very quietly. "I'll get her some aspirin. Be back in a moment."

Dun took her place and leaned over the woman and the man beside her.

"Sorry to hear that," he said sympathetically. "What seems to be the trouble?"

The woman stared up at him. "I—I don't know," she said in a

small voice. "It seemed to hit me all of a sudden. Just a few minutes ago. I feel sick and dizzy and—and there's an awful pain . . . down here." She indicated her stomach. "I'm sorry to be a nuisance— I—"

"Now, now, honey," murmured the man beside her. "Just lie quiet. You'll be better directly." He glanced at the captain. "A touch of air sickness, I guess?"

"I expect so, sir," answered Dun. He looked down thoughtfully at the woman, taking in the perspiration beginning to bead on her pallid forehead, the hair already becoming disarranged, the whiteness of her knuckles as with one hand she gripped the arm-rest of the seat and with the other held on to her husband. "I'm sorry you don't feel well," he said gently, "but I'm sure the stewardess will be able to help you. Try to relax as much as you can. If it's any comfort I can tell you that it looks like being a calm trip."

He moved aside for Janet.

"Now here we are," said the stewardess, handing down the pills. "Try these." She eased the woman's head forward, to help her take a few sips of water from a glass. "That's fine. Now let's make you a little more comfortable." She tucked in a rug round the woman. "How's that?" The woman nodded gratefully. "I'll be back in a few minutes to see how you're feeling. Don't worry about using the paper bag if you want to. And if you need me quickly just press the bell push by the window."

"Thank you, miss," said the husband. "I'm sure we'll be okay in just a little while." He looked at his wife with a smile, as if to reassure himself. "Try to rest, dear. It'll pass over."

"I hope so," said Dun. "I know how unpleasant these things can be. I hope you very soon feel better, madam, and that you both have a good night."

He passed back down the aisle and waited for Janet in the galley. "Who are they?" he asked when the stewardess returned.

"Mr. and Mrs. Childer—John Childer. She was all right fifteen minutes ago."

"H'm. Well you'd better let me know if she gets any worse and I'll radio ahead."

Janet looked at him quickly. "Why? What are you thinking?"

"I don't know. I don't like the look of her. Could be air sickness or just a bilious attack, I suppose—but it seems to have hit her pretty hard." The captain looked faintly worried, his fingers drumming absently on the metal draining board. "Have we a doctor on the passenger list?"

"No one who's entered as a doctor," replied Janet, "but I could ask around."

Dun shook his head. "Don't disturb them now. Most of them are getting down to sleep. Let me know how she is in half an hour or so. The trouble is," he added quietly as he turned to go, "we've got over four hours' flying before we reach the coast."

Making his way to the flight deck, he stopped for a moment to smile down at the sick woman. She attempted to smile back, but a sudden stab of pain closed her eyes and made her arch back against the seat. For a few seconds Dun stood studying her intently. Then he continued forward, closed the door of the flight deck behind him, and slid into his seat. He took off his peaked hat and put on the large earphones and then the boom microphone. Pete was flying manually. Scattered banks of cloud seemed to rush at the forward windows, envelop them momentarily, and then disappear.

"Cumulo-nimbus building up," commented the first officer.

"Getting to the rough stuff, eh?" said Dun.

"Looks like it."

"I'll take it. We'd better try to climb on top. Ask for twenty thousand, will you?"

"Right." Pete depressed a stud on his microphone attachment to transmit. "714 to Regina radio," he called.

"Go ahead, 714," crackled a voice in the earphones.

"We're running into some weather. We'd like clearance for twenty thousand."

"714. Stand by. I'll ask ATC."

"Thanks," said Pete.

The captain peered into the cloudy turbulence ahead. "Better warn Janet to fasten seat belts, Pete," he suggested, correcting with automatic concentration the tendency of the aircraft to bump and yaw.

"Okay." Pete reached for the telephone on the wall beside him. There was a brief shudder as the plane freed herself from a wall of cloud, only to plunge almost instantly into another.

"Flight 714," came the voice on the radio. "ATC gives clearance for twenty thousand. Over."

"714," acknowledged Pete. "Thanks and out."

"Let's go," said the captain. The note of the engines took on a deeper intensity as the deck began to tilt and the altimeter needle on the winking instrument panel steadily registered a climb of five hundred feet a minute. The long window wiper swished rhythmically in a broad sweep from side to side.

"Shan't be sorry when we're clear of this muck," remarked the first officer.

Dun didn't answer, his eyes glued on the dials in front of him. Neither of the pilots heard the stewardess enter. She touched the captain on the shoulder.

"Captain," she said urgently, but keeping her voice well under control. "That woman. She's worse already. And I have another passenger sick now—one of the men."

Dun did not turn to her. He stretched up an arm and switched on the landing lights. Ahead of them the sharp beams cut into the driving rain and snow. He turned off the lights and began to adjust engine and de-icer switches.

"I can't come right now, Janet," he replied as he worked. "You'd better do as we said and see if you can find a doctor. And make sure all the seat belts are fastened. This may get pretty rough. I'll come as soon as I can."

"Yes, captain."

Emerging from the flight deck, Janet called out in a voice just loud enough to carry to the rows of passengers, "Fasten your safety belts, please. It may be getting a little bumpy." She leaned over the first two passengers to her right, blinking up at her half-asleep. "Excuse me," she said casually, "but do either of you gentlemen happen to be a doctor?"

The man nearest her shook his head. "Sorry, no," he grunted. "Is there something wrong?"

"No, nothing serious."

An exclamation of pain snapped her to attention. She hurried along the aisle to where the sick Mrs. Childer lay half cradled in her husband's arms, moaning with eyes closed, and partially doubled over. Janet knelt down swiftly and wiped the glistening sweat from the woman's brow. Childer stared at her, his face creased with anxiety.

"What can we do, miss?" he asked. "What d'you think it is?"

"Keep her warm," said Janet. "I'm going to see if there's a doctor on board."

"A doctor? I just hope there is. What do we do if there isn't?"

"Don't worry, sir. I'll be back straight away."

Janet got to her feet, looked down briefly at the suffering woman, and moved on to the next seats, repeating her question in a low voice.

"Is someone ill?" she was asked.

"Just feeling unwell. It sometimes happens, flying. I'm sorry to have disturbed you."

A hand clutched at her arm. It was one of the whisky quartet, his face yellow and shining.

"Sorry, miss, to trouble you again. I'm feeling like hell. D'you think I could have a glass of water?"

"Yes, of course. I'm on my way now to get it."

"I never felt like this before." The man lay back and blew out his cheeks. One of his companions stirred, opened his eyes and sat up. "What's with you?" he growled.

"It's my insides," said the sick man. "Feels like they're coming apart." His hands clenched his stomach as another spasm shook him.

Janet shook Spencer gently by the shoulder. He opened one eye, then both. "I'm very sorry to wake you up, sir," she said, "but is anyone here a doctor?"

Spencer gathered himself. "A doctor? No. I guess not, miss." She nodded and made to move on. "Just a moment, though," he stopped her. "I seem to remember—yes, of course he is. This gentleman beside me is a doctor."

"Oh, thank goodness," breathed the stewardess. "Would you wake him, please?"

"Sure." Spencer looked up at her as he nudged the recumbent form next to him. "Someone's ill, huh?"

"Feeling a little unwell," said Janet.

"Come on, doc, wake up," Spencer said heartily. The doctor shook his head, grunted, then snapped awake. "Seems that you've got your night call after all."

"Are you a doctor, sir?" asked Janet anxiously.

"Yes. Yes, I'm Doctor Baird. Why, what's wrong?"

"We have two passengers who are quite sick. Would you take a look at them, please?"

"Sick? Yes, certainly."

Spencer stood up to let the doctor out. "Where are they?" Baird asked, rubbing his eyes.

"I think you'd better see the woman first, doctor," said Janet, leading the way and at the same time calling out quietly, "Fasten your safety belts, please," as she passed along.

Mrs. Childer was now as prostrate as the seat allowed. Shivers of pain racked her body. She breathed heavily, with long, shuddering gasps. Her hair was wet with sweat.

Baird stood studying her for a moment. Then he knelt and took her wrist.

"This gentleman is a doctor," said Janet.

"Am I glad to see you, doctor," Childer said fervently.

The woman opened her eyes. "Doctor . . ." She made an effort to speak, her lips trembling.

"Just relax," said Baird, his eyes on his watch. He released her wrist, felt inside his jacket and took out an ophthalmoscope. "Open your eyes wide," he ordered gently and examined each eye in turn in the bright pencil of light. "Now. Any pain?" The woman nodded. "Where? Here? Or here?" As he palpated her abdomen, she stiffened suddenly, choking back a cry of pain. He replaced the blanket, felt her forehead, then stood up. "Is this lady your wife?" he asked Childer.

"Yes, doctor."

"Has she complained of anything in addition to the pain?"

"She's been very sick, throwing up everything."

"When did it start?"

"Not long, I guess." Childer looked helplessly at Janet. "It's all come on suddenly."

Baird nodded reflectively. He moved away, taking Janet by the arm and speaking very quietly so as not to be overheard by the nearby passengers who were staring up at them.

"Have you given her anything?" he inquired.

"Only aspirin and water," replied Janet. "That reminds me. I promised a glass of water to the man who's sick— '

"Wait," said Baird crisply. His sleepiness had vanished now. He was alert and authoritative. "Where did you learn your nursing?"

Janet coloured at his tone. "Why, at the airline training school, but—'

"Never mind. But it's not much use giving aspirin to anyone who is actually vomiting—you'll make 'em worse. Strictly water only."

"I—I'm sorry, doctor," Janet stammered.

"I think you'd better go to the captain," said Baird. "Please tell him we should land at once. This woman has to be gotten to a hospital. Ask to have an ambulance waiting."

"Do you know what's wrong?"

"I can't make a proper diagnosis here. But it's serious enough to land at the nearest city with hospital facilities. You can tell the captain that."

"Very well, doctor. While I'm gone, will you take a look at the other sick passenger? He's complaining of the same sickness and pains."

Baird looked at her sharply. "The same pains, you say? Where is he?"

Janet led him forward to where the sick man sat, bent over retching, supported by his friend in the next seat. Baird crouched down to look at his face.

"I'm a doctor. Will you put your head back, please?" As he made a quick examination, he asked, "What have you had to eat in the last twenty-four hours?"

"Just the usual things," muttered the man, all the strength appearing to have been drained from him. "Breakfast," he said weakly, "Bacon and eggs . . . Salad for lunch . . . A sandwich at the airport . . . then dinner here." A trickle of saliva ran disregarded down his chin. "It's this pain, doctor. And my eyes."

"What about your eyes?" asked Baird quickly.

"Can't seem to focus. I keep seeing double."

His companion seemed to find it amusing. "That rye has got a real kick, yes sir," he exclaimed.

"Be quiet," said Baird. He rose, to find Janet and the captain standing beside him. "Keep him warm—get more blankets round him," he told Janet. The captain motioned him to follow him down to the galley. Immediately they were alone, Baird demanded, "How quickly can we land, captain?"

"That's the trouble," said Dun briefly. "We can't."

Baird stared at him. "Why?"

"It's the weather. I've just checked by radio. There's low cloud and fog right over the prairies this side of the mountains. Calgary's shut in completely. We'll have to go through to the coast."

Baird thought for a moment. "What about turning back?" he asked.

Dun shook his head, his face taut in the soft glow of the lights. "That's out, too. Winnipeg closed down with fog shortly after we left. Anyway, it'll be quicker now to go on."

Baird grimaced, tapping his finger nail with the tiny flashlight. "How soon do you expect to land?"

"About five a.m., Pacific Time." Dun saw the doctor glance involuntarily at his wrist-watch, and added, "We're due to land in three and a half hours from now. These charter aircraft aren't the fastest in the world."

Baird made up his mind. "Then I'll have to do what I can for these people until we arrive at Vancouver. I'll need my bag. Do you think it can be reached? I checked it at Toronto."

"We can try," said the captain. "I hope it's near the top. Let me have your tags, doctor."

Baird's long fingers probed into his hip pocket and came out with his wallet. From this he took two baggage tickets and handed them to Dun.

"There are two bags, captain," he said. "It's the smaller one I want. There isn't much equipment in it—just a few things I always carry around. But they'll help."

He had barely finished speaking before the aircraft gave a tremendous lurch, sending the two men sprawling to the far wall. There was a loud, persistent buzzing. The captain was on his feet first and sprang to the intercom telephone.

"Captain here," he rapped out. "What's wrong, Pete?"

The voice of the first officer was struggling and painful. "I'm . . . sick . . . come quickly."

"You'd better come with me," said Dun to the doctor and they left the galley rapidly. "Sorry about the bump," Dun remarked affably to the upturned faces as they walked along the aisle. "Just a little disturbance."

As they burst into the flight deck, it was only too apparent that the first officer was very sick; his face was a mask of perspiration, he was slumped in his seat, clutching the control column with what was obviously all his strength.

"Get him out of there," directed the captain urgently. Baird and Janet, who had followed the men in, seized the co-pilot and lifted him out and away from the controls, while Dun slipped into his own seat and took the column in his hands.

"There's a seat at the back of the flight deck, for when we carry a radio operator," he told them. "Put him there."

With an agonizing retch, Pete spewed on to the deck as they helped him to the vacant seat and propped him against the wall. Baird loosened the first officer's collar and tie and tried to make him as comfortable as the conditions would allow. Every few seconds Pete would jack-knife in another croaking, straining retch.

"Doctor," called the captain, his voice tense, "what is it? What's happening?"

"I'm not sure," said Baird grimly. "But there's a common denominator to these attacks. There has to be. The most likely thing is food. What was it we had for dinner?"

"The main course was a choice of meat or fish," said Janet. "You probably remember, doctor—you had—"

"Meat!" cut in Baird. "About—what?—two, three hours ago. What did he have?" He indicated the first officer.

Janet's face began to register alarm. "Fish," she almost whispered.

"Do you remember what the other two passengers had?"

"No—I don't think so—"

"Go back quickly and find out, will you, please?"

The stewardess hurried out, her face pale. Baird knelt beside the first officer who sat swaying with the motion of the aircraft, his eyes closed. "Try to relax," he said quietly. "I'll give you something in a few minutes that'll help the pain. Here." He reached up and pulled down a blanket from a rack. "You'll feel better if you stay warm."

Pete opened his eyes a little and ran his tongue over dry lips. "Are you a doctor?' he asked. Baird nodded. Pete said with a sheepish attempt to smile, "I'm sorry about all this mess. I thought I was going to flake out."

"Don't talk," said Baird. "Try to rest."

"Tell the captain he's sure right about my ham-handed—"

"I said don't talk. Rest and you'll feel better."

Janet returned. "Doctor," she spoke rapidly, hardly able to get the words out quickly enough. "I've checked both those passengers. They both had salmon. There are three others complaining of pains now. Can you come?"

"Of course. But I'll need that bag of mine."

Dun called over his shoulder. "Look, I can't leave here now, doctor, but I'll see that you get it immediately. Janet, take these tags. Get one of the passengers to help you and dig out the smaller of the doctor's two bags, will you?" Janet took the tags from him and turned to the doctor to speak again, but Dun continued, "I'm going to radio Vancouver and report what's happening. Is there anything you want me to add?"

"Yes," said Baird. "Say we have three serious cases of suspected food poisoning and that there seem to be others developing. You can say we're not sure but we suspect that the poisoning could have been caused by fish served on board. Better ask them to put a ban on all food originating from the same source as ours—at least until we've established the cause of the poisoning for certain."

"I remember now," exclaimed Dun. "That food didn't come from the caterers who usually supply the regular airlines. We had to get it from some other outfit because we were so late getting into Winnipeg."

"Tell them that, captain," said Baird. "That's what they'll need to know."

"Doctor, *please*," Janet implored him. "I do wish you'd come and see Mrs. Childer. She seems to have collapsed altogether."

Baird stepped to the door. The lines in his face had deepened, but his eyes as he held Janet's with them were steady as a rock.

"See that the passengers are not alarmed," he instructed. "We shall be depending on you a great deal. Now if you'll be good enough to find my bag and bring it to me, I'll be attending to Mrs. Childer." He pushed back the door for her, then stopped her as something occurred to him. "By the way, what did *you* eat for dinner?"

"I had meat," the young stewardess answered him.

"Thank heavens for that, then." Janet smiled and made to go on again, but he gripped her suddenly, very hard, by the arm. "I suppose the captain had meat, too?" He shot the question at her.

She looked up at him, as if at the same time trying both to remember and to grasp the implications of what he had asked.

Then, suddenly, shock and realization flooded into her. She almost fell against him, her eyes dilated with an immense and overpowering fear.

CHAPTER THREE: 0145-0220

BRUNO BAIRD regarded the stewardess thoughtfully. Behind the calm reassurance of his blue-grey eyes his mind rapidly assessed the situation, weighing with the habit of years one possibility against another. He released the girl's arm.

"Well, we won't jump to conclusions," he said, almost to himself. Then, more briskly, "You find my bag—just as quickly as you can. Before I see Mrs. Childer I'll have another word with the captain."

He retraced his steps forward. They were now in level flight, above the turbulence. Over the pilot's shoulder he could see the cold white brilliance of the moon, converting the solid carpet of cloud below them into a seemingly limitless landscape of snow with here and there what looked for all the world like a pinnacle of ice thrusting its craggy outcrop through the surrounding billows. The effect was dreamlike.

"Captain," he said, leaning over the co-pilot's empty seat. Dun looked round, his face drawn and colourless in the moon glare. "Captain, this has to be fast. There are people very sick back there and they need attention."

Dun nodded quickly. "Yes, doctor. What is it?"

"I presume you ate after the other officer?"

"Yes, that's so."

"How long after?"

Dun's eyes narrowed. "About half an hour, I'd say. Maybe a little more, but not much." The point of the doctor's question suddenly hit him. He sat upright with a jerk and slapped the top of the control column with the flat of his hand. "Holy smoke, that's right. I had fish too."

"D'you feel all right?"

The captain nodded. "Yes. Yes, I feel okay."

"Good." Relief showed in Baird's face. "As soon as I've got my bag I'll give you an emetic."

"Will that get rid of it?"

"Depends. You can't have digested it all yet. Anyway, it doesn't follow that everyone who ate fish will be affected—logic doesn't enter into these things. You could be the one to avoid trouble."

"I'd better be," muttered Dun. staring now into the moonglow ahead.

"Now listen," said Baird. "Is there any way of locking the controls of this airplane?"

"Why yes," said Dun. "There's the automatic pilot. But that wouldn't get us down—"

"I suggest you switch it on, or whatever you do, just in case. If you do happen to feel ill, yell for me immediately. I don't know that I can do much, but if you do get any symptoms they'll come on fast."

The knuckles of Dun's hands gleamed white as he gripped the control column. "Okay," he said quietly. "What about Miss Benson, the stewardess?'

"She's all right. She had meat."

"Well, that's something. Look, for heaven s sake hurry with that emetic. I can't take any chances, flying this ship.'

"Benson is hurrying. Unless I'm mistaken there are at least two people back there in a state of deep shock. One more thing," Baird said, looking straight at the captain. "Are you absolutely certain that we've no other course but to go on?"

"Certain," answered Dun instantly. "I've checked and double-checked. Thick cloud and ground fog until the other side of the mountains. Calgary, Edmonton, Lethbridge—all closed to traffic. That's routine, when ground visibility is zero. In the normal way, it wouldn't worry us."

"Well, it worries us now."

The doctor stepped back to leave, but Dun shot at him, "Just a minute." As the doctor paused, he went on, "I'm in charge of this flight and I must know the facts. Lay it on the line. What are the chances that I'll be all right?"

Baird shook his head angrily, his composure momentarily deserting him. "I wouldn't know," he said savagely. "You just can't apply any rules to a thing like this."

He was halted again before he could leave the flight deck.

"Oh, doctor."

"Yes?"

"Glad you're aboard."

Baird left without another word. Dun took a deep breath, thinking over what had been said and searching in his mind for a possible course of action. Not for the first time in his flying career, he felt himself in the grip of an acute sense of apprehension, only this time his awareness of his responsibility for the safety of a huge, complex aircraft and nearly sixty lives was tinged with a sudden icy premonition of disaster. Was this, then, what it felt like? Older pilots, those who had been in combat in the war, always maintained that if you kept at the game long enough you'd buy it in the end. How was it that in the space of half an hour a normal, everyday, routine flight, carrying a crowd of happy football fans, could change into a nightmare nearly four miles above the earth, something that would shriek across the front pages of a hundred newspapers?

He pushed the thoughts from him in violent self-disgust. There were things to do, things requiring his complete concentration. Putting out his right hand he flicked the switches on the automatic pilot panel, waiting until each control became fully orientated and the appropriate indicator light gleamed to show that the next stage of the switching over could be started. Ailerons first, needing a slight adjustment of the compensating dial to bring them fully under electrical control; then rudder and elevators were nursed until all the four lights set into the top of the panel had ceased winking and settled down to a steady glow. Satisfied, Dun glanced at his p.d.i. dial and took his hands off the wheel. Sitting back in his seat, he let the aircraft fly itself while he carried out a thorough cockpit check. To an inexperienced eye, the flight deck presented a weird sight. Just as though two invisible men sat in the pilots' seats, the twin control columns moved slightly forward, backward, then forward again. Compensating the air currents as they gently buffeted the aircraft, the rudder bar moved also, as if of its own volition. Across the great spread of the dual instrument panel the dozens of needles each registered its own particular story.

His check completed, he reached for the microphone that hung on its hook beside his head. He quickly clipped it to his neck and adjusted the padded earphones. The boom mike swung round at his touch so that the thin steel curve almost caressed his cheek. Aggressively, he blew at his moustache, puffing it up so that it practically touched his nose. Well, he thought to himself, here goes.

The switch was at send and his voice sounded calm and unhurried.

"Hullo, Vancouver Control. This is Maple Leaf Charter Flight 714. I have an emergency message. I have an emergency message."

His earphones crackled instantly: "Maple Leaf Charter Flight 714. Come in please."

"Vancouver Control. This is Flight 714. Listen. We have three serious cases of suspected food poisoning on board, including the first officer, and possibly others. When we land we shall want ambulances and medical help standing by. Please warn hospitals near the airfield. We're not sure but we think the poisoning may have been caused by the fish served on board at dinner. You'd better put a ban on all food coming from the same source until the trouble has been definitely located. We understand that owing to our late arrival at Winnipeg the food was not supplied by the regular airline contractor. Please check. Is this understood?"

He listened to the acknowledgment, his eyes gazing bleakly at the frozen sea of cloud below and ahead. Vancouver Control sounded as crisp and impersonal as ever but he could guess at the verbal bomb he had exploded down there on the far western seaboard and the burst of activity his words would have triggered off. Almost wearily, he ended the transmission and leaned back in his seat. He felt strangely heavy and tired, as if lead had begun to flow into his limbs. The instrument dials, as his eyes ran automatically over them, seemed to recede until they were far, far away. He was conscious of a cold film of sweat on his forehead and he shivered in a sudden uncontrollable spasm. Then, in a renewal of anger at the perfidy of his body at such a time of crisis, he flung himself with all his strength and concentration into rechecking their flight path, their estimated time of arrival, the expected cross-winds over the mountains, the runway plan of Vancouver. He had little idea whether it was a few minutes or several before his preparations were complete. He reached for his log book, opened it and looked at his wrist watch. With a dull and painful slowness his mind began to grapple with the seemingly Herculean task of trying to fix times to the events of the night.

Back in the body of the aircraft, Doctor Baird tucked fresh dry blankets round the limp form of Mrs. Childer and tossed the others out into the aisle. The woman lay back helplessly, her eyes closed, dry lips apart and trembling, moaning quietly. The top of her dress was stained and damp. As Baird watched her she was seized with a fresh paroxysm. Her eyes did not open.

Baird spoke to her husband. "Keep her mopped up and as dry as you can. And warm. She must be warm."

Childer reached up and grabbed the doctor by the wrist. "For God's sake, doctor, what's happening?" His voice was shrill. "She's pretty bad, isn't she?"

Baird looked again at the woman. Her breathing was rapid and shallow. "Yes," he said, "she is."

"Well, can't we *do* something for her—give her something?"

Baird shook his head. "She needs drugs we haven't got—antibiotics. There's nothing we can do right now but keep her warm."

"But surely even some water—"

"No. She'd gag on it. Your wife is nearly unconscious, Childer. Hold it, now," Baird added hastily as the other man half rose in alarm. "That's nature's own anaesthetic. Don't worry. She'll be all right. Your job is to watch her and keep her warm. Even when she's unconscious she'll probably still try to throw up. I'll be back."

Baird moved to the next row of seats. A middle-aged man, collar undone and hands clasping his stomach, sat slumped partly out of his seat, head thrown back and turning from side to side, his face glistening with sweat. He looked up at the doctor, drawing back his lips in a rictus of pain.

"It's murder," the man mumbled. "I never felt like this before."

Baird took a pencil from his jacket pocket and held it in front of the man.

"Listen to me," he said. "I want you to take this pencil."

The man raised his arm with an effort. His fingers tried fumb-

lingly to grasp the pencil but it slipped through them. Baird's
eyes narrowed. He lifted the man into a more comfortable position
and tucked a blanket in tightly around him.

"I can't hold myself," the man said, "and my head feels like
it's in a vice."

"Doctor," someone shouted, "can you come here, please!"

"Wait a minute," Baird called back. "I'll see everyone in turn
who wants me."

The stewardess hurried towards him holding a leather bag.

"Good girl," said Baird. "That's the one. Not that I can do
much . . ." His voice trailed away as he thought hard. "Where's
your public address?" he asked.

"I'll show you," said Janet. She led the way aft to the galley
and pointed out the wall telephone. "How is Mrs. Childer,
doctor?" she asked.

Baird pursed his lips. "Don't let's pretend otherwise—she's seriously ill," he said, "And if I'm not very much mistaken there are
others who'll be as bad before long."

"Do you still think it's food poisoning?" Janet's cheeks were
very pale.

"Tolerably certain. Staphylococcal, I'd say, though some of the
symptoms out there could indicate even worse. There again, the
poisoning could have been caused by salmonella bacilli—who can
say, without a proper diagnosis."

"Are you going to give round an emetic?"

"Yes, except of course to those who are already sick. That's all
I can do. What we probably need are antibiotics like chloram-
phenicol, but it's no use thinking about that." Lifting the
telephone, Baird paused. "As soon as you can," he told her, "I
suggest you organize some help to clean up a bit in there. Squirt
plenty of disinfectant around if you've any. Oh, and as you speak
to the sick passengers you'd better tell them to forget the conven-
tions and not to lock the door of the toilet—we don't want any
passing out in there." He thought for a moment, then pressed the
button of the public address system. "Ladies and gentlemen," he
said, "can I have your attention, please? Your attention, please."
He heard the murmur of voices die away, leaving only the steady
drone of the engines. "First of all, I should introduce myself," he
went on. "My name is Baird and I'm a doctor. Some of you are
wondering what this malady is that has stricken our fellow passengers and I think it's time everyone knew what is happening and
what I'm doing. Well, as far as I can tell with the limited facilities

at my disposal we have several cases of food poisoning on board and by deduction—a deduction that has yet to be confirmed—I believe the cause of it to be the fish which was served to some of us at dinner." An excited hubbub broke out at his words. "Now listen to me, please," he said. "There is no cause for alarm. I repeat, there is no cause for alarm. The passengers who have suffered these attacks are being cared for by the stewardess and myself, and the captain has radio'd ahead for more medical help to be standing by when we land. If you ate fish for dinner it doesn't necessarily follow that you are going to be affected too. There's seldom any hard and fast rule about this sort of thing and it's perfectly possible that you'll be entirely immune. However, we *are* going to take some precautions and the stewardess and I are coming round to you all. I want you to tell us if you ate fish. Remember, only if you ate fish. If you did, we'll tell you how you can help yourselves. Now, if you'll all settle down we'll begin right away." Baird took his finger off the button and turned to Janet. "All we can really do now is to give immediate first aid," he said.

Janet nodded. "You mean the pills, doctor?'

"There are two things we can do. We don't know definitely what the source of the poisoning is but we can assume it's been taken internally, so to begin with everyone who had fish must drink several glasses of water—I mean those who are not too ill, of course. That will help to dilute the poison and relieve the toxic effects. After that we'll give an emetic. If there aren't enough pills in my bag to go round we'll have to use salt. Have you plenty of that?"

"I've only got a few small packets that go with the lunches but we can break them open."

"Good. We'll see how far the pills go first. I'll start at the back here with the pills and you begin bringing drinking water to those people already affected, will you? Take some to the first officer too. You'll need help."

Stepping out of the galley, Baird practically cannoned into the lean, lugubrious Lancashire man called 'Otpot.

"Anything I can do, doctor?" His voice was concerned.

Baird allowed himself a smile. "Thanks. First, what did you have for dinner?"

"Meat, thank heaven," breathed 'Otpot fervently.

"Right. We're not going to worry about you then for the moment. Will you help the stewardess to hand water round to the

passengers who are sick? I want them to drink at least three glasses
if they can—more, if possible."

'Otpot entered the galley, returning Janet's rather tired little
smile. In normal circumstances that smile of hers could be guaranteed to quicken the pulse of any airline staff but on this occasion
the Lancashire man could see the hint of fear that lay behind it.
He winked at her.

"Don't you worry, miss. Everything's going to be all right."

Janet looked at him gratefully. "I'm sure it is, thanks. Look,
here's the water tap and there are the cups, Mr—"

"The boys call me 'Otpot."

"'Otpot?" repeated Janet incredulously.

"Yes, Lancashire 'Otpot—you know."

"Oh!" Janet burst out laughing.

"There, that's better. Now, where are t'cups, you say? Come on,
lass, let's get started. A fine airline this is. Gives you your dinner,
then asks for it back again."

It takes a very great deal to upset the equilibrium of a modern
airport. Panic is a thing unknown in such places and would be
ruthlessly stamped out if it occurred, for it can be a highly lethal
activity.

The control room at Vancouver, when Dun's emergency call
began to come through, presented a scene of suppressed excitement. In front of the radio panel an operator wearing headphones
transcribed Dun's incoming message straight on to a typewriter,
pausing only to reach over and punch an alarm bell on his desk.
He carried on imperturbably as a second man appeared behind
him, craning over his shoulder to read the words as they were
pounded on to the sheet of paper in the typewriter. The newcomer, summoned by the bell, was the Airport Controller, a tall
lean man who had spent a lifetime in the air and knew the conditions of travel over the northern hemisphere as well as he knew
his own back garden. Better, in fact, for didn't his onions always
run to seed? He got half way through the message, then stepped
sharply back, cracking an order over his shoulder to the telephone
operator on the far side of the room.

"Get me Air Traffic Control quickly. Then clear the teletype
circuit to Winnipeg. Priority message." The Controller picked up
a phone, waited a few seconds, then said, "Vancouver Controller
here." His voice was deceptively unhurried. "Maple Leaf Charter
Flight 714 from Winnipeg to Vancouver reports emergency.

Serious food poisoning among the passengers, and I mean serious. The first officer is down with it too. Better clear all levels below them for priority approach and landing. Can do? Good. ETA is 0505." The Controller glanced at the wall clock; it read 0215. "Right. We'll keep you posted." He pushed down the telephone cradle with his thumb, keeping it there as he barked at the tele-type operator, "Got Winnipeg yet? Good. Send this message. Starts: 'Controller Winnipeg. Urgent. Maple Leaf Charter Flight 714 reports serious food poisoning among passengers and crew believed due to fish served dinner on flight. Imperative check source and suspend all other food service originating same place. Understand source was not, repeat not, regular airline caterer.' That's all." He swung round to the telephone switchboard again. "Get me the local manager of Maple Leaf Charter. Burdick's his name. After that I want the city police—senior officer on duty." He leaned over the radio operator's shoulder again and finished reading the now completed message. "Acknowledge that, Greg. Tell them that all altitudes below them are being cleared and that they'll be advised of landing instructions later. We shall want further news later of the condition of those passengers, too."

On the floor below, an operator of the Government of Canada Western Air Traffic Control swivelled in his chair to call across the room, "What's in green one between here and Calgary?"

"Westbound. There's an air force North Star at 18,000. Just reported over Penticton. Maple Leaf 714—"

"714's in trouble. They want all altitudes below them cleared."

"The North Star's well ahead and there's nothing close behind. There's an eastbound Constellation ready for take-off."

"Clear it, but hold any other eastbound traffic for the time being. Bring the North Star straight in when it arrives."

Upstairs, the Controller had scooped up the telephone again, holding it with one hand as the other pulled at his necktie, worrying the knot free. Irritably he threw the length of red silk on the table. "Hullo, Burdick? Controller here. Look, we've got an emergency on one of your flights—714 ex Toronto and Winnipeg. Eh? No, the aircraft's all right. The first officer and several passengers are down with food poisoning. I called Winnipeg right away. Told them to trace the source of the food. Apparently it isn't the usual caterer. No, that's right. See here, you'd better come over as soon as you can." He jabbed the telephone cradle again with his thumb and nodded to the switchboard operator. "The police—got them yet? Good, put them on. Hullo, this is the Controller, Vancouver Airport. Who am I speaking to, please? Look, inspector, we have an emergency on an incoming flight. Several of the passengers and one of the crew have been taken ill with food poisoning and we need ambulances and doctors out here at the airport. Eh? Three serious, possibly others—be prepared for plenty. The flight is due in just after five o'clock local time—in about two and a half hours. Will you alert the hospitals, get the ambulances, set up a traffic control? Right. We'll be on again as soon as we've got more information."

Within five minutes Harry Burdick had arrived, puffing into the room. The local Maple Leaf manager was a portly little man with an abundant supply of body oils: inexhaustible, it seemed, for no one had ever seen him without his face streaked with runnels of perspiration. He stood in the centre of the room, his jacket over his arm, gasping for breath after his hurry and swabbing the lunarscape of his face with a great blue-spotted handkerchief.

"Where's the message?" he grunted. He ran his eye quickly over the sheet of paper the radio operator handed to him. "How's the weather at Calgary?" he asked the Controller. "It would be quicker to go in there, wouldn't it?"

"No good, I'm afraid. There's fog right down to the grass everywhere east of the Rockies as far as Manitoba. They'll have to come through."

A clerk called across from his phone, "Passenger agent wants to know when we'll be resuming eastbound traffic. Says should he keep the passengers downtown or bring 'em out here?"

Burdick shook a worried head. "Where's the last position report?" he demanded. A clipboard was passed to him and he scanned it anxiously.

The Controller called back to the clerk, "Tell him to keep them downtown. We don't want a mob out here. We'll give him lots of warning when we're ready."

"You say you've got medical help coming?" asked Burdick.

"Yes," replied the Controller. "The city police are working on that. They'll alert the hospitals and see to the arrangements when we get the plane here."

Burdick clicked a fat finger. "Hey! That message now. They say the first officer is down so presumably the captain passed the message. Is he affected at all? Better ask, Controller. And while you're about it, I should check whether there's a doctor on board.

You never know. Tell them we're getting medical advice here in case they need it."

The Controller nodded and picked up the stand microphone from the radio desk. Before he could begin, Burdick called, "Say, suppose the captain does take sick, Controller? Who's going to ..."

He left the sentence unfinished as the level gaze of the man opposite met his.

"I'm not supposing anything," said the Controller. "I'm praying, that's all. Let's hope those poor devils up there are praying too."

Exhaling noisily, Burdick dug in his pockets for cigarettes. "Joe," he said to the switchboard operator, "get me Doctor Davidson, will you? You'll find his number on the emergency list."

CHAPTER FOUR: 0220-0245

NEARLY four miles above the earth, the aircraft held her course.

In every direction, as far as the eye could see, stretched the undulating carpet of cloud, passing beneath the great machine so slowly as to make it appear almost stationary. It was a cold, empty, utterly lonely world, a world in which the heart-beating throb of the aircraft's engines came rumbling back from the silver-tinted wastes.

Far below, that same powerful pulse of engines, in normal weather, would have reverberated through the desolate valleys of the Rocky Mountains. Tonight, muffled by the ground fog, the sound of her passing was not enough to disturb the scattered communities as they slept in their remote farmsteads. Had someone there chanced to hear the aircraft, he may have disregarded it as an event too commonplace to be worthy of thought. Or he may have wished himself up there, flying to some faraway place and enjoying the solicitous attentions of a crew whose primary concern was his safety and comfort. He could not have dreamed that practically everyone in the aircraft would have gladly and gratefully changed places with him.

Like a monstrous weed, fear was taking root in the minds of most of the passengers. There were some who probably still failed to realize exactly what was going on. But most of them, especially those who could hear the groans and retching of the ones who were ill, felt the presence of a terrible crisis. The doctor's words over the public address system, once they had sunk in, had provided plenty to think about. The hubbub of dismay and conjecture following them had soon died away, to be replaced by whispers and uneasy snatches of conversation.

Baird had given Janet two pills. "Take them to the captain," he told her in a low voice. "Tell him to drink as much water as he can. If the poison is in his system the water will help dilute it. Then he's to take the pills. They'll make him sick—that's what they're for."

When Janet entered the flight deck Dun was completing a radio transmission. He signed off and gave her a strained grin. Neither of them was deluded by it.

"Hullo, Jan," he said. His hand was shaking slightly. "This is becoming quite a trip. Vancouver have just been asking for more details. I thought this lot would shake them up a bit. How are things back there?"

"So far, so good," said Janet as lightly as she could. She held out the pills. "Doctor says you're to drink as much as you can, then take these. They'll make you feel a bit green."

"What a prospect." He reached down into the deep seat pocket at his side and took out a water bottle. "Well, down the hatch." After a long draught, he swallowed the pills, pulling a wry face. "Never could take those things—and they tasted awful."

Janet looked anxiously down at him as he sat before the flickering panel of gauges and dials, the two control columns moving spasmodically backwards and forwards in the eerie grip of the automatic pilot. She touched his shoulder.

"How do you feel?" she asked. His pallor, the beads of perspiration on his forehead, did not escape her. She prayed to herself that it was just the strain he was undergoing.

"Me?" His tone was unnaturally hearty. "I'm fine. What about you? Had your pills yet?"

"I don't need any. I had chops for dinner."

"You were wise. From now I think I'll be a vegetarian—it's safer that way." He turned in his seat and looked over at the first officer, now supine on the floor, his head on a pillow. "Poor old Pete," he murmured. "I sure hope he's going to be all right."

"That's up to you, isn't it, captain?" said Janet urgently. "The faster you can push this thing into Vancouver, the quicker we'll get him and the others into hospital." She stepped over to Pete and bent down to adjust a blanket round him, hiding the sudden tremble of tears that threatened to break through her reserve. Dun was troubled as he regarded her.

"You think a lot of him, Jan, don't you?" he said.

Her golden head moved a little.

"I—I suppose so," she replied. "I've got to like him during the past few months since he joined the crew and this—this horrible business has made me . . ." She checked herself and jumped up. "I've a lot to do. Have to hold a few noses while the doctor pours water down their gullets. Not very popular, I imagine, with some of those hard-drinking types."

She smiled quickly at him and opened the door to the passenger deck. Baird was half way along the starboard side, talking to a middle-aged couple who stared at him nervously.

"Doctor," the woman was saying intently, "that young girl, the stewardess—I've seen her keep going up to the pilots' cabin. Are they well? I mean, supposing they're taken ill too—what will happen to us?" She clutched at her husband. "Hector, I'm frightened. I wish we hadn't come—"

"Now, now, dear, take it easy," said her husband with an assurance he obviously didn't feel. "There's no danger, I'm sure, and nothing has happened so far." He turned baggy, horn-rimmed eyes on the doctor. "*Did* the pilots have fish?"

"Not all the fish was necessarily infected," answered Baird evasively. "Anyway, we don't know for certain that the fish was to blame. You've nothing to worry about—we'll take great care of the crew. Now, sir, did you have fish or meat?"

The man's bulbous eyes seemed about to depart from their sockets. "Fish," he exclaimed. "We both ate fish." Indignation welled up in him. "I think it's disgraceful that such a thing can happen. There ought to be an inquiry."

"I can assure you there will be, whatever the cause." Baird handed them each a pill, which they accepted as gingerly as if it were high explosive. "Now, you'll be brought a jug of water. Drink three glasses each—four, if you can manage them. Then take a pill. It'll make you sick, but that's what it's for. Don't worry about it. There are paper bags in the seat pockets."

He left the couple staring hypnotically at their pills and in a few minutes, progressing along the rows, had reached his own empty seat with Spencer sitting alongside it.

"Meat," said Spencer promptly, before Baird could put the question.

"Good for you," said the doctor. "That's one less to worry about."

"You're having a heavy time of it, doc, aren't you?" Spencer commented. "Can you do with any help?"

"I can do with all the help in the world," growled Baird. "But there's not much you can do, unless you'd like to give Miss Benson and the other fellow a hand with the water."

"Sure I will." Spencer lowered his voice. "Someone back there sounds in a bad way."

"They *are* in a bad way. The devil of it is," said Baird bitterly, "I've got nothing I can give them that's of any real use. You make a trip to a ball game—you don't think to pack your bag in case a dozen people get taken sick with food poisoning on the way. I've a hypodermic and morphia—never travel without *those*—but here they may do more harm than good. God knows why I threw in a bottle of emetic pills, but it's a good thing I did. Some dramamine would be mighty useful now."

"What does that do?"

"In these cases the serious thing is the loss of body fluids. An injection of dramamine would help to preserve them."

"You mean all this sickness gradually dehydrates a person?"

"Exactly."

Spencer rubbed his chin as he digested this information. "Well," he said, "thank God for lamb chops. I just don't feel ready for dehydration yet."

Baird frowned at him. "Perhaps you see some humour in this situation," he said sourly. "I don't. All I see is complete helplessness while people suffer and steadily get worse."

"Don't ride me, doc," Spencer protested. "I meant nothing. I'm only too glad we didn't cop a packet with the fish like the other poor devils."

"Yes, yes, maybe you're right." Baird passed a hand over his eyes. "I'm getting too old for this sort of thing," he muttered, half to himself.

"What do you mean?"

"Never mind, never mind."

Spencer got to his feet. "Now, hold on there, doc," he said. "You're doing a fine job. The luckiest thing that ever happened to these people is having you on board."

"All right, junior," Baird retorted caustically. "You can spare me the salesman's pep talk. I'm not proposing to run out on you."

The younger man flushed slightly. "Fair enough—I asked for

that. Well, tell me what I can do. I've been sitting warming my seat while you've been hard at it. You're tired."

"Tired nothing." Baird put his hand on the other man's arm. "Take no notice of me. I worked off a bit of steam on you. Feel better for it. It's knowing what ought to be done and not being able to do it. Makes me a little raw."

"That's okay," Spencer said with a grin. "Glad to be of some use, anyway."

"I'll tell Miss Benson you're willing to help if she needs you. Once the water is all given out, I think maybe you'd better stay where you are. There's more than enough traffic in the aisle already."

"As you say. Well, I'm here if you want me." Spencer resumed his seat. "But tell me—just how serious is all this?"

Baird looked him in the eye. "As serious as you are ever likely to want it," he said curtly.

He moved along to the group of football fans who had earlier in the evening imbibed whisky with such liberality. The quartet was now reduced in strength to three, and one of these sat shivering in his shirt-sleeves, a blanket drawn across his chest. His colour was grey.

"Keep this man warm," said Baird. "Has he had anything to drink?"

"That's a laugh," replied a man behind him, shuffling a pack of cards. "He must have downed a couple of pints of rye, if I'm any judge."

"Before or after dinner?"

"Both, I reckon."

"That's right," agreed another in the group. "And I always thought Harry could hold his liquor."

"In this case it's done him no harm," Baird said. "In fact, it has helped to dilute the poison, I don't doubt. Have any of you men got any brandy?"

"Cleared mine up," said the man with the cards.

"Wait a minute," said the other, leaning forward to get at his hip pocket. "I might have some left in the flask. We gave it a good knocking, waiting about at Toronto."

"Give him a few sips," instructed Baird. "Take it gently. Your friend is very ill."

"Say, doctor," said the man with the cards, "what's the score? Are we on schedule?"

"As far as I know, yes."

"This puts paid to the ball game for Andy, eh?"

"It certainly does. We'll get him to hospital just as soon as we land."

"Poor old Andy," commiserated the man with the hip flask, unscrewing the cap, "he always was an unlucky so-and-so. Hey," he exclaimed as a thought struck him, "you say he's pretty bad— he'll be all right, won't he?"

"I hope so. You'd better pay him some attention, as I said, and make sure he doesn't throw off those blankets."

"Fancy this happening to old Andy. What about 'Otpot, that Lancashire screwball? You drafted him?"

"Yes, he's giving us a hand." As Baird stepped away the man with the cards flicked them irritably in his hand and demanded of his companion, "How d'you like this for a two-day vacation?"

Further along the aisle, Baird found Janet anxiously bending over Mrs. Childer. He raised one of the woman's eyelids. She was unconscious.

Her husband seized frantically on the doctor's presence.

"How is she?" he implored.

"She's better off now than when she was conscious and in pain," said Baird, hoping he sounded convincing. "When the body can't take any more, nature pulls down the shutter."

"Doctor, I'm scared. I've never seen her so ill. Just what is this food poisoning? What caused it? I know it was the fish, but why?"

Baird hesitated.

"Well," he said slowly, "I guess you've a right to know. It's a very serious illness, one that needs treatment at the earliest possible moment. We're doing all we can right now."

"I know you are, doctor, and I'm grateful. She is going to be okay, isn't she? I mean—"

"Of course she is," said Baird gently. "Try not to worry. There'll be an ambulance waiting to take her to hospital immediately we land. Then it's only a question of treatment and time before she's perfectly well again."

"My God," said Childer, heaving a deep breath, "it's good to hear you say that." Yes, thought Baird, but supposing I had the common guts to put it the other way? "But listen," Childer suggested, "couldn't we divert—you know, put down at a nearer airport?"

"We thought of that," answered Baird, "but there's a ground fog which would make landing at other fields highly dangerous. Anyway, we've now passed them and we're over the Rockies. No, the quickest way of getting your wife under proper care is to crack on for Vancouver as fast as we can, and that's what we're doing."

"I see . . . You still think it was the fish, do you, doctor?"

"At present I've no means of telling for certain, but I think so. Food poisoning can be caused either by the food just spoiling——the medical name is staphylococcal poisoning—or it's possible that some toxic substance has accidentally gotten into it during its preparation."

"What kind do you think this is, doctor?" asked a passenger in the next row who had been straining to hear Baird's words.

"I can't be sure, but from the effect that it's had on the folk here I'd suspect the second cause rather than the first—a toxic substance, that is."

"And you don't know what it is?"

"I have no idea. We don't know until we're able to make proper tests in a laboratory. With modern methods of handling food—and especially the careful way in which airlines prepare food—the chances of this happening are a million to one against. We just happen to be unfortunate. I can tell you, though, that our dinner tonight didn't come from the usual caterers. Something went wrong owing to our late arrival at Winnipeg and another firm supplied us. That may, or may not, have a bearing on it."

Childer nodded, turning the conversation over in his mind. Funny how people seem to find comfort in a medical man's words, Baird reflected in a sardonic appraisal of himself. Even when what a doctor has to say is bad news, the fact that he has said it seems to be reassuring to them. He's the doctor; he won't let it happen. Maybe we haven't come so far from witchcraft, he thought to himself with a touch of anger; there's always the doctor with his box of magic, to pull something out of the hat. Most of his life had been spent in nursing, coaxing, bullying, cajoling—reassuring frightened and trusting people that he knew best, and hoping each time that his old skill and sometimes very necessary bluff had not deserted him. Well, this could be the moment of truth, the final, inescapable challenge which he had always known would face him one day.

He felt Janet standing beside him. He questioned her with his eyes, sensing her to be on the edge of hysteria.

"Two more passengers have been taken ill, doctor. At the back there."

"Are you sure it isn't just the pills?"

"Yes, I'm quite sure."

"Right. I'll get to them straight away. Will you have another look at the first officer, Miss Benson? He might feel like a little water."

He had barely reached the two new cases and begun his examination before Janet was back again.

"Doctor, I'm terribly worried. I think you ought to—"

The buzz of the galley intercom cut across her words like a knife. She stood transfixed as the buzz continued without a break. Baird was the first to move.

"Don't bother with that thing," he rapped out. "Quick!"

Moving with an agility quite foreign to him, he raced along the aisle and burst into the flight deck. There he paused momentarily, while his eyes and brain registered what had happened, and in that instant something inside him, something mocking in its tone but menacing too, said: *You were right—this is it.*

The captain was rigid in his seat, sweat masking his face and streaking the collar of his uniform. One hand clutched at his stomach. The other was pressed on the intercom button on the wall beside him.

In two bounds the doctor reached him and leaned over the back of the seat, supporting him under the armpits. Dun was swearing between his clenched teeth, quietly and viciously.

"Take it easy, now," said Baird. "We'd better get you away from there."

"I did . . . what you said . . ." Dun gasped, closing his eyes and squeezing the words out in painful jerks. "It was too late. . . . Give me something, doc. . . . Give me something, quickly. . . . Got to hold out . . . get us down. . . . She's on auto pilot but . . . got to get down. . . . Must tell Control . . . must tell . . ." His mouth moved silently. With a desperate effort he tried to speak. Then his eyes rolled up and he collapsed.

"Quick, Miss Benson," called Baird. "Help me get him out."

Panting and struggling, they pulled Dun's heavy body out of the pilot's seat and eased him on to the floor alongside the first officer. Swiftly, Baird took out his stethoscope and made an examination. In a matter of seconds Janet had produced coats and a blanket; as soon as the doctor had finished she made a pillow for the captain and wrapped him round. She was trembling as she stood up again.

"Can you do what he asked, doctor? Can you bring him round long enough to land the plane?"

Baird thrust his instruments back into his pockets. He looked at the banks of dials and switches, at the control columns still moving of their own accord. In the dim light from the battery of dials his features seemed suddenly much older, and unbearably weary.

"You are part of this crew, Miss Benson, so I'll be blunt." His voice was so hard that she flinched. "Can you face some unpleasant facts?"

"I—I think so." In spite of herself, she faltered.

"Very well. Unless I can get all these people to a hospital quickly—very quickly—I can't even be sure of saving their lives."

"But that's terrible."

"They need stimulants, intravenous injections for shock. The captain too. He's held out too long."

"Is he very bad?"

"It will soon become critical—and that goes for the others as well."

Barely audible, Janet whispered, "Doctor—what are we going to do?"

"Let me ask you a question. How many passengers are on board?"

"Fifty-six."

"How many fish dinners did you serve?"

Janet struggled to remember. "About fifteen, I think. More people had meat than fish, and some didn't eat at all as it was so late."

"I see."

Baird regarded her steadily. When he spoke again his voice was harsh, almost belligerent.

"Miss Benson, did you ever hear of long odds?"

Janet tried to focus on what he was saying.

"Long odds? Yes, I suppose so. I don't know what it means."

"I'll tell you," said Baird. "It means this. Out of a total field of fifty-five our one chance of survival depends on there being a person aboard this airplane who is not only qualified to land it but who also didn't have fish for dinner tonight."

His words hung between them as they stood there, staring at each other.

CHAPTER FIVE: 0245-0300

CALMNESS, like an anodyne cushioning the shock, descended on Janet as the words of the doctor penetrated her mind. She met his eyes steadily, well aware of his unspoken injunction to prepare herself for death.

Until now part of her had refused to accept what was happening. While she busied herself tending the passengers and trying to comfort the sick, something had insisted that this was an evil nightmare, the sort of dream in which an everyday sequence of events is suddenly deflected into one of mounting horror by some totally unexpected but quite logical incident. At any moment, her inner voice had told her, she would wake up to find half the bedclothes on the floor and the travelling clock on her locker buzzing to herald another early-morning scramble to get ready before take-off.

Now that sense of unreality was swept away. She knew it was happening, really happening, to her, Janet Benson, the pretty twenty-one-year-old blonde who had learned to expect the turning glances of airport staff as she walked briskly along the pine-smelling corridors. Fear had gone from her, at least for the moment. She wondered, in the passing thought of an instant, what her family at home were doing, how it was possible for her life to be extinguished in a few seconds' madness of shrieking metal without those who had borne her feeling even a tremor as they slept peacefully a thousand miles away.

"I understand, doctor," she said levelly.

"Do you know of anyone on board with any experience of flying?"

She cast her mind over the passenger list, recalling the names. "There's no one from the airline," she said. "I don't know . . . about anyone else. I suppose I'd better start asking."

"Yes, you'd better," said Baird slowly. "Whatever you do, try not to alarm them. Otherwise we may start a panic. Some of them know the first officer is sick. Just say the captain wondered if there's someone with flying experience who could help with the radio."

"Very well, doctor," said Janet quietly. "I'll do that."

She hesitated, as Baird obviously had something more to say. "Miss Benson—what's your Christian name?" he asked.

"Janet," she told him in some surprise.

He nodded. "Janet—I think I made some remark earlier on about your training. It was unjustified and unforgivable—the comment of a stupid old man who could have done with more training himself. I'd like to take it back."

Some of the colour returned to her cheeks as she smiled. "I'd forgotten it," she said. She moved towards the door, anxious to begin her questioning and to know the worst as quickly as she could. But Baird's face was puckered in an effort of concentration, as if something at the back of his mind was eluding him. He frowned at the painted emergency-escape instructions on the side of the cabin, not seeing them.

"Wait," he told her.

"Yes?" She paused, her hand on the catch of the door.

He snapped his fingers and turned to her. "I've got it. I knew someone had spoken to me about airplanes. That young fellow in the seat next to mine—the one who joined us at the last minute at Winnipeg—"

"Mr. Spencer?"

"That's him. George Spencer. I forget exactly but he seemed to know something about flying. Get him up here, will you? Don't tell him more than I've just said—we don't want the other passengers to know the truth. But carry on asking them, too, in case there's someone else."

"He just offered to help me," said Janet, "so he must be unaffected by the food."

"Yes, you're right," exclaimed Baird. "We both had meat. Get him, Janet."

He paced the narrow cabin nervously while she was gone, then knelt to feel the pulse of the captain lying flat and unconscious beside the first officer. At the first sound of the door behind him he jumped to his feet, blocking the entrance. Spencer stood there, looking at him in bewilderment.

"Hullo, doc," the young man greeted him. "What's this about the radio?"

"Are you a pilot?" Baird shot out, not moving.

"A long time ago. In the war. I wouldn't know about radio procedures now, but if the captain thinks I can—"

"Come in," said Baird.

He stepped aside, closing the door quickly behind the young man. Spencer's head snapped up at the sight of the pilot's empty seats and the controls moving by themselves. Then he wheeled round to the two men stretched on the floor under their blankets.

"No!" he gasped. "Not both of them?"

"Yes," said Baird shortly, "both of them."

Spencer seemed hardly able to believe his eyes. "But—heavens above, man—" he stuttered, "when did it happen?"

"The captain went down a few minutes ago. They both had fish."

Spencer put out a hand to steady himself, leaning against a junction box of cables on the wall.

"Listen," said Baird urgently. "Can you fly this aircraft—and land it?"

"No!" Shock stabbed at Spencer's voice. "Definitely no! Not a chance!"

"But you just said you flew in the war," Baird insisted.

"That was ten years ago. I haven't touched a plane since. And I was on fighters—tiny Spitfires about an eighth of the size of this ship and with only one engine. This has four. The flying characteristics are completely different."

Spencer's fingers, shaking slightly, probed his jacket for cigarettes, found a packet and shook one out. Baird watched him as he lit up.

"You could have a go at it," he pressed.

Spencer shook his head angrily. "I tell you, the idea's crazy," he snapped. "You don't know what's involved. I wouldn't be able to take in a Spitfire now, let alone this." He jabbed his cigarette towards the banks of instruments.

"It seems to me flying isn't a thing you'd forget," said Baird, watching him closely.

"It's a different kind of flying altogether. It's—it's like driving an articulated sixteen-wheeler truck in heavy traffic when all you've driven before is a fast sports job on open roads."

"But it's still driving," persisted Baird. Spencer did not answer, taking a long draw on his cigarette. Baird shrugged and half turned away. "Well," he said, "let's hope then there's someone else who can fly this thing—neither of these men can." He looked down at the pilots.

The door opened and Janet came into the flight deck. She glanced inquiringly at Spencer, then back at the doctor. Her voice was flat.

"There's no one else," she said.

"That's it, then," said the doctor. He waited for Spencer to speak but the younger man was staring forward at the row upon row of luminous dials and switches. "Mr. Spencer," said Baird, measuring his words with deliberation. "I know nothing of flying. All I know is this. There are several people on this plane who will die within a few hours if they don't get to hospital soon. Among those left who are physically able to fly the plane, you are the only one with any kind of qualification to do so." He paused. "What do you suggest?"

Spencer looked from the girl to the doctor. He asked tensely, "You're quite sure there's no chance of either of the pilots recovering in time?"

"None at all, I'm afraid. Unless I can get them to hospital quickly I can't even be sure of saving their lives."

The young salesman exhaled a lungful of smoke and ground the rest of his cigarette under his heel.

"It looks as if I don't have much choice, doesn't it?" he said.

"That's right. Unless you'd rather we carried on until we were out of gas—probably half way across the Pacific."

"Don't kid yourself this is a better way." Spencer stepped forward to the controls and looked ahead at the white sea of cloud below them, glistening in the moonlight. "Well," he said, "I guess I'm drafted. You've got yourself a new driver, doc." He slipped into the left-hand pilot's seat and glanced over his shoulder at the two behind him. "If you know any good prayers you'd better start brushing up on them."

Baird moved up to him and slapped his arm lightly. "Good man," he said with feeling.

"What are you going to tell the people back there?" asked Spencer, running his eye over the scores of gauges in front of him and racking his memory to recall some of the lessons he had learnt in a past that now seemed very far away.

"For the moment—nothing," answered the doctor.

"Very wise," said Spencer drily. He studied the bewildering array of instrument dials. "Let's have a look at this mess. The flying instruments must be in front of each pilot. That means that the centre panel will probably be engines only. Ah—here we are: altitude 20,000. Level flight. Course 290. We're on automatic pilot —thank the good Lord for that. Airspeed 210 knots. Throttles, pitch, trim, mixture, landing gear controls. Flaps? There should be an indicator somewhere. Yes, here it is. Well, they're the essentials anyway—I hope. We'll need a check list for landing, but we can get that on the radio."

"Can you do it?"

"I wouldn't know, doc—I just wouldn't know. I've never seen a set-up like this before in my life. Where are we now, and where are we going?"

"From what the captain said, we're over the Rockies," replied

Baird. "He couldn't turn off course earlier because of fog, so we're going through to Vancouver."

"We'll have to find out." Spencer looked about him in the soft glow. "Where *is* the radio control, anyway?"

Janet pointed to a switchbox above his head. "I know they use that to talk to the ground," she told him, "but I don't know which switches you have to set."

"Ah yes, let's see." He peered at the box. "Those are the frequency selectors—we'd better leave them where they are. What's this?—transmit." He clicked over a switch, lighting up a small red bulb. "That's it. First blood to George. Now we're ready for business."

Janet handed him a headset with the boom microphone attached. "I know you press the button on the mike when you speak," she said.

Adjusting the earphones, Spencer spoke to the doctor. "You know, whatever happens I'm going to need a second pair of hands up here in front. You've got your patients to look after so I think the best choice is Miss Canada here. What do you say?"

Baird nodded. "I agree. Is that all right, Janet?"

"I suppose so—but I know nothing about all this." Janet waved helplessly at the control panels.

"Good," said Spencer breezily, "that makes two of us. Sit down and make yourself comfortable—better strap yourself in. You must have watched the pilots quite a lot. They've added a lot of gimmicks since my flying days."

Janet struggled into the first officer's seat, taking care not to touch the control column as it swayed back and forth. There was an anxious knocking on the communication door.

"That's for me," said Baird. "I must get back. Good luck."

He left quickly. Alone with the stewardess, Spencer summoned up a grin.

"Okay?" he asked.

She nodded dumbly, preparing to put on a headset.

"The name's Janet, is it? Mine's George." Spencer's tone became serious. "I won't fool you, Janet. This will be tough."

"I know it."

"Well, let's see if I can send out a distress call. What's our flight number?"

"714."

"Right. Here goes, then." He pressed the button on his microphone. "Mayday, mayday, mayday," he began in an even voice. It was one signal he could never forget. He had called it one murky October afternoon above the French coast, with the tail of his Spitfire all but shot off, and two Hurricanes had mercifully appeared to usher him across the Channel like a pair of solicitous old aunts.

"Mayday, mayday, mayday," he continued. "This is Flight 714, Maple Leaf Air Charter, in distress. Come in, anyone. Over."

He caught his breath as a voice responded immediately over the air.

"Hullo, 714. This is Vancouver. We have been waiting to hear from you. Vancouver to all aircraft: this frequency is now closed to all other traffic. Go ahead, 714."

"Thank you, Vancouver. 714. We are in distress. Both pilots and several passengers . . . how many passengers, Janet?"

"It was five a few minutes ago. May be more now, though."

"Correction. At least five passengers are suffering from food poisoning. Both pilots are unconscious and in a serious condition. We have a doctor with us who says that neither pilot can be revived to fly the aircraft. If they and the passengers are not gotten to hospital quickly it may be fatal for them. Did you get that, Vancouver?"

The voice crackled back instantly, "Go ahead, 714. I'm reading you."

Spencer took a deep breath. "Now we come to the interesting bit. My name is Spencer, George Spencer. I am a passenger on this airplane. Correction: I *was* a passenger. I am now the pilot. For your information I have about a thousand hours total flying time, all of it on single-engined fighters. Also I haven't flown an airplane for nearly ten years. So you'd better get someone on this radio who can give me some instructions about flying this thing. Our altitude is 20,000, course 290 magnetic, airspeed 210 knots. That's the story. It's your move, Vancouver. Over."

"Vancouver to 714. Stand by."

Spencer wiped the gathering sweat from his forehead and grinned across to Janet. "Want to bet that's caused a bit of stir in the dovecotes down there?" She shook her head, listening intently to her earphones. In a few seconds the air was alive again, the voice as measured and impersonal as before.

"Vancouver to Flight 714. Please check with doctor on board for any possibility of either pilot recovering. This is important. Repeat, this is important. Ask him to do everything possible to revive one of them even if he has to leave the sick passengers. Over."

Spencer pressed his transmit button. "Vancouver, this is Flight 714. Your message is understood but no go, I'm afraid. The doctor says there is no possibility whatever of pilots recovering to make the landing. He says they are critically ill and may die unless they get hospital treatment soon. Over."

There was a slight pause. Then: "Vancouver Control to 714. Your message understood. Will you stand by, please."

"Roger, Vancouver," acknowledged Spencer and switched off again. He said to Janet, "We can only wait now while they think up what to do."

His hands played nervously with the control column in front of him, following its movements, trying to gauge its responsiveness as he attempted to call up the old cunning in him, the flying skill that had once earned for him quite a reputation in the squadron: three times home on a wing and a prayer. He smiled to himself as he recalled the wartime phrase. But in the next moment, as he looked blankly at the monstrous assembly of wavering needles and the unfamiliar banks of levers and switches, he felt himself in the grip of an icy despair. What had his flying in common with this? This was like sitting in a submarine, surrounded by the meaningless dials and instruments of science fiction. One wrong or clumsy move might shatter in a second the even tenor of their flight; if it did, who was to say that he could bring the aircraft under control again? All the chances were that he couldn't. This time there would be no comforting presence of Hurricanes to shepherd him home. He began to curse the head office which had whipped him away from Winnipeg to go trouble-shooting across to Vancouver at a moment's notice. The prospect of a sales manager's appointment and the lure of a house on Parkway Heights now seemed absurdly trivial and unimportant. It would be damnable to end like this, not to see Mary again, not to say to her all the things that were still unspoken. As for Bobsie and Kit, the life insurance would not take them very far. He should have done more for those poor kids, the world's best.

A movement beside him arrested his thoughts. Janet was kneeling on her seat, looking back to where the still figures of the captain and the first officer lay on the floor.

"One of those a boy friend of yours?" he asked.

"No," said Janet hesitantly, "not really."

"Skip it," said Spencer, a jagged edge to his voice, "I understand. I'm sorry, Janet." He put a cigarette in his mouth and fumbled for matches. "I don't suppose this is allowed, is it, but maybe the airline can stretch a point."

In the sudden flare of the match she could see, very clearly, the fierce burning anger in his eyes.

CHAPTER SIX: 0300-0325

WITH an accelerating thunder of engines the last eastbound aircraft to take off from Vancouver that night had gathered speed along the wetly gleaming runway and climbed into the darkness. Its navigation lights, as it made the required circuit of the airport, had been shrouded in a damp clinging mist. Several other aircraft, in process of being towed back from their dispersal points to bays alongside the departure buildings, were beaded with moisture. It was a cold night. Runway staff, moving about their tasks in the yellow arc lights, slapped their gloved hands around themselves to keep warm. None of them spoke more than was necessary. One slowly taxi-ing aircraft came to a stop and cut its engines at a wave from the indicator torches of a ground man facing it in front. In the sudden silence the swish of its propellers seemed an intrusion. Normally busy Vancouver prepared itself with quiet competence for emergency.

Within the brightly lit control room the atmosphere was tense with the concentration. Replacing his telephone, the Controller lit a cigarette, wreathing himself in clouds of blue smoke as he studied a wall map. He turned to Burdick. Perched on the edge of a table, the plump manager of Maple Leaf Airline had just finished consulting again the clipboard of information he held in his hand.

"Right, Harry," said the Controller. His tone was that of a man running over his actions more to satisfy himself that everything had been done rather than to impart information to another. "As of now, I'm holding all departures for the east. We've got nearly an hour in which to clear the present outgoing traffic in other directions, leaving plenty of time in hand. After that everything scheduled outwards must wait until . . . until afterwards, anyway." The telephone buzzed. He snatched it up. "Yes? I see. Warn all stations and aircraft that we can accept incoming flights for the next forty-five minutes only. Divert everything with an

ETA later than that. All traffic must be kept well away from the east-west lane between Calgary and here. Got that? Good." He dropped the instrument back into its cradle and addressed an assistant who sat also holding a telephone. "Have you raised the fire chief yet?"

"Ringing his home now."

"Tell him he'd better get here—it looks like a big show. And ask the duty fire officer to notify the City Fire Department. They may want to move equipment into the area."

"I've done that. Vancouver Control here," said the assistant into his telephone. "Hold the line, please." He cupped his hand over the mouthpiece. "Shall I alert the Air Force?"

"Yes. Have them keep the zone clear of their aircraft."

Burdick hitched himself off the table. "That's a thought," he said. Great damp patches stretched from the armpits of his shirt.

"Have you any pilots here at the airport?" asked the Controller.

Burdick shook his head. "Not one," he said. "We'll have to get help."

The Controller thought rapidly. "Try Cross-Canada. They have most of their men based here. Explain the position. We'll need a man fully experienced with this type of aircraft who is capable of giving instruction over the air."

"Do you think there's a chance?"

"I don't know, but we've got to try. Can you suggest anything else?"

"No," said Burdick, "I can't. But I sure don't envy him that job."

The switchboard operator called, "The City Police again. Will you take them?"

"Put them on," said the Controller.

"I'll see the Cross-Canada people," said Burdick. "And I must ring Montreal and tell my chief what's happening."

"Do it through the main board, will you?" asked the Controller. "The one in here is getting snarled up." He lifted the telephone as Burdick hurried out of the room. "Controller speaking. Ah, inspector, I'm glad it's you. Yes . . . yes . . . that's fine. Now listen, inspector. We're in bad trouble, much worse than we thought. First, we may have to ask you if one of your cars can collect a pilot in town and bring him here just as fast as possible. Yes, I'll let you know. Second, in addition to the urgency of getting the passengers to hospital, there's now a very serious possibility that the plane will crash-land. I can't explain now but when the ship comes in she won't be under proper control." He listened for a moment to the man at the other end. "Yes, we've issued a general alarm. The Fire Department will have everything they've got standing by. The point is, I think the houses near the airport may be in some danger." He listened again. "Well, I'm glad you've suggested it. I know it's a hell of a thing to wake people in the middle of the night, but we're taking enough chances as it is. I can't guarantee at all that this plane will get down on the field. She's just as likely to pan down short or overshoot—that is, assuming she even gets this far. We're lucky that there are only those houses out towards Sea Island Bridge to worry about—they can be asked to stand by, can't they? We'll route her well clear of the city . . . Eh? . . . No, can't say yet. We'll probably try to bring her in from the west end of the main runway." Another pause, longer this time. "Thank you, inspector. I realize that of course and I wouldn't make the request if I didn't regard this as a major emergency. I'll keep in touch." The Controller clicked the telephone back, his face etched with worry. He asked the man at the radio panel, "Is 714 still standing by for us?" The despatcher nodded. "This," remarked the Controller to the room at large, "is going to be quite a night." He pulled out a handkerchief and wiped his face.

"The fire chief is on his way," reported his assistant. "I'm on to the Air Force now. They ask if they can give any assistance."

"We'll let them know, but I don't think so. Thank them." He returned to his study of the wall map, stuffing the handkerchief away in his pocket. Absently, his fingers probed an empty cigarette pack, then tossed it on the floor in disgust. "Anyone got any smokes?"

"Here, sir."

He accepted a cigarette and lighted it. "You'd better send down for some—and coffee for everyone, too. We're going to need it."

Burdick came back into the room, breathing noisily. "Cross-Canada say their best man is Captain Treleaven—they're ringing him now. He's at home and in bed, I suppose."

"I've arranged for a police escort if necessary."

"They'll take care of that. I've told them we need him in the worst way. Do you know Treleaven?"

"I've met him," said the Controller. "He's a good type. We're lucky he's available."

"Let's hope he is," grunted Burdick. "We can certainly use him."

"What about the big brass?"

"I've put a call in to my president. God help me."

The switchboard operator broke in. "I've got Seattle and Calgary waiting, sir. They want to know if we got the message from 714 clearly."

"Tell them yes," answered the Controller. "Say we shall work the aircraft direct but we'd appreciate them keeping a listening watch in case we meet with any reception trouble."

"Right, sir."

The Controller crossed to the radio panel and picked up the stand microphone. He nodded to the despatcher who threw a switch to transmit.

"Vancouver Control to Flight 714," he called.

Spencer's voice, when he replied, spluttered from an amplifier extension high up in a corner of the room. Since his mayday distress call all his conversation had been channelled through the loudspeaker. "714 to Vancouver. I thought you were lost."

"Vancouver to 714. This is the Controller speaking. We are organizing help. We shall call you again very soon. Meanwhile do nothing to interfere with the present set of the controls. Do you understand? Over."

Despite the distortion, the asperity in Spencer's voice came through like a knife. "714 to Vancouver. I thought I told you. I've never touched a job like this before. I certainly don't aim to start playing damn-fool tricks with the automatic pilot. Over."

The Controller opened his mouth as if to say something, then changed his mind. He signed off and said to his assistant, "Tell reception to get Treleaven up here as fast as hell when he arrives."

"Right, sir. The duty fire officer just checked back," reported the assistant. "He's clearing all runway vehicles and gas wagons well under cover before 714's ETA. The City Fire Department are bringing all the equipment they've got into the precincts."

"Good. When the fire chief gets here, I want a word with him. If 714 reaches us, I don't want our own trucks moving out to her along the field. If we get her down at all, she's not likely to stay in one piece."

Burdick said suddenly, "Hey, with the city departments on to this, we'll have the press at any time." He tapped his teeth with a fat forefinger, appalled at the possibilities. "This will be the worst thing that ever happened to Maple Leaf," he went on quickly. "Imagine it—it'll be front page everywhere. Plane-load of people, many of them sick. No pilot. Maybe civilian evacuation from those houses out towards the bridge. Not to mention—"

The Controller cut in, "You'd better let PR handle it from the start. Get Howard here, at the double. The board will know his home number." Burdick nodded to the switchboard operator, who ran his finger down an emergency list and then began to dial. "We can't duck the press on a thing like this, Harry. It's much too big. Cliff will know how to play it. Tell him to keep the papers off our backs. We've got work to do."

"What a night," Burdick groaned, picking up a telephone impatiently. "What happened to Doctor Davidson?" he demanded of the operator.

"Out on a night call and can't be reached. He's due back pretty soon. I've left a message."

"Wouldn't you know it? Everything has to happen tonight. If he doesn't check in in ten minutes, get the hospital. That doctor in 714 is maybe in need of advice. Come on, come on," Burdick breathed irritably into his telephone. "Wake up, Cliff, for Pete's sake. There's no reason why any one should sleep through this."

On the outskirts of the town another telephone was ringing incessantly, splitting the peacefulness of a small, neat house with its shrill clamour. A smooth white arm emerged from bedclothes, rested motionless across a pillow, then stirred again and groped slowly in the darkness for the switch of a bedside lamp. The lamp clicked on. With her eyes screwed up against the bright light, an attractive redhead in a white embroidered nightdress reached painfully for the telephone, then brought it to her ear and turned on her side. Peering at the hands of the little bedside clock, she mumbled, "Yes?"

"Is this Mrs. Treleaven?" demanded a crisp voice.

"Yes," she said, practically in a whisper. "Who is it?"

"Mrs. Treleaven, may I speak to your husband?"

"He's not here."

"Not there? Where can I find him, please? This is urgent."

She propped herself up on her pillow, trying to blink herself awake. The thought occurred to her that she was dreaming.

"Are you there?" asked the voice at the other end. "Mrs. Treleaven, we've been trying to reach you for several minutes."

"I took a sleeping pill," she said. "Look, who's calling at this time of night?"

"I'm sorry to wake you, but it's imperative that we contact Captain Treleaven without delay. This is Cross-Canada, at the airport."

"Oh." She gathered herself together. "He's at his mother's place. His father is ill and my husband is helping to sit with him."

"Is it in town?"

"Yes, not far from here." She gave the telephone number.

"Thank you. We'll ring him there."

"What's wrong?" she asked.

"I'm sorry—there isn't time to explain. Thank you again."

The line was dead. She replaced the receiver and swung her legs out of bed. As the wife of a senior pilot of an airline she was accustomed to unexpected duty calls on her husband, but although she had grown to accept them as an unavoidable part of his life, part of her still resented them. Was Paul the only pilot they ever thought of when they were in a fix? Well, if he was having to take over a plane in a hurry, he would need to call home first for his uniform and gear. There would be time to make up a flask of coffee and some sandwiches. She drew on a robe and stumbled sleepily out of the bedroom and down the stairs towards the kitchen.

Two miles away, Paul Treleaven slept deeply, his large frame stretched along the chesterfield in his mother's parlour. That determined and vigorous old lady had insisted on taking a spell by the side of her sick husband, ordering her son firmly to rest for a couple of hours while he could. The news from the family doctor the previous evening had been encouraging: the old man had passed the dangerous corner of his pneumonic fever and now it was a matter of careful nursing and attention. Treleaven had been thankful for the chance to sleep. Only thirty-six hours previously he had completed a flight from Tokyo, bringing back a parliamentary mission en route for Ottawa, and since then, with the crisis of his father's illness, there had been scant opportunity for more than an uneasy doze.

He was aroused by his arm being shaken. Immediately awake, he looked up to find his mother bending over him.

"All right, mother," he said heavily, "I'll take over now."

"No son, it isn't that. Dad's sleeping like a baby. It's the airport on the telephone. I told them you were trying to snatch some rest, but they insisted. I think it's disgraceful—just as if they can't wait until a respectable hour in the morning."

"Okay. I'll come."

Getting to his feet, he wondered if he were ever going to sleep properly again. He was already half-dressed, having removed only his jacket and tie so as to lie comfortably on the chesterfield. He padded in stockinged feet to the door and out to the telephone in the hall, his mother following anxiously behind him.

"Treleaven," he said.

"Thank heaven, Paul. This is Jim Bryant," announced his caller rapidly. "I was getting really worried. We need you, Paul, but bad. Can you come over right away?"

"Why, what's up?"

"We're in real trouble here. There's a Maple Leaf Charter—it's an Empress C6, one of the refitted jobs—on its way from Winnipeg with a number of passengers and both pilots seriously ill with food poisoning."

"What! *Both* pilots?"

"That's right. It's top emergency. Some fellow is at the controls who hasn't flown for years. Fortunately the ship is on auto pilot. Maple Leaf haven't got a man here and we want you to come in and talk her down. Think you can do it?"

"Great Scott, I don't know. It's a tall order." Treleaven looked at his wrist watch. "What's the ETA?"

"0505."

"But that's under two hours. We've got to move! Look, I'm on the south side of town—"

"What's your address?" Treleaven gave it. "We'll have a police car pick you up in a few minutes. When you get here, go straight on up to the control room."

"Right. I'm on my way."

"And good luck, Paul."

"You're not kidding."

He dropped the phone and strode back to the parlour, pulling on his shoes without stopping to tie the laces. His mother held out his jacket for him.

"What is it, son?" she asked apprehensively.

"Trouble over at the airport, mother. Bad trouble, I'm afraid. There's a police car coming to take me there."

"Police!"

"Now, now." He put an arm around her for a second. "It's nothing for you to worry about. But they need my help. I'll have to leave you for the rest of the night." He looked round for his pipe and tobacco and put them in his pocket. "Just a minute," he said, stopping in his tracks. "How did they know I was here?"

"I couldn't say. Perhaps they rang Dulcie first."

"Yes, that must be it. Would you give her a ring, mother, and let her know everything is all right?"

"Of course I will. But what is the trouble about, Paul?"

"A pilot is sick on an aircraft due here soon. They want me to talk it down, if I can."

His mother looked puzzled. "What do you mean—talk it down?" she repeated. "If the pilot's sick, who's going to fly it?"

"I am, mother—from the ground. Or I'm going to try to, anyway."

"I don't understand."

Maybe I don't either, Treleaven thought to himself five minutes later, seated in the back of a police car as it pulled away from the sidewalk and slammed viciously into top gear. Street lights flashed past them in ever-quickening succession; the speedometer crept steadily round to seventy-five as the siren sliced into the night.

"Looks like a big night over at the field," remarked the police sergeant beside the driver, talking over his shoulder.

"So I gather," said Treleaven. "Can you fill me in on exactly what's happening?"

"Search me." The sergeant spat out of the window. "All I know is that every available car has been sent over to the airport to work from there in case the bridge estate has to be cleared. We were on our way there too until they stopped us and sent us back for you. I'd say they're expecting a hell of a bang."

"You know what," interjected the young driver. "It's my guess there's a busted-up Stratojet coming in with a nuclear bombload."

"Do me a favour," said the sergeant with heavy scorn. "Your trouble is you read too many comics."

Never, Treleaven reflected grimly to himself, had he reached the airport so quickly. In no time, or so it seemed, they had reached Marpole and crossed Oak Bridge to Lulu Island. Then, bearing right, they crossed the river estuary again to Sea Island and past occasional police cruisers whose crews were already talking to bewildered houseowners in doorways, until they were speeding along the last stretch of Airport Road, the lights of the long, low airport buildings beckoning them on. They braked suddenly, with a protesting screech of tyres, to avoid a fire engine which was making a leisurely U-turn ahead of them. The sergeant swore, briefly but with feeling.

At the main reception building, Treleaven was out of the car, through the doors and had crossed the concourse before the wail of the siren died. Waving aside the commissionaire who hurried across to meet him, he made his way directly to the control room in the administration block. He could move remarkably fast for a man of his size. It was probably that loose-limbed agility which combined with a solidly built physique, lank fair hair and hard lean features, to make him an object of interest to many women. His features, angular and crooked, looked as if they had been inexpertly carved from a chunk of wood. Treleaven had a considerable reputation as a disciplinarian and more than one erring crew-member had had cause to fear the cold light in those pale, almost watery-blue eyes.

He entered Control as Burdick was speaking anxiously and deferentially on the telephone.

". . . No, sir, he isn't qualified. He flew single-engine fighters in the war; nothing since . . . I've asked them that. This doctor on board says . . ."

The Controller stepped quickly over to greet Treleaven. "I'm certainly glad to see you, captain," he said.

Treleaven nodded towards Burdick. "Is that the fellow in the Empress he's talking about?" he asked.

"Yes. He's just got his president out of bed in Montreal. The old man sounds far from happy about it—and so am I. The call shouldn't have come in here. Hurry it up, Harry, will you?"

"What else can we do?" pleaded Burdick into the telephone, sweating profusely. "We've got to talk him down. I've located Cross-Canada's chief pilot, Captain Treleaven—he just walked in the door now. We'll get on the radio with a check list and try to bring him in . . . We'll do the best we can, sir . . . Of course it's a terrible risk, but can you think of something better?"

Treleaven took from the despatcher the clipboard of messages from 714 and read them carefully. With a quiet request, "Weather," he then consulted the latest meteorological reports. This done, he laid the papers down, raised his eyebrows sombrely at the Controller, and produced his pipe which he proceeded to fill. Burdick was still speaking.

". . . I've thought of that, sir. Howard will handle the press at this end—they aren't on to it yet . . . Yes, yes, we've suspended food service on all flights ex-Winnipeg. That's all we know. I called you right away . . ."

"What do you think?" the Controller asked Treleaven.

The pilot shrugged without answering and picked up the clipboard again. His face was set in deep lines as he read the messages again, drawing steadily on his pipe. A young man backed into the room, holding the door open with his leg as he manoeuvred a tray bearing cardboard cartons of coffee. He handed a carton to the Controller and set another down in front of Treleaven. The pilot ignored it.

". . . ETA is 0505 Pacific Time," Burdick was saying with increasing exasperation. "I've a lot to do, sir . . . I'll have to get on with it . . . I'll call you . . . I'll call you as soon as I know anything more . . . Yes, yes . . . G'bye." Putting down the telephone, he blew out his cheeks with relief. Turning to Treleaven, he said, "Thank you very much for coming, captain. Have you got it all?"

Treleaven held up the clipboard. "This is the whole story?"

"That's everything we know. Now I want you to get on the horn and talk this guy down. You'll have to let him get the feel of the airplane on the way, you'll have to give him the landing check, you'll have to talk him on to the approach, and—so help me!—you'll have to talk him right down on to the ground. Can you do it?"

"I can't perform a miracle," said Treleaven evenly. "You know that the chances of a man who has only flown fighter airplanes, landing a four-engine passenger ship are pretty slim, to say the least?"

"Of course I know it!" Burdick exploded. "You heard what I told Barnard. But do *you* have any other ideas?"

"No," Treleaven said slowly, "I guess not. I just wanted to be sure you knew what we were getting into."

"Listen," shouted Burdick angrily. "There's a ship full of people up there, some of them dying, including the pilots. The biggest air disaster in years, that's what we're getting into!"

"Keep your temper," said Treleaven coldly. "We'll get nowhere fast by shouting." He glanced down at the clipboard and then at the wall map. "This is going to be very tough and a very long shot," he said. "I want that fully understood."

"All right, gentlemen," said the Controller. "You are perfectly right to emphasize the risk, captain. We fully accept that."

"What choice is there?" Burdick demanded.

"Very well, then," said Treleaven. "Let's get started." He walked over to the radio operator. "Can you work 714 direct?"

"Yes, captain. Reception's good. We can call them any time."

"Do it then."

The operator switched to transmit. "Flight 714. This is Vancouver. Do you read? Over."

"Yes, Vancouver," came Spencer's voice through the amplifier. "We hear you clearly. Go ahead, please."

The operator handed the stand microphone to Treleaven. "Okay, captain. It's all yours."

"Am I on the air?"

"Go ahead now."

Holding the stand microphone in his hand, its cable trailing to the floor, Treleaven turned his back on the other men in the room. Legs braced apart, he stared unseeingly at a point on the wall map, his cold eyes distant in concentration. His voice, when he spoke, was steady and unhurried, easy with a confidence he did not feel. As he began, the other men visibly relaxed, as if his natural authority had temporarily relieved them of a crushing responsibility.

"Hullo, Flight 714," he said. "This is Vancouver. My name is Paul Treleaven and I'm a Cross-Canada Airlines captain. My job is to help you fly this airplane in. We shouldn't have too much trouble. I see that I'm talking to George Spencer. I'd like to hear a little more about your flying experience, George."

Behind him, the flabby folds of Burdick's honest face had begun to shake in an uncontrollable spasm of nervous reaction.

CHAPTER SEVEN: 0325-0420

SPENCER tensed, shooting an involuntary glance at the girl in the seat beside him. Her eyes, in the greenish glow of the instrument panel, were fixed on his face. He looked away again, listening intently.

Treleaven was saying, "For instance, how many flying hours have you had? The message here says you've flown single-engine fighters. Have you had any experience at all of multi-engined planes? Let's hear from you, George."

Spencer's mouth was so dry when he replied that at first he could hardly speak. He cleared his throat.

"Hullo, Vancouver. 714 here. Glad to have you along, captain. But let's not kid each other, please. I think we both know the situation. My flying up to now has been entirely on single-engine aircraft, Spitfires and Mustangs—I'd say about a thousand hours in all. But that was nine, ten years ago. I've touched nothing since. Do you understand that? Over."

"Don't worry about that, George. It's like riding a bicycle—you never forget it. Stand by, will you?"

In the Vancouver Control, Treleaven pressed the cut-out button on the arm of the microphone in his hand and looked at a slip of paper the Controller held out for him to read.

"Try to get him on this course," said the Controller. "The Air Force have just sent in a radar check." He paused. "Sounds pretty screwed-up, doesn't he?"

"Yes—who wouldn't be, in his shoes?" Treleaven grimaced reflectively. "We've got to give him confidence," he said. "Without that there isn't a chance. Whatever happens, he mustn't lose his nerve. Keep it down, will you?" to the Controller's assistant who was talking on the telephone. "If this guy doesn't hear me clearly he'll be in trouble fast and there will be nothing we can do about it." Then, to the despatcher, "Okay. Make damn sure you don't lose them on the air." He released the cut-out. "714. This is Treleaven. You are still on auto pilot, right?"

"Yes, that's so, captain," came the reply.

"All right, George. In a minute you can disengage the auto pilot and get the feel of the controls. When you've had a bit of practice with them you are going to change your course a little. Listen very carefully, though, before you touch them. When you start handling the airplane the controls will seem very heavy and sluggish compared with a fighter. Don't let that worry you. It's quite normal. You've got a lot of airplane up there so take it nice and steady. Watch your airspeed all the time you are flying and don't let it fall below 120 knots while your wheels and flaps are up, otherwise you'll stall. I'll repeat that. Make absolutely sure at all times that your airspeed doesn't fall below 120 knots. Now, one other thing. Do you have someone up there who can work the radio and leave you free for flying?"

"Yes, Vancouver. I have the stewardess here with me and she'll take over the radio now. It's all yours, Janet."

"Hullo. Vancouver. This is the stewardess, Janet Benson. Over."

"Why, it's you, Janet," said Treleaven. "I'd know that voice anywhere. You're going to talk to George for me, are you? Good. Now Janet, I want you to keep your eyes on that airspeed indicator. Remember that an airplane stays in the air because of its forward speed. If you let the speed drop too low, it stalls and falls out of the air. Any time the ASI shows a reading near 120, you tell George instantly. Is that clear, Janet?"

"Yes, captain. I understand."

"Back to you, George. Take this slowly and smoothly. I want you to unlock the auto pilot—it's clearly marked on the control

column—and take the airplane yourself, holding her straight and
level. George, you watch the inclinometer on the panel. Janet,
you watch the airspeed. 120, remember—keep above that. All
right, then. Start now."

Spencer put down his right hand and grasped the unlocking
device of the auto pilot. His face was rigid. Feet on the rudder
bar and left hand on the gently moving control column, he steeled
himself.

"Tell him I'm switching over now," he told Janet. She repeated
the message. His hand wavered for a moment on the lever. Then,
decisively, he threw it across. The aircraft swung a little to port
but he corrected the tendency gently and she responded well
enough to his feet on the rudder bar. The vibration from the controls seemed to flow through his body like an electric current.

"Tell him okay," he gasped, his nerves taut as cables.

"714 here. We're flying straight and level." Janet's voice
sounded miraculously sweet and calm to him.

"Well done, George. As soon as you've got the feel of her, try
some very gentle turns, not more than two or three degrees. Can
you see the turn indicator? It's almost directly in front of your
eyes and slightly to the right, just by the panel light shield. Over."
Treleaven's eyes were closed with the effort of visualizing the
cockpit layout. He opened them and spoke to the despatcher.
"Listen. I've got a lot of work to do with this man in the air, but
we ought to start planning the approach and landing while there's
plenty of time. Get the chief radar operator up here, will you, and
let me talk to him."

Very gingerly Spencer extended his left leg and eased the control column over. This time it seemed an age before the aircraft
responded to his touch and he saw a faint register on the indicator.
Gratified, he tried the other way; but now the movement was
alarming. He looked down at the ASI and was shocked to see that
it had dropped to 180 knots. Quickly he corrected the swing that
had developed and breathed again as the speed rose slowly to
210. He would have to treat the controls with the utmost respect
until he really understood the time lag; that was evident. Again
he pushed at the resisting weight of the rudder and gradually
felt the ship answer. This time he straightened it up before turning in the opposite direction, so as to maintain speed.

Janet had lifted her eyes momentarily from the instrument
panel to ask in a small voice, "How is it?"

Spencer tried to grin, without much success. The thought passed through his mind that this was rather like his days on the Link trainer all over again, only then nearly sixty lives did not hang in the balance and the instructor was not more than a few feet away in the same room. "Tell him I'm on manual and doing gentle turns, coming back on course each time," he said.

Janet gave the message.

"I should have asked you this before," came Treleaven's voice. "What kind of weather are you in up there?"

"It's clear where we are right now," answered Janet. "Except below us, of course."

"Uh-huh. You'd better keep me informed. Now, George, we have to press on. You may hit some cloud layer at any time, with a little turbulence. If you do, I want you to be ready for it. How does she handle?"

Spencer looked across to Janet. "Tell him—sluggish as hell, like a wet sponge," he said between clenched teeth.

"Hullo, Vancouver. As sluggish as a wet sponge," repeated Janet.

For a few brief seconds the tension at Vancouver Control eased and the group standing round the radio panel exchanged smiles.

"That's a natural feeling, George," said Treleaven, serious again, "because you were used to smaller airplanes. You'll have to expect it to feel even worse when you really throw her around up there, but you'll soon get used to it."

The despatcher cut in, "I've the radar chief here."

"He'll have to wait," said Treleaven. "I'll talk to him as soon as I get a break."

"Right."

"Hullo, George," called Treleaven. "You must avoid any violent movements of the controls, such as you used to make in your fighter airplanes. If you *do* move the controls violently, you will over-correct and be in trouble. Is that understood? Over."

"Yes, Vancouver, we understand. Over."

"Now, George, I want you to try the effect of fore and aft control on your airspeed. To start with, adjust your throttle setting so as to reduce speed to 160 and cruise straight and level. But watch the airspeed closely. Keep it over 120. The rudder trim is just below the throttles on the control pedestal and the aileron trim is under that. Got it? Over."

Spencer checked with his hand, holding the plane steady with the other and with braced legs. "Right. Tell him I'm reducing speed."

"Okay, Vancouver, we're doing as you say."

Time ticked away as the speed slowly dropped. At 160 George adjusted the trim tabs and held up his thumb to Janet.

"714 here, Vancouver. 160 knots on the indicator."

Treleaven waited until he had struggled out of his jacket before speaking. "Right, George. Try a little up and down movement. Use the control column as carefully as if it were full of eggs and watch the speed. Keep it at 160. Get the feel of the thing as you go along. Over." He put the microphone down. "Where's the radar chief?"

"Here."

"At what range will this aircraft show on your scope?" queried Treleaven.

"Sixty miles, thereabouts, captain."

"That's no good for a while, then. Well," said Treleaven, partly to himself, partly to Burdick, "you can't have everything at once. I've had to assume that he's still heading in a general westerly direction. Next call, though, we'll check his heading."

"Yeah," said Burdick. He offered a cigarette, which the pilot refused.

"If he's stayed on the same heading," continued Treleaven, looking at the wall map, "he can't be that much off course, and we can straighten him up when he gets in our radar range. That Air Force check is a help."

"Can't he come in on the beam?" asked Burdick.

"Right now he's got enough to worry about. If I try to get him on the beam, he'll have to mess around with the radio, changing frequencies and a lot of other stuff. I'd sooner take a chance, Harry, and let him go a few miles off course."

"That makes sense," Burdick conceded.

"Here's how we'll handle it," said the pilot. He turned to the radar chief. "I'll do the talking. He's getting used to me now."

"Right, sir."

"As soon as he shows up on your scope, you can feed me the information and I'll relay it. Can you fix up a closed circuit between me and the radar room?"

"We can take care of that," said the despatcher.

"How about the final approach?" asked the radar chief.

"We'll handle that the same way," said Treleaven. "Directly we've got him on the scope and he's steady on course, we'll move to the Tower. You report up there and we'll decide on the runway and plan the approach."

"Yes, sir."

Treleaven picked up the microphone but waited, his eye catching that of the Controller, who was replacing a telephone in its cradle.

"Doctor Davidson is downstairs," the Controller told him.

"What does he have to say?"

"From the information we've got he agrees with the diagnosis of the doctor in the plane. Seemed to wonder at first if it could be an outbreak of botulism."

"What's that, for Pete's sake?"

"Some very serious kind of food poisoning, apparently. Shall we get the doctor up here and put him on the air?"

"No, Mr. Grimsell. It's more important right now to fly this airplane. We'll leave it to them to call for medical advice if they want it. I don't want Spencer's mind distracted from the job if I can possibly help it. I should have Davidson stand by in case he's needed." Treleaven spoke into the microphone. "Hullo, George Spencer. Don't forget that lag in the controls. Just take it steadily. Do you understand that?"

There was a pause. Then, "He understands, Vancouver. Over."

To Spencer it seemed as if the airline captain must have read his thoughts. He had moved the column slowly forward, and then back again, but there had been no response from the aircraft. Now he tried again, easing the stick away from him. Imperceptibly at first, the nose of the aircraft began to dip. Then, so suddenly that he was momentarily paralysed with shock, it plunged downwards. Janet bit hard on her lip to avoid screaming. The ASI needle began to swing round . . . 180 . . . 190 . . . 200 . . . 220. Putting all his weight on the column, Spencer fought to bring the aircraft back. In front of him the instrument panel seemed alive. The climb and descent indicator quivered against the bottom of the glass. The little facsimile of a plane on the artificial horizon had depresssed its port wing and remained in that position, frighteningly. On the face of the altimeter the 100-foot hand whirred backwards; the 1,000-foot hand less quickly but still terrifyingly fast; while the 10,000-foot needle had already stopped, jammed at its nadir.

"Come on, you slug, come on!" he shouted as the nose at last responded. He watched the three altimeter needles begin with agonizing slowness to wind up again, registering gradually increasing height. "Made it!" he said in relief to Janet, forgetting that he was over-correcting.

"Watch it—watch the speed," she exclaimed.

His eyes flicked back to the dial, now rapidly falling again. 160 . . . 150 . . . 140. Then he had it. With a sigh the aircraft settled on to an even keel once more and he brought it into straight and level flight.

"Jeeze, that was nasty," he muttered.

Janet was still checking the ASI. "160. That's all right now."

The door to the flight deck opened behind them and Doctor Baird's voice called, "What's wrong?"

Spencer answered loudly, not removing his eyes from the panel, "Sorry, doc. I'm trying to get the feel of her."

"Well, take it as easy as you can, will you? Things are bad enough back here. How are you doing?"

"Fine, just fine, doc," said Spencer, licking his lips. The door closed again and Treleaven's voice came on the air.

"Hullo, George Spencer. Everything okay? Over."

"All under control, Vancouver," replied Janet.

"Good. What's your present heading, George?"

Spencer peered down. "Tell him the magnetic compass is still showing about 290 and I've been keeping fairly steady on that." She did so.

"Very well, George. Try to stay on that heading. You may be a little out, but I'll tell you when to correct. Right now I want you to feel how the ship handles at lower speeds when the flaps and wheels are down. But don't do anything until I give you the instructions. Is that clear? Over."

Janet got Spencer's nod and asked Treleaven to proceed.

"Hullo, 714. First of all, throttle back slightly, not much, and get your airspeed steady at 160 knots. Adjust your trim to maintain level flight. Then tell me when you're ready. Over."

Spencer straightened himself and called over, "Watch that airspeed, Janet. You'll have to call it off to me when we land, so you may as well start practising now."

"It's on 190," Janet recited. "200 . . . 190 . . . He said 160, Mr. Spencer."

"I know, I know. I'm going to throttle back a bit."

He reached out for the throttles and eased them back. "What is it, Janet? What's the speed?"

"190, 180, 175, 170, 165, 155, 150 . . . That's too low!"

"I know. Watch it! Watch it!"

His hand nursed the throttle levers, almost caressing them into the exact positioning to achieve the speed he wanted,

Janet's eyes were riveted on the flickering needle of the dial.

"150, 150, 155, 160 . . . It's—it's steady on 160."

Spencer puffed out his cheeks. "Phew! That's got it. Tell him, Jan."

"Hullo, Vancouver. Our speed is steady on 160. Over."

Treleaven sounded impatient, as if he had expected them to be ready before this. "Okay, 714. Now, George. I want you to put on 15 degrees of flap, but be careful not to make it any more. The flap lever is at the base of the control pedestal and marked plainly: 15 degrees will mean moving the lever down to the second notch. The flap indicator dial is in the centre of the panel—the main panel. Have you got both of those? Can you see them? Over."

Spencer located the lever. "Confirm that," he told Janet, "but *you'd* better do it. Right?"

She acknowledged to Vancouver and sat waiting, her hand on the lever.

"Hullo, 714. When I tell you, push it all the way down and watch that dial. When the needle reaches 15 degrees, pull the lever up and leave it at the second notch. You'll have to watch and be ready for it. Those flaps come down in a hurry. All clear?"

"We're ready, Vancouver," said Janet.

"Right. Go ahead, then."

She prepared to depress the lever, then jerked her head up in alarm.

"The airspeed! It's down to 125."

"My God!" Spencer pushed the control column forward and roared, "Call it off! Call it off!"

The lurch of the aircraft brought their stomachs to their mouths. Janet almost crouched in front of the panel, intoning the figures.

"135, 140, 150, 160, 170, 175 . . . Can't you get it back to 160?"

"I'm trying, I'm trying." Again he levelled off and jockeyed the controls until the ASI had been coaxed back to the reading required. He passed his sleeve hurriedly over his forehead, afraid to remove his hand from the column for long enough to get out a handkerchief. "There it is. 160, isn't it?"

"Yes, that's better."

"Thank God." Spencer sat back in his seat. "Look, let's relax for a minute, after that." He managed to muster up a smile. "You can see the kind of pilot I am. I should have known that would happen."

"No, it was my job to watch the airspeed." She took a deep

breath to steady her pounding heart. "I think you're doing wonderfully," she said. Her voice shook slightly.

It was not lost on Spencer. He said quickly and with exaggerated heartiness, "You can't say I didn't warn you. Come on, then, Janet. Let's get going."

"Hullo, George," Treleaven's voice crackled in the earphones. "Are your flaps down yet?"

"We're just about to put them down, captain," said Janet.

"Hold it. I omitted to tell you that when the flaps are down you will lose speed. Bring it back to 140. Over."

"Well, I'll be—!" Spencer ejaculated. "That's mighty nice of him. He cut it pretty fine."

"It's probably hectic down there," said Janet, who had a very good idea of the scene taking place at the airport. "Thank you, captain," she said, transmitting. "We're starting now. Over." At a nod from Spencer she pushed the lever down as far as it would go, while Spencer watched the indicator carefully.

"Right. Now back to second notch."

With infinite caution he cajoled the ASI needle until it rested steadily at 140.

"Tell him, Janet."

"Hullo, Vancouver. Our flaps are down 15 degrees and the airspeed is 140."

"714. Are you still maintaining level flight?"

Spencer nodded to her. "Tell him, yes—well, more or less, anyway."

"Hullo, Vancouver. More or less."

"Okay, 714. Now the next thing is to put the wheels down. Then you'll get the feel of the airplane as it will be when you're landing. Try to keep your altitude steady and your speed at 140. When you are ready—and make sure you *are* ready—put down the landing gear and let the speed come back to 120. You will probably have to advance your throttle setting to maintain that airspeed, and also adjust the trim. Is that understood? Tell me if you are doubtful about anything. Over."

"Ask him," said Spencer, "What about propeller controls and mixture?"

At Janet's question, Treleaven said in an aside to Burdick, "Well, this guy's thinking, anyway. For the time being," he said into the microphone, "leave them alone. Just concentrate on holding that airspeed steady with the wheels and flaps down. Later on I'll give you a full cockpit check for landing. Over."

"Tell him, understood," said Spencer. "We're putting down the wheels now." He looked apprehensively at the selector lever by his leg. It seemed a much better idea to keep both hands on the column. "Look, Janet, I think you'd better work the undercart lever and call off the airspeed as the wheels come down."

Janet complied. The arrest in their forward flight was so pronounced that it was like applying a brake, jerking them in their seats.

"130, 125, 120, 115 ... It's too low."

"Keep calling!"

"115, 120, 120 ... Steady on 120."

"I'll get this thing yet," Spencer panted. "She's like the Queen Mary."

Treleaven's voice came up, with a hint of anxiety. "All okay, George? Your wheels should be down by now."

"Wheels down, Vancouver."

"Look for three green lights to show you that they're locked. Also there's a pressure gauge on the extreme left of the centre panel, and the needle should be in the green range. Check."

"Are they on?" asked Spencer. Janet looked and nodded. "Better tell him, then."

"Yes, Vancouver. All correct."

"And say she still handles like a wet sponge, only more so."

"Hullo, Vancouver. The pilot says she still handles like a sponge, only more so."

"Don't worry about that. Now we'll put on full flaps, shall we, and then you'll have the proper feel of the aircraft on landing. You'll soon get the hang of it. Now follow me closely. Put full flap on, bring your airspeed back to 110 knots and trim to hold you steady. Adjust the throttle to maintain the altitude. Then I'll give you instructions for holding your height and airspeed while you raise the landing gear and flaps. Over."

"Did you say 110, captain?" Janet queried nervously.

"110 is correct, Janet. Follow me exactly and you'll have nothing to worry about. Are you quite clear, George?"

"Tell him, yes. We are putting on full flap now."

Once more her hand pushed hard on the flap lever and the airspeed started to fall.

"120, 115, 115, 110, 110 ..."

Spencer's voice was tight with the effort of will he was imposing on himself. "All right, Janet. Let him know. By God, she's a ton weight."

"Hullo, Vancouver. Flaps are full on and the airspeed is 110. Mr. Spencer says she is heavier than ever."

"Nice going, George. We'll make an airline pilot of you yet. Now we'll get you back to where you were and then run through the procedure again, with certain variations regarding props, mixture, boosters and so on. Okay? Over."

"Again!" Spencer groaned. "I don't know if I can take it. All right, Janet."

"Okay, Vancouver. We're ready."

"Right, 714. Using the reverse procedure, adjust your flaps to read 15 degrees and speed 120 knots. You will have to throttle back slightly to keep that speed. Go ahead."

Reaching down, Janet grasped the flap lever and gave it a tug. It failed to move. She bent closer and tried again.

"What is it?" asked Spencer.

"Sort of stiff. I can't seem to move it this time."

"Shouldn't be. Give it a good steady pull."

"It must be me. I just can't make it budge."

"Here. Let me." He took his hand off the column and pulled the lever back effortlessly. "There, you see. You've got to have the touch. Now if you'll just rest it in the second—"

"Look out!" she screamed. "The airspeed!"

It was 90, moving to 75.

Bracing himself against the sudden acute angle of the flight deck, Spencer knew they were in a bad stall, an incipient spin. Keep your head, he ordered himself savagely—*think*. If she spins, we're finished. Which way is the stall? It's to the left. Try to remember what they taught you at flying school. Stick forward and hard opposite rudder. *Stick forward*. Keep it forward. We're gaining speed. Opposite rudder. Now! Watch the instruments. They can't be right—I can feel us turning! No—trust them. You must trust them. Be ready to straighten. That's it. Come on. Come on, lady, *come on*.

"The mountains!" exclaimed Janet. "I can see the ground!"

Ease back. Ease back. Not too fast. Hold the airspeed steady. We're coming out . . . we're coming out! Good Lord God, we're coming out!

"105, 110, 115 . . ." Janet read off in a strangled tone. "It's completely black now. We must be in fog or something."

"Get the wheels up!"

"The mountains! We must—"

"Get the wheels up, I said!"

The door to the flight deck crashed open. There were sounds of crying and angry voices.

"What are they doing?" came a yell from a woman.

"There's something wrong! I'm going to find out what it is!"

"Get back to your seat." This was Baird's voice.

"Let me through!"

The silhouette of a man filled the doorway, peering into the darkness of the flight deck. He lurched forward, grabbing hold of anything to keep himself upright, and stared in petrified disbelief at the back of Spencer's head and then down at the prostrate figures of the two men on the floor. For a moment his mouth worked soundlessly. Then he impelled himself back to the open doorway and gripped the jamb on both sides as he leaned through it.

His voice was a shriek.

"He's not the pilot! We shall all be killed! We're going to crash!"

CHAPTER EIGHT: 0420-0435

WREATHED in woolly haloes, the neon lights at the entrance to the reception building at Vancouver Airport glistened back from the wet driveway. Usually quiet at this pre-dawn hour of the night, except for the periodic arrival or departure of an airport coach, the wide sweep of asphalt now presented a very different scene. At the turn-off from the main highway into the airport approach on the mainland side of the river, a police cruiser stood angled partly across the road, its roof-light blinking a constant warning. Those cars which had been allowed through along Airport Road were promptly waved by a patrolman to parking spaces well clear of the entrance to Reception. Some of their occupants remained out in the damp night air for a while, talking in low voices and stamping the ground occasionally to keep warm, in order to watch the arrival from time to time of fire engines and ambulances as they halted for a few seconds to receive directions to their assembly points. A gleaming red salvage truck engaged gear and roared away, and in the small pool of silence immediately following its noise the sound of a car radio carried clearly across for several yards.

"Ladies and gentlemen, here is a late bulletin from Vancouver Airport. The authorities here stress that although the Maple Leaf

Airline flight is being brought in by an inexperienced pilot, there is no cause for alarm or panic in the city. All precautions are being taken to warn residents in the airport area and at this moment emergency help is streaming out to Sea Island. Stay with this station for further announcements."

A mud-streaked Chevrolet braked harshly at the reception building, swung over to the parking lot, its tyres squealing viciously on the asphalt, and stopped abruptly. On the left-hand side of its windscreen was pasted a red sticker, PRESS. A big man, thick-set with greying hair, and wearing an open trenchcoat, got out and slammed the door. He walked rapidly over to Reception, nodded to the patrolman and hurried inside. Dodging two interns in white medical coats, he looked round for the Maple Leaf Airline desk and made his way over to it quickly. Two men stood there in discussion with a uniformed staff member of the airline, and at the touch of the big man one of them turned, smiling briefly in greeting.

"What's the score, Terry?" asked the big man.

"I've given the office what I've got, Mr. Jessup," said the other man, who was very much younger. "This is Ralph Jessup— Canadian International News," he added to the passenger agent.

"Who's handling it here?" asked Jessup.

"I think Mr. Howard is about to make a statement in the press room," said the passenger agent.

"Let's go," said Jessup. He took the younger man by the arm and drew him away. "Is the office sending up a camera team?" he asked.

"Yes, but there'll be a pretty full coverage by everyone. Even the newsreels may make it in time."

"H'm. Remind the office to cover the possible evacuation of houses over near the bridge. The same man can stay on the boundary of the field. If he climbs the fence he may get one or two lucky shots of the crash—and get away quicker than the others. What about this guy who is flying the plane?"

"A George Spencer of Toronto. That's all we know."

"Well, the office will get our Toronto stringer on to that end. Now grab a pay booth in Reception here and don't budge out of it, whatever happens. Keep the line open to the office."

"Yes, Mr. Jessup, but—"

"I know, I know," said Jessup sadly, "but that's the way it is. If there's a foul-up on the phones in the press room, we'll need that extra line."

His coat flapping behind him, he strode across the concourse, head down like an angry bull, out of Reception and along to the press room. There several newsmen were already foregathered, three of them talking together, another rattling at one of the six or eight typewriters on the large centre table, and a further couple using two of the telephone booths that lined two sides of the panelled room. On the floor were dumped leather cases of camera equipment.

"Well," said Jessup sardonically, "what kept you boys?"

"Hi, Jess," greeted one of the men. "Where's Howard? Have you seen him?"

"On his way, I'm told." Jessup shook himself out a cigarette. "Well, who knows what?"

"We just got here," said Stephens of the *Monitor*. "I put a call in to the Controller's office and got blasted."

"You fellows have it easy on this one," Jessup remarked, lighting his cigarette and spitting out a shred of tobacco. "It's too late for the mornings and in plenty of time for the evenings, unless you put out special mid-morning runs. It's easy to see who's doing the work." He indicated the two men in the telephone cubicles, one from CP and the other UPA.

"Wrap it up, Jess," said Stephens. "To listen to you wire service fellers, you'd think—"

"Quit horsing around," cut in Abrahams of the *Post-Telegram*. "We'd better start shouting up for some action. Pretty soon all the others'll be here and we won't be able to move."

They turned as a youngish man entered, holding in his hand some slips of paper. This was Cliff Howard, high-spirited and energetic, whose crew-cut hair, rimless spectacles and quietly-patterned English neckties were a familiar and popular sight at the airport. He did not smile at the newsmen, although most of them were personal friends of his.

"Thanks for staying put," he told them.

"We very nearly didn't," returned Stephens. The two agency men had hurriedly terminated their calls and joined the others.

"Let's have it, Cliff," said one of them.

Howard looked at Jessup. "I see you've come straight from bed like me, Jess," he remarked, nodding at the pyjamas under Jessup's jacket.

"Yes," said Jessup shortly. "Come on, Cliff. Snap it up."

Howard glanced down at the papers in his hand, then back at

the men gathered round him. There was a film of perspiration on his forehead. "All right," he said. "Here it is. A Maple Leaf Empress was chartered in Toronto to bring supporters to the ball game today. On the Winnipeg leg to here both the pilot and the co-pilot have been taken ill. A passenger is at the controls. He hasn't had experience of this type of airplane before. We're talking him down—Captain Paul Treleaven, Cross-Canada's chief pilot, is on the job—but the authorities thought it advisable to take precautionary measures in clearing the area and bringing in extra help in case of accident."

There was a pause. "Well?" growled one of the newsmen.

"I guess there's not much more I can tell you," said Howard apologetically. "We're doing all we can and I'd sure appreciate it if—"

"For God's sake, Cliff, what are you giving us?" protested Stephens. "How does it happen *both* the pilots are ill?"

Howard shrugged uncomfortably. "We don't yet know for sure. It may be some kind of stomach attack. We have doctors standing by—"

"Now listen," Jessup interrupted tersely. "This is no time to play the innocent, Cliff. There have been enough leaks on this story already to sink a ship. Everything you've just said, our offices knew before we got here. Let's start again. What's the truth about the rumour of food poisoning?"

"Who is the guy who's piloting the ship?" added Abrahams.

Howard breathed deeply. He smiled and made a dramatic gesture of flipping his notes to the floor. "Look, boys," he said expansively, "I'll lay it on the line for you—you know I never hold back from you if I can help it. But if I stick my neck out I know you'll play along with me. That's fair, isn't it? We don't want to get the thing out of perspective. What's happening tonight is a big emergency—why should I pretend it isn't?—but everything that's humanly possible is being done to minimize the risk. The whole operation reflects the greatest credit on the airport organization. Frankly, I've never seen anything—"

"The story, Howard!"

"Sure, sure. But I want you to understand that nothing I say can be taken as an official statement, either on behalf of the airport or the Maple Leaf Airline. The airline is very properly giving all their attention to getting the plane down safely, and I'm just filling in to help you boys along." A telephone shrilled, but no one made a move towards it. "All right, then," said Howard. "So far as my information goes, there has been an outbreak of sickness on the plane which may very possibly be food poisoning. Of course we are taking—"

"Do you mean," someone interposed, "that the food on board the plane was contaminated?"

"No one can answer that question yet. All I can tell you is this, and I want you to get it straight. Fog delayed the departure of the Empress from Toronto and it was late on arrival at Winnipeg —so late that the normal caterers were not available. Food was obtained from another firm instead. Some of that food was fish, and some of that fish, gentlemen, may, I repeat may, have been contaminated. The usual procedure is being carried out by the public health authorities in Winnipeg."

"What about the guy who's taken over?" repeated Abrahams.

"Please understand," continued Howard, "that the Maple Leaf Airline has the very strictest standards of hygiene. An accident like this is a million-to-one freak that could happen despite the most stringent—"

"The guy at the wheel! Who is he?"

"One at a time," said Howard shrewdly, as if warding off a barrage of questions. "The plane's crew is one of Maple Leaf's most experienced teams—as you know, that's saying a lot. Captain Lee Dunning, First Officer Peter Levinson and Stewardess Janet Benson—I've got full details right here—"

"Save that," said Jessup. "We'll pick it up later." Two more newsmen hurried into the room and pushed into the group. "What's the story on the passenger who's flying the crate?"

"My information is that the first officer, then the captain were taken sick. Luckily there was a passenger on board who had piloted before and he took over the controls with the most remarkable smoothness. Name of George Spencer, from Winnipeg I assume—he joined the plane there."

"When you say he has flown before," persisted Abrahams, "do you mean he's an ex-airline pilot?"

"Well, no," admitted Howard. "I believe he flew extensively in the war in smaller aircraft—"

"In the war? That was years ago."

"What kind of smaller aircraft?" Jessup demanded.

"Spitfires, Mustangs, quite a wide range of—"

"Hold it. Those were fighters. Is this man a fighter pilot from the war?"

"Flying is flying, after all," Howard insisted anxiously. "He's under radio tuition from Captain Paul Treleaven, Cross-Canada's chief pilot, who will talk him down."

"But hell," said Jessup almost disbelievingly, "the Empress is a four-engined job. What's its horsepower?"

"Oh, around 8,000, I'd say."

"And you mean that an ex-wartime pilot who was used to single-engine fighters can handle after all these years a multi-engine airliner?" There was a scramble as two or three of the newsmen broke away to the telephone booths.

"Naturally there is some risk," Howard conceded, "which is why the precaution has been taken of clearing the immediate vicinity. The situation is pretty tight, I freely admit, but there's no reason to—"

"Some risk!" echoed Jessup. "I've done a little flying myself— I can imagine what that guy is going through. Let's have more about him."

Howard spread his hands. "I know nothing more about him than that."

"What!" exclaimed Stephens. "That's all you know about someone who's trying to bring in a shipload of—how many people *are* on board?"

"Fifty-nine, I believe, including the crew. I've got a copy of the passenger list for you, if you'll just—"

"Cliff," said Jessup grimly, "if you hole up on this one . . ."

"I've told you, Jess, that's all I have on him. We all wish we knew more, but we don't. He seems to be doing well, on the last report."

"How long have we got before the crash?" Abrahams pressed.

Howard jerked round to him. "Don't assume that," he retorted. "She's due in round about an hour, maybe less."

"Are you beaming her in?"

"I'm not sure, but I think Captain Treleaven intends to talk her down. Everything is fully under control. The airlanes and the field have been cleared. The City Fire Department is moving in extra help, just in case."

"Suppose she overshoots into the water?"

"That's not likely, but the police have alerted every available launch to stand by. I've never known such complete precautions."

"Wow, what a story!" Abrahams shouted and dived into the nearest booth, keeping the door open while he dialled so that he could continue to listen.

"Cliff," said Jessup, with some sympathy for the public relations man, "how long will the gas last in this ship?"

"I can't say, but there's bound to be a safety margin," answered Howard, loosening his tie. He sounded far from convinced.

Jessup looked at him for a second or two with narrowed eyes. Then it struck him. "Wait a minute," he shot out. "If there's food poisoning on board, it can't be only the pilots who've gone down with it?"

"I'll need all the help you can send," Abrahams was saying into the telephone. "I'll give it to you as I get it. When you've got enough to close for the first run, you'd better pull it up both ways —for the crash, and for miracle landing—and hold it. Okay? Switch me to Bert. Bert, you ready? Starts. 'At dawn this morning Vancouver Airport witnessed the worst—"

"Look, Jess," said Howard urgently, "this is dynamite. You can have it all the way, but for pity's sake play it fair to the people upstairs. They're working like crazy. There's nothing that could help the people in the aircraft that isn't being done."

"You know us all here, Cliff. We won't cross you up. What *is* the condition of those passengers?"

"A number of them are ill, but there's a doctor on board who is giving what treatment he can. We have further medical advice available on the radio if required. The stewardess is okay and she's helping Spencer, relaying the messages. You've got the lot now."

"Food poisoning is a mighty serious thing," Jessup pursued relentlessly. "I mean, the time factor is everything."

"That's so."

"If those people don't get down pretty damn soon, they could even—die?"

"That's about it," Howard agreed, tight-lipped.

"But—but this is a world story! What's the position up there now?"

"Well, about ten, fifteen minutes ago—"

"That's no good!" Jessup roared. "A few minutes can change the whole situation in a thing like this. Get the position now, Cliff. Who's duty Controller tonight? Ring him—or I will, if you like."

"No, not for a while, Jess, please. I tell you they're—"

Jessup gripped the public relations man by the shoulder. "You've been a newspaperman, Cliff. Either way this will be the biggest air story for years, and you know it. In an hour's time you'll have a tiger on your back—this place will be stiff with reporters, newsreels, TV, the lot. You've got to help us now, unless you want us busting out all over the airport. Get us the exact present position and you can take a breather for a few minutes while we get our stories through.'

"Okay, okay. Ease off, will you?" Howard picked up an internal telephone from the table. "This is Howard. Control Room, please." He pulled down his lower lip at Jessup. "You'll get me crucified. Hullo, Control? Is Burdick there? Put me on, it's urgent. Hullo, Harry? Cliff. The press are crowding up, Harry. I can't hold them much longer. They want the full situation as of now. They've got deadlines to meet."

"Of course!" snorted Burdick sarcastically in the Control Room. "Certainly! We'll arrange for the flight to crash before their deadlines. Anything for the newspapers!"

"Take it easy, Harry," urged Howard. "These guys are doing their job."

Burdick lowered the telephone and said to the Controller, who was standing with Treleaven before the radio panel, "Mr. Grimsell. Things are boiling up a bit for Cliff Howard. I don't want to leave here. Do you think Stan could take a few minutes out to talk to the press?"

"I think so," answered the Controller. He looked over to his assistant. "What about it? We'd better keep those boys under control. You could make it fast."

"Sure, sir. I'll do that."

"No point in holding back," Burdick advised. "Tell 'em the whole thing—up to and excluding this," and he nodded to the radio panel.

"I get it. Leave it to me." The assistant left the room.

"The assistant Controller is coming down, Cliff," said Burdick and rang off. He heaved his bulk over to the two men at the radio panel, mopping his face with a crumpled handkerchief. "Are you getting anything?" he asked in a flat voice.

Treleaven shook his head. He did not turn. His face was grey with fatigue. "No," he said dully. "They've gone."

The Controller rapped to the switchboard operator, "Teletype Calgary and Seattle, priority. Find out if they're still receiving 714."

"714, 714. Vancouver Control to 714. Come in, 714," called the radio operator steadily into the microphone.

Treleaven leaned against the radio desk. The pipe in his hand was dead. "Well," he said wearily, "this could be the end of the line."

"714, 714. Do you hear me? Come in, please."

"I can't take much more," said Burdick. "Here, Johnnie," to one of the clerks, "get some more coffee, for the love of Mike. Black and strong."

"Hold it!" exclaimed the radio operator.

"Did you get something?" asked the Controller eagerly.

"I don't know . . . I thought for a minute. . . ." Bending close to the panel, his headset on, the operator made minute adjustments to his fine tuning controls. "Hullo, 714. 714, this is Vancouver." He called over his shoulder, "I can hear *something* . . . it may be them. I can't be sure. If it is, they're off frequency."

"We'll have to take a chance," said Treleaven. "Tell them to change frequency."

"Flight 714," called the operator. "This is Vancouver. This is Vancouver. Change your frequency to 128.3. Do you hear that? Frequency 128.3."

Treleaven turned to the Controller. "Better ask the Air Force for another radar check," he suggested. "They should be on our own scope soon."

"714. Change to frequency 128.3 and come in," the operator was repeating.

Burdick plumped back on to a corner of the centre table. His hand left a moist mark on the woodwork. "This can't happen—it can't," he protested in a gravel voice to the whole room, staring at the radio panel. "If we've lost them now, they'll fry—every last manjack of them."

CHAPTER NINE: 0435-0505

LIKE a man in a nightmare, possessed with the fury of desperation, his teeth clenched and face streaked with sweat, Spencer fought to regain control of the aircraft, one hand on the throttle lever and the other gripped tightly on the wheel. Within him, oddly at variance with the strong sense of unreality, he felt scorching anger and self-disgust. Somewhere along the line, and quickly, he had not only lost altitude but practically all his airspeed too. His brain refused to go back over the events of the last two minutes. Something had happened to distract him, that was all he could remember. Or was that an excuse too? He couldn't have lost so much height in just a few seconds; they must have been steadily descending before that. Yet it was surely not long since he had checked the climb and descent indicator—or wasn't that its function? Could it be the gas—"

He felt a violent, almost uncontrollable desire to scream. Scream like a child. To scramble out and away from the controls, the ironically flickering needles and the mocking battery of gauges, and abandon everything. Run back into the warm, friendly-lit body of the aircraft crying out, *I couldn't do it. I told you I couldn't do it and you wouldn't listen to me. No man should be asked to do it—*

"We're gaining height," came Janet's voice, incredibly level now it seemed. He remembered her with a shock and in that moment the screaming in his mind became the screams of a woman in the passenger compartment behind him—wild, maniacal screams.

He heard a man shouting, "He's not the pilot, I tell you! They're stretched out there, both of them. We're done for!"

"Shut up and sit down!" rasped Baird clearly.

"You can't order me about—"

"I said get back! Sit down!"

"All right, doctor," came the adenoidal tones of 'Otpot, the man from Lancashire, "just leave him to me. Now, you—"

Spencer shut his eyes for an instant in an effort to clear the dancing of the illuminated dials. He was, he realized bitterly, hopelessly out of condition. A man could spend his life rushing from this place to that, forever on the go and telling himself he could never keep it up if he wasn't absolutely fit. Yet the first time a real crisis came along, the first time that real demands were made of his body, he fell flat on his face. That was the most savage thing of all: to know that your body could go no further, like an old car about to run backwards down a hill.

"I'm sorry," said Janet.

Still maintaining his pressure on the column, he shot a glance of complete surprise at her.

"What?" he said stupidly.

The girl half twisted in her seat towards him. In the greenish light from the instrument panel, her pale face looked almost translucent.

"I'm sorry for giving way like that," she said simply. "It's bad enough for you. I—I couldn't help it."

"Don't know what you're talking about," he told her roughly.

He didn't know what to say. He could hear the woman passenger, sobbing loudly now. He felt very ashamed.

"Trying to get the bus up as fast as I can," he said. "Daren't do more than a gentle climb or we'll lose way again."

Baird's voice called from the doorway, above the rising thunder of the engines, "What *is* going on, anyway, in there? Are you all right?"

Spencer answered, "Sorry, doc. I just couldn't hold her. I think it's okay now."

"Try to keep level, at least," Baird complained. "There are people very, very ill back here."

"It was my fault," said Janet. She saw Baird sway with exhaustion and hold on to the door jamb to steady himself.

"No, no," protested Spencer. "If it hadn't been for her we'd have crashed. I just can't handle this thing—that's all there is to it."

"Rubbish," said Baird curtly. They heard a man shout, "Get on the radio!" and the doctor's voice raised loudly to address the passengers, "Now listen to me, all of you. Panic is the most infectious disease of the lot, and the most lethal too." Then the door slammed shut, cutting him off.

"That's a good idea," said Janet calmly. "I ought to be reporting to Captain Treleaven."

"Yes," agreed Spencer. "Tell him what's happened and that I'm regaining height."

Janet pressed her microphone button to transmit and called Vancouver. For the first time there was no immediate acknowledgment in reply. She called again. There was nothing.

Spencer felt the familiar stab of fear. He forced himself to control it. "What's wrong?" he asked her. "Are you sure you're on the air?"

"Yes—I think so."

"Blow into your mike. If it's alive you'll hear yourself."

She did so. "Yes, I heard all right. Hullo, Vancouver. Hullo, Vancouver. This is 714. Can you hear me? Over."

Silence.

"Hullo, Vancouver. This is 714. Please answer. Over."

Still silence.

"Let me," said Spencer. He took his right hand from the throttle and depressed his microphone button. "Hullo, Vancouver. Hullo, Vancouver. This is Spencer, 714. Emergency, emergency. Come in, please."

The silence seemed as solid and as tangible as a wall. It was as if they were the only people in the world.

"I'm getting a reading on the transmitting dial," said Spencer. "I'm sure we're sending okay." He tried again, with no result. "Calling all stations. Mayday, mayday, mayday. This is Flight 714, in serious trouble. Come in anybody. Over." The ether seemed completely dead. "That settles it. We must be off frequency."

"How could that have happened?"

"Don't ask me. *Anything* can happen, the way we were just now. You'll have to go round the dial, Janet."

"Isn't that risky—to change our frequency?"

"It's my guess it's already changed. All I know is that without the radio I might as well put her nose down right now and get it over. I don't know where we are, and even if I did I certainly couldn't land in one piece."

Janet slid out of her seat, trailing the cord from her headset behind her, and reached up to the radio panel. She clicked the channel selector round slowly. There was a succession of crackles and splutters.

"I've been all the way round," she said.

"Keep at it," Spencer told her. "You've got to get something. If we have to, we'll call on each channel in turn." There was a sudden, far-away voice. "Wait, what's that!" Janet clicked back hurriedly. "Give it more volume!"

". . . to 128.3," said the voice with startling nearness. "Vancouver Control to Flight 714. Change to frequency 128.3. Reply please. Over."

"Keep it there," said Spencer to the girl. "Is that the setting? Thank our lucky stars for that. Better acknowledge it, quick."

Janet climbed back into her seat and called rapidly, "Hullo, Vancouver. 714 answering. Receiving you loud and clear. Over."

With no perceptible pause Vancouver came back, the voice of the despatcher charged with eagerness and relief.

"714. This is Vancouver. We lost you. What happened? Over."

"Vancouver, are we glad to hear you!" said Janet, holding her forehead. "We had some trouble. The airplane stalled and the radio went off. But it's all right now—except for the passengers, they're not taking it any too well. We're climbing again. Over."

This time it was Treleaven speaking again, in the same confident and measured manner as before but clearly with immense thankfulness. "Hullo, Janet. I'm glad you had the good sense to realize you were off frequency. George, I warned you about the danger of a stall. You must watch your airspeed all the time. There's one thing: if you've stalled and recovered, you obviously haven't lost your touch as a pilot."

"Did you get that?" Spencer asked Janet unbelievingly. They exchanged nervously strained smiles.

Treleaven was continuing: "You've probably had a bit of a scare, so we'll take it easy for a minute or two. While you're getting some height under you I want you to give me some readings from the instrument panel. We'll start with the fuel tank gauges ..."

While the captain recited the information he wanted, the door to the passenger deck opened and Baird looked in again, about to call to the two figures forward. He took in their concentration on the instrument panel and checked himself. Then he entered, closing the door behind him, and dropped on one knee beside the forms of the pilot and first officer, using his ophthalmoscope as a flashlight to examine their faces. Dun had rolled partly out of his blankets and was lying with his knees drawn up, moaning softly. Pete appeared to be unconscious.

The doctor readjusted the covers, wrapping them in tightly. He mopped the men's faces with a damp hand-towel stuffed in his pocket and remained crouched in thought for a few seconds. Then he rose, bracing himself against the tilt of the deck. Janet was relaying figures into her microphone. Without a word the doctor let himself out, carefully sliding the door closed.

The scene outside resembled a vast casualty ambulance rather than the passenger deck of an airliner. At intervals along the crowded cabin, their reclining seats fully extended, sick passengers lay swaddled in rugs. One or two were quite motionless, scarcely breathing. Others were twisting in pain while friends or relatives watched them fearfully or replaced damp cloths on their foreheads.

Bending forward, the more effectively to render his homily to the man he had recently thrust back into his seat, 'Otpot was saying, "I don't blame you, see. 'Appen it's better sometimes to let off steam. But it don't do to start shouting in front of the others who're poorly, especially the ladies. Old doc here is real champion, and so are the two up front flying. Any road, we've got to trust them, see, if we want to get down at all."

Temporarily subdued, the passenger, who was twice the size of 'Otpot, stared stonily at his own reflection in the cabin window by his seat. The perky little Lancashire man came along to the doctor, who patted his arm in thanks.

"You're quite a wizard, aren't you?" said Baird.

"I'm more scared than he is," 'Otpot assured him fervently, "and that's a fact. Heck, if you hadn't been with us doctor. . . ." He shrugged expressively. "What d'you make of things now?" he asked.

"I don't know," Baird replied. His face was gaunt. "They had a little trouble up front. It's hardly surprising. I think Spencer is under a terrible strain. He's carrying more responsibility than any of us."

"How much longer is there to go?"

"I've no idea. I've lost all sense of time. But if we're on course it can't be long now. Feels like days to me."

'Otpot put to him as quietly as he could, "What d'you really think, doc? 'Ave we got a chance?"

Baird shook the question off in tired irritation. "Why ask me? There's always a *chance*, I suppose. But keeping an aeroplane in the air and getting it down without smashing it to a million pieces, with all the factors that involves, are two mighty different propositions. I guess that much is obvious even to me. Either way, it isn't going to make much odds to some of the folk here before long."

He squatted down to look at Mrs. Childer, feeling inside her blanket for her wrist and noting her pinched, immobile face, dry skin and quick, shallow breathing. Her husband demanded hoarsely, "Doctor, is there *nothing* we can do for her?"

Baird looked at the closed, sunken eyes of the woman. He said slowly, "Mr. Childer, you've a right to know the truth. You're a sensible man—I'll give it to you straight. We're making all the speed we possibly can, but at best it will be touch and go for your wife." Childer's mouth moved wordlessly. "You'd better understand this," Baird went on deliberately. "I've done what I could for her, and I'll continue to do it, but it's pathetically little. Earlier on, using morphia, I might have been able to ease the pain for your wife. Now, if it's any consolation to you, nature has taken care of it for us."

Childer found his voice. "I won't have you say that," he protested. "Whatever happens, I'm grateful to you, doctor."

"Of course he is," interposed 'Otpot heartily. "We all are. No one could've done owt more than you, doc. An absolute marvel, that's what."

Baird smiled faintly, his hand on the woman's forehead. "Kind words don't alter the case," he said harshly. "You're a man of courage, Mr. Childer, and you have my respect. But don't delude yourself." The moment of truth, he thought bitterly; so this is it. I'd known it was coming tonight, and I knew too, deep down, what the answer would be. This is the salty taste of the real truth. No romantic heroics now. No coloured-up and chlorophylled projection of what you *think* you are, or what you like others to think you are. This is the truth. Inside another hour we shall all very probably be dead. At least I shall go exposed for what I am. A rotten, stinking failure. *When the time came, he was unequal.* The perfect obituary.

"I'm telling you," Childer was saying with emotion, "if we get out of this, I'll have everyone know what we owe to you."

Baird collected his thoughts. "What's that?" he grunted. "I'd give plenty to have two or three saline drips aboard." He rose. "Carry on as before, Mr. Childer. Make sure she's really warm. Keep her lips moistened. If you can get her to take a little water now and then, so much the better. Remember she's lost a very critical amount of body fluids."

At that moment, in the Control Room at Vancouver, Harry Burdick was in the process of replacing some of his own body fluid with another carton of coffee. In addition to the microphone held in his hand, Treleaven now had on a telephone headset and into the latter he was asking, "Radar. Are you getting anything at all?"

From another part of the building the chief radar operator, seated with an assistant before a long-range azimuth scanner, answered in a calmly conversational tone, "Not a thing yet."

"I can't understand it," Treleaven said to the Controller. "They ought to be in range by now."

Burdick volunteered, "Don't forget he lost speed in that last practice."

"Yes, that's so," Treleaven agreed. Into his headset he said, "Radar, let me know the instant you get something." To the Controller, "I daren't bring him down through cloud without knowing where he is. Ask the Air Force for another check, will you, Mr. Grimsell?" He nodded to the radio operator. "Put me on the air. Hullo, 714. Now, listen carefully, George. We are going through that drill again but before we start I want to explain a few things you may have forgotten or that only apply to big aeroplanes. Are you with me? Over."

Janet replied, "Go ahead, Vancouver. We are listening carefully. Over."

"Right, 714. Now before you can land certain checks and adjustments must be carried out. They are in addition to the landing drill you've just practised. I'll tell you when and how to do them later. Now I just want to run over them to prepare you. First, the hydraulic booster pump must be switched on. Then the brake pressure must be showing about 900 to 1,000 pounds a square inch. You'll maybe remember something along these lines from your fighter planes, but a refresher course won't hurt. Next, after the undercart is lowered you turn on the fuel booster pumps and check that the gas feed is sufficient. Lastly, the mixture has to be made good and rich and the propellers set. Got all that? We'll take it step by step as you come in so that Janet can set the switches. Now I'm going to tell you where each of them are. Here we go...."

Janet and Spencer identified each control as they were directed.

"Tell him we have them pinpointed, Janet."

"Hullo, Vancouver. We're okay on that."

"Right, 714. You're in no doubt about the position of each of those controls, Janet? You're quite sure? Over."

"Yes, Vancouver. I've got them. Over."

"714. Check again that you are in level flight. Over."

"Hullo, Vancouver. Yes, flying level now and above cloud."

"Right, 714. Now, George. Let's have 15 degrees of flap again, speed 140, and we'll go through the wheel-lowering routine. Watch that airspeed like a hawk this time. If you're ready, let's go...."

Grimly Spencer began the procedure, following each instruction with complete concentration while Janet anxiously counted off the airspeed and operated the flap and undercarriage levers. Once again they felt the sharp jolt as their speed was arrested. The first tentative streaks of dawn were glimmering to eastward.

In the Control Room Treleaven took the opportunity to gulp some cold coffee. He accepted a cigarette from Burdick and exhaled the smoke noisily. He looked haggard, with a blue stubble around his chin.

"How do you read the situation now?" queried the airline manager.

"It's as well as can be expected," said the captain, "but time's running dangerously short. He should have at least a dozen runs through this flap and wheels drill alone. With luck we'll get about three in before he's overhead—that is, if he's on course."

"You're going to give him practice approaches?" put in the Controller.

"I must. Without at least two or three I wouldn't give a red cent for his chances, not with the experience he's got. I'll see how he shapes up. Otherwise. . . ." Treleaven hesitated.

Burdick dropped his cigarette to the floor and stepped on it. "Otherwise what?" he prompted.

Treleaven rounded on them. "Well, we'd better face facts," he said. "That man up there is frightened out of his wits, and with good reason. If his nerve doesn't hold, they may stand more chance by ditching off-shore in the strait."

"But—the impact!" Burdick exclaimed. "And the sick people —and the aircraft. It'd be a total loss."

"It would be a calculated risk," said Treleaven icily, looking the rotund manager straight in the eyes. "If our friend looks like piling up all over the field, your aeroplane will be a write-off anyway."

"Harry didn't mean it like that," broke in the Controller hurriedly.

"Hell, no, I guess not," said Burdick uncomfortably.

"With the added danger," continued Treleaven, "that if he crashes here, fire is almost certain and we'll be lucky to save any-one. He may even take some ground installation with him. Whereas if he puts down on the ocean he'll break up the aero-plane, sure, but we stand a chance of saving some of the passengers if not the very sick ones. With this light mist and practically no wind the water will be pretty calm, reducing the impact. We'd belly-land him by radar as near as we could to rescue craft."

"Get the Navy," the Controller ordered his assistant. "Air Force too. Air-sea rescue are already standing by. Have them put out off-shore and await radio instructions."

"I don't want to do it," said Treleaven, turning back to the wall map. "It would amount to abandoning the sick passengers. We'd be lucky to get them out before the plane went under. But it may be necessary." He spoke into his headset. "Radar, are you getting anything?"

"Still nothing," came the even, impersonal reply. "Hold it, though. Wait a minute. This may be something coming up. . . . Yes, captain. I have him now. He's ten miles south of track. Have him turn right on to a heading of 265."

"Nice work," said Treleaven. He nodded to be put on the air

as the switchboard operator called across, "Air Force report visual contact, sir. ETA 38 minutes."

"Right." He raised the microphone in front of him. "Hullo, 714. Have you carried out the reverse procedure for flaps and undercart? Over."

"Yes, Vancouver. Over," came the girl's voice.

"Any trouble this time? Flying straight and level?"

"Everything all right, Vancouver. The pilot says—so far." They heard her give a nervous little laugh.

"That's fine, 714. We have you on radar now. You're off course ten miles to the south. I want you to bank carefully to the right, using your throttles to maintain your present speed, and place the aircraft on a heading of 265. I'll repeat that. 265. Is that clear? Over."

"Understood, Vancouver."

Treleaven glanced out of the window. The darkness outside had lightened very slightly. "Thank God they'll be able to see a little," he said, "though not until the last minutes."

"I'll put everything on standby," said the Controller. He called to his assistant, "Warn the Tower, Stan. Tell them to alert the fire people." Then, to the switchboard operator, "Give me the city police."

"And then put me on to Howard in the press room," added Burdick. He said to Treleaven, "We'd better explain to those guys about the possibility of ditching before they start jumping to their own conclusions. No, wait!" he suddenly remembered, staring intently at the captain. "We can't admit that would mean writing off the sick passengers. I'd be cutting my throat!"

Treleaven was not listening. He had slumped into a chair, his head bowed with a hand over his eyes, not hearing the confused murmur of voices about him. But at the first splutter as the amplifier came alive he was on his feet, reaching for the microphone.

"Hullo, Vancouver," called Janet. "We are now on a heading of 265 as instructed. Over."

"714. That's fine," said Treleaven with an assumed cheerfulness. "You're doing splendidly. Let's have it all again, shall we? This will be the last time before you reach the airport, George, so make it good."

The Controller was speaking with quiet urgency into his telephone. "Yes, they'll be with us within the half-hour. Let's get the show on the road."

CHAPTER TEN: 0505-0525

SPENCER tried to ease his aching legs. His whole body felt pummelled and bruised. In his anxiety and the effort of concentration he had expended almost unnecessary energy, leaving him, the moment he relaxed, utterly drained of strength. He was conscious of his hands trembling and made no attempt to check them. As he watched the unceasing movement of the instruments, a fleck of light rose constantly in front of his eyes, slowly falling again like a twist of cotton. All the time that interior voice, now every bit as real to him and as independent as the one in his earphones, kept up its insistent monologue, telling him: *Whatever you do, don't let go. If you let go, you're finished. Remember, it was like this many a time in the war. You thought you'd reached the end then —completely bushed, with not another ounce left in you. But every time there was something left in the bag—one last reserve you never knew you had.*

He looked across to Janet, willing himself to speak. "How did we make out that time?" he asked her. He knew he was very near to collapse.

She seemed to sense the purpose of his question. "We did pretty well," she said brightly. "Anyway, I thought Captain Treleaven sounded pleased, didn't you?"

"Hardly heard him," he said, turning his head from side to side to relieve the muscles in his neck. "I just hope that's the lot. How many times have we done the flap and wheel routine now—is it three? If he asks us to do it once more, I'll . . ." *Steady on,* he admonished himself. *Don't let her see what a state you're in.* She had leaned over to him and wiped his face and forehead with a handkerchief. *Come on now, get a grip. This is only nervous reaction—blue funk, if you like. Think of Treleaven: what a spot he's in. He's safe on the ground, sure enough, but suppose he forgot something—*

"Have you noticed, the sun's coming up," said Janet.

"Why sure," he lied, lifting his eyes. Even ahead to the west the carpet of cloud was tinged with pink and gold, and there too the vast canopy of sky had perceptibly lightened. To the south, on the port beam, he could see two mountain tops, isolated like islands in a tumbling ocean of cotton wool. "We won't be long now." He paused.

"Janet."

"Yes?"

"Before we go down, have a last—I mean, another look at the pilots. We'll probably bump a bit—you know—and we don't want them thrown about."

Janet flashed a grateful smile at him.

"Can you hold on there for a moment?" she asked.

"Don't worry, I'll yell quick enough."

She slipped off her headset and rose from her seat. As she turned to get out, the door to the passenger deck opened and Baird looked in.

"Oh—you're off the radio," he observed.

"I was just going to have a look at the captain and co-pilot, to make sure they're secure."

"No need to," he told her. "I did it a few minutes ago, when you were busy."

"Doctor," called Spencer, "how are things with you back there?"

"That's why I looked in,' said Baird tersely. "We're running out of time—but fast."

"Is there any kind of help that we can get you on the radio?"

"I'd like to have had a diagnostic check with a doctor down there, but I guess it's more important to hold the air open for flying the machine. How long is it likely to be now?"

"Well under the half-hour, I'd say. How does that sound?"

"I don't know," Baird said doubtfully. He held on to the back of Spencer's seat, weariness apparent in every inch of his posture. He was in shirt-sleeves, his tie discarded. "There are two patients in a state of complete prostration," he went on. "How much longer they can last without treatment, I can't say. But not long, that's for sure. And there are several others who'll soon be just as bad, unless I'm very wrong."

Spencer grimaced. "Is anyone giving you a hand?"

"You bet—couldn't possibly manage, otherwise. One feller in particular—that Lancashire character—he's really turned out a—"

The earphones came to life. "Hullo, 714. This is Vancouver. Over."

Spencer waved Janet back into her seat and she hurriedly donned her headset.

"Well, I'll get back," said Baird. "Good luck, anyway."

"Wait a minute," said Spencer, nodding to the girl.

"714 here," Janet acknowledged into her microphone. "We'll be with you in a moment."

"Doctor," said Spencer, speaking quickly, "I don't have to fool you. This may be rough. Just about anything in the book is liable to happen." The doctor said nothing. "You know what I mean. They may get a bit jumpy back there. See that they're kept in their seats, huh?"

Baird seemed to be turning words over in his mind. Then he replied in a gruff tone, "Do the best you can and leave me to take care of the rest." He thumped the young man lightly on the shoulder and made his way aft.

"Okay," said Spencer to the girl.

"Go ahead, Vancouver," she called.

"Hullo, 714," responded the clear, confident voice of Treleaven "Now that you've had a breather since that last run-through George, we'd better press on again. You should be receiving me well now. Will you check, please? Over."

"Tell him I've been having a few minutes with my feet up," said Spencer. "And tell him he's coming in about strength niner." *Strength niner*, he thought. *You really dug that one up.*

". . . a short rest," Janet was saying, "and we hear you strength niner."

"That's the way, George. Our flying practice has slowed you down a bit, though that's all to the good as it will be getting light when you come in. You are now in the holding position and ready to start losing height. First I want to speak to Janet. Are you listening, Janet?"

"Hullo, Vancouver. Yes, I hear you."

"Janet, when we make this landing we want you to follow the emergency crash procedures for protection of passengers. Do you understand? Over."

"I understand, captain. Over."

"One more thing, Janet. Just before the landing we will ask the pilot to sound the emergency bell. And, George—the switch for that bell is right over the co-pilot's seat and it's painted red."

"Can you see it?" asked Spencer without looking up.

"Yes," said Janet, "it's here."

"All right. Remember it."

"Janet," continued Treleaven, "that will be your warning for final precautions, because I want you to be back then with the passengers."

"Tell him no," Spencer cut in. "I must have you up front."

"Hullo, Vancouver," said Janet. "I understand your instructions, but the pilot needs me to help him. Over."

There was a long pause. Then, "All right, 714," Treleaven answered. "I appreciate the position. But it is your duty, Janet, to see that all emergency crash precautions are taken before we can think about landing. Is there anyone you can explain and delegate this to?"

"What about the doctor?" suggested Spencer.

Janet shook her head. "He's got enough on his plate," she said.

"Well, he'll have a bit more," he snapped. "I've got to have you here if we're to stand any chance of getting down."

She hesitated, then pressed the stud to transmit. "Hullo, Vancouver. Doctor Baird will in any case have to keep a watch on the sick passengers as we land. I think he's the best person to carry out the emergency drill. There's another man who can help him. Over."

"Hullo, Janet. Very well. Detach yourself now and explain the procedure very carefully to the doctor. There must be no possibility of error. Let me know when you're through." Janet laid laid aside her headset and climbed out of her seat. "Now, George," Treleaven went on, "watch that you keep to your present course: I'll give you any corrections as necessary. Right now, as you approach the airport, I'll give you a cockpit check of the really essential things. I want you to familiarize yourself with them as we go along. Some of them you'll remember from your old flying days. Be certain you know where they are. If you're in any doubt this is the time to say so. We'll have as many dummy runs as you like but when you do finally come in the procedure must be carried out properly and completely. We'll start on the first check directly Janet gets back on the air."

In the Control Room at Vancouver, Treleaven took a dead cigarette from his mouth and tossed it away. He looked up at the electric wall clock and back at the Controller. "How much gas have they got?" he demanded.

Grimsell picked up the clipboard from the table. "In flying time, enough for about ninety minutes," he said.

"What's the angle, captain?" asked Burdick. "You figure there's plenty of time for circuits and approaches, don't you?"

"There's got to be," said Treleaven. "This is a first-flight solo. But keep a strict check on it, will you, Mr. Grimsell? We must have plenty in hand for a long run-in over the ocean, if I decide as a last measure to ditch."

"Mr. Burdick," hailed the switchboard operator, "your president is on the line."

Burdick swore. "At this time, he has to get back! Tell him I can't speak to him now. Put him through to the Maple Leaf office. Wait a minute. Put me on to the office first." He picked up a telephone and waited impatiently. "Is that you, Dave? Harry. Surprise for you—the Old Man is on the line. Hold him off as best you can. Tell him 714 is in holding position and his prayers are as good as ours. I'll ring him directly the—directly I have something to tell him. Then I suppose he'll jump a plane here. Right, boy."

The assistant to the Controller, his hand cupped over a telephone, was saying to his chief, "It's Howard. He says the press are—"

"I'll take it." The Controller seized the telephone. "Listen Cliff. We're accepting no more non-operational calls. Things are far too critical now. . . . Yes, I know. If they've got eyes, they'll see for themselves." He replaced the receiver with a bang.

"I'd say that boy was doing a pretty good job," grunted Burdick.

"He is, too," agreed the Controller. "And those newspapermen wouldn't be doing *their* job by keeping quiet. But we can't be distracted now."

Treleaven stood by the radio panel, his fingers drumming absently, his eyes fixed on the clock. Outside the airport, in the first light of dawn, the emergency measures were in full swing. At a hospital a nurse hung up her telephone and spoke to a doctor working at an adjacent table. She handed him his coat, reaching also for her own. They hurried out and a few minutes later the overhead door to the vehicle bay of the hospital slid up, emitting first one ambulance and then another.

In a city fire station one of the few crews to be held to the last minute on reserve slapped down their cards and raced for the door at the sound of the bell, snatching up their clothing equipment on the way. The last man out skidded back to the table and lifted up the cards of one of his opponents. He raised an eyebrow, then dived after his colleagues.

At the little group of houses near Sea Island Bridge, which lay in direct line with the airfield, police were shepherding families into two buses, most of the people with street clothes thrown hastily on over their night attire. A small girl, staring intently at the sky, tripped over her pyjamas. She was picked up instantly by a policeman and deposited in a bus. He waved to the driver to get started.

"Hullo, Vancouver," called Janet, a little breathlessly. "I've given the necessary instructions. Over."

"Good girl," said Treleaven with relief. "Now, George," he went on quickly, "the clock is running a little against us. First, reset your altimeter to 30.1. Then throttle back slightly, but hold your airspeed steady until you're losing height at 500 feet per minute. Watch your instruments closely. You'll have a long descent through cloud."

Spencer spread his fingers round the throttles and gently moved them back. The climb and descent indicator fell slowly and a little unevenly to 600, then rose again to remain fairly steady at 500.

"Here comes the cloud," he said, as the gleams of daylight were abruptly blotted out. "Ask him how high the cloud base is below."

Janet repeated the question.

"Ceiling is around 2,000 feet," said Treleaven, "and you should break out of cloud about fifteen miles from the airport."

"Tell him we're holding steady at 500 feet a minute," instructed Spencer.

Janet did so.

"Right, 714. Now, George, this is a little more tricky. Don't break your concentration. Keep a constant check on that descent indicator. But at the same time, if you can, I want you to pinpoint the controls in a first run-through of landing procedure. Think you can manage that?"

Spencer did not trouble to answer. His eyes rooted on the instrument panel, he just set his lips and nodded expressively.

"Yes, Vancouver," said Janet. "We'll try."

"Okay, then. If anything gets out of hand, tell me immediately." Treleaven shook off a hand someone had laid on his arm to interrupt him. His eyes were screwed up tightly as he looked again at the blank spot on the wall, visualizing there the cockpit of the aircraft. "George, this is what you will do as you come in. First, switch the hydraulic booster pump *on*. Remember, just fix these things in your mind—don't do anything now. The gauge is on the extreme left of the panel, under and to the left of the gyro control. Got it? Over."

He heard Janet's voice reply, "The pilot knows that one, Vancouver, and has located the switch."

"Right, 714. Surprising how it comes back, isn't it, George?" Treleaven pulled out a handkerchief and wiped the back of his neck. "Next you'll have to turn off the de-icer control. That's bound to be on and will show on the gauge on the right of the panel, just in front of Janet. The flow control is next to it. That one's easy, but the control must be off before you land. Watching the descent indicator, George? Next item, brake pressure. There are two gauges, one for the inboard brake and one for the outboard. They're immediately to the right of the hydraulic boost which you've just found. Over."

After a pause, Janet confirmed, "Found them, Vancouver. They're showing 950 and—er—1,010 pounds—is it per square inch?—each."

"Then they're okay, but they must be checked again before landing. Now, the gills. They must be one-third closed. The switch is right by Janet's left knee and you'll see it's marked in thirds. Are you with me? Over."

"Yes, I see it, Vancouver. Over."

"You can work that one, Janet. Next to it, on the same bank of switches, are the port and starboard intercooler switches. They're clearly marked. They will have to be opened fully. Make sure of that, Janet, won't you? Open fully. The next and most important thing is the landing gear. You've been through the drill, but go over it thoroughly in your mind first, starting with the flap movement and ending with the wheels fully down and locked. Full flap should be put on when the plane is very near touchdown and you're sure you're going to come in. I shall direct you on that. Is this understood by both of you? Over."

"Tell him yes, thanks," said Spencer, his eyes not leaving the panel. His shoulder had begun to itch abominably, but he blanked his mind to the irritation.

"Okay, 714. When you're on the approach, and after the wheels are down, the fuel booster pumps must be turned on. Otherwise your supply of gas might be cut off at the worst moment. The switch for these is at five o'clock from the auto pilot, just behind the mixture controls."

Janet scanned the panel in a daze. *"Where?"* she almost whispered to Spencer. He peered at the board and located the switch. "There." His finger stabbed at the little switch, above the grooved bank that held the throttle levers.

"All right, Vancouver," she said weakly.

"Now the mixture is to be changed to auto rich. I know George has been itching for that, so I won't say any more—he'll handle that all right. Then you have to set the propellers until the green lights under the switches come on. They're just about touching George's right knee, I should think. Got them?"

"Pilot says yes, Vancouver."

"Lastly, the superchargers. After the wheels are down, these must be set in the take-off position—that is, up, on your aircraft. They are, of course, the four levers to the left of the throttles. Well now. Any questions about all that? Over."

Spencer looked at Janet despairingly. "It's all one big question," he said. "We'll never remember it all."

"Hullo, Vancouver," said Janet. "We don't think we'll be able to remember it."

"You don't have to, 714. I'll remember it for you. There are some other points, too, which we'll deal with when we come to them. I want to go over these operations with you thoroughly, George, so that when I give the word you'll carry out the action without too much loss of concentration. Remember, this is just a drill in flipping over switches. You still have to fly the aircraft."

"Ask him about time," said Spencer. "How much have we got?"

Janet put the question to Vancouver.

"As I said, George, you've got all the time in the world—but we just don't want to waste any. You'll be over the airport in about seven minutes. Don't let that bother you. There'll be as much time as you like for further practice." A pause. "Radar reports a course adjustment necessary, George. Change your heading five degrees to 260, please. Over."

Treleaven switched off his microphone and spoke to the Controller. "They're well on the glide path now," he said. "As soon as we've got visual contact, I'll level them off and take them around for circuits and drills. We'll see how they shape up after that."

"Everything's set here," said the Controller. He called to his assistant, "Put the entire field on alert."

"Hullo, Vancouver," came Janet's voice over the amplifier. "We have now changed course to 260. Over."

"Okay, 714." Treleaven hitched up his trousers with one hand. "Let's have a check on your height, please. Over."

"Vancouver," answered Janet after a few seconds, "our height is 2,500 feet."

On his headset, Treleaven heard the radar operator report, "Fifteen miles from the field." "That's fine, George," he said. "You'll be coming out of cloud any minute. As soon as you do, look for the airport beacon. Over."

"Bad news," Burdick told him. "The weather's thickening. It's starting to rain again."

"Can't help that now," rapped Treleaven. "Get the Tower," he told the Controller. "Tell them to light up—put on everything they've got. We'll be going up there in a minute. I'll want their radio on the same frequency as this. Spencer won't have time to fool around changing channels."

"Right!" said the Controller, lifting a telephone.

"Hullo, 714," Treleaven called. "You are now fifteen miles from the airport. Are you still in cloud, George? Over."

A long pause followed. Suddenly the radio crackled into life, catching Janet in mid-sentence. She was saying excitedly, ". . . lifting very slightly. I thought I saw something. I'm not sure. . . . Yes, there it is! I see it! Do you see it, Mr. Spencer? It's right ahead. We can see the beacon, Vancouver!"

"My God," said Treleaven to Burdick, "they're through. All right, George," he called into the microphone, "level off now at 2,000 feet and wait for instructions. I'm moving to the Control Tower now, so you won't hear from me for a few minutes. We'll decide on the runway to use at the last minute, so you can land into wind. Before that you'll make some dummy runs, to practise your landing approaches. Over."

They heard Spencer's voice say, "I'll take this, Janet." There was a broken snatch of conversation, then Spencer came on the air again, biting off his words.

"No dice, Vancouver. The situation up here doesn't allow. We're coming straight in."

"What!" shouted Burdick. "He can't!"

"Don't be a fool, George," said Treleaven urgently. "You've *got* to have some practice runs."

"I'm holding my line of descent," Spencer intoned deliberately, his voice shaking slightly. "There are people up here dying. Dying! Can you get that into your heads? I'll stand as much chance on the first run-in as I will on the tenth. I'm coming straight in."

"Let me talk to him," appealed the Controller.

"No," said Treleaven, "there's no time for argument." His face was white. A vein in his temple pulsed. "We've got to act fast. I say we've no choice. By all the rules he's in command of that airplane. I'm going to accept his decision."

"You can't do that," Burdick protested. "Don't you realize—"

"All right, George," Treleaven called, "if that's the way you want it. Stand by and level off. We're going to the Tower now. Good luck to us all. Listening out." He ripped off his headset, flinging it down, and shouted to the others, "Let's go." The three men leapt out of the room and raced along the corridor, Burdick bringing up the rear. Ignoring the elevator, they bounded up the stairs, almost knocking over someone who was coming down, and burst into the Tower Control Room. An operator stood at the massive sweep of window, studying the lightening sky through night binoculars. "There he is!" he announced. Treleaven snatched up a second pair of glasses, took a quick look, then put them down.

"All right," he said, panting. "Let's make our decision on the runway."

"Zero-eight," said the operator. "It's the longest and it's pretty well into the wind."

"Radar!" called the captain.

"Here, sir."

Treleaven crossed to a side table on which appeared a plan of the airport under glass. He used a thick chinagraph pencil to mark the proposed course of the aircraft.

"Here's what we do. Right now he's about here. We'll turn him so he begins to make a wide left-hand circuit, and at the same time bring him down to a thousand feet. I'll start the pre-landing check here, then we'll take him over the sea and make a slow turn around on to final. That clear?"

"Yes, captain," said the operator.

Treleaven took a headset that was handed to him and put it on. "Is this hooked up to the radar room?" he asked.

"Yes, sir. Right here."

The Controller was reciting into a telephone-type microphone: "Tower to all emergency vehicles. Runway is zero-eight. Zero-eight. Airport tenders take positions numbers one and two. Civilian equipment number three. All ambulances to positions numbers four and five. I repeat that no vehicle will leave its position until the aircraft has passed it. Start now."

Leaning down on the top of a control console, the captain flicked the switch of a desk microphone. At his elbow the spools of a tape recorder began to revolve.

"Hullo, George Spencer," he called in a steady, even tone. "This is Paul Treleaven in Vancouver Tower. Do you hear me? Over."

Janet's voice filled the Control Room. "Yes, captain. You are loud and clear. Over."

Over the telephone, the calm voice of the radar operator reported, "Ten miles. Turn to a heading of 253."

"All right, George. You are now ten miles from the airport. Turn to a heading of 253. Throttle back and begin to lose height to one thousand feet. Janet, put the preliminary landing procedure in hand for the passengers. Neither of you acknowledge any further transmissions unless you wish to ask a question."

Removing his hands one at a time from the control column, Spencer flexed his fingers. He managed a grin at the girl beside him. "Okay, Janet, do your stuff," he told her.

She unhooked a microphone from the cabin wall and pressed the stud, speaking into it. "Attention please, everyone. Attention please." Her voice cracked. She gripped the microphone hard and cleared her throat. "Will you please resume your seats and fasten your safety belts. We shall be landing in a few minutes. Thank you."

"Well done," Spencer complimented her. "Just like any old landing, eh?"

She tried to smile back, biting her lower lip. "Well, not quite that," she said.

"You've got plenty of what it takes," said Spencer soberly. "I'd like you to know I couldn't have held on this far without. . . ." He broke off, gently moving the rudder bar and the wheel, waiting to feel the response from the aircraft. "Janet," he said, his eyes on the inclinometer, "we haven't much more time. This is what we knew must happen sooner or later. But I want to make sure you understand why I must try to get her down—somehow—on the first shot."

"Yes," she said quietly, "I understand." She had clipped her safety belt around her waist and now her hands were clenched together tightly in her lap.

"Well, I want to say thanks," he went on, stumblingly. "I made no promises, right from the start, and I make none now. You know, if anyone does, just how lousy I am at this. But taking turns around the field won't help. And some of the folk in the back are getting worse every minute. Better for them to . . . to take their chance quickly."

"I told you," she said. "You don't have to explain."

He shot a look of alarm at her, afraid in the passing of a moment that he stood exposed to her. She was watching the airspeed indicator; he could not see her face. He glanced away, back along the broad stretch of wing behind them. It was describing with

infinite slowness the tiny segment of an arc, balancing on its tip
the misty blue-grey outline of a hillside twinkling with road lamps.
Sliding under the body of the aircraft, on the other quarter, were
the distantly blazing lights of the airport. They seemed pathetically small and far away, like a child's carelessly discarded string
of red and amber beads.

He could feel his heart thumping as his body made its own
emergency preparations, as if aware that what remained of its life
could now be measured in minutes, even seconds. He looked
critically at himself, a man apart, performing the movements to
bring the aircraft back to level flight.

He heard himself say, "Here we go, then. This is it, Janet. I'm
starting to lose height—*now*.'

CHAPTER ELEVEN: 0525-0535

HARRY BURDICK lowered his binoculars and handed them back to
the Tower Controller.

From the observation balcony which girdled the Tower, the
two men took a last look over the field, at the gasoline bowsers
pulled well back from the apron and, clearly visible now in the
half-light, the groups of figures watching from the boarding bays.
The steady throb of truck engines from the far end of the field
seemed to add to the oppressive, almost unbearable air of expectancy which enveloped the whole airport.

Searching in his mind for any possible fault, Burdick reviewed
Treleaven's plan. The aircraft would arrive overhead at something below two thousand feet and carry on out over the Strait
of Georgia, descending gradually on this long, down-wind leg
while the last cockpit check was executed. Then would follow a
wide about-turn on to the final approach, giving the pilot
maximum time in which to regulate his descent and settle down
carefully for the run-in.

A good plan, one which would take advantage too of the slowly
increasing light of dawn. It occurred to Burdick what that would
mean to those of the passengers who were well enough to care.
They would watch Sea Island and the airport pass beneath them,
followed by the wide sweep of the bay, then the island getting
shakily nearer again as their emergency pilot made his last adjustments to the controls. Burdick sensed, as if he were up there with

them, the suffocating tension, the dreadful choking knowledge that they might well be staring death in the face. He shivered suddenly. In his sweat-soaked shirt, without a jacket, he felt the chill of the early morning air like a knife.

There was the sensation, quickly passing, of being suspended in time, as if the world were holding its breath.

"We are on a heading of 253." The girl's voice carried to them distinctly from the radio amplifier. "We are now losing height rapidly."

His eyes shadowed with anxiety, Burdick glanced meaningly into the face of the young man at his side. Without a word they turned and re-entered the great glass surround of the Control Tower. Treleaven and Grimsell were crouched before the desk microphone, their features bathed in the green glow from the radar monitor set into the control console in front of them.

"Wind still okay?" asked the captain.

Grimsell nodded. "Slightly across runway zero-eight, but that's still our best bet. It's the longest."

"Radar," said Treleaven into his headset, "keep me fed the whole time, whether or not you can hear that I'm on the air. This won't be a normal talk-down. Scrap procedure the instant 714 runs into trouble. Cut in and yell."

Burdick tapped him on the shoulder. "Captain," he urged, "what about one more shot at getting him to hold off—at least until the light's better and he's had—"

"The decision's been made," said Treleaven curtly. "The guy's nervy enough. If we argue with him now, he's finished." Burdick shrugged and turned away. Treleaven continued in a quieter tone, "I understand your feelings, Harry. But understand his too, surrounded by a mass of hardware he's never seen before. He's on a razor edge."

"What if he comes in badly?" put in Grimsell. "What's your plan?"

"He probably will, let's face it," Treleaven retorted grimly. "If it's hopeless, I'll try to bring him round again. We'll save any further arguments on the air unless it's obvious he doesn't stand a chance. Then I'll try to insist he puts down in the ocean." He listened for a moment to the calm recital of radar readings in his earphones, then pressed the switch of the microphone. "George. Let your airspeed come back to 160 knots and hold it steady there."

The amplifier came alive as 714 took the air. There was an

agonizing pause before Janet's voice intoned, "We are still losing height. Over."

Like a huge and ponderous bird, the Empress moved slowly past the western end of the Lansdowne Race Track, hidden now in the early-morning mist, and over the arm of the Fraser River. To the right the bridge from the mainland to Sea Island was just discernible.

"Good," said Treleaven. "Now set your mixture controls to take-off—that is, up to the top position." He fixed his eyes on his wrist watch, counting the sweep of the second hand. "Take your time, George. When you're ready, turn your carburettor heat controls to cold. They're just forward of the throttles."

"How about the gas tanks?" Burdick demanded hoarsely.

"We checked earlier," replied Grimsell. "He's on main wing tanks now."

In the aircraft Spencer peered apprehensively from one control to the next. His face was a rigid mask. He heard Treleaven's voice resume its inexorable monologue. "The next thing, George, is to set the air filter to ram and the superchargers to low. Take your time, now." Spencer looked about him wildly. "The air filter control is the single lever below the mixture controls. Move it into the up position."

"Can you see it, Janet?" asked Spencer anxiously.

"Yes. Yes, I have it." She added quickly, "Look—the airport's right below us! You can see the long main runway."

"*Plenty* long, I hope," Spencer gritted, not lifting his head.

"The supercharger controls," continued Treleaven, "are four levers to the right of the mixture controls. Move them to the up position also."

"Got them?" said Spencer.

"Yes."

"Good girl." He was conscious of the horizon line dipping and rising in front of him, but dared not release his eyes from the panel. The roar of the engines took on a fluctuating tone.

"Now let's have that 15 degrees of flap," Treleaven instructed. "15 degrees—down to the second notch. The indicator dial is in the centre of the main panel. When you have 15 degrees on, bring your airspeed back slowly to 140 knots and adjust your trim for level flight. As soon as you've done that, switch the hydraulic booster pump on—extreme left, by the gyro control."

Through Treleaven's headset, the radar operator interposed, "Turn on to 225. I'm getting a height reading, captain. He's all over the place. Nine hundred, up to thirteen hundred feet."

"Change course to 225," said Treleaven. "And watch your height—it's too irregular. Try to keep steady at 1,000 feet."

"He's dropping off fast," said the operator. "1,100 . . . 1,000 . . . 900 . . . 800 . . . 700. . . ."

"Watch your height!" Treleaven warned. "Use more throttle! Keep the nose up!"

"650 . . . 600 . . . 550. . . ."

"Get back that height!" barked Treleaven. "Get it back! You need a thousand feet."

"550 . . . 450 . . ." called off the operator, calm but sweating. "This isn't good, captain. 400 . . . 400 . . . 450—he's going up. 500. . . ."

For a moment, Treleaven cracked. He tore off his headset and swung round to Burdick. "He can't fly it!" he shouted. "Of course he can't fly it!"

"Keep talking to him!" Burdick spat out, lunging forward at the captain and seizing his arm. "Keep talking, for Christ's sake. Tell him what to do."

Treleaven grabbed at the microphone, bringing it to his mouth. "Spencer," he said urgently, "you can't come straight in! Listen to me. You've *got* to do some circuits and practise that approach. There's enough fuel left for nearly two hours' flying. Stay up, man! Stay up!"

They listened intently as Spencer's voice came through.

"You'd better get this, down there. I'm coming in. Do you hear me? *I'm coming in.* There are people up here who'll die in less than an hour, never mind two. I may bend the airplane a bit— that's a chance we have to take. Now get on with the landing check. I'm putting the gear down now." They heard him say, "Wheels down, Janet."

"All right, George, all right," said Treleaven heavily. He slipped the headset on again. He had recovered his composure, but a muscle in his jaw worked convulsively. He closed his eyes for a second, then opened them, speaking with his former crispness. "If your undercarriage is down, check for the three green lights, remember? Keep your heading steady on 225. Increase your throttle setting slightly to hold your airspeed now the wheels are down. Adjust your trim and keep all the height you can. Right. Check that the brake pressure is showing around 1,000 pounds— the gauge is to the right of the hydraulic booster on the panel. If the pressure's okay, don't answer. You with me? Then open the gills to one third. D'you remember, Janet? The switch is by your left knee and it's marked in thirds. Answer me only if I'm going too fast. Next, the intercoolers. . . ."

As Treleaven went on, his voice filling the hushed Control Tower, Burdick moved to the plate glass window, searching the sky low on the horizon. The dawn light was murky, retarded by thick cloud banks. He heard Treleaven instruct a gentle 180-degree turn to the left, to bring the aircraft back for its last approach, impressing on Spencer to take it slowly and easily while the last checks were carried out. The captain's precise monotone formed a sombre background to the thoughts of the frantically worried airline manager.

"This," he said to an operator sitting nearby, "is a real tight one." The operator grimaced. "One thing's for sure," said Burdick. "Whatever happens in the next two or three minutes, there'll be hell let loose around here." He patted his trousers for cigarettes, thought better of it, and wiped the back of his hand across his mouth.

"Now advance your propeller settings," Treleaven was saying, "so that the tachometers give a reading of twenty-two fifty r.p.m. on each engine. Don't acknowledge."

"Twenty-two fifty," Spencer repeated to himself, watching the dials closely as he made the adjustment. "Janet," he said, "let me hear the airspeed."

"It's 130 . . ." she began tonelessly, "125 . . . 120 . . . 125 . . . 130. . . ."

In the Control Tower Treleaven listened on his headphones to the steady voice from the radar room. "Height is still unsteady. Nine hundred feet."

"George," said Treleaven, "Let your airspeed come back to 120 knots and adjust your trim. I'll repeat that. Airspeed 120." He looked down at his watch. "Take it nice and easy, now."

"Still turning, but losing height," reported the radar operator. "800 feet . . . 750 . . . 700. . . ."

"You're losing height!" rapped out Treleaven. "You're losing height. Open up—open up! You must keep at around one thousand."

Janet continued her reading of the airspeed: "110 . . . 110 . . . 105 . . . 110 . . . 110 . . . 120 . . . 120 . . . 120 . . . steady at 120. . . ."

"Come up . . . come up!" gritted Spencer between his teeth, hauling on the control column. "What a lumbering, great wagon this is! It doesn't respond! It doesn't respond at all."

"125 ... 130 ... 130 ... steady on 130. ..."

"Height coming up to 900 feet," intoned the radar operator. "950 ... on 1,000 now. Maintain 1,000."

Treleaven called to the Tower Controller, "He's turning on to final. Put out your runway lights, except zero-eight." He spoke into the microphone. "Straighten out on a heading between 074 and 080. Watch your airspeed and your height. Keep at a thousand feet until I tell you."

In one series after another, the strings of lights half-sunken into the grass beside the runways flicked off, leaving just one line on either side of the main landing strip.

"Come out of your turn, George, when you're ready," said Treleaven, "and line up with the runway you'll see directly ahead of you. It's raining, so you'll want your windshield wipers. The switch is down at the right on the co-pilot's side and is clearly marked."

"Find it, Janet," said Spencer.

"Hold your height at a thousand feet, George. We've taken you a long way out, so you have lots of time. Have Janet look for the landing light switch. It's in the panel overhead, a little left of centre. Hold your height steady."

"Can you find the switch?" asked Spencer.

"Just a minute . . . yes, I've got it."

Spencer stole a quick look ahead. "My God," he breathed. The lights of the runway, brilliant pinpoints in the blue-grey overcast of dawn, seemed at this distance to be incredibly narrow, like a short section of railway track. He freed one hand for an instant to dash it across his eyes, watering from their concentration.

"Correct your course," said Treleaven. "Line yourself up straight and true. Hold that height, George. Now listen carefully. Aim to touch down about a third of the way along the runway. There's a slight cross wind from the left, so be ready with a gentle right rudder." Spencer brought the nose slowly round. "If you land too fast, use the emergency brakes. You can work them by pulling the red handle immediately in front of you. And if that doesn't stop you, cut the four ignition switches which are over your head."

"See those switches, Janet?"

"Yes."

"If I want them off it'll be in a hurry," said Spencer. "So if I shout, don't lose any time about it." His throat was parched; it felt full of grit.

"All right," Janet replied in a whisper. She clasped her hands together to stop them shaking.

"It won't be long now, anyway. What about the emergency bell?"

"I hadn't forgotten. I'll ring it just before touchdown."

"Watch that airspeed. Call it off."

"120 . . . 115 . . . 120. . . ."

"Begin descent," said the radar operator. "400 feet a minute. Check landing gear and flaps. Hold present heading."

"All right, George," said Treleaven, "put down full flap. Bring your airspeed back to 115, adjust your trim, and start losing height at 400 feet a minute. I'll repeat that. Full flap, airspeed 115, let down at 400 feet a minute. Hold your present heading." He turned to Grimsell. "Is everything ready on the field?"

The Controller nodded. "As ready as we'll ever be."

"Then this is it. In sixty seconds we'll know."

They listened to the re-approaching whine of engines. Treleaven reached out and took a pair of binoculars the Controller handed him.

"Janet, give me full flap!" ordered Spencer. She thrust the lever down all the way. "Height and airspeed—call them off!"

"1,000 feet . . . speed 130 . . . 800 feet, speed 120 . . . 700 feet, speed 105. We're going down too quickly!"

"Get back that height!" Treleaven shouted. "Get back! You're losing height too fast."

"I know, I know!" Spencer shouted back. He pushed the throttles forward. "Keep watching it!" he told the girl.

"650 feet, speed 100 . . . 400 feet, speed 100. . . ."

Eyes smarting with sweat in his almost feverish concentration, he juggled to correlate speed with an even path of descent, conscious with a deep, sickening terror of the relentless approach of the runway, nearer with every second. The aircraft swayed from side to side, engines alternately revving and falling.

Burdick yelled from the Tower balcony, "Look at him! He's got no control!"

Keeping his glasses levelled at the oncoming aircraft, Treleaven snapped into the microphone, "Open up! Open up! You're losing height too fast! Watch the airspeed, for God's sake. Your nose is too high—open up quickly or she'll stall! Open up, I tell you, *open up!*"

"He's heard you," said Grimsell. "He's recovering."

"Me too, I wish," said Burdick.

The radar operator announced, "Still 100 feet below glide path. 50 feet below glide path."

"Get up—up," urged Treleaven. "If you haven't rung the alarm bell yet, do it now. Seats upright, passengers' heads down."

As the shrill warning rang out in the aircraft, Baird roared at the top of his voice, "Everybody down! Hold as tight as you can!"

Crouched double in their seats, Joe and Hazel Greer, the sports fans, wrapped their arms round each other, quietly and composedly. Moving clumsily in his haste, Childer tried to gather his motionless wife to him, then hurriedly leant himself across her as far as he could. From somewhere mid-ship came the sob-racked sound of a prayer and, farther back, an exclamation from one of the rye-drinking quartet of, "God help us—this is it!"

"Shut up!" rapped 'Otpot. "Save your breath!"

In the Tower, Grimsell spoke into a telephone-type microphone. "Crossing the perimeter now. All fire-fighting and salvage equipment stand fast until the aircraft has passed them. She may swing." His voice echoed back metallically from the buildings.

"He's back up to 200 feet," reported radar. "Still below glide path. 150 feet. Still below glide path. He's too low, captain. 100 feet."

Treleaven dragged off the headset. He jumped to his feet, holding the microphone in one hand and the binoculars in the other.

"Maintain that height," he instructed, "until you get closer in to the runway. Be ready to ease off gently. . . . Let down again. . . . That looks about right. . . ."

"Damn the rain," cursed Spencer. "I can hardly see." He could make out that they were over grass. Ahead he had a blurred impression of the beginning of the runway.

"Watch the airspeed," cautioned Treleaven. "Your nose is creeping up." There was a momentary sound of other voices in the background. "Straighten up just before you touch down and be ready to meet the drift with right rudder. . . . All right. . . . Get ready to round out. . . ."

The end of the grey runway, two hundred feet across, slid under them.

"Now!" Treleaven exclaimed. "You're coming in too fast. Lift the nose up! Get it up! Back up the throttles—right back! Hold her off. Not too much—not too much! Be ready for that cross wind. Ease her down, now. Ease her down!"

Undercarriage within a few feet of the runway surface, Spencer moved the control column gently back and forth, trying to feel his way down on to the ground, his throat constricted with panic because he now realized how much higher was this cockpit than that of any other plane he had flown, making judgment almost impossible for him.

For what seemed an age, the wheels skimmed the runway, making no contact. Then with a jolt they touched down. There was a shriek of rubber and a puff of smoke. The shock bounced the aircraft right into the air again. Then the balloon tyres were once more fighting to find a purchase on the concrete.

A third bump followed, then another and yet another. Cursing through his clenched teeth, Spencer hauled the control column back into his stomach, all the nightmare fears of the past few hours now a paralysing reality. The grey stream below him jumped up, receded, jumped up again. Then, miraculously, it remained still. They were down. He eased on the toe brakes, then held them hard, using all the strength in his legs. There was a high-pitched squeal but no sudden drop in speed. From the corner of his eye he could see that they were already more than two-thirds down the length of the runway. He could never hold the aircraft in time.

"You're landing too fast," roared Treleaven. "Use the emergency brakes! Pull the red handle!"

Spencer tugged desperately on the handle. He hauled the control column back into his stomach, jammed his feet on the brakes. He felt the tearing strain in his arms as the aircraft tried to slew. The wheels locked, skidded, then ran free again.

"Cut the switches!" he shouted to the girl. One by one, she snapped them off. The din of the engines died away, leaving in the cabin the hum of gyros and radio equipment, and outside the screaming of tyres.

Spencer stared ahead in fascinated horror. With no sound of engines, the aircraft was still travelling fast, the ground leaping past them in a blur. He could see now a big checkerboard marking the turn at the far end of the runway. In the fraction of a second his eyes registered in the picture of a fire truck, its driver falling to the ground in his scramble to get away.

Treleaven's voice burst into his ears with the force of a blow.

"Ground-loop it to the left! Ground-loop it to the left! Hard left rudder!"

Making an instantaneous decision, Spencer put his left foot on the rudder pedal and threw all his weight behind it, pressing it forward savagely.

Veering suddenly from the runway, the aircraft began to swing in an arc. Flung from one side of his seat to the other, Spencer struggled to keep the wings clear of the ground. There was a rending volume of noise, a dazzling flash, as the undercarriage ripped away and the aircraft smashed to the ground on its belly. The impact lifted Spencer clean from his seat. He felt a sharp pain as his safety belt bit deeply into his flesh.

"Get your head down!" he yelled. "We're piling up!"

Gripping their seats against the maniacal violence of the bouncing and rocking, they tried to curl themselves up. Still under momentum, the aircraft continued to slither crabwise, ploughing the grass in vicious furrows. With a screech of metal it crossed another runway, uprooting the runway lights, showering fountains of earth up into the air.

Spencer prayed for the end.

Like a prisoner in some crazy, helpless juggernaut, blood appearing in the corner of his mouth from a chance blow as yet unfelt, he waited for the inevitable tip-over, the upending, splintering crash that would, for him, disintegrate into a thousand fiery pinpoints of light before they were swallowed into darkness.

Then, quite suddenly, they were moving no longer. Spencer seemed to feel the same crazy motions as if they were still careering across the field; but his eyes told him they had stopped. For the space of seconds there was no sound at all. He braced himself against the awkward sideways tilt of the deck and looked over at Janet. Her head was buried in her hands. She was crying silently.

In the passenger compartment behind him there were murmurs and rustlings as of people who unbelievably awake to find themselves still alive. Someone laughed, shortly and hysterically, and this seemed to let loose half a dozen voices speaking at once.

He heard Baird call out, "Is anyone hurt?"

The noises melted into confusion. Spencer closed his eyes. He felt himself shaking.

"Better open up the emergency doors," came the adenoidal tones of 'Otpot, "and then everyone stay where he is."

From the door to the flight deck, jammed open in the crash, he heard the doctor exclaim, "Wonderful job! Spencer! Are you both all right?"

"I ground-looped!" he muttered to himself in disgust. "We

turned right around the way we came. What a performance—to ground-loop!"

"Rubbish—you did magnificently," Baird retorted. "As far as I can tell, there are only bruises and a bit of shock back here. Let's have a look at the captain and first officer—they must have been thrown about some."

Spencer turned to him. It was painful to move his neck.

"Doctor—" his throat was hoarse, "are we in time?"

"Yes, just about, I'd say. It's up to the hospital now, anyway. You've done your part."

He tried to raise himself in his seat. At that moment he became aware of the sound of crackling. He felt an upsurge of alarm. Then he realized that the noise was issuing from his headset which had slipped to the neck. He reached down and picked it up, holding one phone to his ear.

"George Spencer!" Treleaven was calling. "George Spencer! Are you there?"

Outside there was now a rising crescendo of sirens from crash tenders and fire trucks and ambulances.

"Yes," he said, "I'm here."

Treleaven was jubilant, caught in the general reaction. Behind his voice there were sounds of excited conversation and laughter.

"George. That was probably the lousiest landing in the history of this airport. So don't ever ask us for a job as a pilot. But there are some of us here who'd like to shake your hand, and later we'll buy you a drink. Now hold everything, George. We're coming over."

Janet had raised her head and was smiling tremulously.

"You should see your face," she said. "It's black."

He couldn't think of a thing to say. No witticism; no adequate word of thanks. He knew only that he was intolerably tired and sick to the stomach. He reached over for her hand and grinned back.

THE LION CALL

R. A. J. Maguire

HE squatted in the shade of a tree behind the District Office, the grubby book held closely to his face. One spatulate finger moved slowly along the line of large print. Concentration creased his brow and he squinted slightly as he mouthed the little words.

"*Ka—!*" he said, deep from his chest, the black skin stretched around the cavern of his mouth in which white teeth gleamed. "*Ka—,*" and then, triumphantly, "*Kat!*"

"Kat!" he repeated.

"*Paka!*" he added, referring laboriously to the parallel column in which the Swahili words were printed.

"*Paka!*" he said with relish. "*Kat!*"

He was a lean man of perhaps thirty years. The loose khaki blouse he wore was cut low, giving prominence to the Adam's apple in his scrawny neck. His bony knees, shining knobs on either side of his face, tapered down to slim ankles ending in enormous feet, splayed on the sand. His name was unpronounceable, and everyone in Jato, from Wright the District Commissioner downwards, knew him as *Twiga,* which means a giraffe.

Absorbed in his study he was unaware of the approach of Benson, the District Foreman, until the latter came to a halt a few paces away. Twiga looked up and scrambled hastily to his feet. Benson regarded him in silence.

Twiga smiled diffidently. "Master," he said, "there is a word here I do not understand. Could you——"

"Give me the book," interrupted Benson.

Twiga handed it over.

"Are you aware," said Benson venomously, "that I've been shouting for a messenger for ten minutes, while you were sitting here, doing damn all?" His voice quivered with rage. "What the hell d'you mean by it?"

Twiga remained silent. He glanced at Benson and looked away quickly. Lifting one foot off the ground, he began to scratch the back of his calf with the big toe.

"There's not the slightest use in trying to talk to you!" snarled Benson. He tore the flimsy book across and threw the pieces on the ground in front of Twiga.

Twiga cried out in protest, stooped and began to gather the scattered bits of paper. Benson drew back his foot and launched a kick that sent the angular figure sprawling. "Perhaps that'll teach you not to waste so much of the time you're paid for!" he shouted, and walked away, his young face dark with anger.

A roar of belly-laughter came from a gang of Africans, working on a wall at the far side of the compound, who had been watching every move. Twiga looked at them sourly, picked himself up and went on collecting the torn paper. "*Oie!*" he lamented, as the full extent of the disaster became apparent. "*Oie!* Truly he is a foul one, that Benson!"

He looked carefully around and spat between his teeth. "A snake was his mother!" he muttered.

"You know," said Wright, "if you don't mind my saying so, I think you have the wrong slant on things."

"I don't know what you mean," said Benson, uneasily shifting his feet. He faced Wright across the table in the District Office. Behind Wright the open window framed an immense view. For mile on mile the tree-clad foothills of the Black Mountain rolled and dipped towards the horizon. Scattered patches of cultivation stood out like gashes in the mountain's flanks. To the east the forest was unbroken where the long ridges piled up to the summit, wreathed in mist. The afternoon sun shone metallically in the rain-washed atmosphere.

"I mean simply this," said Wright. "You're working among Africans—you're with them every day—but there's no real contact between you and them, and there should be. We're pretty isolated here and when the rains set in we'll be more so. I've always thought that there's a lot to be got out of these people, primitive though they are. After all, they're the only human beings about the place. Why don't you——"

Benson snorted. "Grease-balls!" he said explosively. "How can you think they're human—creatures who never wash and cover themselves with ochre and mutton fat. Stinking louts! What do they know?"

"Maybe they haven't the sort of knowledge that you would value," said Wright, "but what they do know they've learned through the struggle for existence. They live hard, you know; it's a hard country and I think their knowledge is to be respected." To himself he thought, *God! You're being pompous! But how the hell do you get anything across to a fellow like this?*

"All right, then!" said Benson. "You're talking to me as if I was a kid, but I'll tell you one thing—when I've been here another six months I'll know as much as any of them about—about hunting, for instance. I admit I haven't had the practice at tracking, but I'm learning, and in my own way, too!"

"Good for you!" said Wright, "but wouldn't you learn quicker if you talked things over with them, sometimes? You'll find them all out to help and there are some first-rate hunters about the place. Now, Twiga——"

"Twiga!" broke in Benson. "I've already told you he squats on his stern all day, buried in a damn book, instead of doing the job he's paid for. What does an African messenger want with reading?"

"I might reply by asking what *you* want with hunting," said Wright. "As a matter of fact, his father has some cattle and I think Twiga's idea is that if he can learn to read and, perhaps write, he'll be able to help the old man keep his end up with the cattle-traders. But that doesn't matter," he went on, "Twiga is learning the hard way, like you are. The difference is that *he* hasn't the chance of being helped, for there's no one here with the time to teach him."

"There's nothing he or any of them can teach me that I can't teach myself, and I'm doing it," said Benson stubbornly.

"Y'know, I'm not so sure," said Wright slowly. "You remember that lion-skin I sent home for setting-up, just about the time you came here?"

"What of it?"

"I never told you that the lion was called to me," said Wright.

"Called to you—what on earth do you mean?" said Benson, staring at the other.

"I mean just that," said Wright. "I'd never shot a decent lion and I wanted one pretty badly. They all knew this, of course. But I was a bit surprised when they offered to call one for me. They don't do it often."

"I don't understand," said Benson. He swallowed. "How did they——"

"Well," Wright began, "you know what the country over at Kalaita is like—mainly scrub, with patches of forest and a few small glades. Twiga went across to Kalaita early one morning and got hold of a goat from the villagers. He——"

"Oh, so Twiga was in it!" interrupted Benson.

"Yes," said Wright mildly, "he and a fellow named Kintet, of the same tribe, who used to work here. Kintet brought me to a glade where we found that Twiga had slaughtered the goat, out in the open. He was scattering the entrails about when we came on him. 'There has to be blood,' he said. When he'd finished his arrangements he told me to sit down under a tree where I had a clear view of the glade. Then he and Kintet climbed the tree."

"And then?" said Benson, with an indulgent air.

I could take a running kick at you, you little blighter, thought Wright. "Oh, Twiga told me to keep still and then they began calling, in turn," he went on patiently. "So far as I could see, each man put his forefingers on either side of his nose and made a muffled, bleating noise into the hollow formed by the palms of his joined hands. It wasn't a very loud noise. I had them do it for me afterwards. They explained that 'to the lion, it is a goat', although I must say it didn't sound much like a goat to me.'

Wright put his hands to his face and made a nasal sound.

"It was something like that," he said. "I waited under that tree for about half an hour, I suppose. Nothing happened except that some vultures, probably attracted by the dead goat, arrived and sat in a tree near by. D'you know, they were the first to warn me? I was watching them—filthy-looking brutes—when a ripple of movement went through them; they all seemed to shift a little at the same instant. I looked across the glade, and just as I did so there was a surge in the grass and the best lion I have ever seen trotted out into the open. The two up in the tree went on calling and the lion moved forward a few steps. I shall never forget how he looked —his black mane stood out from his head and neck, making his face seem as small as a monkey's. Whether he saw me or not I don't know, but he paid no attention to me."

Benson, his eyes glistening, said eagerly, "So you got him?"

"I shot him in the chest. I could hardly have missed, for the range was about ten yards and he went over without a kick," said Wright. "I was just going across to have a look at him when Twiga hissed from above, 'Don't move! Another will come!', and they went on calling."

Wright looked at Benson and raised his eyebrows.

"I must say, what with the noise of the shot and the disturbance made by the vultures as they flew away, I didn't believe strongly in the second lion, but within a few minutes she was there. I saw her coming, bounding through the grass a little to the left of the spot where her mate was lying. She stopped when she came into the open, and as she stood, head up and almost broadside on, her tail whipping up and down, I swear to you she looked as if she was waiting for the bullet."

Wright ceased speaking and looked down at his desk.

"It was an odd business," he said slowly. "I may be imagining it, now, but I think . . . it seemed to me there was a feeling of *compulsion*—I can't describe it in any other way—in that place. Somehow, everything that happened *had* to happen . . . and yet the two Africans, although they were very pleased about the male's black mane, appeared quite unconcerned otherwise."

"I don't believe it!" said Benson. "I mean," he added, flushing, "I mean there must be some explanation. How could a lion be called, to order? It doesn't make sense!"

"I'm not giving you any explanation," Wright said. "I haven't got one. I'm merely telling you what happened to support my statement—theory, if you like—that these people have knowledge that we haven't got. They also have pride and self-respect, although perhaps you may not think so."

"So I'm on the mat because I booted Twiga, am I?" said Benson truculently. He stood up.

"Oh, for God's sake!" Wright groaned. "I'm trying to help you to get the most out of your job, that's all. Think it over."

"I'm sorry, but I don't agree with you," said Benson primly. "I'm here to tell these people what to do; it's not their business to instruct me. If you don't want me, you needn't renew my contract when the year's up."

He walked out of the office.

"You young ass!" murmured Wright wearily, reaching for a cigarette.

Twiga crouched in the low doorway of his hut in a corner of the compound. The fading light made his task, already difficult, harder still. With an almost hairless brush and the dregs of a bottle of gum, borrowed from the District Clerk, he was mending his book. His hands were accustomed to less delicate tasks and it was proving a messy business.

Muttering to himself, he worked patiently at the tattered pages that were growing slowly into a sodden mass. It would be solid in the morning and unreadable for the most part, but he knew nothing of that. For the moment, he was engrossed in the problem of arranging the pages in sequence—no easy matter when you are but dimly familiar with figures above nine. He worked on doggedly. It was important to bring the book back to life, for had not the District Clerk, who was a highly educated man, said that there was much knowledge in the pages he hadn't yet studied?

"Enter!" called Wright.

The door opened half way and Twiga slid round it into the

room, retaining a firm hold on the door handle. As the gaunt figure stood before him in the lamplight, Wright's thought was that Twiga, indoors, always succeeded in looking as if he were poised for flight.

"I have called for you because I am worried about Bwana Benson," Wright said.

Twiga was silent.

"It's two hours beyond sunset and he hasn't got back. What do you think?"

"He has shot his game, maybe," said Twiga woodenly.

"Perhaps," said Wright, "but he told me he was going down to Milola on his *pikipiki* and he should have been back by now, whether he saw game or not. *I* think," he paused and looked at Twiga, "*I* think he's got into trouble. In the Milola bush there would be no one to see, or to hear him if he called."

"He could call by firing the rifle," said Twiga. "*Kaa! Kaa!* Like that! People would come."

"I suppose he could," said Wright, "but if he hasn't returned by the first light, we must look for him."

"I can go now, Master," said Twiga. "There is a moon."

"I hoped you'd say that," said Wright, smiling. "For one thing, you'll travel quicker on your own." He thought for a moment. "Now listen, if there's no news by, say, midday to-morrow, I'll come out with some men. We'll follow the edge of the Milola forest, where it meets the plain, until we contact you. Is it understood?"

Twiga grunted.

"This is the last time I'll let Benson go off by himself," muttered Wright. "Damn the stubborn fool!"

Twiga looked down his nose and left the room without speaking.

The moon had set and the grey half-light that comes before the dawn lay over the land like a thin blanket when Twiga came on Benson's motor-cycle, standing to one side of the rough track and covered neatly with a canvas groundsheet. He walked around the machine two or three times, his eyes on the ground, and then squatted on a corner of the canvas. He reached into the front of his blouse and produced a lump of charred meat. He bit into the meat, and, holding it in his teeth, neatly cut off a piece with his broad-bladed spear. He chewed slowly, his eyes fixed on the bush.

When the first glimmer of the coming daylight was in the sky, he picked up the spear, rose to his feet and struck off into the bush. The leaves, heavy with dew, slapped at his face and hands and closed behind him.

The sun was high when he came to the end of his search.

Benson lay on his back in the middle of a rocky clearing, his rifle beside him. His shorts were rucked up and his bare legs were covered with scratches from knee to ankle. His right shin was a mess of blood and shattered tissue through which protruded splintered fragments of bone. As Twiga bent over him his eyes opened and focused slowly.

". . . don't know how it happened," he murmured through colourless lips, ". . . running . . . must've tripped . . . stone turned under my foot . . ." his voice rose to a scream. "Get me out of this, for Christ's sake!" Tears rolled down his cheeks.

Twiga picked up the rifle and examined it. The bolt was open, the magazine full and a cartridge was jammed in the breech. It had been fired. Twiga put his nose to the muzzle of the rifle, sniffed and shook his head. With the edge of his spear blade he levered at the rim of the cartridge which presently came loose and lay in his hand. It was a misfire, complete with its bullet. He stood motionless for a moment. Then he rammed the misfire back into the breech, put the rifle on the ground beside Benson and walked over to the edge of the clearing.

Benson began to swear. In a bitter monotone he cursed himself, his ill-luck and Twiga, while he shifted uneasily on the ground, groaning with pain as the jumbled words left his lips. Steam rose from his soaked clothes into the sunlight.

Twiga took off his sandals, knotted the thongs together and hung them around his neck. With his spear wedged in his armpit, he placed one foot against the trunk of an acacia tree, reached up and was presently astride a low branch. He climbed upwards without haste, avoiding the thorns, until he found a smooth crotch. Deliberately he placed his spear in a fork near to hand, adjusted his body to the crotch and found a convenient branch for his feet. He parted the foliage and looked down at the figure in the clearing. Now Benson lay still. His voice had sunk to a drone in which the words were not distinguishable.

Impassively, Twiga let the leaves fall back into place. Then he cupped his hands in front of his face and began to send his nasal call out over the bush.

A PRAYER FOR THE SHIP

Douglas Reeman

"A Prayer For The Ship" is published by
Jarrolds Ltd.

The Author

Douglas Reeman always had a great ambition to serve in the Navy, which he joined at an early age. He saw service in destroyers, but eventually made a final "home" in small craft and saw service in the Atlantic, North Sea and the Mediterranean. He has always been interested in human problems and he now works for the educational department of the L.C.C. He is married and lives on a small motor yacht. *A Prayer for the Ship,* his first novel, was written in his free evenings. As a member of the Royal Naval Sailing Association he is a keen and regular yachtsman.

CHAPTER ONE

THE whole of the naval anchorage seemed subdued and cowed by the relentless, sleety rain which drove across the estuary, whipping the grey waves into a turbulent, white-capped frenzy. As the wind moaned through the mean little streets around the port, and swept the soaking jetties, the various ships-of-war strained and tugged at their cables and wires, while huddled figures in glistening oilskins sought cover and protection behind the gun-shields or flapping canvas dodgers. Across and beyond the boom-gate, a few barrage balloons plunged and staggered like drunken whales, as their cursing crews somewhere in the muddy fields fought with the creaking moorings. The sea itself looked even greyer than usual, and it was difficult to discern the break with the racing clouds which was the horizon, where a lone trawler fought into the teeth of the gale, one minute hidden by the steep, jagged waves, and the next instant showing her streaming keel, more concerned with staying afloat than listening for a prowling U-boat.

The tall, rust-streaked sides of the Coastal Forces Depot Ship *Royston* shuddered as the gale punched her, but she remained the steadiest vessel in the harbour, her cables fore and aft stretched bar-taut, and her deck-planking patterned with little humps of blown salt. Her charges, Motor Torpedo Boats and Motor Gunboats, were strung in uncomfortable trios around her, banging and lurching together, rope fenders and old motor tyres doing their best to ease the jolting motion. Up on the main deck, the Quartermaster peered out towards the railway wharf, and cursed unsympathetically at the ship's motor-boat which had just left the shelter of the wall, and was bounding over the stream towards him. He saw the Coxswain lift his hand in a half-hearted sign and then withdraw into the tiny wheelhouse. The Quartermaster turned to the other figure sharing his vigil, the Officer-of-the-Day, who was endeavouring to read a signal, already soggy with rain, in the shelter of his oilskin.

"Motor-boat returning, sir," he yelled. "One officer aboard."

Lieutenant Pike waved the tattered signal in acknowledgement.

"Turn out the Duty Watch, I am going to bring the boat aboard, no more trips today."

As the Quartermaster pulled out his silver call and switched on the Tannoy microphone, Pike watched with narrowed eyes as the motor-boat swung up to the main gangway and hooked on with its usual precision. His glance shifted to the nearest Motor Torpedo Boat, the only one showing a sign of life, as a handful of the Depot Ship's maintenance party scurried round repairing and replacing the scars of a running battle two nights before, when the young First Lieutenant had been killed, as so many had been from this flotilla.

As usual the replacement was arriving in the motor-boat. Pike returned the salute of the slim officer who stepped over the gangway, his too-new greatcoat gleaming with rain.

"Sub-Lieutenant Clive Royce, come aboard to join," he shouted.

They shook hands, and Pike ushered him to the first doorway, while two disgruntled members of the Duty Watch collected the baggage of the latest arrival.

"Go below to the wardroom," said Pike. "The Commander is in there at the moment and he'll want to see you right away."

Royce nodded, and stepped into the passageway. Immediately, the sounds of the storm were muffled, and a feeling of security surrounded him. He stripped off his greatcoat and cap, straightened his uniform, and had a quick glance in the mirror outside the old-fashioned door marked "Wardroom". He had a pleasant face, with eager, grey eyes, and a firm but generous mouth. His hair, now flattened by cap and rain, was dark almost to the point of being black. Taking a deep breath, Royce slid the door to one side and stepped in. The wardroom had once been the first-class saloon in the old ship's early days as a small passenger and cargo vessel, and had a prosperous, rather Edwardian look about it. The sides and deckhead were oak-panelled and carved in ornate designs, and a long, polished bar completely lined one end. The whole room was littered with dumpy, red-leather chairs and sofas, all well-worn but comfortable looking, and most of them were occupied by youthful officers who lounged about reading magazines, listening to the radio, or just dozing.

A round-faced, cheerful-looking Commander leaned against the bar listening to a serious Lieutenant, who kept pounding the bar as if to emphasize a point that was beyond anyone else's comprehension.

Royce coughed nervously. "I was told to report direct to you, sir. My name is Royce."

"Well now, I'm Commander Wright, and I do all the 'crewing' of the boats here, so I'll get you fixed up right away." He beamed. "And this is your Commanding Officer, Lieutenant Harston, so I'll leave you to get acquainted, while I arrange your orders."

At twenty-three, Harston was already a veteran of the East Coast and Channel warfare, and the first signs of strain were beginning to show on his pale, rather artistic face. Coolly he offered his hand in a surprisingly strong handshake.

When he spoke, it was with a soft, careful deliberation.

"I've taken the trouble to look up your particulars in advance, because in this racket we don't seem to find the time as we go along."

He paused while he made a gesture to the barman with his glass, which was ignored in favour of two elderly officers at the other end of the bar.

With a shrug, he continued, "Terrible service here. Now, let me see. You're twenty years old, been commissioned three months. Sea experience, three months in an Asdic trawler. You'll probably notice the difference when you find three and a half thousand horsepower under your feet. Correct me if I'm wrong, but I believe you were beginning to be a marine draughtsman before you joined, any connexion?"

"Well, I've always been keen on the sea, small boats, and that sort of thing," finished Royce lamely.

"What you mean is, you haven't a clue, but you're a hard-working boy, and willing to learn. I only pray you get longer to learn than your predecessor," he added grimly.

At the sight of Royce's crestfallen expression, he relented, in fact his whole personality changed, and a warm, friendly grin spread across his face.

"Never mind, tomorrow morning I'll take you over the boat, and tomorrow night I'm afraid we go out again. In the meantime, we'll grab this blasted steward and drink to War Savings, or something!"

As that first evening wore on, Royce had plenty of time to study his superior, and to observe his quick, breath-taking changes of mood and manner. He would re-tell some of his experiences in the flotilla on the East Coast convoy routes, or the mad dashes through the night with the enemy coast only a few yards abeam, telling how and why each operation was a success or a failure, speaking in his soft, precise voice, his blue eyes distant and apparently unseeing, then with a jerk, he would become a boy again, as he recounted incidents like the occasion when he and his friends stole a fire-engine and drove it madly round the town, hotly pursued by the military police. He lay back in his chair and gave his queer, high-pitched laugh, "There was hell to pay over that. But they never caught us. In fact, old Benjy over there has still got a hose in his cabin."

Every so often he introduced Royce to his new team-mates, as they drifted in and out of the bar, and he appeared satisfied with the way that he answered the very mixed selection who made up the flotilla's Commanding Officers. There was Ronnie Patterson, a young, red-faced north countryman, whose language was apt to appal strangers, but who was obviously a great favourite with everybody. Artie Emberson had been a barrister, and looked it. When he spoke in his drawling voice to the steward on the question of drinks, it sounded as if he was questioning a rather dumb witness. "Benjy" Watson was the inevitable practical joker, who had missed many a court-martial by sheer good luck—the last occasion being when he dressed in a captured German officer's uniform and went to a local cinema. His pointed, pink face split into a beaming smile as he re-told the story.

"Not a blessed soul took any notice of me," he roared, "and if I hadn't given a Nazi salute when I passed two army types, it would all have been a waste of a run ashore!"

Jock Murray was another whom Royce liked instantly. A small, hard-faced ex-fisherman from Aberdeen, whose family had been trawling the North Sea for generations, he was a man of few words and only one interest, the sea.

One thing they all had in common, they were old before their time, aged by experiences that Royce could only guess at, and imagine.

When the bar-shutters fell with a bang that brought a roar of protests, Royce floated, rather than walked, down to the tiny, box-like cabin which was to be his home while in harbour. A newly cleaned and emptied place, where his predecessor had once slept and thought and hoped, and although only dead forty-eight hours, the last of his earthly traces had already been swept away.

So Clive Royce went to war, and with the relentless rain lashing the side of his cabin, he fell into a deep, dreamless sleep.

Royce's first morning with the One Hundred and Thirteenth

Flotilla dawned fresh and clear, the gale had blown itself out during the night, and only the smell of damp oilskins and a few puddles on the canvas awnings gave a hint of the torrential rain. The whole harbour bustled with activity, as if to make up for a lost day, and as motor-boats and harbour launches scurried to and fro between their parent vessels, ships' companies and base staff got down to the daily business of preparing their charges for sea.

As he swung himself down the catwalk from the depot ship on to the first M.T.B., Royce was aglow and eager to start, inspired perhaps by the easy confidence of the other officers at breakfast, plus a somewhat ponderous speech delivered by the base Operations Officer about the "nation depending upon these young men in its hour of need", while Royce shifted impatiently at the top of the gangway. Ah, there she was! Low, grey and sleek, Number 1991 painted in large numbers on her bow, her decks crammed with overalled figures, one of whom straightened and saluted. A short, chubby, little man, with a battered Petty Officer's cap tilted rakishly over unruly ginger hair, he put down an enormous wrench.

"Petty Officer Raikes, sir, Coxswain. I expect you'll be the new officer?"

He had a faint Liverpool accent, and seemed amused by Royce's immaculate uniform.

"The Captain's aft at the moment, sir, I think he's expecting you."

Was there a hint of sarcasm in his voice? Royce couldn't be sure. Perhaps it was the hidden bitterness of a junior professional to a senior amateur.

"Very well, Cox'n," he nodded, and stepped aft. "That was it," he thought, "be brief and to the point."

He found Harston sitting on a smoke float, deeply engrossed in a conversation with a large man in a bowler hat, the sign of dockyard authority.

Royce smiled, "Reporting for instruction, sir, and a fine morning it is too, after the drenching I got yesterday."

Harston stood up quickly, like a cat: "When I want your views on the weather, I'll let you know," he snapped. "It may interest you to know that I've been here since six-thirty, trying to get these repairs finished, and while you no doubt have been indulging in a bit of gossip, and enjoying an excellent breakfast, I've also been arranging your duties for you!"

Royce flushed and stammered, completely taken aback by this

unexpected attack. "The Operations Officer stopped me, sir, he was telling . . ."

"I'm not interested. If you want to be a big pin in a little ship instead of tea-boy in a battle-wagon, you'll have to get down to it, and forget this barrack routine stuff. We don't start at nine here, with three hours for lunch, we keep going till the job's done, and the job right now is to get this boat ready to go out at 2000 tonight!"

He swung back to the stolid dockyard manager, who had taken a sudden interest in the guard-rails during this tirade.

His voice now sounded heavy and tired: "Righto, Angus, you'll do that for me, then? Bless you." And without a further word, he strode to the catwalk. As he heaved himself over the other M.T.B., he turned and called for the Coxswain.

"Get those men at work on the guns as soon as you can, I don't want any more jamming. And get some overalls for Sub-Lieutenant Royce, and then show him the boat, every bit. I'm going to have breakfast, if there's any left now."

Royce watched him scramble up the ladder and out of sight; he was completely shattered.

"Phew, was that the chap who told me last night not to worry," he muttered. "Well, I can see this is going to be just fine."

The portly Angus coughed at his elbow, "I'm off, just got to see about some new bolts, an' that. Now, don't you worry about him, son, he's the best that comes, I've seen a few, too. Trouble is, he's been at it too long. I think the poor bloke's just about had it." And with a heavy thud on the shoulder, he too disappeared.

For the next hour, Royce and the Coxswain crawled and scrambled over every inch of the M.T.B.'s eighty-five feet, the latter pointing out this and that he felt would be of immediate interest, but reserving his more personal observations until he found out with what sort of an officer he had to deal.

As he confided to the Petty Officer Motor Mechanic, "Pony" Moore, later in the morning over their "tots", "You never know with these Wavy Navy types, some of 'em listen like babes while you try to stop them making fools of themselves, and the next thing you know you're on Defaulters 'cause you haven't done the job to their liking!"

"When will you learn, Tom, all officers are bastards," was Moore's only comment.

Royce did find out, however, that the flotilla was engaged in assisting the two other main East Coast groups operating from Harwich and Yarmouth, with the result that their patrols were more varied and uncertain, and the whole base was kept on a mobile footing.

Eventually they arrived back at the tiny, open bridge. The Coxswain pointed to a speaker in one corner.

"That's our latest bit of gear, sir, an R.T. link between the group. It enables the Senior Officer to get right on to you at once about the form of attack, etc. It's a big help at night, I can tell you, 'specially when you can't use lights, and most likely can't even see the next ahead."

"Have any of the boats got Radar yet?"

"Blimey, no, sir!" laughed Raikes, "there's a queue from Pompey to Benghazi for that lot. The next war'll be over before we even get a smell!"

He suddenly tensed, "C.O.'s coming aboard, sir, I'll be off after the guns' crews, the starboard Oerlikon is bloody bad!"

Harston stepped briskly on to the bridge. "How's it going, Number One?" he drawled. "All buttoned up?"

"Yes, sir," said Royce coldly, "I'm trying not to make an ass of myself."

He received a searching glance. "Take it off your back, Number One, we've all got to learn. Now shove off to the depot ship and get your issue of special clothing, and then report to the Flotilla Commander's office at eight bells. He likes to meet all his new boys. Before they make asses of themselves," he added drily.

The office was situated in what had once been the Purser's room, and he was shown straight in to the presence of Lieut.-Commander Arnold Paskins, R.N.V.R., ex-author, yachtsman, and mountaineer, and now in command of the flotilla, with twenty skirmishes and two D.S.C.s to his credit. He rose from his desk, littered with signals, serial photographs, and charts, a tall, lanky, but wiry figure, topped by a sharp-featured, well-informed, aristocratic face, with clear, steady eyes.

"Sit down, Royce," he offered. "I thought that it would be only fair for you to get to know as soon as possible the sort of job you've landed in. There's no other branch in the Service where so much responsibility falls on the most junior officers, chaps like yourself, who only a few months ago were at home doing respectable jobs, or going to school, or like me," he grinned, "just enjoying life. I've studied your reports and I'm satisfied with what I've read, so provided the Hun gives you time, there's no reason why you shouldn't make the grade. As you know, we're going out tonight, and if anything goes badly, you might find yourself in command by morning. Could you do it?" Those piercing eyes bored into him.

Royce thought to himself, "After this morning's episode, I think it would be comparatively simple!" But he could only answer: "I'll do my best, sir."

The interview was ended, and as he left the cabin, Paskins returned to the endless mass of the paper war.

The Operations Room in *Royston* was crowded and noisy as was usual before every sailing-time, and the chairs which were lined in front of the big wall-maps and charts were already filled with Commanding Officers and their "Number Ones", chatting, or shouting lustily to each other, or making notes and alterations on their own charts. Harston and Royce found a couple of chairs at the front, and having greeted everybody and settled down, the former pointed out the patrol areas on the big master chart. A hush fell on the gathering, and the officers rose to their feet as Commander Wright, Paskins, and an R.A.F. Officer entered the room.

"Sit, gentlemen," boomed Wright. "You may smoke."

There was renewed rustle of scraping matches, and clicking lighters, and when all were settled and the pipes were going well, Wright continued: "This is the patrol area for tonight." He pointed with a long cane. "You will observe that at approximately midnight the local coastal convoy passes the main north-bound convoy about here, and as it shows every sign of being a dark and cloudy night, you can expect some trouble."

The R.A.F. Officer was next. Royce discovered that he was the representative from Coastal Command who gave details of the local flying and air cover in the area. He had a dull, uninteresting voice, and as he droned on, Royce thought over the events of the day, and in spite of himself, he had to smile. The C.O. had been more than helpful and friendly all the afternoon, and had apparently forgotten the morning's clash of temperaments, and he now sat hunched forward on the edge of his chair, listening intently to everything the officer on the rostrum had to say, his face alight with boyish enthusiasm and keen understanding, apparently unaware that he had nearly caused Royce to lose faith in himself.

The Air Force officer sat down, and the irrepressible Commander Wright jumped to his feet. "Any questions, gentlemen?"

One by one the various Commanding Officers rose and fired their queries. Weather report, enemy shipping movements, recognition signals, and a score of other details, which Royce and the other "second-hands" scribbled on their pads. Eventually the conference ended, and in groups they hurried back to the boats which now rode easily in the gentle swell, as if resting before their ordeal.

As Royce changed into his one-piece waterproof "Ursula suit" he felt himself trembling with excitement, his mind awhirl with the instructions and taut with a determination to give his C.O. no new cause for complaint. There was nobody he could turn to for advice or guidance now, all that was behind him, this was it, the "front line", and right at that moment he would not have changed places with any other living creature, even considering the great overshadowing sinking feeling caused by fear. Fear of what? He couldn't be sure whether it was of death, or of not making the grade. He gave the zip-fasteners a final jerk, clapped on his cap, and stepped out on deck.

Harston leaned over the side of the bridge, having a shouted conversation with Artie Emberson in 1993, moored alongside. The latter waved a copy of the *Daily Mirror*.

"I see that some chappie in the House of Commons says we are expendable, so we have to keep our petrol engines, diesels are too expensive for us apparently. So in future, old man, when you burst into flames, remember, nobody loves you!"

Harston grinned: "I'd like to have had some of those perishers with me on the last trip, they might have learned what it's like to float about on top of a time-bomb!"

"Come, come," drawled Emberson, "you really mustn't be so bitter, don't you realize there's a war on?"

Harston's next remarks were drowned by a deafening roar, as Emberson's engines came to life, and Royce smelt the powerful fumes of the high-octane spirit, as smoke enveloped the boats, then the roar toned down to a steady pulsating throb as they ticked over confidently. Emberson wound a bright yellow scarf about his throat, and giving the thumbs up sign to Harston, he turned away to make final preparations for sea.

"Right," snapped Harston, as Royce appeared. "Single up to springs and stand by to slip." He smiled briefly: "Old Artie's got the fastest boat in the flotilla, and won't let you forget it, but we'll show him when we get out."

On the cramped fo'c'sle, Leading Seaman Parker, a tough, capable man in oilskin and thick leather gauntlets, was supervising the business of preparing the wires for a quick get-away, as he had done so often before, and he shot a steely glance at the new First Lieutenant as he came forward. Like the Coxswain, he wondered how the new boy would behave.

Royce returned the casual salute: "You're Parker, I believe," he said. "Carry on and single up to springs, and stand by to slip."

He was going to add that he wouldn't interfere with Parker's routine task, but at that moment he felt the boat shake, and with a series of coughs and snarls the main engines shook themselves awake. He had no idea that these frail craft would stand such a shaking, and he noted with some amusement that Parker's whole burly frame quivered like a jelly on a plate.

Parker waited until the engines settled to a steady rumble, then shouted: "Is it right we're goin' to get a refit this trip, sir?" His hoarse, Cockney voice easily drowned the din, and Royce was even able to appreciate the slightly anxious note in his tone.

"Worried, Parker?" laughed Royce, and the three other seamen who lounged against the guard rails, chuckled.

"I've been in this boat long enough to be bleedin' worried," answered Parker defiantly, and spat over the side.

Royce coloured at this unexpected outburst, and saw the other seamen tense with expectancy.

"That's enough of that," he barked, surprised at the sound of his own voice. "You've obviously not been in it long enough to learn to control yourself, now just you stand by those wires!"

"Aye, aye, sir," answered Parker heavily, and turned his angry eyes away.

Royce turned to the bridge, where the C.O. was peering through his glasses at the signal tower, furious with Parker, and himself. It was becoming more and more obvious to him that there was a great deal more to being an officer than just wearing the uniform. How could he show he wanted to learn, without appearing stupid, and how could he adopt Harston's easy manner with the crew if it only made him seem weak?

His jumbled thoughts were cut dead by the insistent winking of a powerful lamp from the tower, and Harston's terse orders.

"Let go springs, bear off forward," and to the voice-pipe at his side: "Slow ahead together. Starboard ten."

As Royce watched, the greasy wires were released by the depot ship hands and splashed briefly into the water, from where they were eagerly snatched, before they could wrap themselves around the churning screws, and with a quickening vibration at his feet, the boat swung away from her moorings in a wide arc, to take her place at fifth in the line of the eight boats which were all manoeuvring into an orderly procession heading for the boom-gate. Lieut.-Commander Paskins, the Senior Officer, led in his newly-painted craft, her bold 2001 shining in the setting sun. Royce could see him scanning the flotilla through his glasses, and felt vaguely reassured by his presence. As he returned to the bridge, and reported that the boat was fully secure for sea, the R-T speaker crackled into life.

"Hallo all Captains, this is Leader calling. Keep close station on me, and watch for convoy recognition signals round about midnight. No moon tonight, so don't creep on to my quarter-deck!"

The speaker popped and went dead. Harston grinned, he seemed more at ease now that he was at sea again.

"What a useful gadget, much better than the lamp, the blessed signalman always gets excited in action anyway, and squirts the signals all over the place!"

The boats slid over the full but gentle swell, into a glorious blood-red sunset, that painted the glittering waters with a mil-lion rich and changing hues, and as it grew darker, the boats became dull, uneven blobs on this heaving travesty of colour.

"I'm going to get a couple of hours shut-eye now," said Harston. "That'll give you time to get the feel of her, and I'll be fresh later on when I'm needed." He smiled: "Alright, Number One, she's all yours." And suddenly the bridge was a lonely place.

Royce peered over the darkening fo'c'sle, where the pom-pom crew, in their bulky clothing, hunched around the gun, and away over the bows, at the twisting stern of Emberson's boat, and the white froth which seemed to link all the boats together.

From out of space, a tinny voice rattled: "Able Seaman Lewis relieving on the wheel, sir." Royce groped his way to the now invisible voice-pipe, and acknowledged the message. That meant that the reliable Coxswain had left the wheel and handed over to the usual Quartermaster.

"Cocoa, sir?" a youthful murmur at his elbow steadied the wave of nerves which threatened to make him recall the Captain to his aid, and the signalman, Mead, a slender, seventeen-year-old who had joined the boat only a month before, thrust a steaming mug towards him. Royce drank gratefully, and felt the thick chocolate radiating through his whole body.

"I needed that, 'Bunts'," he smiled. "You're new here too, aren't you?"

"Yes, sir, finished my training last month, and came straight here. I had hoped for a chance to get a commission, but I suppose nobody thought I was the right type," he grinned ruefully.

Royce, determined to make a success of this encounter, reassured him hastily, and was on the point of promising to take the matter up, when he happened to look ahead again, and with a sickening shock, realized that Emberson's boat had vanished from view. With a hasty glance at the compass, which told him that they were on the correct course, he yelled down the voice-pipe:

"Full ahead together, and watch your course!"

To the horrified Mead he barked: "Make to the next astern. Increase speed and keep station on me."

Even as the lamp began to clatter, the boat leapt forward with staggering force, throwing up twin banks of foam from either bow, as the high-speed hull lifted from the water like a dolphin. He peered out ahead into the darkness, straining his eyes, and sweating with fear. If he lost the rest of the flotilla on his first trip out, Harston would definitely get rid of him. Damn the cocoa, and the signalman, if only he had . . . a frantic shout came from the pom-pom.

"Boat dead ahead. Dead ahead!"

And there it was, fine on the port bow, with the distance shortening at an alarming rate. His head was suddenly clear, and he felt strangely resigned.

"Hard a-starboard. Stop. Full astern together."

The boat reeled round to starboard, and the engines screamed in protest. Vaguely from below he heard the crash of breaking crockery, but still they rushed on, until every detail was visible on the other boat. Then, when a crash seemed inevitable, the engines began to tell, and with maddening slowness she slewed round and glided up along the other boat's starboard quarter.

Saved! He licked his lips, now trembling. "Slow ahead together, Quartermaster, resume previous station."

Emberson's loud-hailer clicked on: "Mother, there's someone at the back door!"

Royce waved to him with relief, and watched anxiously as the other boats astern sorted themselves out and resumed patrol in an orderly line.

He was then aware of Harston's dark figure below the bridge, and he stiffened for the onslaught.

Instead: "Well done, nothing like livening things up a bit!" and he was gone.

When the Captain returned to the bridge, just before midnight he found the new Number One with his eyes glued to the next ahead, his lesson learned. He smiled to himself, it would not do for Royce to know that the Coxswain had shaken him awake to inform him that the new officer was rushing at full speed into the rest of the flotilla, apparently out of control!

In the far distance, a pin-point of light stabbed at the blackness, and the Senior Officer replied to the challenge, which had come from one of the convoy's escorts, and the next instant the slowly moving merchant ships were looming past. Coasters, oil tankers, freighters, and all the rest, huge, and yet so helpless, and dependent on the anxious escorts which dashed backwards and forwards around the convoy like ferrets smelling out a rabbit.

Harston jerked his head in their direction. "Rather them than me. Look at those blessed escorts. One destroyer, vintage about 1917, two converted trawlers. It makes you sick; you've got your politicians to thank for this state of affairs."

In a few moments, the convoy was swallowed up by the night, and the anxious business of station-keeping began again, but now Harston remained on the bridge, which was now whipped by a keen breeze that removed all traces of drowsiness from the watchkeepers, and with an unlit pipe clenched between his teeth, he constantly swept the starboard beam through his night glasses.

"Not much to worry about with that little convoy," he observed. "It's the big northbound we've got to watch out for. They break up the convoy here to take it through the swept channel, and the E-boats sometimes have a go for the stragglers." Then he stiffened. "Ah, there she is, right on time."

And there was another light flashing, far away on the starboard bow, and soon the familiar, hulking shapes of the groping merchantmen were gliding past, their empty hulls rising like giant forts, and their half-exposed screws churning white patches of froth against the inky backcloth. Again the escorts raced back and forth, through their cumbersome charges, but a stronger guard this time, two destroyers, and some corvettes—taking no chances.

Ship after ship rolled past, till Royce lost count, and then, with a final protesting hiss of steam from an ancient freighter, they too were gone.

The flotilla swung about to steer north-east, the "top leg" of the patrol area, slackening speed over the dark swell, so that their engines just seemed to be ticking over, and it was again possible to talk without shouting above the din.

Harston rested his chin on folded arms, as he leaned across the screen. "Sorry you joined, Number One?" he grinned.

The other looked up quickly from the dimly-lit compass. "I guess I'll be alright," he said thoughtfully. "I must say I wish I had the knack of being fierce enough to get things done without worrying about their feelings." He nodded towards the huddled gun's crew. "It's difficult to get people to look up to you without giving them the impression that you're looking down on them, if you follow me," he finished lamely.

"Heavens, what a complicated mind you've got." The muffled figure shook with soft laughter. "But I think I know what you mean; it happens to all of us at first. Take my advice, don't try to be too definite in your ideas until you've got to know the lads as individuals, you'll be right on top line then."

They lapsed into contented silence as a can of hot, sweet tea was heaved on to the bridge, the scalding liquid running through Royce like a fresh confidence.

One of the bridge lookouts lowered his glasses. "Leader's turning, sir, comin' back down the line."

Paskins' boat cruised slowly down the line and as he came abreast of them, he shouted through his megaphone, "We'll stop here for a bit, in case Jerry's sending anyone across to intercept the convoy." And as he raced back to the head of his flotilla, the boats cut their engines, and rolled uneasily in the freshening breeze. With legs braced, the two officers stood back to back with their glasses trained into the blackness, Royce noting with sympathy the dismal retching of the young signalman as he fought his private battle with the sea.

Half an hour passed. Their eyes smarted, their bodies ached with the constant readjustment to the irregular pitching of the slender hull, and only Harston seemed cheerful and alert. Without warning, a bright orange flash lit the horizon, and seconds later a dull boom echoed across the water, yet before it had died away, the R-T speaker crackled into life.

"Leader calling. General chase!"

Harston's orders jerked Royce back to reality. "Full ahead, steer due West."

All round, the eager engines coughed and roared to life, and with a mighty flurry of foam they were off, their graceful high-speed hulls surging and leaping over the steep, little waves towards the distant fire which slowly ebbed and then died, as if extinguished by a giant hand. Emberson's boat was well out ahead of the pack, throwing up two solid sheets of spray as she tore into the night like a grey avenger.

Royce scrambled down to the pom-pom platform on the bucking fo'c'sle, as the gunners stripped off the spray shields, and trained their weapon round. His heart thumped madly, and he felt the sour taste of vomit forming in his throat, the icy fingers of real fear clutched at his inside, until he felt his head reeling. With an effort he steadied himself against the rail, and then noticed that Leading Seaman Parker was the gunlayer, his face hard and set, his large, red hands controlling his gun with ease and practice. For a moment their eyes met, and Parker's heavy face twisted into a grin. "Now d'you see why I want a bloody refit?" he yelled, and Royce found himself laughing crazily in return, his voice sounded unnatural too, as he called back, "I'll need one myself after this!"

He found himself falling through space as the boat rolled to her beam, the tiller hard over, but Parker's vice-like grip pulled him up with a jerk, and as if in a dream he caught a brief glimpse of a lump of wreckage in the water that Harston had narrowly avoided, and two upturned white faces that were immediately lost in their boiling wake. As they swung back on course, they caught up with the rear ships of the convoy, and Royce had many blurred impressions of gleaming black hulls and rusty plates skimming past within feet of his touch. A destroyer was firing rapidly across the head of the columns at a twisting, silver-grey shape brilliantly framed by a well-placed star shell.

"E-boat, Green one-one-oh!" yelled the rating wearing the head-set, and the pom-pom swung round farther still, but the target was blotted out by a madly zig-zagging tanker, which broke away from the neat line of ships.

"For Christ's sake, what's he doing?" cursed Parker, and as if in answer, a fresh explosion rent the night in two, and a blinding flash lit up the stricken tanker's bridge and rigging like a hideous monument, and a searing pain shot through Royce's eyeballs, as he cringed back from the shock. Already the ship was rolling in her death agony, and in the light of the fires on board they could clearly see small, pathetic figures scrambling down the sloping decks. As they crossed her bows they saw the killer turning towards them, the long, low shape gleaming in the flickering light from the tanker. With a deafening rattle the starboard Oerlikon opened fire, the red tracer clawing over the rapidly shortening range, then the heavy thud, thud, thud of the pom-pom joined in, as the two boats closed each other. Then Royce saw the green tracer climbing, apparently lazily, from the E-boat's guns, and pitching down straight for him. He felt a sudden, hot breath on his cheek, and heard the clang of metal behind him, while somewhere on the bridge he heard Harston's cool voice shout: "Watch your steering, Coxswain, there's another ship dead ahead!"

At the swing of the wheel, the M.T.B. swerved again across the path of the E-boat, the range dropping to twenty yards, before another looming merchantman hid the E-boat from view. In the distance, they saw Emberson's boat take up the chase, and the tracers intermingled in a fresh, deadly pattern, as the German captain twisted and turned in desperation to break off the action. Yet another M.T.B. burst out of the convoy and opened fire immediately, and in the concentrated cross-fire, they saw the enemy stagger and lose speed as small orange flashes rippled across her bridge and decks, and pieces of the hull broke away as the cannon shells struck home. Without warning the E-boat ploughed to a stop, and burst into flames, burning petrol spewing out of her like life-blood. Within seconds she flopped on to her side, and with a searing hiss slid under the surface. The silence which followed seemed to burst the eardrums, and even the racing engines appeared quieter. Shakily Royce drew his glove across his cold, wet face, gulping in the keen air to rid his throat of the tang of cordite and fire.

"Alright, sir?"

He was aware of Parker peering at him through the gloom, a look of concern on his large face. He nodded shakily, feeling incapable of speech, and only dimly conscious of his surroundings.

Parker rounded on his gun's crew who were watching Royce with interest. "Come on you lazy lot!" he bawled. "There may be some more of the perishers about yet, so don't look so ruddy cocky!"

The pale blob of Harston's head appeared over the bridge

screen. "Very nice shooting," he called. "You can secure now and get rid of the empties; Jerry has broken off the action. Come on to the bridge, Number One."

As Royce clambered over the glittering shell cases to the ladder, he forced himself to think straight, and to try to piece together the violent events of this unreal and nightmarish encounter with the enemy, and immediately his mind was assailed with fresh doubts as to his competence in such a terrible situation.

Making a great effort to keep his voice steady, he nodded in the direction of the convoy, "What happens now, sir? Do we stick with them, or press on after the E-boats?"

Harston was studying him keenly. "Well, I'm happy to say, neither. They'll be quite safe now, and Jerry got a bloody nose. One E-boat sunk by that lucky old lawyer, Artie, and the destroyer mauled another. Pity about those two ships," he added, "but at least they were empty, except for their crews, and God only knows where they are now, poor devils. There are a couple of trawlers looking for them."

He glanced up at a pinpoint of light ahead, and focussed his glasses. After a moment he turned, his face suddenly tired. "Make a signal with the lamp to the next astern, 'Resume formation'. We're returning to base."

Royce forced a smile. "Bunts still seasick?"

Harston stared at him for several seconds before replying, then waved vaguely to the darkened corner of the bridge. "Afraid he's bought it," he said harshly.

Royce lurched over to the small figure sitting awkwardly against the signal locker, and knelt down at his side. The young signalman's legs were sticking straight out in front of him, his hands still clutching his Aldis lamp against the oversized duffle coat. His face was thrown back, and the fair, curly hair rippled gently in the cold breeze, as the glazing blue eyes stared up at the scudding clouds, as if amazed at what he saw. Through the thin plating at his back was a small, round hole.

Royce, suddenly ice-cold, choked back the lump in his throat, very gently prized the lamp from the stiff, chilled hands, and blindly triggered the signal to the dark shape astern.

As the flotilla reformed into line, Harston swore softly out to sea. "Damn them to hell! He was just telling me that he wasn't afraid!"

He pounded his fist on the rail, then seemed to go limp. "You did well, Number One, but don't ever worry about being afraid, the man who says he isn't is either a liar, or a bloody lunatic!"

The Coxswain stepped out of the darkness and touched his cap. "Everything's secure below, no damage," he reported. "I'll get a couple of the lads to give me a hand with young Mead here." He fumbled under his oilskin, and produced a bottle and two enamel mugs. "I brought you a couple of tots of neaters, sir. I reckon you can do with it up here."

Harston downed his rum with one gulp, and walked stiffly to the compass. "I'm going below to write my report, Number One. It saves a bit of time when we get in. Do you think you can handle her now?"

Royce nodded.

"Call me when you sight Outer Spit buoy, that'll be about 0500."

He paused as he passed to the bridge ladder. "It's all so bloody futile, isn't it?" and then he was gone.

Royce checked the course, and leaned against the screen, his chin pillowed on his hands, suddenly desperately tired and cold, his face stiff with salt spray, and the towel wrapped around his neck soggy and raw against the skin. On and on thundered the boats, and still he stood as if in a trance, only once stiffening when he heard the Coxswain supervising the removal of Mead's body, his watchkeeping companion of how long ago? Only four hours, it seemed like a lifetime.

Far ahead he saw the steely grey fingers of the dawn creeping almost cautiously across the horizon, and the dim shapes of the other boats took on a hard realism. Up and down the weaving line, red-rimmed eyes peered out for friends, and weary, muffled figures waved and sighed with relief. As far as Royce could see, Emberson's boat was the only one with visible damage. A line of holes above the waterline, and one larger gash in the deck just aft of the port torpedo tube, not too bad, in fact.

"Outer Spit buoy on the starboard bow," reported the lookout, and Royce peered at his watch, 0445.

He leaned to the Captain's speaking tube. "Captain, sir," he called. "In position, Outer Spit ahead."

Harston joined him, and silently, side by side, they stood and watched the landmarks taking shape in the growing light. First the dull hills at the back of the port, then, more sharply defined, the long, low harbour walls, the boom-gate, now open to receive them, and a couple of outward-bound trawlers, jauntily thrusting their blunt bows into the choppy sea, their spindly funnels belching smoke, their tattered ensigns fluttering defiantly as any cruiser. The hands fell in for entering harbour, silently this time, only dimly aware of their surroundings, and only thinking of sleep, the sailor's cure for everything.

Through the harbour mouth, and up the stream, past the heavy cruiser *Leviathan*. On the cold morning air they heard the shrill notes of a bugle sounding Reveille, "Wakey, wakey, lash up and stow," and as they threaded their way between the moored vessels, unnoticed, except by the vigilant signal tower, the anchorage roused itself for another day.

First to the petrol jetty to take on fuel, then, while the other boats made for the depot ship, they pulled over to the railway wharf, where Royce saw a khaki ambulance waiting to take young Mead on his last trip. They watched it drive away, then slipped once more, and in the harsh, bright morning sunlight they tied up alongside the *Royston's* catwalk. Seven o'clock exactly.

The depot ship's maintenance men, wide awake and freshly shaved, hurried aboard and went to work. Royce dismissed the hands and sleepily watched them scramble up the steep side and disappear. Then, together, the two officers went over the main gangway, where Harston handed his brief, scribbled report to a messenger, and they were confronted by Artie Emberson, his reddened face creased into a smile. He slapped two hands on Harston's shoulders, and pulled him towards him.

"So you're still here, you old devil, and I thought I'd be able to have your breakfast this morning!" But his obvious relief shone in his eyes.

Breakfast was a hurried, silent meal, as the grubby officers mechanically warmed their chilled insides with the carefully prepared food, and then, with a tired smile here, and a pat on the shoulder there, they dragged themselves to the same, quiet privacy of the little cabins. As Royce closed his door behind him, he caught a glimpse of himself in the mirror and was shocked at the grey, lined and suddenly aged face which stared back at him. He didn't remember undressing, or dabbing his sore skin with the steaming water, he just managed to heave his body between the gentle sheets and switch off the light, and the next instant he was safe from the sea, from patrols, and from himself.

CHAPTER TWO

In the months that followed, the war at sea, as far as Royce was concerned, pursued a regular, wearying pattern. Night after night they patrolled their scattered areas of the North Sea, covering the vital convoys which crept up and down the East Coast, and sometimes there was the variation of the hit-and-run dash across to the mud flats of the Dutch coast in search of the enemy's supply ships. Like the men who manned them, the little ships knew every stress and strain as the momentum of war quickened, and the carefully-laid rules were overlooked or savagely broken. Often in foul weather, and always at faster speeds than their engines were expected to tolerate, they pushed into the night, their wooden hulls twisting and bucking, while the cold North Sea winds moaned through every crack and crevice, making the watch below groan, and clutch their damp blankets closer to their chilled bodies. On watch, these men fought against sleep, and off watch, rest was denied them by the cold nights, and the uneven motion of the mess-decks, which took every opportunity to bombard them with crockery, wet clothing, and the ever-penetrating sea water, which slopped about them, and made their lives a misery. Even the prayed-for refits became scarcer and shorter, as the cry went out for more ships, and more men. In the middle of these confused circumstances, Royce grew up, and became a useful and efficient member of their little world which was cut off from the rest of the fleet, and, in fact, from any other way of life. He now knew the life history of every member of the crew, their likes and dislikes, and their weaknesses. Their hopes and fears he shared.

It was not, as he repeatedly told himself, quite as they had said it would be when he left the training establishment at Hove. Apart from that breath-taking encounter on his first patrol, he had not caught even a smell of the enemy. His war so far had mainly been against the weather, plus a steadily mounting struggle with the boat's technical and domestic affairs, of which the latter was becoming rather out of hand. It was, as far as he could see, a case of a good crew overworked and pushed to breaking-point, with little prospect of improvement. His opposite numbers in the flotilla assured him that all would be well in action, but as that seemed a cruel justice to him, he painstakingly carried out his duties ashore and afloat, in a great effort to avoid a queue of defaulters at the Captain's table, or the miserable collection of leave-breakers and deserters, which some First Lieutenants were having to contend with. The result, although not startling, was gratifying, and was not unnoticed by Harston, who left more and more tasks to his assistant, in the safe knowledge that they would be carefully and intelligently carried out, without the fear of an aftermath of furious signals from base, or disgruntled comments from the Coxswain. The other result was that Royce's social life was now at a standstill. With the exception of brief visits to a giant Nissen hut in the harbour limits, lavishly called the Officers' Club, he had confined his activities to the depot ship. With these thoughts in mind, he sat in his cabin half-heartedly concocting a letter to his parents. He found it difficult to write in a matter-of-fact way that would please his mother, and yet find suitable information about the war, of which he knew little, for the sake of his invalid father, who was, in his own way, a keen strategist. In addition, he knew that any one of these letters might well be his last. Both the other East Coast groups had been encountering heavy opposition of late, and it seemed likely that their turn would come again soon.

He finished the letter with a flourish, and a sigh, and reached for his pipe. At that moment, the door slid open, and Harston and Artie Emberson were framed in the light.

"Well, well, well," drawled the latter, "so this is where your little slave hangs out!" He surveyed the spartan cabin, which resembled all the others in the ship to an exact degree.

"Hmm, most tastefully furnished too. As you have stated, John, this is a very adaptable lad."

Harston grinned. "Sorry to upset your solitude, Number One, but you'll doubtless be horrified to know that S.O.O. has granted the flotilla a night in harbour. Apparently they want the whole area cleared of small fry so that our larger friends can get in some sea time!"

Emberson interrupted. "And as the junior partner, we thought you might be interested in having your education extended by a run ashore to the old White Hart with us. You like?"

Royce was already buttoning his jacket, and searching for his respirator. "Thanks very much; two pieces of good news in one evening is more than I can resist."

Emberson winked. "Not only a keen lad, but eager!"

The White Hart was situated half-way along the port's High

Street, between the food office and a musty-looking restaurant, its high, ornate façade giving the appearance of vulgar opulence amongst the other neglected and weather-beaten buildings. As the three officers pushed open the swing doors and fumbled through the heavy blackout curtains, the brassy, cheerful noise, coupled with the mixed aromas of beer and tobacco, over-whelmed them. The evening was young, but already the bar was half filled with early drinkers, mostly naval officers from the local flotillas, with a pale blue sprinkling of the Air Force Coastal Command base nearby. Here and there, in the odd corners of the vast lounge, were the seemingly misplaced regular customers, their dowdy suits making a sharp contrast with the uniforms. They too were mixed, either elderly, sitting quietly with their friends and watching the young sailors' friendly horseplay, or young and loud-mouthed, the product of the port's reserved occupations. These latter were usually overpaid and, therefore, overconfident of their new surroundings.

The long bar of dark wood, shiny with bright lights and spilt beer, was ably controlled and easily dominated by a cheerful bar-maid of supreme proportions, who scurried to and fro with pots and glasses, her plump face split into a permanent grin, and her speedy service punctuated with giggles and nods to her thirsty court, and a hurried, "Sorry, love, no spirits", to any strange face which hovered near her domain. The landlord, a rotund and grizzled little man, in a shabby tweed suit, remained at the end of the counter, passing the time with his cronies, and keeping a watchful eye on the busy scene.

Emberson shouldered his way through the crowd. "Ah, Grace, my beloved," he called, "could my friends and I have three large pints, and three halves of your very best cider."

Grace beamed. "Oo, sir, I thought you'd be out tonight, what a nice surprise."

"So much for security," said Emberson, with mock sadness.

Royce eased his way through the crush, and plucked at his sleeve. "I don't like cider, thanks, the beer'll do."

"Shurrup, nitwit!" hissed Emberson. "It's Scotch! What do you want to do, start a riot in here?"

They found a small table, conveniently abandoned by the R.A.F., and sat back, stretching luxuriously.

Harston drank deeply. "The friendliest joint in town," he smiled, "and with Artie's influence over the queen there, we are more or less well in for the duration."

"Dear me," replied the lawyer. "A most unfortunate expression. When will you realize that my feelings for the wee Grace are just platonic." He regarded Harston solemnly. "You, sir, have no soul. How can you keep the respect of young Clive here, if you can't learn to moderate your approach to the fair sex."

Royce relaxed in his chair, enjoying the wrangling of his companions, and feeling for the first time accepted into the close fraternity which he had chosen a year? a lifetime ago.

The evening wore on, and the bar filled to its uproarious capacity, while from the radio Vera Lynn did her best to comfort the nation's young men elsewhere. Here in the White Hart her efforts seemed wasted. Royce's mind swam happily, and he seemed vaguely unable to prevent his face from slipping into a vast smile of good fellowship. His detached thoughts were shattered by a mighty slap on the shoulder which made him cannon into the table, nearly causing a disaster.

Benjy Watson's shiny pink face floated over them, and behind him two other officers of the flotilla struggled manfully with a large parcel.

"My dear old soaks!" he boomed. "I've had the most ghastly night; these two dreadful characters have been leading me astray." He silenced their protests with a wave of a huge fist. "You know I wanted the 'Save for Victory' banner from the post office to go round my bridge? Well, these silly baskets got me so flustered, I got the wrong one. It's all about a Dog Show! I ask you, a Dog Show! I haven't got a dog!" He pulled a bottle from one jacket pocket, and a glass from the other, while the others howled with laughter at this latest crazy episode.

"You lunatic!" roared Harston. "No wonder we're always at sea, this town isn't safe from you!"

With the arrival of the irrepressible Watson and his accomplices, the quiet party was shattered, and Royce's sides ached, as he found himself caught up in an act that would have made a small fortune on any variety stage.

The lights had just been dimmed to herald "Last Orders"-shouted announcements would have been useless, when the curtains parted, and above the milling bodies, a blue steel helmet, with the word "Police" painted on the front, could be seen making its way to the bar.

Benjy's jaw dropped, and a look of complete horror crossed his face.

"Christ! I've been rumbled at last, and caught with the loot too!"

He wheeled rapidly to his grinning companions. "Don't stand there like a shower of silly oafs, get rid of that banner, and let's get out of here!"

As one man they downed their drinks, the parcel skidded beneath the legs of two startled airmen, and in a compact, if unsteady, body they forced their way to the doors. Even as they reached the curtains the policeman yelled out above the din, "An air-raid warning has just been sounded, so be careful you don't show any lights when you leave."

Benjy was hustled protesting up the street.

"But what about my banner?" he implored. "All that trouble for nothing. I'll do that silly copper if I ever see him again."

Harston chuckled. "Time for bed, little man, it definitely was not your day for carrying the banner."

Still laughing, they arrived at the barbed-wire enclosure of the harbour area, and automatically straightened themselves as they produced their identity cards to the weary sentries. Benjy was still muttering and bewailing his loss when they reached the windswept pier, and only when they split up and went to their cabins on the depot ship did he start to smile.

"You just wait, I'll get you something really worthwhile next time," he promised.

Royce was past caring. He was happy, and the Navy was just too wonderful for words.

The flotilla swept gaily through the boom-gate, weaving and dipping in the easy swell, as they picked up their stations on the Leader. A keen breeze swept over the tiny bridge of M.T.B. 1991, as Royce listened to the hands in the various parts of the boat reporting that they were "Closed up to exercise action", the normal practice when leaving harbour, to ensure that all sections were working correctly. As the last reported, "Port Oerlikon closed up, sir," Royce informed the Captain that all was well.

Harston hardly seemed to notice, he was visibly excited, and in fact, new life seemed to have crept into the whole crew, as this was not just another patrol, not another aimless battle with the weather. The sweep by the destroyers on the previous night had broken up three enemy convoys off the Dutch coast, and the R.A.F. had reported that they were making an effort to reform and press on up the coast, doubtless loaded with vital supplies for the armies in Denmark and Norway, and for the German Baltic fleet. The flotilla's job was to intercept and destroy the rearmost convoy. All morning they had laboured with the maintenance staff to get everything in first-rate order, and extra care had been taken as the long, evil-looking torpedoes had been greased and slid into the tubes on either side of the boat, and now, as the low coastline was swallowed up in the dusk astern of them, they all knew that this was to be another supreme test of their skill in the handicraft of war.

"Defence stations now," said Harston, "and make sure everyone gets a good whack of food during the next two hours. And we'll get some corned beef sandwiches laid on for the return journey too. I think they'll have earned it by then."

Harston went below for his customary cat-nap, and half of the crew followed his example, in order that they could be fed in two watches. No longer did Royce tremble at the loneliness of the bridge, in fact, he enjoyed the feeling of complete power that he had over the lithe, trembling hull beneath his feet. As Harston had told him that first day, he now knew the difference between a trawler and this three and a half thousand horsepowered killer.

On and on they went, and as the sky darkened they met a solitary destroyer on patrol, creeping along like a great grey shadow, in the hopes of surprising a raider, or assisting some convoy straggler.

The new signalman, Collins, a stolid north-countryman, turned his head, "Signal, sir, from destroyer, 'Should you be out alone so late?' Any reply, sir?"

"Make, 'If we had been E-boats, we'd have been picking you out of the drink by now'!" snapped Royce.

There was a chuckle, as the lamp clattered away in the corner of the bridge.

"No answer, sir."

An hour later they were reinforced by a strong flotilla of Motor Gunboats from Harwich, the "pocket battleships" of Coastal Forces. Their purpose was to cover the withdrawal after the attack had been pressed home. Signals flashed, and the boats jockeyed to and fro, until the M.T.B.s had formed into two parallel lines ahead, with the M.G.B.s three miles astern, then silence enveloped the flotilla, and no more signals were made or required, as each captain knew what was expected; it was all just a matter of time. The mighty engines purred obediently as they were throttled down to a minimum speed, and the tiny ships crept stealthily forward, searching, probing. Royce swung his night-glasses in a wide arc, and decided it was time to call the Captain, and seconds later Harston climbed up beside him, fresh and apparently unworried. He took in the situation at a glance. His boat led the starboard column, and Paskins in the leader, led the port column at a distance of about a thousand yards.

"Action Stations," he said quietly, and Royce pressed the button that had called sailors from their rest, and to their deaths, the world over.

Even before the bells stopped ringing, the last man heaved himself into his allotted space, which, for the next few hours at least, would probably decide the fate of the whole boat. The slim barrels of the Oerlikons, and the menacing muzzles of the pom-poms swung back and forth through their maximum arcs, as the crews tested them, and reported automatically to the bridge. The steel hatches clanged shut over the engine room, imprisoning the mechanics in what was at best a shaking, roaring helter-skelter of noise and fumes, and at worst a blazing hell from which there could be little chance of escape.

"If we can pull this off all right tonight, Number One, I think we can get that refit you want so badly, plus a bit of leave, of course."

"That'd be really something, sir," replied Royce feelingly, for he knew that the boat's maintenance was becoming a little bit out of hand. A good slipway in the dockyard was what she required now.

At the prospect of leave, they lowered their glasses and grinned at each other like schoolboys. Royce had long ago decided that Harston should have a rest from active service for a bit.

"Enemy coast ahead!" sang out the bridge lookouts together, and as they peered across the dark, oily water, they could make out only vaguely the black finger of land which was the start of the low-lying mudflats which abounded in these waters.

For another half-hour the boats felt their way forward, but no convoy steamed out to greet them, no targets loomed before the gaping torpedo tubes, and the tension on the decks could be felt. Here a man rubbed his eyes savagely, and stared again into the sombre blackness, and there another cursed his mate softly as their bodies touched on the gently rolling gun-platform.

Royce was not the least affected, and he felt a childish rage consuming him, causing him to rebuke the signalman for lowering his glasses for a few seconds.

"Those damned airmen have made a mistake," he muttered. "There's no convoy, and if there was, they slipped out this morning, blast them!"

"That'll do, Number One!" The voice was mild, almost disinterested.

Royce swore again under his breath, and peered over towards the Leader's blurred shape on the port beam, and then he saw a shaded signal lamp blinking astern: he must be worried too, to use a lamp so close to the enemy coast.

"Leader's signalled supportin' gunboats to sweep to the southeast, and to report if there's anything at that end of the coast," reported Collins. His voice sounded doubtful.

Still Harston seemed unsurprised and apparently preoccupied with his own thoughts. Royce could faintly make out his outline in the front of the bridge, leaning across the screen on his folded arms, an unlit pipe clenched between his teeth, which suddenly gleamed white in the gloom as he smiled.

"Number One," he spoke softly so that the lookouts and signalman should not hear. "Don't let this sort of thing get you down; this war's like a great, stupid puzzle. If we work like hell, and have lots of actions, the boats crack up, and we need boats, more and more of them. If we don't get a shot at anything, and have patrols, then it's the crews who go round the bend. You just can't please anybody."

He paused and studied his First Lieutenant's gloved hand as it pounded the rail, softly yet viciously, in a steady rhythm.

"It's not that I'm a crack-brained, death-or-glory character, or that I don't realize that ninety-nine per cent of finding and knocking seven bells out of Jerry is just plain luck," explained Royce, the words tumbling out of him. "It's just this constant waiting, and not knowing." His voice trailed away, and he shrugged his shoulders helplessly.

Harston moved swiftly across the bridge, with his quick, cat-like step and gripped his sleeve urgently, pulling him close to his pale face. When he spoke again, his tone was strange, quite unlike anything Royce had heard from him before, almost fanatical.

"Never, never feel that you're wasting your time. Everything we do helps to tie them down, even when we're not killing them! That's why I rode you hard when you were sent to me, war is a hard business. Now you've made the grade, our grade, otherwise I wouldn't be telling you this." Here he paused and waved his arm towards the hidden coast, and when he continued, he spoke slowly as if spelling out the words: "But I hate those bastards more than any other crawling creature on this earth. I've seen what they can do, have done, and'll keep on doing until we——"

He broke away with a jerk, as a dull boom and blue flash lit the slowly cruising clouds. Immediately the R-T speaker crackled into life: "Leader calling, the M.G.B.s have struck oil, maximum speed!"

The night split open as the engines roared into life, and Royce saw their own bow lift before him, as all boats raced off in perfect twin lines, throwing up the great, curving streams, their stems slicing through the water. He flung himself down the ladder to the gun platform, with a brief impression of Harston hanging over the bucking torpedo sighting mechanism. He seemed to be laughing.

Now the sky was criss-crossed with tracers, and a small fire blossomed into a full, orange glow, showing a small ship burning and listing on to her side. As they closed the battle, they saw the M.G.B.s circling four trawlers, firing rapidly, and even as they watched, another of them burst into flames, throwing up a fountain of sparks.

Harston leaned over the screen, beckoning urgently, and as Royce climbed up, he shook his fists wildly. "For Christ's sake, what are those fools doing? Look at them! They've broken formation, and for what?" His voice rose almost to a scream. "Four bloody trawlers! There's your convoy, Number One! Are you satisfied? No? Well *they* apparently are!"

Royce was dumbfounded. "But I don't see——"

"Do you want me to spell it for you? They are a decoy! A decoy, and our so-called escorts fell for it, and now we're in the trap!"

Royce's heart went cold as he realized the implication of this new menace, and tried to force his mind to function, but he seemed numb, until Harston seized his arm roughly.

"Get aft and stand by to jettison smoke floats, and get ready for some fancy shooting."

Paskins, too, fully realized their position, and unless he acted promptly there was nothing to prevent the hunters becoming the hunted. Frantically he signalled the jubilant gunboats to reform and cease fire, and then formed the torpedo boats into one line, his own boat leading, and Harston's now fifth, with Emberson following in the rear. There was only one thing to do now, get out into the open sea as soon as possible.

It was at the very moment of decision, even as the boats began to move off, that the trap was sprung.

There was a sullen detonation astern of the flotillas, and many thought that it was a trawler blowing up, but doubts were short, as a star shell burst with savage brilliance in the sky at their backs. In a split second the night became day, as they were silhouetted and sharply defined to anything that lay ahead. Blinded, the gunners hugged their weapons, a lifetime passed, in fact four more seconds, then the black wall ahead of them flamed into life, a mad, whirling cone of red and white tracer shells, that screamed overhead and hissed into the churning waters around them, with such a crescendo of noise that they were stunned. Two seconds later, Paskins' boat reached the maelstrom, and was ablaze from stem to stern, sharp little flames licking out of the bridge superstructure joined those which were eagerly consuming the upper deck. There were two sickening explosions which shattered the craft into a hundred sections, and sent flaming wreckage whirling skywards, and she was gone! Before they could recover from this awful spectacle, they were all in it, twisting and turning to avoid the probing, searching avalanche of fire which flew about their ears! Royce sent the smoke floats thudding into the sea, and soon a pall of smoke would be forming to provide cover or confusion for friend and foe alike. He scrambled to the gun platform, as the twin pom-poms groped blindly for a target, his head splitting with the crash and rattle of the enemy salvoes. Then, for the first time, they all saw their hunters, for the sea seemed full of them. E-boats, their long, dark hulls gleaming with spray as they tore down towards them, and astern of them were half a dozen armed trawlers, not in the accepted sense, but floating gun batteries, protected by steel plates and huge blocks of concrete, behind which the German gunners fired and reloaded as fast as a combination of training and hatred would allow.

"Open fire, first trawler!" yelled Royce, and the pom-poms joined in the tattoo with a steady bang-bang-bang, their twin tracers lifting and dropping towards the hunched, menacing shape of the trawler. The range closed rapidly, five hundred yards, two hundred, one hundred, until they saw their shells rippling along her sides. The Oerlikons and machine-guns added their ear-shattering rattle, as if in desperation, but still the trawler came on, her decks a mass of spitting muzzles.

Royce felt the boat lurch beneath him as white-hot metal tore into her sides, and something clanged against the gun-shield and screamed away into the night. Another violent flash illuminated the boat, and he saw the mast and aerials stagger and pitch across the bridge. Simultaneously a deafening explosion came from aft, the shock sending him spinning to the deck. He scrambled to his feet, dimly aware that the pom-poms had ceased fire. Leading Seaman Parker sat moaning softly by the ready-use ammunition locker, his face a bloody mask. The other gunners were twisted together in a distorted embrace by the guns. With horror he saw a white hand on the already darkening decks, like a discarded glove.

Of the trawler there was no sign, although her gunfire roared and whined through the steep bank of smoke forming astern, which was tinged with pink and orange hues, making it look a real and solid thing.

He realized too that they were maintaining their speed, but turning in a wide circle. Forcing his way behind the port Oerlikon gunner, who fired steadily into the smoke, he pushed his way into the shuttered wheelhouse. Even as the door opened, he smelt the cordite fumes, and above the rattle of the guns, he could hear a persistent, shrill screaming.

As his eyes became adjusted to the feeble light, he realized that the interior of the wheelhouse was a complete shambles. Pieces of equipment were scattered about the deck, and he could see the flashes from the starboard Oerlikon's intermittent bursts through a six-foot gash in the plating. Petty Officer Raikes was on his knees by the wheel, hard at work with a screwdriver, which he was using like a jemmy, as he used all his strength to free the steering gear, which was jammed tight by a corner of a steel plate, bent over like wet cardboard. Royce noticed that his unruly hair was speckled with little pieces of paint which had been torn from the deckhead. Lying pinned under the twisted metal of the gash in the bridge side was the wretched creature whose spine-chilling screams made Raikes fumble and curse, and turn an imploring eye to Royce.

"Carn you stop 'im, sir?" he gasped. "God knows what's keepin' 'im alive!"

Indeed, there seemed little resemblance to a man in the twisting bundle of rags which caused Royce to step back with horror. Able Seaman Lund, already wounded, had been dragged to the bridge for safety, only to be pounded into human wreckage by the last salvo of cannon shells, which had raked the boat from stem to stern. With a final jerk, the Coxswain freed the wheel, and clambered to his feet, spinning the spokes deftly in his scratched and bleeding fingers, and as if that was the awaited signal, the awful cries ceased, for ever.

"I'm on course, now," shouted Raikes, "but if you can get me a relief, I'll give you a hand on deck." He sounded cool and confident.

Royce nodded dumbly, and went outside into the cold air, to pull his aching body on to the bridge. With despair he saw the tangle of wires and halyards wrapped round the mast, which pointed over the side like a broken limb, and under it, the shattered chart table, wood splinters, and the upended signal locker spewing out its cargo of coloured bunting. Harston knelt in the pose of a runner waiting for the starting pistol, moaning softly, and trying to pull himself to the voice-pipe, each movement causing him to clench his teeth and close his eyes with pain. In two strides, Royce reached him, and eased the weakly protesting body back against the screen.

"It's all right, Skipper, just take it easy, we'll have you fixed up in no time. Now just you lie quiet."

Harston seemed to hear, but he couldn't be sure, and he glanced wildly round for assistance. For the first time he saw the large sea boots of the signalman protruding from beneath the chart table. One of them twitched faintly, and then, with a sudden heave, Collins rose from the wreckage like a huge dog, apparently unhurt, but shaking his head, and repeating slowly, "Gawd, what 'appened?"

Royce yelled madly: "Quick, Collins, relieve the Coxswain, and steer," he twisted round to the compass which was, by a miracle, intact. "Steer north-west, and send him up with the first aid gear." He stared at the signalman anxiously. "Can you do that?"

"Yessir, I'm okay, just a bang on the 'ead. Gawd!" and he limped down the ladder.

Harston's eyes opened, and he seemed to be trying to focus on Royce's worried face. A gloved hand patted feebly at his shoulder, and a small voice croaked, "Leave me, Number One, I've had it. Get the boat out of here."

His chest shook to a violent fit of coughing, and Royce held him close, hugging him until it stopped.

The pale face twisted into a smile, and Royce bent his head to hear.

"You're all right, Clive, the best I've ever——" He coughed again.

Royce felt a sudden fierce grip on his arm as Harston tried to pull himself forward.

"Look after my boat, and the lads for me, will you?"

Royce nodded. "Don't say it, I'll get you back," he choked.

"Tell Artie he can have my breakfast, and tell him that . . ." He quietly lowered his face on to Royce's shoulder, and he felt his body give a long shudder and go limp.

For several seconds he sat holding him, until the Coxswain appeared with two seamen. Then he turned his head away, so that they should not see his tears, and rasped, "The Captain has just died. See to the others."

Gently he freed himself from the embrace, and stood stiffly at the rail, then he called down the engine room voice-pipe, "Everything all right down there, Moore?"

The tinny voice rattled back, "Aye, aye, sir, no damage. There were two holes forrard below the waterline in the mess-decks, but I've had 'em plugged. I can still give you maximum revs, if you're wanting to get out of it, sir."

Royce could well imagine Moore squatting down in the smoke and din of the engines, surrounded by tanks of high-octane spirit, and wondering what on earth was happening above his head, but taught by his nine years in the navy to ask no questions.

"Very good, stand by for full speed after the Coxswain has made his report."

Ten minutes later, Raikes reported the findings of his hurried tour. "Five dead, including the Captain," he paused and lowered his eyes. "Three wounded, one seriously, that's Banks, port Oerlikon," he added.

Royce then remembered the huddled gunner firing wildly into the smoke screen. Alone, wounded and frightened, he had fired until his magazine was empty.

"As to damage," continued Raikes, suddenly brisk. "Two shot holes below the line, now plugged. 'Bout two hundred holes in the port side, and half that on this side. Pom-poms jammed, machine-guns smashed, and motor dory in bits. Most of the gear below is buggered-up too."

"In other words, she'll float but not fight. Right, keep the Oerlikons closed up, and try to get the wounded comfortable. Oh, and a good cup of rum all round."

He turned to the voice-pipe. "Steer west-north-west, full ahead!"

He was aware that the Coxswain was still standing there. "Well?"

"I just wanted you to know, sir, that I'm sorry about the Captain. He was the finest man I've ever served under." For once he seemed at a loss for words.

Royce nodded. "Thank you, 'Swain, I know what you mean."

Collins had resumed his place, and was sorting out his flags in an aimless and fuddled manner, and as he worked, muttering and humming to himself, Royce stood looking at the empty corner of the bridge, the dark stains on the planking, the cruel pattern of bullet holes in the thin plating that had plucked down a man, a leader, who even at the gateway of death had thought of his duty to others.

Furiously Royce dashed his hand across his face and eyes, and stared hard across the grim, heaving waters, the reaction of the last soul-tearing hour causing him to tremble violently, and his stomach to heave until he felt faint and ice-cold.

Of the battle there was no sign, in fact, as far as he could ascertain, there was no other vessel at sea, and a great peace had replaced the flaming crescendo which had nearly engulfed them. Far across the dim horizon the sky broke, and displayed the silver fangs of the dawn, which were reflected and magnified by the twin sheets of white foam cascading from each side of the sharp bow, as it lifted and pointed towards home. Beneath his feet he felt the thud of hammers as the Coxswain's party shored up the splintered planks, and sorted out the usable gear from the debris and confusion. The sounds of their activity, and the smell of cocoa from the galley steadied his nerves, and he felt himself stretching, and exercising his taut muscles for the first time. Wearily he raised his glasses, and as he swept the bleak area on the port side he tensed as into the lenses flitted a small, white feather, surmounted by a fast moving hull, and even as he watched, the shape shortened, turning towards him, moving fast.

Already his hand groped for the button which caused the alarm's clamour to call its urgent message throughout the boat, and brought the men running once again to their stations, except that this time there were only the two Oerlikons, with little ammunition, the huge torpedoes that lay in their tubes like useless passengers, and of course, they were quite alone.

"It's one of the gunboats, sir!" Collins's keen eyes had recognized the speeding shape, even at that considerable distance.

And a gunboat it was, flashing a challenge, which Collins promptly answered. She tore down in a wide arc to run parallel with them, but fifty yards away.

"Reduce speed, and keep station on me," boomed the loud hailer, and Royce caught a glimpse in the grey light of the Senior Officer of their escort surveying their damage through his glasses.

As Royce made no comment—his own loud hailer was in several pieces—the sharp voice crackled again: "The rest of your flotilla are coming up astern. You are the last one to be accounted for."

Royce waved heavily, and ordered the Coxswain to reduce speed. The Senior Officer had set him wondering. "The last one to be accounted for." What did that mean? That all but Paskins' boat were safe? But what of the casualties? At that thought, a fresh pang of grief shot through him, as he saw starkly in his mind's eye Harston groping weakly across the deck where he himself now stood, and he remembered anew his helplessness as he felt the last spark of life die, the vital, ever-boyish spirit vanish in a split second.

It was all so unreal, so nightmarish, that he shook himself violently, without realizing that this nightmare would live with him forever.

He suddenly observed that all the terrible scars of battle were now visible on the gallant little ship's upper deck, and the horizon had taken on a hard, grey line, as a new day broke, slowly at first, as if reluctant to display the night's tragedy, then with the full, bright glare of a watery sun, it was upon them. And with it came the little band of brothers, limping painfully out of the early morning mist, one behind the other, closely bunched, seeking comfort and protection in what, at any other time, would be a dangerous formation.

Emberson's boat led, and as she drew near, an intricate pattern of holes could be seen down the side, and the barrel of one Oerlikon was missing. From the bridge, a bright yellow scarf waved like a defiant banner. Next, Benjy Watson's 2007 came into view, towing another boat stern first, and making very heavy going of it, as the reluctant charge, which was Jock

Murray's 3007, yawed awkwardly from side to side. Watson stood high on the bridge screen, watching the tow-rope with red-rimmed eyes, and constantly barking changes of speed to his Number One, who sat on the chart table, having his hand bandaged. Murray's boat was a mess, blackened by fire, riddled with shot, she was down by the head, the pumps clanking monotonously to stop the sea which poured hungrily through the torn planks. The Captain slumped moodily by the compass, breathing heavily, and cursing the slow passage. Half his crew lay dead below, and his Number One had been blinded.

Still the procession came on, M.T.B. 1815, commanded by Lieutenant Deith, the suave, dark ex-car-salesman from Kensington, was steering a very erratic course; her rudder gone, she was using just the engines. She, too, had plenty of debris, human and otherwise, to show as evidence of defeat.

Lieutenant Cameron's 2015, the flotilla's newest addition, was least damaged, except for a torn upper deck, and hovered in the rear, keeping a watchful eye on her companions.

And that was all; two boats missing, Paskins's and 1917, Lieutenant Ronnie Patterson, the youngest of the captains.

By this time, Emberson had drawn close alongside and was waving happily with a megaphone.

"Get John up here, will you!" he yelled. "I knew you'd turn up all right."

Royce swallowed hard, and gripped the rail with desperation. "I can't," he faltered. "He was killed last night."

He wanted to say so much, but what was there to add to this bald statement, that now sounded so cold and indifferent?

Emberson's smile of welcome vanished, and he seemed turned to stone.

"I see," he nodded slowly. "I see." And he added something which sounded to Royce like, "my friend".

He pulled off his cap, and lowered his head, his hair ruffling in the cold breeze. He stood like that for some seconds, but it seemed a frozen eternity. Then with a brisk jerk he replaced his cap, and squared his shoulders.

"You and I'll have a talk later," he called. "I'm glad you're safe."

With a roar of engines he swerved away to lead the line again.

Royce never forgot the voyage back, every little detail, and each crisis forcing him to strain himself to the utmost of his ability, and by the time they were challenged by the destroyer patrol sent out to guide them to safety, he was near mental and physical collapse.

In silence they landed their dead at the railway jetty and handed over the boats to the waiting dockyard men. Then, bundled together in a harbour lighter, they made their way back to the *Royston*, unaware of the curious and anxious faces that lined the rails, feeling nothing but a deep despair of pain and defeat.

CHAPTER THREE

The hard, bright glare of a spring morning sent a powerful shaft of light sweeping across Royce's tiny cabin, as the steward deftly unscrewed the deadlight, and laid down a large cup of tea at the side of the bunk. The bunched figure wrapped in the blankets lay quite still, like the others that the steward had been busily tending, and even the scattered array of salt-stained clothing, sea boots, and other gear bore a marked similarity. Gently but firmly, in a manner born of long practice, he found a shoulder, and shook it. The figure groaned, and stirred slightly.

"Morning, sir, pusser's tea for one!" he chirped brightly, and then stood back to await results. Like the rest of *Royston*'s ship's company, he knew quite well about the last battle of the M.T.B. flotilla, and of the losses sustained. He knew, too, that this young officer had refused help and rest after his ordeal, until he had made sure that his crew were safe in their hammocks. And even then, he had forced himself to write letters to the relatives of the dead, and telephone the hospital to inquire of the wounded. As he had handed in his report to the Operations Officer, he had been told that fourteen days' leave would be granted to all the boats' crews, as from the following morning. This morning.

Royce blinked, and heaved himself on to one elbow. Dazzled by the bright sunlight, he squinted at the steward.

"Thanks. What's the time?" His voice sounded thick.

Swiftly the steward moved into the attack. "Now don't you worry about a thing, sir," he said quickly. "It's eight o'clock now, and it's a lovely morning to be starting your leave. I've pressed your best uniform, and Stripey Muddock has done four shirts real smashing for you. Oh, and I've looked up the trains to London just as you asked. Breakfast is spam, but Cookie has doctored some powdered eggs, special. I'll bring it in to you."

Royce didn't remember asking about trains, and suspected he was being pampered, but the door closed before he could muster a comment, so he rolled off the bunk, and sipped the sweet tea.

Later, as he munched his breakfast, he thought about leave, and wondered if his parents would see any difference in him or whether his mother would persist in treating him like a school-boy. The thought of the Surrey woods, now green and fresh, the feel of springy turf under his feet, and the excited barks of old Bruce as he lumbered about in the bushes, sent a queer thrill through him, and a warm excitement made him determined to close his mind tightly on the previous forty-eight hours.

As he dressed slowly and carefully, his ear picked out the usual shipboard noises which he had come to know so well. The measured tread of the Quartermaster above his head, the clank-ing of a winch, the appealing mew of the gulls, and the twitter of the pipes throughout the ship, as the hands were invited to muster on the fo'c'sle to perform a task.

In bustled the little steward, and surveyed his charge carefully, then nodded. "Very smart, if I may say so, sir, and just in time for the nine-ten to London. Gets in at about eleven thirty, and there are plenty of trains out from Waterloo for your manor."

Royce thanked him, and picked up his case and respirator. "Tell the Quartermaster to hold the post-boat. I've just got to call in to the Wardroom."

The handshakes were firm, and the good wishes genuine, as he parted from his friends, all of whom were looking forward to their leave, as a starving man sees his first meal. Emberson fol-lowed him on deck, and together they looked down into the duty boat, hooked on at the main gangway, the Coxswain obviously impatient to be off.

"Well, so long, Clive," he said quietly. "Have a good leave and forget everything else. I'm following you in about an hour."

Royce watched the lonely figure at the guard-rails until the motor-boat turned the railway jetty, and the *Royston* was hidden from view.

He made a smart figure in his best doeskin jacket, the gold wavy stripe gleaming on the sleeve, as he strode briskly up the ramp to the station. A naval patrolman hurried from the R.T.O.'s office, and saluted.

"Beg pardon, sir. Sub-Lieutenant Royce is it?"

When the officer nodded, he continued: "Dockyard gate 'ave just 'phoned through to say there's a Wren trying to get through to see you. I don't know no more, the line's gone dead again, but I expect it's some message from the Signal Tower."

Royce paused, one eye on the clock. "Hm, I guess it'll wait till I get back. I don't want to wait an hour for another train."

"Aye, aye, sir. I'll tell them you've gone if they get through again."

Royce settled himself in an empty compartment, and proceeded to fill his pipe with duty-free tobacco. Ten minutes to wait, and then the war and the navy would be left behind.

His line of thought was interrupted by a screech of brakes in the station forecourt, where he saw a grey dockyard van jerk to a halt, and immediately a small figure in blue jumped out, and hurried up the platform, apparently peering in each window, to the obvious delight of the sailors in some of the compartments.

"Good God," he thought. "It must be an urgent message after all."

He went cold at the thought of a possible recall to duty, but in order not to prolong the agony, he thrust his head out of the window.

"Are you looking for me?" he called.

She reached him, and stood looking up, breathing fast. He saw by her badges that she was in the signals branch, but at once his attention was taken by the girl herself. She had quite the most attractive face possible, he thought. The eyes, which were now looking anxiously into his, were of the darkest brown, which contrasted with the smoothest skin Royce had ever seen. From beneath her jaunty cap, dark curls were rebelling against naval uniform, and completed this enchanting picture.

He realized he was staring, and coloured slightly. "I'm Royce," he explained. "Are you looking for me?"

"Yes, I wanted to ask you about Lieutenant Harston," she said quickly, her voice soft and warm. "I was hoping you could wait for me."

Royce tensed, taken aback. "I didn't know he had any friends outside the flotilla here." He felt vaguely angry. "I expect the *Royston* can tell you the full details."

The rather sad little face tightened. "I'm Julia Harston, his sister," she said quietly.

Royce was completely shattered, this unexpected turn of events made his mind whirl, and he struggled to put right the damage his hasty words had done.

"I, I'm terribly sorry, I didn't understand," he stammered.

"You see I thought, I thought Harston had no relatives . . ." He coloured when he realized he had referred to her brother by his surname.

"I thought a great deal of him, he taught me everything about this job, and when you came up to ask about him, well, I just felt I didn't want to share . . ." He broke off helplessly.

She studied his face for a few seconds, and when she spoke it was with slow deliberation, as if she wanted him to feel the impact of every word.

"We have no parents, they were killed in an air-raid on London last year." She paused, and for a split second her lower lip trembled. "Now I'm the only one left."

Somewhere down the platform, a hundred miles away, a voice shouted: "Hurry along there! Close all doors!" And a warning whistle sounded.

Royce was torn by violent and previously unknown emotions. She stood there alone and small on the now empty platform, and he felt he wanted to jump down and hold her close to him, to comfort her, and to protect her.

The words came tumbling out of him. "Look, can I see you again? I'll be back soon; I can come back earlier."

"I shouldn't think so. I'm going on draft tomorrow," she answered simply.

A shrill whistle called urgently, and the engine gave a violent hiss of steam, and the train shuddered.

"Please, I must see you," implored Royce, leaning right out of the window, until her face was but a foot away. "Where will you be going?"

The train jolted, and began to trundle out of the station.

Her small chin jutted defiantly. "I expect the Powers That Be can tell you the full details!"

With that she turned and walked quickly down the platform, and as the train gathered speed Royce still hung precariously from the window and watched the tiny blue figure until smoke from the ancient engine blotted out the station, and the scenery became squalid rows of small houses on the outskirts of the port.

He sank down on the worn cushions, a feeling of helplessness overcame him, and he knew for the first time the ache in his heart. All the way to town he sat restlessly staring out of the window, picking out the old landmarks, and trying to free his mind of the large brown eyes of Julia Harston. Julia: he repeated her name over and over in his mind, until it kept time with the clickerty-click of the wheels. If only he hadn't sent the telegram to his mother saying what time he'd be arriving, he could have stopped just a little longer. When the train pulled up with a last protesting lurch, he had determined to find her, wherever she was, whatever she thought of him.

He only vaguely remembered Waterloo as he struggled across its busy concourse, the blaring loudspeakers, and hundreds of hurrying servicemen. The joyous reunions, and the brave and tearful farewells, that were commonplace in a Britain at war.

An hour later he stepped down from another slow train on to the little station on the edge of Oxshott woods that he knew so well, and, as if in welcome, the daffodils in the stationmaster's garden made a colourful fanfare. The next instant, his mother's arms were about his neck, and his father pumped his hand, while Bruce, older and fatter, but just as boisterous, lolloped about his legs. In the background, old Arthur the porter, who had been there for a lifetime, nodded and smiled.

"You're looking well, Clive," said his father gruffly, and his mother merely nodded, her eyes shining.

And so, in a specially hired taxi—they had never gone in for a car—arms linked and Bruce perched on a suitcase beside the driver, Clive Royce came home. Not the callow youth in the proud uniform who had set out less than a year ago, full of worried anticipation and eager hopes, but a quieter and older person, self-confident, an officer.

The first week of his leave was made up in dashing round visiting old family friends, as much to please his parents as anything else. In the evenings, he walked contentedly through the woods, smoking his pipe, and throwing sticks for the dog, but always at the back of his mind lurked the fears of the previous week, and once in the night he sat up in bed sweating, hearing again the rattle of the machine-guns and the awful cries of the dying. When he thought of Harston, he thought of Julia, and when he thought of her, he was always filled with the same desperate longing. He had to find her, to see her again.

The second week dwindled all too quickly, and as the days passed, his mother seemed to shrink, and become more and more attentive, and although he had never told her of the horrors of battle, she was quick to understand what had changed her son.

On the last Thursday they sat round the fire in the evening, after a late dinner, Royce feeling sure he had been forced to eat half of their rations, and talked of the future, after the war, when his father glanced at his watch, and reached for the radio.

"Won't do to miss the news, will it, dear?" he smiled. "Clive'll feel he's getting out of touch."

It was all the usual information, an advance here, a retreat there, air raids in the Midlands, air raids on Germany. And then at the end: "During the night, our light coastal forces have been active off the Hook of Holland, and actively engaged a number of enemy E-boats. One E-boat was sunk, and several damaged. Two of our vessels sustained some damage and casualties. Next of kin have been informed."

His mother switched it off, and said too cheerfully, her face averted, "What about the last of the sherry. I'll go and get it for you lazy old things." And she hurried out to the kitchen.

The two men faced each other, then his father patted his knee. "You mustn't mind Mother, you know how she worries," was all he said.

But the next day on that same platform, he thought of those words, as they stood in silence until the train was actually running into the station, then the good-byes were hurried, the hugs so brief, and as he was borne rapidly away from the sun-drenched little station, the picture of the two seemingly frail figures, and the rough worried-looking dog, were imprinted firmly on his mind.

After many wearisome hours of travel, consisting mainly, he thought, of changing trains every few minutes, and trying not to leave his respirator on the rack, he observed the now familiar landmarks of the low-lying Essex coast, and soon the deserted marsh flats, and the rich, fresh fields began to give way to scattered houses and cottages, and eventually the train ground to a stop in the bustling harbour station.

As he strode to the barrier, he picked out several faces from the flotilla, who either saluted or smiled, according to their rank or disposition. Petty Officer Moore, spruce and dapper in immaculate uniform and gold badges, so unlike his usual greasy overalls and woollen cap, was apparently loaded down with mysterious parcels from doting relatives—he came from a vast family—and seeing Royce, he nodded awkwardly, and fell in step beside him.

"Afternoon, sir," he greeted affably, "I 'ope you 'ad a good leave?"

Without waiting for an answer, he plunged into the full story of his own achievements, which appeared to consist of mainly visiting as many pubs as possible, with his family, all of whom were employed at the docks, and as he put it, "the bleedin' cash was flying about like peas on a pusser's blanket!"

As they strolled along the railway jetty, they saw the boats lying once more alongside the depot ship. In two weeks the dockyard had done marvels. Planking patched and replaced, all the hulls repainted a very dark grey, which improved their rakish lines, and even now their decks swarmed with overalled figures as the maintenance staff completed the work of restoring and putting final touches to their craft.

In the *Royston*'s wardroom, the bar was just opening as Royce hurried in, and soon he was firmly embedded in a tight circle of old friends, and eagerly they exchanged gossip, and pumped the other officers for the latest news of operations.

A small, wizened R.N.R. Lieutenant, bearing the purple stripe of an Engineer, and known to all affectionately as "Fixer" Martin, because of his magical powers with the M.T.B.s' engines, looked sadly at his empty glass, and shook his head.

"I'm afraid you poor boys have a shock in store." He sighed deeply, and continued: "Have any of you fly-by-nights heard of a Lieutenant-Commander Aubrey Kirby, Royal Navy?"

He made "Royal Navy" sound like an illuminated address.

"Good Lord, yes," answered Benjy Watson, who looked rather haggard after a violent leave spent chiefly in the West End of London. "He's the Captain of the old destroyer *Wycliffe*, a bit of a bastard to all accounts. Why?"

Martin smiled crookedly. "*Was* the Captain of *Wycliffe*." He paused. "You will be delighted to learn that this straightlaced, regimental, self-opinionated lump of peacetime navy is now Senior Officer of the flotilla!"

He was not disappointed by the gasps of amazement.

"And as our plump friend here says, he is one big bastard!"

"But look here, old man," drawled Emberson, "we've always had an R.N.V.R. chappie, that was the whole point, I mean, with all due respect to our regular brothers, we don't want a fellow who's thinking of his career all the time. Dash it all Fixer, you must be mistaken."

Deith, the quietest of the flotilla's commanders, pondered thoughtfully, and signalled the steward to fill Fixer's glass. As he wrote out a chit for another round of gins, he smiled.

"Well, thank you so much for cheering us all up, you old

pirate, he may not be as bad as all that, why, he might even get to like us."

Martin laughed outright. "I heard him talking to the Operations Officer, by accident of course, and he said, quote: 'Coastal Forces are an important arm to the Service.' Wait," he warned, as a cheer was raised. "He then said, quote: 'It's too important to be run by a lot of irresponsible yachtsmen and week-end sailors.' Unquote! What! no more cheers?"

"Hm, and I see that there's a conference in the forenoon at two bells tomorrow. I imagine that's so we can get acquainted," said Emberson, rubbing his chin. "Steward! Same again, and we'll drink to a short war!"

A blue, choking haze of tobacco smoke swirled and eddied around the operations room, as the flotilla officers made themselves comfortable for the conference, and as Royce glanced about him he saw everywhere the visible signs that the fortnight's leave had performed wonders, and a new life had been pumped into the fresh, eager faces. He felt a quick pang inside when he remembered that no longer would he sit with his ear cocked for Harston's quick and witty observations, and the careful and patient explanations of these conferences, and he wondered sadly what his new C.O. would be like. It was strange that he had not yet met the replacement, as he had already seen several new faces who had taken the places of the wounded and the dead. Except for his own boat, the flotilla was again up to full strength, with two new Vosper boats in the place of those which had become tombs for their crews. Even Jock Murray's 3007 was back, complete with a new bow, and as the slow-speaking Scot had said, "It was the neatest bit of plastic surgery you could wish for!"

A hush fell, as two figures strode on to the raised platform.

"All right, gentlemen," said Commander Wright cheerfully, "carry on smoking, and I'll bring you up to date."

But all attention was rivetted on the other officer who sat down briskly behind his superior. Lieutenant-Commander Aubrey Kirby was all that you would expect a regular naval man to look. His uniform neat, a gleaming white shirt, its starched cuffs protruding sharply from beneath the sleeves bearing the two and a half gold symbols of authority. He was so true to pattern that it was difficult to determine the man himself. He was rather short and stocky, with a pink, round face. His hair, which was cut short to regulation length, was brushed straight back, but it had no definite colour, and even his features were very ordinary. But the eyes, they were a different matter. Like two pieces of pale blue glass, and as he sat erect and self-contained, with his small hands folded in his lap, he looked for all the world like a smug Siamese cat, or so Royce thought.

He was not alone in this somewhat discouraging opinion. Benjy leaned over his shoulder, his warm breath smelling faintly of gin.

"Don't you feel sorry for the feller? The pekingese in the pigsty!"

He shut up quickly, as the cold eyes flickered in his direction for the briefest instant.

Commander Wright rambled on, apparently unaware that anything was amiss, and Royce realized that the speech of introduction was coming to a close.

"And now, gentlemen, I'll leave you to your new S.N.O., who will tell you about the next operational patrol."

With that, he withdrew, a trifle too hastily.

Kirby rose slowly, and walked to the middle of the platform, exactly the middle, and stood with his hands behind his back, like the guest conductor at a promenade concert. When he spoke, his voice was sharp and clear, but unexpectedly high, and he got straight down to business.

"In a few moments we'll go over the plan of action for tomorrow night, but first I want to bring a few points, merely matters of personal discipline, to your notice."

He paused, and a twinge of uneasiness ran through his audience.

"Firstly, some of you appear to imagine that uniform is unnecessary in Coastal Forces. Those of you who feel this way will most certainly be crossing swords with me in the near future. From now on, aboard the depot ship, and at any time in harbour, number fives will be worn, without the trimmings. No fancy scarves, or funny hats, and not battle dress. If you are personally neat and smart, you will set a good example to your men."

Emberson stood up quickly, his face half amused and half angry.

"But, sir, you can't treat the men here as if it was barrack routine," he drawled. "Why, it can be dangerous in this job, and a little laxity in some ways helps a lot."

For the first time a gust of laughter ran round the officers. Kirby was unmoved and quite expressionless.

"My orders stand," he snapped, "and I'll trouble you to keep your personal opinions to yourself."

Emberson cursed under his breath, and sank down to his seat.

"That scuttled you," grinned Benjy. "First round to the Little Admiral!"

Kirby then proceeded to list the orders and regulations which would in future be enforced in every boat of the flotilla, which seemed to cover every eventuality from the colour schemes of the hulls, to the lengths of beards worn by the crews.

He finished up his offensive in the same unemotional, crisp tones, pausing only to flick a speck of dust from his sleeve.

"Remember," he ended, "you have not been outstanding in the past. I intend to see that this is the best flotilla on the East Coast, and if you all co-operate, my task will be easier. If not," he shrugged, "some of you will have to be transferred."

Royce only vaguely heard the details of the patrol for the following night, his head was whirling with indignation; he felt hurt, not for himself, but for his friends, who now sat silently listening, while the clear, flat voice continued to rattle off the facts and figures, as if they were a crowd of backward schoolboys.

"One final point. I shall be taking over 1991, with Royce as my Number One, so all my personal orders will be passed through him. That is all, gentlemen, I trust you will see to your duties."

They rose and moved for the door, but the voice had not quite finished.

"Sub-Lieutenant Royce report to me."

Royce was left in the empty room facing his superior, and a feeling of resentment filled him, but he took the proffered hand, which was cold and soft.

"Well, Number One," said Kirby cheerfully. "Took it well, didn't they?"

"They're wonderful chaps, sir," mumbled Royce hotly. "They've been through hell, and I wouldn't wish to be with a finer lot."

Kirby's face hardened.

"Let's hope you don't have to. In the meantime, I want a list of all defects from the engineer over the last six months, and the results of all practice gunnery shoots over the same period. On my desk tomorrow morning."

He turned on his heel and strode off. Royce felt as if the whole private, happy atmosphere of his little kingdom had been sud-

denly shattered by this interloper. When he reached the wardroom he found that the others were of the same opinion.

"Strewth!" roared Benjy. "If I tell my boys to put number
threes on, there'll be a ruddy riot!"

Emberson smiled quietly.

"Not to worry, I think I can say without offending any grey-
beards present, that I am now the oldest inhabitant here, and I
can further pronounce that within a few months this chap will
be as good as gold, after all, be patient, he *is* R.N.!"

"Oh yes," nodded Murray from the corner of the bar, "I've
heard of them. They look after the navy in peacetime!"

A howl of laughter went up, and the ice was broken.

The following afternoon, however, Royce stood uneasily on
the bridge of the M.T.B. awaiting his new Commander, and
having slaved for twenty-four hours to get the boat ready, he was
in no mood for laughing. The boat gleamed from stem to stern,
the smell of new paint pervaded everywhere, and all visible signs
of the last action had been wiped away, like an unpleasant
drawing from a blackboard. When he had first mounted the
bridge, he had not been thinking about Kirby and his regulations, but wondering how he would react to going into action
again, and whether his nerve might have gone, like so many, who
had been labelled "bomb-happy". In the warm sunshine the
bridge looked quiet and peaceful, and the fresh steel plates
gleamed dully in their grey paint, while the brass of the binnacle
and voice-pipes shone cheerfully in welcome. It was difficult to
imagine this place as the roaring, shell-torn hell that it had been
just a couple of weeks ago. He had checked the charts, the stores
and ammunition. The guns had been tested and the torpedoes
stripped and prepared, until he was quite satisfied. He had even
done the returns that Kirby had wanted for some purpose or
other, and he was feeling the strain now of waiting to see his
superior's reactions to his efforts. He had not long to wait. Kirby,
in a spotless new duffle coat and white scarf, swung over the side
and marched up to him, and even as he returned his salute, his
eyes darted everywhere, taking in every small detail.

"Quite good, Number One," he conceded at length. "We proceed to sea at 1630 as ordered. Make a signal to that effect.
Although it's a more or less routine patrol off the Dutch coast,
we might be lucky, and in any case it'll get the cobwebs blown
away."

The Coxswain mounted the bridge to report all hands aboard

for sea, and Royce was pleased to see that he had made a special effort to smarten his appearance. His cap, usually worn after the style of Admiral Beatty, perched carefully on the unruly, carroty hair, and his sweater was almost white.

"I understand that you, at least, are a regular?" questioned Kirby. "That is a good thing indeed."

"Yes, sir," answered the Coxswain, cautiously, "and I bin in this boat for two years, since she was built."

"I see."

And as Raikes turned to leave, "See that I'm piped aboard on every occasion in future, and I don't want to see the men lounging on the guard-rails. Keep them busy. A busy ship is an efficient one. I shall be watching you, Coxswain."

"Aye, aye, sir," answered Raikes, in apparent amazement.

"Good," thought Royce, "even the R.N. aren't used to this sort of thing."

In due course the time of departure drew near, and with special care Royce watched as the hands singled up the wire springs, ready to slip. Around him the other boats were busy, and Royce felt a glow of affection as he watched the familiar figures scurrying to and fro. On the bridge, Kirby stepped from one side to the other, swinging up his glasses and examining his flotilla from every angle.

Collins, the signalman, lowered his glass. "Signal from tower, sir, 'Preparative, five minutes'."

Kirby rang down "stand-by" to the engine room, and listened angrily, as the other boats began to rev their motors vigorously.

"If the engines are in proper order," he barked, "you don't need to start them until that Preparative is lowered."

With a rush the tiny flag dipped, and Royce yelled, "Let go all lines. Bear off forrard!"

Fortunately for Petty Officer Moore, the engines roared to life at the crucial moment, but as he said later, "Never before, and never agin!"

Carefully, and gracefully, the eight boats swung into line and picked up their distances, making a proud picture in the bright sun. The new ensigns fluttered defiantly from the gaffs, and on every deck the crews stood in neat lines for leaving harbour.

As he stood on the fo'c'sle with his men, Royce's heart lightened with pleasure at the sight, and he felt bound even closer to these wild young men, upon whom so much depended.

Through the boom-gate they threaded, and round the bell-buoy, towards the inviting but hostile sea, over which a million shimmering lights sparkled, and not even the faintest breeze ruffled its gleaming surface. He wondered what it would be like in peacetime. The small beaches packed with perspiring families, no doubt. Sand castles and toffee-apples. Laughing girls and carefree men. It was a world that didn't exist. He sighed, and dismissed the hands, and returned to the bridge.

"As soon as it's sunset, the flotilla will go to action stations," ordered Kirby, "and as I said at the conference, nobody fires a shot or breaks station without a signal to that effect from me."

Royce took over the watch, realizing it was useless to argue or make suggestions, and Kirby retired to his cabin. It seemed obvious to him that Kirby still thought he was running a destroyer, and didn't really grasp the significance of this close fighting, where individual action counted for so much.

As the light faded, and the boats bowled forward at a steady, medium speed, Royce leaned pensively on the screen, and thought again of Julia. It was wonderful to have someone to think about in that way, and he decided that as soon as he could get ashore, he would start making inquiries to try and trace her, without making it too obvious. He wished that there was someone he could consult about such matters, someone who would be able to give him the benefit of experience that he himself lacked. Before he had volunteered for the navy, he had been far too wrapped up in his work, and studying for seemingly impossible exams, to even consider investing some of his meagre allowance on the pursuit of the opposite sex. It was all very worrying; she might at this moment be getting engaged, or even married, without his getting another look at her. He shook himself, this was absurd, he told himself, why, even if he ever found her again, she might be quite unlike the girl of his constant thoughts, and he would make a fool of himself once more. But the image of the large brown eyes persisted, and again all doubts and appeals to reason were dispelled.

Two ungainly corvettes, their sides streaked with rust and red lead, steamed sedately past, no doubt on their way back home from convoy duty, and as is the custom of the navy, the signal lamps got busy.

"Signal from *Rockrose*, sir," grinned Collins. " 'What yacht club are you?' "

Royce laughed. "Make 'East Coast Cruising Club. What are you doing?' "

For a few seconds the lights winked back and forth across the darkening water.

From *Rockrose,* "Joining the Wrens, Good night!"

With a cheery toot on the siren the battered pair made off towards Harwich.

Kirby stood by his side, apparently drawn from his cabin by the sounds.

"What was happening, Number One?" he queried. "What signals were they? Have they sighted something?"

"No, sir, just the usual light chatter, otherwise all quiet."

"I don't approve of these silly signals, Royce, they're quite unnecessary, and only encourage slackness. The only signals to be sent are those you put in the log. Do you understand?"

"Aye, aye, sir," said Royce heavily, while Collins suddenly busied himself with the flag locker.

You absolute pig, he thought to himself, and turned his attention to the compass.

Kirby, who looked pale and drawn, stood fidgeting for some moments, his calm temporarily upset by all these unorthodox goings on, then giving Royce and the signalman another glare, he stalked from the bridge.

Collins's soft, tuneless whistle wafted quite clearly above the rumble of the engines, "All the nice girls love a sailor——"

"Oh, for Christ's sake stow it, will you!" he barked, then realizing it useless to take it out of the unfortunate Bunts, "See if you can get some kye laid on, it's getting a bit chilly now."

"It certainly is, sir," muttered Collins with heavy irony, and hurried off before he could receive another rebuke.

At the clamour of Action Stations, the hands poured up from below, and settled themselves once again around their weapons, muttering and cursing about what they considered to be an unnecessary precaution. Able Seaman Roote, who had relieved Parker as gunlayer on the pom-pom, while he was in hospital with his badly cut face, made no bones about voicing the opinion of the mess-deck.

"It's ruddy daft, that's what! 'Oo does 'e think 'e is, I want to know? In this tub already I bin in twenty scraps, and nobody's ever asked me 'ow I was dressed before! But 'is bleedin' lordship up there says, 'Hall thet his a-goin' to be quate different in the footure.'" He mimicked in a high, falsetto voice.

"Lofty" Poole, his "oppo", showed his strong teeth through

the gloom. "Watch out Rooty, 'e'll 'ave you in cocked 'at and spurs afore long!"

The ex-milkman from Hackney laughed mirthlessly.

"You 'eard what old Bunts said? Poor old Jimmy-the-One was fair fumin'. Bunts reckoned 'e was goin' to poke the Old Man in the chops!"

"Yeh, old Jimmy's not a bad bloke for an officer; 'e was proper busted up about the Old Man catching it. The real skipper, I mean."

They huddled together for extra warmth, and lapsed into a companionable silence born of long training.

Bunched abaft the squat bridge, the torpedo party too were going through their usual fumbling paces with their twin giants, their bodies rolling to the easy motion of the throbbing hull. The L.T.O., a small, unhappy-looking man from Cornwall, called Petroc, kicked one of the tubes savagely.

"You'm a big useless lump o' metal, that's what yew are!"

As the torpedo showed no sign of having heard this outburst, he continued, "If yew don' sink summat this time, oi'll stuff the ol' man in yew, an' foire 'im instead! Reckon yew won' loike that!"

Overhead the sky was a ceiling of black velvet, sprinkled with a million stars of every size and shape, which made their little ship seem unimportant and fragile. The short, stumpy mast revolved in a tight circle, pointing first at one group of stars, and then another, like a dark finger.

Royce thrust his head and shoulders beneath the waterproof blackout curtain covering the private world of the chart table, and with the aid of the dim light, he got to work with parallel rulers and dividers on the well-worn chart showing the approaches to the Hook of Holland.

The principle of inshore fighting is to creep among the treacherous sand-bars, where the convoys and their escorts cannot reach, and then pounce out at full speed, every man for himself. It usually worked.

Now at a dead slow crawl, the lithe shapes of the flotilla crept forward against the ebb tide. Station-keeping was no great difficulty on this occasion, as all the boats were leaving long phosphorescent trails astern, like fiery comets, but even so, carelessness, as they all knew from experience, could result in sudden, crippling damage, or the prospect of being left high and dry on a mud-bank for the enemy to collect at leisure.

Kirby stood very erect by the chart table, shrouded in his duffle coat, his eyes fixed on an invisible mark ahead. What schemes were passing through his thoughts Royce could only guess, but in his own mind the usual combination of cold excitement, and the tugging grip of fear, had already got to work. He shivered violently, and worked his shoulders vigorously, he wanted to stamp his feet too, but knew that this was probably the moment of decision, calling for complete watchfulness and silence. On the other hand, it would quite likely be just another empty patrol.

"Stop engines," ordered Kirby curtly, and as the boats lapsed into silence, one after the other, the gentle slap, slap of the small waves against the mahogany sides sounded loud enough for even a dead German to hear.

Royce kept a careful eye on the compass, trying to determine their drift on the sluggish current, and the nearness of the other craft, and he jumped violently when Kirby suddenly jabbed him in the ribs.

"There," he hissed, pointing over the port bow. "D'you see?"

For the moment he could fix his eyes on nothing, and then for the tiniest instant, far away it seemed, he saw a minute flicker of light, then blackness. Yes, there it was, a faint beam of light, then it had gone again.

"What is it, sir?" asked Royce. "It's no buoy, there are none about here. It was rather like a signal, but it was almost regular, wasn't it?"

Kirby raised his glasses again, and Royce heard him chuckle.

"I've seen that before on other slack ships. That was a loose deadlight over a port."

He waited for the significance to sink in.

"Each time the ship rolls, the deadlight opens, and out shines the light. Probably some stupid officer in his cabin. Oh yes, Number One, there's a nice big ship on the end of that light. Stand by to engage with torpedoes!"

Royce flung himself down towards the torpedo party, hearing briefly as he did so, the click of a shaded Aldis lamp to the other boats. The engines purred to life, and they crept forward once more, this time in earnest.

Peering round the side of the wheelhouse, Royce saw the darkness ahead lose its silky smoothness, and slowly but surely a new, hard shape began to emerge. It was like a wild dream, it was so unreal and almost frightening, as this great ship moved silently across the water ahead of them. The range was still about a thousand yards, and yet the strange vessel rose like a factory, high above them.

"Phew, it must be the *Queen Mary*!" muttered Petroc.

The voice-pipe rattled, "Stand by, tubes."

They waited.

Still they cruised towards each other, on a course which could end in a collision if nothing happened. Surely the enemy captain must see them soon.

Petroc checked with his sighting bar. "Three hundred yards, sir," he whispered.

Then, quite clearly and crisply across the water, they heard the urgent clamour of a klaxon hooter, and a split second later there was a flat explosion from the bridge, as a snowflake rocket was sent on its journey over the surprised vessel. When it burst, in a gleaming, eye-searing glare, they saw before them, as if engraved on a black backcloth, a vast oil tanker of some twenty thousand tons, every detail clear and bright from her tall, tapering derricks and lofty bridge, to the neat lifeboats stacked under their davits. In answer to the alarm, tiny figures scurried aft to a shrouded gun platform, while the great ship began to turn away from the attackers. A fresh, creamy froth rose from her stern, and she surged forward, the bow wave rising against the proud, raking stem. But in vain, even at the Tactical School at Portsmouth, no target could be better placed for a kill.

They all heard the harsh orders on the R-T, as Kirby flung his force to the assault. As their own bows lifted, and they swung on the new course, their engines screaming with hate, Kirby gave the signal to fire. With a cough of yellowish smoke, the great fish pounced from the gaping mouths of the tubes, ungainly and ugly, but as their sharp fins and propellers dug into their natural element, the sea, they shot forward remorselessly, gathering a fiendish speed. Instantly, the M.T.B. heeled over, lightened from her burden, scudding round and away, to leave the way clear for the next boat in the line.

They could clearly see the sharp bows of Emberson's boat cleaving rapidly on the same course as they had just taken, and when he fired his fish, it looked all the more impressive and terrible. The German gunners had been forgotten in the excitement, but now, above the noise of the engines, they heard the sharp bang of the twelve-pounder as they got the first shell away. Where it went they never knew, for at that instant, their torpedoes struck home, biting deep into the bowels of the engine room.

They exploded as one, and the night was torn in two by the great roaring detonation. A tall column of water rose high above the masts, followed by a terrifying orange flash, more powerful than even the rocket had been, and before their shocked minds could readjust themselves, the centre of the main deck dissolved into a mass of writhing flames, the heat of which could be felt harsh on their faces. Another deafening bang heralded the arrival of one of Emberson's torpedoes, the other had apparently missed, and before their eyes, the vast bows dropped into the sea, as if sheered off by an invisible knife. Kirby signalled to break off the action, and withdrew from the new menace of the blazing oil which was pouring in thousands of gallons from the shattered tanks. It spread over the waves in a great fiery apron, stripping the paint from the ship's scorched sides, and causing the jagged plates to glow red, and to buckle into fantastic shapes. Slowly and majestically she dipped her head in submission to the savage onslaught, the great flames hissing and darting along the whole length of the decks, and above all other sounds could be heard the bellow of scalding steam, and more internal explosions, as her very entrails were torn to shreds. The propellers, now still, rose dripping and shining in the glare, whilst in a shower of sparks, the main derrick tore free from the tormenting fire and plunged over the side. More quickly now, the glowing carcass that had been a proud ship but a few moments before rose steeply, until it hung, apparently motionless, while the awful sounds of tearing metal and heavy equipment breaking through the length of the hull, ground across to the watchers. With a great sigh, and another sullen explosion as the boilers split asunder, she took the final plunge, pulling up with another jarring crash as she struck the bottom of the channel, and rolled over on to her side, to disappear in a flurry of foam and burning oil.

They watched in silence, as if in homage to the dying ship, the old hands with a hard feeling of satisfaction, the others, like Royce, in shocked wonderment. They cruised for a while around the creeping patch of flaming oil, knowing in their hearts that there would be nobody left to save from such a holocaust, but peering into the greasy water just in case. Only the pitiful oddments remained, a life-raft, a few pieces of smouldering deck planking, and a smoking bundle of charred rags and flesh, face down, a despairing shoulder turned against the desperate land of the living.

Kirby found it difficult to conceal his jubilation, and paced impatiently back and forth, until, with a hasty glance at his watch, he ordered his flotilla to reform, and continue north-east up the coast.

"That'll show them, Number One," he said, rubbing his hands. "Now we'll see what else we can find."

Royce glanced at him in surprise.

"Surely we're not going to stay here, sir?" he asked. "That ship must have been waiting for her escorts, and in any case, the local support groups will have been alerted by now, and they'll be down on us like a ton of hot bricks. It's happened before like that to this flotilla."

The pale blob of Kirby's face turned towards him for some moments.

"Getting cold feet, Royce? There's no need to go to panic stations yet, you know."

Royce felt his face burning, and remembered his own foolish remarks to Leading Seaman Parker before that first patrol.

"Certainly not, sir, it's just that we've always pulled away from this coast after an attack; there's no room to manoeuvre."

"I think I know this business better than you," snapped Kirby. "I would be very much obliged if, in this instance, the amateurs would stand fast, and try to learn something for a change."

He jerked his head back in the direction of Emberson's boat.

"Take him for example. Wasted two torpedoes, mine would have been quite sufficient. And in any case, he missed altogether with one!"

"We might have missed with ours, sir, then it would have been very different."

"Really, that's very interesting," Kirby's voice was heavy with sarcasm. "I'm not in the habit of wasting valuable equipment. I'm not in the Service just for a lark while there's a war going on; I'll trouble you to remember that!"

Royce choked back the hot fury that made his eyes swim with rage.

"Aye, aye, sir," was all he dared allow himself to say.

As he lay against the side of the bridge, steadying his glasses, he found it difficult to believe that anyone could be so utterly callous and pompous, to be able to give a lecture about his career, quite calmly, after having just destroyed a valuable enemy ship. It was quite fantastic, all the more so, because he was so sure of himself, so self-reliant.

For two hours they cruised through the night, the dark coast-line never far abeam, and then, quite suddenly, they saw the two trawlers coming straight towards them. Royce's heart sank. It seemed inevitable that they should meet again with the "floating forts", and that this would be another wall of destruction.

"They might be the flak-boats!" he shouted, above the in-creasing roar of the engines, "Covered with guns and concrete!"

Kirby paid no heed, but headed straight for the nearest vessel.

Both trawlers were flashing lights wildly, and turning away from each other, their shapes lengthening, their stumpy funnels clearly visible.

"Open fire!" shouted Kirby, and the bridge rattled and vibrated as the tracer shells clawed towards the nearest dark shape. The Oerlikons joined in with their ear-shattering rattle, and at once a flurry of splashes churned the water around the trawler into a white frenzy, moving steadily, until a ripple of flashes tore along the decks, to hover, and then hold the high bridge in a deadly cross-fire. Pieces of wood flew in every direction, and faintly the sounds of breaking glass were heard, as the wheelhouse windows flew to fragments, carving the helmsman to ribbons. She slewed round and stopped, steam pouring from her, and flames beginning to take hold of the superstructure, and as they turned round her stern, Deith's 1815 shot into view, his tracers swamping the other trawler with a deluge of fire, and like her sister, she began to settle down, a dense pall of smoke rolling over the sea towards them.

Kirby snatched the hand-set of the loud-hailer, his crisp voice carrying clearly above the crackle of burning woodwork and exploding ammunition.

"Get back in station," he yelled, "I can finish this one off."

Deith's speeding boat turned in a creamy circle, and the whole flotilla must have heard his angry voice boom across the water.

"My bird, I think, sir!"

"Impudent young puppy," fumed Kirby. "We'll see about that!"

He flounced up and down the bridge, to the obvious delight of Collins, and then calmed himself with a supreme effort.

"Steer west-south-west, and take up course for base," he snapped.

Then, as if to let off steam, "So much for your 'Floating Fort-resses'. It seems I've come along just at the right time!"

As the flotilla sped for home, and even until the horizon began to lighten, Royce stood silent and fuming beside his superior, not daring to speak, and conscious only of a helpless feeling of frustration at the unfairness of Kirby's remarks, and at the ruthless way he was so obviously determined to capture as much of the limelight as possible for himself.

He mellowed a little at the sight of the glorious, glowing ball of the sun, rising in all her splendour over the horizon, and bringing life and colour to the flat glassy sea. It was a rare experience for them to sail in the sunlight, and as they felt the little early morning warmth fan their tired faces, they felt that the fangs of the night had been temporarily drawn.

"Aircraft, sir. Red nine-oh!"

The gunner's warning cry made heads turn skywards as one, and soon the glasses of the flotilla focused on the minute black speck which had appeared from between the high, fleecy clouds.

"There's another, and another, by God, there's 'alf a dozen of 'em!" muttered Collins.

The hunt was on, and already these planes would be calling their base for reinforcements.

The six aircraft turned in a wide semi-circle, their wings glinting, until the sun was behind them, and then in a perfect line they screamed down to the attack.

Again the M.T.B.s' armament rattled into life, as every boat sent a barrage of shells and bullets to meet the attackers. Down, down, down they came, until the black crosses were clearly visible on their wings, and then the first in line, garishly painted in yellow stripes, opened fire with his battery of wing-mounted machine-guns, and a shower of woodwork and loose gear flew from one M.T.B.'s deck. But the concentrated barrage was too much for the others, and they pulled violently out of their dive, one with a light plume of smoke streaming behind it.

Marshalled by Yellow-Stripes, they reformed and headed for the clouds, and it was only then that they saw the five Spitfires zooming low over the water, rolling their wings in welcome.

"I'm going below now," informed Kirby. "Signal the Spitfires, 'About time too'," and he stamped down the ladder.

Collins picked up his lamp, but Royce shook his head.

"Make 'Pleased to see you'," he grinned. "That sounds a bit better!"

The fighters streaked off after the Germans, and the sea became an empty glassy mirror of reflected morning glory.

"Signal from 3007, 'That bugger has made a mess of my new deck'," repeated Collins with a broad smile.

Poor old Jock, but still it was a relief no one was hit.

They had a big welcome back to the base, when they cruised slowly and carefully alongside the depot ship, the hands fallen in at their stations, and ensigns fluttering bravely. Kirby had made signals in every direction as they had crossed the boom, so that no doubt would be left in the minds of the naval staff as to whose victory it really was.

When the depot ship bugler was sounding "Sunset" that evening, they gathered together in the bar, where another piece of news was awaiting them.

Benjy Watson burst excitedly into their midst, his face beaming with pleasure.

"Guess what, old Artie's half-stripe has come through; the Little Admiral's got a rival now!"

Deith raised his glass, "Good old lawyer, he's damned well earned it too!"

Emberson entered the wardroom at that moment, his face thoughtful, and in seconds his back was being thumped, and a large glass put in his hand.

Royce smiled, and called above the din, "I'm very pleased, Artie, how does it feel?"

"Yes, what's it like Lootenant-Commander?" quipped Benjy.

Emberson looked sadly at each one in turn, before speaking, as if to memorize each friendly face.

"It's not as easy as all that, chaps. I'm being drafted to Harwich as Senior Officer of a flotilla of Fairmile M.T.B.s, so you see, this is the end of the road for us," he ended quietly.

Their faces fell. It didn't seem right to break up the old crowd like this. Up to now, only death or disablement had parted them.

"Och, that's a raw deal." Jock Murray was the first to speak. "We'll miss you, lad."

Emberson straightened up. "I'm off tomorrow afternoon, so tonight let's have the mother and father of all parties!"

That was a cheering thought, especially as they knew that they were not required to go to sea for at least two more days.

"Right, but where'll we have it?" queried Lieutenant Cameron. "Can't have it aboard here, without Kirby and other outsiders horning in, with all due respect to your C.O.," he added with a grin, turning to Royce.

"No," agreed Emberson. "We'll have it aboard my boat, and Benjy's, as he's right alongside me."

He turned to Benjy. "Now you've got work to do. Get some Wren types laid on, tell them it's a farewell party, so they don't think we're up to anything. And you, Jock, you're in charge of bonded stores. Scrounge all the booze you can. And get some beer as well from the White Hart. I think that just about covers everything."

One hour later, the Quartermaster was treated to the happy spectacle of some sixteen officers threading their way along the catwalks to two of the M.T.B.s, each carrying an assortment of bottles, and hastily prepared snacks that the chief cook had been heavily bribed to prepare, whilst across the water floated feminine laughter, as the duty boat arrived from the signal tower. Benjy had made a good haul, somehow or other; not one presentable Wren officer now remained on duty in the port.

The atmosphere in Artie's tiny wardroom, which measured about eighteen by ten, was close, to say the least, but as the guests arrived it was evident that the cramped quarters would be a help rather than a hindrance.

Lieutenant Peter Page, Artie's Number One, had done well. In about half an hour he had folded up the bunks, put down a borrowed carpet, produced flowers, and still found time to fix up a kind of buffet, of which he was now in charge.

After the usual shouted introductions, which nobody heeded anyway, the party really got started, and very soon, with the aid of a battered gramophone, some sort of dancing was in progress, consisting mainly of swaying back and forth over the precious carpet, bumping heads on overhead pipes and treading on each other's feet. When exhausted, it was customary to take your partner on to the upper deck and sample the cool night air, before plunging back into the fray. It was in the latter position which Royce now found himself, with a ravishing blonde Third Officer called Sylvia, who now persisted in calling him "old solemn-face".

Royce, who by this time was feeling slightly light-headed, proceeded to marshal his thoughts, and like all men who have had one too many, broached the question of Julia Harston, with what he fondly imagined was superb cunning, but what in fact sounded as if he was comparing the romantic Sylvia with one of many conquests.

"Really, darling," she breathed, her expensive perfume

mingling evenly with the scent of one of Benjy's gin-slings, "don't tell me you're one of those awful men of the world that mother warned me about?"

Royce tried again, but it was quite useless, so after a somewhat wet kiss, he piloted his charge back to the party, where he passed her over to Cameron, who, being a Romeo of the first water, was quick to take advantage of the situation, and together they took a further stroll on deck.

Emberson shouldered his way through to him, with yet two more glasses.

"Enjoying yourself, Clive?"

"Yes, thanks, Artie. That damned girl Sylvia whatsit, I was trying to pump some information out of her, about a girl I want to find, John's sister. She was in the signals here, but went on draft, after——"

"Good heavens, I knew he had a sister, but I didn't know she was here," Emberson was plainly amazed. "Nice, is she?"

"She's wonderful," sighed Royce. "Hates me though."

Emberson laughed until he shook from head to toe.

"It sounds fine. Please don't mind my laughter, old friend, it's just the way you come out with things."

Royce smiled self-consciously. "I know, but I can't get her out of my mind."

"Leave it to me. I wish you'd asked me earlier, as I happen to know their drafting type, but she's on leave at the moment. Tell you what, I'll write to her next week, and get the gen for you, how's that?"

Royce's face showed plainly how it was.

"There's one other thing I wanted to tell you." He dropped his voice. "I think we both get on well, and I've never known old John take to a chap as he did to you, so I'd like to have you with me at Harwich, as soon as you get a command. Don't laugh, it won't be long, in fact, I think it'll be when you pick up your second ring."

Royce was touched. "It'd be fine by me," he said sincerely.

"I've spoken to old Wright, and he says he'll do what he can for you. I gave him a load of bull about you, of course. Seriously though, I'd ask for you now as Number One, but that'd foul your chances of an appointment. So remember, all you've got to do is pick up the stripe, don't fall foul of Kirby, whatever he does, and find Julia. I'll do the rest."

After that, the world seemed a finer place to be in, and Royce's pent-up feelings burst forth with such enthusiasm and hitherto unsuspected gaiety that the already successful party was brought to a most happy and boisterous conclusion. In twos and threes, they ambled up to the darkened decks, and even the dismal wail of distant air-raid sirens failed to curb the full-throated, if unmelodious, singing. Having got the Wrens safely embarked upon their motor-boat, to the amused grins of the seaman on duty, they proceeded to march up the catwalks to the *Royston's* main deck, with Emberson perched shakily on their shoulders. The Officer-of-the-Day, already warned in advance, stood by the shaded police-light, at a solemn salute, as to the tune of "Don't Put Your Daughter On the Stage, Mrs. Worthington", the revellers voiced the famous Coastal Forces ditty, in honour of their comrade.

> *"Don't send my boat out to sea, Senior Officer,*
> *Don't send my boat out to sea.*
> *She's a bit of a roaring gash-boat*
> *Of that we'll all admit,*
> *Her boost is far too phoney,*
> *The Captain's a bit of a Twit."*

For such a sad occasion, all of them had done their best to make the night a memorable one.

CHAPTER FOUR

WHAT a short summer it seemed to Royce, so full of activity and not a little danger, that he did not have much difficulty in avoiding Kirby, who, as autumn sent her icy messengers scurrying through the rising winds of the Channel and North Sea, became more and more wrapped up in himself, rarely speaking to his crew, except in the line of duty, and avoiding his officers in their spells ashore. He walked like a man possessed of some weird driving force, unable to trust his so-called amateur crews, he spent every moment of his spare time poring over the flotilla orders, and studying reports of other groups' activities. It was well known that he was persistently badgering Commander Wright about their patrol areas, almost openly accusing him of giving his flotilla the worst areas to cover. This was mainly due to the fact that the record of successes rarely seemed to come his way, and as he was quite unable to see it was due to the fact that his method of operations was far too fixed, and lacking in the necessary reckless dash, he and the redoubtable Wright soon began to get on each other's nerves.

Emberson had been true to his word with regard to Julia Harston, but there success ended. She had been drafted to Rosyth —it might have been Greenland for all the use it was to Royce— and as he didn't wish to open operations by writing to her, in case she stopped him dead in his tracks, he spent hours of his watch-keeping time dreaming and hoping for the chance to get leave, and make the long pilgrimage to Scotland. When he confided these matters to Deith, he nodded sagely, and merely said, sadly, "Must be love, old man."

Around the world the tides of war ebbed and flowed, and time after time the dark clouds of near destruction seemed to hang over the British forces. While the armies of the Commonwealth fought and died in the steaming swamps, or the parched deserts, or trained and waited around the coasts of England, politicians wrangled and argued about expenditure and wastage almost as though the war was a private enjoyment of the forces, not to be encouraged unless from a political angle.

Fortunately, the majority of bomb-torn and rationed Britain faced the grim future with realism and fortitude, and found time to give a thumbs-up at any announcement of a hard-won victory, and should it be a reverse, they just shrugged, and hung grimly to the old supposition that we could always win the last battle.

The war at sea meant convoys, and still more convoys. Hard-pressed ships, many of which would have retired gracefully to the breakers' yards but for the war, battled every mile of ocean, bringing the life blood to the nation, and carrying men and material to a score of battle-fronts. Alongside the Royal Navy, the men of the merchant fleets carried on the grim struggle without complaint, the ultimate prey and target for every submarine, E-boat and bomber that the enemy could hurl against them, while the pitifully thin escorts hunted blindly around their helpless charges, shooting, depth-charging, and dying.

Unlike the army, they rarely saw their enemy. He was just another menace, like the howling gales which scattered the convoys' straight lines, and made navigation on a pitch-black night a screaming nightmare; or the hidden mine, lurking in the grey waters, inert and still, until touched by an unwary ship, with the terrible aftermath of the thunderous explosion, inrushing seas, and the pitiful cries of doomed sailors trapped within. No, to the men of the Navy, the enemy rarely had a personality. He was everywhere and nowhere, the constant menace, who made them think only of the next minute, of the next hour. Tomorrow was too improbable.

News from the other sea battle-grounds seemed bleak. In the Atlantic, the mounting fury of the U-boat assault was taking terrible toll. In one month, over a quarter of a million tons of allied shipping had been sent to the bottom, and while British yards were building more and more sorely needed escort vessels, corvettes, frigates and destroyers, so too the enemy pushed a stream of underwater killers across the sea routes. At night the Royal Air Force gamely endeavoured to bomb all sources of production, as well as the bases, but their efforts bore little fruit, for apart from the fact that all such places were strongly defended, the German war machine now had the choice of a vast coastline stretching from Norway in the north, to the Bay of Biscay. So, as usual, the brunt was falling on a handful of rust-streaked ships, held together by the determination of their crews, and driven by the fierceness of those who knew their backs were to the wall.

In the Mediterranean the story was the same, too few ships, too many of the enemy. And yet here, too, they were somehow holding their own. Fighting the convoys every mile of the way to beleaguered Malta, and covering and supplying the army in the desert, pausing only to pray, or die.

With increasing pressure by enemy heavy units in these spheres, it was obvious that it was just a matter of time before they tried a new method of attack in the restricted waters of the narrow seas. Intelligence reports had brought the disquieting news that many new E-boats and destroyers were being harboured in Ostend, Flushing and Calais, possibly with a view to making the movement of coastal convoys impossible, and thereby pave the way for an invasion. Already, by day and night, heavy guns fired at regular intervals across the Channel, causing casualties and destruction in and around Dover, and occasionally destroying a slow-moving coaster.

Fortunately, these grave matters rarely caused much concern amongst the seamen, whose duty it now befell to face all these fresh dangers, and their intimate worries usually proved more absorbing.

The 113th Flotilla was no exception, and as the winter broadened into a grim reality, Lieutenant-Commander Kirby fussed and grumbled, until the main worry—of the sailors at least—became that of keeping their kit clean and properly marked and worn, regardless of what operation their boat might be engaged on, or the problems of drying damp clothing on the tiny, overcrowded mess-decks. As for the officers, they struggled on, bearing the main responsibility and hoping that Kirby would drop dead.

On this cold autumn morning, the little wind-swept boats cruised bumpily over the steep, sand-flecked waves of the Belgian coast, although that unhappy country lay invisible just under the horizon. To make matters more uncomfortable, a fine, penetrating drizzle was blowing gustily in grey sheets, reducing the visibility to about two miles, and making watch-keeping a nightmare. As was his custom, Kirby refused to allow any man a break from his action station, with the result that everywhere Royce looked he saw his men crouched miserably by their guns, trying to take advantage of any scanty cover available.

His plight was probably the worst, for as he stood on the open bridge, bracing his legs against the boat's uneasy motion, he was a free target for anything the weather could throw at him. He shuddered, as he felt the first icy trickle penetrate his left boot, and his thick sock, recently received from his mother, was soon a soggy mass. About his neck a tightly wound towel was heavy and cold with rain and spray, and his glowing cheeks stung with the drizzle, which pattered across him like needles.

Kirby was perched on the stool in the corner, the hood of his oilskin suit shrouding his face, like a brooding monk, his sharp eyes darting ahead, and then back at the other boats, as they weaved forward into the grey seas.

Royce gently patted his face with the back of a glove, and peered at his watch. Eight-thirty, and they had been at sea for about ten hours. He smiled miserably at the thought of the warm glare of the bar in the White Hart, a hot meal, and bed, and then winced again as a steely needle of water penetrated his collar, and between his shoulder blades.

"Could I dismiss one watch, sir?" he asked. "Could get some cocoa on the move and a bite to eat."

The hunched figure appeared not to have heard, so he started again.

"Come over here, Number One. Look at that fool on the Port Oerlikon, what's his name?"

Royce leaned over, resigned to no cocoa. "It's Weeks, sir, only joined two days ago. He's an Australian."

"Yes, yes," snapped Kirby testily, "I remember. Well he's asleep!"

He bent over the voice-pipe.

"Cox'n, come to the bridge, and bring Weeks with you!"

The tinny voice rattled up the brass tube: "Is he ill, sir?"

"No, you fool, he's bloody well asleep!"

There was a scraping of feet as the Coxswain handed over the wheel, and a minute later he appeared on the bridge, followed by Able Seaman Weeks. The latter was a tall, gangling individual, what the average person pictures as the typical Australian. His face which now stared sulkily from beneath a woollen cap, was deep-lined and tanned, quite out of place in such a climate, and the wide grey eyes, which had once checked countless sheep on a Queensland farm, glowered rebelliously at the Captain.

Kirby didn't waste any time.

"Weeks, you were asleep on watch. That makes you useless to me, and a potential danger to this ship!"

The tall figure stiffened. "That's a damn lie!" he retorted hotly. "I was restin' me head on the blessed magazine!"

His lazy drawl struck an unnatural note in the tense scene.

Kirby went white.

"Silence!" he shouted. "Don't be so impertinent. I know your type too well, in and out of the detention barracks, and proud of it I suppose!"

Royce felt sick.

"Excuse me, sir," he pleaded, but Kirby spun on him.

"Attend to your duties, sir! Don't interrupt!"

Weeks took a step forward, and stuck out his craggy chin.

"I come umpteen thousand miles to fight the Jerries, and I'll damn well fight you an' all if it comes to that," he said slowly. "This is a crook ship, and fer your information, you are the worst god-damned Pommy bastard I've yet had the pleasure of meetin'!"

"That's enough of that!" barked the Coxswain, and stepped smartly forward.

For a moment there was complete silence, but for the steady patter of rain across the chart table, and the signalman's sharp intake of breath. The main figures of the drama stood facing each other, like actors who have forgotten their lines, Kirby, white-faced and quivering with rage, and Weeks, now relaxed and defiant. Royce and the Coxswain stared helplessly at both of them.

Kirby shook himself, as if unable to believe his ears.

"Get back to your station, Weeks." His voice was almost inaudible. "Coxswain, I'll see this man when we return to base. Dismiss!"

He shouted the last order almost wildly, and Royce prayed that Weeks wouldn't start anything more.

Surprisingly, he saw the two figures shuffle from the bridge, Raikes in front, obviously shaken, and the Australian on his heels, his face expressionless.

Royce's discomfort at the weather was quite forgotten, and he peered hastily through his glasses, but his mind was so much of a whirl, that he saw nothing.

When he heard the voice again, it was flat and toneless.

"In all my service, I've never seen such an insolent, mutinous lout. Just wait until I've had time to deal with him!"

And that was all. Royce gave an inward sigh of relief.

The boats turned in a half circle and continued the eye-aching search for prey, the wind and rain now beating over the starboard quarter, and causing them to roll and twist uncomfortably.

"By the way, Number One, you'll be surprised to hear that your second stripe has been recommended," remarked Kirby casually.

Royce jerked out of his reverie, startled.

"Gosh, this is a surprise, sir," he gasped. "Thank you very much."

He hadn't thought a great deal about promotion, but now that it was so close, he found himself grinning like a schoolboy.

Kirby permitted himself to smile thinly.

"As flotilla leader, I think I should have a full lieutenant with me. Although I'm not saying you've earned it by any manner of means," he added.

Even such a dampening remark was lost on Royce, and he hummed happily, waving to Watson's boat astern for no apparent reason.

Kirby shrugged, and shook his head.

"Really, Number One, perhaps I shouldn't have told you."

Royce smiled, "Sorry, sir," and to himself he said, "It's taken you nearly a whole day to tell me anyway!"

"Aircraft, dead astern!" yelled the signalman, and they saw the warning lights flickering along the line of boats.

The deck throbbed as they increased speed, and the slim

muzzles swung round to cover the approach of the plane, which could be seen vaguely through the scudding clouds.

A voice piped up from the waist.

"Sunderland, sir!"

And they relaxed, as the fat, friendly shape of the Coastal Command aircraft took on a sharper line through the driving rain. Having seen them and exchanged recognition signals, it began to circle, an Aldis lamp busy.

The signalman lowered his lamp.

"Three E-boats coming up astern fast," he reported. "About eight miles."

They waited, while Kirby quickly pored over the chart.

"Hmm, they're making for Flushing, I don't doubt. Must have been in the Channel raiding our shipping. Hoist Flag Five. We'll attack in two groups as planned."

Jock Murray's boat led three of the M.T.B.s away to the west, turning in line abreast in a flurry of foam, while the others worked up to full speed abreast of Kirby. On every boat the men tensed at the signal, flag five, "Attack with guns", and for most it would be a new experience to get to grips with E-boats in broad daylight. Usually they were but fleeting grey shadows, spitting death through the darkness.

Royce clambered down to the pom-pom, where the well-greased shells lay inert and waiting. Leading Seaman Parker, back again from the hospital, his red face criss-crossed with small, white scars, grinned confidently.

"We'll give 'em what-for nah!"

"I don't expect they'll be thinking of anything but bed," shouted Royce excitedly. "Just as we do on our way home."

Sure enough, three shapes could be seen approaching fast from the south-west, great bow-waves creaming away from the long, rakish bows, the silver-grey hulls low in the water, and hardly visible. The leading boat swung over to port, and a flat stream of green tracers cruised over the wave tops towards them. The other two boats took up station in line abreast of the leader and also opened fire.

Again and again the pom-pom at Royce's side banged, and they saw the shells beat the sea into a savage froth around the second E-boat, while the machine-guns got into a steady, screaming rattle. Twice he felt the hull shudder beneath him, and a smoke float aft was cut to ribbons. But the Germans had fallen into the trap, as Murray's quartet came roaring up from astern, every gun belching orange flames, and the E-boats were caught between a devastating cross-fire.

With a bang, the leading E-boat stopped dead and slowly capsized. The second one was ablaze from the bridge to the bow, and several tiny figures could be dimly seen through the sheets of rain, hurling themselves overboard.

For an instant the M.T.B.s slowed down to re-form, and seeing his chance, the remaining German captain dashed for the gap, his guns blazing fiercely. Royce saw that the torpedo tubes on the E-boat's decks were empty. Some British sailors had died during the night.

Benjy's loud-hailer boomed across the water, "Tally-ho!" and with a roar of throttle they streaked in pursuit, the tracers knitting a deadly pattern between them.

Kirby shouted down from the bridge.

"Three more E-boats ahead, Green four-five! Range about a thousand yards. Look to it, Number One!"

He was looking savage.

The newcomers were obviously from the same flotilla as the others, and had apparently taken another route home.

Now the battle became fierce, the Germans fighting a delaying action back to base, no doubt praying for help to arrive.

It was then that it happened. Royce found himself lying on the slippery deck, his head and ears roaring. Shakily he scrambled to his feet, and stared round. He had heard and felt nothing, yet the boat had received a direct hit on the port bow, a stream of shells exploding the full length of the fo'c'sle. Parker was cursing, and struggling with the gun, it had jammed solid, while the loading number knelt at his side, wheezing and retching painfully.

Already the boat had a definite list, and as Royce ran to the bridge he saw smoke pouring from the after hatch. The bridge was untouched, and Kirby was dancing up and down with impatience, while the signalman called up the nearest M.T.B.

"Get below, and deal with the damage, then come back here!"

Royce dashed aft past the tubes, and reached the choking smoke cloud, where Petty Officer Moore and his mechanic were hard at work with the extinguishers.

"Nothin' bad, sir," gasped Moore. "It's the paint store. 'It with a tracer."

Below it was a shambles, and as the lights flickered on, he saw jets of water pouring in through the shattered mahogany sides, the double skin of the sides bent inwards like brown teeth.

The Coxswain appeared on the scene with Weeks and two more hands, and with hammers and plugs they got to work, slipping and cursing in the icy water.

When he returned to the bridge he found the other M.T.B. coming alongside, Deith's red face peering anxiously over the screen at them.

"I'm continuing the fight aboard her," snapped Kirby. "I've got to bag those other Jerries before they get within range of the coast."

Royce stood dazed and not understanding.

"You mean you're leaving us?" he stammered.

"Of course I am. You make for home as best you can, we'll catch you up."

As he threw himself down towards the other boat, he turned, a smile on his face.

"See if you can earn that other stripe!"

With a roar, and a puzzled wave from Deith, the boat turned away in pursuit of the running battle, while Royce stood helplessly on the bridge, which suddenly became a lonely and terrible place.

For some moments he stood staring after the fast-moving boat, until its shape became obscure in the curtain of fine rain, still uncomprehending, and slightly shocked by the suddenness with which his boat had been reduced from a swift, living creature, to a heavy, listing hulk, in which he was now the captain.

His scattered thoughts were interrupted by the Coxswain, and Petty Officer Moore, who appeared at his shoulder.

"I've just finished me rounds," announced Raikes calmly, "and I've got all the bad leaks patched up, except for those more'n a foot or so above the waterline. I'm afraid the automatic pump 'as been sheared right off by a splinter or something. That'll be a dockyard job to put it right."

"Yessir, but we've got the hand pumps goin' like a fiddler's elbow, so provided you can keep 'er down to about five or six knots, we might be all right," added Moore.

Royce pulled himself together, and studied their competent faces with a feeling of new confidence, and inner warmth, but he knew that the responsibility, given to him by the thin wavy line on his sleeve, was his alone, and that they were waiting for his own deductions and orders. Unbeknown to them possibly, they had made his burden considerably lighter.

"The fact is," he said with a rueful smile, "we have to get the hell out of here before it gets too hot for us, and fast as we can with safety. We're very much alone, I'm afraid, and mustn't depend too much on the rest of the boys finding us again."

He led them to the chart, and they stood politely watching while he outlined their approximate position. When he had finished, Moore pushed back his greasy cap and scratched his thinning hair with an oily finger.

"I dunno much about navigation an' all that lark, sir, but I must say there seems to be an awful lot 'er North Sea between us an' the old *Royston*!"

They laughed, and each felt relieved that the situation still allowed them such licence.

Raikes, a professional seaman, craned forward, and tapped the stained chart with a pencil.

"If you don't mind me saying so," he said in his clipped and forthright manner, "it'd be better if we forgot all about the others, who as you say'll probably miss us anyway, and took the plunge due west, straight across to Blighty, and hope to be picked up by a patrol."

Royce saw the logic immediately. If they kept to their present course the enemy would probably pick them off as stragglers, whether they were with other M.T.B.s or not, whereas the lonely route would quite likely bring them into contact with a destroyer to cover their painful withdrawal.

So due west they went, slightly down by the head, and listing to port, the engines roaring and thudding as they pushed the hull along at a snail's pace, the uneven trim making their task doubly difficult. From either side came the monotonous clank, clank of the heavy pumps, as half the hands toiled to keep the bilges free, and the engine-room safe from the relentless waters, while the others, now fully alert, stood against the wind and rain, fingering their guns, and peering at each horizon.

Alone by the pom-pom, Parker laboured with his tools to get his clumsy charge unjammed and ready for firing again.

His assistant, who had been flung against the ammunition lockers by the force of the explosions, lay quietly behind the bridge, freed from the pain of his shattered ribs by the Cox-swain's morphia, and wrapped carefully in two lifejackets. He slept the sleep of one who has already departed from the fears of battle. Old Petroc, resting for a moment from the pumps, shook his head dolefully, as he jammed a rolled pair of overalls under the injured man's head.

" 'Ee's a lucky un, 'ee is, recon he done it for the purpose. Loik 'e as not knew the bloody pumps'd fold up!"

Then, spitting on his blistered hands, he turned back to his job.

Royce, alone on the bridge, he had sent the signalman to help on deck, lay across the screen, the glasses gripped in his wet chafed hands, while the icy trickles of water explored the only warm place in the small of his back. Already it seemed as if they had always sailed this sea alone, and that there was no foreseeable end to the voyage.

Clank, clank, clank, went the pumps, while Parker's hammer beat out a steady tattoo below him. His senses became dulled by the noises, while his shivering body seemed to cringe at the onslaught of the rain. He forced his tired eyes down to his watch, and marvelled at the fact that three hours had already passed since Kirby had gone off to search for fresh laurels.

An oilskinned figure, barely recognizable as Able Seaman Roote, appeared at his side, guarding something under his streaming coat. He peered uncertainly at Royce's face.

"Me an' the boys thought yer might like a bit of Chinese weddin' cake, sir," his cockney twang sounded eager and somehow comforting. "We nipped in the galley an' warmed it up a bit, an' thought you might like a bit an' all."

His voice trailed away, as he whipped out a small basin of hot rice pudding. Royce vaguely remembered it from two days before, and he took the basin in his hands, revelling in its warmth.

"Thank you very much, Roote," he said, touched. "Just what I need."

Roote grinned, his sharp, knowing face creased with pleasure, and as he hurried away he added, "Beggin' yer pardon, sir, but we wouldn't er' done it fer someone 'oo shall be nameless!"

He was off before Royce could think of a suitable comment. Instead, he lifted the basin to his lips, there being no spoon, or any other instrument for that matter, and as he did so, he smelt and tasted the deep, rich fragrance of service rum. He laughed aloud, and gratefully swallowed the hot, glutinous substance. The old so-and-so's, he chuckled, they didn't miss a trick. He imagined Kirby saying, "Storing rum is a punishable offence, Number One!" or "A sober ship is a happy one!"

He pondered over his recent life in the game little ship that struggled along beneath him: of how the Coxswain who now shared his every confidence, had at first openly showed his contempt for him. Harston's death had drawn them closer together perhaps. Even a character like Roote, who, until he had volunteered for Coastal Forces, had been fighting a constant war with authority in general, and officers in particular, had shown him the meaning of loyalty, and the acceptance of leadership. It was funny, he had bullied them, punished them, and driven them beyond the barrier of comfort, yet, because of his fairness, which he was inclined to take for granted, they had accepted him as their own leader, and personal property.

Another hour passed, and the unpredictable weather of the North Sea changed again. The rain broke off with an angry flurry of gusty squalls, which made the wounded boat stagger in her stride, and the wind force became stronger, veering round astern, so that the waves became longer and heavier, their great, grey peaks, unbroken as yet by white horses, rolling menacingly up under the transom in long, even ranks, each crest lifting the box-like stern clear of the water, and causing the overworked screws to screech a protest as they whirred free into thin air. Then, with a heave, they would drop again into a trough, and the boat would shudder, and lurch forward, always fighting the man at the wheel, as he tried to stop the sagging bows from broaching the boat round into the broadside position of danger. The wind, laced with salt, found its way through the damp clothing, chilling the flesh, and making their faces raw, while the ensign at the gaff grew steadily more and more tattered, blowing straight forward like the banner of a departed warrior.

Even the spirits of the seamen began to flag, as they toiled at the pumps, or stood on watch, wet, cold, and hungry. The Coxswain scurried from one end of the boat to the other, issuing a rebuke here, and a word of encouragement there, and later, a tot of "neaters" to all hands.

To reduce the rolling as much as possible, Royce had most of the unusable gear on deck heaved overboard. The smashed smoke-float, the motor dory, new but a month before, and now riddled with holes and damaged beyond repair, and countless articles which only made the boat struggle harder by their presence. The torpedoes were the main disadvantage, especially as they could no longer be fired with the bows at such an angle, but Royce decided against sending over four thousand pounds worth of machinery to the bottom.

It was about fifteen-thirty when they saw a dark shape smudging the horizon on the starboard quarter, and anxiously they strained their eyes even harder to catch a glimpse of the stranger, while Royce gritted his teeth, and opened the throttles a little further, making the boat slightly steadier, but causing some of the makeshift plugs in the shot holes to weep and squirt water each time she bit into a wave.

The wind was still freshening, and the ugly, grey hills were now tinged with curved, angry white crests, and as they plunged into each trough, the boat shuddered and groaned, then shaking the salt froth from the streaming decks, she would stagger up on the next roller, while every man peered aft at the other vessel, which was growing rapidly larger. Royce jammed his glasses against the rattling signal locker, and wedged his aching shoulders into a sharp voice-pipe cover, while he endeavoured to get a good look at the ship which was obviously overhauling them. As he angrily dashed the salt from his streaming eyes, and wiped the lenses of the glasses on a piece of sodden tissue, he saw that the faces of his men were now turned up towards him, waiting for a verdict.

Slowly, gently, but firmly, he moved the powerful glasses along the top of the heaving locker, seeing the tumbling waves magnified to a horrible and larger distortion, then into his vision came the close-up picture of the newcomer. In the seconds that he held her, he saw a large, rakish trawler, of the ocean-going type used by the Norwegians before the war, now painted a dark grey, with a thin plume of smoke trailing from the squat funnel, lifting and plunging over the tumbling water towards him. The high, knife-like fo'c'sle rose at all times clear from the sharp bow-wave, and it was possible to see the powerful gun mounted high up, close to the stem head, in the manner of all converted trawlers.

Royce thought furiously and quickly, it was possible that the other ship had not seen them, as they were so low in the water, and should she be an enemy, and it was unlikely to find a lone British trawler this far from base, she might well be on a hurried mission to another part of the coast. It was worth a try, and shakily the little M.T.B. turned into a quarter sea, away from the trawler. Royce watched tensely, and his heart sank, as he saw the other ship's silhouette shorten as she turned bows-on again in their direction.

Having informed the engine room to expect a last minute dash, he called Petroc to the bridge.

"Get the remaining smoke float ready to lower," he ordered. "It won't be too wonderful in this wind, but it may help. And loosen the life-rafts, in case we have to ditch."

Petroc turned his worn face to the angry waters, and shuddered.

"Like as not we'm needing 'em afore long," he muttered.

A light winked across the water, and Royce snatched up the Aldis lamp, flashing the first letters that came to his mind. The trawler waited a moment, then repeated the challenge. Again Royce flashed a meaningless garble in reply. God, if only it would get darker, but even with the prevailing weather conditions and threatening clouds, they had another hour at least to dodge and elude their powerful adversary. As he watched, he saw a red ball mount to the trawler's gaff, and break out stiffly to the wind. The bold, red flag, with the black cross and swastika, which they knew so well.

At once there was a puff of smoke from her bows, blown immediately to nothing by the wind, and seconds later the flat, heavy boom echoed across to them. Even as they stared round, a tall, spindly column of water rose about a hundred feet ahead of them. Another bang, this time the shot was nearer, making their hull wince, as if struck a body-blow. Frantically Royce signalled aft, and the tub-shaped smoke float thudded into the water, the black, greasy vapour already pouring out in a steady stream, low across the wave tops. The wind plucked at the fringes of the pitiful smoke-screen, and tore the life from it, leaving only the core, and a fast-moving vaporous mist between them and the German.

"Open fire when your guns bear!" ordered Royce, and following on his words came the clatter of the starboard Oerlikon, as Able Seaman Poole sent a stream of tracer spinning through the smoke, the shells seeming to bounce across the waves as they groped for the enemy.

The next shell fell so close that a deluge of water cascaded into the bridge, making Royce splutter and cough, the salt water tinged with the stink of cordite.

Over went the wheel and the M.T.B. swung crazily to starboard, as another shell burst in the very spot where she would otherwise have been. Poole gave a wild whoop, as he saw his tracers spatter across the trawler's bridge, and they watched as she turned away, drawing out of range. Bang—and the awful scream passed close overhead, making them duck, and the ghostly waterspout rose a cable's length beyond them. If only the pom-pom would fire, cursed Royce; this was hopeless. Although the trawler had been hit, and had temporarily lost the range, it was just a matter of time.

The strength of the smoke-float was rapidly diminishing, and he decided that soon the time would arrive for him to decide how best he could use his engine power to try to make good an escape. The weather was steadily worsening, and the harsh sweep of the wind was approaching gale force, and the boat was beginning to get into real difficulties, which even without the appearance of the enemy, would have been critical enough.

He reeled to the engine-room voice-pipe, shouting hoarsely above the spasmodic bursts from the Oerlikons, which were now pointing straight astern, and the rising shriek of the wind, whose icy hand plucked the words from his mouth and flung them seawards.

"Chief!" he yelled. "Do all you can, I'm going to make a run for it!"

Moore's steady voice carried clearly up to his waiting ear.

"Good luck, sir!"

Royce snapped down the cover of the voice-pipe, and rang for half speed, and felt an increasing rumble beneath him, as the boat thrust her stem into the grey and tempestuous seas. The bows, cracked and splintered, abetted by the mounting water in the flooded bilges, plunged heavily into every trough, throwing up great sheets of spray over the gun platform, and swamping the bridge. But still the revolutions mounted, and they thrust forward, the seamen on deck slithering and falling across the streaming salt spume, as they manfully fought with the pumps. Only the Oerlikon gunners, strapped in their guns by leather harnesses, remained firm in the onslaught, and Weeks at the port gun could faintly be heard cursing as he fumbled with freezing hands to fit a fresh magazine.

Another shell hissed into the sea off the port side without exploding, but it was very much closer than the last, so once more they lost valuable headway, as the boat clawed away from the tell-tale splash in an effort to elude the next shot.

It was obvious that the trawler was still overhauling them, and even with the poor visibility her shape was taking on a sharper outline, as she dipped and plunged in relentless pursuit.

Royce sent Parker below to report on the state of the repairs, as the pom-pom was now definitely classed as unserviceable, and when he reappeared, breathless and wild eyed, Royce guessed that the cards were stacked against him.

"S'no use, sir!" bawled Parker, snatching violently at the rail to stop himself from being pitched back down the ladder. "The water's two feet over the mess-deck, an' still comin' up fast."

He paused for breath, watching the officer's taut face anxiously.

"The sea is tearin' the outer skin right off the port bow, just under the tube!"

Royce could well visualize the scene. The havoc wrought by the savage cannon shells would soon be exploited by these heavy seas.

He reached across to the voice-pipe again.

"No good, Chief, slow her down, just give me steerage way!"

He toyed with the impossible idea of going full astern, to try to save the strain on the bows, and lowered his head again to the brass bell mouth of the pipe. As he did so, he heard a sharp, abbreviated whistle of higher pitch than before, followed in the tiniest fraction of a second by a deafening crack behind him. Simultaneously, a blast of hot air struck him in the mouth. Dazed and incredulous, he realized that the voice-pipe was streaming smoke in his face.

He straightened, and stared aft, his stomach retching violently. Angry, red flames clawed along the stern, and a thick pall of black smoke rolled away on the wind.

It had been a direct hit on the boat's small quarter deck, the shell pitching down against the after bulkhead before exploding with sickening impact below, sending a stream of razor-sharp, white-hot splinters in every direction, and making the after flat a raging furnace.

With a sudden, almost fatalistic calmness, Royce gave his orders.

"Coxswain! Hand over the wheel, and come on deck. Get every extinguisher to work aft!"

Parker still stood at his side, his honest face white with shock.

"Come on Parker!" he snapped. "Get all hands except the gunners down to that fire!"

Then urgently, he called the engine room.

"Chief! Moore! Can you hear me?"

A tired-sounding voice answered.

"Aye, sir, I'm here."

A pause and a bout of violent coughing.

" 'Fraid I can't get you any more revs. The fire's in here now, and one of my lads has bought it!"

"Right, Chief, clear out! Bring the other chap on deck. We'll have to ditch!"

A longer pause.

"Aye, aye, sir, we'll do that!"

Overhead another shell screamed like a mad thing, but the German gunners were shooting wildly, their aim ruined by the M.T.B.'s death pall.

Royce leaned over the side of the bridge, trying to get a glimpse of the trawler, but she was invisible through the smoke. He looked into the upturned face of Able Seaman Poole, who hung suspended in his gun harness, his arms swinging to the motion of the boat. His eyes were open wide with amazement. There was very little of him from the waist down. Royce sobbed, and was violently sick, his lungs aching and sour.

Raikes appeared below him, his face worried.

"Sir! The engine-room hatch is jammed solid. Pony can't get out! Can you come, sir?"

For the first time in a century, or so it seemed, Royce left the bridge, walking as if in a dream, stumbling across the splintered decks to where the hands hacked and slashed at the deck casing around the metal hatch of the engine room. Feathers of smoke streamed from every crack, and from the tiny, grill-like ventilator, where two of the hands were squatting. They moved away as Royce knelt down to the small, barred opening, and beneath it he could plainly see the dull red glow within.

As if out of the flames, a frantic, terrified voice, high-pitched and desperate, made Royce recoil with horror.

"God! Get me out of here! Please, will someone help me. Please, don't leave me!"

Then they heard Moore's harsh tones.

"It's all right, son, I'm here!"

There was an audible thud and the cries ceased. As the crackle of flames rose to an all-engulfing roar, they heard Moore coughing violently, then there was nothing.

Royce stood up, his nerves screaming, and he looked wildly at the white faces around him. Each one set in its own clear caste, but bonded together with their common suffering.

"All right, lads, lower the rafts!"

He forced himself to say those fearful words.

"Abandon ship! And good luck!"

He noticed that one seaman was crying.

The knives flashed dully, as two seamen slashed at the rafts' lashings, and the cumbersome objects splashed alongside secured only by a thin line.

Some of the men went eagerly, and some gazed fearfully at the heaving waters, unwilling to leave the apparent security of the boat. But eventually they leapt down, shouting each other's names, and peering dazedly at the slanting deck. The boat was already much lower in the waves, but as the after part flooded, the trim was gradually corrected, as if in a final defiance.

Royce and the Coxswain stood side by side, holding grimly to the guard-rail, when a fantastic idea formed in Royce's racing brain.

"We're on even keel for a bit!" he shouted, his eyes smarting with the smoke. "What are the settings on the torpedoes?"

"Ten feet, sir," answered Raikes, puzzled.

"Right, just check they're both ready for firing, then over you go!"

Raikes, numbed by the loss of his friend, didn't seem to be able to grasp his meaning.

"What are you going to do?" he stammered.

"I'm going to blow that bloody trawler to hell. That's what!" yelled Royce wildly. "She'll be up here in a minute to have a look round, and with luck, I'll be able to get both fish running even now.'

Raikes stiffened.

"I'll stop an' give you a hand," he announced stolidly.

"Like hell you will, Coxswain! You look after the men and pick me up afterwards."

They both knew there was little chance of that. Already the flames licked the deck near the fuel intakes, under which lay the high-octane spirit.

He pushed the Coxswain towards the tubes, and when he saw him checking the firing mechanism, he ran to the bridge, and threw the confidential books overboard in their weighted bag.

The Coxswain hovered by the rail, his face blackened and scratched,

"So long, sir, don't leave it too long!"

As he jumped into the nearest raft, they severed the line, and shoved off, staring silently back at the boat.

Royce waved and laughed crazily, "Thank you, lads! Now get clear!"

He staggered back into the choking clouds, stepping over the abandoned articles of clothing, and pathetic possessions, the boat dead already but for the crackling flames, and the rattle of loose gear and empty shell cases as she rolled heavily with a stricken stagger. Grimly he squatted by the sighting bar, forcing himself to concentrate on the small, dark patch of sea ahead, fenced off by a long, sullen bank of oily smoke. Frantically he shut his ears to the distant sound of paddles, as the rafts moved away, fighting the rising feeling of panic within him. Supposing the trawler had gone away, or came up too late, he would be fried alive for nothing. It was madness, terrifying madness, which held him in its grip. He lowered his sweating forehead against the ice-cold metal, and his body shook with a paroxysm of uncontrollable sobbing. It didn't matter any more. There was no Kirby to criticize him, no seaman to watch his weakness with contempt. Only Poole swinging gently at his gun, one of his arms now alight like a torch. Petty Officer Moore and his two mechanics burning below would no longer be interested, and Able Seaman Lake, the injured man, doped with morphia, had been cut to pieces while he slept, he too would shed no tears.

Desperately he turned his mind to home, and he imagined his mother getting the telegram. And Julia, he had not seen her again, to tell her, to tell her what? He lifted his head in his anguish, and there in front of him lay the trawler.

She was motionless, and barely half a mile away, her shiny sides reflecting and glistening with the white-capped waves, the menacing muzzle of the gun still trained on him, and several figures lining the decks. Gritting his teeth, and smearing the tears from his smarting eyes, he peered along the sights. Behind him, a sudden burst of machine-gun fire made him cry out, but it was only an ammunition belt burning. A great hissing roar came from below, as the seas poured in to quench the fires in the tiller-flat. There was a crack as the plate glass of the chart table succumbed to the heat, and the carefully folded charts were reduced to ashes. But slowly and remorselessly, the trawler drifted into the sights, the raking stem, the gun, with its vigilant and victorious crew, then the tall bridge, and the arrogant swastika flag, the emblem hated the length and breadth of enslaved Europe. His breath hissed, and with a silent prayer he squeezed the triggers. There was a puff of smoke, a dull thud, and the two slim shapes slid from the tubes, hardly making a splash, so close was the deck to the sea. Fascinated, he crouched, and watched the puffs of foam as the little propellers bit into the water, and the well-greased and intricate mechanism guided the two monsters down to the depth of ten feet. Suddenly there was a frantic flurry at the trawler's stern, as the engines roared into full speed; slowly she swung round, gaining speed, while Royce shouted curses to the winds.

Then it happened. One minute he saw her clearly ahead of him, escaping the M.T.B.'s final challenge, then there was a deafening roar, and a blinding flash, that sent great shock waves rolling towards him. A vast pillar of water rose two hundred feet in the air, and when it had settled, falling slowly like majestic white curtains, there was not one stick or spar to be seen. Shakily he staggered to the side, deafened and half blinded, his clumsy fingers fumbling with his lifejacket. He didn't remember jumping, only the great, icy, choking water closing over his head. Vaguely his spinning brain recorded the bitter taste of salt and petrol, and a terrible pressure on his lungs and stomach, as an underwater explosion tore the clothes from his body. Then a great, engulfing blackness swept over him, shutting out everything.

CHAPTER FIVE

THE thriving naval base of Harwich lay cradled by the twin arms of the rivers Stour and Orwell, the great concourse of turbulent water, never still or easy at any time, now shimmered and heaved in the watery sun of the late afternoon. Whichever way you cast your eye, could be seen the vast numbers of lean, weathered grey shapes of destroyers, moored in twos and threes at their buoys; paunchy little corvettes in their breathtaking dazzle-paint; overworked minesweepers; and scores of tiny harbour craft scurrying about on their urgent business. At the far end of the anchorage lay the lithe hulls of the local submarine flotilla, watched over by the ugly hulk of their depot ship, whilst to the south, around Parkeston Quay, a light cruiser was enjoying an overdue boiler clean.

The pale glow glittered around the pierheads of the huge naval training establishment, H.M.S. *Ganges,* whose towering mast dominated the harbour. Around the piers, the heavy, clumsy cutters were pulled by their sweating young amateur crews, while leather-lunged Petty Officers strode up and down between the oarsmen, shouting, watching, and hoping for the best. These were the Navy's raw material, who now under the eyes of the main East Coast striking force, struggled manfully with the mysterious commands of "Oars" and "Give way together!" Carrying out these orders was even more of a mystery to most of them, at the moment.

Up and behind Landguard Point lay Felixstowe, its sheltered waters looking like a sheet of tarnished pewter, and here nestled the hornet's nest of the Coastal Forces Group: M.T.B.s, Motor Gunboats, and the Motor Launches, maids of all work. Most of them were painted in the popular bizarre stripes and waves of dazzle paint, while one flotilla sported black hulls, with red shark-like mouths and gleaming white teeth painted around their stems. Not "pusser" perhaps, but very effective by night.

From all these points and creeks of bustling activity, one landmark could always be seen with ease and clarity, the imposing red-brick buildings of the Royal Naval Hospital at Shotley. Once past the wrought-iron gates and the naval orderly in white gaiters and belt, and up the wide gravel drive flanked by the air-raid shelters, a feeling of great peace and business-like calm pervaded the very air.

The long wards, with their neat rows of iron beds stood like soldiers on a polished parquet parade ground. All seemed to be occupied. Some of the inmates lay quietly sleeping, or gazing at the ceilings, and some hobbled painfully along the floor on sticks or crutches, their pale blue jackets clashing with a variety of pyjamas. Behind screens at one bed, an Able Seaman lay in a coma, moaning very softly: two of his shipmates, conspicuous and uncomfortable in their blue uniforms and gold badges, sat quietly watching, waiting for him to die.

These, and many more, were the harvest of the unsung war at sea, who were now fighting their greatest battle.

Down yet another airy passage, identical to all the others, but for its numbering, where two young nurses sat sewing up a rent in a blackout curtain, to the small wards, where the post-operational cases were watched and treated, where a wounded man's slender life-line could be strengthened, or cut. The window of one of these rooms looked out across the harbour, and an elderly naval sister, her face lined and worn, stood idly watching a fussy frigate manœuvring towards her buoy, where the two half-frozen buoy-jumpers sat waiting to receive the picking-up rope. On the fo'c'sle, tiny figures in shiny oilskins waited stolidly, while upon the open bridge, her captain eased the ship forward against the treacherous and powerful tide. Behind the sister, in a darkened corner of the white-walled room, a still figure lay straight and stiff on the bed, his chin resting against the neatly turned sheet; his skin pale and transparent. Above the eyes, and covering the rest of his head, was a complicated criss-cross of bandages, whilst at waist level, the bed blossomed out in an ungainly bulge, where wire cages protected the motionless body from all contact. The sister shifted her weight to the other foot, and sighed deeply, and, as if in sympathy, the frigate hooted impatiently on her siren.

Noiselessly the door opened, and a tall Surgeon-Commander, with bushy black eyebrows and heavy jaw, strode purposefully to the bed, his stethoscope glinting in the fast fading light.

At his elbow the duty sister reached for the record card and chart from a shelf, and for some moments there was silence, but for the rustle of the papers, and the chink of bottles as the other sister tidied the small bedside table.

"Hmm, not much progress here, sister," said the Commander at length, rubbing his chin with his thick, capable fingers.

"It's forty-eight hours now, sir, and Doctor Anderson said we should have seen some change, one way or another, by today."

The gold and red braided sleeve reached under the sheet, and felt the pulse.

"Hmm," he said again. "Have his parents been sent for?"

"Yes, sir. Mr. and Mrs. Royce will be arriving some time this evening. The Wardmaster has just finished arranging transport at the station."

The Commander sighed deeply; it was all conforming to the too-familiar pattern. Their torn, burned, shocked and shattered bodies came to him in a steady stream, but he was still unable to view the situation with the callous indifference often expected of his trade. This one, for instance, a mere boy, who had done heaven knows what deeds out there in the North Sea, now lay like a piece of stone before him, the mechanism of life ticking only feebly. He sighed heavily. He had just finished one surgery case, when the Matron had bustled in to his office in her usual brisk manner, with news of more survivors landed by a destroyer at the base. The usual pathetic procession had followed, led by the shock cases, their hair matted with oil, their shivering bodies covered by heavy blankets; then the stretcher cases, including this one, with his hastily bandaged body and blackened skin. He studied the chart again: severe burns to arms and chest, head

injuries and an aftermath of shock. If there was to be an aftermath.

As if he had come to some decision, he straightened and
glanced at his watch.

"I'm going for tea now. Call me at once if there's any change
at all. Anything."

And he strode out of the room. As he passed one of the wards,
he heard the strident voice of one of the sisters, obviously
rebuking someone.

"I don't care, do you hear?" she snapped. "You just get back
to bed while I get your tea. I'll jolly well report you if you don't
behave!"

The Commander stepped into the ward, now brightly alight,
the long curtains drawn.

Sister Adams smiled wearily.

"Good evening, sir. I wish you'd have a talk with Bed Five; he
keeps wanting to go out. But he'll have to see the doctor in the
forenoon tomorrow before I can let him move."

He walked slowly across to the offender, who sat defiantly
upright against his pillows.

"What's the trouble, my lad, and who are you anyway?"

"Petty Officer Raikes, sir, Coxswain of M.T.B. 1991. I just
wanted to see my officer."

He paused, his face creased with worry.

"Will you tell me, sir, is he going to be all right?"

The Commander was touched, and his frown faded.

"I've heard about you, Raikes," he said, and squatted on the
edge of the bed. "You went back for him, didn't you? The
Captain of the destroyer told me all about it; how you took a
raft through blazing petrol to save that officer's life."

Raikes flushed and squirmed with embarrassment.

"Is he going to live, sir?" he persisted.

"You've done your part, and now we'll do ours. Try to rest for
a bit, and leave the worrying to us."

As he got up to leave, he turned: "Raikes, I'm proud to have
met you."

Raikes lay back, heedless of Sister Adams, who clucked impatiently as she straightened his sheets and patted his pillows,
and let his mind drift back to that moment of decision.

He shut his eyes tightly, and once more he felt the crazy rocking motion of the tiny raft. They had seen their boat drift away
in a pall of flame and smoke, with the hunched, blackened figure

alone on her deck, and they had forgotten their own suffering, even their will to survive, as with shocked eyes they watched the grim drama unfold before them. Suddenly the trawler had hove in sight, like another actor making an entrance, and they had seen the torpedoes streak on their errand of death. Hoarsely they cheered and cursed, as the explosion died, and then they had been shattered by the roar as their own little ship had burst asunder and plunged down. He forced his mind back, making sure of every detail, just as he had told the destroyer's officers. It was Able Seaman Weeks who had shouted: "Jeez! Jimmy-the-One's back there! I saw his lifejacket!"

For Raikes that had been the moment of decision.

"What's it to be, lads?" he had croaked, as an angry wave smote him across the shoulders. For a brief instant they had peered across the heaving sea, at the blazing wall of petrol left by the dying M.T.B., but only for an instant.

Weeks had heaved himself up on his knees, causing the raft to rock dangerously.

"Too right we go back! Now gimme a ruddy paddle!"

Frantically they made the nightmare journey within feet of the licking flames, fighting every bit of the way. Somehow they found him, and pulled him across the raft. The half-naked body, torn and bleeding, and the fearful burns, swollen horribly by the salt water. And somehow they had got clear of the fire, huddling together for warmth and comfort, singing, cursing, and holding desperately on to life. Three hours later, the riveted side of the destroyer loomed like a wall beside them, the scrambling nets, the strong arms and helping hands, and the murmured words of encouragement. He remembered the feel of a soft towel dabbing at his tender skin, and the harsh fire of rum in his throat. The destroyer had circled the spot slowly, looking for the other raft. They found it an hour later, but only one figure lay tied to its pitching frame. The ship's doctor had tried to keep them away, but they had seen Leading Seaman Parker lifted tenderly aboard. He had smiled vaguely at them, and spoken in a strange voice. As they had watched, shocked to silence, Parker said, "I'm home, Dad, I couldn't get in the cinema, so I come home early." He started to laugh wildly, as they forced the needle into his arm.

Raikes breathed out hard, and opened his eyes. Poor old Parker, what a waste.

Faintly across the cold air drifted the plaintive note of a bugle, Sunset, and Raikes slept.

Out and across the uneasy stretch of swift-moving water, the light faded. The newly arrived frigate swung peacefully at her buoy, her engines still. On her quarter-deck, the duty signalman folded up the ensign, and made his way to the bridge, while the Officer-of-the-Day, having attended to the brief but permanent ceremony of Sunset, turned his mind to the string of details which awaited him, and every other Duty Officer in the harbour. Libertymen, Defaulters, Rounds, Darken Ship, Duty Watch, Working Parties, and all the rest. War or peace, it made no difference to his tight routine. On scores of other ships too, the vigilant Quartermasters paced their gangways, checked their moorings, and thought of home.

Threading her way in and out of the moored, darkened shapes, the destroyer's liberty tender panted her way towards Parkeston Quay, her small deck space overloaded with sailors, who were looking forward to a brief run ashore. As she grazed to a standstill alongside the slimy piles of the jetty, and long before the first lines were made fast, the noisy, jostling throng were scrambling up on to the concrete ramps, lighting cigarettes, and adjusting caps at a more rakish angle, and keeping an eye open for the Customs Officers, who might not take too kindly to the packs of duty-free tobacco stored in the useful respirator haversacks. One or two of them glanced curiously at the elderly couple who stood looking small and lost by the entrance to the railway station, and so utterly out of place, but in a very short while, the blue-clad throng had split and vanished, leaving these two alone.

But not for long. There was a splutter of a fast motor-boat at the jetty stairs, and a Petty Officer's head, followed by a stocky, duffle-coated body, rapidly appeared over the edge.

He hurried over.

"Mr. and Mrs. Royce?" he queried, leaning forward.

Mr. Royce nodded. "What a train journey we've had, haven't we, dear? Had to change three times."

His wife smiled at him, but the Petty Officer, a pensioner, recalled to the Navy, saw that there was little mirth behind those anxious eyes.

"Well, follow me if you please. There's a nice supper laid on for you at the . . ." he faltered. "At the hospital."

Slowly they climbed down the slippery steps, guided by a torch, to where the sleek, blue launch throbbed and squeaked against her fenders. Once settled, the Petty Officer shouted, "Let go!

Shove off forrard!" And with a growl they slid into the darkness.

The passengers sat quietly in the tiny cockpit, shielded from the spray, and stared at the strange and alien surroundings of their son's world, hitherto but an unreal picture painted by the B.B.C. and Clive's regular letters.

Mrs. Royce turned her head, and could dimly make out the reassuring profile, always at her side.

"Do you think——" she started, for the hundredth time, and stopped helplessly.

"Don't worry, my dear, I told you before, they've asked us down just to help his recovery a bit."

He squeezed her arm in the darkness.

As they stepped ashore at the smart, white-painted landing stage, flanked by the brass dolphins, another figure stepped forward to greet them, and following the steel-helmeted sentry, they entered the hospital grounds. The motor-boat swung away to her berth at the boats' pool, the old P.O. wondering sadly how long he was expected to make these heartbreaking journeys, backwards and forwards, with parents and wives and friends. He spat over the side of his boat, and turned his attention to the bowman.

"Your turn to wet the tea when we've tied up, Nobby!"

The waiting-room where Mr. and Mrs. Royce found themselves five minutes later, was already occupied and Mr. Royce gave an inward sigh of relief, knowing that further conversation at this stage would be impossible. As they sat on the well-worn sofa, he studied the two officers sprawled in the chairs by the radiator. One, a languid Lieutenant-Commander, with a keen but tired face, was idly glancing through an ancient magazine, while the other, a stocky, hard-faced Lieutenant, was scraping out his pipe with slow deliberation. The former suddenly looked up, his clear eyes questioning. Having apparently made up his mind, he nudged his companion, and stood up.

"Good evening. Have I the pleasure of addressing Mr. and Mrs. Royce?" His voice was a well-modulated drawl.

Mrs. Royce smiled, and nodded shyly.

"Well, bless my soul." The Lieutenant stepped up to them with outstretched hand. "I'm Murray, Jock to you both, if you will, and this is Lieutenant-Commander Emberson. We are great friends with your son."

The ice was broken, for both names at least were familiar and often mentioned in Clive's letters.

Emberson drew up a chair. "What a shame your having to come all that way by train—it's no joke in this part of the world."

"No, it's one helluva journey, if you'll pardon the expression, ma'am," added Murray.

Before Mr. Royce could make a similarly casual remark, he heard his wife's voice, with the merest quaver in it, and he steeled himself.

"Tell me quite truthfully," she said quietly. "Does it seem that we—that Clive——" She faltered and stopped.

Emberson and Murray exchanged quick glances.

"Now just you stop worrying."

His assurances were halted by the sudden entrance of the Surgeon-Commander, and both the officers stood to attention.

"I'm Commander Lloyd, and I'm very glad you got here all right," he said gruffly. "Now just come along and see your boy and then we'll fix you up with a real unrationed dinner."

Without speaking, they hurried down the bare corridors to the private ward.

As the Commander reached for the handle, the door was wrenched open, and he nearly collided with the sister.

"Where are you going?" he hissed. "What's happening?"

Mrs. Royce felt faint, and held her husband's arm, watching the sister's face, who was clearly put off her guard.

"It's all right, these are his parents," barked Lloyd, trying to conceal his fears.

"It's the young officer, sir," she stammered, glancing from one to the other. "He spoke to me!"

"Good God! Did he?" and the bulky Commander pushed past her, closely followed by the others.

Mrs. Royce let out a soft cry as she saw the figure in the bed, but the doctor paid no heed to either of them, until he had finished his examination. Eventually he drew himself up, and let out a great sigh.

"Your son," he said slowly, "has done the impossible. He has, in fact, turned the corner quite safely." He turned to the door.

"You may sit here for ten minutes; I'll arrange for your meal. Come with me, sister." The door closed.

An ambulance drove noisily up the gravel approach to the hospital, and somewhere in the far distance sounded the wail of an air-raid siren, but in that small room, at that moment, there was complete peace.

When the sister returned, she found them still sitting there, and with a great smile she laid a tray of tea at the bedside.

"Thought you might like a nice cup of tea to be going on with."

Mrs. Royce's eyes shone. "Bless you for taking so much trouble. Could you please tell me what he said to you?"

The sister paused, puckering her brow.

"Well, I was just sitting there by the window, when I heard him move, so I went over. As I reached him, he opened his eyes and looked me straight in the face and said, 'Are the others all right?' So I said, 'Yes' or something, and he smiled at me, and sort of relaxed. You know the rest."

"My poor Clive, his face looks so thin."

"Don't you worry. Commander Lloyd says it's going to be just fine."

"By the way," Mr. Royce's voice was a little unsteady. "What did happen to 'the others'?"

The sister busied herself noisily with the cups.

"There were only eight survivors, I'm afraid."

Reluctantly they had to go, and after an enormous meal, which they scarcely noticed, they were taken to a room in the annexe, where, for the first time since receiving the telegram, they slept.

The following morning was bright and crisp, with a keen, steady breeze sweeping the estuary into a million tiny white-caps. The sky was, for once, completely clear, a fine if rather hard blue. The vessels tugged impatiently at their cables, as if to jerk their crews awake for such a refreshing day, and already from countless galley funnels, faint wisps of smoke, and mixed aromas of frying bacon or utility sausages, blended invitingly with the more prevalent ship odours of oil and men. The Preparative flag mounted the gaff of the port signal tower, two minutes to Colours, and on the newly swept and scrubbed quarter-decks, the signalmen waited to hoist their ensigns, so that another naval day could be officially started. One minute later, Royce opened his eyes, and slowly, very slowly, his brain and senses battled to find some common understanding. At first he had the impression that he was suspended in space, a feeling of unreality and disembodied detachment deprived him of any sort of realization. There was only a bright haze surrounding him, no feeling yet of self-possession, or in fact, the will to bring himself back to his real world, so recently a world of torment.

Out on the vast parade ground of H.M.S. *Ganges*, an unknown boy bugler was to start the wheels turning once more, was to give

Royce his cue, his reintroduction to the land of the living. The bugler raised his shining instrument, and moistened his lips. The Officer-of-the-Day roared hoarsely, "Make it so!" and as the gleaming flag mounted the mast, the strident notes rang out round the sombre buildings, causing the dozing gulls to rise in squawking protest, and echoing and ebbing until they eventually penetrated the subconscious barrier of Royce's mind.

He squinted, closed his dry lips, and tried to move, and as the stab of pain lanced his back, he became, in that split second, fully aware of everything but his surroundings. At first, he was filled with fear, and then curiosity, as he painfully twisted his head towards the source of the light, where, sitting by the window with her head nodding, he saw a nurse. So he had made it. The very effort of trying to marshal his thoughts made him weak, but silently he struggled back over a period of blankness, until he saw with sudden clarity the enemy ship. It was so real that it seemed to shut out the light, to fill the room. He felt his body go clammy; it was the first time he had really noticed the presence of his limbs, and he tried to move his legs. He could not. Gritting his teeth, he tried again, holding his breath and contracting his stomach muscles with the effort. Little red and green dots jumped lightly before his eyes, and he lay back gasping, while in the back of his head a hammer began to pound mercilessly. So this was it, someone had rescued him, but for what? To be a helpless cripple? He shut his eyes tightly, and bit his lip to prevent a whimper of self-pity. Even his arms refused to rise above the sheets, and a surge of sudden panic made him fling his head from side to side on the pillow, each movement making the pain worse, until eventually he heard himself cry out, a sort of gurgle. Instantly, there was a patter of footsteps, and a cool hand pressed gently but firmly across his brow, and with it came a peculiar feeling of security. He stared up at the concerned grey eyes, and was dimly aware of a smell of soap, and the squeak of starch in the white uniform. He opened his lips, which felt like old leather, and tried again.

"Where am I?"

He halted, frightened, surely that wasn't his voice? It was too high, too cracked.

He cleared his throat, and felt the taste of petrol. Instantly, as if sparked by an explosion in his mind, the terrible memories came flooding back, tumbling over themselves, in wild and horrible confusion. Crackling flames, gunfire, and rushing water, tore round within his brain, like a symphony from hell, with a background of screams, some of which were his own.

How long this paroxysm lasted he didn't know; he only became dimly aware of strong hands holding him, and soothing voices, soft, yet persistent.

He lay limp and quiet, his mind dead once more, until one of the voices penetrated and held him in its grasp.

"Now come on, old fellow, wakey wakey, it's high time you sat up and took a little nourishment!"

Frantically Royce gathered himself together, and found himself looking into the heavy, confident face of the surgeon.

"Sorry, sir, everything went a bit rocky," he stammered. "But I feel a lot better now."

As he said that, he really did feel a surge of life pulsate through him, and he tried to smile.

"Well now, since you've decided to stay with us, you'd better hear what's wrong with you."

He raised one hand hastily, as Royce flinched.

"Now don't get worried, I promise you that you'll be all right and about again in a few weeks. Provided you're a good boy of course. Just the odd burn, and a scratch or two; you've been very lucky. Comparatively speaking that is," he added with a broad smile.

The surgeon's matter-of-fact manner began to have the desired effect. All the perfectly normal service catch-phrases and casual slang made Royce feel more at ease, and he found himself thinking of things and happenings outside his own personal torment.

"Tell me, sir," his voice was quiet and tense. "How did I get here? Are the others safe?"

The big figure settled itself comfortably on the edge of the bed, and slowly and carefully the surgeon retold the story of Raikes's gallant rescue, of the destroyer's arrival on the scene just at the right moment, and lastly he came to the piece that he could personally vouch for, the survivors' arrival at the hospital.

Royce listened with amazement. It seemed impossible now that he had ever been involved in such happenings, let alone been the principal character. The other man's voice stopped, but Royce knew that he must have omitted much, just to spare him. He smiled grimly.

"And there were only eight of us left, you say? Are they getting on all right now?"

"Fine! Why, you're the only one who's caused any panic so far, so you just think about getting better, and going on some leave! Besides, we need your bed!"

Royce lay back, and for the first time he felt relaxed, his worst fears had been dispelled. He had been tested, and he had made it.

In his opinion, the next three hours of his new-found life were the most difficult, when with his parents sitting by his side, he tried desperately to make light of all his experiences, and to prevent his mother from taking complete control from the sister, who smiled at some of her suggestions, which made Royce blush with embarrassment. Eventually they had to go, and he felt suddenly tired and weak, as his mother lingered by the bed, watching him anxiously.

"The doctor says you'll be able to come home soon," she said. "So look after yourself, my dear, and don't worry about not being able to write to us. We'll send you some things to replace the ones you have lost."

Royce looked down at his heavily bandaged hands, the thought of not being able to do all the usual little jobs, writing, shaving, filling a pipe, or even opening a door, had not occurred to him.

Mr. Royce saw the look of dismay on his son's face.

"We'll be off now, Clive. It was grand to see you again. Your mother and I are proud of you."

"Proud? I did what I had to do, Dad." His voice too was getting weaker.

"Now you get some rest; we're off to get that train, and start getting the house ready for you."

As they stood looking back from the open door, he cleared his throat.

"Yes, proud, that's what I said. We saw two of your officers this morning. They told us everything. Cheerio, son."

The sister immediately took charge again, straightening the blankets, and making him comfortable, in the manner of nurses the world over, muttering dark threats, and grumbling at her patient. Unfortunately, it was not difficult for anyone to see she adored her latest patient, as the surgeon pointed out.

The days which followed were difficult for Royce, cut off from the life he knew and trusted, and constantly forced to endure the pain and discomfort of his injuries, and their treatment. He was not allowed any visitors, for fear that too much conversation would weaken him, but the letters and messages of good wishes and congratulations which had poured in from the *Royston* moved him beyond words.

The one exception to the rule was Raikes, who had been so persistent, and who had kept up his stream of inquiries to such a degree, that he was permitted to sit in the room for most of the afternoon, provided he didn't make Royce too excited. It worked beautifully, and most of the time the two men were quite content to sit and lie in silence, each sharing the richness of comradeship and achievement.

At the end of the first week, their little routine was interrupted by the sweeping entrance of the matron, in a high state of excitement, an unusual occurrence for that particular pillar of strength.

"Good Heavens alive!" she boomed, her starched cuffs waving. "This place is a pigsty, it won't do at all!" She then proceeded to readjust every article in sight, until it seemed to be to her liking, although to everybody else the room looked just as usual, spotless.

Royce creaked his head round on the pillow, in the way he had now perfected.

"What's up, Matron? The Admiral coming?"

She shook her finger at him, frowning. "Now, how did you know? I only knew myself ten minutes ago!"

Royce paled. "You mean an admiral *really* is coming? To see me?"

"He certainly is," she consulted a tiny watch on her plump wrist, "and he should be here any minute."

Raikes stood up, his eyes shining.

"Well, sir, I'm sorry to say this, but I'm desertin' you this time. Admirals aren't in my line!"

And with a wicked grin he vanished.

"Phew, what's gone wrong now, I wonder," he muttered, staring hard at the ceiling. "Surely they're not going to put me through it again."

Vice-Admiral Sir John Marsh, Flag Officer in Charge of the base, was a small, unassuming figure, so that many persons had been shattered by his unexpectedly forthright, and often harsh, manner. And as he stepped lightly into the small room his sleeves ablaze with gold lace, his sharp eyes darting round, Royce could almost feel the energy given off by this miniature volcano. The Admiral wasted no time.

"My boy, I'm pleased to meet you," he barked. "I expect I'll be seeing more of you later, but right now I have to get on with the war."

"Yes, sir," agreed Royce lamely.

"However, I wanted to tell you personally, that I think you've done a grand job. A really fine piece of work."

"But it was only a trawler, sir, I——"

"I know what happened, and I know what you did, exactly."

"What the Admiral means," Royce became aware that the Admiral's languid Flag Lieutenant, a very overworked young man, was hovering at the rear, "is that some award——"

"Shut up, you fool," snapped the other testily. "What I mean is that you have been recommended for the Distinguished Service Cross. Suit you?"

Royce stuttered. "Suit me, sir?" he gasped. "I'm so, so . . ." He struggled for words. "I just don't know how to thank you, sir."

"I'm thanking *you*, Royce. Now I have to be off, but we shall meet again soon. Come, Roberts."

The door swung behind them.

"Did you hear that, Matron, or am I dreaming?"

"Yes, but you don't deserve it. Look at your dressings; keep your head still!"

But before she bustled out she gave him a little hug.

So regular and efficiently planned is hospital life and routine, that even small things become highlights in the patient's life, and Royce found himself becoming more and more restless, as his strength increased, and he eagerly looked forward to any unusual happening, such as his somewhat dangerous shave, which an attractive, if inexperienced, V.A.D. gave him every other day. Or the re-making and changing of sheets, when the whole operation was completed without moving the patient. Quite an extraordinary feat. And finally, after the doctor's casual permission, the day when he was allowed to get up. Gingerly he eased his feet into his slippers, and lurched to an upright position, at least that was what he had planned. But for the ever-vigilant sister, he would have fallen. He was quite determined, however, and step by step, he wobbled to the window, his sore limbs and bandages giving him a weird top-heavy feeling.

If the journey was painful, the reward was great. As he stood, breathing jerkily, and leaning one shoulder against the wall, he saw the whole harbour laid out like a shimmering chart before him, and once more he felt at home, reassured. For a whole hour, despite the sister's threats, he stood eagerly drinking in every detail, and studying every vessel in sight, trying to follow the many activities of the bustling harbour craft, and the ponderous cranes lining the busy jetties. He felt more determined than ever to leave the hospital in record time, especially as all the others had already been released, and had gone on leave. Raikes had seemed almost reluctant to leave him, but he too had now left. Royce smiled inwardly. Good old Raikes, thank God he was going to get a D.S.M. for his selfless bravery.

He laughed aloud when he remembered his last letter from Benjy Watson, for even though it was a little exaggerated, and rather colourful, it seemed certain that Kirby was not just a little displeased by Royce's good fortune. But the mood passed, when he remembered the others who had been less fortunate.

Emberson visited him as often as his exacting duties permitted, and kept him fully informed of the local flotillas' activities and sorties against the enemy, and whenever possible he brought him brief items of news about his own boats, or of Benjy's latest episode.

"You got the other stripe, a D.S.C., and a reputation," he drawled, his lined young face breaking into a warm smile, "so I think you're booked for that command. Don't scoff, my lad, you wait and see."

"Oh stop, Artie, you're driving me up the wall," laughed Royce. "Don't you know what it's like to be cooped up in here with all this"—he waved his arm towards the harbour—"going on just under my nose."

Emberson regarded him thoughtfully for a while.

"Tell you what, Clive, come down to my boat next week; we'll have a wee party. Nothing vast, of course, your doc wouldn't like it."

"Could I? Will they let me?"

"You leave it to me, old friend. It'd be a sort of recuperative holiday, a health-cure, in fact. After all, nothing's too good for a wounded hero!"

Royce almost danced. "If you can fix that, *I'll* pay for the party!" he laughed gaily.

He could think of nothing else, and even when they removed his head bandages, and he saw the bare patches where his scalp had been neatly repaired, he merely remarked, "It'll soon grow again."

Eventually the day of the promised outing arrived, and as he stood by the Wardmaster's office, where that harassed individual struggled with the vast amount of paperwork required of a hospital at war, he felt rather like a small boy who, having recovered from mumps, is about to take his first glimpse of the outside world.

"I dunno what the Commander's thinking of, letting you go gallivanting off into the town like this. It'll be downright bad for morale, that it will!"

Royce looked at himself in the full-length mirror on the wall, and smiled ruefully. He certainly was a weird sight, with his loose, blue hospital overall, and scuffed battledress trousers. Even if his new uniform had been ready for him, he would have been unable to encase his bandaged arms in the sleeves, while his healing body would certainly have taken unkindly to any sort of stiff jacket. He was even more appalled by his face. All youth seemed to have been drained from it, and left instead a haggard, almost shrunken imitation of its former self. The eyebrows had not yet fully grown, and his forehead still bore the angry marks of the fire's caress. The crudely clipped hair was disguised and held in place by a brand-new cap, with glittering badge, which he had purchased for the occasion, and now seemed to accentuate and magnify his wild appearance.

"Well, I'm going anyway," he said firmly. "I look dead already, and I will be if I stop here much longer."

A taxi stood ticking over in the driveway, and the driver thrust his head out of the window.

" 'Ere y're, sir, Commander Emberson told me ter pick yer up and deliver yer safe to 'im."

Royce grinned, and levered himself in to the back seat, and with a roar they were off.

Whether it was the jolting of the cab, or the excitement of being out again and still alive, or whether it was just the fact that he did not fully realize the inner extent of his injuries, he could not say, but after about ten minutes he was hanging on to the side-straps, and swallowing hard, to prevent himself from being violently sick. The aged driver had been watching him in the driving mirror and suddenly stopped the cab.

"I think I'd better be taking yer back. It don't do no good to kill yerself like this."

Royce didn't trust his voice, but shook his head vigorously, and painfully scrambled out on to the pavement.

"I'll be okay, but I think I'll walk for a bit; you just follow me up, if you don't mind."

"Lor' bless you, I don't mind, if you don't!"

So with the slim figure in the flapping blue coat, striding with great concentration down the pavement, and the old taxi growling along the kerb behind, they continued the journey.

Royce felt he could breathe better, and even the giddiness was a bit easier, although every so often he would pause as if to study a shop window, while the street swam in a mist around him. In this way he was able to fool the driver, and gather strength for the next stretch.

By the time they reached the wired gate of the Coastal Forces mooring area, he was shaking from head to foot, and desperately he manoeuvred his bandaged hands across his face, now shiny with sweat. A Petty Officer wearing a Naval Police armband stepped from a small hut, and saluted, his eyes wide with obvious amazement.

"Look *here*, sir," he sounded concerned. "It's none of my business, but I think I should telephone the P.M.O."

"No, it is none of your damned business!" snapped Royce. "D'you think I've come this far to be held up by a lot of blasted red tape!"

The Petty Officer was unmoved.

"Very well, sir, then I shall take it upon myself to escort you to Commander Emberson's boat. Fortunately, it's not far."

Royce relented, and smiled.

"Sorry, P.O., I think I must be getting a bit edgy."

They reached the foot of the gangway without further incident, and Royce leaned against his escort, while he let his eye travel along the seemingly enormous length of the M.T.B. She was one of the new Fairmiles, and almost twice the size of those in his own flotilla. Vicious looking muzzles peeped from every direction, while the torpedo tubes visible from the jetty, pointed menacingly at the Fleet Mail Office. Her decks were suitably busy with overalled seamen, under the direction of a fresh-faced Sub-Lieutenant, smart in blue battledress and a gleaming white sweater. Very right and proper for the Senior Officer's boat, he thought. Must be some of old Kirby's influence. He watched the young Sub moving purposefully about the deck, attending to his duties, and compared him with the image he had seen in the hospital mirror, half an hour or so previously. Was it possible that he had looked so full of youthful high spirits when he had first reported to

Harston? About the same age too, but only in years. His inner searchings were cut short, the Sub having stepped lightly to the jetty without his noticing. Must be losing my grip, he thought fiercely.

"Lieutenant Royce?"

He straightened automatically. It was the first time he had been addressed by his new rank, and it sounded strange, and rather formal.

"We weren't expecting you so soon, sir, this is very nice. The C.O.'ll be tickled pink. He's got some friends to celebrate your return, as it were."

He paused, and peered at him, his face clouding. "D'you feel all right, sir?"

Royce sucked in a lungful of salt air and nodded. "Yes, lead on, it takes a bit of getting used to, that's all."

"I see, sir," but he obviously didn't.

"By the way, my name's Bird, with all the obvious disadvantages, and after I've finished on deck—we're just going to test our new Browning—I'll be in the wardroom drinking up the experiences of my betters!"

"Bitters, you mean!"

Emberson strode forward with hands outstretched.

"Clive, you crafty old devil, you made it then, and thwarted my reception committee."

Royce held out his hand, and then they both looked at the shapeless bandages, Emberson with his hand half raised for the automatic handshake.

"Sorry, Artie, I forgot. We must bow to each other!"

The problem of getting him down the steep ladder to the wardroom had already been discussed, and two seamen stood below, guiding his feet, while the Coxswain and Emberson dealt with the top half. Royce didn't have to do a single thing for himself.

The wardroom was long for an M.T.B., and narrow, with all the usual varnished fittings, and pipes criss-crossing the deckhead. The sight of the rippling reflection of the quiet water on the rough anti-condensation paint, the gentle movement beneath his feet, and the accompanying shipboard smells and noises, were a welcome indeed.

A tall seaman in a tight white jacket was laying tea, and pulled up the most comfortable chair.

Royce sat on the edge gingerly, and grimaced.

"Nearly didn't make it, but it was worth the effort. I can't tell you what it's like to be back."

"I know, I know, it's not much, but it's home."

"Where are the others that your Subby was telling me about?"

"Don't fret, they'll be back. They've just gone over to the *Kitson* to look at this new radar gadget. All the new ships have got it in Harwich."

The curtain was thrust aside from the door, and Benjy Watson, Jock Murray and three other officers entered.

"Here he is!" yelled Benjy. "Who told me he had resigned?"

Royce looked from face to face, wondering what they thought of his crumpled appearance, and realizing just how much he had missed them.

"Too tough, that's me," he grinned.

They enjoyed to the full the carefully prepared tea—goodness only knows where so much rationed stock had been filched, but it was marvellous. Then with pipes well alight, they talked and yarned until they were hoarse, and Royce felt again the creeping faintness and sudden giddy lapses, which caused him to speak quickly and nervously, as if afraid he would be forced to break off and leave.

The others knew full well what was happening, and several meaning looks were exchanged. Emberson would have sent for the taxi earlier, but his main surprise was still to come. He glanced at his watch anxiously.

"I'm very much afraid your probation is running out, Clive," he said quietly. "You have to be back in half an hour. That was the arrangement with the old Doc."

Royce rose unsteadily, knowing that his reserve was beginning to fail. The faces around him blurred, and he blinked to clear his vision. He had been holding a cup between his muffled hands, as a dog will hold a bone, and the effort of setting it on the table was unbearable. He vaguely noticed that the others were silent. Even Benjy looked strange, and worried.

"Thank you for having me, gentlemen," he forced a crooked smile. "It's been just what I needed."

It was at that moment that the Browning machine-gun on deck fired a practice burst, and although he had been forewarned, he was seemingly unprepared for its violence, and his own reaction. The wardroom, the officers, everything dissolved in front of him, all his racing brain could follow was the dreadful staccato rattle, that in a split second made his sick mind lurch, and with a gasp, he threw his body to the deck.

Even as they jumped to his aid, Emberson swearing horribly at the unseen gunners, the curtain by the door jerked aside once more, and the small figure of a Wren stepped hurriedly inside.

"I'm late, I'm afraid, sir, the bus——" she broke off, her eyes widening at the scene, her face suddenly white.

"What's happened? Is he all right?"

Emberson looked up, "Blast, just too late," he said. "Quick, hold his head, and keep his shoulders off the deck!"

Royce lay on his side, only dimly aware that he was alive. Everything was dark, he heard a voice yelling, "Coxswain, make a signal, urgent, send ambulance!"

Ambulance? At sea? Impossible. Weren't we in action? Yes, that was it, the guns, must keep them firing. He turned his body, but someone was holding him, stopping him. He struggled feebly, and tried to get his eyes in focus.

From far away he heard his voice protesting. It was at that instant he saw Julia looking down at him, close enough to touch, and then he felt content, the pain and urgency seemed to slowly disperse.

"Julia, my darling," he whispered. "You shouldn't be here, it's not safe . . ." his voice trailed away.

He was only dimly conscious of the white jackets, and the stretcher, but the vision of that face, with the tear-filled eyes, made him suddenly desperate, some hidden strength made him cry out, urgently, and as the mist closed over him, he heard that voice once more, just as it had been at the railway station, soft and sweet. "It's all right, Clive, everything's going to be fine now."

As the ambulance tore towards the hospital, its gong sounding shrilly, he felt a great peace sweeping over him. The Cease Fire bell, that was it. Yes, everything was going to be fine now.

Royce sat by the window in his dressing-gown, the pale yellow glow of the afternoon sun lighting his face, and easing away the lines of strain. For once, he paid little heed to the activities of the harbour, and even yesterday's visit to the M.T.B., with the dreadful aftermath of delirium, and this morning's stern rebukes from both the doctor and the matron, had faded into insignificance, and all because of the letter, which he had read and re-read half a dozen times, and which now lay in his lap. When he had recovered from his drugged state of semi-collapse, he had been half fearful that the one bright spot, the one brief moment of pure happiness, had been but another dream, a figment of his tortured imagination, but the letter, hastily written on N.A.A.F.I. notepaper and handed to him by the nurse, had dispelled all his fears, and left him with a feeling of excitement, and a trembling anticipation. The letter was brief, and in her firm, neat hand Julia Harston had done her best to cram as much as she could into its construction, while apparently keeping one eye on an impatient railway clock. He started to read it again, smiling secretly to himself, and still unable to realize his good fortune.

She explained fully how Emberson had made a long-distance telephone call to her, and had in fact told her how Royce had been on the danger list, and had been asking for her in his moments of semi-consciousness, and he thought she might well be able to improve and encourage his recovery. A hurried explanation to an understanding Second Officer, a quick sub by one of the other girls at the signal station, a fast train south, and she had arrived in time to see his suffering, and to understand the pain and shock which he had endured so bravely. He found himself feeling rather pleased at that piece, for he knew in his own mind that if he looked ghastly when he had left the hospital, he must have been a gibbering wreck when she had made her entrance. Altogether a bad impression to make under the circumstances. Reading this, he felt considerably better. She continued by telling him that she had had to hurry off back to Rosyth, but not before the hospital had informed her, rather coldly, that the patient was "as well as could be expected, in view of his escapades". He grinned, that was more or less what the matron had said to him. It was the end of the letter he really liked.

I'm so very sorry about the way I treated you when we last met, but I now know that we both understand. If you still want to see me, I shall be very happy, and I shall look forward to hearing from you. Please look after yourself, and give my thanks to Commander Emberson, who has told me so much about you.

Yours sincerely, Julia.

That was the piece that made him glow. And she had signed herself simply Julia. It was only a written word, on the cheap paper, but to him it was a breath of true intimacy. Once it had been only a dream, something to think about during the wearying hours of watch-keeping, but in a flash, or so it seemed, there had been a series of breathtaking and terrifying changes in his life, and the dream had changed to something real, and the future had been given life and hope. All the same, he mused, it would have to be handled extremely carefully, for up to now, the initiative had been in the hands of others, and if he wasn't going to make another mess of it, he would have to give the matter a great deal of thought. The first thing was to get his service life rearranged, and straightened out, and that meant he would have to get well clear from the hospital. He immediately got down to the latter problem, with his usual keen and methodical way, and the doctors and nurses, overworked though they were, were quick to notice his sudden interest in his treatment, and a new impatience at any delay or setback.

Within two weeks, he had discarded most of his outward signs of injury, and took pleasure in striding about the hospital grounds, and occasionally walking down to the base to see Emberson, and on one otherwise dismal morning, he carefully put on his new uniform, said his farewells to the hospital staff, and headed for home, for three weeks' leave.

As usual, he enjoyed his leave to the full, and was pleased to be able to make his parents happy by being home again, but this time there was a difference, within himself he was a changed person. At first he ignored it, and tried to overlook something which might be only fancy, but as the days of enforced idleness wore on, he began to realize that Lieutenant Clive Royce, D.S.C., was a completely different being from the worried, but easy-going young officer who had once muddled and struggled through the early intricacies of life in an M.T.B. The harder he thought about it, the more baffling it became, he could not even place the exact time of the change. After all, he told himself repeatedly, he had not had an easy war so far, so it wasn't that, it was something far deeper.

He had written twice to Julia in Scotland, telling her of his progress, and now he hoped to be able to visit her as soon as possible. And he told her of his strange feeling, and fears. Her letters were, as always, witty yet soothing; friendly, but not showing a great deal of sympathy for his broodings. At first he felt rather hurt by her apparent sharpness, but as he strolled through the woods, ignoring the constant drizzle that seemed fated for his leave, reading her words over and over again, trying to find hidden meanings in every one, he realized that her approach was the right one. The past was history, but others would be looking to him from now on, relying upon his experience for their very existence. He knew then how he had changed. By responsibility to others. It was as if a curtain had been lifted, the way was now clear, and when the buff envelope was handed to him by his mother, four days before his leave was due to end, he felt in some way relieved.

"I have to report back to the *Royston*," he announced simply. "I don't quite understand it, I have to appear before a Board."

His parents quietly helped him pack his newly bought kit, when Royce suddenly jerked up as if he had been shot. "Good God!" he burst out. "Surely they don't think I'm round the bend!"

So often, he had seen officers classified as unsuitable for Coastal Forces, and even for any seagoing duties; men who had once been hardened fighters, and seemingly indispensable, had suddenly become shattered wrecks, grey-faced ghosts, who shied from any decision, and jumped at every sound. Such was the price of danger.

"Oh no!" he groaned. "They couldn't do that to me now. I must make them see that I'm all right now!"

It was a miserable journey back to the base, and seemed to take twice as long as usual, and even the first glimpse of the *Royston's* ungainly bulk was now an anti-climax.

He hurried into the wardroom to pump his friends for information, only to find that the flotilla was at sea, covering a convoy, so there was nothing else to do but walk straight to the Commander's office, and get it over.

Commander Wright looked up with surprise, as a thin-lipped Royce was shown in.

"Good heavens, man, you're back early," he roared jovially. "It's damn good to see you again. Oh, and congratulations, me boy."

Royce stood stiffly. "I'd like to know if I may, sir," he faltered. "The Board tomorrow morning, can I appeal against it?"

"Appeal against it? Appeal against it?" Wright bellowed so loud that the Writer in the next office shuddered. "What the devil d'you mean, sir? After all this trouble, don't you want a command? Damn and blast my breeches, explain yourself, sir!"

Poor Royce was past any explanation.

"Command?" he said weakly.

"Yes, don't you know anything about it?"

"No, sir. I thought it was the Old Crock's Rush they were giving me, you know, the Axe."

Wright lay back in his chair, and laughed till his eyes were wet, looking rather like a newly boiled lobster.

"Oh, Royce, you'll be the death of me!" he wheezed. "Here's me, pulling every damn string under the Old Pal's Act to get you fixed up with a command, and to be serious for a moment, we need experienced M.T.B. men badly, and you come in here nattering about being bomb-happy!"

He pulled a bottle and two glasses from a side drawer.

"Here, me boy, let's drink to it. I've done all I can, you just give Captain Marney the right idea tomorrow, and you'll be all set."

Royce sat dazed in the chair, and scarcely noticed the neat gin, yet another phase was unfolding, seemingly beyond his control. A command, well.

As he left the office, walking on air, he could still hear Wright laughing.

CHAPTER SIX

CAPTAIN REGINALD MARNEY, D.S.O., Officer-in-Charge Coastal Forces at the base, paced impatiently up and down the spotless interior of his stateroom-cum-office. A Writer, and the *Royston*'s Yeoman of Signals stood discreetly at one end, motionless, but for their eyes, which followed the great man back and forth on his journey.

Captain Marney was an imposing man in his late forties, his face brown and lined by years of service from Iceland to Shanghai, and his short hair greying rapidly under the weight of his many responsibilities.

"Well, that about covers it for this morning," his voice was clipped. "Make another signal to F.O.I.C., Yeoman, repeated 'Staff Officer Operations and all Commanding Officers'."

He paused, and let his keen blue eyes drift through the well-polished scuttle, and finally rest on an M.T.B. which was manoeuvring alongside the Gun Wharf. Young fool, he thought, too much rudder. The M.T.B. appeared to stop rather suddenly, as it bounced off the rubber fenders of the jetty, and the Captain felt vaguely satisfied that his observations had not been mistaken. He cleared his throat, and the Yeoman licked the point of his pencil.

"During the next month, maximum effort is to be made

against all enemy coastal shipping, in order to withdraw as many of the German Forces as possible from our own convoy routes. It will be appreciated if Base and Operations Staffs will co-operate with Commanding Officers to the best of their ability during the next decisive period. Send that off Restricted, as usual," he ended.

He had been dictating letters and signals for two hours, as was his usual custom each morning. As the other two turned to leave, he added, "And, Yeoman, make a signal to M.T.B. 7784, er, 'Suggest change of rudder at the right time may prevent change of command at the wrong time'."

He smiled drily, these Wavy Navy chaps, ah well, it was all new to them. He sighed heavily.

His Chief Writer, a ferrety man called Slade, entered stealthily.

"Commander Wright and Commander Thirsk, for the Board, sir."

"Very well, Slade, table, chairs, etc. The usual."

He was a man of few words.

The "Board" assembled every so often, to arrange replacements for commanding officers, to fill the vacancies caused by death, promotion, new boats, and the many other nerve-racking problems of supply and demand. At this moment, with ships being lost left and right, the demand was very great, and the supply was getting less and less experienced.

When Royce eventually sat down facing the grim-faced trio, he felt the first qualms of possible defeat, but he steeled himself, and took consolation from Wright's nod of encouragement.

Captain C-F came quickly to facts.

"Read your history, Royce. Quite like it, but I want you to tell me the story again. Right from when you first reported here."

They listened in silence, studying the younger man's face, understanding the full impact of his words. When he finished, they sent him out of the room, to wait in maddening solitude. Not for long, and he studied their faces, especially that of the Captain.

"I think you'll be pleased to know that we're satisfied, and I am quite sure you'll do your best to make up in resourcefulness and courage, what you lack in training."

He paused while Royce mumbled his thanks.

"Don't thank me, Royce, remember it's a great task you have before you. You must realize that you will be quite alone in your small way, just as I am here. There will be many difficulties which you must face without a pause, and without consultation with others. Your men will be mostly new to the trade, much more amateur than you ever were. And the reason I have selected you for the task, quite apart from your technical qualifications, which are obvious, is because you have not lost your sense of humanity, you have not allowed yourself to become hard. Remember, to become too hard, even in war, is to become too brittle."

"I'll try to live up to that, sir."

"Well, good luck. Now off you go, and get that well-needed drink. Commander Wright will give you all the details this afternoon."

As the door closed behind him, the three regular officers relaxed, and looked at each other.

Commander Thirsk, a ruddy-faced destroyer captain, shook his head. "Poor little beggars! In peace-time it'd have been years before we heard what that young man has just heard. Now they're expected to take a command when they can hardly salute properly."

"Don't forget, Harry, it was harder to get killed then," said Captain Marney soberly.

The somehow derelict-looking end of the port installations, known as the repair yards, was as usual a wild, carelessly distributed tangle of discarded machine parts, and uneven piles of rusting sheets of armour plate, while here and there, panting diesel generators chugged and roared, as they pumped power along the snaking cables, which wriggled away in every direction. Along the slipways, running with a potent mixture of green sea-slime, and oil, various small ships of war were suffering the many indignities of repair and destruction heaped upon them by the dockyard workers, who, in boiler suits and cast-off clothing, ambled from one job to the other, in a manner, which to the uninitiated, appeared to have neither planning nor reason.

It was difficult to connect the stripped or slimy hulls, which loomed uncomfortably on the trestles, their intimate parts strewn around the ramps in wild profusion, with the graceful grey shapes which rode at their moorings in the harbour. They were apparently lost, doomed to lie for ever amid chaos. The maintenance staff, however, took all despair and criticism in their stride, and in the manner of all dockyards, went their own peculiar way, and completed most of the work to schedule.

One particular boat caught Royce's eye as he and Commander Wright strode through the winding cobbled fairway, their chins tucked into greatcoat collars, to stop the penetrating north wind from undoing the good work of an excellent breakfast. She lay on the second slipway, her paint stripped from her sides, the mahogany planks sharp and bright, like a naked wound. Various wires and power cables trailed over her sides, and a small army of men hammered and scraped, sawed and painted, with workmanlike indifference. A lifebuoy lay on the ground by her side, the flaked gilt lettering still showing boldly, M.T.B. 1993, Emberson's old boat. The two men stopped for a while in silence, as if paying homage.

"Getting a well-deserved spruce up," muttered Wright at length. "Should have had it long ago."

A harassed-looking Lieutenant, in dirty flannel trousers and battledress blouse, stepped out from behind a pile of oil-drums, his greasy hands clutching impressive bundles of official forms and lists. Wright returned a fumbled salute cheerily.

"Hallo there, Page, how's the jolly old refit progressing?"

Page grimaced. "Up the wall! That's what I'll be before long. I don't know when she's more trouble, in the water or out!"

As they left him, Wright glanced keenly at Royce who trudged purposefully at his side, his eyes peering ahead.

"That's what you'll be like after today, my lad. The grandeur of command. Oh, my hat!"

Royce nodded, but hadn't really heard, his mind, brain and soul were captivated and controlled by one thought, one swelling desire, to get to his new boat as soon as possible. He and Wright had pored over her facts and details, dimensions and builder's claims, until the early hours of this morning, and even then he had tossed and turned in bed, running over every last piece of available information about H.M. M.T.B. 9779. This was his greatest moment, or very soon would be, and he prayed silently that he would be equal to it. He had been vacantly munching his breakfast, when Wright had strolled in, and announced casually that the boat, fresh from the builder's yard, and her hurried trials, had just arrived at the repair yard, to have her final armament fitted. She was ready for him.

The crew had been drafted aboard her at Dover, the nominal list and other eagerly perused details lay in his greatcoat pocket within easy reach, and as he unwittingly quickened his pace, he felt like the new boy joining his first boarding-school.

"Here, slow down a bit!" puffed Wright. "She won't disappear before you get there!"

He had been at the game too long not to recognize the symptoms, and he rested his hand on Royce's arm.

"Take a piece more of advice from an old hand, if you think it's worth anything. Remember one really important thing, and that is, the crew are much more worried about you, and what you're going to be like. And they are, for the most part, real amateurs, green as grass; you'll have to be really patient, and work for them, show them the way. And that goes for the officers too."

Royce smiled gratefully. "Thanks, sir, I was beginning to get in a flap, but what you said has helped more than you'll ever know."

At that moment they turned the corner of the giant edifice of the machine shops, and the whole northern sweep of the headland came into view, and they shuddered at the vicious punch of the wind. Below them, pointing out into the stream like a rugged stone monument was the loading-wharf, along which trundled vans and cranes, trucks and wheelbarrows, packed with the essential materials for keeping a ship at sea, from rope fenders to toilet paper.

Most of the vessels were store ships, or tenders to larger vessels lying out at the deep anchorages, but Royce had eyes for only one craft, which shone in her new grey paint, gleaming and confident of her powerful beauty. She seemed aware of the bright splash of colour she made among the bustling shapes of the hard-worked launches and lighters, a slender, graceful creature, a living thing.

Royce stopped dead in his tracks, causing Wright to stagger backwards.

"Good God, what's up?"

"Oh, sorry, sir, I was a bit swamped by all this. She's a beauty!"

As they drew nearer, and lower down the sloping road, Royce began to realize how vast his new command was, compared to the rest of the flotilla. Like the boats he had seen at Harwich, she was one of the latest, powerful additions to the Mosquito Fleet, and to him at that moment she looked enormous. He forced his mind over the details again. She was nearly one hundred and fifteen feet long, and her engines generated over four thousand horse-power, giving her well over thirty knots. Although she only carried two torpedoes like her smaller sisters, she positively bristled with guns, ranging from a Bofors on the fo'c'sle, to heavy Brownings aft, while around the bridge pointed the familiar, slender snouts of two Oerlikons. A very tough customer, if properly handled. That thought made his mind turn to the crew, which, apart from the officers, consisted almost completely of Hostilities Only ratings. A sobering thought.

Of the officers, apart from their names, and brief service records, he knew nothing. Sub-Lieutenant John Carver, a twenty-one-year-old ex-professional photographer, was to be his Number One. He had been eleven months in the service, three months in an Atlantic destroyer, the rest under training of one sort or another. The other officer was an eighteen-year-old Midshipman, Colin Leach, who, nine months before, had still been at college.

They halted a discreet distance from the gangway, where a young seaman lounged, an enormous revolver hanging from his belt.

Royce smiled grimly. I'll have to do a "Kirby" on him, he thought.

"Well, Royce, this is as far as I go. I think it's important for a new C.O. to have this moment all to himself. Cheerio!" and before Royce could protest, he was gone.

He flicked open the collar of his coat, took a deep breath, and walked slowly towards the boat.

Several things happened at once. First, the sentry jerked to attention, and caught the lanyard of the revolver in the gangway rail, causing him to wriggle awkwardly, and prevented him from saluting at all. Royce gave him a suitably cold stare. The next thing was the sudden appearance of an officer in immaculate uniform and white muffler at the guard-rail.

He saluted stiffly as Royce climbed to the deck, feeling like an ancient mariner. This must be Carver. A tall, striking young man, with a long, handsome face and fair hair, whose general appearance was only marred by rather protruding eyes, which gave him a haughty, if not actually arrogant look.

Returning the salute, Royce shook him by the hand, his eyes darting quickly round the decks. Clean and neat, but then, of course, it was a new boat. Too early to judge yet.

"So sorry we haven't finished loading stores," Carver's voice was surprisingly low and pleasant. "I'm afraid I've succeeded in upsetting the gentleman in the bowler hat over there."

Royce glanced at the gentleman in question, who squatted grimly on his lorry by the boat's side, smoking his pipe.

"He said his tea-break came first or something. The war could, er, 'bloody well wait!'"

Whether this was true or not, the joke was extremely well timed, and Royce decided to allow himself to be drawn slightly from his protective wall of authority. He grinned, and clapped the other on the shoulder.

"He's setting us a good example, let's go below and have a cup, that is if you've managed to get all that installed yet?"

The wardroom was long and slender like that on Emberson's boat, but there the similarity ended. The newly varnished furniture, and clean white paint, gave it an unlived-in atmosphere, bordering on discomfort.

"We'll have to get some gear in town, Number One, and make the place like home."

A curly-haired seaman, in the conventional white jacket, clumped in with a tray of tea.

Royce studied the man's impassive face, as he laid the table. One of his crew.

"What's your name?" he queried pleasantly, and the man jumped.

"Er, Trevor, sir, Able Seaman." The north-country burr was strong. "Starboard Oerlikon gunner, sir."

For a brief instant, Royce felt a chill run down his neck, as he saw again the mutilated body of A.-B. Poole hanging from the starboard Oerlikon, swinging gently in the flames.

He shuddered, then nodded. "Thank you, Trevor, I hope you shoot as well as you handle a teapot!"

Carver was watching him closely, and when the seaman had departed behind the serving hatch, he coiled himself down in a shining new chair.

"What's it like, sir, going into action, in one of these boats, I mean. It's hard to visualize somehow."

Royce looked at him hard. This was the first sign of Captain Marney's words coming true. He now had to show he was able to control his own emotions, and those of his men as well.

"Don't try, Number One. It's never so bad or good as you expect anyway. I'll keep you so busy that you'll probably not even notice."

Carver smiled, and examined the toe of an elegant shoe.

"When I was training we were told about your last boat. I'm very glad to be learning under you." He was quite sincere.

There was a scuffle, and a crash outside the door, and a youthful voice was raised in anguish.

"Blast the ladder! Ouch, my blessed leg!"

A new cap flew in the door, and landed neatly on a chair, and there were further sounds of heavy packages being put down.

"I say, Number One, has the Old Man blown in yet?" piped the voice.

Carver flushed, and rose awkwardly, but Royce silenced him with a wave.

"Lord, I've got so many Confidential Books to correct, I'll never be done," and with a bang, Midshipman Leach burst in.

"I've just seen a boat all shot up on one of the slipways, I——" he stopped, his jaw dropping. "Gosh, sir, I'm sorry, I didn't know . . ."

"As you see," said Royce drily, "the Old Man has arrived!"

At the same time he was thinking, how incredibly young, he makes me feel like a grandfather.

Leach certainly looked every inch a midshipman, but the uniform seemed to accentuate his youth. His round, pink face, blue eyes, now wide with horror, and unruly hair, gave him the appearance of a startled schoolboy.

Royce smiled. "It's all right, Mid, have some tea, relax."

"It'll probably be too strong for him," said Carver severely.

As they chatted, and Royce fired questions concerning the crew, he knew that this was going to be a happy wardroom, and as they would not be living aboard the *Royston*, leaving her to the cramped crews of the little boats, it was just as well.

He spent the afternoon exploring the boat, and checking the lists with Carver who, although most willing, was lamentably uncertain of practically all the normal procedure. He would have to be led for some time. Leach's duties were confined at present to correcting A.F.O.s, charts, and all the other books and papers required of even this small warship, and this he did, with an enthusiasm which made Royce chuckle.

The Coxswain had not yet joined, and a Leading Seaman called Denton accompanied Royce on his rounds. He was a burly Londoner, a peacetime R.N.V.R., and a reliable influence on the mess-deck.

He piloted Royce into that long, homely space, now deserted while the hands worked on deck, and he saw with affection the neat lockers, with the garish pin-ups already in evidence. The built-in cupboards, the lines of damp dhobying, and rolled towels, gave the appearance of packed habitation, the discomfort borne by most sailors.

Next, Royce met the Chief, a P.O. Motor Mechanic from

Derby, named Anderson. A lively young man, with a long face like a racehorse, he nevertheless impressed him by his knowledge and love of his giant charges.

"They make the boat fly, sir," he rubbed his hands. "You'll see, when we get out."

Royce left him in the engine room, feeling confident of one other good man. But for the most part, the men he questioned were seamen by training, and not by experience. Gunners according to their badges, although they had shot at nothing but reliable and condescending targets towed by aircraft trawlers. "Give me time!" he muttered.

Eventually he found himself alone once more in the strange surroundings of his new cabin. He was amazed that so much could be jammed into such a minute space. From the neat bunk to the built-in bureau, it had an air of quiet efficiency. He unpacked his cases, which had been spirited aboard by some unseen hand, and changed slowly into his seagoing rig, listening while he did so, to the orderly chain of noises over his head, the full impact of his grim task of training and using the boat only dawning on him as his eye caught the brief sign on the open cabin door. It stated simply, "Commanding Officer". He sat heavily on the bunk, feeling suddenly deflated, staring at it for some moments, weighing up his chances of success, and the apparent possibilities of a horrible failure. There was now no one to give him guidance, no detached feeling that all he had to do was obey orders. He would be giving them. For once, he felt at a loss, and that he ought to be rushing on deck to see what his officers were doing. He restrained himself, and began to think slowly and deliberately, as he was to do many times in the future. Peering out of his small scuttle, he was able to see the *Royston*, and the Coastal Forces' moorings, about half a mile away. His orders stated that he was to take the M.T.B. alongside the *Royston* as soon as he had finished taking on stores, i.e. about 1200 hours. Such a narrow piece of water, comparatively clear of shipping, as most of the harbour craft had tied up ready for the midday meal, but to him, in a strange craft, with the prospect of going alongside under the eyes of the flotilla, it may well have been the North Atlantic. He was suddenly aware of a hush in the shipboard sounds, and as he stood with his head cocked, Carver clattered down the ladder to his door. He was now clad in a bright new duffle coat, and had his cap under his arm. He was obviously more than a little worried.

"All stores aboard, and ship ready to move," he announced breathlessly. "The Coxswain is waiting in the *Royston*. I've just had a signal," he added.

"Blast!" thought Royce savagely. "Not even an experienced coxswain," but to Carver he said as evenly as he could manage, "Stand by to slip."

Pulling on his duffle, and slinging his glasses round his neck, he climbed to the bridge, where Leading Seaman Denton stood stolidly by the wheel. Unlike the other boats, this type had the steering position on the open bridge, and although it meant that the coxswain was more prone to injury in action, it had the advantage of allowing the captain to be able to direct operations with the minimum of wheel orders, which was so essential when a vessel of this nature was employed twisting and turning at high speed, and the captain was required to supervise and control the firing of torpedoes. He nodded to him briefly, and noted with satisfaction that the bridge was clean and sensibly laid out. A young signalman was fiddling with halyards behind him, and on the fo'c'sle he could see the hands taking the slack off the wires. He checked with the engine room, and rang down "stand by", and was startled by the immediate roar of the giant engines, which settled down to a steady confident rumble. The air was faintly tinged with exhaust fumes. Only when there was absolutely nothing more to do on the bridge, did Royce steel himself to begin the operation of actual movement.

"Let go forrard!" he bawled, and he saw a dockyard worker heave their bow rope into the water, and Carver seemed to be coping all right there.

He craned over the screen. "Let go aft!"

Vaguely he saw Leach nod, his face anxious, and then scurry right aft to watch the dripping wire snaking aboard.

When satisfied that there was no wire in the water to foul the screws, Royce rang down for "Slow ahead".

The strong current which was eddying round the end of the jetty had swung out the bows just nicely. Royce had allowed for it without conscious thought, and as the engines snapped into gear, the boat thrust purposefully out into the open.

"Steer straight for the depot ship," he said, not wishing to complicate matters.

"Aye, aye, sir," and Denton spun the wheel in his hard hands, his eyes squinting against the glare on the water.

Royce's heart had stopped pounding quite so horribly, and

he felt instead a wild sensation of elation. He had actually started the ship himself, his own craft. He rubbed his hands.

Carver was looking up at him for instructions.

"Hands fall in fore and aft for entering harbour!"

Carver saluted, in a rather theatrical manner, and a second later Royce heard the twitter of the pipe, and the padding of feet on the wooden decks, as the hands fell in.

To the onlooker, she made a brave sight in her new paint and gleaming guns, with the white-jersied figures standing in two neat lines on deck. From beneath her cut-away stem, twin rolls of foam creamed away behind her, while from the gaff a starchy new ensign flapped in the slight breeze.

Carver stood in the eyes of the boat, staring ahead, and thinking goodness only knows, while little Leach stood aft, dwarfed by the seamen.

On down Fenton's Reach, to the destroyer flotilla leader, bearing the broad black band of Captain (D).

As they drew abeam, Royce yelled "Pipe!" and again the shrill notes of the call echoed across the water.

They paid their respects to the Senior Officer. She, too, replied with a clear, trilling precision.

Royce beamed with pleasure, and wished he could confide with someone about his childish delight. At that moment the signalman shouted, and pointed over the port quarter.

"Ship closing sir!"

Royce swung round, and saw with amazement the lumbering hulk of an ancient freighter, with black smoke gushing from her spindly stack, steering straight for him. She was still a good fifty yards away, and must have steamed round the point while they had been busy with salutes. Royce checked the marks, and found that he was in the correct channel, and had the right of way.

"Bloody fool," he muttered, and Denton grinned.

The M.T.B. held her course for some moments, until in fact it became obvious to everyone on board that either Royce broke the rule of the road, or there would be an unpleasant collision.

"Hard a-starboard, and cut across her wake," he snapped, and then switched on the loud hailer. He noted that the paint was hardly dry. He heard it squeak into life, and directed his attention to the towering, rusty bridge of the freighter.

"*Flying Lantern* Ahoy!" The harsh vibrations brought two

little heads to the bridge rail, one wearing a battered, gold-braided cap, and the other a rakish trilby.

"Don't you know your regulations?" roared Royce, and waited.

The trilby vanished, then reappeared with a megaphone, which was handed to the captain.

"What's the matter? 'Fraid we'll scratch your wee yacht?"

Some of the seamen tittered, and Royce flushed.

"No, we're scared you'll capsize in our wash!"

The captain called back an unprintable word, and went into his wheelhouse and slammed the door.

Royce felt better, and realized that he was practically up to the *Royston*'s buoys. More piping, then the delicate touch astern on the engines, as the heaving lines went to the waiting seamen on the pontoons. "Stop engines"; it was over.

As the boat shuddered into silence, and creaked against her fenders, he swung down to the fo'c'sle.

"I'm going aboard, Number One. Don't forget what I told you about Dress of the Day. Commander Kirby is probably watching even now. I see that the rest of the flotilla are now back. I'm going to find our new coxswain, P.O. Banks, or whatever his name is."

"What shall I do now?" Carver sounded lost.

"Feed the brutes, and see that they get their tots," grinned Royce, and started up the catwalk.

The first person he saw was the familiar, stocky figure of Raikes.

"Petty Officer Banks, reporting for Coxswain," he said without a smile.

"What? Have you gone up the wall?"

Raikes smiled, and Royce felt a glow of friendship.

"Well, sir, this Banks chap did a silly thing. He found that some rotten perisher had mixed up the draft chit, an' he got 'imself sent to Scapa; cruel, ain't it, sir?"

Royce laughed loudly. "Now I wonder what rotten perisher did that? It's good to have you back. Quite frankly, I need your services badly."

"I watched you come alongside, sir, and quite frankly, I think the Navy's gettin' some very queer seamen nowadays. Still, we'll soon lick 'em into shape."

Royce walked on air as he strode to the wardroom. He felt that now, at least, he had someone upon whom he could rely, to help the unkind process of training the crew to run more smoothly.

The very first person he saw in the wardroom was Kirby. Somehow he seemed smaller and older. He was leaning against the bar talking to Deith, who looked distinctly uncomfortable.

"Good grief!" said the latter, with a relieved smile. "Here he is at long last," and ignoring Kirby he shook him by the hand.

"Good afternoon, Number One; or rather I should say Lieutenant Royce now, shouldn't I?" Kirby's voice was flat. "It's all working out for you, isn't it? Promotion, and a command. Well done."

But his tone showed no warmth. As he turned and left the room, Deith shook his head.

"God, what a man. We've just been out on a practice run, and I missed the target. You'd think I'd tin-fished the *Nelson* for all the fuss he's making!"

The other familiar faces drifted in, tired and thirsty, and upon seeing Royce, they seemed to come to life. Benjy positively beamed.

"My boy, you're a hero, you're absolutely magnificent, you do credit to us all!" he thundered.

Royce grinned, for although he, too, was proud of the blue and white ribbon on his breast, he knew that at least six of the flotilla's officers already held that decoration. Benjy was one.

"I'm back all right," he smiled, "and I have a feeling that there is a party in the offing."

There was indeed.

Viewed from the sea, the East Coast has probably less personality than any other part of the British shoreline, with its constant blue misty lowland, and the patchy fen district, a silhouette only broken here and there by the squat shapes of villages, church spires, and the occasional navigational aid. In winter, it becomes even more bleak, and the making of an exact landfall or fix becomes all the more difficult, especially when the compass binnacle is swinging through a jerky arc of eighty degrees or so.

Alone, on the angry, white-crested sullenness of the North Sea, with the half-hidden hump of land reaching away from the port beam, M.T.B. 9779 rose and fell uncomfortably, as she ploughed forward into the vicious little waves. Every so often, her sharp stem fell into an unsuspected trough, and there would be a flat smacking noise, and a sheet of salt spray would fling itself high over the tiny bridge, and make the decks stream and glisten. Up, down, up down, with a correspondingly sickening motion from side to side, until it seemed as if the whole world had always been built on this crazy pendulum.

In his cabin, Royce lay fully dressed on his bunk, one foot jammed against his bookshelves, to prevent a sudden passage to the deck, his hands were clasped behind his head, and he stared moodily at the blank face of the clock. He had been in command for exactly a week now, and every day, without exception, he had been forced to manoeuvre his beloved boat back and forth across the harbour, practising his crew at all the evolutions of seamanship, and trying to make them perform all the seemingly tiresome and unnecessary details of ship ceremonial, and all to Kirby's whims and desires. Only once had he been outside the boom-gate for a practice shoot, and that had been shortened by bad weather.

It must be impossible, he told himself, but all the same, it did seem as if Kirby was going out of his way to be awkward and unhelpful, as if he didn't want him to be part of his flotilla on patrol.

Commander Wright, in all his wisdom, had watched these happenings with anxiety and distaste, and at last, in desperation, he had approached Kirby on the matter. Kirby had stood complacently in his office, his neat hands inserted in the pockets of his monkey jacket, those piercing eyes cold and sceptical.

Wright had turned his eyes away, determined not to show his dislike.

"It's like this, Kirby, we've got to get these boats out on the job, every boat we can muster, provided it'll float."

Kirby was unmoved.

"There's no point in putting an untrained crew to sea with the flotilla. They'd only be a liability."

Wright turned, his eyes hard. "Damn it, man, they're all untrained! We haven't got time, don't you see? This isn't peacetime!"

"Some are more untrained than others."

Was there a trace of a sneer on Kirby's face. Wright studied him thoughtfully, fully aware he was making little progress.

"As Senior Officer of the flotilla, I must take all the responsibility for my captains," continued Kirby, speaking softly. "And frankly, the reputation of the whole Group is being damaged by this influx of second-rate seamen."

Like an ancient knight circling an adversary, Wright saw the small chink in the armour, and mercilessly he lunged.

"I've been as reasonable as I know how, but it seems to me that you're only interested in your own damned reputation," he grated. "These are good boys, all of 'em. I should know, I've been watching them die long enough. And, quite off the record, of course, if you can't make something of your flotilla, I'll bloody well see that we get someone who can!"

He sat down heavily, breathing fast, glaring at Kirby, who had paled.

"May I remind you, sir, that what you're suggesting constitutes a threat to me, personally?"

Wright smiled, but there was no mirth. "Yes, I'm threatening you. What do you propose to do about it?"

Kirby stood stiff and shocked, like a man hearing sentence at a court martial, unwilling to yield, yet unable to find a way out of this unforeseen predicament.

Wright followed up the attack, by turning to his wall-chart, covered with coloured pins and numbered darts.

"Look here, there's a small convoy of three ships leaving Yarmouth tomorrow, they're stragglers of the last north-bound. Young Royce can go as their escort. It'll give him time to break in his boat and crew, in his own way. All right?"

"Very well," snapped Kirby, "and I'll take him with me on the next sweep."

He stood looking at Wright, his gaze now uncertain.

"All right, Kirby, carry on, and for goodness sake try to understand that it's harder for them than it is for you."

"I hope I know my duty, sir!"

"I hope so, too," answered Wright meaningly.

As the prompt result of that meeting, Royce was now at sea, his own master at last. With another glance at the clock, he heaved himself off the bunk, and adjusted his body to the uneven roll, then with a deep sigh he made his way to the bridge.

His head and mind were cleared in an instant by the keen air, and the sharp edge of the salt, and without speaking he checked the chart, while from the corner of his eye he saw Carver clinging to the voice-pipe, his face like death.

"Well, Number One," he said eventually. "How's it going?"

"I feel ghastly. And I've not picked out the ships yet."

Royce swung his glasses shorewards. "Hmm, where was your last fix?"

"Er, Lowestoft lighthouse."

"Well, that should be all right. Give them another ten minutes or so then we'll turn in a bit, and see if we can pick them up."

It was like listening to another person, just to hear his own voice giving orders, making prophecies, with a calm, confident manner he had not believed possible. He chuckled to himself.

"How are the hands shaking down?"

"Fifty per cent are fighting sea-sickness, I'm afraid. So am I," added Carver miserably.

"Right, go below, and have a warm. I'll hang on here for a bit."

When the grateful Carver had departed, Royce leaned happily across the screen, humming to himself, completely disregarding the retching of the helmsman's stomach.

Sure enough, a few moments later, the signalman reported three ships closing from the north-east, so increasing speed the M.T.B. steered to intercept. To any seasoned captain they appeared the usual sweepings of the Convoy Pool, but to Royce, the three battered coasters represented his first personal convoy, and for the next quarter of an hour he weaved around them, jockeying them into a semblance of order, and generally getting them sorted out.

Then they steadied down on the starboard side of the little procession, and the awful motion started again. When Carver returned, still looking slightly green, Royce went below once more.

Half concentrating on the latest Admiralty Fleet Orders, and half on a corned beef and pickle sandwich, he sat in his solitary chair, wedged in one corner of the cabin, a feeling of contentment and confidence making his tired body relax. Eight bells, young Leach would be taking over his first watch at sea from the First Lieutenant. He cocked his head back, the sandwich poised in mid-air, imagining the scene. The hurried confidences, the whispered instructions, then the eighteen-year-old boy would take over command of the bridge, with the care and protection of the M.T.B. and three merchantmen in his hands alone. A frightening thought, although on this route, through the swept channel of the vast East Coast minefields, there was not a great deal of sudden danger. Too light for E-boats, too dangerous for submarines. Aircraft were the main worry. Royce shook his head when he remembered the shooting of his gunners. They would have to get in a lot more practice.

He jumped nearly out of his skin as the voice-pipe at his elbow whistled urgently.

Leach's voice was shrill: "Sir, there's an object in the water. 'Bout a mile on the starboard bow!"

Royce didn't wait for a lengthy description; he flew up the ladder. Training his glasses round, while Leach fidgeted nervously at his elbow. It was a small, yellow shape, barely visible above the little waves. A rubber dinghy.

Lifting to the full throttle, the boat tore down to the fragile craft, the sailors momentarily forgetting their seasickness, and curiously gathering at the guard-rails. They slowed and circled warily.

The three airmen sat bunched in the pitching circular dinghy, their legs entwined in the centre, their heads jerking and nodding to the waves' cruel rhythm. Facing the M.T.B., one of the leather-clad figures stared blankly, his mouth hanging open.

A seaman shouted, his voice breaking the silence: "'Ere y'are mates, catch a line!"

The fools, thought Royce savagely, what a lot they've got to learn, then to Carver who had appeared hatless below him on the fo'c'sle: "Get them aboard, quick as you can. Lay them out by the tubes!"

Leach caught his breath sharply. "Are they . . . ?"

"Yes, dead as mutton," said Royce shortly. "Exposure."

In shocked silence the seamen watched, while Raikes supervised the grisly task. Eventually they had finished, and with a roar the boat tore off in pursuit of the coasters. Royce sighted the bridge Lewis gun and squeezed the trigger angrily. The bobbing dinghy vanished in a cloud of spray and bullets. No trace remained of yet another small part of the nation's sacrifice.

He sighed, and looked at Leach, who was standing staring back across their creaming wake.

"All right?" he queried sharply.

"Yes, sir, it shook me a bit, that's all. I've never seen—I never realized they looked like that."

Royce softened. "Forget it, Mid. I'm afraid there'll be others, before we're finished."

The hours dragged by, with little to take the hands' minds off that little drama. Two weary trawlers passed them, heading for the Channel, and in the far distance a corvette patrolled her allotted beat, otherwise the sea was theirs.

The three merchantmen kept in their steady, ponderous line, moving through the water at less than five knots, until eventually the novelty and tension of Royce's new authority began to sag, and he decided that the opportunity was ripe for getting through his impressive pile of ship's correspondence. Also, with him absent from the bridge, the other officers would be able to practice their capabilities as seamen.

He took a last look round the wintry scene.

"I'm leaving you in charge, Mid. Call me if there's any difficulty with navigation, or handling the boat"—he knew full well that he'd rather die first—"and I want to know about any strange aircraft, or ships. All right?"

"Oh yes, sir, I'll be all right now." The young face was eager.

With a smile Royce clumped below, and as he spread the papers across his desk, he noted with relief that the violent motion of the boat had eased considerably, and there was now merely a heavy roll, and a slow-moving M.T.B. will roll on wet grass.

Every so often he heard the soft creak as the rudder was put hard over, and he smiled, knowing that Leach was cautiously practising altering course, just as he had once done, when standing his first watch alone.

"Captain, sir!" The voice-pipe rattled.

"Yes, what's the trouble?"

"Wind has dropped, and there's a bit of a mist coming up from the east."

Royce digested this information carefully.

"Very bad is it?"

"Well, sir, I can't see *Bentaur*."

"What!" Royce leapt for the door.

Bentaur was the leading ship of the line.

As soon as his head cleared the hatch, he saw the thick yellow mist billowing like smoke across the water on their starboard bow. This was no mist, this was the real thing.

With five bounds he reached the bridge, and then as he scrambled up he steadied himself. No point in letting everyone see he was worried. Taking a deep breath, he strode to the front screen, where Leach's duffled figure peered anxiously forward.

By heaven, it was going to be a real pea-souper all right. He had seen it so often on this coast. One minute you have the damp, blustering wind, then a lull, and up comes the fog. The real enemy. He glanced at the other ships quickly, plodding along, confident and indifferent, but the leader had completely disappeared, wiped out by a sudden thick, swirling fence. What a dreadful business. He cursed inwardly. He could not tell the other two to anchor, and leave the *Bentaur* steaming on her own. In a couple of hours, his charges would be all over the place.

"Signalman!" he barked. "Signal both ships to reduce speed, and stream fog buoys. Port lookout, fetch the Coxswain!"

As the Aldis clattered, he assembled his thoughts. There was just a chance he could catch the other ship, and shepherd her round to the rest of the flock, before darkness fell.

Raikes appeared, imperturbable as ever.

"Take over, 'Swain. I'm going straight up the line after the leader."

"Aye, aye, sir."

With a deep-throated roar, the boat surged forward into the the gloom. In a second the fo'c'sle was hidden from them in a thick, choking cloud and reluctantly they throttled down, edging forwards jerkily, every man straining his ears and eyes.

Without warning, the deep-toned squawk of a fog-siren boomed out ahead, and Royce switched on the loud-hailer. Again, a bit nearer this time.

"That's queer, Raikes," he muttered. "He must be stopped, we're getting near to him so quickly."

Raikes nodded, his keen eyes scanning the steep bank of yellow which surrounded them. The M.T.B. seemed to be suspended in space.

Then they heard it, the steady pulsating beat of engines, thud, thud, thud, getting louder and louder.

"Stop engines!" His throat was dry.

Gently rocking on an invisible sea, they waited, their eyes smarting in the thick vaporous clouds.

Royce saw it first, fortunately, an imperceptible darkening of the fog-bank ahead, then with awful suddenness, two anchors zoomed into view, about thirty feet above their heads, like two huge eyes peering down at them. As he jumped for the voice-pipe, he got a blurred impression of the high, rust-streaked stem aiming straight for them.

"Full ahead port, hard a-starboard!" His voice sounded strained.

The engines roared to life, and the slim hull tacked round, as the giant iron bulk of the *Bentaur* reared over them, her siren deafening them. Helplessly they watched the full length of her dull sides sheer past, missing by mere inches. Then she was gone.

Sweating inwardly, Royce remembered the loud-hailer, his voice boomed and re-echoed around them.

"*Bentaur*, ahoy! Stop your engines! Anchor immediately!"

As if in answer, there was a sickening, tearing crash, and the sound of screaming metal.

"God, she's hit one of the others," hissed Raikes.

Carver had also appeared by this time, and stood awkwardly in the background, not quite sure of what was happening.

With Royce tense and full of foreboding, the boat crept back along her course. A dark shape loomed ahead.

The loud-hailer squeaked. "Are you damaged?"

A hoarse voice floated down to them.

"Nay, but ah bluidy well will be if I stop here with all these bluidy lunatics!"

They pressed on until eventually, guided by bangs and frantic shouts, they discovered the two ships, locked together, with twenty feet of *Bentaur*'s stem firmly sliced into the other's fo'c'sle. Faintly they could hear the sounds of an anchor cable running out.

They scraped alongside.

"*Bentaur* ahoy! What's the damage?"

There was a pause.

"Nothing much to us. But I'm afraid the other chap's lost a bit of weight!" came the cheery reply.

Royce fumed.

"Get aboard, Number One, and get them sorted out!"

Carver was relieved to be doing something, and went forward to await a rope ladder.

Royce paced up and down, deep in thought. Of all the damn fool things. It was obvious what had happened. The Officer-of-the-Watch on the *Bentaur*, seeing the fog, and realizing the others had vanished, had lost his head, and had come charging back to look for them.

Leach's face was at his elbow, almost imploring.

"It's all my fault, sir. I didn't know a fog could gather so quickly."

"Well, you know now." He didn't trust himself to go further, and Leach slumped miserably by the compass.

When Carver reappeared, breathless and rather grubby, Royce expected the worst.

"She's not making much water," he announced, "and the Captain says the fog's lifting already."

It appeared to be as thick as ever.

Royce shrugged. "I hope you've gained a bit of experience from all this, Number One?"

"Rather, I wouldn't have missed it for anything!"

Royce didn't know whether to laugh or swear.

"Dammit, you'll do, go back and keep an eye on things, before I lay you out with something heavy!"

He shook his head. What could you say to a man who thought a predicament like this was an interesting spectacle?

The merchant captain knew his weather lore, for within half an hour the fog began to move. It didn't lessen in density, it simply moved on, propelled by a languid breeze which obligingly wafted in from the north-east.

It was a sorry sight, like two jungle giants in a death struggle. *Bentaur* had come off best, but the other ship, an aged freighter with the strange name of *Madame Zest,* had a gap in her bows large enough to drydock the M.T.B.

The third ship had anchored of her own accord, and lay about a mile off, a cheerful spectator.

"Do you require a tug?"

Madame Zest considered for some moments.

"No thank you. We will be able to make about three knots. All damage above waterline."

"I'm sorry it had to be you."

"I'm not. We'll get a damn good refit out of this!"

Slowly and painfully they weighed anchor, and formed up in line, *Bentaur* slinking guiltily behind her wounded adversary.

Night fell, but it was clear enough to make station-keeping easy, although at that speed it would be difficult to do much more damage.

Raikes was humming softly.

"With your permission, sir, I'll carry on below to check that the ship is properly darkened."

It was a polite way of reminding Royce that he should not still be on the wheel.

Royce grinned, and as the Quartermaster took over the helm, he remembered Leach.

"Good God, Mid. You're quiet."

Leach stammered: "I thought I'd said enough, sir," he faltered.

"Forget it. I have. And when you've been at it a bit longer you'll come to expect this sort of thing every day of the week!"

Leach's face filled with gratitude. "Gosh, thank you for saying that, sir, you don't know what it means to me."

"But that's just it, I do. Now go and rustle up some cocoa," said Royce gruffly.

As the small figure scurried below, he chuckled.

"You're getting pompous already."

"Pardon, sir?" queried the helmsman.

"Oh, er, I said keep an eye on the leading ship," muttered Royce, flushing.

This was proving to be a better test for the ship's company than Commander Wright had visualized, apparently. Throughout the boat, there was a brittle air of jittery expectancy, as the seamen pondered and voted for what was going to happen next. Royce observed, with grim amusement, that few of his amateur crew would pass the port torpedo tube on their comings and goings, where, in the dim light, the dark canvas-covered bodies of the airmen lay lashed together, comrades to the bitter end. They will have to learn.

A pinpoint of light flickered ahead, the leading merchantman was making an announcement.

"Southbound convoy ahead, about two miles," repeated the signalman.

"How the devil," began Royce, then he remembered that from the freighter's lofty bridge, on such a comparatively calm sea, the dark shapes would be clearly discernible.

"Quick, make the challenge!" he snapped, but already the leading escort was creaming towards them, flashing menacingly.

As the lamps clattered, Royce reflected how different this type of procedure was to his normal round, where every ship seen in the night was an enemy.

Soon the silent, dark shapes had passed, and they had the sea to themselves again, and when dawn found them, cold and stiff, they were all longing to be rid of their heavy companions, who ambled so comfortably abeam of them.

Royce decided it was time to get a little sleep.

"Call me if anything happens, Mid, anything, you understand?"

It seemed as if the bunk had barely taken his weight, when the voice-pipe whistled again.

"Sorry, sir, but there's a destroyer coming up fast." The voice was nervous.

Again he mounted the bridge. The sea was a dull grey, tinged with blue blotches, sullen and heavy, but in contrast the sky had cleared and had been left drained of any colour whatever. The destroyer was approaching fast, and when only a cable clear, she slewed round, making an impressive wake, which made the M.T.B. roll heavily.

The metallic voice boomed across to them.

"Come alongside, I have fresh orders for you."

Royce came to life, putting off tiredness like an old coat.

"Leading Seaman Denton, stand by to collect orders! Coxswain report to the bridge. Mid, Starboard Watch stand by with fenders, we're going alongside."

The orders fell from his lips automatically, it seemed, without thought.

With engines growling, Raikes steered the boat under the lee of the dark grey hull, while Royce hung anxiously over the screen, watching the gap of water narrow between them. One good bang and a lot of written reports would be called for.

At the destroyer's rail, a Sub-Lieutenant waited with a canvas bag, which he lobbed neatly at Royce's feet as he passed.

The voice of authority boomed once more.

"I am detaching one of my corvettes for your little brood; you proceed to Rosyth and refuel. I understand you've got to take the Press to sea on your return trip. Cheerioh, we must get on with the war. It's still on, you know!"

Royce was at a loss for a witty answer. His mind was in a whirl. Rosyth, it was a miracle. Julia. A miracle! Feverishly he tore the envelope open. It stated baldly that he was to return to base after refuelling, and join the flotilla without delay. In order not to waste a journey, however, three war correspondents were to be given a ride down. To gain the right "atmosphere", no doubt.

Royce hummed gaily, as he bent over the chart, all his worries seemed unimportant now. Julia, at last.

"Steer north, forty-five west, half speed. Yes, what is it, Mid? What's the matter?"

Leach was hopping. "It's Number One, sir, he's still aboard the *Madame Zest*!"

Carver was still quivering when he swung aboard from a dangerous looking ladder.

"Strewth, I thought you were cross with me," he laughed. "Strewth! Didn't fancy stopping with those chaps. They're *real* sailors!"

With paintwork still gleaming, and the hands fallen in at their stations, the M.T.B. cruised easily alongside the oiling wharf, between a grubby corvette, and two M.L.s.

As the last rope snaked ashore, and the boat trembled to a halt, Royce called his officers to the bridge, and informed them of his new orders.

"The point is, that we've got to get down to it. Drill them till they drop if necessary. You saw how they reacted to those airmen?" He could have added, 'and you too.' "I have a feeling that we'll be seeing quite a bit of action when we rejoin the flotilla, so get 'em down to it."

"What time do the Press arrive, sir?" Carver's face was quite straight.

"Any time now, so you look after them till I get back. I'm just going up to the Signal Station."

"Would you like me to go, sir?" Leach was eager.

"Er, no, this is something special."

Was there a glimmer in Carver's eye? I'll stop that.

"Right, Number One, you can start now while you're waiting to fuel. Turn the hands to Damage Control Drill, and see if you can knock five minutes off the Fire Drill, too!"

"Aye, aye, sir!" But he still smiled.

In feverish haste, Royce shaved, and flung on a decent uniform, then hurried ashore, in search of the signal station.

After a somewhat agonizing route, between oil pipes, mountains of wooden crates, and a squad of Home Guard drilling, he eventually found the lofty, whitewashed building, overlooking the graceful sweep of the anchorage.

He was taken aback by the bustling efficiency of this vast establishment. In every direction messengers scurried, carrying important-looking signals, while from the various offices came the clatter of typewriters and teleprinters. He examined the doors carefully. The first stated, "Staff Officer, Communications, Please Enter". He gingerly opened it. Directly inside he saw a hatstand, upon which hung three caps, liberally covered with "scrambled egg". Quietly, he pulled the door to, and moved farther along the passage. The next door had nothing on it, so he opened it hopefully. A Wren stood facing a wall-mirror, and turned as he appeared.

"The Officers' Heads are at the end of the passage!" she announced hotly.

Mumbling apologies, Royce withdrew.

"Can I help you, sir?"

Royce turned, blushing, to face another Wren, who stood smiling at his side. She was obviously bound for the forbidden room.

"Well, yes," he answered thankfully. "To be perfectly honest, I'm looking for Wren Harston. She's in the signals branch here."

"That's right, she's in my watch. Just go up the stairs to the Tower, and ask the Second Officer. Her name's Mannering."

Royce was overcome. "Thanks very much; I've never been here before."

She gave him an old-fashioned look. "So I just gathered!"

The door swung behind her.

He started to climb the stairs, his heart heavy with excited and painful anticipation. This was to be an important moment, but his confidence had taken wings.

The S.D.O. and Signals Office presented to his anxious eyes a violent maelstrom of Wrens in white shirts and rolled sleeves, and millions of fluttering pieces of paper. The noise was overpowering, at least six of the girls were reading or repeating signals over an imposing battery of telephones, while others called mysterious numbers and references to each other. At an overladen desk, a buxom Second Officer was also using her telephone, it seemed for an argument, although she managed to drink a cup of tea at the same time. No one took any notice of him. He was invisible. He noticed that the back of the room was made of glass, and opened on to the signal "Veranda", where several girls, well wrapped up against the weather, were manipulating a ponderous signal projector. From another small door, a rosey-faced Chief Yeoman emerged, puffing at a pipe. It was comforting to note that he at least was surprised to see another man in the room.

"Lost, sir?"

"I'm looking for——" He stopped, his glance travelling across the Chief's massive shoulder. She had just come in from the veranda, stripping off her oilskin and cap, shaking out the dark curls, and rubbing her cheek with a mittened hand. Quite clearly, he heard her say to another girl, "There's an M.T.B. at the quay. What's she doing right up here?"

Blindly, he pushed past the astonished Yeoman, brushing a sheaf of signals from a desk, until he was right behind her.

"She's my boat. Care for a cruise?" he gulped.

She swung round, the large brown eyes wide with astonishment.

"Heavens! Clive! What on earth?" Her small hands fluttered about her grubby shirt, and patted her wind-blown curls. "What a way to find a girl."

"Only just got in. Got to leave in two hours. Can I see you somewhere?"

The words tumbled out of him.

"It's awfully nice to see you again. You're looking much better; a command suits you."

She studied his face. "It's difficult. But I'll see the Two-Oh."

Dazedly, he saw her hurry to the desk, where the telephone argument was progressing well. The Wren Officer glanced in his direction, and said to the telephone, "Hold on, Flags, but I still say you're mistaken!" and dropped the instrument heavily. It must have cracked "Flags'" eardrum.

"Don't be long, Lieutenant; you can have her for ten minutes. It's only because you're a stranger. Or are you?" The Wrens tittered.

Julia plucked his sleeve impatiently. "Come on," she whispered. "I'll get you out of here while you're still safe!"

Outside, a thin drizzle had started, and they found themselves walking quickly away from the building, yet in no particular direction. Royce was torn by many emotions. He was happy beyond words to find himself in her company again, but worried and uncomfortable because it was not working out as he had planned it in dreams, so many times in the past. It was like saying goodbye to someone very dear on a railway station, a scene which is enacted every day of the year. The two persons wait, saying nothing, unless it is to remark on the weather, or some such triviality, although their hearts are bursting. Then, as the train begins to move, out comes the pent-up flood, the hopes and fears. Too late, the precious time has been wasted.

Desperately, he turned, "Isn't there anywhere we can get a cup of tea or something? There's such a lot I want to say."

"Only a canteen hut the dockyard maties use." She pointed. "Over there."

The drizzle was getting heavier, and thankfully they pushed open the ill-fitting door of the little Nissen hut, and glanced round its spartan interior.

It was barely furnished with scrubbed tables, where the work-men could eat their sandwiches, and boasted a small canteen counter, and a pot-bellied stove which glowed warmly. Two men in overalls leaned against the counter, gossiping to the blowsy woman behind it. They all looked up in surprise, as the worried-looking young officer, and an attractive Wren in a rain-soaked oilskin, burst in on their private world.

Royce guided her to a bench by the stove, all the time drinking in every little detail about her. She took off her cap and shook it, hissing, over the fire, running her fingers through her hair.

"Phew, I'm afraid I'm not looking my best. I wasn't expecting company. I expect you're sorry you came?"

"Good Heavens, you look wonderful, really fine," he burst out.

She looked at him, the little secret smile playing round her lips.

"I believe you mean it, too," she said.

"I certainly do mean it, I——"

A harsh voice interrupted him.

"If you're wantin' anything t'eat, you'll 'ave to get it at the counter. We got no posh waiters 'ere!"

The two workmen grinned.

Royce fumbled in his pocket and banged down a sixpence.

"Two teas then."

He hurried over to her, slopping most of the tea on the floor. He heard the awful woman say something about "show 'em where they get off". He didn't realize the reason for her hostility, or care.

Julia warmed her hands on the cup, her large brown eyes thoughtful.

"I would have liked to get a closer look at your boat. It's like old times to see an M.T.B. again," she added wistfully.

She brightened suddenly, and for a brief instant he saw her brother's quick change of mood in her. "Still, never mind, tell me all about yourself. How have you been getting on?"

Royce took a deep breath. The initiative had been passed to him.

"Never mind about me." He leaned forward, looking into her eyes earnestly. "It's you I'm worried about."

No, that was no good. He tried again.

"I wanted to see you again, so much, you'll never know how much I've been thinking about you."

He waited for a rebuke, none came. She was listening closely, her eyes lowered. He noticed the dark curve of her lashes.

"You see, I don't think it's right. You're right up here, and I'm stuck down at the other end of the line. I want to be able to see a lot more of you," he ended lamely.

She smiled up at him, showing her even, white teeth. "But you hardly know me."

He suddenly seized her hand, desperately; this was it, now or never.

"Believe me when I tell you that I'd like to remedy that. I want to know you very much better, if you could put up with me."

He was aware that she hadn't withdrawn her hand from his, nor had she raised any objection. He trembled, quite unaware that the three characters at the counter were watching closely.

"I'd like that," she said softly, "but what shall we do about it?"

Royce's heart gave a leap, his inside felt like rubber.

"Do about it?" His voice rose with excitement. "You must come back to the old flotilla!"

"Shh!" she raised her finger. "You must keep calm."

He grinned sheepishly. "Sorry, but I'm a bit in the air. I'm not used to being with a beautiful girl."

"That's a good one. I'm in a mess at the moment!" But she was touched by his boyish sincerity.

He dragged his eyes to his watch.

"Lord, I'll have to be going," he groaned.

Together they stood up, buttoning their coats, and with obvious reluctance went outside to the din of the dockyard.

The canteen manageress sniffed.

"Didn't even drink their blessed tea!"

They were back by the signal station again, and they stood sheltering in the deep doorway.

"You didn't mind my coming here to see you?" he asked.

"I'm very glad you did. Now what have we decided?"

"Well, look, it's Christmas soon; what are you doing? Have you any leave to come? Were you going home?"

She waved her hand, embracing the harbour. "This is my home now," she said flatly.

He could have bitten out his tongue. "I'm a fool; I didn't mean that. Could you come down south?"

"To do what?" she questioned.

He laughed vaguely. "I don't know. I don't even know if I shall be out on Ops or not. But you could stay at the White Hart or something. Could you?" His voice was imploring. "It would be wonderful."

She wrinkled her nose. "I'd like that very much. Leave it to me."

She knew full well that if any other person had made such a suggestion it might have implied one thing only. But she knew that this anxious face was harbouring no such thoughts. Having decided that, she felt very much better, as if she had been given a new lease of life.

"I must be off now. My Number One is probably having fifty fits already."

He held her hands in his, unwilling to leave.

"Think of us sometimes, won't you?"

She nodded, her eyes serious. "Look after yourself, won't you?"

He released her, and stepped back, as if to sever the bond between them. Then he started to back away, while she still stood uncertainly in the doorway, her face wet with the rain.

He went suddenly hot, and he found himself clenching his fists. I must, he told himself, I'm not going without holding her just once. He squared his shoulders and marched back to her. She opened her mouth in an unspoken question. Taking her elbows in his hands, he gently pulled her towards him.

"Good-bye for now, Julia," his voice was shaky. "God bless you."

And with that, he bent and kissed her quickly on the mouth. For one brief instant he felt the smoothness of her skin, and tasted a new compelling warmth. Then he turned and blundered away. He then realized that she had not spoken a word. Fearfully, he looked back, but she was still there, her face shadowed by the doorway. She waved to him slowly, then she was gone.

He found himself climbing aboard, without realizing he'd made the journey back through the yard. Vacantly he returned Carver's salute, and walked blindly to the bridge. He wanted desperately to be left alone.

Carver pattered after him, pouring out details in a steady stream. Fuel on board; boat ready for sea; war correspondents in wardroom swigging gin; etc., etc.

He forced his mind to cope.

"Everybody on board, then? Right, make to Tower, 'Request permission to proceed', then start engines."

Thankfully he leaned against the chart table, his back to the signalman, who was busy flashing.

She didn't stop me, she didn't tell me I'm a fool, he repeated. "Julia," he said deliberately. He glanced round quickly, but no one had noticed his weakness.

"From Tower, 'Affirmative', sir."

The little ship slid carefully from her moorings, and with her decks glinting in the rain, and a growing white froth at her rakish stem, she steered down the channel.

"Signal from Tower," reported the signalman, surprise in his voice.

"They say, 'Happy Christmas', sir."

"What on earth do they mean? It's only November," muttered Raikes, as he spun the spokes of the wheel.

But Royce plunged across the bridge, swinging up his glasses. In an instant he had found, and focused on the signals veranda. The small, gleaming figure stood by the searchlight, waving.

With his glasses raised, Royce waved, until the Tower was hidden finally by a towering cruiser.

He swung round, and even the seamen fumbling with the wires on deck seemed to him to be perfect.

"A very nice trip, Cox'n."

Raikes sucked his teeth, and studied the line of buoys.

"All right for some, sir," he grinned.

CHAPTER SEVEN

THE return trip was successful, in that it was quite uneventful, for Royce at any rate. The crew still talked with misgivings about the first part of the trial run, the stiffened airmen, and the charging menace of the merchantmen in the fog, but Royce knew that it would change to a casual boast when they were ashore, in suitable company, and eventually it would warrant no comment at all. They would fall into the pattern and shape of the navy at war, provided they were allowed to live long enough.

He was thankful to be rid of the war correspondents, for to him they seemed somehow shallow and patronizing, with their ready flow of first-hand experiences, apparently from every battle-front but this one. They were ever ready to give full vent to such sentiments as, "you chaps are doing a magnificent job" and "nothing'll be too good for the boys in blue, when this lot's over". Of the merchant navy, too, "the heroes of the little silver badge". The last one made poor Raikes hurry from the bridge, pleading a stomach upset.

Royce had the impression that so many of these people, whose sole job it was to present the war news to the bewildered general public at home, did little to understand it themselves. He knew that this was a completely unfair assessment, it was just unfortunate that he had been blessed with such encounters as these. In addition, he wanted to be able to combine the running of his new ship, with thinking about Julia, and whereas at any other time, a new face, and a different viewpoint were more than welcome, these two great obsessions excluded all other possibilities.

He watched with anxious anticipation, as the seamen hooked on to their buoy astern of the *Royston*, keeping the engines ready to roar to the rescue should one of them develop a case of stage fright, and drop the lines in the water. The manoeuvre was successful, and thankfully, he shook hands with the "gentlemen of the Press", and saw them scramble into an immaculate pinnace which had been sent to collect them. Perhaps it was unfortunate that the cruise had been a blank, from their point of view, but no doubt imagination would rally to their support.

Within a quarter of an hour, he found himself aboard *Royston*, along with all the other C.O.s of the flotilla, assembled in the Operations Room. He was glad to see the old faces again, and to welcome the new. It was like doing something useful after being on the shelf. As he entered, Kirby, who stood by the wall charts, cleared his throat noisily.

"Ah, Royce, you're late. Your E.T.A. was thirty minutes ago. Was it not a straightforward run?"

The tired young faces turned towards him. He felt absurdly like a schoolboy, arriving after class had started.

"Had to drop my passengers, sir," he said shortly.

"Well, well, first things first, I suppose."

He turned his back, and stared at the charts, while Royce sank gratefully into a vacant chair.

"What ho, chum, how's the wee boat behaving?"

He glanced sideways into the wrinkled grin of Jock Murray.

"Fine, but I know now what a nitwit I must have been when I first started!"

"Who says you're not now?" Benjy hissed over his shoulder, grinning hugely.

"When you're settled, gentlemen?" Kirby's voice was sour.

He waited till they had given him what he considered to be suitably intelligent expressions, then continued. Royce thought he was looking much older.

"I think you're all fully conversant with this chart." They noticed with interest that it showed the approaches of Ostend, with a riot of colours depicting minefields, patrol areas, and other local data. He really had their attention now.

"Intelligence reports that the fast minelayers which have been playing havoc in the Channel, and across all the local shipping lanes, are now based here. Tactics, as we know, are to dash out at high speed by night, get rid of the mines, and hurry back before dawn. What we didn't know was how they cleared our destroyer patrols."

He paused, and dabbed his mouth with an immaculate handkerchief.

"We know now. Certain information is being wirelessed by agents here, in England, direct to France, concerning local convoys. Immediately the enemy receives this information, he dispatches minelaying aircraft to the Thames Estuary, or Southampton Approaches, or the south-west corner, 'E-Boat Alley' as some of our newspapers deign to call it, or sometimes all three at once. Immediately, all commands concentrate the sweepers, plus escorts, to keep the ports open, while the patrols are needed to cover the convoys from attack while all this is going on."

He surveyed them with a cold stare.

"It is at that moment, gentlemen, that the real menace slips from Ostend, and does its work."

They exchanged meaning glances.

"As the sea-distances are so small, yet our patrol areas so large, it is obvious, therefore, that we must destroy them as they leave the base. No other vessel can do it. No other vessel has the speed to get in and out before the enemy's air cover can be used. The task is ours."

A babble of murmurs broke out, and Kirby raised his hand.

"If you please, I suggest you would do better to address your comments to me. Now." He sat down.

Benjy scrambled to his feet, his jovial face slightly perplexed.

"How do we know when they are out, sir? I mean, they aren't going to drop us a wire, are they?"

There was a chuckle.

Kirby studied him pityingly.

"We will patrol in pairs, off this area, on every convoy departure night. Intelligence is giving us every support."

There was a loud groan, and Murray rose hastily.

"Would it not be better to get them when they're well clear? We could perhaps bag all of them."

"It would not."

It was quite obvious that Kirby was running true to form. He was tight on all other information. It was his party, and that was all there was to it.

As they leaned against the bar, sipping their gins, they discussed the matter at some length. One thought was uppermost in their minds, "Just so long as it doesn't mess up Christmas!"

The following day, while Carver exercised all hands, Royce sat in his cabin composing a letter to Julia. He was so full of the prospect of seeing her again, and in the foreseeable future, that he found it difficult to put into words such details as the weather, the food, and the state of his health. Eventually, he took the plunge, and told her exactly how he had felt as he waved her good-bye, and almost guiltily he popped it into an envelope and dashed on deck to catch the postman. As the duty boat chugged away, he sighed, the letter was on its way, he had made a start.

He leaned for a while against the port tube, and listened to Raikes patiently instructing five seamen in the use of a scrambling net.

"It's like this. You sling it down over the side, and then you send two of the strongest lads down on it. One at each end. They 'elp to keep the net steady, an' they can yank the survivors outer the water. Any questions?"

A spindly youth, named Cleavely, whom Royce knew already, as he had been earmarked as a potential officer, stepped forward.

"But if they're badly injured, you're not supposed to handle them like that, surely?" His voice was shocked.

"Either you gets 'em up, or you leaves 'em!" Raikes was final.

"It seems a bit antiquated to me. Why not rig a davit, or something?"

" 'Cause you'll be too busy, I shouldn't wonder," answered the Coxswain mildly.

Royce walked away, smiling. Raikes always had been one for understatement.

But altogether, as he made his tour, he found the hands very willing to learn their new trade, and obviously much awed by the other battle-scarred boats which lay around them.

An M.T.B. swung away from the sweeping arms of the loading jetties, and crept carefully out into the stream, feeling its strength, then having made up her mind, she gathered way and headed for the *Royston*. As she turned her wet, shiny sides towards him, he read her large, white numbers quite clearly. It was Watson's boat. With her huge engines purring magnificently, she cruised gently past, too close as usual, her sweeping fo'c'sle barely five feet clear. Benjy's red face, rising from a peculiar yellow flying suit and red scarf, was a tonic, and made up for the day's lack of sunshine.

" 'Ow do, chum?" he bellowed. "Coming up to the White Hart tonight?"

"Rather. Haven't been up there for ages."

The M.T.B. coasted round, the seamen professionally standing by with wires and fenders, and Benjy raised his megaphone.

"Don't look so envious. We can't all have good crews!"

Royce shook his fist, laughing. It was good to be back.

The White Hart was crowded that night, and already the air was thick and friendly when Royce, Watson, Deith and Murray strolled in. They somehow found an empty table and sat surveying the scene, and their glasses.

"Who's going out first on this crazy patrol stunt?" asked Murray absently.

"Guess," smiled Deith. "The Guvnor himself, of course, just to be sure that it's quite safe for us!"

Royce put down his empty tankard, and darted a quick glance at them.

"D'you think I can book a room here? Round about Christmas, for a friend, I mean."

There was an ominous silence, then Murray leaned across with an air of assumed confidence.

"Is it a wee bit of fun you're contemplating, me boy?"

Royce grinned uncomfortably. "No, it's nothing like that, you'll be sorry to hear. As a matter of fact I met a girl, but then you know her. What the devil am I trying to explain it to you for?" he exploded.

"Come, come, it's a Christmas wedding we'll be having!" Benjy was jubilant. "Drinks all round!"

"Oh, for Pete's sake, you're like that Coxswain of mine. You can't tell him anything about personal matters without getting a peculiar look!"

It turned out, however, that the hotel boasted six rooms to be exact, and the landlord, after studying Royce carefully, said he would keep one vacant until further notice. That wasn't too difficult for him, as he rarely had any paying guests at all, but somehow he made it sound like a gracious favour. As he said later to his wife, it was most unusual for a sailor to book a room for one. Ah, well, things were changing all the time.

By the time Royce got back to his table, he found Benjy in earnest conversation with two well-painted, and somewhat middle-aged ladies, who were sipping large gins, and giggling loudly, flashing their eyes round the bar, as if to announce their new conquest to all and sundry.

"Blimey, dear, you are the bleedin' limit, you are!" cooed the first, whose make-up appeared to have been applied with a paint brush. "What d'you take us for?"

Benjy shot a broad wink at the others, and patted her plump knee.

"Ah, here he is. I was just telling them you've been trying to find two bridesmaids for your wedding!"

Deith grinned wickedly. "One of 'em was Miss Chatham of 1918 too!"

"Saucy little bugger, ain't he?" sniffed the second lady, who was definitely swaying a little.

But, like all women of their type, they took the rough humour like a kitten takes cream.

As they rolled happily back to the pier, Royce was still being ragged unmercifully, and was almost thankful to feel his own deck under his feet once more. He would have to protect his Julia from all that, he decided. She might get the wrong impression.

Early morning showed a trio of corvettes, and three Asdic trawlers, slipping their moorings, and making their way to the boom-gate. The local escort group were on the move, quite unaware that Intelligence had forecast their routine task as being the mainspring of the trap. Somewhere out across the grey, mist-shrouded horizon, perhaps even now, the fast minelayers were loading their deadly eggs in readiness. Royce watched them go, listening to the slap of their wakes against his boat, and then resumed his breakfast. We shall see, he mused.

The morning was uneventful, except that an air of eager readiness hung over the flotilla. All the boats were fully ammunitioned, stored, and had fuel tanks well topped up. Only essential work took any of the men ashore, and then only within the dockyard.

Royce and Carver stood side by side on the tiny quarterdeck, smoking their pipes, and watching the sea-gulls, swooping and screaming as the cook emptied his gash-bucket over the side.

"What sort of photography did you do before you joined, Number One?"

"Oh, all sorts, free lance, dress models, anything really. If I could have done some of this stuff," he waved towards the ships, "I'd have made a packet."

"I suppose you met plenty of women on that work?" Royce was casual.

"Oh Lord, yes, I've had my moments!" He laughed bitterly.

"Nice, were they?"

Carver turned towards him, his eyes glinting. "Some of them. But if I may say so, none of them compared at all favourably with your Wren, from what I could see through my glasses!"

Royce looked astounded, and coughed hastily. "Oh, er, yes."

Carver grinned unhelpfully. "The sun is over the yardarm, sir, allow me to buy you a gin!"

Leach was slumped in a chair reading yesterday's paper.

"Two pinks, Mid, and make it snappy. And have a lemonade yourself!" said Carver affably.

"Soon be time to get the wardroom decorated, chaps," said Royce, making himself comfortable. "I think we'll have a few guests aboard."

They were discussing the possibilities, when the Quartermaster appeared at the door.

"General recall, sir. All boats to report when all hands on board."

Royce put down his glass carefully, digesting this information.

"Very good. Have we anyone ashore?"

The Quartermaster, a raw youth from Plymouth, with the peculiar name of Sax, frowned. "Only the postman, sir, an' he's due back now."

So this was it; something more than rumour was on the wind.

One by one the boats reported "Ready for sea" to an impatient Kirby, and after a further exchange of signals they slipped quietly, and fell in line behind the Leader, making for the open sea.

Once clear of the boom, they opened up their throttles, and snarled away from the local traffic, making an impressive and much-resented wash.

On the bridge, Royce was making last-minute arrangements for all emergencies which might arise with his unblooded crew.

Carver was making a great show of station-keeping, and taking careful note of the other boats. As junior ship, they held the position of last in the line; quite satisfactory really, as it meant that at night you only had to keep station on the next ahead, without the additional panic of some ambitious skipper hitting you hard in the rear. Royce smiled to himself, as he knew from experience that Carver was watching his every action, so that when left in sole command of the bridge he would overlook nothing. So long as I don't forget anything as well, he mused.

Eight shining hulls, keeping perfect formation, they scudded along the choppy, grey surface, throwing back a dirty yellowish spume, which rose crisply from the sharp bows and rolled away on either beam, flattening and mingling with the uneasy waters. Kirby, in his newly arrived boat, 2002, led the flotilla, and Watson, as Second-in-Command, was fifth in the line. Royce levelled his glasses ahead, trying to catch a glimpse of Kirby's new First Lieutenant, a young ginger-haired fellow called Crispin, but the small forest of stumpy masts and flickering ensigns obscured everything but an indistinct blob. Poor chap, he thought, not a very nice appointment for a new boy.

"It'll be dark in about an hour and a half," he said, glancing round, "I expect Kirby'll order 'Test guns' soon."

"D'you think we'll be all right if we meet this little lot?" Carver lowered his voice.

"Oh sure, we'll be all right. But you must impress on your gunners to hold their fire until they're quite sure of a target. Otherwise it's so damned confusing for the bods on the other boats."

Kirby's lamp began to wink.

"Test guns, sir," reported the signalman quickly.

Royce glanced at him sharply. This was Paynton, an under-sized boy of about eighteen, his wide eyes nervous already. That wouldn't do, so much depended on him at all times. Royce made a mental note on future morale-boosting, and then nodded to Carver.

"Right-ho, Number One, I want every gun to fire a short burst on a safe bearing, but until they get used to it, I want each gun to fire separately. Check 'em yourself."

"Aye, aye, sir."

For some reason he started with the heavy Browning machine-guns aft, probably to be out of vision from the bridge. After a pause they burst into life, a muffled and insistent rattle, like a million woodpeckers hard at work. Next the port Oerlikon. A bit wild here, the burst was much too long. That was A.-B. Rush, a big, pimply-faced man from Kent. Rather a sullen type he appeared to Royce. Trevor, on the starboard Oerlikon, behaved like a concert pianist. He caressed his well-greased gun like a delicate instrument, then with a final pat, he fired a short, steady burst, the tracers whistling smokily away towards the horizon. A cool enough gunner there, all right. Leading Seaman Denton performed comparatively well too on the big Bofors cannon on the fo'c'sle. It was an intriguing weapon, which had its ammunition inserted in clips like a giant rifle, and fired in a sharp, remorseless series of ear-splitting cracks. Denton would be all right anywhere. A little old for Coastal Forces perhaps, but very dependable. His crew, an A.-B. named Manners, who looked for all the world like a jovial hippopotamus, especially now, in his shiny oilskin, and Larkin, a little Ordinary Seaman from Ireland, also seemed happy enough, and had already neatly christened the gun "Vera" with bold, imposing lettering.

Carver came back smiling.

"All right, were they? I thought they were quite good really."

"Bloody awful!" answered Royce cheerfully. "Now you take over the con, I'm going to have a word with the torpedo crew."

And relishing the open-mouthed expression of dismay on Carver's face, he lowered himself to the deck.

The L.T.O., Currie, saluted. "Tubes correct, sir." He was a ruddy-faced young man, with the easy confidence of the mechanically-minded. His two assistants, Barlow and Ash, both very new and very young, stood silently watching their Captain, as his quick glance took in the long, slender tubes poking out from either side of the bridge, their intricate mechanism coyly shrouded with little canvas spray hoods.

"Very good. I just wanted to impress on you that, although the guns do a helluva lot, you are the chaps I want to carry right up to the Jerry's front door, where you can get rid of your babies."

He let his words sink in. He remembered the trawler crossing his sights, the noise and the pain. God preserve these three from all that.

"Where d'you come from, Ash?" he asked suddenly.

The short figure in the Ursula suit stiffened.

"From Surrey, sir," he faltered.

"Oh, what part?"

"Dorking, sir. I was a delivery boy at the big butcher's there, sir."

"I'm a Surrey man, too," said Royce pleasantly. "And what about you, Barlow?"

"I was a runner, sir," he grinned apologetically.

"A what?"

" 'E means a bookie's runner, sir," explained the L.T.O. "A good skive before the war."

Royce returned to the bridge. What a delightful occupation, a bookie's runner, but what would be shown at the labour exchange, I wonder?

Leach had joined Carver, and they both turned to greet him.

"It's getting awfully cold," observed Leach, wrinkling his freckled nose distastefully. "I wonder if I could arrange some kye?"

"Yes, and fix it for all hands, on and off watch, while you're at it," added Carver.

Royce nodded approvingly. The lessons were being learned.

Leach scurried below to organize the glutinous mixture beloved by all British sailors, and Royce stood by the screen, narrowly watching the next ahead, 2003, another new Fairmile, commanded by a hatchet-faced Lieutenant named Mossbury. He had been transferred from Harwich, and was already showing signs of strain. A bit "bomb-happy" they said. He saw with interest that his crew were exercising at the smoke floats or something. Didn't believe in slackness anyway.

Whatever lay ahead, on the sullen horizon, the boat felt good, growling away beneath him, making all the bridge fittings chatter in harmony. Sax, the Quartermaster, gripping the wheel in gauntletted hands, whistled softly through his teeth, his mind elsewhere, while Paynton was clumsily splicing a new flag halyard, apparently engrossed.

"Going to be a clear night, Number One," he announced at length. He looked at his watch. "We'll split into pairs at sixteenthirty. Kirby and Page are going in first, to smell out the ground."

Carver rubbed his hands vigorously. "Let's hope something starts soon then."

More cocoa, more signals, and they found themselves beginning to lose sight of details on the next ahead: the ominous signs of a sudden nightfall were making themselves apparent.

At the prearranged time the boats split up and, like the tentacles of an octopus, they moved from a central pivot, reducing speed, and coasting smoothly over their allotted areas.

Their own companion was to be Deith, in 1815, and as the others faded like shadows into the deepening gloom, the latter swung his boat parallel and hailed them.

"We'll keep about two cables apart! If anything happens it'll come from the south-east."

That was now on their port quarter.

"Just the night for them, too!" shouted Royce. "Three local convoys out, no moon, but nice and clear!"

With a few more comments, they drew apart, and settled down on their lonely patrol. Somewhere behind them, Kirby would be manoeuvring into position to get behind any enemy vessel which ventured into this area of the Channel.

"If they come out, won't they be heavily escorted?" Carver's face was a dark shadow by his side.

"No, they depend on speed. If they're spotted they beat it without dropping a thing. They don't want half the sweepers in the Home Fleet up here undoing all the good work."

Leach appeared. "Well, how far in do they expect to get?"

"Oh, they've managed to get pretty close to the coast before now, I understand. It's not so much the number of ships they sink, in actual fact, it hasn't been many, but they tie up every blessed thing while the poor sweepers are going over the whole blessed area."

"Hmm, what a waste," observed the thoughtful Carver. "I suppose if we catch them, they'll send out some more?"

"Maybe." Royce sucked on an unlit pipe. "But if we don't catch 'em, well, it might mean that the Mid here'll miss his Christmas in harbour!"

"And my C.O." said the Midshipman quickly. They laughed.

"Split up, and check all the guns. I know it's been done, but I want to be sure that the loading numbers keep a steady flow of ammo, if required, that is."

Having got rid of them, he turned his attention to the signal-man.

"How d'you feel, Bunts? Bit different from the Signal School, eh?"

"Yes, sir, but I think this is just fine. It's just that actually being on active service is rather queer. I mean, sir, it's so unlike any other sort of feeling, isn't it?"

Royce could sense the boy staring at him through the gloom.

"Yes, indeed. You should be quoted in the House of Commons, my lad. I can just hear the Honourable Member for Somewhere-

or-Other saying, 'Active service is rather queer!' Yes, I think it would go down very well," He laughed.

"Oh, I'll be okay when I'm doing something," said Paynton earnestly, "I've got to be."

" 'Course you will, Bunts," said Royce casually. "I'll have the hide off you if you run up a dirty ensign, or something!"

He turned to the dim compass. He'll be all right. I don't wonder at his being jumpy, he thought. You feel so naked and unprotected on an open bridge.

"Aircraft about somewhere," muttered Sax, glancing overhead at the vast ceiling of stars.

"Not much good, even if it's a Hun," observed Royce. "We can't fire at anything but our special target, I'm afraid."

"Glad they don't know that too," said the Quartermaster dourly.

A brisk breeze had arisen, whipping the black, heaving carpet around them into uncomfortable, hard little waves, whilst above them the velvety sky was sprinkled with millions of pale stars, which seemed higher and smaller than usual. Not even a puff of cloud was to be seen, and no moon pointed her finger across the dark surface to guide them. It was perfect for aircraft, but a naval game of hide-and-seek would be extremely chancy. As he ran a gloved hand along the port screen, Royce felt a crunchy crispness under his palm. A sea-frost was forming early, in readiness to make the gunners lose their feet, no doubt. Those gunners, would they keep their heads? he mused. It was comforting to see the brief wake of Deith's boat in company.

Overhead, the aircraft droned hollowly, as if lost, and then slowly faded away. There was a flurry of foam, as Deith's boat moved closer again.

"We'll drift a bit, I think!" he shouted. "We're most likely to hear something than see any blasted ship in this blackout!"

The motors died away, and they jogged up and down, the silence only broken by the slap of the waves against the hulls, and the rattle of loose equipment on the invisible decks.

Carver had taken up his station on the fo'c'sle, and on both boats the hands were closed up at first degree of readiness. Raikes, who had taken over the wheel, drove one fist into the other, and said nothing. Paynton, his face an oval blob, leaned purposefully over his locker, focusing his glasses astern. Occasionally there would be a cough, or a nervous laugh from the deck beneath them, followed by a quick rebuke from some equally well-hidden authority, then there would be only the sea noises once more. A large fish jumped violently out of the water close to the boat, and fell with a heavy plop, before any comment could be made. The flag halyards shook and rattled in the keen breeze, and a pencil rolled off the chart table with the clatter of a tree falling. Royce's taut stomach began to settle. It looked as if it was to be a fruitless business after all. In a way, he felt vaguely relieved. Royce dived his head under the apron of the chart table, and switched on the feeble light. Here, shielded from the cold spray, and the electric air of taut vigilance, with the familiar and homely figures, and pencilled lines, a few inches from his nose, he felt the private security and comfort of an ostrich with its head in the sand. The absurdity of this comparison made him relax slightly, and even smile, and picking up his dividers he began to measure up the narrow distances from the enemy coast. Was it possible that, just a few miles away, Belgian people lay in their beds, or plotted against their invaders, or even stood looking out to sea, hoping for freedom? It was a strange thought.

He shifted his glance up across the grubby chart, chafed by wet oilskins and disfigured by mugs of cocoa, until he found the familiar names of the English coast: Ramsgate, Newhaven, and poor Dover, which daily shook to the thunder of the German cross-channel artillery. So many little people, all trying to live, and make the feeble strands of life spin out just a bit longer. He straddled his legs wider, to steady himself, and he felt a cold draught penetrate up the rear of his oilskin and explore his nether regions. He started again to examine his pencilled marks, and again his mind wandered happily away. What of Julia? What would she be doing now? The reality of seeing her had already drifted into a dream-like mist of a fairy tale. He sighed, and rubbed his cheek, already sore from the salt.

"Oh sir! Sir! There it is!" Payton positively squeaked. "The signal!"

Royce came back to the present with a jerk, and cracked his head on the side of the table. Cursing, he swung his glasses to his eyes, but they were unnecessary. Away to the south-east four stars were falling slowly and gracefully from the heavens. Two red over two green, the signal. Somewhere between these flares and his own ship lay the enemy. His mind raced, and his ear dimly recorded Raikes saying gruffly, "You just remember to report properly next time, Bunts. This ain't no fireworks display."

A shaded light winked across the water, as Deith excitedly prepared for the chase, then, with a steadying rumble, the engines took control of the resting craft, and pushed them gently forward, with just enough force to raise a small bow-wave, and start the hull quivering with life and power.

The trap was sprung, as somewhere around the black wastes of the Ostend approaches, eight M.T.B.s converged, like the mouth of a poacher's bag, secure in the knowledge that a fast force of Motor Gunboats would by now be hovering on the horizon, in case support would be required.

As they crawled slowly forward, like hunters after game, every eye, ear and muscle was strained, until the very nerves cried out in protest. Men swallowed hard, their throats suddenly dry, others fought off waves of sickness, or cursed helplessly at the black wall ahead of them. It was almost a relief when the horizon lit up in a savage, white glare, which made their eyes jerk in their sockets, and, seconds later, a dull roar boomed hollowly around the cave of night. The glare died slowly into a flicker, which left a red carpet draped across the horizon, getting smaller and smaller. In that mere tick of time, before the light completely died, Royce's powerful lenses caught the briefest hardening of the shape in the dull red glow, almost as if someone was standing in front of him, half blocking his view. He blinked, and lowered his glasses. Nothing, not even the glow any more to guide him.

Below him, he could hear Carver chattering excitedly with his gunners.

"Silence!" he grated savagely, and darted a quick look at the compass, his brain working furiously.

He raised his glasses again, but the ebony seas mocked him.

"There was something peculiar about that," he muttered. "There must have been something just about to cross in front of the fire. If only the glare had held a bit longer!"

Suddenly, he took a deep breath, his mind made up. There had been something, there was a ship out there, slinking stealthily back home, hoping that the confusion of the fire would take all attention from her. It was now or never.

"Bunts, signal to Lieutenant Deith, 'I am going to engage', got that? Coxswain, full speed, steer south-forty-five east!"

It seemed an age, but in fact seven seconds passed and then, with a vast, ear-shattering snarl, the torpedo boat leapt forward, the beast unleashed. Royce grabbed wildly at a support, as the bows rose up in front of him, sending two great banks of solid white foam roaring away on either beam. Aft, the narrow stern buried itself deeply, as the whirling screws bit down deeper, and harder, until the rushing waters cascaded past and over it like walls of solid snow, gleaming starkly against the black nothingness beyond.

Deith's boat fanned out to run parallel with them, and a brief glance showed Royce that the boat's keel was visible as far back as her bridge. His own boat must be like that too, he marvelled, meaning that every so often, as she bounded over the waves, he and the bridge were suspended in space. It was incredible.

"Stand by tubes!" he barked, his voice harsh and unnatural, and to Carver he bellowed, "Open fire as soon as your guns bear!"

Heaven only knows what Leach is thinking about down on the bucking stern, with his machine-guns, he thought, probably trusting to luck, and the ability of his skipper, as he had once done.

A fine thing it would be if his eyes had played him false, and they were tearing down on nothing, or another British boat. There could be no second chance. Their engines would already have warned any ship within miles of their attack.

On and on, blindly, with teeth gritted, and eyes smarting. Perhaps the bearing had been wrong, perhaps they had overshot the target, perhaps—God! What was that? The M.T.B. bucked and reared like a mad thing, recovered, and thundered on. He lurched to the rail and peered away across the port beam. Just briefly, before their wake surged down and obliterated everything, he saw a white-crested bank of water roll away astern. What the—then, like a shaft of light, his brain cleared. They had just crossed the wake of another vessel, moving fast!

"Hard aport!" he yelled, and the boat reeled round, engines screaming, the blurred shape of Deith's boat following suit.

They straightened up and scudded after the invisible ship.

Still they saw nothing but their own glittering cascades of foam, heard nothing but the eager bellow of power beneath them, which mingled with their own heartbeats, and own silent prayers, and shouted curses.

They were quite unprepared for the next move, which was to be made by the enemy.

Without warning, a sharp, pale blue beam of light sprang out of the darkness, wavered, and then fixed on to Deith's boat. One minute there was nothing, and the next instant, this terrible searchlight had sprung across the water, pinioning the startled M.T.B. in its eye-searing glare. Although the little boat twisted and turned desperately to shake it off, the light held them pitilessly, until to Royce it looked as if the boat was held stationary on the end of a pillar.

"Quick, Carver! Open fire! Get that light!"

Desperately he pressed the bell switch by his waist, and heard the tinkle echo round the boat.

Instantly the Bofors came to life, and the rapid crack-crack made his head sing. The port Oerlikon and Browning quickly followed, and Royce almost wept with rage and helplessness, as he saw the lazy tracers climbing wildly clear of the target.

Deith's gunners, mesmerized and blinded by the great, unblinking blue eye, fired but a few shots, no one knew where they fell, and when the German eventually decided that the drama was being prolonged unnecessarily, he too opened fire, making a red and white triangle of fire, the apex of which centred upon the M.T.B.'s bridge. Royce saw the pieces of woodwork whipped into the air by a hail of bullets, and a tattered sheet of armour plate rose like a spectre in the harsh light, and vanished over the side. He saw, too, the tiny figures fall from the guns, one running wildly, flapping at the air, before pitching through the rail into the boiling waters.

"Hard over, Raikes, round on her other beam. I'm going to engage with torpedoes!"

Moving with the grace of a bounding leopard, they swung in a semi-circle, Royce speaking carefully and slowly to the torpedomen, ignoring the spasmodic fire of the guns, and concentrating every fibre in his body, shutting out the horror of the other boat in its death-agony. Once on the ship's disengaged side, he saw her clearly silhouetted by her own gunfire, more like a small destroyer than a minelayer. But as they tore towards her, the great searchlight began to swing round, seeking them out, and as it crossed her own deck, he saw the dull gleam of the mines in their trestles aft. This was the target, their goal.

"Fire!"

And even as the beam deluged them with light, Royce knew within his heart the torpedoes would run true. Automatically, his brain sorted out details, discarding the unnecessary.

"Hard a-port, drop smoke floats." That was it, just like the instruction books, just like he'd heard Harston and Kirby say so many times before.

The dense smoke rose from the float, and hung ghost-like over the searchlight's beam, making the scene unearthly, which it indeed was. Raikes hadn't moved except with his hands, as he manoeuvred the boat towards safety. Paynton beat the screen with his fists, and shouted wildly, "Why don't they hit? Please make them hit!" His prayer was answered, as the gleaming fish struck home into the entrails of the minelayer.

Surprisingly enough, the noise seemed deadened. It was more like a vast, hot breath, which engulfed the whole boat, making their throats retch and choke, their faces sear. Already blinded by the searchlight, they missed the vast, red column of water which towered over the stricken ship, and as the light was suddenly extinguished, so too the ship was removed from their vision, blasted into oblivion. For a shocked period of several minutes they kept moving, while the sea hissed and splashed with flying and falling fragments, then when all was still, Royce swung the boat and headed back at maximum speed, making for the tiny, flickering beacon in the far distance.

Deith's boat was well down by the stern, and blazing fiercely. They could quite clearly hear the roar and crackle of woodwork, and the sharp bang of exploding ammunition, as they speeded desperately to help. Within a hundred yards of their sister, it happened, a billowing yellow cloud of flame, a crackling roar, and the hiss of steam, as the cold waters hungrily engulfed the shattered hulk.

Royce stared dully, numb.

"Stop engines. Stand by scrambling nets!"

His voice was far away. He knew he would never see Deith again, never hear the gay laugh, or feel the warmth of companionship. The pattern was still falling into place.

A shout from the fo'c'sle.

"Two men in the water! Port bow!"

Clumsily, they scrambled aboard, two of Deith's seamen. Bleeding, coughing out the raw fuel, and whimpering softly. Royce saw Leach's set face, as he guided them gently below. There were no others.

"Another explosion, dead astern!" yelled a voice, and they saw a queer glow, shaped like a pine tree, rising higher and higher, until its power finally faded, and it was wiped away for ever.

The three minelayers had been removed, as ordered.

Royce forced himself to concentrate his full attention to the boat, and shut out all personal feelings, and he listened with an almost detached air, as Carver and Leach reported to the bridge.

"I can't understand it," muttered Carver shakily. "Not one casualty, not one blessed man! Just three small holes aft, one through the transom, and the others on the starboard quarter. All above the waterline."

"What about you, Mid?"

"No damage, sir." Leach's voice was trembling. "Gosh, you were wonderful, if I may say so, sir, I thought we'd had it!"

Raikes coughed. "Another signal, sir. 'Re-form'." He pointed over to the flashing light.

Royce stretched, feeling suddenly cold and stiff.

"See what I meant about gunnery, Number One?" But he was no longer angry; he knew that after this they would shoot straight. For their own sakes, and for him.

"Yes, I feel badly about that. But they tried, sir; it wasn't their fault."

"I know." Royce forced a tired smile. "We were lucky really."

Carver swayed slightly to the boat's motion. "It wasn't luck. You pulled it off on your own."

"Don't be such an ass!" said Royce crossly. "Get some hot fluid sent round. We're getting out of here fast!"

The stormy dawn found them streaking rapidly for home. Kirby led his flotilla, and several of the boats bore signs of battle, but apart from Deith and his men, the casualties had been very few. To the great men at Whitehall, it would appear to be a clean-cut operation, and the public might not even hear about it.

Kirby's boat turned, and wallowed heavily down the weaving grey line of boats, his loud-hailer calling loudly for reports of damage and casualties. As he drew level, Royce strained his aching eyes across the narrow gap, and tried to ascertain the extent of Kirby's operations. He noted that both his torpedoes had been fired too, and part of the boat's side was marked in long claw-like scars. He was not left in doubt for long.

"Been busy, Royce? I hear you bagged the second ship?"

"Yes, sir." A pause. "Deith bought it, I'm afraid."

He cursed himself and the unreality of this life which forced him to speak with studied indifference of a true friend, butchered before his eyes.

"They come and they go, and I'm sure he would have preferred it this way. I got the first minelayer, and Mossbury took the other. Quite a good show, really."

Royce fumed. Had the man no feelings? As if any breathing,

sane, or intelligent being would choose to be fried alive! He choked back the hot words. Instead, he merely lifted one glove in acknowledgement. As far as Kirby was concerned anyway, the incident was closed.

Kirby turned away, and increased his speed towards the head of the line, while Royce watched him go with smouldering eyes. What this war is doing to us, he thought bitterly.

Although dawn should have made its full appearance, a heavy, wet mist, mingled with a soaking drizzle, kept the visibility down, and darkened the skies with a fast-moving blanket of grey vapour. It was very depressing, but typical.

With the first light, came a visible change too in his command. Instead of an air of woolly indecision, the hands grouped silently by their guns, matured and woven together as a crew overnight.

The only openly cheerful face was that of Paynton, who had taken part in, and recovered from, his first action like a nervous patient after a difficult operation. He was, literally, glad to be alive. Even as Royce slumped moodily against the port screen, he could hear the boy's soft humming, as he busied himself, oiling his Aldis lamp. He had taken to the "trade", but as Kirby had put it, "They come, and they go." Royce laughed aloud, and Raikes twisted his head sharply, his eyes shrewd.

"Told yer they'd learn, didn't I, sir?"

"You did, 'Swain. I thank the high heavens we had the chance."

"Aircraft dead astern!" yelled Paynton suddenly.

As the signal rippled up the line of boats, the men forgot their chilled bodies, and numb fingers, and reached for the tools of their new profession. As he raised his misted glasses, Royce heard Denton's gruff voice from the Bofors.

"Nah then, *proper* shootin', this time!"

There it was, a black beetle, whose shape expanded and contracted as it felt its way through the gaps in the cloud.

"What do you make of her, Number One?" he called.

In his bright new duffle coat, and gleaming cap, with the fair hair curling from under the peak, Carver looked every inch the film star, about to make a momentous action or statement, which would bring an empire crashing.

Instead, after a long look, he said lamely, "I think it's a Wellington. But then again, I——"

"She's divin'!" snapped Raikes suddenly, and pulled himself protectively against the wheel.

Out from the cloudbank now, gathering body and menace, the plane skimmed lower.

Royce sighed. "Take your time, gunners, then open fire!"

The plane was pointing straight at him, its twin propellers making silver circles on either side of the bullet nose. Then a throaty rattle filled the air, and a hail of cannon shells changed the oily waters into a frenzied dance of flying spume. Then it was gone, darkening their decks for a brief instant with bat-like wings, the black crosses directly over the masthead.

With a roar of engines the pilot pulled out of his dive, and turned for the safety of the clouds.

Crack-crack-crack! went the Bofors, and in jealous haste the Oerlikon joined in, sending a spray of shells after the intruder. Above the thunder of their own power, they could still hear the more resonant note of the German circling, apparently dissatisfied with his first efforts.

"*That* wasn't no Wellington, sir!" shouted Trevor, from behind his gun. "Gave me quite a turn!"

There was a snigger, and Carver turned to the bridge for support. "Rather like one though, don't you think?" He was never at a loss.

"I think she's coming back!"

The aircraft zoomed into view, this time from the port quarter, her guns spitting as she dived at them. The rattle was so sharp, that it deprived their brains of power or motion.

Brownings first this time, then the others, and from the wreaths of smoke around Cameron's boat, it was plain to see they were being well supported.

"Two aircraft, bearing red four-five!"

Lower than the first plane, the twins swept in barely a hundred feet off the sea, their wing-edges afire with yellow, spitting flames. For God's sake, Kirby, do something, he cursed.

"Ninety degree turn to starboard!" yapped Paynton.

Thank heavens, Kirby was bringing his boats into line abreast, giving maximum fire-power to the aircraft. There would be no unhappy straggler to be picked off at leisure. They surged round, working up to full speed, the air splitting with their full-throated snarls, the water burst asunder with a vast wall of twisted bow-waves and rolling wakes. Every boat came to life, the professional and the amateurs, old hands, and the new. Butchers' boys, clerks, bus conductors, and fishermen, with eyes narrowed, teeth gritted, and stomach muscles pulled in tight. Royce pulled the stripped

Lewis into his shoulder, and squinted into the sights. It was all blurred. The grey background, the dark bottom-edge of torn water, and then into line the speeding, wafer-thin silhouette. He squeezed the trigger, and felt the ancient weapon pummel his shoulder. The first plane swung wildly away from the mounting cone of destruction, but the twin held his course. Something thudded into the bridge deck, and a chorus of shouts broke out from aft, and the plane was over them, revealing the shark-like underbelly. Twisting and turning, she swung away, but lacking the support of the other, she was done, for as she passed free of the boats, a savage line of bursts rippled her from nose to tail, making her stagger. Then, with a forlorn cough, one engine died, and a thin plume of black smoke billowed out of her cabin. Lower and lower, and the drizzle almost blotted her out, when at the point where sea met sky, she struck, bounced, and pancaked heavily, in a shower of spray, and vanished.

Of the other two planes there was no sign. There was only the flotilla, now needlessly speeding in their determined little line.

"Detach from group, and pick up survivors, if any," read Paynton.

"Blast!" He's done this deliberately, he thought furiously. Probably thinks I'll go off my head, because of Deith.

"Acknowledge!" he snapped.

It was lonely being away from the others so soon, and with the throttles down, they pushed back into the teeth of the weather. He called the officers to the bridge again.

"What was all that damn shouting aft, Mid?"

Leach smiled nervously, his pink face pinched and haggard.

"Sorry about that, sir. The Brownings were running short of ammo, and the loader, Cleavely, didn't arrive. Both my chaps reckoned they could have finished that Jerry, if they could have given him the whole magazine-full."

"Well, have a word with him. I won't have anybody going chicken in the middle of a stunt like that!"

Was that me talking? The harsh captain? What price nervousness now?

He turned quickly to Carver, lowering his eyes.

"Well?"

"Oh, jolly good, sir. I said this is a lucky ship. Just a few more holes for the Chippy, and that's the lot! I'll get the Jerry airmen to clean the boat up, if we find them!" He laughed.

"I can manage without your humour, thank you!" he snapped. He saw Carver's face stiffen. "And I'll trouble you to brush up your aircraft recognition. Make yourself useful!"

He stalked to the front of the bridge, furious with Carver, and more so with himself. They think I'm jumpy, too hidebound, that's what it is. He looked quickly at Raikes, but the Coxswain's face was quite expressionless. He was aware that Leach had gone forward to supervise the scrambling nets, and noted with childish satisfaction that he looked extremely miserable.

Raikes glanced over his shoulder. "Go and fetch the new ensign, Bunts, you'll find it in my cabin."

Captain and Coxswain stood alone, side by side, as they had on the sinking M.T.B., Royce thin-lipped and strained, and Raikes steady-eyed and thoughtful.

"You remember that time we shot up the oil-tanker, off the Bight, sir?"

"I remember. I hadn't been aboard very long at the time."

"That's right, sir. I recall the C.O. saying afterwards that he thought you'd make a very good officer. You know why, sir?"

"You tell me."

Raikes looked steadfastly ahead, at the small white horses. His face was grimly determined.

"Beggin' your pardon, sir, but he said it was because you'd managed to joke about it, although you'd been through a private hell of your own."

Royce felt a lump in his throat.

"That was quite the politest telling-off I've ever had! Blast you, Raikes!"

"Aye, aye, sir."

"And thanks very much, too."

"S'all right, sir. I've served long enough to know that whatever ship you're in, gashboat or flagship, the junior officers always think their C.O.'s past it! You'll never change the Andrew."

Royce felt fresh and clean, and forgot his inner pain, and when the signalman returned to say he couldn't find the ensign, he was very tempted to say that he had only been sent out of the room while his captain got a fatherly "bottle". Instead, he said, "Well, get some cocoa then!"

They eventually found the airmen floating in their brightly-coloured life jackets, their faces turned up towards the boat in a trio of shivering, coughing wretchedness.

The scrambling net splashed down, and two seamen, Jenkins

and Archer, climbed down until their legs were lapped by the icy water. Denton kept a watchful eye from the rail, while Carver and Leach made up the reception committee. Royce noted with great satisfaction that the gunners maintained a vigilant watch on the skies while the boat lay motionless, although their curiosity must have driven them frantic. Yet another lesson learned.

The three airmen stood dripping on the deck, gazing round in ill-concealed astonishment. They must have thought it unlikely they were going to be found.

One of them, a small, pudding-faced youth, held his shattered hand inside his tunic, his features twisted in agony.

The tall one, fair-haired and tight-lipped, snapped at him angrily, and then drew himself very straight, as Royce stepped down from the bridge.

"I shut be greatfull ef you gould attend to mein unter-officer, Captain. He is slightly vounded!" he said stiffly.

Royce nodded, and Leach stepped forward with the first-aid satchel.

The other German, a hard-faced brute of a man, with a shock of dark curls, snarled angrily.

"It's a pity ve dedn't get you first!" he snapped. His accent was slightly American.

The officer rattled a string of obvious harsh comments, and the airman stood stiffly to attention, looking rather ridiculous.

The officer bowed slightly. "The man is a fool, Captain. Ignore him. He has not learned to, er, how do you say, play the game?" He smiled briefly.

"Take them below, Mid, with an armed guard."

As the strangers were led below, Royce shook his head and sighed.

"I don't know, Number One. I thought they'd look different somehow. You know, the Master Race and all that. They're very like us to look at, aren't they?"

"If I may say so, the comparison ends there. Cocky little bastards!"

Leach came back panting. "All tucked up nicely. Two survivors and three Jerries. In the wardroom and P.O.s' mess respectively."

Royce climbed the bridge ladder, then stopped, his foot poised halfway, and looked down into their expectant faces.

"By the way, I think you both did very well. Oh, and Number

One, I'm sorry I bit your ears off. It was completely unjustified, so forget it."

Carver beamed. "I'm sure I deserved it, sir!"

"No, I forgot something. But I was reminded of it just in time," he said quietly, and hurried up the ladder.

They had an inspiring welcome at the base, complete with sirens, and witty signals from every direction.

Not the least of Royce's pleasures was to see that as the three captured Germans were being escorted ashore, one of the war correspondents of his Rosyth trip was standing open-mouthed on the jetty, and looking suitably impressed.

He joined the other two in the wardroom as soon as they had snugged down.

"Won't worry you now, blokes, but there's just one little bit of advice I can give you to save any embarrassment in the future. If you get yarning with the other officers, never mention those who've 'had it'. No matter how much they meant to you."

He felt suddenly tired and heavy, and looked dully from Carver to Leach, trying to fathom out their reactions to his words, which to him already seemed meaningless and pointless.

Carver was holding out one slim hand, studying it thoughtfully.

"Look at that, shaking like a jelly!" he mused, and for a moment, Royce imagined he had not heard.

"I think that idea you've just mentioned is a damn good one. When a chap has been through what you've put up with in the past, I think it must be extremely necessary to sever all strings, and especially when you've lost a friend or two."

He nodded several times, like an old man, his fair hair flopping over his high brow.

Leach looked up defiantly.

"I wasn't a bit scared! I couldn't see a blessed thing from down aft! But that M.T.B. burning like that . . . I kept thinking, it might have been us!"

Royce shrugged heavily.

"Anyway, it wasn't us. And by God it never will be if I can do anything about it!" he said savagely.

Carver stood up slowly, unwinding himself like a cat, and stretched himself languidly, wringing from his tall frame all the discomforts of cold, tiredness and anxiety.

"It's my humble opinion, sir, that we've nothing to worry about, so long as we have a professional for a C.O."

Royce looked glassily at him, trying to think of an answer, trying, too, to fight off the fear that he was letting the strain of command crush his will power. He felt so very, very tired.

There was a tap on the door, and Paynton stepped in.

"Signal from Senior Officer, sir. 'All First Lieutenants to exercise hands at Fire Fighting at eight bells'."

"Very good," smiled Royce. "Acknowledge."

Carver fell back into his chair, like a deflated balloon, his face crimson.

"Well, damn me!" he exploded. "I mean to say, that really is a bit too much, sir! Doesn't he think we need a bit of rest?"

Leach stood up, yawning.

"Well, I'm for forty winks. Don't let the Fire Brigade make too much noise, will you, Number One?"

"Oh Hell! What shall I do?" Carver was desperate.

"When I was a First Lieutenant, I used to ask that very question," grinned Royce, feeling slightly better. "Call me if you need inspiration."

Carver flung his slippers across the wardroom at the departing Midshipman, who turned and eyed him sadly.

"Quos deus vult perdere prius dementat," he quoted solemnly.

"Come again?" gurgled Carver.

"A rough translation is, 'Those whom the gods wish to destroy, they first send mad!'" And he ducked quickly away round the door.

As Royce lay back in his bunk, he smiled contentedly to himself. With a crew like this he had to be all right. They were too precious to be sacrificed without a battle. He closed his eyes.

CHAPTER EIGHT

ROYCE sat comfortably at the wardroom table, a cup of tea at his elbow, methodically checking and re-reading the impressive piles of ship's correspondence, and demand-notes. He leaned back, and started to fill his pipe, noticing as he did so, the bowed head of Leach on the opposite side of the table, apparently engrossed in correcting the Admiralty Fleet Orders.

Outside the warm shell of the low cabin, he could hear the steady swish of icy rain against the wooden hull, and the squelchy thud of the Quartermaster's measured tread above his head. Every so often, a powerful squall would rake the harbour reaches, lashing the sheltering vessels, and he would hear the mooring wires groan a protest, as the boat jerked back sharply. He tried to shelve the problem that had been gnawing at his mind since they had returned to base. He glanced again at the bulkhead calendar. Ten days to Christmas. That was it. Julia's present. The great problem. It had to be something special, but what? He frowned.

"Something wrong, sir?"

"Er, no, Mid, I was just thinking about Christmas," he said, truthfully.

Leach dropped his scissors and glue brush.

"Yes, it'll be my first in the Navy," he said excitedly. "Will we have a party?"

"We will indeed. We'll ask everyone if necessary. Just to please you. Commander Wright has stated that the flotilla will be in harbour for Christmas. Unless there's a flap on, of course."

Carver entered, and hurried to the stove.

"God, it's parky on deck," he shivered. "Just got the last of the stores stowed away. I've sent the hands to tea."

Royce nodded, "Ah, Mid, I want you to go to the Coxswain, and ask him about getting some turkeys for the lads. See if he's got it in hand."

"Aye, aye, sir."

"Look, Number One," he said, when Leach had left them, "I want your help rather badly."

"Oh sure," answered Carver airily, "Anything you name. Except Fire Fighting, of course!"

"Ass! No, this is rather serious."

He paused, searching for words, while Carver studied him, his face expressionless.

"My, er, Christmas guest. Well, she, that is—— Oh damn it! What I mean is, I want to give her a decent present, and really I haven't a clue about these matters."

The other man eyed him shrewdly.

"And as a loose-living sort of character, I might be able to advise you, eh?" he laughed.

"Good heavens, I didn't mean that! But you did say you'd had quite a bit of experience in this field."

"You haven't anything in mind, I suppose?"

Royce coloured slightly, "Well, I did think of a nightdress. You know, something special," he mumbled.

"Leave it to me. I know a chap in London who can get just the thing. Black Market of course, but as money is no object," he lowered one eyelid dramatically, "I dare say it will be something special all right!"

"You don't think that she'll get the wrong idea, do you?" Royce was anxious, and no longer cared if it showed, "I mean, you know how it is."

"Well, I think I know how it is. But you shouldn't have to worry too much. Much better a present like that, than a set of knitting needles or something!"

"Phew, what a relief! You really are a pal. When can you go?"

"I'll 'phone the bloke tomorrow morning, and fix it up. I've no doubt he'll post it to me. We've done quite a bit of business in the past.

He smiled wickedly.

"How will you know her size?" queried Royce suddenly. "I don't know myself."

"Not to worry. It doesn't matter a lot, and I got quite a good look at her. Of course, I may want her to come over for a fitting!"

"You blighter, that'll cost you a large pink gin," shouted Royce, "But thanks, anyway, and I give you full control of my purse."

Leach came back, shivering.

"Raikes said you'd already got the turkeys fixed up with the N.A.A.F.I. manager," he said peevishly, "I got all wet for nothing!"

"Oh, er, yes, Mid, I forgot. Captain's privilege, you know."

He and Carver exchanged a quick glance of mutual understanding. The manœuvre had been completed with success.

Ordinary Seaman Jenkins poked his head round the door, the light reflecting from his gleaming oilskin.

"Air-raid warning's just gorn ashore, sir," he croaked, his eyes darting round the warm comfort of the wardroom. "Wind's rising from the nor'-east, an' the rain's gettin' worse," he added gloomily.

Royce desperately wanted to say, have a drink to warm your inside, but custom and discipline prevailed.

"Very good. Tell the Coxswain to close up the gunners as soon as it's a Red warning."

It was customary for the flotilla to assist the town's anti-aircraft guns when the enemy came too near to the port.

Shortly after the Quartermaster's announcement, *Royston* signalled, "Air-Raid Red", and Carver mustered his guns' crews around the dripping weapons. Away across the town could be heard the rumble of ack-ack fire, and on the dark, storm-wracked mantle of the horizon, they saw the red flashes of their exploding shells. Tiny pin-pricks of light.

Then steadily, above all other sounds, above the slap of water, the moan of the wind, and the pattering of rain, rose the uneven beat of powerful engines. The too-familiar, Berrum-Berrum-Berrum, that night after night heralded the approach of death and destruction to men, women and children. It was peculiar to think that thousands of feet above them, on this bitter evening, dozens of human beings squatted on little stools, and peered at complicated instruments, solely intent upon this one devilish purpose.

There was a dull roar from the town, and a bright flash, followed by an echoing rumble of falling masonry. The first bomb had fallen. Another and then another, and dimly across the dark anchorage they heard the clamour of fire bells. Slowly the bombers faded away, out of reach of the probing guns, and the *Royston* signalled, "Stand Down".

"Too high for us, anyway," mused Royce, as he squinted upwards against the driving rain. "I think the party's over for tonight. They were probably on their way back home, and had a few bombs to get rid of."

As the hands clattered thankfully back to the warmth of the messdecks, the three officers stood watching the flickering fires ashore.

"Not much of a raid, anyway," muttered Leach, "The A.R.P. seem to have it all under control."

"Yes, I think I'll take the First Lieutenant ashore for a pint," said Royce suddenly, "We're not wanted tonight, and it'll do us good to stretch our legs."

"Hmm, yes, and I could make an important 'phone call, I suppose," answered Carver drily.

"What, leave me out here at the buoy alone?" squeaked Leach. "Never mind, Daddy won't be long. . . ."

As Carver remarked, as they sped swiftly across the dark waters of the harbour in the motor dory, Leach was really tickled pink at the idea of playing Captain for a while.

While the confident Carver made his way to a telephone box, to make the all-important arrangements, Royce wandered around the squalid, little streets which backed the dockyard in an uneven semi-circle. In one, there was an unusual disturbance, as firemen, air-raid wardens and police, hacked and pulled at the shattered remains of one small house, the front of which lay scattered across the roadway. In the poor light of shaded hand-lamps and torches, he saw the pathetic, broken furniture, stripped wall-paper, and a picture hanging at a peculiar angle, whilst the air was thick with the smell of recently extinguished fires. Even as he watched, he saw two uniformed figures carry a small, limp bundle into the lamplight, and as they laid it carefully down on the pavement, he saw the old lady's silver hair moving faintly in the breeze. It was he knew, the only movement she would ever make again. He turned away bitterly, and strode back to the yard gates, where Carver was just leaving the booth.

"All set," he grinned, "He'll send the loot as soon as he can. But in any case, he promises to have it for you in time for Christmas."

Royce shook himself, and felt suddenly cold, "Thanks a lot, let's go and get that drink."

"Have you by any chance noticed, Number One, how the Jerries have been stepping up their raids in this area?" he asked, as they crunched blindly over some broken glass.

"Well, I had got the idea that it's been worse since the time I came here," confessed Carver thoughtfully. "Any reason, d'you suppose?"

"The way I see it is, that we've been doing so well over the other side in the last few months, and Jerry's determined to cut us off at the roots, so to speak. The dockyard, oil tanks, and I suppose they'll also be after the poor old *Royston!*"

They pushed open the doors of the White Hart, and Carver paused, "So long as they don't get any more accurate, I don't care!"

Royce thought of the little figure, with the silver hair, it was likely that a lot of people would be better off if the bombers had found their real objectives.

The hit-and-run raids on the East Coast by day and night, did little to slow up the mounting offensive by Coastal Forces against enemy shipping, however, and even four days before Christmas, after a long patrol, which necessitated the flotilla's refuelling at Harwich, with a taut Kirby in the lead, they had sent a German destroyer to the bottom. The flotilla's biggest warship kill so far. While the other officers celebrated the victory aboard the *Royston*, Royce paced impatiently up and down his cabin, six paces either way, as he waited for Carver's return from shore. Disaster was staring him in the face. The promised gift for Julia had not arrived from London, and Carver had dashed ashore to get to the bottom of the delay. After an age had passed, he heard the splutter of a motor-boat alongside, and he forced himself to sit staring at the door.

Carver's face, however, was cheerful.

"He gave me a terrific line about the hold-up. Said it was his partner's fault. But he promises definitely it'll be here tomorrow evening."

Royce sighed deeply.

"Thank the Lord for that!"

"He's not a bad chap, really, he won't let me down. Never has yet, anyway."

"Hmm, it would appear that you're a pretty fast lot!" said Royce gravely.

"Yes, as a matter of fact, I had thought seriously of writing a book about my experiences. Complete with photographs, of course. 'How to be Happy Though Married' might make a good title!"

As they were not intending to put to sea during the Christmas period, unless "so required by a given emergency", all the youthful captains got down to cleaning and decorating their boats, in order that the entertaining of guests might be all the more satisfactory. As Royce, followed anxiously by Leach, poked and pried into messdeck and engine room alike, he felt satisfied that his own boat had never looked better. Brass gleamed, and grey paint shone brightly, while the gay contrast of paper chains and coloured home-made lanterns brought gaiety and humanity to both the crew's quarters and the wardroom. He laughed aloud, when he saw an open cookery book, displaying a sizzling turkey, lying in the galley. He turned to Petty Officer Raikes, who was hovering in the rear.

"D'you know, I've never seen such a thing in a galley before, Cox'n."

"An' neither 'ave I, sir. We must be makin' naval history!"

In the wardroom he congratulated his exhausted First Lieutenant, who lay limply in his chair.

"Thank you," he groaned, "I feel as if I'd done the perishing boat on my own."

"That'll be the day," muttered Leach.

"I thought we'd get all the routine over tomorrow, Christmas

Eve," interrupted Royce hastily, "We'll do the whole thing ourselves, we'll even have a pukka Divisions, on the fo'c'sle, if it's
fine, and on the mess-deck, if it's wet. Then Christmas, we'll have
a very gentle routine, Number One, with heaps of food for the
lads. How does it strike you?"

"Fine," answered Carver, brightening, "I'll get the gramophone working again, and we'll get a couple of hymn records
from the Base Padre. By the way, sir, what time does your guest
arrive?"

"Oh, er, about twelve hundred. She'll go to the hotel first, and
then I'll bring her straight aboard for a drink. See that the Gin
Pennant is flying. We might as well have a few characters here
for her to see."

"And to give you a little support?" queried Carver innocently.

"Hah, a fat lot of support that'd be!"

"And what about Christmas Day, are we having any guests
then?"

Leach was already making mental calculations.

"Oh sure, the flotilla and *Royston* will hold Open House all
day, I believe. So you'll be all right, Mid. She can come."

The boy blushed to his eyebrows, and Royce thought, "I'm a
fine one to talk."

That evening they arranged their cards around the wardroom.
From other ships, from parents, distant relatives, and friends. It
was a pointed fact that Leading Seaman Denton, and Campbell
the Telegraphist, were the only married men out of the whole
ship's company, and as Royce carefully pinned Julia's neat card
over the boat's photograph, he reflected that he would like to be
the third.

Voices sounded outside, and the Quartermaster peered in.

"Officer's mail, sir, an' one parcel for the First Lieutenant.
Registered."

A silence fell in the wardroom as the seaman left, and all eyes
were on the package in Carver's hands.

"Well, here it is. Open it, sir," grinned Carver, and thrust it
towards him.

Royce took it awkwardly, and turned it over and over in his
grasp. Leach produced a knife, and he found himself tearing off
the wrappings. He never knew quite what he had expected, but
the article which suddenly came to light, left him speechless.

"Good God!" he gasped, "Look!" he sounded helpless, which
he was, "I can't give her this. There's nothing of it!"

It lay on the polished table, across an open copy of Admiralty Fleet Orders. It was black, a thing of beauty, but almost transparent. In fact, as the round-eyed Leach leaned forward, he gasped, "Gosh, I can read the new A.F.O.'s about fire buckets right through both sides of it!"

Carver was a little shaken, but did his best not to show it.

"Well, that's it," he said defiantly, "It happens to be the best that cash can procure. I didn't know the old blighter was sending me quite such a passionate outfit, but now that he has, believe me, any girl'd give her eyes for it!"

"Blast your eyes, this isn't any girl!" spluttered Royce. "She'll get the wrong idea completely. And now the shops are all shut till after Christmas! What have you done!"

He sat down heavily, staring at the nightdress, while the others stood uncertainly by the table. Carver, as usual, rose to the occasion.

"I think some very excellent pink gins are called for. And a great deal of thought."

"Make mine a very large one," said Royce weakly.

"What are you going to do?" Leach was hopping with excitement.

Royce reached for the glass, "God only knows!"

"I can't imagine what you're worried about," said Carver evenly, "After all, she won't be expecting a present at all, so you can say you got it in Ireland, that you won it, or something."

"But I've never been to Ireland, and in any case, you don't just win things like this!"

He reached out cautiously, and touched it. It was beautiful. In fact, the thought of Julia actually wearing it made his head swim.

"Blast it!" he croaked, "I'll have to think of something."

Funnily enough, it was Leach who settled the matter, when Royce had practically acknowledged defeat.

"Why not tell her the truth? Tell her what really happened."

The other two stared at him, and slowly their faces relaxed. It was a solution. Not quite what Royce was looking for, but a solution. The decision was made, the box and wrapping produced, and the contract was sealed.

The rest was up to him.

The morning of Christmas Eve was a memorable one, both for the weather, and for the spirit of friendly comradeship which hung over the boat. Normally, the idea of Divisions, and a church service, with all the necessary business of changing into best uniforms, and other forms of regimentation, is repellent to sailors serving in small craft, but today, as they fell in by watches on the long fo'c'sle, Royce sensed a feeling of oneness with these men, whom he led, and who trusted him. Curiously enough, he had never seen them all together on his own boat before for such a ceremony, as normally in harbour, Church Parties went to the Depot Ship, which boasted all the facilities, and he felt pride and affection, as he saw the Petty Officers, and Leading Seamen, reporting their men to Carver. Even Leach, immaculate in his new uniform, looked a different person from the tousle-headed boy he normally saw about his duties.

Carver had mustered the hands, and called them to attention. He turned smartly about and saluted.

"Divisions mustered for Church, sir," he snapped.

Royce returned the salute, and for a brief moment they stood eye to eye. Carver alert, and waiting for the next order, and Royce wondering what it was that the Navy had, what tradition or quality made these men, who had been raw amateurs like he had been, into part of the Service. Had made them a team, proud and jealous of their heritage, although if questioned, all would have denied it. He could not find the answer. Instead, he said, "Carry on."

Carver turned, and carried on.

As the order "Off caps" was given, the Church Pennant broke out smartly from the yard, and a silence fell over the boat. Tucking his cap under his arm, Royce stepped forward, his eye taking in the scene as if it was a picture.

The seamen stood in their straight lines, rolling gently to the slight harbour-swell. Here and there, a blue collar flapped in the crisp air, and a lock of hair moved. Overhead, a high-flying gull screamed angrily, and somewhere, in the far distance, there was a rumble of cable, as a frigate dropped anchor.

His clear, steady voice gave strength and realism to the prayers, in which sailors have joined for many generations. He lifted his eyes from the book, as he came to the lines which he knew by heart, and looked at the lowered heads, and the proudly curling ensign.

". . . be pleased to receive into Thy Almighty and most gracious protection, the persons of us Thy servants, and the Fleet in which we serve. Preserve us from the dangers of the sea, and from the violence of the enemy. . . ." It was all there.

After the short service, he carried out his inspection, speaking to every man, and trying to fathom the mysteries of each moulded face. Raikes, the calm professional, compact and steady as a rock, and in the line behind him, Manners, looking more like a hippopotamus than ever with his bulging stomach. Ash, the ex-butcher's boy, Archer, the Newfoundlander, with his permanent grin, and Petty Officer Anderson, looking quite out of place without his overalls and grease-gun.

Finally it was over, and the hands were dismissed, with a Christmas greeting, to go for their rum.

Royce stood in his cabin, eyeing his reflection in the glass. It was nearly time to leave for the station, and he could feel the excitement rising within him.

He gave his jacket a final brush, and went on deck, where his two officers waited by the ladder.

"Motor-boat just put off from the railway jetty to collect you, sir," announced Leach.

"Good luck," smiled Carver, "Bring her back safely."

"I'm going to need all the boat's share of luck, that you're always talking about," said Royce, eyeing the distant railway. "Still, thanks all the same."

The station was practically deserted, as all the people with Christmas leave had long since departed for their homes, and as Royce strode up and down the grimy platform, with nervous impatience, he wondered what stroke of fate had decided that he and Julia should have met on this very place, such a short time ago.

He stamped into the unheated waiting-room, with its smell of carefully preserved dirt, and looked unseeingly at the security posters. "Careless talk costs lives" announced one, and "A loose lip means a lost ship" said another. He frowned and looked at his watch, for the twentieth time. I wonder if—he pondered, and then he heard it, the distant, shrill whistle of the engine. He wrenched open the door, and watched the little train wheeze into the station, and stop with a final shudder. Porters shouted hoarsely, doors opened and banged, and several passengers alighted. A few workmen from the aircraft factory outside the port, some marines, several sailors, and then, when his heart was beginning to sink, he saw her step down from the end carriage, and stand quite still on the platform. For a full moment, he stood rooted to the ground, watching her, once again thrilled by her nearness, and filled with the desire to protect her from everything, and everybody. The next thing he knew, his legs were hurrying him towards her. She turned, and recognition forced the frown from her face. Instead, she smiled, and Royce, remembering their last good-bye, was, for a moment, completely flustered.

"Why, hello, Clive, I thought you'd forgotten, and I'd be left here stranded," she laughed.

"I may forget a lot of things, but I'm not likely to do that," said Royce softly.

"You look very well, Clive. It's nice of you to ask me down like this, although I'm quite sure I'm wrong to accept."

Then seeing the look of consternation on his face, she smiled up at him.

"I'm only joking, I'm jolly glad I came. Really."

He seized her by the arm, and picking up her case, steered her to the waiting taxi, the words falling over themselves, as he told her of the ship, the hotel, the fact that he wanted her to go aboard for lunch at once, and a hundred other things.

She was touched, he was so obviously pleased to see her, and so eager to make her happy. She had not known much happiness since the death of both her parents, and then her brother, but now, as she sat beside this taut, young officer, with the worried eyes, she felt in her heart, that a real, warm happiness was returning.

"Here we are. The White Hart," announced Royce, bundling out of the cab, "How long will it take you to get ready?"

"Give me ten minutes," she laughed, "After all, a girl needs about that, after coming all the way from Scotland!"

He watched her being taken up the wide staircase to her room, unable to take his eyes from her, drinking in the easy grace of her body, as she stepped up the worn carpet, leaving the aged porter breathless. The landlord came out of his little office, and nodded a greeting.

"So she's arrived, has she?" he cracked his lined face into what to him meant a smile, "I hope you're going to behave yourself, although I wouldn't blame you if you didn't."

Royce met his watery gaze, "Don't worry, I'm afraid you'll probably see more of her than I will. Look after her, won't you? I don't care what it costs."

"Oh, the real thing, is it, young feller?"

"I sincerely hope so," said Royce fervently.

The old man put his hand on his shoulders.

"Thank you for saying that. You've done quite a bit to restore my faith in human nature. Come and have a whisky while you're waiting. She'll be half an hour, if she says ten minutes."

Royce knew that it was a rare event for the landlord to "push the boat out", and he knew too that he was now officially out of the mere "customer" status.

The whisky was as genuine as the old man's good wishes, and he leaned against the bar, feeling the spirit warming his inside.

An army Lieutenant suddenly looked up sharply, and sucked in his breath, and the soldier, even as Royce was looking at him, put down his glass, nudged his companion, and said quite audibly, "Gosh, Tom, what a lovely girl!"

Royce turned his head casually, and froze. Julia stood uncertainly at the foot of the stairs, one small hand resting on the rail, looking round the large room. But a new, different Julia. He had never seen her in civilian clothes before, and had never really considered the matter. She had changed into a close-fitting green tweed costume, with a sort of yellow scarf about her throat. Her black hair shone and reflected the many bright lights in the room, and as her eyes found his, they lit up with such beauty, that he heard his own heart pounding.

She walked quickly towards him, her whole body seeming to revel in the freedom from uniform. No one spoke, but Royce knew that every eye was upon them, admiring her, and envying him.

"There, fifteen minutes exactly. Well, twenty, anyway. I hope you didn't mind my changing?"

"Mind? Good heavens, no, you look marvellous," said Royce loudly.

Colour rose in her cheeks, and her eyes softened.

"Shh, Clive, you're as bad as you were at Rosyth, except that this time we're not drinking tea!"

"Shall we go, Julia?" he said her name carefully, like a jeweller handling a precious gem, "I'd like you to meet my friends."

As they left the bar, the landlord refilled his glass, and drank it straight down. Then, refilling it yet again, he raised it to the swinging doors. "Happy Christmas to you both," he said huskily.

The harbour made a brave sight in the watery sunshine, as they reached the jetty, and Royce was surprised to find the motor-boat already waiting for him. Carver was to be congratulated. As they swept up the line of mooring buoys, he pointed gaily to the M.T.B. which swung easily at her wires.

"There she is!"

"Oh, very tiddley, she looks quite big from here."

They motored alongside, and the bowman hooked on. Royce guided her carefully up the ladder, and on to the deck. His own deck. Another surprise awaited him there, for Carver and the Quartermaster, both in their best uniforms, stood at the salute, while Leach and Raikes stood a little farther inboard, at attention. Obviously Carver was putting on a good show.

He now stepped forward, bowing slightly to the girl who stood at the gangway, an amused smile on her lips.

"Welcome aboard," he said solemnly, "May I, on behalf of 9779, bid you greeting, and wish you a Happy Christmas, in advance."

"This is my dreadful assistant," grinned Royce, and waving the others forward, "And this is Colin Leach, the Third Hand."

They shook hands warmly, and then Julia turned to Raikes.

"You, I know, don't I?" she said softly, "It's just like old times, isn't it?"

Raikes took her hand in his large paw, and studied her carefully.

"It's good to see you again, Miss Harston," his voice was gruff, "It'll be better'n old times now."

"If I may make a suggestion, sir," there was a slight edge in Carver's suave manner, "Could the Mid take your guest round the boat? the Cox'n can be Chief Guide."

"Well, I thought that was to be my privilege," Royce was puzzled.

"Ah yes, sir," said Carver smoothly, "But there is a small service matter which now requires your attention. I think you will be able to clear it up soon, and then I'll get the cocktail shaker out."

"Er, very good," answered Royce, "Would you care for a quick tour, Julia? I'm afraid I've got some little job to do."

"Ah, the weight of command," she smiled, "All right, but I warn you, I might hear some awful things about you!"

As she was ushered away by her attentive escort, Royce turned in bewilderment.

"What the devil's gone wrong now? We haven't got a flap on, have we?"

Carver looked uncomfortable.

"Well, no, sir."

"Come on, spit it out!"

"The S.O.'s on board. In the wardroom."

"What, Kirby? That's a bit unusual, but what the hell, nothing's gone wrong lately, has it?"

"I think you'd better see him yourself, sir, if you don't mind."

Royce strode impatiently to the hatch, and as he swung down the gleaming ladder, he swore hotly to himself. If Kirby thought he was going to mess up his biggest moment, he'd get a shock, why, it was unthinkable—he jerked aside the curtain, and stamped in. Kirby was sitting awkwardly in one of the big chairs, and for a moment, Royce couldn't think what was different about him. His uniform was as impeccable as usual, and his head just as well groomed, but when he tried to rise to his feet, it became all too obvious. He was completely drunk. Royce was so aghast, that he just stared. It was unbelievable. It was as if he had discovered a curate in a disorderly house.

Carver was breathing heavily behind him.

"You see, I didn't know what to do with him," he hissed.

"What the blazes are you two gabbling about?" Kirby swayed sideways, and clutched at the scuttle for support. His eyes were no longer piercing, in fact they were glazed, and he seemed to have the greatest difficulty in focusing them.

"I just wanted to, wanted to——" He stopped, and fell back against the side, his hair flopping over one eye, while his mouth opened and shut noiselessly.

Royce snapped into action.

"Quick, get the coffee to work, before the others come," and to Kirby, "Very nice of you to take the trouble, sir, I'm sure. Please take a seat."

It was like a dream, it seemed impossible that this could be the perfect, self-contained superman, that they had come to loathe. He was fumbling inside his jacket, and mumbling.

"Saw you bring a, hic, bring a young lady aboard," he paused, and looked up at him glassily, "Thought you might like to shee a picture of my wife?" He wrenched out his wallet.

Royce fumed impatiently for the coffee. For once he felt quite at a loss. The Commander was waving a faded photograph towards him, and he got a blurred impression of a frail looking lady standing on a beach, squinting into the sun, and waving at the camera. Royce had no idea what had brought the man out to the boat, but he suddenly felt terribly sorry for him.

"Very nice, sir," he said at length, "I hope we shall have the pleasure of meeting her one day."

Kirby didn't appear to hear, but carefully poked the picture back into the wallet.

"Well, thash all, Royce!" and he stood up with a jerk, knocking an ashtray to the deck. "I jush wanted you to know," and he leaned heavily on Royce's arm, "that I've made something of thish flotilla, an' I'm bloody well proud of it." His stomach bubbled menacingly. "And whash more, I'm bloody well proud of all of you. Thash all!"

And grabbing his cap from the peg, he lurched to the door, where he wheeled round colliding with Julia and Leach, to whom he bowed.

Leach went white, and Julia looked from one to the other in amazement.

"Oh, this is Lieutenant-Commander Kirby, our Senior Officer." Somehow the explanation seemed unsatisfactory, and Royce hurried on.

"Is his boat alongside?"

"There was a motor-boat approaching," said Leach, his eyes fixed to Kirby, as if mesmerized. "Shall I help the Commander on deck?"

"No, I'll see him over the side," said Royce hurriedly, and guided Kirby to the ladder, where, with Carver's assistance, he struggled on deck. Commander Wright's red face beamed up at them from the motor-boat.

"So there he is, the rascal! Led me a proper dance he has!"

And he reached up to assist a safe descent into the boat. As Kirby slumped into the cockpit, Wright craned up to the M.T.B.'s deck.

"This is your friend Watson's doing. Slipped him a Mickey Finn! All the same, he did mean to give you all a Christmas Greeting, you know."

"Yes, sir, I know he did. And if I may say so, I think he'll be respected for this lapse, rather than criticized."

"Hah, we've not finished yet, there's still two more boats to go!" roared Wright, and with a wave, the boat sped away.

Royce rejoined the others, and accepted a glass shakily.

"Phew, I never thought I'd ever see a thing like that. Poor old Kirby!"

Carver raised his glass. "Here's to our guest. I might tell you, you're the first of the fair sex ever to set foot on these sacred decks."

"I'm honoured," answered Julia. "Why is that?"

Carver smiled at Royce. "Our Captain wanted you to be the first."

Royce felt himself colouring.

"That, plus the fact I didn't hear anything horrible about you during my tour of inspection, makes you quite the nicest captain in the Fleet." She raised her glass to him, her eyes warm.

"Thank you for being the first," mumbled Royce, and drained his drink, without noticing any taste.

He was, in fact, completely happy, and was content to leave the lunchtime conversation to Leach and Carver, while he sat and simply devoured her with his eyes.

"We're having the big eats tomorrow at fourteen hundred, or thereabouts," Carver was saying. "After the lads have had theirs. That gives us time to serve them with their grub for a change. Very democratic ship this. When will you be coming?"

Julia laughed, "I haven't been asked yet!"

"You must come just as soon as you can," blurted Royce. "I've made arrangements with the N.A.A.F.I. boat to run you over whenever you arrive."

"I'd love it anyway. Will there be many others?"

"Oh, just a few," Carver was vague. "And now you've christened the boat, Mid'll be able to bring his young lady too!"

How quickly the hands of the wardroom clock flew round, and soon it was time to think about Julia's transport arrangements. As he helped her down into the motor dory, the anchorage was in darkness, the stars hidden by scudding banks of cloud.

The engine coughed into life, and the helmsman steered the boat skilfully between the moored vessels. A keen, icy breeze whipped the water into angry little white caps, and Julia shivered.

Royce sensed rather than saw the movement, and without further thought he stood in the swaying boat, and stripped off his greatcoat, calling to her above the clamour of the engine.

"Here, put this on, or you'll end up on the sick list!"

She nodded thankfully, and slipped her arms into the coat, drawing its thick folds around her body.

"Thank you, that was very sweet of you," she called. "But what about you?"

He laughed happily. "Not to worry, I've got sort of used to this sort of thing."

"Oh, have you? I thought I was the first female visitor you'd had aboard?"

"Gosh, I didn't mean it that way!" he stammered hastily.

She found his arm, and squeezed it gently. "It's all right, I'm only teasing again."

The boat squeaked against the jetty, and together they ran quickly up the slippery stairs.

"Shan't be long, Cox'n! Go and get a cup of tea at the Guard-house, I'll call for you in about ten minutes."

The muffled figure at the tiller nodded, "Aye, aye, sir."

As they walked briskly along the cold, deserted streets, towards the hotel, Royce slipped his arm through hers, conscious of her nearness.

"I like the way you always think of your men," she said suddenly.

"No more than anyone else. After all, they don't get a lot of luxuries, do they?"

"It's a lot more than some officers I could mention. There's one who calls in at the Signal Station sometimes, he's always boasting that he never speaks to anybody below a Petty Officer!"

"I'll bet his men just love him!" said Royce, for some reason feeling a pang of jealousy.

How could he possibly hope to win her affection, when they were to be separated by the length of the whole country, and she would be back at the vast naval base, surrounded by dashing and eligible officers, many of whom were shore-based, and had apparently little else to do, but pay visits to the Signal Station.

"Penny for them?"

"Oh nothing," he answered mournfully. "I was just thinking how very quickly this Christmas leave is slipping away."

They turned into the High Street, only a hundred yards to go now. A searchlight cut half-heartedly into the night sky, swung in a small arc, and then went out. Two policemen passed them, pushing their bicycles, their chins tucked down into their capes.

Royce stopped suddenly, pulling Julia up short. He looked round searchingly, but was confronted by the blind eyes of the darkened windows.

"What's the matter?"

"Sorry, but d'you know, I've been looking forward to seeing you again so much, and I've hardly had a moment alone with you since you arrived. And now there's nowhere to go."

He looked down at her upturned face.

"I know, it's just one of those things. Never mind, perhaps we'll manage tomorrow."

Royce groaned inwardly, he knew what his boat would be like on Christmas Day.

"Look, there's something I must say, even at the risk of upsetting you, and I wouldn't willingly do that for the world," he said quickly, "You might have guessed that I'm more than just fond of you."

She started to speak, but he hurried on desperately.

"No, let me finish, I've got to get it off my chest. The fact is, and believe me, I've thought about it a lot, I knew when I first saw you on that dreadful station, that there could never be anyone else, never be another girl who would make me feel as I did then, and as I have been feeling ever since. You see Julia, I love you."

For a moment, there was silence, then she took his arm, and together, they walked on, slowly. At length she spoke, and her voice was so low that he had to bend his head to hear.

"What can I say, Clive? Of course, I'm not upset. How could I be? I'm very flattered. But you have known me such a short time. Why, I may be quite different from what you expect."

His heart plunged, and the night became darker. He realized then that they had stopped outside the White Hart, and at that moment he hated the sight of it.

"But," she went on, her voice serious, "there's another reason."

Further and further, his soul spiralled into the bottomless abyss.

"Do you really think it's wise to talk of this so seriously, when any day or hour, one or both of us may be taken, like John was?"

The side door of the hotel opened slightly, and the porter poked out his head.

"Ah, thought I 'eard you, miss. I've got yer key ready."

She nodded to him, and turned to Royce, who stood back limply.

"Please, Clive," she whispered, "I'm tired, it was so unexpected, I must think. You do understand?"

"Yes," he answered miserably. But he didn't.

"Do you still want to see me tomorrow?"

"More than anything in this life. I'm grateful that you didn't just box my ears for being impertinent," he said, trying to smile.

She took his hands in hers. "I'll be there. Now take your greatcoat, before you freeze."

He took the coat dumbly, and struggled into it.

"Well, good night, Julia."

He couldn't tell what expression the darkness was concealing, he could only see the pale outline of her face. Without warning she reached up, and he felt her warm, soft hands on his neck.

"Dear Clive," she said softly, and kissed him lightly on the cheek. Then she was gone.

He walked across the road, and looked up at the hotel's darkened windows. How long he stood there he didn't know, but eventually he moved off towards the harbour, kicking blindly at a paper bag which blew along the pavement.

What else had he expected, he asked himself. What could she see in him anyway? Damn and blast, he swore, she was just letting him down gently. Still, she hadn't actually said no. And she had kissed him. If only there was more time.

He found the boat's crew waiting by the jetty, and clambered into the tiny cockpit.

"All right, sir?" questioned the coxswain.

"No, all bloody wrong!" snapped Royce. Then relenting, "Sorry, Cox'n, you know how it is."

"Yes, I know, sir."

The others were waiting up for him, sleepy and rosy-faced. There was a strong scent of gin in the air.

"All right?" asked Carver brightly.

"No, all bl——" he checked himself, and smiled half-heartedly.

"I'm afraid our side didn't do too well," he confessed. "Perhaps our second innings tomorrow will be better."

"Yes," piped up Leach. "You wait until she sees her present."

"God! The present!" gasped Royce, his jaw dropping, and his eyes met Carver's. "I think I'll have to call that off."

"Check the moorings, Mid," said Carver distantly.

Leach smiled, "Aye, aye, I get it."

When he had gone, Carver tapped out his pipe, and looked thoughtful.

"You're wrong, you know. About her, I mean."

"How the hell do you know?" said Royce irritably.

Carver shrugged. "Call it my intuition, if you like, but look at it this way. She's a very lovely girl, and a very intelligent one too. It stands out a mile that she could get any man she wanted." He grinned crookedly. "She could get me any time. Yet she comes all the way down here, to put up at an hotel, and to spend Christmas in acute discomfort with us on this boat, which, although we love it, is no yacht. And all this at your suggestion and bidding. Do you want me to go on?"

Royce nodded, and Carver poured himself a large gin from a bottle which stood at his elbow, two-thirds empty. He took a long sip, and grimaced.

"Well then, in my opinion, she's not exactly indifferent to you."

"Mind you," interrupted Royce, "she used to be stationed here when her brother was my C.O. She wanted to look round, and to see the boat," he ended lamely.

"If I may say so, at the risk of being court-martialled or something, you're talking bloody rubbish!" His eyes were beginning to look glassy.

Royce said nothing, a faint shaft of hope was penetrating his heart.

Carver drained his glass, and stood up, unsteadily.

" 'Sides which, you'd be good for each other."

"Thanks, Number One, you've been a big help. It's good to have a Father Confessor aboard."

" 'S'all right, Skipper, any time. She's a wonderful creature. And, again if I may make so bold, you're a bloody wonderful chap yourself, so there!" He finished defiantly. "Now I'm going to bed, and when I awake, I'm going to have a very merry Christmas!" And he wobbled out of the wardroom.

Royce relaxed, and lay back in the chair. He felt as if he had been put back together again.

CHAPTER NINE

CHRISTMAS morning was one mad rush. And by the time the crew had been served with their monstrous dinner, and the officers had sampled the puddings, and had "sippers" on the mess-deck, and in the P.O.'s Mess, they were feeling more in the seasonal mood themselves.

Royce changed into his best uniform, and entered the wardroom. His two officers were already fussing around the table's cramped seating arrangements, and consulting the steward.

Suddenly, a red-faced Raikes and Able Seaman Sax appeared at the door. Raikes was obviously full of the unlawfully bottled rum from the P.O.'s Mess, and was looking very solemn.

"Yes, Coxswain," said Royce, surprised that they should leave their own respective celebrations.

Raikes pushed Sax forward roughly, and for an awful moment

Royce thought the bluff seaman had been up to something.

"Come on, me boy, spit it out!" barked Raikes, grinning.

The other officers drew aside—they had obviously been expecting this—and Sax drew a deep breath.

"Sir, I 'ave been selected by the ship's company," he began carefully, "to be the one to present you wiv' this little gift." He held out a small parcel in a large hand. "An' we want you ter know that we 'ope you like it." He stopped.

"Go on," prompted Raikes.

"Oh yes, an' what's more, we want you ter know too, that we've got the best skipper in the 'ole blasted Andrew!" He finished breathlessly.

Royce took the parcel, and eventually a thin box came to light. He opened it shakily, and took out a pipe. Not an ordinary pipe, but one produced by a leading London firm. It had cost them plenty.

Able Seaman Manners piped up from the back: "If you don't like it, we can change it for you, sir?"

Royce looked up at the circle of rough, anxious faces.

"Like it?" He held it carefully in his hands. "Like it? I'll take great care of it. Thank you very much, lads." He cleared his throat. "Thank you very much," he said again.

"Come on, lads," said Raikes roughly, "back to yer debauchery!" And the laughing, noisy throng clattered away to the fo'c'sle.

"Well, what do you think of that?" said Royce quietly.

"Bribery, that's what it is!" laughed Carver. "There's been more trouble getting the right sort of pipe than I had getting the nightdress!"

Royce walked out on to the deck, into the keen north wind, and stood at the rail, just looking at the new, shining pipe.

The Quartermaster, Ordinary Seaman Elton, stamped his feet, and cleared his throat noisily.

"All right, annit, sir?" he said cheerfully. He was still looking forward to his Christmas dinner, which would be waiting for him as soon as he was relieved. "Reckon yer won't be wantin' to drop that in the 'oggin?"

Royce smiled. He was too overcome by the crew's unexpected kindness, to voice much comment, and merely assented quietly.

The Quartermaster's red-rimmed eyes suddenly sharpened.

"'Allo, 'ere comes the 'Fisherman' agin!"

The Fisherman, as it was known, was the R.A.F. Air-Sea Rescue launch, stationed at the base, and commanded by a jovial little Yorkshire Flying Officer, who was renowned for his success at finding his colleagues, floating in their rubber dinghies and Mae Wests, or just holding on to their shattered aircraft, wherever they might be. At this moment, the graceful black and yellow hull was just swinging out into the fairway, away from her moorings, and after a noisy gear-change, she threw up a sheet of foam from her raked stem, and steered purposefully for the boom-gate.

As she drew abeam, the skipper, dressed as usual in his battered grey cap and kapok jacket, raised his megaphone.

"Just like the blessed navy! You lie stinking in harbour, while we go out on the job!"

Royce cupped his hands. "Nuts! What the hell are you going out for? I didn't think there had been much local flying lately, because of the weather."

"Nah! But Coastal Command have reported an empty dinghy floating off the Mullion Flats, so Joe Soap here has got to investigate. Christmas Day, too. I ask you!" His other remarks were drowned by the increased roar of engines, as the boom-defence vessel dropped her flag, to announce that the front door was open.

Royce waved cheerfully after him, and shivered in the sudden squall which ruffled the water.

"Bit of a blow coming up, I think, Elton."

"Aye, sir. Signal Tower report gale warning in the channel for tonight."

Their attention was taken by the blunt shape of the N.A.A.F.I. boat, puffing manfully round the bend, her decks crammed with unlawful passengers, who were cadging lifts from one vessel to another. She was heading straight for the M.T.B. moorings.

"Ah, some of the guests. Stand by to help them on board, Q.M., and tell the hands below, there's a free lift to the *Royston* going, if they want to go over for a game of Tombola, or something."

"Aye, aye, sir."

Long before the boat had clumsily manœuvred alongside, he had seen Julia. She was standing in the wheel-house by the skipper, wrapped in a duffle coat. As he waved to her, he felt the now familiar lurch of his inside, the overpowering sense of longing. He saw her wave back to him.

The next instant, he found his small decks crammed with visitors. Benjy Watson and Jock Murray were well to the fore, in company with two Wren officers from the Operations Section ashore. Page and his Number One, and young Crispin, Kirby's new Second Hand, whom Royce had made a special point of inviting. It was extremely rare for Kirby to allow him much free time, and by the look of extreme joy on his pale face, it looked as if he was going to make the most of it. A brightly-painted little girl, in a somewhat improbable fur jacket, and a tall, aristocratic W.A.A.F. Officer, completed the party, so far. Carver bustled around, and shepherded the uninitiated below, away from the probing fingers of the rising wind. Royce muttered welcomes in every direction, but made straight for Julia.

"Welcome back," and he took her hands in his, "let's get below quickly."

Coats and caps were shed, and the ladies retired to Royce's cabin, which was to be the unofficial 'powder room'.

Bottles clinked, and the men lifted their glasses thankfully.

"Blimey, I need this," gasped Benjy. "Blessed wind took me breath away!" He drained it at a gulp, and looked round approvingly.

"Glad we decided to come here, Clive. Can't get many bodies in my little paint-pot."

Page, who was carefully examining the Christmas cards, chuckled suddenly.

"Heard about you and old Kirby, this morning, you rascal! Fancy you managing to get him bottled. Little Mister Perfect!"

Benjy's eyes creased. "Yep, gave him a treble gin with a drop of high-octane in it. Boy, he went off like a bomb! Still," he sighed heavily, "he got it on me this morning. He's made mine the Duty Boat!"

"But for Pete's sake, all your lads are as drunk as coots!" exploded Murray. "Ye're a fine Duty Boat. Suppose the *Tirpitz* comes out to bombard the White Hart. A fine protection you are!"

Royce laughed. "Have you seen the weather? There'll be no Jerry activity today. Old Benjy knows his onions!"

The tall Waaf entered, guiding the small girl, who smiled shyly at the wardroom in general.

Carver and Leach hurried forward.

"This is Jean Mannering, an old friend," announced Carver, as he introduced the girl in immaculate air force blue. "Used to be a model, didn't you, dear?"

Benjy's eyes lit up with sudden interest.

"Well, now, that's very interesting. I'm sure we shall find a lot to talk about later on!"

She smiled, and looked faintly bored.

"I can imagine. By the way, this young lady is Ann Hardwick."
She pushed the young lady into the limelight, and Royce realized
that this must be Leach's latest conquest.

"Pleased to meet you, I'm sure," she cooed, and took the gin
from Leach's hand with alacrity, while he studied her with dumb
admiration.

God, that must be what I look like, thought Royce ruefully.

The two Wrens were on familiar ground, and quickly made
themselves at home, but Julia seemed to bring all festivities to a
temporary halt. When she entered, Royce knew that, like himself,
the others were just standing, drinking in her beauty. She was
wearing a plain, flame-coloured cocktail dress, which was devoid
of jewellery, but whose simplicity accentuated the breath-taking
curve of her body.

She paused, a little uncertain of her reception.

"Thank goodness, my guest has arrived!" roared Benjy suddenly, and ushered her solemnly to a chair. "I'm afraid you aren't
going to get a look in, Clive!" he laughed, with a wink.

"I was afraid of that," groaned Royce feelingly.

Already he had the impression that events were moving too fast
for him to keep control. He turned to the messman, who was carefully tasting a large bowl of punch. He jumped, as a slim, brown
arm slipped through his, and turned to look into her laughing
eyes.

"You see, I'm here, Clive. Don't look so gloomy," she said softly.
"Happy Christmas to you."

Royce was transformed. He wanted to seize her, here and now,
instead he grinned sheepishly. "Sometimes I feel just like a blessed
schoolboy!"

"And so you are. And that's just how I like you!"

"Here, you two!" bellowed Benjy. "That'll keep till later.
Here come the eats!"

The ice was broken, if it had ever existed, and noisily they
jammed themselves around the table, and its extension, which
was constructed of disguised ammunition cases.

How they struggled through the mountains of food, Royce
couldn't say, but eventually they lay back in their chairs, sighing
contentedly.

"That was a real fine do," sighed Murray, as he glassily watched
the messman whisking away the table, and piling the plates
through the pantry hatch.

The gramophone was lifted into place, and Carver and the

messman soon had the air ringing with suitable background music.

Through the scuttles Royce saw that the sky was darkening angrily, and the bucking water was turning into an unreal purple. He turned away, feeling unnaturally snug and contented.

Carver brushed by him, and hissed in his ear. "Don't forget the present!"

Royce nodded, and turned to Julia, who was having a deep conversation with Page.

He let his glance caress the warm, soft curve of her slender neck, the smooth cheek framed by a raven's wing of shining jet hair, and he swallowed hard.

Benjy lurched to his feet, and grabbing one of the Wrens, heaved himself over to the gramophone.

"C'mon, Dorothy, let's shake a foot!"

"I'd love to, Benjy. But my name's Alice!"

Royce leaned forward. "Care to take a chance, Julia?"

Together they moved across the tiny cleared space, while the others called encouragement. He was not only aware of her nearness, but of her elusive lightness in his arms. A breath of perfume made his head spin, and coupled with the uneasy sway of the M.T.B.'s deck, he wanted only to hold her close.

He was aware that some of the others had started to dance, and now, the pressure of bodies around them forced them together.

Protectively his arm encircled her waist, and through the thin material of her dress, he felt her body stiffen. Then, as he wondered whether to release her or not, she suddenly relaxed, and moved in close against him. He could sense the gentle pressure of her body willingly cradled in his arms, and the overpowering feeling of desire which engulfed him at that moment made him bury his cheek in her hair. He didn't trust himself to look into her eyes.

The music screamed to a halt, as a sudden lurch by the boat made the needle screech across the record. Benjy and his gasping partner collapsed, helpless in a chair, hooting with laughter, while the others sorted themselves out by the gramophone. Leach was trying to pacify his small friend, she was already looking a little the worse for wear. Only Royce and Julia remained, motionless, in the middle of the throng, and he knew then, that he would never let her go. He put his hands on her shoulders, to steady her against the roll of the boat, and she lifted her eyes to his. They were very large and very near to his. They seemed to be filled with violent and mixed emotions, as if she too felt as he did, yet at the same time imploring him to use his control, for both of them. He felt hot and cold in quick succession, and then, with a quick, almost apologetic smile, he dropped his arms to his sides, and motioned her to the settee berth at one side of the wardroom.

"Phew, let's take a breather," he said unconvincingly.

She nodded, without speaking, her eyes shining.

With a squawk, the music started again, and immediately the others proceeded to sway noisily together in the semblance of a dance. They sat in silence, watching, Royce not daring to look at her. She put a cool hand on his, but when he stole a glance in her direction, she was staring ahead. Seeing nothing but her thoughts.

He listened to the faint but persistent moan of the wind against the wooden hull.

"Pity it's not summer, we could have had a walk round the upper deck."

As he said it, he saw a distant vision of a lonely, sun-drenched beach. He was lying at her side, while she lay in a sleek bathing costume, her head pillowed on his arm, gazing up at an azure sky. It was a long time since he had dared look so far ahead. Any future had always seemed far too improbable.

Without realizing it, he said quietly: "I've got a present for you, Julia."

"Clive! What a terrible thing to do! I didn't bring you one. How sweet of you."

She was smiling at him, her eyes searching his face. He stood up stiffly, the drinks and the atmosphere making his head whirl. He felt reckless.

"It's in my cabin. Will you come and see it? I can't let you open it here." He gestured towards the others.

"All right, but I shall feel awful about not bringing you anything."

You'll feel awful anyway when you've seen it, he thought desperately. He helped her to her feet, and as her hair brushed his cheek, the feeling of longing stabbed him, so that he wanted to cry out.

As they pushed their way to the door, Carver, who was slopping gin into the Waaf's glass, looked up sharply, but his look of encouragement was wasted. Royce didn't see him. Nor did he heed Benjy's throaty, "Oi, oi, then?" He hurried her into the comparative quiet of the narrow passageway, feeling his way past the familiar obstructions, until he felt the door of his cabin. The light revealed the piled clothing of his guests, littering his bunk and chair, and for a moment he blinked uncertainly. It was as if his one private place had been invaded.

"I like your little hide-out, Clive. It's quite cosy."

She stood framed against the white bulkhead, a vision of flame and cream, touching the simple fittings lightly, while he looked at her dumbly.

His eye fell on the bureau at her side, and hurriedly he jerked open a drawer, and held the parcel delicately in his hands.

"Before I give you this, there's one thing I must make you understand," he started, watching her face. "I wanted to give you this, but . . ." he faltered. "It's a present that you might take offence at, if you didn't know that I'm no hand at this sort of thing, and that my intentions, all my intentions where you are concerned, are completely sincere."

That was not what he had wanted to say at all, but he stopped; his mind had dried up. He held out the parcel to her.

She put it on the bunk, and carefully untied the wrapping, a loose lock of hair falling over her smooth brow.

Royce braced himself, and watched, fascinated, as with a gentle movement she drew the nightdress from its paper. He heard her quick intake of breath, as she held it at arm's length, her face entranced. Slowly she lifted her head, and then he saw that there were tears in her eyes.

He clenched his teeth. "You're not too angry, are you?"

She shook her head violently, and suddenly held the black wisp against her body.

"Angry?" she asked, and there was a sob in her voice. "I think it's wonderful. And I know exactly what you were thinking when you got it. Oh, Clive. It's beautiful, and I love it."

A surge of elation lifted him, and he took two steps across the cabin towards her. When he put his arms round her, she buried her face in his chest, crying quietly, while he stood happy but uncomprehending.

"Don't mind me, Clive, just hold me. It's just that you make it so difficult . . ."

He stroked her hair gently, and held her close, shutting his eyes with a feeling of great contentment.

There was a sudden and violent commotion outside the door, and he heard Benjy's loud voice calling him. He cursed inwardly, and giving the girl a reassuring pat on the arm, he stepped into the passage.

"Well?" he asked, trying to appear more normal than he felt. "What's the matter now?"

"Matter? Matter?" Benjy's face was purple, and for once, worried. "I'll tell you the matter. My dear old chap, I've just had a signal." He brandished a soggy piece of paper. "I've got to go to sea! Now!" He paused, gasping for breath. "As you know, I'm the duty boat," he added, as if that explained everything.

Murray appeared behind him.

"Ah told you, Benjy boy, you shouldn't have let your boys get bottled, even for Christmas," he said grimly.

Royce mustered his thoughts. "But what the blazes have you to go out *for*? The weather's like hell."

"That ruddy R.A.F. rescue launch has broken down off the Mullion Flats, an' I've got to tow her in!" he wailed. "What the hell am I going to do?"

Royce took the signal from his limp hand and glanced at it, a wild plan forming in his brain.

"Leach, get the Quartermaster and the Coxswain," he shouted. "I'll go, Benjy, and as I'm on the end buoy, we can get out without disturbing anyone. Make a signal to *Royston*, Number One. Explain that Benjy's developed an engine defect, or something."

The others were looking at him in wonderment.

"Man, ye're a marvel," muttered Murray. "But what about the guests?"

Royce rubbed his chin thoughtfully. "Hmm, well, we can drop those on Page's boat by the oiling wharf as we go out. We'll only be about half an hour, all being well. Unless——" He looked at Julia, his eyes bright and slightly wild. "Care for that trip I promised you?"

She had her hands behind her, concealing her present from the others, but her face lit up, and she nodded.

"It'd be wonderful, but wouldn't you get into trouble?"

"If he's found out, he will," grinned Murray, "but he has the luck of the devil. Anyway, we'll be coming too, to see that he doesn't get up to anything!"

Raikes stepped forward, his hair dishevelled.

"Do I understand we're going out, sir?" His voice was quite steady.

"Can we, Cox'n? How are the hands?"

"'Bout fifty-fifty, sir. But enough to get to the Mullion an' back all right."

"Right, tell Anderson to start the engines now, and take as

many sober blokes as you can find on to the fo'c'sle, and get ready to slip. Don't worry about those on the *Royston,* let 'em enjoy themselves." He waved his hand towards the other officers. "We've pressed some more help into service!"

Raikes chuckled, and shook his head sadly. "If you don't mind me sayin' so, sir, I don't think the Andrew'll ever be the same after the temporary gentlemen 'ave finished with it!" And grinning hugely, he hurried away.

Benjy wiped his face. "Gosh, I need a drink. That was a narrow shave!"

"You always need a drink," said Murray wryly, and led him back to the wardroom.

Royce slipped on an oilskin, and wrapped a towel round his neck.

"Here, put on a duffle, and an oilskin, and anything else you can find suitable in the cupboard, and I'll go and explain to the other girls."

As he turned to go, his head spinning with calculations, she checked him, but as he looked questioningly at her, she stepped back, her expression one of suppressed excitement.

"No, no, you go now," she said quickly. "You're a captain again. I'll tell you later."

He gave her a puzzled smile, and ran for the wardroom, colliding with Leach.

"*Royston* says 'Proceed,' sir," he gasped.

"Very good. Now you tell your friend Ann to get her coat and hat. I'm dropping the guests on Page's boat until we get back. You go with them, and keep the party going until we get back."

Leach was aghast. "But all those women!"

"It's all right. Page's Number One'll be coming with you. If he can still walk!"

He laughed wildly as he hurried for the bridge, at the excited squeaks from the girls, at the sight of a glassy-eyed seaman standing on the rain-lashed deck in his underpants, and, above all, at himself.

The engines roared belligerently into life, and the boat trembled with anticipation.

Carver stood at his side. "Which chart, sir?"

"Don't want one," he shouted. "It's only round the corner!"

He peered over the screen at the dim, shining figures on the fo'c'sle. One of them waved. "Ready to slip, sir!" Raikes' voice carried like a foghorn.

"Here, Number One, take the wheel. Leave old Raikes to manage that lot down there."

The night was as black as pitch, and the rain was driven like icy darts into their faces, as it lashed the exposed decks.

"Slip!" he yelled hoarsely, and as the wire rasped back through the fairleads, he felt the boat borne sideways by the wind, wallowing uncomfortably.

"Ahead together, half speed," ordered Royce carefully, and was rewarded by the engines' change of tempo, as with a purposeful thrust they pushed the boat forward into the teeth of the weather.

Squinting into the darkness, he could just make out the dim shape of the solitary M.T.B. against the wharf, and slowly he jockeyed towards her.

He took a quick glance down to the waist, where he saw the huddled groups of guests waiting to change boats. Page's Number One waved what looked like a bottle in his direction. "Ready to go!" he called. Right, this had to be just so, and with great precision he brought the boat under the lee of the stonework, and alongside the other vessel, where the forewarned crew gathered eagerly to welcome their visitors.

"All gone, sir!" And with a throaty growl they swung round and motored for the boom-gate. A green light winked brightly ahead, and Royce grabbed the Aldis to shutter a reply. Then, gripping the rail and rocking back on his heels, he let the weather hold him in its grasp.

"Here we go, then. Full ahead both!"

Once outside the shelter of the headland, the boat shuddered to the wind's mounting punch, and solid sheets of spray swept up and over the masthead. It was like racing into a solid black void, with nothing to guide them but the swinging compass card, and a distant winking wreck-buoy.

Raikes clambered on to the bridge, breathing heavily, his oilskin streaming.

"All secure on deck, sir."

"Very good, take over the wheel."

Carver willingly relinquished the helm, and steadied himself against the chart table, wiping his face with a sodden handkerchief.

" 'Strewth, what a night! Still, it's better than going out for a game of 'catch' with Jerry," he called.

"Better go below, and make sure the wardroom's all right. We don't want everything smashed before we get back!"

Carver waved, and ducking his head, scrambled down along the glistening deck.

"You know the place, 'Swain?" asked Royce, peering at Raikes's bulky shape.

"Aye, sir, we'll be up to it in about ten minutes, I should think."

"Right, we'll get the new towing hawser out on deck. And a few fenders too. Just in case!"

"Already done it, sir," chuckled Raikes.

It was at that moment Royce became aware of the girl standing at the rear of the bridge, clutching with both hands at the signal locker for support. He reached her in a bound, and helped her to the lee side, behind the glass screen.

"Did you come up alone?" he yelled, his voice anxious.

"No, it's all right. A sweet little seaman wanted to help me, but I practically had to carry *him*!"

He shook his head admiringly. She made a heartening sight, clad in an oversize duffle coat and oilskin. Protruding from beneath these billowing garments, he saw an ungainly pair of rubber boots. She stood now, laughing at him, her hair whipped back by the wind, her face running with spray, while she struggled to keep her feet.

"Well," he said at length, when he realized he was staring rather hard. "What do you think of her?" And he waved his arm, embracing the darkened boat.

"Marvellous! She's all you said, and more. I never realized how fast they were, before. But you will be careful, won't you?"

He smiled. "Don't worry, I'll not take any risks with you aboard."

An extra-big wave slapped angrily at the boat's lifting bows, and Julia slipped sideways across the canting deck, her clumsy boots skidding helplessly. Royce roughly encircled her waist with his arm, while he grabbed the rail with his other hand, pulling her safely against his body. Then he stood behind her, gripping the rail on either side of her, and acting as a cushion for any further sudden lurches.

"Phew, thanks very much," she laughed shakily. "You nearly lost your passenger, just then!"

He smiled happily and pulled her close, peering over her head at the angry waters approaching them, while her damp hair rippled against his chin. Her nearness, the boat, and the wild exhilaration of the weather intoxicated him.

He gripped her tighter, and pointed suddenly, as a lazy red flare arched over the black wastes, and fell slowly, spluttering into the sea.

"There she is! Right on the button!"

She twisted in his grasp, looking back at him.

"What are you going to do now?"

"Tow him. That's about all we can do at the moment."

Carver and Page had joined the knot of seamen behind the bridge, and Royce could vaguely hear their shouted orders, as they struggled with the heavy hawser, which, like all its breed, had a mind of its own. He turned his attention back to the Rescue Launch, for as Raikes swung the M.T.B. round in a semi-circle, with the engines' roar slowly diminishing, he could plainly see her bright yellow upperworks swaying sickeningly, as the helpless boat jerked to a canvas sea-anchor, her decks awash.

The girl felt his body tense, and when he spoke to Raikes, his voice, too, was different, hard and cool.

"Near as you can, Cox'n. Don't crowd her. I'm going to speak to the skipper."

"Aye, aye, sir." The hands turned the spokes, almost gently.

Royce blew into the mouthpiece of the loud-hailer, and it whistled plaintively.

"D'you hear, there? Are you still intact?"

"I think so!" The answering voice was distorted by the wind. "Thank you for leaving your party just for little old me!"

Royce could easily read the agony of worry behind that jocular greeting. He knew too well the shortcomings of such a boat, left engineless in such a sea.

"I'm going round again, then I'm passing a line to you, for the towing warp. O.K.?"

"Aye, but watch you don't get it round your screws!"

His next remarks were drowned by the roar of the M.T.B.'s engines, as Raikes swung her neatly away, to avoid being flung against the other boat's side by a white-hooded wave which reared with sudden fury.

Unconsciously, Royce had taken out his pipe, and clenched it grimly between his teeth, while he weighed up the situation. Julia moved away, and clung quietly in the corner, watching him, heedless of the spray which stung her cheek.

"Port side to! Get ready with the lines!" bellowed Royce, hoping that Carver's head was now properly clear. He found time to smile at the thought of Benjy, who, shorn of responsibility, now lay comfortably in the wardroom with Murray, singing discordantly.

There she was again. He could see the white numbers on her flat stern, rolling through a ninety degree arc.

"Stand by!"

The boat moved in fast, like an experienced boxer, then, as they stood stem to stem, barely twenty feet apart, the engines stopped, and a burly seaman sprang to the rail, gauging the distance.

"Let her go!" roared Royce, and the seaman's arm soared, sending the line snaking into the darkness. There was a faint tinkle of glass.

"Right through her blasted wheelhouse winder!" breathed Raikes admiringly. There had been a seven pound wrench on the end of the line.

"Heave away lads! Roundly!"

He was rewarded to see the airmen whipping in the slack of the line as fast as they could manage under such desperate conditions. It seemed an age before the eye of the hawser was reluctantly swinging across the gap, and all the time, Captain and Coxswain used every knack and every trick of engines and rudder, to stop the boats colliding.

"All fast, sir!" Carver waved his dripping cap wildly.

Slowly, painfully, they drew ahead, holding their breath as the hawser rose out of the sea, tightened, throwing off a shower of drips like a wet dog, and then settled down to take the strain. The Rescue Launch veered round, fell in behind them, and obediently allowed herself to be taken home.

Royce didn't take his eyes off her, however, until they crawled through the protective arms of the boom, and under the shelter of the wind-swept jetties of the base.

They eased their charge alongside, and as the lines snaked ashore, the M.T.B. slipped the tow, and made for her own moorings.

"Many thanks, Navy!" The 'Fisherman' waved after them thankfully.

"It was a pleasure!"

Royce breathed out deeply, and stretched.

"Not too bad, eh, Cox'n?"

"Not bad, sir."

Carver and Page appeared on the bridge, grinning like schoolboys.

"What an original party you give," Page chuckled, "Nothing

like a bit of excitement. I wonder what old Kirby would have said about it?"

"Funny you should say that. I was just thinking, a few months ago we couldn't have done anything like it. Any of us. You've got to hand it to old Kirby, he's taught us a lot, and I think he's learned a bit from us."

He watched narrowly, as the seamen picked up the buoy-ring, and hooked on.

"Stop engines."

The tide gripped the boat, and swung her firmly into line with the other moored craft.

"You're probably right," confessed Page, "but I still say he's an awkward cuss."

"Well, let's go and finish the party," said Royce sadly, "I think I see our other guests coming over in a motor-boat. Number One, make to Royston, 'Mission Completed'." In his heart he knew he was only trying to spin out the time, to put off the moment of her departure.

"Come below, Julia. You must be frozen."

She shook her head vigorously. "Not a bit of it. I'll bet the others will be terribly jealous."

Below, in the snug atmosphere of the wardroom, Royce suddenly wanted to be rid of his friends, of everyone else but Julia, but he grinned ruefully, and submitted to the mounting noise of enjoyment.

Julia's face was fresh and alive from her boisterous sea trip, and she hung back from the door, a finger on her lips.

"I'm not coming in like this," she whispered, "I'm going to put a new face on, and get rid of your sea-going robes." She faltered, and turned back to him, her face suddenly serious, and Royce stepped into the passage, his face inquiring.

"I think you were superb," she said, her eyes warm, "I shall always remember you like that. It helps me to understand, to realize what you are going through, when you are out there——"

"I was just trying to make an impression on you," he grinned awkwardly. "After all, I did promise you a trip, when I came up to Rosyth."

She wrinkled her nose prettily. "Don't try to fool me. Now you go and fix me a nice drink, because I expect I shall suddenly start to feel a bit weak, in a minute."

He stared after her. "I feel a bit weak now," he thought.

They sat for the rest of the time, side by side, hardly speaking, yet each fully conscious of the other, and only dimly aware of the din and clamour.

Murray was trying grimly to stand on his head in one corner, and drink a pint of beer at the same time, until Benjy took the opportunity to empty a soda syphon down his leg, to the hilarious delight of the two Wren officers.

Leach and the small girl, now looking completely dazed, were dancing slowly and dreamily in the middle of the wardroom, although the gramophone had long since ceased to play. Of Carver and the Waaf there was no sign.

Page lurched happily over to them, and sat heavily on the table. He grinned vacantly at Julia.

"Some party, eh?" He helped himself to another drink, and nodded drowsily. Then, with a jerk he looked at her again.

"By the way, are you coming to see the boy here get his gong next week?"

"Gong?" she queried, looking strangely at Royce. "Tell me about it."

Heedless of Royce's frown, he chattered on. "Well, he's going to get his medal officially from the top brass, that's what," he confided.

She looked at Royce seriously. "Is that true?"

"Yes, I forgot to mention it," he mumbled uncomfortably.

She let her eyes fall to the small ribbon on his chest.

"I'd very much like to be there," she said quietly. "But I don't think I can manage it so soon after my leave."

"Between you and me, it terrifies me," he confessed. "And I'd put it out of my mind for a bit, thanks to you."

"Write to me about it, won't you?"

"About everything, Julia, it's been so wonderful, having you here."

They sat looking at each other, and only came back to reality when a red-faced Petty Officer thrust his head into the doorway.

"Anyone for the shore, please?" he boomed. "I'm collecting all guests, and this is the last boat."

"Give him a drink, quick!" hissed Royce, banging Page to life with his elbow.

He stood up heavily, the joy draining out of him. "I'll help you get your things."

He watched her putting on her borrowed duffle coat, and tying the silk scarf over her head, heedless of the other girls, who were laughing and chattering gleefully.

Carver had appeared, a trifle sheepishly, with the tall Waaf, and he noted that his collar was smeared with lipstick.

They let the others go ahead, both dreading the moment of departing.

"What time do you leave tomorrow?" he asked, although he already knew the answer.

"Eleven o'clock. I shall get back to Rosyth in time for the forenoon watch the day after."

The keen night air seemed hostile.

He put his hands on her waist, and pulled her to him.

"I do so wish you'd reconsider, Julia. Please believe me when I tell you that there'll never be anyone else. Ever. I know I've only known you such a short time, and I know too that you could get any man, just by raising your little finger. But I want you, so very much."

For a moment she stood still in his arms, then, with a sudden force, she put her arms round his neck, pulling herself closer, her eyes bright.

"That was what I was saving to tell you," she murmured, "I know now what I want."

He felt her body tremble, and her hands gripped his neck fiercely, "I do love you, Clive, I love you so much."

A starshell seemed to burst before his eyes, blinding him, and there was a great roaring in his ears, and the next instant they were clinging to each other, and she was kissing him hard. As she broke away from him, he tasted the salt from her cheek, the spray or tears, he couldn't say.

"No, don't hold me again, Clive, I must go," she cried. "But if you want me, I'll come to you again, somehow."

Blindly, they ran out on to the deck. A fat harbour launch, crammed with noisy passengers, was bumping alongside, while her coxswain leaned impatiently over the rail.

She was half-laughing and half-crying, and Royce was in a dream. She stepped down on to the crowded boat, and immediately the ropes were cast off, and a widening gulf of water grew between them. He shouted wildly, following the boat the full length of the M.T.B., to the delight of the passengers.

"I'll try to get to the station tomorrow!"

But he couldn't be sure if she had heard him, although she waved until the boat was swallowed up in the blackness. He was sure of only one thing. He was the happiest, luckiest man alive.

CHAPTER TEN

WHEN a country decides to go to war, it is not just the people who, willingly or unwillingly, take on a new and uncertain guise, and as in the case of England, draw together in some sort of uniform and hopeful tolerance of enforced discipline, its very way of life alters. From Buckingham Palace to the humblest home with its blackout curtains and pathetic backyard air-raid shelter, from the schoolhouse which has become a casualty station, to the church hall which has changed overnight to a Home Guard headquarters. Or the Southend paddle steamer now sweeping mines, alongside the millionaire's yacht marshalling a convoy in Weymouth Bay. All these, and more, become part of the pattern.

What had once been the rambling clearing house for fish, brought in by the trawler and drifter fleets of the east coast, had suddenly suffered such a transformation. It was a high-roofed building, over a hundred yards in length, with a smooth concrete floor, and two of its walls open to the elements and the wharf fronts. The comfortable peacetime untidiness had been changed to one of ordered neatness, with whitewashed bricks, loading bays for lorries, carefully marked with coloured signs and helpful arrows. At the far end, where the girls of the port used to tear with gory relish at the vast piles of herrings, a mountain of ammunition boxes awaited disposal, while in a dark corner on trestles, a headless torpedo, liberally smeared in golden grease, was nearing the end of its long journey.

Normally, the "Shed" as it was known by the naval population, was a turbulent centre of activity, a constant whirlpool of men and material which swept from office to shipyard, and from ship to sea. Today was different. It was one of those special days, which every so often the Navy earmarks, and puts aside for a suitably special occasion. One moment the Navy's private world is full of bustle and noise, with sweating men in shabby clothes working desperately, always with time against them, and then, quite suddenly, all that is changed. Here, at this moment, all those same men are drawn up in neat lines, smartly dressed in their best uniforms, the blue ranks forming three sides of a square. A silvery sun is forcing its way through the unsettled banks of cloud, to settle briefly on the set faces, and to reflect but momentarily on the gold badges, and the gleaming bayonets of a Marine guard.

They have come together just for this short while, knowing full well that in a few hours they will be back at their work again, cursing the Service, and the war. There are all sorts of sailors present, ranging from the base personnel, to the hardened veterans of the destroyers and mine-sweepers, whose shore-time can be counted in hours. The bulk of the men, however, are the Light Coastal Forces, lined up with their officers, and quietly waiting to witness the nation's appreciation of their valour. For although but a few medals are to be presented, every man here knows, be he captain or signalman, gunner or cook, stoker or lieutenant, that he can share in their winning, and feel a just pride in the deed which has gained the small piece of gleaming metal.

Royce and the others stood in a self-conscious line, abreast of the dais, he with his heart in his mouth. He tried to focus his eyes ahead, on the slender mast of a distant frigate, but each time he found himself glancing furtively at the sea of seemingly unfamiliar faces around him, or at the single squad of Wrens, as if to gain their moral support.

Vice-Admiral Sir John Marsh, as Flag Officer, was representing the king for the purposes of the presentation, and he stood small and erect on the dais, his head thrust slightly forward, the pale eyes darting piercingly and searchingly over the faces before him. He was in the process of winding up a brief but carefully worded speech.

"And so," he barked, his voice echoing round the iron girders of the roof, "we have come to the bitterest part of the struggle, when all, each and every one of us, has to make the all-important decision." He paused, allowing his words to sink in. Across the harbour came the clank of a winch, and somewhere overhead an aeroplane droned lazily. "We must decide, here and now, to work harder, longer, and if necessary, to give the last drop of blood to the common end. Many of us have fallen, and will fall on the way, but that is the way to victory." He stopped, and cleared his throat.

Royce's eye fell on Benjy, standing at the head of his crew, a tight-lipped, grim-faced Benjy, looking old before his time.

The Admiral turned to his Staff Captain, who held a sheaf of papers in a leather folder. Royce steeled himself. This was the moment. The other two lieutenants who were with him were first, they were both Motor Gunboat captains. Royce found himself listening with awe, as the Admiral read the citations. Surely these two youthful figures could not have achieved so much. He saw the Flag Lieutenant step forward and hand the little box to the Admiral. There was a great hush, as if the world was holding its breath, and then he pinned the small silver cross on the first officer's jacket, and shook him by the hand. Royce chilled as the second man stepped up. One side of his face was like a wax mask, smooth and dead. The one remaining eye stared steadily ahead, as the cross was pinned to his chest, but as the Admiral began to speak to him in a low voice, the lieutenant lowered his head, and his body shook violently with a paroxysm of violent sobs. Royce turned his face away, as the two sick-bay attendants led the officer gently from the building. Such was the price.

"Lieutenant Clive Royce," the sharp voice broke into his thoughts, and clenching his teeth he marched quickly to confront the Admiral. The pale eyes regarded him coldly, as the Staff Captain read loudly from his papers, but Royce was only dimly aware of the context. He was still thinking of that other lieutenant. It might have been him. "Did, in the face of extreme danger, under the aforementioned circumstances, and without regard for his personal safety, carry out the destruction of the enemy, in a manner over and above the line of duty." The voice had stopped, and he felt, rather than saw, the Admiral affix the decoration.

"Well, my boy, I said we should meet again, eh?" The eyes were now smiling, the lined face relaxed. "Congratulations."

"Thank you, sir."

It was all a dream. He saluted and marched to the side, where, with real pleasure, he watched as Raikes received his hard-earned D.S.M.

The base padre said a few words. The Marine band struck up "Hearts of Oak", and with an almost eager haste the blue ranks wheeled round and marched out into the salt air. Back to the war.

Royce and Raikes walked slowly along the main jetty, towards the landing-stage, each immersed in his own thoughts.

"Didn't take long, did it?" said Royce at length.

Raikes thought for a bit, his eyes dreamily watching the gulls dancing over the water, swooping and screaming at the flotsam.

"I dunno, sir. I aged about ten years in there!"

Royce slapped him across the shoulder, brought back to reality by Raikes's simple forthrightness, which had done so much to draw them together.

"Bit of luck the Admiral doesn't know about our Christmas escapade," he laughed. "I don't suppose he'd approve of Wrens in M.T.B.s!"

Raikes whistled shrilly and waved in the direction of the idling motor dory.

"I shouldn't bank on him not knowing!" he answered wryly. "That's 'ow you become an Admiral, knowing them things!"

"Starboard twenty."

"Starboard twenty, sir. Twenty of starboard wheel on."

"Steady."

"Steady, sir, course south-thirty east."

"Steer south-forty east."

There is a pause, and the steering chain rasps and rattles, as the Quartermaster, his eyes straining to watch the dancing compass card, floating under its feeble lamp, eases the wheel over spoke by spoke. When he speaks, his teeth are clenched because of the cold, and because the dawn is still a whole night away.

"Course south-forty east, sir." The whisker of the lubber's line has halted opposite the required point.

"Very good." Carver's tone is one of strain. He levels his glasses ahead, searching the invisible horizon.

Jenkins, on the wheel, curses quietly, as a feather of white spray jumps the screen and plunges itself wetly beneath a gap in his muffler. He is thinking about his mother and her fish shop in Brighton. They'll just be closing now, and the air will be filled with vinegar and hot fat. He smiles secretly, and licks his lips.

"Watch your helm." Carver is worried and angry. Somewhere ahead is the Motor Gunboat flotilla they have been sent to contact. Somewhere astern, Kirby will be fuming impatiently.

Paynton hums happily amid his flags and lamps, while Leach is invisible, save for his buttocks, as he pores over the chart. Thinking of his girl, thinks Carver, allowing his mouth to soften.

The bridge is like a small stage in a vast, empty and darkened theatre, where the players are waiting for a final rehearsal. Except that here there is no time to rehearse.

Above the spiralling mast, the clouds are solid black things, slashed with silver valleys, as a baffled moon tries to show them the way. As it sheds its beams briefly, the sea too is revealed, a powerful, menacing desert of heaving jet dunes, with the occasional white crust torn free by the biting wind. This is the North Sea.

There is a sharp clink from the Bofors mounting, and a scuffle of feet. Someone laughs, and Denton's throaty voice quells them with threats.

"Bridge?" A tinny voice floats questioningly up a voice-pipe.

"Bridge," snaps Carver, wondering what it must be like, bouncing about in the engine room, between those thundering giants.

"Permission to send Stoker Barker to the mess-deck to bandage 'is 'ead, sir? 'E's bumped it on number one pump."

"I suppose that makes a difference from, say, number two pump?" Carver's voice is heavy with sarcasm.

"Pardon, sir?"

"Skip it. Yes, send him up."

God, I'm tired, he thinks. That girl'll kill me. There is a soft snore from the chart table, and Carver kicks savagely at the Midshipman's curved stern.

"Wake up, Colin! You lazy bastard!"

The watch is proceeding as normal.

Below in his cabin, Royce lay lazily and dreamily in his bunk, his mind and body unwilling to return to the ways of duty. He squinted down his fully-clothed body to his large sea-boots, which stuck into each corner of the bunk, to stop him rolling on to the deck. From a hook on the door, his dressing-gown hung out at an angle of forty-five degrees, as if on a bracket, and then swung back eerily to another improbable position. Royce watched it idly for a while, and then returned to Julia's letter, which he rested on his chest, to catch the light from his bunk lamp. He sighed contentedly, and started to read it again:

". . . and so the transfer has been arranged. I shall be moving down to Harwich, almost at once, to attend an advanced signal course there. I don't even mind that. Any excuse to be near you again."

He smiled, and felt the strong stirring within him. He turned over the page, drinking in her round, neat writing.

"I shall come and see you as soon as I can, to let you know the arrangements at Harwich. As I said before, we all saw your picture in the paper the other day, getting your medal. I was very proud, and cried a little bit. Must close now, as I am certainly not going to miss getting transport to the station, to come to you again."

It was signed, simply, "with love, Julia". He stretched contentedly. It was still like a miracle. He wanted to have some little thing of hers to touch and hold, just to prove he was not dreaming. He glanced round the disordered cabin. She was here in this place, just a week ago, he marvelled. He could still picture her, still sense her perfume, her nearness.

"Captain, sir?"

He swallowed hard, and rolled over to the voice-pipe.

"Yes?"

"Gunboats ahead. 'Bout half a mile."

"Very good. Get the Coxswain on the wheel. I'm coming right up."

He swung his legs to the deck, and slipped his glasses round his neck. At the door he paused. Her vision was still there and, smiling inwardly, he climbed the ladder to the main-deck.

He nodded to the others, and followed his usual painstaking routine. Compass, chart, weather, speed. Right. He turned his attention to the dark shapes, revealed only by their creaming bow-waves, which were looming on the port bow.

"Made the challenge?"

"Yes, sir. Their Senior Officer is coming alongside to get the gen."

Even as they waited, one of the gunboats swung out of line, and sidled alongside, her engines idling. Royce could see the white blobs on her bridge, and shining oilskins.

"Ahoy there! This is S.N.O. here. Give me the message, and we'll get cracking!"

Royce raised his megaphone. The loud-hailer would be a bit too much, in the enemy's back garden as it were.

"Lieutenant-Commander Kirby's compliments, and he says for you to go straight in now, without waiting for any further confirmation. As you know, the story is that the two enemy transports are coming up the coast fast, with one escort ship. A Hans-Lody class destroyer." He paused; the salt was making his throat like sandpaper.

"What about the bloody E-boats?" The booming voice was testy.

"Yes, they'll be in a covering sweep, about five miles ahead of the convoy. You're to go in, as if you were making a normal sweep, and draw the E-boats off. You're to start the sweep at oh-one-oh-oh."

There was a pause, while the water swished and slopped between the two boats.

"Okay! I hope the Intelligence reports are right for once! Good huntin'!"

The gunboats milled round their leader and then, after much gear-changing, they prowled off into the night, in a tight arrowhead formation.

To Carver's ill-concealed relief, Royce took over the con, and when they eventually picked up Kirby's cautious signal, he breathed a deep sigh of admiration.

"Jolly good, Skipper. I don't know how you manage to get the exact rendezvous like that."

"It's dead easy, Number One. He signalled, so we know it's the S.O. If he'd fired, we'd have been at the wrong place, see?" said Royce drily.

They cruised steadily towards the hidden coastline, the engines throttled down, and grumbling throatily.

Raikes, who had been moodily studying the bobbing stern of Cameron's boat, started suddenly.

"Good 'eavens, I forgot!" he exploded.

The others peered at him uncertainly.

"A 'Appy New Year, gentlemen!" he said solemnly.

Carver laughed. "So it is. God bless us, every one!"

They reached round in the darkness and shook hands. Carver called out the news to Leach, who had gone aft to his Brownings, and there was a stifled cheer.

"The last year of war, perhaps," said Royce thoughtfully. "Who knows?"

On the horizon there was a sharp crackle of automatic fire, and an impressive display of tracer shells. The gunboats were putting on their show.

"We've struck oil!" jerked Carver excitedly. "Now where is the——"

He was cut short by Kirby's action lamps flashing urgently, and the quickening roar of engines.

"Full speed ahead! Stand by torpedoes!" barked Royce. "Okay, John, get forrard. And keep your head down!"

The convoy was completely taken by surprise, as the lean hulls tore down upon them. They had confidently watched the E-boats tear after the gun-boats, and settled down thankfully behind the powerful bulk of the destroyer.

Kirby's blackboard tactics swung smoothly into operation. The destroyer was to be first, and less than twenty seconds after the first gun had fired, two torpedoes burst in her engine-room, and another reduced her fo'c'sle to a flaming hell.

Frantically she fired her secondary armament at the M.T.B.s

as they flashed into the gleam of her own funeral pyre, and the night was ripped apart by the clatter of machine-guns and cannon. Yet another steel fish struck home, and with an eye-searing flash, she rolled on her beam-ends, the fires hissing and shooting out great geysers of scalding steam.

Royce saw the tracers rippling and bouncing along her upturned and streaming bilge keel, and then, with a frightful scream of rending metal, she vanished, leaving a small, glittering pool of burning oil.

The two transports were turning for the coast, but the leading vessel was hit twice by torpedoes before her rudder could be brought round. She listed heavily, and was shrouded in escaping steam.

Royce brought the boat slewing round, and fired his own sleek charges into the blackness. As he altered course, the engines racing, the night lit up with a thousand multi-coloured hues, as the ship broke in two and exploded.

The remaining ship was firing her guns frantically, and appeared to be out of control.

One M.T.B. was also in difficulties, with flames flickering out of her bridge.

Another great roar, and the last of the transports lifted her bows, and slid to the bottom.

In a welter of plunging wakes, the M.T.B.s tacked back into line, the sea dark again, but for the blazing M.T.B., now two miles astern.

Benjy's boat went about, and his voice boomed across the water. "Kirby's bought it! Nip back and take off the blokes, will you? But don't hang about, Clive!"

Royce waved, and watched grimly as Benjy took over command of the flotilla, and led them, roaring away, towards safety.

"Stand by on the fo'c'sle, Number One. I'm going alongside. Get ready to pull the wounded aboard. We won't have a lot of time. The fire's got a good hold!"

He swung to the aft rail. "First-aid party, Mister Leach! Lively now!"

Raikes sucked his teeth, his eyes fixed on the blazing boat, looming closer and closer.

"Gently does it," breathed Royce. The stench of petrol, and the warm breath of fire on his cheek, made his throat contract.

The seamen lined the rails, and he saw Carver leap on to the other boat's slanting deck as they scraped alongside.

The bridges of the two boats were side by side, and as the other one listed over, slowly and wearily, he saw the shambles clearly revealed by the growing flames.

Men were leaping wildly across the narrow gap to safety, while others were dragged ruthlessly over the rails, their injuries making them cry out pitifully.

He saw Kirby step stiffly from the wrecked bridge, his clothes in rags, his face a torn nightmare.

He seemed to see Royce looking down at him, and for a moment he stood there motionless. Then, he slowly bent forward, in a grotesque curtsy, his torn scalp gleaming dully, and pitched over the side between the two grinding hulls. Royce retched.

"All off, sir," yelled Carver, and with a quickening tremble they moved clear and, with bows lifting, speeded after the others.

Commander Wright strolled along the deserted jetty, sniffing appreciatively the crisp morning air.

In the harbour, a bugle sounded sadly, and one small harbour launch scudded across the anchorage, disturbing the nodding gulls perched on the buoys. He could taste the coffee on his tongue, and he hummed absently to himself as he scanned the clear, colourless sky. It had the makings of a fine day. When he reached the steps at the foot of the Signal Tower, he stared across to the heavy bulk of the *Royston*. Her moorings were still empty. He frowned, and consulted his watch, then looked out at the glittering line of the sea, towards which a dirty trawler puffed with slow, graceless rolls. They should be back now, he thought, and strolled into the signals office. The Yeoman was sitting back in a chair, his eyes puffy from too little sleep. Wright waved to him cheerily.

"Don't get up, Yeo', I'm just going to wait in the office here for a bit. The 'T.B.s'll be back soon. Any news?"

"As you know, sir, they got their objective all right. We had a signal from the gunboats two hours ago. I expect the M.T.B.s took a bit longer to find the destroyers that were going to escort 'em back." The man yawned.

"Hmm, quite so," mused Wright, and walked out on to the steps again.

A naval bus drew up by the gates, with a squeal of brakes, and Wright smiled, as about twenty Wrens climbed down, and made their way to the dockside canteen.

The pensioner driver called lustily after them: "Nah don't you be long, my cherubs. 'Alf an hour fer breakfast, an' we're off."

He noted with surprise that one of the girls had detached herself from the group, and was walking uncertainly in his direction. As she drew close, his smile of admiration was replaced by one of recognition. She saluted, and he noted warmly how her jaunty cap had difficulty in controlling her delightful curls.

"And a very good morning to you, my dear," he boomed jovially. "A Happy New Year, too."

"Good morning, sir." Her smile transformed her face. "I hope you don't mind, but I've got something to send over to Lieutenant Royce's boat."

He saw she was holding a brown paper parcel.

"We're just passing through, you see," she explained. "Going to the new Signals School."

Wright grinned roguishly. "He told me you were coming down. The lucky young devil! But I'm afraid he's out on Ops at the moment. Should be back any time. Then you can give him the parcel yourself."

Her face clouded, and her eyes glanced fearfully to the vacant buoys by the *Royston*.

"Nothing too dangerous, is it, sir?" There was an edge to her voice.

"Course not, my dear. Now you come into the S.D.O. and have a cup of tea, and I'll send someone to fetch you something to eat. Then we can wait for him together."

She smiled gratefully, but he saw the haunted look in her eyes. As he leaned through the signals, he watched her standing by the windows, her slim body taut. He shook his head and sighed. If he had a girl like that, now—— A bell jangled harshly.

"Captain C-F on the 'phone, sir," said a rating, his hand over the mouthpiece.

"What the devil—oh, all right." He took the instrument and listened intently. The Captain's voice was crisp.

"Had a signal from Coastal Command, you'll be getting it about now, but I can't wait. One of the boats has bought it, so you'd better arrange for all the usual stuff."

"Was there some trouble then, sir? I thought the operation was pretty clear cut."

The girl turned from the window, stiffening, her face white.

"Don't know anything else yet, Commander. But inform the hospital at once to get ready."

The line went dead, and he slowly replaced the receiver.

"Bad news, isn't it?" Her voice was hoarse.

"We don't know yet," he said grimly. "Come on, we'll get up to the main jetty where they come in."

In silence they hurried along the foreshore, the plump, red-faced Commander, and the small Wren at his side, until they arrived at the old harbour entrance. There was a strong smell of seaweed and fuel oil.

Wright tensed, a string of flags rose to the yard of the boom vessel.

"Damn my eyes! They must be able to see the boats. Can you see 'em, girl?" He gripped her arm tightly.

The sea was smooth and glassy, and in the far distance she saw the fast-moving craft sweeping defiantly across the early-morning stillness, ploughing up great rollers of crested foam. The air trembled and slowly filled with the vicious snarl of the racing engines, until all other sounds were swamped, and the very wharf seemed to vibrate under their feet. Nearer and nearer they came, in a perfect formation, the ensigns flapping wildly, making a splash of colour against the sombre grey hulls.

Wright was counting, "Five, six, seven. Just one missing."

She clenched her hands until the nails bit into her palms. It mustn't be, it can't be, her heart cried out. Not now. Oh God, spare him. Her eyes smarted, so that she could hardly see the slim shapes as they roared round the headland and into the harbour reach. The first boat bore a line of scars along her fo'c'sle, and two still shapes lay on her stained deck, covered by their blankets.

Good old Benjy, thought Wright, he's made it again.

One by one they nosed up to the jetty, where the ambulances stood patiently.

"By God!" roared Wright deafeningly. "There he is! There's your boy!"

M.T.B. 9779 screeched alongside the rubber fenders of the jetty, and the ropes snaked ashore to the waiting hands. The engines sighed away to stillness as the stretcher-bearers went aboard.

She was running now, blindly stumbling over the slimy, uneven stones, her eyes bright, and her lips parted.

Royce stepped slowly on to the jetty, his waterproof suit stained and blackened, his shoulders heavy, as he watched the wounded survivors going away.

Then, with a gasp of dazed recognition, he saw her. She didn't stop running until she fell breathless into his outstretched arms.

"Julia, what are you doing here?"

He held her tightly, shielding her from the scene behind him.

"I brought you your present, darling." There was a sob in her voice, as she pulled the parcel from under her arm.

"You're safe, you're safe," she murmured.

With his free hand he tore open the parcel. It was a bright yellow scarf. He laughed and wrapped it round his neck, then gently, he lifted her chin, and studied her face seriously.

"Are you happy now, darling?"

She nodded, and together they walked up the jetty.

Behind them, the little ships lay quiet and still.

THE TASTE OF ASHES

Howard Browne

"The Taste of Ashes" is published by
Victor Gollancz Ltd.

The Author

Howard Browne was born in Nebraska. After
one year of college he left and began his
writing career, which is almost unbelievably
prolific. He was a magazine editor for thirteen
years, but has now become a full-time writer.
He began writing in 1940, with magazine
fiction-detective, Western, science-fiction, fan-
tasy and adventure stories. He has written
seven novels, 700 radio plays, 15 hour-length
filmed TV plays and three feature-length
motion pictures. Needless to say, with this
enormous productivity, Mr. Browne has never
had time to travel outside the U.S.A. He now
lives in California, writing under the names of
John Evans and Howard Browne.

CHAPTER ONE

Out in the Risewood Terrace section of Olympic Heights the streets run heavily to curves and circles and dead ends. Along them live the captains of industry, in bright new homes of face brick and fieldstone and redwood, very modern, very functional, with assembly-line lawns transplanted trees and shrubbery and exactly the right amounts of carefully draped ivy to kill that too-new look. On the front seats of late model sedans each morning are shiny dispatch cases filled with sales campaigns and cost analyses and corporation law.

The time was around eleven in the morning of a warm half-cloudy June day. I had driven out from Chicago in response to a phone call the previous afternoon from a Mrs. Serena Delastone, who thought she might require the services of a nice polite private detective who could be trusted to keep his hands off the parlour maid and the family silver, although not necessarily in that order. At the moment I was behind the wheel of the Plymouth, parked at the kerb in front of the address she had given me and looking at it.

Alongside the ranch-house and picture-window neighbours it was as out of place as hip boots on a Madonna. A lumpy frame mansion that had gone up about the time the *Maine* was going down, sitting solidly in the centre of a quarter acre of cool-looking lawn under a pair of giant oaks and behind a ragged box-elder hedge. Three floors and no less than twenty rooms. A gabled, slab-shingled roof, too many dormers and spindle turrets and big-bellied windows, loaded to the lightning rods with ginger-bread trim—all in a weathered blue-grey.

And sitting on the steps of a wide shadowy veranda, a small somebody watching me.

I pinched out my cigarette and got out on the parkway side of the car and went over to the opening in the hedge and through it.

The small somebody was a girl.

She was on the top step. She sat with her chin propped on her fists, elbows on her knees, watching me come along the flagstone walk. I got as far as the foot of the steps, stopped there and said, "Good morning."

She didn't say anything. She didn't move. Her very dark blue eyes were round and direct and unblinking, as eyes in a seven-year-old face so often are.

"Nice day," I said, showing her my teeth.

You needed more than a bright smile to dent her. The very round, very blue eyes stayed on me as steady as the eyes in a painting. She was all slicked up. Her dress was a bottle-green challis, high in the yoke, lace insets, pearl buttons here and there, and fifty years behind the times. Full length white ribbed stockings. Black patent leather shoes with twin straps shone like dark mirrors. Straight brown hair, held behind the ears by tortoise-shell barrettes, fell to her thin shoulders and not a strand out of place.

But most of all that analytic stare. I began to feel like a guy with two left feet and a crooked eye. I said, "Well, watch out for draughts," and started up the steps. And that was when she took her chin off her fists and in a high clear treble said, "Uncle Edwin went up to Heaven."

That stopped me. Now it was my turn to stare. The thin too-white face went on holding all the animation of a breakfast egg. "I know about Heaven," I said, just to be saying something. "Seraphim and cherubim and lotto for the ladies."

"You talk funny," she said politely. "So does Aunt Karen. Lots of times. Do you like Aunt Karen?"

"We get along," I said. "No real fights, you might say."

Her face began to melt into what could pass for shy interest. She looked at the fresh shine on my shoes, at the new crease in my trouser legs, at the small dent that high-school football had put in the bridge of my nose too many years before. She moved a hand to scratch an ankle. She scratched with slow methodical thoroughness. She said, "I don't believe I know your name."

"Well," I said, "in a way it's kind of a small secret. But I guess I could tell you."

"Mine is Deborah Ellen Frances Thronetree," she said.

"Not a name to be spoken lightly," I said.

She almost smiled. "You're funny. You know why I like her?"

"Who?"

"What?"

"Why you like who?"

"Well, my goodness. Aunt Karen. You know."

"Oh, that one," I said. "What's so special about her?"

"Well, my goodness. She plays with me. Lots of times. And she's been up in a airplane and she sneaks comic books in so's Grandmother Se'en won't find out and puts them under my pillow so's I can find them when I go up to take my nap like I have to do every single afternoon almost. She cries sometimes."

I traced back until I figured I had it. "That would be Aunt Karen? The one who cries sometimes?"

Her expression indicated that I was certainly slow on the uptake today. "Well, my goodness. I *said* that. Shē locks her door. But I can hear her. Once I wanted to come in but she wouldn't let me. She says I have bad dreams only I mustn't talk about them or even think about them because they aren't really and truly true. Grandmother Se'en always takes them away from me."

"Takes?" I said.

"My comic books, silly! I *told* you!"

"Why," I said, "would she do that?"

She moved a shoulder. Ethel Barrymore couldn't have done it better. "She just does, I guess. She says the killing ones are bad for little children. I don't see why, do you? Just the bad people get killed, and bad people get killed all the time in the Bible when they're bad, and Grandmother Se'en says I have to read the Bible, and she listens. Some every day. Do you read the Bible?"

"I got as far as the begats," I said.

"You didn't tell me your name," she said.

"An oversight," I said. "I ask your pardon."

I sat down next to her on the worn wood. She started nervously and slid quickly away from me, putting most of the step between us. I stretched out my legs and found a cigarette and lighted it. She watched every move. "Some people," I said, "call me Paul. The ones I can talk to. Like you, for instance."

Her small mouth tightened primly. "Grandmother Se'en says it is not polite to call grown-up people by their first name."

"Pshaw," I said, "I bet she still wears a stomacher."

"He was my real uncle," she said.

I needed only a couple of seconds this time. We were back to Uncle Edwin. The one who had gone to Heaven.

"He was killed," she went on in the same quiet, detached way. "With a gun."

I blew some smoke out into the soft June air. "You mean on purpose? Or was it an accident?"

She stared at me gravely. "Lots of policemen came and one

stepped on Grandmother Se'en's pansy bed and she scolded him."

"They never did know where to put their feet," I said.

She looked away from me and didn't say anything. In the silence I drew deeply on my cigarette and watched a bluejay rooting around in a wet spot on the lawn. His heart wasn't actually in it, as if he'd eaten too much already and this was just for practice.

A car turned the corner and drifted slowly on down past my Plymouth. A two-tone Mercury, black and grey, apparently just off the washrack. A buggy-whip aerial quivered at the rear bumper and the words OLYMPIC HEIGHTS POLICE DEPT. were neatly painted on the side facing the house. One of the two harness cops in the front seat put his head all the way out the window and stared hard at the Plymouth's rear licence plate. That kind of attention seemed a little unusual, I thought.

A patent leather shoe moved sharply on the wooden step. Deborah Ellen Frances Thronetree said, "Why is it secret?"

There was that in her tone which hadn't been there before. I turned my head and blinked at the older-than-seven-years-face. The shy friendliness had gone out of it, replaced by a brand of off-key suspicion.

"Why is what a secret?" I said.

"Well, my goodness. You said your name was."

"Oh, you know," I said, remembering. "I was just talking. You might say it's a way I have. I didn't mean anything by it."

Her blue eyes went from round to narrow and moved quickly over the bumps and hollows of my face. She knew an evasion when she heard one, and this clearly was one. When the words did come, they came fast and shrill. "You didn't either come to see Aunt Karen! You're just a old policeman! I don't even *like* you!"

Her green skirt swirled and she was on her feet and down the steps and out of sight around a corner of the house before I could get my tongue untangled.

"Well, my goodness," I said.

The bluejay went on poking at the ground as though nothing had happened. I looked at it, at my cigarette, at the watch on my wrist. Four minutes past eleven. Four minutes late for my appointment with Mrs. Serena Delastone. We can't have that, Mr. Pine. Private inquiry agents are punctual. Or would that be the Boy Scouts?

I put out my cigarette with slow care and dropped it behind a

rose bush where it wouldn't show before next winter and rubbed
a hand across the slope of my jaw and sniffed at the tobacco smell
on my fingers. I looked at the fingers. They were pretty good
fingers, those fingers. I had four of them on that hand. Not counting the thumb, in case you didn't want to count thumbs. That
should be about par for an old policeman.

"Why would they shoot Uncle Edwin?" I said aloud.

Nobody answered me. Nobody was listening except the bluejay
and he couldn't be bothered with private detectives. I got off the
step and wandered across the porch and hunted up the bell.

CHAPTER TWO

A BOLT turned and the door moved back just far enough to show
a length of blue apron, a pointed nose and a gimlet eye behind
half a pair of wire-rimmed eyeglasses with a bifocal hump. A high
cracked voice said, "Well, what is it you want, young man?"

"The name," I said, "is Pine. To see Mrs. Serena Delastone.
I'm expected."

"She ain't hardly up yet," the voice complained. "You some
kind of salesman or something?"

I could make out a face now, a flabby old face under some
blotchy white hair. I showed the face my hands, empty except
for one not very new hat. "No sample cases," I said. "The lady
sent for me. I have an appointment. Eleven o'clock. Today."

"You don't need to yell," the old woman whined. "What you
say the name was?"

I repeated the name. All of it this time. She chewed it over and
said I could wait. Outside. The door was shut harder than necessary and the bolt snicked back into place. That would keep me
from sneaking in and swiping the chandeliers.

The minutes marched by. I put my hat back on and went over
and leaned against one of the porch pillars and listened to the
grass grow. A boy went by on a bicycle, whistling a loosely
arranged version of the Notre Dame *Victory March*. A dog
barked. From far off down the sky came the drone of a plane.

The door pulled back again, not much wider than before, and
the old woman said, "You can come in." Her tone let me know it
wasn't her idea.

I squeezed through and followed her along a dim reception
hall and on into a big square parlour panelled in varnished-over

mahogany and crammed with late Georgian junk. Most of the upholstered pieces were covered with a stiff pictorial tapestry that would be murder to sit on. The carpet had the look of a very old, very fine Aubusson, but was just old. Lamps with tasselled silk shades and ornate finials stood on marble-topped tables with cabriole legs. There was a wide marble fireplace that didn't look as if there had been any fires in it lately, and over it a white mantel kneedeep in dust-catchers, the ugliest a brass clock under a glass dome.

And over everything hung the odour of age and respectability, and the silence was the silence of a bankrupt funeral parlour.

We went on down the room to where a wide staircase slanted upward along the wall. Near the foot of the stairs was a tall narrow doorway to another room, and through the doorway came the wet bubbly sound of somebody gargling. It wasn't any of my business. So I slowed down a little and looked in there.

A huge man was sitting in a huge barrel chair with his legs resting on a huge Turkish ottoman. His massive head was thrown back at an impossible angle and he was snoring, not gargling. He looked to be past sixty, with a wide square face, quite a lot of coarse grey hair worn the way William Jennings Bryan used to wear his, and features that would have been called aristocratic once but were just heavy now. On an octagonal table alongside him were two tall brown bottles that didn't have milk in them, and one glass. He would only need one glass. I couldn't smell the stuff but it was there all right. In the bottles, in the glass, in him. And at eleven o'clock in the morning.

He made a noise like a boot coming out of the mud and turned his head and mumbled thickly. Abruptly he brought up a hand and pawed the air with fingers the size and colour of peeled bananas. He didn't wake up. At the moment a twenty-one-gun salute couldn't have waked him.

The old woman was giving me the steely eye. "The Colonel ain't been well," she said. Her tone dared me to make something of it.

"He should be," I said. "Look at all the medicine he's taking."

She glared at me and turned away. We went on up the stairs and along a wide hall to a corner and around that. I didn't see any ghosts and no chains were being rattled. Presently the old woman stopped outside a closed door, knocked on it, opened it and I went through.

CHAPTER THREE

It was a large room, shadowy in the corners and not enough light anywhere else, although there were windows along one wall. It was furnished from the same period as the downstairs parlour, just as overloaded with gimcracks and with a canopied bed against a side wall big enough to turn a honeymoon into a treasure hunt.

Mrs. Serena Delastone wasn't in bed. Not formally anyway. She was over near a wide casement window open to the morning air, an open newspaper on her knees, propped up on pillows on a bright chintzy chaise longue that clashed badly with the Sheraton and Chippendale. There was a low table next to the chaise and on that a lacquered black tray holding what was left of a once sizeable breakfast.

I took a winding path through the antiques and came out in front of her and stood there holding my hat. She looked me over, not saying anything, taking her time, not smiling and not frowning. I had the feeling she expected me to tug at my forelock and ask if this wouldn't be the day for fertilizing the petunias.

"Good morning, Mr. Pine," she said finally. Her voice had the hard flat bite of a drill sergeant's. "You may sit down. A little closer, please. I'm not a well woman and talking tires me."

I hoped the melon, scrambled eggs, bacon, toast, marmalade and coffee hadn't overtaxed her. I put my hat on a nearby lamp table and drew up an armchair with a tall back and no comfort and sat on it and stared at her.

She was around sixty, I judged, and not a small woman. She was wide in the shoulders and deep in the chest and high in the nose. She had her share of wrinkles but all they did was give her that seasoned look. Her jaw was prominent in a no-nonsense way, her mouth large and stubborn, her eyes direct and without warmth. She had black hair, although there was grey sprinkled through it, set in perfect ridges that looked hard enough to crack walnuts on. She was wrapped in a blue silk robe that didn't reveal much and wasn't intended to. A light checkered wool afghan covered her from the waist down. She was holding a showy lace handkerchief in blunt spatulate fingers. They had the look of fingers that would dig in and hold on.

She pushed the newspaper aside and drew herself slightly

higher on the pillows. Her breathing was slow and even and faintly audible in the quiet room. She said, "I assume you have credentials. I should like to see them."

I rooted the photostat of my licence out of my wallet and put it in her hand. It got the same fish-eyed going-over I'd been getting, front and back. She returned it and waited for me to tuck it and the wallet away. Her expression went right on being no expression at all.

"Frankly I'd expected a somewhat older man," she said. "Still I must say you look capable enough. I hope that you are. This will not be an easy assignment."

I nodded to show I was listening. A light breeze came in at the window and twitched the wrinkled napkin on the breakfast tray. Behind me a clock ticked away with quiet authority.

"This concerns my youngest daughter," she said in her firm baritone. "Karen is twenty-six, very pretty in the flashy way girls are pretty these days, and utterly spoiled. At the moment she appears to be in some sort of trouble and I want her out of it. Even though I'm confident that it's trouble of her own choosing. Naturally what I'm telling you is to be kept completely confidential."

"Naturally," I said.

She moved the hand holding the handkerchief around vaguely and cleared her throat. It was not a gentle sound. "Five days ago," she went on, "a man calling himself by the unlikely name of Pod Hamp telephoned me. He sounded quite mysterious. Here are his exact words: 'It's about your daughter, Mrs. Delastone. She's got herself mixed up with a guy and there are some pictures and letters—stuff like that. Not what either of you'd like to see floating around—if you get what I mean.' Then he laughed, Mr. Pine. A nasty revolting laugh which left no doubt as to the type of pictures and letters they were.

"I demanded to know what he expected me to do about it. He said he thought he might be able to get hold of the things for me, provided I was willing to pay out some money, of course." She paused to lift a solid eyebrow at me. "In short, blackmail."

I nodded and crossed my legs the other way. "You say this concerns your younger daughter. That would mean there's an older one. Since Hamp didn't mention any name, he might not have meant Karen at all."

Her mouth moved in what she would call a smile. "You haven't met Martha, of course. She's not a girl to get herself involved in anything questionable. Certainly not the kind of unspeakable situation we have here." Her mouth went back to a straight line. "I'm not one to mince words, as I'm sure you'll discover for yourself. Martha is past thirty and not attractive in a physical sense. Her interests are confined to public affairs, charities, and her work as the Colonel's assistant at the City Hall. Beyond a desire for a great deal more money than I'm willing to give her, she is no problem to me." She moved a hand in a gesture that closed the subject. Permanently. "You may take my word, Mr. Pine, that Martha is not mixed up in anything as—as slimy as what we're talking about."

"Okay," I said. "If you're satisfied, I am. How much is Hamp trying to pry out of you?"

"Twenty thousand dollars," she said harshly.

"Uh-hunh. Anything like this ever happen before where Karen's concerned?"

Serena Delastone bent to the breakfast tray and poured coffee from the shiny squat electric percolator into the only cup. She took the stuff black and unsweetened, the way she took life. She settled back among the pillows and brought up the cup with a steady hand and sipped a careful sip and went on watching me out of pale opaque eyes.

"No," she said, answering my question. "Not that I haven't expected it. The girl has been a trial to this family for years. There have been several men, all of them worthless. One night, just recently, I found her asleep across her bed, fully clothed and simply reeking of cheap whisky. Her bag was open on the floor with over fourteen hundred dollars in it. I hesitate to imagine where she got her hands on that kind of money. Not from her father or me, I can tell you. And judging from some of the phone calls she gets, her friends are as common as dirt."

I got out a cigarette and moved it around in my fingers, letting her get used to the idea of tobacco in her boudoir before I reached for a match. "About this call from Hamp," I said. "How far did you get with him?"

"Of course he had it all worked out," she said. "I was free to send around somebody I could trust to examine the material, as he called it. He left a number where he could be reached as soon as I was ready to do business."

"There's the police," I said. "They can take this over for you. A score like this is their meat. They arrange a payoff in marked money—then blooie! He wouldn't know what hit him. And you won't have to worry about whatever it is he's got on your daughter. That they know how to handle too."

Her mouth pulled down at the corners. "I thought of that, of course. I have no intention of letting the police get hold of those pictures. They can't help but be utterly disgusting. Let the police get so much as a glimpse at anything of that order and tongues would start wagging all over town. Evidently you fail to realize the position this family holds in Olympic Heights, Mr. Pine. Another scandal so soon could ruin us."

"Uncle Edwin being scandal number one?" I asked, not really caring.

It had an effect. Her whole body jerked and her face turned a dirty shade of white. "Just exactly what do you know about my son's death?" she demanded in a voice like a cross-cut saw.

"It was in the papers," I said, shrugging.

She put the cup she was holding down with slow care. Then she patted the firm lines of her lips with the hunk of lace. Then in a tightly controlled voice she said, "Let me make this perfectly clear to you, young man. You're here to do exactly what I tell you to do. What happened to my son is over and done with and not to be discussed. With me or with anybody else. Do you think you can remember that?"

"I'll try hard," I said.

She leaned into the pillows and smoothed the afghan across her rock-ribbed knees. Colour began to crawl back in among her wrinkles. "Now perhaps we can get on with the subject. No, Mr. Pine. I have no intention of calling in the police. I'm frankly surprised you even suggested it."

"Me too," I said. "But I'm learning fast. What does your daughter have to say about Hamp's call?"

She moistened her lips. "I—well, I haven't mentioned it to her. It would only lead to more of her lies and another display of her disgraceful temper. Actually I fail to see what telling her would accomplish."

"Maybe nothing," I admitted. I lighted the cigarette and stood up to snake an empty saucer off the tray. I put it on the table next to my hat and dropped the matchstick in it and sat down again. "But it might keep her from making the same mistake later on. If she's still seeing the guy."

Her mouth curled in a grim unpleasant smile. "Don't let that concern you in the slightest, Mr. Pine. Once I get my hands on those things she'll toe the mark. I promise you."

I stared down at the clean white length of my cigarette. In my line of work you didn't meet many like Serena Delastone, but even one of her went a long way. "About this phone call from Hamp," I said. "It came through five days ago?"

"Yes."

"No word from him since?"

"Not directly. No."

"It's not something he'd be likely to stall around on," I said. "What do you mean—not directly?"

She looked at me woodenly. "It happens you're the second man I've called in on this matter, Mr. Pine. Quite recently I found it necessary to engage a private detective to recover a rather valuable diamond brooch for me. An heirloom. He was successful in getting it back, so naturally I called him in to deal with this Hamp person. A man named Jellco. You may even know him."

"I know a Sam Jellco," I said. "Not well, but I know him."

A lot she cared who I knew. "Yes, I believe that was his name. Not that it matters now. He proved incompetent and I didn't hesitate to dismiss him."

"Incompetent in what way?"

"No backbone at all, for one thing. And insubordinate. Wanted to do things the easy way. Despite my instructions."

"That doesn't make a man incompetent, Mrs. Delastone. There are times when the easy way is the smart way."

That didn't get me admired either. "You might as well get this straight," she said in a tough voice. "When I hire a man I expect him to take orders. Regardless of whether he agrees with them or not."

"That's fine," I said. "Provided you want a tyre changed or the lawn seeded. But this happens to be something a little more strenuous. When it comes to dealing with attempted blackmail I don't want some amateur breathing down my neck."

She flushed solidly. "See here, young man, do you want this job or don't you?"

"Not if it comes to using your head instead of mine, Mrs. Delastone. If you're looking for a messenger boy, ring up Western Union. They come a lot cheaper than I do."

She sucked in her breath sharply, nearly strangled on it and let loose with a coughing fit that filled the room with a harsh tearing sound. I sat there and watched her fight for air. Maybe I had gone too far. A hell of a lot I cared. We weren't meant for each other to begin with.

"Get out!" she roared hoarsely. "Get out of this house before I have you thrown out!"

I stood up, yanked my hat off the table and headed for the door, not running and not crawling either. I got all of ten feet before her voice snapped at my back. "Come back here, Mr. Pine!"

It was another one of her orders and the tone was still pure granite. I swung around, not coming back. "What for?" I growled. "When I want an arm chewed off I'll try the zoo."

"Oh for heaven's sake," she said impatiently. "Come back here this instant and sit down. For a supposed businessman you certainly have bad manners."

Coming from her that staggered me. I walked over and sat on the chair and there was some silence while we tried to stare each other down. Finally she turned her head and reached for the coffee cup. Maybe that meant I had won. Or maybe it meant she wanted more coffee.

"There's no reason for us to quarrel," she said, calmly enough. "I don't have the time or the inclination to look for another man, and besides I suppose all you private detectives are pretty much alike. Where were we?"

"You had hired Jellco. Did he see Hamp?"

She nodded. "He saw him, all right. Then he telephoned me and advised that I pay the full price immediately and close the matter. While he didn't say so in so many words, I gathered that the pictures and letters were completely disgusting. I told him, of course, that I had no intention of paying out twenty thousand dollars or anything even faintly close to such a fantastic amount. He started to give me an argument and I dismissed him then and there."

"Couldn't you raise that much?" I asked.

"That's got nothing to do with it," she snapped. "You don't think for a minute I intend to let some cheap crook hold me up, do you? There must be other ways to get those things. Only it has to be done quick, before they can do any real harm. It so happens that my husband, Colonel Delastone, is a member of the Olympic Heights Board of Commissioners, as well as being very active in political circles. He had a great deal to lose by having something like this get out. As does the rest of this family, for that matter."

I put some ash in the saucer, keeping my thoughts off my face. "Sure," I said. "I can imagine. It wouldn't do Karen much good either."

All that did was add to her impatience. "That's something she should have thought of. I've certainly warned her often enough about her conduct. If she were the only one to consider, I would be inclined to let her take the consequences. It might cure her of running around with the disreputable crowd she's so fond of."

A lovely old slab of cement, this one. A kind word for everybody except people. Maybe that steel-trap mouth and the rocky face and the crowbar fingers and the hard eyes and the disagreeable voice were things she couldn't help. Maybe there was a heart of gold under that prissy robe and the soul of a saint behind whatever souls hide behind. Maybe she loved her children in her own crude way and endured her husband's drinking and didn't bet the grocery money on the horses. I didn't know any of that and I didn't want to know.

She polished off the rest of the coffee and snapped the cup back on the tray. Her hand was as steady as General Motors. I blew out some smoke and said, "What is it you want me to do, Mrs. Delastone?"

"I want you to see this Hamp person," she said flatly. "I want you to get hold of this—this evidence and bring it to me. All of it. There are to be no loose ends turning up later on. And I want you to work fast."

"The man still wants his twenty thousand dollars, Mrs. Delastone."

She humphed hard enough to rattle the fixtures. "Well, you don't expect he's going to get it from me, do you? Why do you think I'm hiring you? If I intended to pay out that kind of money I would deal with the man myself, not risk letting a third party get his hands on those pictures."

I stared at her foolishly. "You wouldn't like to make a suggestion or two on how I'm to swing it without money, would you?"

"You have a gun, I presume," she said icily. "Use it to scare him into handing them over. Blackmailers are cowards to begin with or they wouldn't be blackmailers. I thought you were an experienced man."

"I thought so too," I said. "But that was before I met you. And if Hamp gets real stubborn I could always shoot him a little. You think that would do it?"

Her throat moved. Her eyes were like the windows of an

empty house. "You'll be well paid," she said doggedly. "You've got to get those things for me."

"Why?" I said rudely. "Just to keep the Colonel in good with the boys down at the fire house? You don't really need the stuff, lady. Just get your daughter killed off quick before she disgraces everybody, give her a nice funeral so the neighbours won't talk, and your troubles are over. Only don't expect me to kill her for you."

Blood poured into her face. It took a lot of blood because there was a lot of face. She reared back and opened her mouth to blast me through the wall.

But this time I beat her to it. I scooped my hat up once more and stood in front of her, hitting the hat lightly against my leg over and over. "No thanks, Mrs. Delastone. Nice of you to call me in, and don't think I couldn't use the dough. But some jobs I don't take. This is one of them. Thanks again and I'll be running along now."

This time she didn't call me back. I could feel her eyes boring into my spine all the way to the bedroom door. I shut the door softly behind me and walked slowly on down the wide carpeted hall, past closed doors with the look of decaying dreams behind them, to the top of the solid darkwood staircase with its massive balusters and the heavy rail worn satin-smooth by generations of hands.

Halfway down was a small landing where the stairs made a sharp-angled turn. I stopped there and listened to the brooding silence and tried to picture the place alive and gay with bright voices and easy laughter and the rustle of petticoats under stiff party dresses, with pale yellow flames from candelabras gleaming on bare shoulders and black broadcloth, and maybe a duel shaping up in one of the bedrooms.

It had all been too long ago.

The Colonel and his bottles were gone. I let myself out the front door and put my hat back on and blinked at the bright June sunlight. The air smelled of today and growing things and young love. The bluejay was missing and Deborah Ellen Frances Thronetree nowhere in sight and except for my car the street was empty.

It was getting on toward noon. Almost time to tuck away some lunch. I threw away what was left of my cigarette and got in behind the wheel and drove off. I didn't took back. Why should I? There was nothing back there for me.

CHAPTER FOUR

THEY had been having one of those late spring heat waves out Iowa and Nebraska way, and early the next morning it came panting in to turn the city into a steam bath. By evening the papers were running pages of air-conditioning ads and the movie houses bragged about it being twenty degrees cooler inside.

It was late when I got home. I turned the bedside radio on and was down to my shorts, drinking a mild bourbon and water and thinking lazily of getting under the shower, when the phone rang.

"Is this Mr. Pine?" A woman's voice, light and hurried and with a vague thread of worry underneath. "Mr. Paul Pine?"

I said it was.

"I don't know you personally," the voice said, "but you know my husband, I understand. At least he knows a Paul Pine and you're the only one in the book."

"It's possible," I said. "That I know him, I mean. Maybe if you tell me his name . . ."

"Well, of course. Please don't think me silly. I'm afraid I'm a little—well, my husband is Sam Jellco. I'm Linda Jellco. Sam happens to be in the same business you are. You *are* a private detective?"

I said, "Hold on a minute, Mrs. Jellco." I put down the receiver and switched off the radio in the middle of a friendly credit jeweller's commercial. Yesterday morning an elderly battle-axe had mentioned Jellco as the private detective I was supposed to take over for; thirty-six hours later his wife was calling me on the phone. A coincidence? They happen. They happen all the time. I lighted a cigarette from the open pack on the night table and sat on the edge of the bed and picked up the phone again.

"All clear," I said. "Sure, I know Sam, Mrs. Jellco. We happened to testify before the Grand Jury one day last winter and there was a little drinking done afterwards."

"He told me about it," Linda Jellco said. "You made quite an impression on him. He told me if he ever needed a private detective you'd be the man. Of course he laughed when he said it, but he did say it and the name stayed with me."

There had been a small catch in her voice towards the end: the sound a woman makes when she's not far from tears. I said, "You think he needs one now, Mrs. Jellco? Is that it?"

Her released breath came to me along the wire. "Well . . . I—I'm not sure. It's just that too many . . ." She tried out a laugh but it fell to pieces on her. "Around eight-thirty this evening a woman named April Day telephoned here asking for Sam. From Olympic Heights. You may know the town—about forty miles north, on the lake."

"I know the town," I said.

"Anyway," she went on, speaking very fast, "this woman told me Sam was supposed to meet her at eight and hadn't shown up. He wasn't at the hotel either, according to her, and while she didn't come right out and say so, I could tell she was quite upset."

I put down the cigarette and drank some of my drink, listening to the rush of words, thinking that it was late and that I was tired and sweated up and that a shower was going to be like a week-end on the Yukon.

". . . would be calling me at ten tonight," Linda Jellco was saying, "and if she'd care to leave a message I would see that he got it then. She said no, never mind, she was sorry she had disturbed me. Before I could get any more out of her she hung up."

There was a longish pause. Into it I said, "I'm still here, Mrs. Jellco. Did you tell Sam about it?"

"No," she said quietly. "I didn't hear from him at ten after all. I might not have thought much about it—although it wasn't like him—if it hadn't been for this April Day thing. When I hadn't heard from him by ten-thirty, I telephoned the hotel where he was staying.

"They had to ring several times. Then, when he did answer, he sounded odd—cold and distant. Simply said he was busy and to try him again in twenty minutes. You would have thought I was some stranger!"

"You called him back?" I asked.

"At eleven. This time there was no answer at all. The desk said no message had been left for me. I couldn't believe it, Mr. Pine. Sam wouldn't do anything like that to me. I even had the clerk send a boy up while I held the wire. Sam wasn't in his room."

That, it seemed, was as far as she could take it. I looked at the clock on the nightstand. 11:47. I said, "It would seem fairly obvious. Your husband's on a job, and I don't have to tell you the kind of hours you run into in this business."

"Don't you think I keep telling myself that?" she said sharply. "Don't get the idea I'm one of these rattle-headed women who gets the vapours every time her husband stops off for a drink.

You can laugh if you like but I'm positive something's wrong. Terribly wrong."

"I'm not laughing. You left a message for him?"

"Of course I left a message. And two more messages since then."

"Is he on a case out there, Mrs. Jellco?"

"Yes."

"What's the nature of it?"

"He didn't tell me and I didn't ask."

"Uh-hunh. You know the name of the client?"

"No, Mr. Pine. It may not sound like it but I'm not one to pry into my husband's affairs."

I said, "Does the name Delastone mean anything to you?"

She hesitated. "No-o. I don't think so."

I didn't say anything. Outside the open window beyond the bed the trees whispered softly in the night air and a June bug hammered endlessly against the screen. The day had been close and sticky with far too much sun, and I had spent most of it baking behind the wheel of my car parked near the entrance of an apartment house on South Shore Drive while waiting for a missing patent attorney to contact his current sweetie. His wife wanted him back for some reason of her own and was willing to pay to have him found, but he hadn't showed. Not that day nor the next. Not, in fact, until four months later when one of the national agencies located him working a gas pump on West Pico, in Los Angeles.

In a sudden rush of words Linda Jellco said, "Would you go out there for me, Mr. Pine? I know it's late and I'm probably acting very silly and all that, but I'm asking you just the same. I'll pay whatever you think it's worth. Sam knows you and he likes you and you can make him understand how worried . . . I don't want to bring the police in; I'm sure you realize why. I'd go myself except that I don't have the car and—well, would you go?"

It was what I had expected all along and I had my answer ready—the only answer that made sense. "I don't think so, Mrs. Jellco, and I'll tell you why. In the first place, where would I go? He's not back at the hotel or you would have heard from him by now. It's a long drive and by the time I get there the chances are he'll have had your messages and called you. I'm not saying he hasn't run into some trouble, but this is a business that tests high on trouble and from what I've seen of your husband he can take care of himself. I know this isn't what you want to hear from me but it's the best I have to offer. Okay?"

She was polite, waiting until I had run down and even a few heartbeats beyond that. "I see," she said finally, and the way she said it dropped the temperature considerably. "You've made it very clear. Forgive me for having bothered you."

"No both——"

I was holding an empty wire. I hung up slowly and stared at my bare feet. Maybe I was aces with Sam Jellco, but to his wife I was now a busted flush. Private dicks had no business being married. Private dicks should live with nothing except a few books and a bottle or two on the pantry shelf and a small but select list of phone numbers for ready reference when the glands start acting up. Private dicks should be proud and lonely men who can say no when the hour is late and their feet hurt.

The bug buzzed at the window. The night breeze stirred the curtains and lifted some of the ashes from the tray beside the telephone. I was free to step under the shower and flush away the honest sweat of a hard day's toil and crawl into bed and sleep the free and easy sleep. Mrs. Jellco might have a little trouble dropping off, but she should have thought of that before letting a guy in her husband's line buy the ring.

I had my shower, not enjoying it as much as I expected, and twisted a towel around my middle and went into the kitchen and brewed a pot of coffee. I drank two cups, strong and black and hot, stirring in a little black molasses rum to give it body. I was wide awake and fidgety now, knowing the reason and not wanting to know it.

Back to the bedroom again. The breeze through the window was a little stronger, cool against my naked chest. The clock said 12:32. It seemed very late to be that early. I lay on the bed and looked at the ceiling a while and a hell of a lot of good that did. I flipped on the radio and listened to what the guy tried to tell me was genuine Dixieland jazz, mostly barrelhouse piano and bad trumpet. I spun the dial and in came Debussy. Five minutes of him was four over par. I shut the thing off entirely and sat up and looked at the clock. 12:48.

I thought of that nice light hurried voice as it had come across the distance, trying hard not to show panic and showing it just the same. I thought of the woman behind that voice, maybe in bed now and finding it as restful as a slab of concrete, staring at the clock every minute or two, waiting for the phone to ring and

make everything right again. Or maybe it had already rung and
he had said, "What's all the shooting, honey?" and got back ten
minutes' worth of the edge of her tongue as a reward.

I rolled over and groped for a cigarette. Go ahead, Pine.
You've got a big soft heart and a head to match. Go ahead and
ring her up and find out. If she's heard from him, then that's the
end of it and go to sleep. And if she hasn't heard from him—
well, you know Olympic Heights. You were out there just yesterday—remember? Forty-two miles out and forty-two miles back.
Two hours for the round trip, not counting the time needed to
fluff up his pillow and button his pyjamas. You may have to
pry the bottle out of his fist first, but then that ought to be easy
for a capable guy like you. And then you can buzz the little
woman and let her know hubby is fine and dandy so she can get
her beauty sleep and rise up bright and early the next morning
and go out buying a hat or two to teach him not to worry her
after this.

Unless I could come up with a short cut.

The downstairs switchboard dialled Information for me. I told
her what I was after and she said, "One moment, please," and
there was the sound of pages being turned.

A moment was all it took her. "I'm sorry, sir. I don't find an
April Day listed in Olympic Heights."

"How's the weather out there?"

Her voice stayed flat and impersonal, the way Mr. Bell insisted
they all sound. "If you will dial——"

"Skip it," I said. "I already know. Hot as the devil's bathtub
and with about as much breeze as you find in a vacuum tube.
I'll bet you on it."

"Will there be anything else, sir?"

I said there wouldn't and thanked her and put back the
receiver and took the Chicago directory off the nightstand shelf.
It showed an office number for Jellco in the Loop and a residence
number under her name. On Jeffery Avenue, far out on the
southeast side of town.

She must have been sitting there with the phone in her lap.
Her voice shook with relief and unshed tears. "Sam! My God,
I've been nearly out of my——"

"No," I said. "Paul Pine again, Mrs. Jellco. No word, hunh?"

She needed a moment before she could trust her voice. "No,"
she said thickly. "No word. Nothing."

"All right. What hotel and what room number?"

"Then . . . you're going?"

"Why else would I be calling you, Mrs. Jellco?"

"I— It's the Olympia House. Room 304. This is awfully——"

"Isn't it? It'll take me an hour to get there. At least. He'll have called you before then and everything will be just peachy, and the bill you'll get will have you on beans and rye bread for the rest of the month. And don't think I'm kidding."

"I'm very grateful to you," she said in a small voice.

"It's just that I need the money," I said and hung up.

CHAPTER FIVE

OLYMPIC HEIGHTS. A spread-out town with a population just short of the fifty-thousand mark. It ran to wide streets and a network of boulevards, a lot of fancy municipal landscaping that would show up big on the tax bills, and a nice shiny modern downtown district on the lake front. From there the town fanned out in three directions, with the stately homes and the big estates dotting the hills to the north and west.

It was shortly before two o'clock when I drove into the business section. Bars and an all-night restaurant or two were doing fine, judging from the noise and lights, but everything else was closed down for the night. A native reading a paper under a corner street lamp gave me directions, and I drove around a few corners and nosed into a diagonal parking slot half a block below the Olympia House.

A brightly lighted marquee of stainless steel and frosted glass ran the full length of the hotel front. Milling around under it were fifty or sixty solid citizens, all shapes and sizes, all sporting big blue celluloid badges that read: CENTRAL STATES REALTY ASSOCIATION in white letters not quite a foot high. A warm friendly crowd, most of it getting along in years and weight, full of noisy greetings and cigar smoke, the men in business suits, the women decked out in evening dresses that went in heavily for lace insets and bare shoulders.

I edged through them and on through one of the revolving doors and up a short flight of maroon-carpeted steps to a large square brightly lighted lobby loaded to the gunwales with more of the blue-badge set. This was the big night. Stray wisps of perfume, the pharmaceutical bite of Scotch, more cigar smoke, more powdered backs. A vortex of voices and a great deal of laughter, most of it shrill. A Mr. Lanihan was being paged by a middle-aged bellhop in a maroon-and-silver monkey suit. No activity to speak of for the registration clerk or the cashiers, but a double line in front of the key-and-mail desk.

I circled the mob, hunting the elevator bank and finally finding it around a corner in time to get swept into a waiting car by a rush of conventioneers ready to call it a night. I had my hat dented and my shine ruined and the smell of Sen-Sen breathed in my face. I took it all without a murmur. Not taking it could have earned me a belt over the head with a mortgage.

Six of us got off at the third floor. I stopped to light a cigarette, letting the others get ahead of me. One of the men had a pot belly and an orchid in his teeth and his audience was dying at the top of its lungs. All except a hard-bitten red-head who kept saying, "George is *so* funny," in a voice you could chop a cord of wood with.

And then they were gone and their noise with them and I was walking down a long silent hall, past dark brown doors with raised metal numbers on them in an off-white shade. Number 304 was all the way back, near a fire exit. A thin line of light showed below the door, indicating that Mr. Jellco had finally wandered in and solved everybody's problem. Or maybe he simply had left without turning off the lights, as any hotel manager could tell you guests have a bad habit of doing.

No door buzzers at the Olympia House. That didn't slow me down. I knocked.

No feet hit the floor, no voice barked a question, no lock snicked back. I tried a second time, putting a little more muscle behind it, with the same result. I shrugged and breathed in some more cigarette smoke and looked back along the deserted corridor. An old, old story. Another night, another hallway, another door knocked on with nothing to show for it except bruised knuckles and the memory of a distant echo.

Mr. Jellco wasn't in. Mr. Jellco was out, likely in some corner pub and a tall frosted glass to lean on. If he was a man given to drink. He had nibbled two or three with me six months or so before, but you couldn't rightly hold that against him. Two or three drinks on a cold winter afternoon don't make a man a lush.

Well, I could go back down to the lobby and sit among the realtors and wait. That would be the easy way. Only there might be something in his room to furnish a lead: an address jotted down on the desk blotter, a crumpled phone message in the waste basket. If Linda Jellco was going to pay me I might as well earn the money.

I tried the knob. It was a freshly polished brass knob and it yielded the way a bank vault yields at two in the morning. You don't get in, friend. Not without the key you don't. And this was a modern fireproof hotel, recently built, and there would be none of this cute business of clicking back the lock with a nail file or a tough strip of plastic, neither of which I had on me at the moment anyway.

Nothing left except to leave as quietly as I had come. I walked back to the elevators and rode down with an operator who was asleep on his feet. The lobby still looked like fight night at the stadium. There was a grouping of couches, chairs and rubber plants across from the desk. One of the chairs was empty. I beat an upholstered female to it and sat down. The lady didn't like it but I looked too healthy to hit.

Some time creaked by. I continued to sit. The rustle of feet, the surf-sound of voices, the lights—all were tugging at my eyelids. I shook my head and tortured a cigarette and watched the key clerk. He was a harassed little man with a company smile pasted on his face, handing out keys, answering questions, hating every minute of it. Behind him was the key-and-mail rack, and even my heavy eyes could make out the numbers across the distance. In the slot marked 304 were some slips of paper. And a key.

I left the chair and went over and joined the knot of guests and added my palm to those already under his nose. I said, "304," in a bored voice. A tagged key and four message slips were slapped into my hand. I turned away, not quick and not slow, and strolled towards the elevators. It had been easy. Anybody could have done it.

Another crowd was waiting for an up car and I waited with it. At the third floor two men got off with me and moved away, around a corner and out of sight. I dropped my cigarette into a sand jar and drifted on down the hall, meeting no one, hearing nothing that meant anything. I stopped outside 304 for the second time that night, knocked again for no reason except it's the way it is done, got the same answer as before, slid the key into the lock, turned it and pushed the door open.

CHAPTER SIX

HE was on the floor at the foot of the bed, lying on his belly under the hot glare of the ceiling light, fully dressed, his arms at his sides, his face turned toward me. His eyes were half open with only the whites showing, his square not unhandsome face the colour of library paste, his thick black hair rumpled. A pool of blood had formed under him and crept out at the side to leave a dark jagged stain on the tan broadloom carpeting.

I stepped in and closed the door softly and leaned against it, feeling the muscles of my face slowly tighten and the taste of metal forming in my mouth. Maybe this was something I had expected all along. Maybe at a time like this the phantom fingers of prescience reach out ahead of you, preparing you, cushioning the shock. Maybe I was a little nuts.

No sound. No sound at all. My eyes flicked around, getting everything in. The bathroom door was open and darkness beyond it. I slid over and reached in and felt along the wall until my fingers hit a switch that turned on a light above the mirror. Nobody lurking behind the door, nobody soaking in the tub. A crumpled hand towel on the sink had no bloodstains or powder burns on it. A glass shelf below the medicine chest held shaving tools and a toothbrush. Nothing in the chest except hotel soap and a supply of toilet tissue. I used my handkerchief to wipe what I had touched and backed out of there.

Directly across from the bathroom was the door to the room's one closet. An oversized black leather suitcase stood against the back wall, a couple of "Fly United" airline labels pasted on the side towards me and a leather tag attached to the handle. A neatly typed card under the tag's glassine window read, "Samuel G. Jellco, 7498 Jeffery Ave., Chicago, Ill." I wondered what the "G" stood for. A suit and raincoat on hangers on the closet rod, another suit on the floor looking stepped on. I left it there.

I crossed to the body. Jellco, all right, and no mistake. Wearing a summer-weight suit, light grey, and a porous white shirt. I couldn't see his necktie. The jagged white scar across the back of his right hand had been there last winter. I remembered him running a thumb lightly across it and saying something about never starting up with a guy holding a broken beer bottle.

I bent down and felt along the side of his neck, hunting the big artery and not finding it, knowing all along I wouldn't find it. A thin red bruise behind his left ear disappeared into the hairline. He might have hit the foot of the bed there on his way down. Anything was possible. The flesh was cool but not yet cold. On a warm night it takes longer.

Beyond the body was the bed and beyond the bed one of these small table desks they give you in hotels in case you have to write home for money. Light glinted on metal near the far leg of the desk. Dull bluish metal. A gun.

I unkinked my back and stepped across the body and squatted down next to the gun, looking at it, not touching it. It was a .32-calibre Smith & Wesson revolver, the short barrelled model that weighs about a pound. Deadly accurate up to fifty yards. Only Sam Jellco hadn't had any fifty yards. A few feet at the most. Without touching the gun I sniffed at the muzzle and caught the bright tang of burned cordite. Not overpowering but it was there just the same.

I rose up again. One window, closed tight, behind figured green-and-grey drapes and a tilted eggshell Venetian blind. On the desktop a cheap glass ashtray holding the dottle from a pipe and nine cigarette stubs, three of them showing faint traces of lip rouge. Two highball glasses side by side, each with a little clear water at the bottom that could have been left there by melted ice cubes. Nothing else on the desk except the standard items found on hotel desks everywhere, and under it a small oval-shaped wastebasket.

I plunked the basket on the desk chair and dipped into it. The Cellophane from a cigarette pack, a crumpled square of grey wrapping paper, a broken length of red string, another sheet of wrapping paper, quite good-sized, that had the words *Olympic Florists* worked into it over and over like a visible water mark. Under that was an oversize glossy-black matchbook cover with nothing printed on it except the initials CCC in tall thin sans-serif letters. I refilled the basket, set it under the desk and went back to the body.

It was important not to move him, which made getting into the pockets difficult at best. But it had to be done. Or I thought it had to be done.

His wallet held the usual identification and credit cards, a driver's licence and over a hundred dollars in tens and twenties. I put the wallet aside. Next a very good straight-stemmed briar pipe, an import, with SGJ engraved in Old English script on the gold band. A leather keycase, an initialled handkerchief with a smear of lipstick on it, seventy-four cents in change, a pocket comb, a battered tobacco pouch almost empty. That was all. If any of it added up to a clue, I wasn't bright enough to interpret it.

By this time I knew a little more than when I first opened the door to 304. Not enough, however—not nearly enough. I finished putting the stuff back and stood there for a long time, thinking of the day I had first run into Sam Jellco.

The wooden benches outside the Grand Jury room had no comfort in them that snowy January afternoon. Just the two of us sitting there, smoking his cigarettes while waiting to be called in. We had talked, easy aimless talk about nothing in particular, and afterward we stopped off at a bar on Twenty-sixth Street for an hour or so. I remembered him as a soft-spoken, alert-eyed man in his early thirties who evidently read a lot, who knew a good deal about music, and who had been booted off the Salt Lake City police force for insubordination. Something had been said at the time about our keeping in touch, but I never saw him again.

Until tonight.

Well, he was dead now. Dead on the floor of a hotel room, his blood staining the carpet and his dreams as dust, while the woman who loved him walked a distant floor.

The telephone was on the night stand waiting. Waiting for me to put through a call to the local law and break the big news. Pine finds another body. His first in Olympic Heights, but then he's only been in town forty minutes or so. Tune up the chapel organ, oil those catafalque rollers, dust off the lilies, ring up Local 22 of the Grave Diggers Union. Pine is abroad in the land and the mortality rate starting to climb.

That wasn't getting me anywhere either.

The phone made me think of the message slips I had been handed along with the room key. I brought them out and smoothed them carefully. The wording on all four was identical: "Mr. Jellco, call your wife, urgent" and signed with scrawled initials I couldn't decipher. Not that it mattered. Each slip showed the imprint of a time-stamp in purple ink, with the first at 11:02, the last at 1:44. I put all four on the desk and laid the room key on top of them and reached a hand up and rubbed it hard along the side of my jaw.

I remembered the number, or thought I did, and the hotel operator put my call through. Linda Jellco had the receiver up before the first ring was all the way out. She said, "Hello." Only the one word, and that not very robust, and in it a war between hope and anxiety.

I bit down on my teeth. "Paul Pine again, Mrs. Jellco."

A small sound I couldn't identify. Then: "I was beginning to think you'd never call. Have you found Sam?"

"Yeah," I said. "Yeah, I found him."

A small pool of silence and then her voice coming out of it. "I don't like the way you sound, Mr. Pine."

"I don't like it either," I said. "I ought to come in and tell you what I have to tell you, Mrs. Jellco, only there's no time for that. Not now."

"You're frightening me," she said quietly. "Please tell me the truth."

"Sam is dead, Mrs. Jellco."

A small shuddering cry, very brief, and then nothing. Nothing at all. I could have done it better perhaps. Afraid I have bad news and you must be brave and if there's anything I can do. Only in the end it would be all the same anyway. The shock would be just as great and the pain just as sharp, and when the tears came there would be just as many tears.

I went on holding the receiver, waiting. When finally she spoke, there were no tears, no hysteria. Only her voice, suddenly strong and clear. "Where is he? How did it happen?"

"At the hotel," I said. "In his room. He was shot."

"He was . . . you mean he was m-murdered?"

"Looks that way. Did Sam have a gun? A ·32 Smith & Wesson?"

"He has a gun. I'm sure I wouldn't know what kind . I'm coming out there."

"Sure," I said. "But not to the hotel. Go directly to Police Headquarters."

"They . . . know about it?"

"You were the first," I said. "I'm sorry about this, Mrs. Jellco. I don't know who is responsible or why. Maybe the cops can come up with the answers. If that makes it any easier."

"Easier?" she repeated bitterly. "I—I can't talk any more, Mr. Pine. Not right now. Goodbye."

A faint click told me I was alone. I cradled the receiver and took out my handkerchief and wiped my forehead and hands. The whites of the dead man's eyes glistened in the harsh light. I went over and drew the blind up a little and raised the window about a foot. Red neon in a bar window across the way spelled out *Miller's High-Life Beer*. A side street, quiet and empty at this hour.

I came back across the room and reached for the phone again. This time it would be the guardians of law and order. They would come over quick enough and tromp in, their hands close to the butts of their guns, and see what there was to see. Then they would haul me in and breathe in my face and yell in my ear and ask eight thousand questions, some of them sensible, and get sore at the cute way I had got into Jellco's room. There would be hard eyes and furrowed brows and an acre of suspicion and far too much tough talk about locking me up and mailing the key to their representative in Tierra del Fuego. It would be like that. It had never been any other way.

The girl on the board said, "At your service"—the Olympia House idea of good public relations.

"Get me the police," I said.

It threw her for a loss. "The . . . police?" She sounded young and unsure of herself.

"They have police in this burg, don't they?" I said.

"Why, yes sir. I'll ring the manager. He'll—"

"The hell with the manager," I said. "If you'll pardon the expression. The cops is what I asked for and the cops is what I want. And don't go chasing any hotel dick up here either."

"Yes sir." There was the uneven clicking of a number being dialled, a buzz, then a polite masculine voice said, "Police Department. Sergeant Chalmers speaking. May I help you?"

I took the receiver away from my ear, stared at it in disbelief, then put it back again. Olympic Heights must have had something I didn't know about.

"I want to report a shooting," I said.

CHAPTER SEVEN

THEY made it in twelve minutes flat. No siren howled in the street, no feet clomped along the corridor, no impatient voice bellowed, "C'mon, open up in there." Just a quiet knock at the door, and when I drew it back two slender well-dressed men looking in at me, their expressions sober but not at all unfriendly.

The taller of the pair had a lean tanned intelligent face and a confident manner. He looked past my shoulder, then at me. "Mr. Pine?"

"That's right."

"I'm Detective-Lieutenant Fontaine, Olympic Heights police."
He brought out a small leather folder from a side pocket of his
coat, flipped it open to show me an enamelled blue-and-gold
buzzer, flipped it shut again and dropped it back into the same
pocket—all of it done with a kind of negligent grace. "My
associate, Sergeant Gillian."

"Pleased to meet you," I said.

They came in and the door was closed. Lieutenant Fontaine's
bright blue eyes circled the room casually, missed nothing. He
was almost too handsome and not at all soft. He wore a dark grey
tropical worsted, not a wrinkle in it, a pale pink shirt with the
collar points buttoned down, a black knit tie held in place by
a gold clasp. His black shoes were loafers, over black nylon
socks. No hat, and his dark hair was clipped down almost to a
crew-cut. He looked like a college boy who had got into ad-
vertising and was doing all right. Except that he was no longer
a boy.

He said, "I should like to see your identification, sir."

I got out the photostat for him. He memorized it and handed
it back, nodded sharply and walked past me with a quick light
step and went down on one knee beside Jellco's body. He put the
back of a hand against the dead man's cheek, moved one of the
arms to check the degree of rigor, touched the blood on the rug
with the tip of one finger. Next he located the wallet and eased
it out, checked the cards in it, counted the money, then put the
wallet back. He stood up, dusted his knee and came back to where
the sergeant and I were standing.

"A Samuel Jellco," he said. "A Chicago private investigator.
In your line, Mr. Pine. A friend of yours?"

"We met once a few months back," I said.

"You reported that he was dead when you found him, I understand. How long ago was that?"

"That I found him? I guess half an hour to forty minutes."

He smiled pleasantly. He couldn't have been nicer if he owed
me money. "These are simply preliminary questions, you understand. As soon as the coroner and the laboratory technicians
arrive, we'll run down to the station and take a statement from
you. If you don't mind."

I shrugged. "I don't mind."

"Fine. We like to do these things in the right way. This is
all unofficial, of course—at the moment, anyway—and you may

speak freely." He gave me another helping of his smile. "How was it you happened to find him?"

"I spoke to Mrs. Jellco earlier tonight," I said. "She'd had a phone conversation with her husband that didn't sound right. When she called him back there was no answer and that really worried her. So I agreed to drive out here and see what was wrong, if anything. Incidentally, Lieutenant, she's been told about this and she's on her way out. I hope that was all right?"

"Certainly. Saves us——"

A knock at the door interrupted him. The sergeant opened up and three men came in loaded down with bags and cameras. Two were on the youngish side with the look of crime-lab men about them; the other was much older and had the tired face and calm eyes of a small-town G.P. He would be the coroner.

They went past us to the bed and put their bags down on the nice clean counterpane and catches were snapped open. Lieutenant Fontaine put a friendly hand on my shoulder. "Perhaps you had better wait in the car, Pine. This shouldn't take long. At least I hope not. Sergeant."

Gillian gave him a snappy salute and the two of us stepped into the corridor. The sergeant got out his cigarettes, gave me one and held a match. He had sandy hair cut the same way as the the lieutenant's, a square good-humoured pink face with a sprinkling of freckles across it, and a crooked grin. "Your jaw's been hanging down on your necktie for ten minutes," he said conversationally. "This the first time you ever saw a police officer at work?"

"You can't kid me," I said. "That guy's no cop. Where's the beetling brow and the heavy scowl? Where's the suspicious manner and the tough language?"

He waved out the match, dropping it in his pocket instead of on the hotel carpet. "You been meeting the wrong kind of fuzz, mister. I've heard of the boys you're talking about. Not in Olympic Heights. The Colonel wouldn't stand for it. Mostly college men here, a lot of us cum laude. B.A., myself. University of Pittsburgh."

" 'Though Birnam wood be come to Dunsinane,' " I said.

" 'And thou opposed, being of no woman born,' " he said.

We traded grins. "Nuts," I said. "You're no cop either."

"B.A. is what I said, pal. What the hell, I know a guy on the force who can quote you the entire fifth act. And does, with a few drinks in him."

"Not the lieutenant," I said. "Tea would be his drink."

"Don't kid yourself about Fontaine. No dopes on this force and no pansies. The Colonel has 'em screened mighty careful before any badges get handed out."

"That's the second time you've mentioned the Colonel," I said. "That would be Colonel Delastone?"

The last of his grin disappeared. "What are we standing around here for? The lieutenant said to wait in the car. Let's go, hunh?"

It was a long room, not very deep, fronting on the Chestnut Street side of the Olympic Heights' City Hall. Soft fluorescent light from three evenly spaced aluminium fixtures overhead bathed the pale green walls and heavy-duty grey linoleum. The same brand of humid air I'd been breathing most of the night came in through screened windows, smelling of gasoline and hot rubber. That would be from the department garage around the corner.

The time was a quarter past four. In the morning. An hour ago they had sat me on a hardwood bench with a slatted back across from an oak railing with a swinging panel. Behind the railing were a few desks and beyond them a low bank of olive-green filing cases against the wall between windows. A bare-headed young cop in a tan uniform blouse, a Sam Browne belt and tan trousers sat at a desk and whispered into a telephone. Behind him, at another desk, a plain clothes man read a newspaper, a summer-weight brown suit-coat draped carefully along the back of his chair. Next to the filing cabinets a teletype stuttered fitfully between long stretches of silence.

Not much doing around headquarters this time of morning. Only one murder, and the boys in the back room were working on that. Any minute now I'd be telling my part in it. My head ached dully, the floor of my stomach rose and fell like a leaky rowboat in a choppy sea, the bottoms of my feet burned from wearing shoes at too long a stretch.

Half a cigarette later a door opened in the rear wall and a wiry looking harness bull stuck his head out and nodded to me. I got up stiffly and walked in past him and we went down a short stretch of hall to a door that was mostly frosted glass. Black letters on the glass said *Private* but that was only meant for law-abiding citizens who didn't go around getting messed up in murder.

My escort opened the door and I followed him in. This was a fair-sized office, only one desk and that had a glass top and the things you find on most desks. There was a four-drawer filing cabinet with a white vase of artificial flowers on top, and here and there about the room three straight-back chairs. One wall held a couple of framed prints, the kind you get in any chromo shop on any street anywhere.

Nobody waiting to welcome me. The harness cop circled the desk and drew the window up halfway, then dug into a drawer of the filing cabinet and took out a steno's shorthand notebook. He said, "Might as well take a load off your feet, sir."

I couldn't get over hearing a cop say "sir" as though he meant it. "I'll just do that little thing," I said and took one of the chairs near the desk. The cop sat in a chair under the two pictures and turned back the cover of the notebook and brought a mechanical pencil out from somewhere under his uniform jacket. Nobody could be as bored as he looked.

Some more time passed. My companion moved his feet around on the linoleum and yawned hugely behind a polite hand. A newspaper truck went by in the street beyond the open window, a kid in levis and a Hawaiian shirt riding the tailgate. Over to the east the sky grew slowly pink. Another hot day coming up. I remembered reading somewhere how hospital records showed that most terminal cases breathed their last at this hour. Nobody would have to tell me why.

And then the sound of brisk steps in the hallway, the door opened and closed and Detective-Lieutenant Fontaine was settling into the swivel chair across the desk from me.

He snapped on the lamp and moved it a few inches to one side to get an unobstructed view of me. "Sorry to keep you waiting around this way, Mr. Pine. But you know how it is."

I said I knew how it was. He liked me for saying it. He didn't look quite as chipper as he had earlier and the collar of his pink shirt had wilted a little. But he still had his smile. Nothing could take that away from him.

He took out a fresh pack of cigarettes, tore away the wrappings with quick graceful movements of his tapering fingers, shook a couple loose and offered me one. I showed him the lighted one I was holding and he nodded pleasantly and used one of these windproof lighters to get his burning. He inhaled deeply, enjoying it, and said, "Nasty business, Pine. We don't get many killings in Olympic Heights. Now and then one in the Mulberry

Square section, but that's usually no problem. How old a man are you, by the way?"

"Thirty-four," I said.

"You seem a bit older than that."

"I usually do at five in the morning."

Light from the lamp gleamed along his teeth. "You've got a point there. We'll try to make this brief." He sucked in more smoke and blew it out in a thin streamer. "What we'll need is a statement from you. Of course we can't demand that you make one . . ."

"Glad to co-operate, Lieutenant."

He let me see that I occupied a high place on his list of favourites. "I knew you'd feel that way about it, Pine. Bentley, here, will take it down and transcribe it. If that's all right with you."

"Whatever you say," I said.

"Good. Now if I might see that licence of yours again . . ."

I dropped the photostat on the deskpad in front of him. He left it lay and swivelled his chair toward Bentley and put his elbows on the armrests and made a tent of his finger-tips. It gave him the look of a third vice-president about to dish out a little dictation to an ash-blonde secretary with a thirty-eight-inch bust and hotcha hips.

"Suppose," the lieutenant said cheerfully, "we start it off this way: 'My name is Paul Pine. I am a private detective, licensed by the State of Illinois and at present residing at—' " he crooked his neck to look at the photostat—" 'the Dinsmore Arms Apartments, 6912 Wayne Avenue, Chicago, Illinois. The following is, to the best of my knowledge and recollection, a true and complete statement, made by me freely and without duress or promises of any kind.' "

Bentley's pencil danced across the page, leaving a trail of pothooks. Fontaine turned back to me, beaming. "I think that sets it up. Suppose you take it from there, Pine. Starting with your call from Mrs. Jellco and on to where I arrived at the hotel room. Get in the time of each development—or as close as you can approximate the time."

It took me four minutes. Some of it I left out: how I managed to get into the room in the first place, the fact that I had searched the body, my spotting the gun on the far side of the desk. If you read the statement with your eyes instead of your head, it sounded as though I had breezed up to 304, pushed open the door, found Jellco dead, rushed straight to the phone, rang up the widow and broke the news, depressed the cut-off bar, dialled the cops and yelled for help, then gone over and waited with my nose against the wall until the boys bearing badges showed up.

Everything nice and simple. No complications to start them fingering their chins and hoisting their eyebrows and talking of holding me for investigation. And they could hold me, too. It wouldn't take much. Give them a smidgin of doubt, a breath of suspicion, and I would wind up sharing a detention cell with the town drunk.

My cigarette had gone out. I got up to drop it into a small silver bowl on the desk for that purpose and sat down again and used my handkerchief to dry my wrists and forehead. Not yet five in the morning and already a scorcher.

Lieutenant Fontaine brought his eyes down from a dreamy contemplation of a corner of the ceiling that had gone on while I was talking. He turned his head and looked at me along the line of his shoulder. "Is that all of it, Mr. Pine?" he asked mildly.

"Pretty much," I said.

"Well, sir, you certainly know how to streamline a report," he said, not hiding his admiration. "Not a wasted word. Concise." He hesitated, then added delicately, "Perhaps a bit too concise."

I didn't ask him what he meant by that. I didn't shrug my shoulders to indicate that I was sorry but I couldn't give him any more than what I had. I just sat there.

He picked his cigarette off the edge of the desk's glass top. It had burned down past the edge and there was a yellow stain on the paper. He made an expression of distaste and dropped the butt into the silver bowl. He swung his chair around and tucked his legs under the desk and ran a hand across the short dark hair above his right ear. "A few questions," he murmured.

"Sure, Lieutenant."

"You knew Jellco, I think you said."

"I met him once. We spent a couple hours getting acquainted."

"A likeable chap?"

"I thought so. We had some mutual interests, it seemed."

"Such as?"

"Nothing worth repeating, Lieutenant. Music, books, things like that."

"At any time did you see him after that first meeting?"

"No."

"Anybody ever mention his name to you since them?"

I thought of my conversation with Serena Delastone. There seemed to be no reason for me to go into that. Not now, anyway, and not to him. "No."

"When did you first meet Mrs. Jellco?"

"I haven't met her. Not personally. I thought I told you that." He moved a hand. "Perhaps you did. I'm sorry. Last night was the first time you ever spoke with her?"

"That's right."

"She knew of you, however. Inasmuch as she telephoned you for help."

"She explained that to me. Jellco had told her of meeting me, and the name stuck."

He glanced at the watch on his wrist. He seemed a little tired. You couldn't blame him for that. "As I understand it," he said smoothly, "Mrs. Jellco asked you to make the trip out here because she felt that her husband was in some sort of difficulty. He had failed to call her at a previously arranged time, and when she telephoned him half an hour later he sounded troubled. At his request she called him back a bit later and received no answer, whereupon she requested your help."

"That sums it up, Lieutenant," I said.

"Did it strike you that she was unduly alarmed? Frankly, from what you've told me of your conversation with her, I'm a little surprised that you'd agree to drive all the way to Olympic Heights."

"I charge for my services, Lieutenant. The lady was worried and she was willing to pay to get some peace of mind. So I took the job. I've taken sillier jobs."

He flashed his teeth. They were fine teeth, no plugs in them that I could see. "We all have. Where did she call you from?"

"Her home. An apartment, I gather. On the South Side of Chicago."

"How do you know she was calling from there?"

"Maybe she told me," I said. "Or I might have assumed it. I've forgotten. Anyway, when I called her back she answered the phone."

"You mean from the hotel? That was sometime later."

"Not from the hotel. From my apartment. Before I started out here."

His interest sharpened. "What time was this?"

"Shortly before one o'clock. Maybe a quarter to."

"You didn't mention that before, Mr. Pine," he said chidingly.

"I didn't intend not to. When she first called I was reluctant to make the trip. Then I changed my mind and called her back to say I'd go."

"At what time did she originally call you?"

"It's in my statement, Lieutenant. Around 11:40."

"An hour," he said, nodding slowly, not smiling now. "She could have travelled quite a distance in an hour."

You could almost hear the wheels turning behind that high tanned forehead. I said, "What are you getting at, Lieutenant? If it's all right to ask?"

His eyes were half closed. He drummed the fingers of his right hand lightly on the glass. "We try to account for all the possibilities," he said. "You can understand that, I'm sure."

"Like measuring Linda Jellco for the murder of her husband?"

"Well, now." He opened his eyes very wide. "That's a bit premature, wouldn't you say? Let's move along to another matter. Let's talk about the four message slips found on the desk in Jellco's room. With the key to room 304 on top of them. You may have seen them there, Mr. Pine."

"I saw them," I said.

He fished in the inner pocket of his coat and brought out a small memorandum book with a black leather cover and leafed through it to the page he wanted. "Those slips show," he said, reading aloud, "four calls from Mrs. Jellco between 11:02 last night and 1:44 this morning. The operator took down each message and passed it on to the desk clerk. It can be assumed that he put them in the right slot, although he doesn't remember and can't be expected to."

He raised his head and looked at me. I was supposed to say something. "It figures," I said.

He closed the book gently and placed it gently on the desk and patted it gently. "He was shot around 10:30, Pine. Give or take fifteen minutes. Doc Levy puts it between 9:30 and 11:30, but a couple in the room across the hall heard what they thought was a backfire at 10:30. Or very close to it."

"Correction," I said. "Linda Jellco called the hotel at eleven. When she didn't get an answer to 304, she had the clerk send up a boy. He reported nobody in the room."

He was already shaking his head. "Mrs. Jellco showed up here at headquarters over an hour ago. She told us about that. The hotel has no record of sending anybody up to that room."

"Doesn't mean they didn't," I said. "There's a convention going on and the place is jumping. The help over there is too busy to keep records."

"We're checking the bellboys to make sure," Fontaine said. "If any of them did go up there, he'll remember it. And that brings us to something else. How did those slips get in that room in the first place? All of them show they were made out *after* Jellco's death. The key would be in the room, of course. But not those messages. And since the last one was made out at 1:44, they would have had to be put there between then and the time you walked in. What we want to know is, by whom? Certainly not by one of the hotel employees."

The phone on the desk rang before I could say anything. The harness cop jumped up to answer it but Fontaine waved him away, picked up the receiver and said, "Yes? . . . How are you, Ira? . . . Not yet. Where are you? . . . Make yourself comfortable and I'll be out. . . . Not too long, I think. You might check with Captain Brill. . . . I see. . . . Yes. . . . Yes, of course."

He hung up slowly and looked at me. I said, "About those messages being in the room, Lieutenant. You can write that one off."

His face, once so open and friendly, went slowly blank. "How is that?"

"I left them there."

He made a small gesture with one hand and the cop, back in his chair, poised the pencil, ready to take down my confession. I said, "When I got there the door was locked and nobody answered. I went downstairs to wait. The key to 304 was in the box. Keys were being handed out wholesale so I asked for Jellco's. I got it, along with the messages."

"There are laws against that kind of action, Mr. Pine," he said sternly.

"No criminal intent involved, Lieutenant," I said. "Besides, I was acting for Mrs. Jellco. That means something."

"This is a murder case, sir. I'm afraid I'm not entirely satisfied with your story. Nor with that of Mrs. Jellco. It will be necessary to hold you."

"On what grounds, Lieutenant?"

He sighed faintly. "As a material witness, let us say. I——"

The phone rang again—a longer ring that sounded even shriller than the first. The lieutenant almost dropped the receiver getting it to his ear. "Fontaine speaking. . . . Oh yes, Captain, I——"

He stopped abruptly, listening. His face slowly flushed, then as slowly paled again and grew a little pinched around the mouth. It was a half a minute before he was allowed to speak again. He said, "Yes. . . . I understand, Captain. . . . Certainly."

He laid the instrument gingerly back in its cradle. His eyes seemed to veil over. He reached for a cigarette and lighted it, not offering me one. His fingers were not altogether steady. He swivelled his head toward the young cop. "Type up Mr. Pine's statement, Bentley," he said in a neutral voice. "In triplicate. And hurry, please."

Bentley saluted smartly and left the room, almost running. The door banged behind him. Fontaine got out of his chair and walked slowly over to the open window and stood there with his back to me. His shoulders weren't quite as square as they had been. Smoke drifted up from the cigarette in his hand.

Beyond him the street was coming to life. Cars drifted by. A coloured porter was using a garden hose to flush yesterday's dust from the walk in front of a dress shop directly across the way. I yawned and rubbed my eyes and yawned again. I wondered what it would be like to sleep a week.

When Fontaine turned around again he was his old self once more. He came briskly back to his chair, gave me a brilliant smile and reached for the telephone. "Have Mr. Groat come in," he said into it. "He's around there somewhere."

He broke the connection and reached out with the hand holding the cigarette and tapped ash into the bowl. No more shakes, at least not in that hand.

We were sitting there not saying anything when the door was opened and a tall thin bird came in. He was under forty but not very far under, wearing a shapeless brown suit, a white shirt open at the neck, a loosened and badly wrinkled tan Palm Beach tie, and a last year's panama shoved far back to show light brown hair that had started to recede. He had a thin sallow face filled with what I took to be a cynical humour, a bony chin, and a pair of moist brown eyes under drooping lids.

He said, "Hiya, Lieutenant," and gave me a glance that would have penetrated a six-inch oak board.

"This is Mr. Pine," Fontaine said heartily. "The man who found Jellco's body. Ira Groat, Pine. Member of the local press."

"Private dick, hunh? I got there right after you left. Sure messed up the rug this friend of yours." He swung one of the chairs around and straddled it, resting his arms along the back. "Any idea who pulled the trigger on him?"

Lieutenant Fontaine cleared his throat, getting our attention. He leaned back in the chair and looked at a spot four inches above the top of my head. "Captain Brill phoned me a few minutes ago," he said. "The investigation has been completed. There was no murder, gentlemen. Mr. Jellco committed suicide."

Ira Groat closed his eyes, opened them, picked up one of his hands and stared fixedly at the palm. "Well, now," he said in a curiously hushed voice. "Fancy that. I guess you just never know. What motive, Lieutenant?"

"I'm afraid we don't have the answer to that," Fontaine said. He spread his hands and moved a shoulder. "Perhaps we may never know. He left no note in the room and the widow could advance no explanation."

My face felt stiff. I reached up slowly and touched it. Stiff was hardly the word. Even my throat felt stiff. Maybe I was stiff all over. Stiff and sore and filled with a useless fury. I said, "Ha, ha," in a voice I had never heard before.

Both of them were staring at me blankly. They were still staring when the door opened smartly and Bentley came through with some sheets of paper in one hand. He crossed in front of me, murmured an apology and placed the papers in front of the lieutenant.

Fontaine glanced at the top sheet, nodded to show he was satisfied and pushed all three over to my side of the desk. He took a pen from the socket of the desk-set and held it out to me with a steady hand. "Your statement," he said. "Would you mind signing all three?"

"Why bother?" I said. "You don't really need a statement from me. Not any more you don't. You ought to know that."

"We need your signed statement, Mr. Pine," Fontaine said patiently. "Not that we can force you to sign it, of course. Perhaps you'd like to read it over first."

"You read it to me," I said. "Let the words roll out. I'll bet Mr. Groat here would love to hear it. All about finding a guy who shot himself and bled on the rug. Oh hell. Just give me the pen. My fingers are probably a little stiff but not stiff enough to keep a broad-minded, public-spirited guy like me from doing his civic duty. Not to mention law-abiding and be sure to send flowers on Mother's Day."

His hand had a hard capable look. I snatched the pen out of his fingers and scrawled my name at the foot of each of the three sheets. A blot of ink fell on the last of the three. I laid the pen down carefully and pushed the papers over to Fontaine and picked the photostat of my licence off the desk where he had dropped it.

I stood up. "Will that be all, Lieutenant?"

His face was a dull red. It took him a few seconds before he could trust his voice. Even then it could have been steadier. "I think so. Yes. That will be all."

"I'll be running along then," I said. "It was nice meeting you. I can't think of anything nicer. Not right now I can't. You too, Mr. Groat. Great little city you've got here. I'll be running along now."

I went over to the door and opened it. I looked back for no reason. They hadn't moved. They weren't looking at me or at each other. They were just sitting there in the silence.

I closed the door gently and went away.

CHAPTER EIGHT

AT 6:20 I had the keys out and was unlocking the apartment door. The blinds were still down from the night before and the living room dim and shadowy and somehow unreal, needing only a lurking figure with the blueprint of Bulgaria's new battleship under his cloak to complete the picture.

I grunted and went on through, into the bedroom, and shucked off what I had worn for too long and crawled under the shower. After that I shaved and got back into the shower to rinse off what was left of the lather and got out again and walked into the bedroom without drying myself and lay down on the bed.

Time to rest, to put aside the cares and tensions, to pick up a little shut-eye. Only there was too much in me that had sharp edges and a gritty feel. Too much that was anger and frustration and the savage memories of the night. A body and too much blood and a woman's small shuddering cry. A cop in a swivel-chair, his face a dull red, his eyes evasive. The knowledge that cities are run like cities and not germ-free sections of Utopia. Crimes—even crimes the size of murder—swept under the municipal rug because somebody upstairs wanted them hidden for reasons of his own. The Fix. Always the Fix.

Traffic sounds filtered in through the screened window and died on the floor. The world was awake and up and out. But not Pine. He was safe abed, nursing his wounded ideals, dwelling on the flaws of Life. Think nothing of it, pal. Get on out and make the big money, eat the rich food, sleep with the pretty girls. Like the man says, it's a world you never made.

The bedside clock ticked away. The heat grew slowly unbearable. In the kitchen, the icebox lurched and whined. And then I was out of bed and getting dressed and drinking my coffee, and by nine o'clock I was behind the wheel of the Plymouth on my way downtown.

The rest of the morning was taken up with just sitting. In my office, behind the scarred oak desk, with my heels on the big blotter and the blind tilted against the sun and a cigarette burning in my fingers or the groove of the ashtray. I had a suite— reception room and inner office—on the eighth floor of the Clawson Building: twelve floors of red brick crammed in between two aristocratic skyscrapers on the south side of Jackson Boulevard, a few doors below Michigan Avenue. The halls were forever gloomy and not very clean, and there was a built-in odour of disinfectant and what I imagined to be wet hay, although I had never seen any of either around. The other offices held such going concerns as cut-rate dental laboratories and typing services and obscure correspondence schools, along with a few doctors and dentists who had flunked the course on how to get into the heavy sugar.

At ten-thirty the mailman came by and shoved three envelopes through the letter drop: a perfumed note on pink paper from a woman in Forest Park asking me to telephone her for an appointment; a badly typed letter from a college senior who intended to do a thesis on the place of the private investigator in our modern society and would I give him a few pointers; and a two-colour ad. for an air-conditioning unit for the office or home, no expensive installation necessary and guaranteed to turn any room into an Alaskan playground complete with dogsled and a month's supply of whale blubber.

I got up and opened the blind and breathed in some of the heat and watched a thin dark girl in an office across the way combing out a new permanent, her mouth full of bobby pins. I lighted a fresh cigarette and came back to my chair and tried the

Forest Park number. I got a woman who gushed. It was all a mistake, she said. She had fired a maid a day or two before and missed a diamond watch immediately afterward and had intended hiring me to get it back instead of reporting it to the police and getting all involved in a lot of horrid publicity, only her husband had found the watch under the bed where it must have slipped during the night—"can you imagine!"—and would I please disregard her letter and forgive her for being such a nuisance. I forgave her and found a pencil and scribbled a few lines at the foot of Joe College's letter, saying that if there was a place for private detectives, which I doubted, Siberia was it and I would contribute modestly to a fund for that purpose.

The air-conditioning ad. went into the wastebasket.

After lunch I stopped off at a music shop and pawed the new arrivals at the record counter. Nothing except a lot of long-play noise. Through the glass walls of a demonstration booth oozed the corn syrup of Number One on the Hit Parade: a female sobbing in B flat about her guy walking out while she was changing the sheets. Progress is our most important product.

Back upstairs again. If any customers had dropped in during my absence they had given up. I shed my coat and sat down and turned back my cuffs. It was even too hot to smoke. A fly buzzed in, circled the room once and buzzed out again.

The day wore on. I finished reading the paper and threw it in the basket under the desk and wondered if there were any bars left where they sprinkled sawdust on the floor. I cleaned some of the accumulation out of the centre drawer. I was bored. Nobody came in, nobody called up, there was nobody for me to call.

Twice I caught myself thinking of Linda Jellco. Why think of her? She was just a voice on the phone. Every day men died and wives wept while picking up the insurance money with a firm hand. A hard blow, but she would ride with it. A man like Sam Jellco would hardly marry a bowl of mush. Only that was a lot of hooey. Nobody knows the kind of woman a man will marry. Until he marries her.

At 2:30 the phone rang. Over it came the voice of a woman named Cawthra, at an address in one of those swank co-ops along East Delaware Place on the near North Side. She said she had a confidential matter that needed attention and could I arrange to be at her home at three that afternoon. She sounded calm enough. No, she would prefer not going into details over the phone. A friend had recommended me, saying that I was trustworthy and reasonably intelligent. She didn't say who the friend was. I told her I'd be there at three and thanks for calling.

I closed the window. The girl across the way had finished with her hair and was now painting her nails. The typing might not get done but she would look very glamorous not doing it.

I got as far as the corridor door, then turned around and came back fast and dialled Linda Jellco's number with hard quick jabs of my finger before I could change my mind.

There was no answer.

It turned out that Mrs. Cawthra's husband, the senior partner of a Loop wholesale jewellery firm, had been missing for two days now, and like most of them, she didn't want to go to the police about it. It seemed this was my week for missing husbands. Mrs. Cawthra said it wasn't his first "dereliction"—that he was "inclined" to drink heavily on occasion and that she was quite sure this was simply one more occasion. She looked so cool and self-contained in a high-bred antiseptic way that just saying hello to her was like a shot of penicillin.

I did a little low-key snooping in the right places and turned up an address in Michigan City that might be productive. I drove out there. Mr. Cawthra was on hand, all right, very drunk and in a decidedly unantiseptic bed with a blonde as hard as a jail-house door. I snaked him out of the place without having to show my machine gun, sobered him up some with black coffee at a local drive-in, listened to his troubles, and took him home. His wife was glad to see him in a molybdic way, accepted the old amnesia gag—in front of me anyway—paid me a day's wages and expenses, and by nine that evening I was having cold cuts and salad at the Red Star Inn on North Clarke Street.

It was nearly eleven by the time I got home. No messages at the switchboard, but in one of the lobby chairs, her shapely legs crossed and a white watered-silk box-bag in her lap, was Linda Jellco.

CHAPTER NINE

WHEN I came out of the kitchen lugging a pair of drinks, she was in the big lounge chair, her head back and her eyes closed. Under the lamplight her face had a pale drawn look and her hair was the colour of a wheat field about the time they're getting out the reaper.

"Try this for size," I said.

The eyes opened slowly. Even with the hard core of pain I could see in them they were lovely eyes, wide-spaced and a cool blue-green, beneath a bold sweep of dark brows. She was a step past thirty, I judged, tall and slender and nicely rounded. What she wore was right for this time of year, with the look of quiet simplicity that always runs up the price.

She took the glass I held out to her, thanked me gravely and drank from it. Deeply. A touch of colour seeped into the clear skin drawn tightly over her high cheekbones.

She lowered the glass and rested its bottom on the palm of her other hand. Her smile was ragged. "I needed that. You have a nice place here."

"Uh-hunh." I sat on the couch across from her and took a long pull at my own glass. Some of the day's accumulation of heat in me drew back under the ice-chilled bite of whisky. "Sorry you had to find me out. I was working."

"I should have called first. It simply never occurred to me. I'm not keeping you from anything?"

"A shower and a drink were all I had in mind. The shower can wait. Hot, isn't it?"

"Terribly." She drank some more of the Scotch and water she had asked for. She put the glass on the coffee table next to her bag and gloves and straightened slowly. Light from the lamp caught the shine of her eyes. It was not the shine of tears. Tears were something she would shed in private, if at all.

"A friend drove me out there," she said suddenly. "I went straight to the police as you suggested. They were very polite."

"They don't come any politer," I said.

"I spoke to a Captain Brill. He asked me a great many questions, with a man taking down everything I said. Finally they let me see Sam. I almost wish now that . . . They had put him on a stone slab in a horribly cold basement room. There was a sheet over him and a big yellow tag wire to one of his t-toes. . . ." A lip started to quiver and she bit it for quivering. "I—wasn't feeling well, so they let me lie down for a while on a couch in one of the offices upstairs. Later—I don't know how much later—Captain Brill came in and talked to me again. He was very sympathetic. He said Sam's gun had been found under his body, that a test bullet showed he'd been shot with the same gun. He explained about it being a contact wound and that something he called a paraffin test had brought out nitrates on the right hand.

Sam, he said, had killed himself. My husband had committed suicide."

"Only," I said, "you don't believe it was suicide at all."

Her mouth became a hard thin line. "No," she said evenly. "I don't believe it. I don't believe it at all. And I don't think you believe it either."

Her words seemed to hang in the air between us. I sat there holding my glass, not saying anything, remembering a blued-steel .32 lying behind a desk leg instead of under the body of the man it had killed, as it now seemed the police were claiming. And that brought back the flushed face and evasive eyes of Lieutenant Fontaine and the strangely hushed voice of a reporter named Ira Groat saying, "Well, well, fancy that." They were hard and unlovely memories, like paving stones along mean streets, leading nowhere and to nothing.

Linda Jellco said, "You yourself said it was murder. When you telephoned me. You must have had a reason."

"The cops have their reasons too," I said. "They just don't take a fast look around and let it go at that. They have the boys with cameras and rulers and comparison microscopes. They dust for fingerprints and vacuum the rugs and peer into test tubes. Maybe I made a mistake. I make a lot of mistakes. I'm a private detective—just as your husband was. I serve a smooth subpoena and dig up divorce evidence when it's not too smelly and locate missing persons. Now and then I run across somebody dead. Not as often as they do in books or at MGM, but it has happened. When it does I don't like it and I get out from under like a goosed ballet dancer. What I'm trying to tell you is that I'm no expert on police matters. Just let me try posing as an expert and any law-school freshman could tie me in knots and read Blackstone on Search and Seizure at the same time. Can I get you another drink?"

"You sound like a man with a bad conscience," Linda Jellco said calmly.

I laughed shortly and stood up and carried my glass into the kitchen. I used more bourbon than usual and splashed in some soda and dried my hands on a dish towel. It was a hot night. I couldn't remember a hotter one. There was a dampness under my arms and my feet were on fire and I didn't smell like fresh-cut flowers. I brought my drink into the living room and sat down again.

She was waiting for me to say something. I had nothing to say.

She reached for her handbag and turned back the flap and took out a cigarette. One of those built-in filter things. Five cartons and you can cancel your Blue Cross. She used a pale gold lighter about the thickness of her thumbnail and blew a pale plume of smoke into the room's close air before dropping the lighter into the bag and snapping it shut. Small movements, meaningless in themselves, forming a bridge to span an awkward pause.

"There wasn't any reason for it," she said doggedly. "That has to mean something. Sam was in the best of health, not a care in the world, no debts except on the car and I think the television set. He had no—no *motive*. Can't you see that? Or is it you just don't care? Why should you? He was just a man you had a drink with once."

I said, "What would you like me to do, Mrs. Jellco?"

She didn't even hear me. "We had four years together. That doesn't sound like much, does it? Four years of happiness out of a lifetime? And then there's a phone call in the night telling you your husband is dead. Only that's not bad enough. They try to convince you he did it himself, only he didn't even think enough of the woman he loved to leave a note saying *why* he did it. What am I supposed to think? That he'd done some terrible thing and couldn't face up to it? Or that he hated his wife so much he would rather be dead than live with her? What *am* I supposed to think?"

She was beginning to edge toward hysteria. I got off the couch and pried the forgotten cigarette from her fingers and knocked the ash into a tray on the coffee table and put the cigarette back in her hand.

"The maid on this floor's very fussy," I said. "She's crazy about Verdi and hates Stephen Foster. Try telling her ashes are good for the moths and she'll spit in your eye."

Her mouth dropped open a little, then closed slowly. She moistened her not-too-red lips. Her eyes were deep and dark and filled with hurt. "I thought you'd be the one to—come to. There didn't seem to be anyone else."

"Okay," I said. "What would you like me to do?"

"There is some money," she said, staring up at me. "A few hundred in the checking account, almost two thousand in bonds, a policy for ten thousand that Sam took out last year. I'm ready to spend all of it if I have to."

"To do what, Mrs. Jellco?"

"Why, to—to make them admit it. I mean, make them tell the

truth, that somebody murdered Sam. Then they'd have to make an investigation, wouldn't they?"

"Admit what? That a mistake's been made. I can see you don't know much about cops, Mrs. Jellco. Those boys never admit anything. Not without an ocean of proof they don't—and mostly not even then."

"Very well. Then get the proof for them!"

I sighed a small sigh. "They wouldn't want it, Mrs. Jellco. Take my word for it."

"Not want it?" she repeated incredulously. "Are you trying to tell me they'd deliberately—" She stopped short and got a little white around the mouth. "I refuse to believe it!"

I turned and went back to the couch and drank some of my drink and sat there turning the glass in my hand and looking at it instead of her.

I said, "You wouldn't know this, Mrs. Jellco, but a few years back I worked as an investigator for the State's Attorney's office in Chicago. I'm not saying that makes me an authority on law and order but it did teach me some of the facts of what goes on behind police blotters. Such as now and then a murder being officially written off as suicide. It happens too often at the precinct level in big cumbersome cities like New York and Chicago. In a town the size of Olympic Heights it's not so easy, but that doesn't mean it can't be done . . . and is done if there's a big enough reason. You've got to get support from the top: the right word from the City Hall, a quiet nod from the local State's Attorney. Without at least both of those any police cover-up would fall flat on its face."

"You mean that's what's happened this time?" Her voice shook. "But why Sam? What could he possibly have to do with that filthy little town?"

"That would be guessing," I told her. "In the first place we'd have to know what he was doing out there. Private detectives have been known to find out too much about the wrong people. It might be he pried open a closet door and had a skeleton fall on him."

"Just like that," she said, her voice bitter. She bent to rub out the cigarette and pick up her neglected glass. "Now I suppose it's up to me to bury him nice and quiet, arrange with the cemetery for what they call Perpetual Care, then sneak back to the apartment and stare at the four walls and keep my mouth shut. Just so some small-town pillar of society with the right connections won't have any trouble sleeping nights. No, thank you! You can sit there and tell me it's not going to bring Sam back or make things any easier for me, but I want whoever killed my husband found out and punished. I can't do it myself. You can."

"I wouldn't know where to start, Mrs. Jellco."

Her eyes flashed at me. She was no weeping willow, this one. "Very well. Then I'll find somebody who will."

"It won't be hard," I said. "The phone book's full of them. They'll charge you all the traffic will bear and run up the old expense account and fill out yards of neatly typed reports that add up to ten per cent of nothing at all. And then about the time your patience wears thin or your money runs out you'll be told, 'Sorry, lady, but it looks like the police had it right all along,' and you'll be right back where you started. A lot poorer and probably no wiser."

"Nice of you to be so concerned, Mr. Pine," she said stiffly. "Only it happens to be my money and my patience. And I might be lucky, you know. I might find somebody who's not afraid to take a job just because it means a little hard work. Or even a little danger. Somebody who hates to see anyone get away with murder."

We stared at each other across the width of the coffee table. She was giving me both barrels, working on me in the way a woman works on a man, the only way they know how to work. Challenging me, goading me, showing her contempt in advance in case I turned out to be yellow and without a noble soul. All she was leaving out was the sex angle. I didn't think Linda Jellco would use that one. Not as a weapon she wouldn't.

"Don't try so hard," I said, before I knew I was saying it. "I'll take your money. Just like the boys I was telling you about would take it. You'll get results if there are any to get, but you'll get no guarantees. Fifty bucks a day, Mrs. Jellco. And expenses."

Her face got a little pink. "You'll get your money, Mr. Pine," she said coldly. She took a sip from her glass and put it down and picked up her bag and asked the way to the bathroom. When she came back there was a fresh drink waiting for her on the table.

"Sit down," I said. "Now that I'm working for you I'll need answers to some questions."

She leaned back and crossed her legs. She had freshened her make-up and some of the tension was gone from her expression. I watched a pulse throb slowly at the base of her throat.

I said, "When was it Sam went out there? To Olympic Heights?"

"The same day I called you. He left the apartment shortly before noon."

"He tell you earlier that's where he was going?"

"Why . . . yes. He mentioned it the night before."

"Can you remember what he said? Exactly, I mean."

She thought about it. I watched a frown put a small uneven line in the clear skin above her eyes. "It wasn't much really. Just that he would be in Olympic Heights for a day or two and I could reach him at the Olympia House if anything important came up. Then the next morning he . . . kissed me good-bye and said he'd be sure to call me at ten that same night."

I swallowed some more of the bourbon and lighted a cigarette. "Okay," I said. "Let's take it a little further. Would you say he was on his way to take a job? Or that he already had the job and was going to work at it. Sometimes you can pick up an impression about such things, you know."

"I'm afraid I formed no impression," she said slowly. "Sam was often out of town on cases, and this seemed to be just one more of his trips. I can tell you this much, though: he was out there for two days less than a week before. And again for three days late last month. I don't know why. Except that he was working for somebody who lived in Olympic Heights."

I nodded, remembering what Serena Delastone had told me about hiring Jellco on two separate occasions. "You any idea this last job had something to do with the first two?"

"I couldn't answer that, Mr. Pine." She moved her shoulders with infinite weariness. "I know you wouldn't be asking if it wasn't important but I simply don't know."

"You're doing fine. Think back: did he leave a number both times where you could reach him?"

"I . . . He must have. There wasn't a night when he was away that I didn't know where to reach him." A small smile moved her stiff lips. A smile for what used to be, a smile that went back to the days before a bullet turned the man she loved into a length of cold meat filled with embalming fluid.

The room seemed hotter than ever. I took out my handkerchief and sponged my forehead. "You still have those numbers around, Mrs. Jellco? They might help."

She started to shake her head, no. Instead she said, "It's barely

possible. I know I wrote them down. I could look when I get
back to the apartment."

"Do that." I took in some smoke and washed it down with the
liquor. "Tell me a little about Sam. His habits, his likes and dislikes, his hobbies. Sometimes knowing such things comes in
handy."

She bent her head, hiding her eyes from me. But when she
spoke her voice was firm and unhurried. "Sam was thirty-six years
old. He drank in moderation, smoked a pipe, and loved to bowl.
He read a great deal, thought Puccini was the greatest composer
in history, and hated modern art. He could make a woman feel
she was necessary and important."

She took a deep breath and lifted her head. "Does that answer
your question, Mr. Pine?"

"What about your husband's office? If he was a man to keep
files they might give us a lead."

Her face brightened a little. "Why yes, of course. Room 1203
Seaboard Exchange Building. I haven't been near the place since
he took it three or four months ago. Do private detectives keep
files?"

"In my case, two. Full of atmosphere and a couple of dirty
shirts."

Her smile was lopsided. "Sam's are probably no different.
You'll want the key." She drew the box-bag to her and took out
a worn leather keycase and handed it to me. "That was his. I
don't know which one is for the office, so you might as well take
them all."

I unsnapped the catch. Seven lengths of metal glittered in the
yellow lamplight. I raked them with a finger. Two were for a
General Motors car, two others for tumbler locks, a short thin
one with a number stamped on one side. A mailbox key and a
skeleton job completed the set.

"That about does it," I said. "Unless you can come up with
those phone numbers we talked about."

I closed the keycase and placed it on the table. When I looked
up again she had a blue pinseal wallet out. She slid four
fifties into view and across the glass to where I could reach
them without straining. "When that's gone," she said in a
brittle voice, "let me know."

"This could be a fool's errand, Mrs. Jellco. What it boils down
to is go fight City Hall."

"You're not a fool," she said evenly. "If there's nothing you can learn, then that's that and come back and tell me so. Not that I'll believe it, you understand; it'll simply prove that the police have buried the truth too deep to dig up. But at least I'll have the satisfaction of knowing I did what I could."

She tucked the wallet deep in the bag and closed the bag with a sharp little click. She picked up the white gloves and drew them on and smoothed the fingers carefully. Then she stood up with easy grace and looked across the table at me, her face blank, her eyes opaque.

"After the inquest this morning," she said in an edged voice, "I went back to see Captain Brill. He had two of his bright young men with him. You think for a minute they wanted to hear my side of it? They just leaned back in their nice upholstered chairs and blew pipe smoke around and said suicide was always hard for the family to believe and why didn't I get some sleep. And all the time they were wishing I had the good sense, if not the decency, to get up and walk out and forget it."

"None of that proves anything, Mrs. Jellco."

"I'm not saying it does. I'm saying you could smell the cynicism, the lack of honesty, in that room. They *knew* Sam hadn't killed himself. Don't take my word for it. Go on out there and see for yourself."

I said, "I'm working for you, Mrs. Jellco."

She scooped up the bag with a swift hard motion. "I hope so. Just try keeping an open mind. That seems little enough to ask."

I went as far as the door with her. She said good-bye and thank you and walked off down the hall to the elevator, her back stiff and her shoulders squared. She was closer to the breaking point than she realized. I closed the door and came back to the coffee table and lined up the edges of the four fifties and looked at the engraving of Ulysses S. Grant on the top one. Unless I was mistaken the old gentleman's beard seemed a little more tangled than usual.

The bills went into my wallet along with what little was already in there. I blew ashes off the table and emptied the ashtray into the waste basket. There was the faint ghost of perfume in the air. I sniffed at it, thinking it was like the woman who had just left. Not exactly cool and aloof but no prairie fire either. And decidedly not cheap.

After a while I picked up the late Sam Jellco's key container and bounced it lightly on a palm. 1203 Seaboard Exchange Building. It sounded like an easy place to start. Far easier than a police station that ran to upholstered chairs, handmade ties and good English.

CHAPTER TEN

THEY were tearing up a strip of Clark Street that morning, between Monroe and Adams. Yellow-and-black sawhorses outlined the wounded pavement, and in the humid air workmen used their picks and shovels and air hammers, puffing on their pipes and counting the hours until quitting time.

The Seaboard Exchange Building was at the corner. A chain shoe store and a religious goods supply house flanked the recessed entrance, and inside, beyond revolving doors, was a magazine-and-cigar counter in charge of an enormous Italian woman with gold hoops dangling from her ears. The air was almost cool and scented with Lysol and printer's ink.

I waited for an elevator. There were three of them, two in use. A very tall starter in a powder-blue uniform and military cap to match stood by, clutching a gadget that made sounds like castanets. He looked as remote as a West Point upperclassman. One of the floor indicators swung down through the low numbers, a chain rattled deep in the shaft and the metal doors whooshed apart, spilling out somebody's secretary and two men with briefcases.

I rode up to the twelfth floor and stepped out. The doors slid shut with a soft hiss, leaving me alone in the centre of a wide and cheerful corridor lined with pebbled-glass doors. A framed floor chart on the opposite wall indicated I would find 1203 around the corner to my right.

I walked along the hall, my heels clicking briskly against the silence, and stopped outside of 1203. It was in between Borland & Son, Attorneys at Law, and the Playtime Novelty Co. Neat black letters on the frosted glass read, SAMUEL G. JELLCO, *Investigations*. A smart brisk efficient air about it all, with no hint that Mr. Jellco was all through investigating.

I fished out Jellco's keycase and bent to try for the right one . . . and froze, seeing something for the first time and not liking what I saw. Scratches, several of them, in the metal in front of where the latch would be. Fresh scratches, with a tiny new scar where a sliver of paint had flaked away, and beyond that enough of a crack to admit a very thin steel blade, say, to press back the lock bar.

It could have happened last week. Or five minutes ago. I tried the knob with all the delicacy of a husband hearing a man's voice in his bedroom. The knob turned easily under my hand and the door retreated noiselessly an inch or two. Enough for me to see a Nile green wall, a section of picture frame, the arm of a tan leather chair.

I straightened slowly and dropped the keys back in my pocket. Now was the time for getting the .45 out and clicking the safety menacingly a time or two. In case the prowler was still in there. Only mine was a Colt .38, no safety to click and at this very moment under three shirts in the bottom dresser drawer.

No sound of laboured breathing from within. No furtive movements, no squeaking shoes. I shoved the door all the way back and walked in.

A square reception room, furnished sparingly and in good masculine taste. A leather couch and three matching chairs to sit on in case the detective was busy and you would care to wait. A few magazines scattered along the top of a blondwood table in one corner under a twisted-looking modern lamp.

And in one of the chairs, surveying me coolly above the open pages of a copy of *Life*, a slim young woman in an unflashy grey-blue linen suit and a thin jewel-necked white sweater, her legs crossed carelessly and a king-sized cigarette burning between the ringless fingers of her left hand. Within easy reach was a perfectly clean ashtray, and shoved down next to her on the couch a black patent-leather bag and white cotton gloves.

"Good morning," she said casually. "Are you Mr. Jellco?"

I took off my hat and let it hang along my leg. I said, "What can I do for you?" It didn't answer her question, unless she thought it did.

She closed the magazine and dropped it on the table with the others. "Are you always this late? I've been waiting over half an hour. I'm here for a friend."

"A friend." I nodded and didn't look at her legs, although they were arranged to be seen. "How did you get in?"

She lifted an eyebrow at me. It was a nice eyebrow, as was its twin, not plucked like a Christmas goose and not an exaggerated curve, either. "What an odd question. I walked in. Shouldn't I have? The door wasn't locked or anything."

"Usually," I said, "it is. Locked, I mean. I'm very careful about locking doors."

She thought about it, then shrugged lightly and went on looking cool and elegant. "Well, I haven't touched anything except your magazines. If that's what's worrying you."

She had that monied look. A fashionable Eastern finishing school, a year in Europe, a coming-out ball at the best hotel, with a name orchestra and a three-column spread in the Sunday roto-gravure. Her hair was a rich reddish-brown set by an expert and topped off with a hat of sparkling white material you could have lost under a hangnail.

She looked to be twenty-four and could have been a year or two past that. Her face tended to be round, high in the cheeks and not all sharp angles the way so many of them are these days. Her skin was flawless and she knew enough to use cosmetics as a guide instead of a crutch. She had a firm jawline, a small nose, full lips that seemed a little hard and unrelenting. Her eyes were brown and wide-set, slanting a little at the outer corners to give her a vaguely oriental look. Those eyes alone would get her a lot of attention.

The door to the inner office stood open, with dust notes dancing in a bar of sunlight across one corner of a blond desk. I nodded toward the door and said, "Let's go in where we can talk sitting down. About your friend."

She rose gracefully, snubbed out the cigarette, picked up the bag and gloves and went in ahead of me, her black sandals sound-less against the broadloom.

The room didn't appear to have been ransacked. I tugged the one window open a crack from the bottom to fight the dead air and lowered the Venetian blind far enough to cut off some of the glare. In addition to the desk there were a pair of green leather chairs for the customers and a matching swivel job for the boss. Also three green metal filing cabinets, a coat tree with a woman's umbrella hanging from one of its pegs, a framed licence on one wall between two smeared reproductions of what had been nothing much to start with. Put everything together and you had all you would need for a small business with a reasonable overhead and no sinking fund.

She was already in one of the green chairs, the desk between us, her legs crossed again and her bag and gloves resting on a knee. She gave the place a lot of distinction. I tried the swivel chair. It didn't squeak like the one in my office, but then it was much newer, as was everything else in sight.

I tested the middle drawer, found it unlocked, and took out a scratchpad and a freshly sharpened pencil and put them on the glass top and gave her my professional smile. "Nice of you to throw a little business my way," I said. "Let's start off with the name."

She seemed faintly amused in a well-bred way. "That really won't be necessary, Mr. Jellco. I told you I'm acting for a friend."

"So you did," I said. "Her name will do. Assuming your friend's a woman."

"Yes. However, we can leave her name out of it. At least for the time being. She may need the services of a private investigator but first she would want some information. You know what I mean. Such as your rates and whether you do the kind of—well, the kind of investigation she has in mind."

"I'm very reasonable," I said. "Cut rates if you send in box tops. What does your friend want done?"

I got the lifted eyebrow treatment again. "Nothing very complicated. Are you always so flippant?"

"I slept well. Just how uncomplicated would you say?"

"Well . . ." She covered her hesitation by fumbling her bag open and taking out a wafer-thin cigarette case that looked to be worth more than my wardrobe. "Do you handle divorce work?"

"You mean a little polite shadowing and keyhole peeking? Or just a heavy foot to kick in the bedroom door?"

Colour climbed in the lovely column of her throat. "I'm sure I wouldn't know the details," she said frostily. "She's the one to tell you that. I'm simply asking if you take on such work and what your charges are."

"You could have found out that much over the phone."

She lighted the cigarette with flame from a lighter that matched the case. The initials K. D. were worked into one of the corners in what wouldn't dare be anything less than diamond chips. She put away the lighter and case and breathed out some smoke. Anger was beginning to gather in her face.

"We seem to be wasting a lot of time," she said. "I'm aware that I could have telephoned. In something like this you want to have a look at the kind of man you're dealing with. Otherwise you may find yourself involved with some ratty little blackmailer. Or worse."

"Uh-hunh. How do I stack up so far?"

"Well, at least nobody'd call you little." She ground out her cigarette, although she'd taken only a puff or two from it, and immediately lighted another. "What puzzles me is this cagey routine of yours. I see no need for it at all."

"It's part of the tradition," I said. "Like an Indian rain dance. Do you always smoke so much?"

She started to laugh, but frowned instead. "Are you trying to be funny? What's my smoking got to do with this?"

"I just asked," I said.

"I smoke a great deal," she said impatiently. "I also take a drink when the clock is right, and I'm told my dancing is flawless." Her fingers moved over the gloves and bag, gathering them up. "It's obvious you're not the slightest bit interested in talking business, so I'll be getting along."

"Not yet," I said. "Let's visit some more. Let's discuss a few things that need discussing."

She stabbed her chin at me. "I've been telling you right along what I came here to talk about. If you don't want a client, there's no point in my staying."

I left the swivel chair and came around the desk and stopped in front of her. "Let's talk about how you got in here. The outer door was locked, lady. Somebody kind of forced it a little. It wouldn't be hard if somebody had the right thing to work with. A long thin nail file and a reasonable amount of perseverance would do the trick. You wouldn't happen to have a long thin nail file on you by any chance?"

She started to get up but she'd have had to knock me down to do it. She sank back, her eyes blazing and no fear in them. "Either I walk out of here this instant," she said in a cool unhurried way, "or you're in for more trouble than you can get out of."

"Stop trying to scare me," I said. "We were talking about the door. On it I found some scratches—marks made in forcing the lock. I don't know that you put them there. Maybe, like you been telling me, you just happened to drop around this morning to do a good deed for a friend. You tell it well and everything being equal I probably would have believed you. Only you had to go and dress it up. That made me suspicious. Of you."

She looked away from me, then back again. Her bosom rose and fell under even breathing. She was as flustered as the Third Army.

"Right off the bat," I went on, "you mentioned you'd been waiting in the other room more than half an hour. But right next to you was an ashtray. An ashtray without a flake of ash in it. That didn't fit in with a half-hour wait. After that long it should've had at least a couple of cigarette stubs in it. The way you eat cigarettes."

She didn't quite laugh in my face. "So on the strength of that you're willing to accuse me of breaking into your office. Is that your idea of proof?"

"I don't expect to take it to a court of law," I said. "What I'm after is whether your being here is a part of the puzzle I'm working on."

"Puzzle?" she repeated, making it a question.

"Yeah. Puzzle. The puzzle of who murdered Sam Jellco."

Her lips parted and her eyes got very wide and her breathing snagged. Her way of registering a reasonable amount of shock. "But I thought . . . Aren't you—I mean, I thought you were Mr. Jellco."

I continued to stand over her, leaning a hip against the edge of the desk to rest my legs. "It's possible you didn't think anything of the kind. You could know that Jellco was dead. There's been time enough for it to get into the papers. Not that knowing it would prove you had anything to do with his being dead. Let's say that you did know all along, that you came up here to get something from his files. Something you couldn't afford to let fall into the wrong hands. Only I showed up before you had time to hunt for it. So, knowing all along I wasn't Jellco, you tried to bamboozle me into thinking you came here for a friend, found the door conveniently unlocked and sat down to wait. I made enough noise coming along the hall for you to set the stage."

There was some silence. An air-hammer dug into paving on Clark Street twelve floors below the window. It sounded as though the paving wasn't giving up easy. Some ash fell off the girl's cigarette and landed on the rug between her shoes.

And then she moved, reaching past my hip to drop the cigarette into the tray. "I'm sure this has gone far enough," she said, drawling the words. "I don't know who you are and I'm sure I care even less. Please get out of my way. I'm leaving. Right now."

"Sure," I said and bent down and took the bag out of her lap.

All her carefully built calmness disappeared instantly. She lunged from the chair, rage twisting her face. "You—you— Give me that!"

I gave her my back instead. She grabbed my arm and tried to yank it out by the roots. "Lay off," I growled, "before I belt you one."

I made it sound authentic. She backed away a step and stood there panting, her face red but still beautiful, her body trembling with fury, while I put the desk between us and upended the bag on the glass top.

The usual junk they all carry—and one item they usually don't. A short length of strong spring steel, rounded at one end and ground down almost to razor thinness. Just the thing for putting scratches in locked doors.

I picked it up and held it out for her to see. "Shame on you," I said. "Keep on this way and you can end up making licence plates for the State."

Words fought their way out of her throat. "I've had about all of you I can take."

I smiled sadly and put the junior jimmy to one side and took a woman's wallet off the heap. It was of ostrich skin, with gold corners and a design in gold sequins worked into one side. In it were some bills I didn't bother counting and five or six transparent identification panels containing a driver's licence, a press pass issued by the Olympic Heights' *Daily Journal,* three credit cards, and a picture. I stared hard at the picture. It was of a man's face—a man about thirty-five, I judged, a little too regular in the features but with a brand of hard competence impossible to miss. I decided he would have the olive skin and hot black eyes and flashing teeth you find all over the south of Italy. His hair was black with a suggestion of curl to it, and he sported a moustache —one of those pencil-line jobs Rafael Sabatini's heroes wouldn't be caught parrying a riposte without.

Everything that had a name on it was made out to Miss Karen Delastone, 25 New Cambridge Drive, Olympic Heights, Illinois. I folded the wallet and let it slide back into the bag and scooped the rest of the stuff in on top of it.

Karen Delastone hadn't moved. She stood with her arms stiffly at her sides, her back painfully straight, holding herself in. Even a slight touch would twang her like a harp string.

I set the bag on the desk, resting my hand on it. "I've heard of you, Miss Delastone. Too bad about Uncle Edwin."

It shook her like a shot to the chin. The colour fled from her face, leaving it haggard and filled with naked terror. One hand groped blindly at the desk for support. As a strictly random remark, mine had been a dilly.

"Who are you?" she almost whispered. "What do you know about my brother's death?"

"He was shot," I said. "So was Sam Jellco. A few miles apart. Is there a connection, Miss Delastone? A connection like the same finger pulling the trigger on them both? Would that be it?"

"You're crazy!" she said wildly. "Edwin killed himself. If you know anything at all, you know that."

"That's what they say happened to Jellco. Suicide. What are you doing here, Miss Delastone. What did Jellco have on you that was worth turning burglar to get?"

"I've no intention of telling you anything," she said between her teeth. "Give—me—that—bag!"

"You're going to have to tell somebody sometime," I said. "And it might as well be me. We could even be on the same side and not know it." I got out one of my business cards and dropped it in her bag. "Think it over."

Wordlessly she put out a not very steady hand. I shrugged and put the bag in it. She whirled around and tramped over to the inner door and through it. I heard the hall door slam and then I was alone with the silence and the sunlight and the rattle of air-hammers from far below.

Karen Delastone. A girl who, according to an unknown named Pod Hamp, had been a target for the wrong kind of lens-snappers. Well, she was certainly what the loose-lipped set would drool over. Maybe her acting as a model for smutty art made a twisted kind of sense. A girl with a mother like Serena Delastone could get rebellious in some mighty unusual ways.

I spent twenty minutes digging through the dead man's files and desk. He kept records, all right, and they had the look of having been ransacked by somebody in a hurry. Nothing left that I could use. Nothing with the name Delastone on it and nothing at all on what Jellco had been doing in Olympic Heights. If Karen Delastone had removed anything, she must have pinned it to her brassière. It meant that any lead I got would have to come from some other source.

Such as the Olympic Heights City Hall.

CHAPTER ELEVEN

THE desk sergeant looked tired and a little harried. But he couldn't have been more polite. No, Lieutenant Fontaine wasn't on duty and wouldn't be until eight o'clock tonight. Captain Brill? Why, certainly. I could find his office on the second floor, north wing, of the city hall. Use the main entrance around the corner on Maple Street. You're entirely welcome. Sir.

The Olympic Heights City Hall had a couple of wings and a central shaft of Indiana limestone that went up six floors. A bronze plaque said it had been erected in 1947, with Mayor Orville Bedenkamp laying the cornerstone. A line of heavy brass doors stood open in the bright humid air, and on the way in I got the careful eye from the usual collection of bright boys who do nothing except hang around such places waiting to get their feet in the public trough.

Inside was a wide cool very clean and cheerful corridor, with offices opening off it where you could arrange to get married, buried, open a business, drive a car, own a dog, build a house or tear it down. Halfway along were two elevators, a building directory on the wall between them. Only one elevator was running. I rode up with an operator in shirtsleeves and with a mouthful of Doublemint. I could smell the stuff clear across the car.

The second floor had wide halls in three directions. I followed the correct one around a corner and down some more hall. I saw no one and the only sound came from my shoes against the composition floor. It seemed a lot of building for so little business.

Twin frosted-glass doors lettered OLYMPIC HEIGHTS POLICE DEPARTMENT marked the corridor's end. I went through, into a good-sized square room divided by a counter-top railing with a swing gate, and behind the railing a uniformed lieutenant sitting at an uncluttered desk. On the wall behind him was a steel engraving of George Washington signing something or other below crossed American flags, and in one corner a plain clothes man pored over the tape in a teletype machine.

The lieutenant looked up as I approached the desk. He was still in his twenties—a nice open face, black curling hair with a widow's peak, and what amounted to almost a shy smile. He said, "Good afternoon, sir. May I be of assistance?"

It was the last in a whole series of last straws. I said, "Look, do you say it because you were brought up to say it, or do they insist on it? The mayor, I mean—or would it be the City Council by any chance?"

He looked baffled. In a polite way. "Insist on what, sir? I'm afraid I——"

"Never mind," I said. "You just did it again. Sir—I mean you said 'sir.' There is such a word, but it never sounds right coming from a cop. I mean an officer. You *are* an officer? I mean a police officer? Never mind answering that one, either. You're wearing a uniform and this wouldn't be the fire department, because the sign on the door said—" I took off my hat and scratched behind my left ear and put my hat back on again. The plain clothes man at the teletype had straightened up and was staring at me.

The lieutenant laughed pleasantly. "You seem a little confused, sir. What can we do for you?"

"Yes," I said. "I mean, yes, you can do something for me. I hate to impose but I'd like to see Captain Brill. If it's not too much trouble."

Some of his bright cheerfulness seemed to fade, leaving his expression blank but not hard the way most of them get. "That would be the Detective Bureau. Next floor up. Through that door for the stairs."

I followed directions until I reached an open door with DETECTIVE BUREAU *Walk In*, on the glass.

I walked in. It was the anteroom to three inner offices. Two young men in plain clothes sat at opposite sides of a wide desk with a green linoleum top. One was smoking a pipe over a crossword puzzle, the other was reading a paperback novel. Evidently nobody around there ever bothered making out reports.

The guy with the book looked up, showing me a sunburned face and direct brown eyes. "Yes, sir?"

"Captain Brill," I said.

"What did you want to see the captain about?"

"There was a homicide at a local hotel a couple of nights back. I'd like to speak to him about it."

Nothing changed in his face but his eyes were sharper than when they first came off the book. "That would be this Jellco suicide?"

"Yeah. That would be the one."

"The newspapers had the details."

"So they did. That doesn't mean they had them all. Which is why I'd like to see the captain. If it's all right with you."

He dog-eared his page and closed the book. "It's fine with me. The captain's the one to object. What's the name?"

I gave him the name. He was halfway out of his chair when a sudden thought stopped him short. He settled slowly back, a frown carving a vertical line between his eyes.

"Just a moment," he said sharply. "Pine, you said. Aren't you already tied into that case in some way?"

"At least I didn't shoot him," I said. "Any more than he did."

"Any more than *who* did?"

"Jellco. These pronouns can throw anybody."

He seemed surprised that I should know about pronouns. "Are you trying to tell me Jellco wasn't a suicide?" he demanded.

"I wouldn't try to tell you anything," I said patiently. "You're just somebody standing between me and Captain Brill—the man I came here to see."

He flushed a little. "Perhaps we can remedy that," he said silkily. "Have a seat while I'm finding out."

"This is fine," I said. "If it's okay with you I'll just stand here and count my blessings."

He lunged to his feet, almost upsetting the chair, stalked over to one of the inner offices, knocked on the door, then opened it and went in, closing the door with almost exaggerated care.

The minutes passed. The cop at the crosswords threw down his pencil, tapped out his pipe and put it away, yawned, went over to the watercooler and had a drink. He stared at me over the edge of the paper cup while emptying it, then crumpled the cup and tossed it into a wastebasket and went past me without a glance, leaving the room.

I was alone. I turned my hat in my hands and sniffed at the warm air and listened to the faint mumble of voices from behind the closed door. Feet passed along the corridor a time or two but nobody came in.

And then the door opened and the young cop was standing there jerking his chin at me. I walked past him, into cool air as soothing as a bishop's benison, and he said, "This is Mr. Pine, Captain," in a respectful voice.

A sea-green carpet, walls a cocoa-brown, a bank of files the same colour as the walls, several armchairs in a shaggy brown material. The kind of desk that sits on low runners instead of legs took up the centre of the room, its furnishings mostly leather and burnished copper.

Behind the desk, his back to a window air-conditioner, was a tall rangy number in his late thirties. He had crisp black hair shot through with touches of silver above tight-set small ears, strong regular features under a coat of tan, a jaw like the side of a cliff, and calm blue eyes with fine lines radiating from their outer corners An open face, an intelligent face— the face of a man who would be quick and competent and maybe even ruthless if the occasion called for it.

Maybe this would be the occasion.

He said, "How are you, Pine? I'm Benton Brill. I saw your statement on this Jellco suicide. Sit down, won't you?"

I sat in a chair next to the desk. The young cop had closed the door and was standing with his back to it, his expression solemn. I said, "Mind if I smoke, Captain?"

He shook his head, which I translated as permission. I lighted a cigarette and leaned toward the desk to drop the match into a bright copper ashtray with the Olympic Heights city seal worked into the bottom.

Captain Brill was letting me see that he was baffled. "The sergeant, here, says you want to talk to me about the Jellco case. I can't imagine why. You know it's closed?"

"So I was told, Captain. Only the widow isn't satisfied to let it stay closed. She insists Jellco had absolutely no reason to kill himself."

"I talked to her personally," Brill said, his tone casual. "Damned attractive woman. Naturally she finds it hard to believe." He leaned back and swung one leg over the other. He wore a grey basket-weave shirt with button-down tabs, a solid maroon tie, and a dark grey summer suit a good tailor had sweated over. The insignia of a Greek-letter fraternity was worked in gold into his tie clasp. "We may be only a small-town force, Pine, but there are no better ones. The physical evidence was there for trained men to see and they saw it: contact wound, position of the gun, nitrates on the right hand, no signs of a struggle, and his own gun. We're satisfied, the State's Attorney is satisfied, a coroner's jury is satisfied, and not an hour ago the Grand Jury reaffirmed the finding. That's enough for us; it should be enough for Mrs. Jellco. I can understand her grief and shock, but she must get used to the realization that her husband is dead—by his own hand."

I said, "Knock it off, Captain," in a sour voice.

For what seemed a long time he sat as though cut from stone. Then he uncrossed his legs slowly and leaned forward slowly and put his hands palms down on the desk top and skewered me on the blue blade of his eyes.

"Perhaps," he said in a below-zero voice, "you'd be kind enough to enlarge on that remark, Mr. Pine."

"I'll enlarge on it all right," I said. "Just don't go handing me any of this whale manure about contact wounds and nitrate tests and no signs of a struggle. What you left out is the part about the key to Jellco's room being left at the hotel desk *after* he was shot, the hotel's statement to his wife that nobody was in that room half an hour *after* the couple across the hall heard the

gun go off, and this hanky-pank of planting the gun under Jellco's
body. I've been in this business nine years now, Captain. I never
yet saw a coroner's jury that knew a nitrates test from a leg of
lamb. But let one get its teeth into the kind of physical evidence
I'm talking about and see what verdict you get."

The air-conditioning unit hummed quietly to itself. No other
sound in the room. Captain Benton Brill went on trying to
stare me down. Only I wasn't having any. Not from him I
wasn't.

He cleared his throat finally and a small cold smile touched his
mouth. "I wouldn't want to misunderstand you, Pine," he said
almost gently. "You are accusing this department of tampering
with evidence—in this case changing the position of a gun to
support a finding of suicide. Is that correct?"

I nodded. "You're reading me fine. That gun was six to eight
feet from the dead man. I saw it there, near a leg of the desk.
It was still there when your boys arrived. Suppose you tell me
how it got under the body."

The chill smile was still pasted to his lips. He bent and drew
open a desk drawer and brought out a sheaf of papers and
flopped them down on the glass. The one on top was his meat.
He skimmed it across the desk towards me with a sharp movement of his wrist. "Your statement," he said. "Exactly as you
dictated it and bearing your signature. Show me where it
describes the position of the gun."

I made no move to pick it up. "Let's cut the comedy. My
statement contains what it should contain: the circumstances
leading to my finding Jellco's body. You know damn well if I
had tried to stick in stuff like where the gun was, Lieutenant
Fontaine would've yelled his head off. In a polite way, naturally."

By this time any other cop in my experience would be reaching
for a blackjack. Captain Brill reached for a pipe and an oiled-skin
tobacco pouch instead. Filling the bowl leisurely, he tamped it
tight with a thumb and picked up a packet of paper matches.
His face was as calm as a Sunday afternoon in Tulsa, although
I thought his fingers trembled a little. Maybe I thought that
because I wanted to think it.

He leaned back and puffed out a cloud of bluish smoke and
watched it fall slowly to pieces and drift away. His small smile
indicated that a good police officer tries to humour the cranks.
He took the pipe out of his mouth and rubbed the bit lightly
along his cheek and said:

"You've brought up some interesting points. I don't know of any reason why they shouldn't be answered. Take this matter of Jellco's hotel key. I'll admit it bothered us too. Until we went to work on it."

He was going to powder me on that one. I could see it coming. And he was going to relish every second of it.

"A bellboy," he went on, "noticed the key sticking in the lock to 304 shortly after eleven that same night. It happens rather often, I'm told: a guest drinks too much or has something on his mind or simply is careless. Under those circumstances it's the hotel's custom not to disturb the occupant, but simply to remove the key and turn it in at the downstairs desk until it's reported missing. The bellboy followed those instructions. Does that answer your question?"

"Uh-hunh. Leaving two to go. The hotel told Mrs. Jellco nobody was in 304 at eleven o'clock. Lieutenant Fontaine mentioned that Jellco was shot between 10:15 and 10:45. Somebody's got to be wrong."

He was shaking his head before I finished. "Far as we can determine, sir, Mrs. Jellco made no request to check on 304."

"In short, she's lying?"

"Not necessarily. When a guest fails to answer his phone it's generally safe to assume he's not in. It was a busy night at the Olympia House. As I see it, there was no bellboy available at the time, so after a decent interval whoever took the call simply said there was no one in 304."

"You know who took the call," I pointed out. "It would have to be the same party who wrote out the message time-stamped eleven o'clock."

He turned up the palm of one hand. "The man doesn't even recall filling out the slip. As I said before, it was rather a hectic night over there."

"Which," I said, "brings us back to the gun."

"The gun," he said flatly. He looked down to where his hands were resting on the desk-top, the pipe held firmly in one of them. They were strong hands, lean and brown like his face, with sworls of coarse black hair between the knuckles. After what seemed a long time he looked up at me again and now his eyes were as cold as Alpine peaks.

"That one," he said, weighing each word, "I'm throwing out. You can't make it stick—not with me or anybody else."

"Not even with the Attorney General in Springfield?"

His expression indicated I needed a keeper. "I guess that leaves us with nothing more to talk about, Pine."

"Would it be all right if I looked over the exhibits?"

"The exhibits?" he repeated sharply.

"Yeah. You know. Like lab reports and the autopsy results. Along with the statements of the hotel help and the couple who heard the shot. Maybe I could jog a few memories."

His jaw locked. "Just what are you getting at?"

"The inquest put it down as suicide," I said. "Only the widow isn't satisfied and she's the one I'm working for. It's no skin off your pelvis, Captain. Since it's no longer police business I won't be getting in your way. And if it does turn out to be murder, you'll naturally want to be the first to see justice done. Which is why I mentioned the exhibits."

"You're wasting your time, Jellco shot himself."

"Don't worry about my time," I said.

His smile flickered. "Then I'll worry about mine. Good morning, sir."

I didn't move. "How," I said, "would I go about seeing the Chief?"

"Well, now," he said, dragging out the words. He put the pipe down with slow care and leaned back in his chair, studying me. Across the room the young plain clothes man cleared his throat in a shocked manner. I'd forgotten he was still around.

"The Chief," Brill said finally. "I assume you mean the Chief of Police. In other words you intend going over my head."

"It must have happened before this, Captain."

His jaw muscles were beginning to bulge and his hands were turning into capable-looking fists and he couldn't seem to take his eyes off me. Captain Brill was losing his temper. I liked that. I liked that fine. When their tempers begin to go they start making mistakes, and mistakes were what I was after.

"Yes, sir," he said, clipping the words off short. "It has happened before. By residents of Olympic Heights. Taxpayers, as they called themselves. But not by three-for-a-nickel private dicks from out of town."

"I may be cheap," I said. "But not that cheap. What I'm trying to get across to you is that I don't discourage easy. According to the inquest Jellco killed himself. I think he was murdered. I intend to prove he was murdered, if I can. Letting me see the evidence might possibly help me prove it."

"And if I say no, you go to the Chief?"

"Yeah. And if he says no, I go to the State's Attorney."

He looked past my shoulder. "Andrews."

The plain clothes man came over to the desk and stood at attention, avoiding even a sidelong glance in my direction. "Yes, Captain?"

"Mr. Pine would like to see Chief Maller. Take him right up."

"Yes, sir." He wheeled smartly on the ball of one foot and marched over to the door and opened it and stood there like a palace sentry.

I got up slowly and rubbed out my cigarette on the city seal. "One thing more."

"Well?"

"I never met a cop yet who wasn't overly sensitive about the department. If you thought I was lying about the position of that gun, how come you let me get away with it?"

He frowned up at me, puzzled. "What would you suggest? That I have a couple of my men work you over?"

"I've been worked over for a lot less," I said. "It's not that I'm asking for my lumps, you understand. But me being a cheap private eye from out of town and not a taxpayer, I'm surprised you didn't try your luck."

He let out a slow breath. "I'm afraid we don't operate that way, Mr. Pine. Visitors are welcome in Olympic Heights. As long as they mind their own business and don't break any laws."

"Uh-hunh." I swung my hat against my leg. "How about visitors who go around prying open closed police cases?"

He didn't say anything, but his eyes veiled over, giving me my answer. I said, "I'll go along now and see the Chief. Maller, you said his name was. Thanks for your time, Captain."

He nodded without speaking and picked a report off the pile and started reading it. Only I didn't think he was reading. His ears were too red and his teeth too tightly clamped for real concentration.

The young plain clothes man closed the door for me. He knew his place, that boy.

CHAPTER TWELVE

CHIEF MALLER wasn't in. Not to me anyway. I found that out while standing on his sculptured rose-grey broadloom in an outer

office taken from a four-colour illustration out of last month's
Fortune Magazine.

The man who broke the news to me was a neat small-boned
number wrapped up beautifully in pale tan gabardine and with
eye-glasses in dark shell frames across a thin sliver of face. He was
behind a typewriter, transcribing shorthand into letters on engraved official stationery with the Chief's name and title nice and
big so nobody would overlook them.

I looked past the top of his slick black hair at the closed door
to the private office. "When's he expected back?"

He sneered without moving a muscle of his face. "I'm sure I
wouldn't know. He's out on an important appointment that
quite possibly may take up the rest of the day."

"Do tell. Dedicating a whorehouse, I expect."

He turned a violent pink. "What," he said, straining the words
through his teeth, "was it you wanted to see him about?"

"I need a ticket fixed," I said. "Would two bucks be all
right?"

Another crack like that and I'd have a typewriter thrown at
me. If he could lift it. "It's obvious we're not getting anywhere,
Mr.—ah—Pine. Unless you care to tell what——"

"Don't give me that," I said. I bent down and pushed my face
at him. "You know goddam well what. Brill must've been on
that phone before I got halfway to the elevator. I'll bet he's not
out at all. I'll bet he's in there right now. Suppose I open that
door and prove it to you."

He didn't give an inch. "You'll do nothing of the kind," he
snapped. "I told you Chief Maller was out. As far as you're
concerned he's still out. Now, do you want to leave a message or
do I have you tossed out of here on your ear?"

I straightened, grinning. "You forgot to say 'sir'. Okay, I'll
leave a message. Tell him I was here about a murder. Tell him
I'll be back. Tell him to go fry a derrick."

The phone on his desk rang sharply before he could yell at
me. He snatched up the receiver and barked, "Yes?" into it.

What he got back was one of those voices whose whisper can
rattle the dinner dishes. The anger fell off his face like a stained
bandage. "Why, yes, sir," he said, anxious to please. "As a matter
—Of course. . . . Yes, sir. . . . Right away, sir."

He replaced the instrument and lifted his eyes to me. The
voice on the phone had taken the starch out of him. "That was
Colonel Delastone, Mr. Pine. The Colonel is on the Board of

City Commissioners. He would like you to stop by and see him for a moment."

"You don't say," I said. "What's on his mind?"

"He didn't explain, sir."

"How come he knew I was here?"

He looked away from me, shrugging.

"That Captain Brill," I said admiringly. "He knows what a telephone's for, I'll say that for him. All right, where do I find the Colonel?"

First an anteroom a lot of money had been turned loose in, then an inner office where a fragile lovely left off caressing the keys of an electric typewriter long enough to announce me in a fragile voice, then still a third office that made everything before it only fit for the slums. A blending of pastels, filtered light from the windows, artificially cooled air, the rich sheen of expensive woods.

And in the centre of it all, the Colonel rising ponderously from behind a king-sized desk to welcome me.

"How do you do, Mr. Pine?" he said in a voice that filled the room. "I'm Colonel Delastone—Colonel Quentin Delastone, to be exact. Mighty kind of you to drop in, sir."

"Not at all, Colonel," I said.

We shook hands. His was mammoth and meaty and moist, manicured to the hilt. The diamond on his left little finger would have derailed a freight.

Still gripping my fingers, he made a quarter-turn and waved his free hand toward a rather tall unattractive woman sitting on a couch with her legs drawn up and what appeared to be a volume from a law library open in her lap. "This is my daughter, Martha, Mr. Pine. My right-hand man, so to speak." He rolled out a laugh that rattled the windows. "Knows more about running a city than I do myself. And believe me, sir, that's considerable."

Martha Delastone gave me an uninterested nod, said, "Good morning," in a voice as colourless as the rest of her, and put her eyes back in the book. Inviting me in was clearly the old man's idea, not hers.

The Colonel lowered himself into his chair and pointed out one for me that was mostly foam rubber. He looked pretty much as I remembered him from the day I called on Serena—the mane of greying black hair, an acre of paunch, the square face with features beginning to sag with age. No brown bottles in sight this time, but there would be at least two in the deep drawer.

I refused a cigar from a carved mahogany box lined with cedar. He fished one out for himself and sat there rolling it between his fingers and eyeing me over it, not saying anything, trying to judge how difficult I was likely to be.

"They tell me," he said finally, making it sound jovial, "you've been kicking up quite a fuss downstairs."

"The word is 'stink'," I said.

His smile was as big as Omaha, his face as open as Las Vegas, his small brown eyes as sharp and searching as a surgeon's scalpel. "Fuss is a politer word, Mr. Pine," he said reproachfully. "Thing is, I'm what you might call the Police Commissioner here in Olympic Heights—unofficially, that is—and I hate to see my boys picked on. At least, without cause. Now if you've got a complaint of some kind, why not just sort of trot her out and let me have a look?"

"No complaint, Colonel. All I'm after is a little co-operation from the department."

"Well now." He made a sweeping motion with the hand holding the cigar. "Co-operation is something we're always happy to furnish. What did you have in mind?"

"A free hand in investigating a murder."

A shadow seemed to come and go in his eyes. "Murder," he rumbled. "A word that falls strangely on the ear in our quiet little community, sir. I know of no such crime here within the past two or three years."

"That's possible," I said. "This one your boys closed out as suicide—as did the inquest. But that doesn't necessarily mean it was suicide."

From his reaction I could have been talking about the weather. "I assume you're referring to the death of this man Jellco over at the Olympia House. A tragic affair."

"How true," I said.

"As I understand it," he went on evenly, "Jellco was found shot to death by his own gun—found by a private detective." He paused to arch a thick greying eyebrow at me. "A man named Pine, as I recall. That would be you, of course."

"So it would," I said.

He brought up his cigar and bit the end off between large square teeth and spat it clear across the room. It travelled like a bullet, hit the wall and bounced halfway back. "Frankly, sir,' he said, reaching for a match folder near the lamp, "I don't see what you're driving at. Captain Brill and his men made a thorough investigation. They found Jellco had died of a self-inflicted wound. I've certainly no reason to doubt them *or* their finding. They're trained, efficient men. Otherwise they wouldn't be on the Olympic Heights force."

"And when they found the gun to be too far from the body to support a finding of suicide," I said, "they planted it under the body. That makes them efficient, all right."

He sat there clutching the matches and staring incredulously at me. In his face the storm clouds were beginning to gather.

"You don't seriously expect me to believe that, Mr. Pine? Where's your proof?"

"I was hoping I wouldn't need proof," I said. "In my trusting way I sort of hoped you'd be willing to do a little checking up on your own. Just on the off-chance that somebody around here had tried to pull a fast one by covering up for somebody else. Without your knowledge, of course."

His eyes were hard and bright with anger. "That may be standard practice in Chicago, sir, but we don't operate that way in this town. I know every man in this building and there's not one of them I don't trust completely and without reservation. And yet you've got the colossal gall to walk in here and make these wild accusations without a stick of evidence to back them up. You may not have good sense, by God, but there's nothing wrong with your nerve!"

"This isn't anything I can argue you into, Colonel," I said patiently. "If you think I'm making all this up as I go along, that's your business. If you think wide streets and flower-filled parks and a bunch of neatly tailored Ph.D's for cops make a city corruption-proof, that's also your business. All I'm asking is the chance to do a little investigating on my own. Without interference."

"No!" he barked, redfaced. "Absolutely not! I refuse to damage the morale of my men by supporting any such un-warranted action."

"The hell with their morale," I said. "Sam Jellco was murdered and we both know it. As Police Commissioner you would almost have to know it. For my money you either ordered the fix put in yourself or you know who did. I aim to find out why. With or without your blessing."

I reached for my hat.

"Hold it!" he ordered sharply. "I've got some questions to ask you."

"Why waste your time?" I said. "I don't have any answers."

He was still holding the folder of matches. He tore one loose with a savage jerk of his fingers and was lighting the cigar when the phone rang.

There was an extension next to the couch. Martha Delastone put aside her book and took the call. She listened, raised her eyes and gave me a level stare while she listened, then said, "Just a minute," and put her hand over the mouthpiece. "For you, Father."

She hung up when he answered and went on staring at me appraisingly and with a complete lack of self-consciousness. I stared back, figuring I could get away with it.

She was nobody's pin-up, this one. Lifeless brown hair drawn severely back into a bun at the nape of a short thick neck, sallow skin, mismatched features, and a figure with too many pounds in the wrong places. Her tobacco-brown shantung suit had looked better on the rack than it did on her. About thirty-five, although she could have passed for forty without much effort.

I thought of Karen Delastone as she had looked in Jellco's office a few hours earlier. Judging from the rest of the family, she had lapped the field when it came to looks.

Martha Delastone s gaze swung idly from me back to her book. She picked it up casually and was settling back when the Colonel said, "Sounds good to me. Go ahead and handle it that way."

He cradled the receiver. The cigar he had been holding all along came slowly up and settled in one corner of his full-lipped mouth. He put his elbows on the desk and hunched his heavy shoulders in my direction, still sore at me and now ready to do something about it.

Abruptly he said, "I'm through being patient. What's the real reason you're in Olympic Heights?"

That one I hadn't expected. "I thought I told you that. Maybe you dozed off, or something."

"You told me a pack of lies," he said in a voice that came from the bottom of his chest. "Jellco, you said. You lied. You've been snooping around here for days. I want to know what you were doing at my home three mornings ago."

"You fooled me on that one," I said. "I'd have sworn you were sleeping it off."

For a wild moment I thought he was coming across the desk at me. "The truth, you son of a bitch!" he shouted. "The truth, or by God you'll wish you'd strangled on your bib!"

I gave him a tired leer and shoved back my chair. "Will that be all, Colonel?"

He didn't say anything. He couldn't say anything. He was three inches from a stroke and moving fast. In the loud silence Martha Delastone turned a page. I got off the foam rubber and went toward the door.

"Pine."

After the way he'd been carrying on, I was surprised at how calm he made my name sound. I turned around. His face was still the colour of a slaughter-house floor but he seemed safely past the apoplexy stage.

"My son is dead." His voice was very loud, very clear. "I will not have anyone stirring up muddied waters over his death. Your friend Jellco found out as much."

I looked at him open-mouthed. "That's quite an admission. You telling me that's why he was killed?"

I wasn't sure he even heard me. There was a crazy shine to his eyes and his hands were trembling. "You're not wanted in this town, sir. Get in your car and drive away from Olympic Heights. Go back to Chicago and stay there. Right now. Today. There is nothing here for you. Nothing but trouble. Believe me."

It sounded theatrical. Such things often do when they're meant. I shook my head. "I'll stay, Colonel. At least long enough to do what I came here to do. Thanks just the same." I put on my hat and glanced over at the couch. "Nice meeting you, Miss Delastone."

She looked up, deadpanned, but didn't say anything. The Colonel had turned to stone. I opened the door and walked out.

The fragile lovely at the typewriter gave me a timid smile as I went past her. She had heard the Colonel's side of the conversation. She would have needed ear plugs not to hear it.

CHAPTER THIRTEEN

IT was the noon hour. I had my lunch farther uptown, at a spotless cafeteria full of stainless steel and whirring fans and run with the rigid efficiency of an assembly line.

Over a second iced coffee I thought about Colonel Delastone.
Why out of a clear sky that crack about his son's death? Stirring
up muddied waters—to quote him. And that right on the heels
of demanding to know what I was doing out at his home two
days before. So far as I knew there was no connection between
the deaths of Jellco and Edwin Delastone. So far as I knew—
which was about four inches.

I smoked a cigarette, ignoring the pointed sniffs of a snooty-
looking dame at the next table, and went on thinking. You
couldn't write the Delastone clan out of this even if you wanted
to. Serena had hired Jellco, then fired him. For incompetence.
The uppity Miss Karen Delastone had been caught burglarizing
his office. The Colonel more than likely had a hand in writing
his death off as suicide. And now it appeared that dear dead
Uncle Edwin belonged in there someplace.

The time had come to find out just where that someplace was.

A soft hand touched my shoulder carefully. I looked up. A
thin man with a chinless face and narrow shoulders was standing
behind my chair, his expression pained. "I beg your pardon, sir,"
he murmured. "You shouldn't be smoking that cigarette, you
know."

The snooty-looking dame was smirking triumphantly at me
over a dish of tapioca pudding. I looked back at the man. "You
mean you believe all this talk about cancer?"

He pointed to a sign on the wall ten feet away. It said NO
SMOKING in letters a foot high. "Perhaps you failed to notice
the sign," he suggested.

"I noticed it," I said. "I don't need a sign to tell me when to
watch my hat. Take that fat dame over there. A hatsnatcher if
I ever saw one."

She heard me and her face got red. But not half as red as his.
"I'll have to ask you to extinguish your cigarette," he said stiffly.
"The other diners are complaining."

"She ought to lay off puddings," I said. "No wonder she looks
like Edward Arnold. That's the trouble these days. Too many
people digging their graves with their teeth."

His dignity was going fast. "I'm telling you to put out that
cigarette," he said, too loudly. Heads turned in our direction.

"This?" I said in a surprised voice, holding up the cigarette.
"I just lit it. You any idea what these things cost? What with
taxes and the middleman, you damn near got to have a rich old
aunt on her deathbed to take a chance on buying a pack. Not

that it's always been like that. I remember here a few years
back——"

He made a grinding sound with his teeth and turned around
and left. He left quickly. I grinned at the woman and got back a
look you could heat a ten-room house with. I stood up and took
my hat off the rack and went over to her. "You stooled on me,
lady. Lucky for you I don't have my gat along today."

She bristled. "*I* beg your——"

"So okay," I said. "So you made a mistake. It could happen
to anyone. Only after this don't try stealing a guy's hat."

I stopped at the cashier and paid my check and helped myself
to a toothpick. It came wrapped in thin paper and had a mint
flavour. I didn't see the chinless bird around. Likely out in the
alley sneaking a smoke.

There was a cigar store at the corner. I used its phone book
and learned there were two newspapers in Olympic Heights.
One—*The Daily Telegram*—ran its listing in boldface type and
on the strength of that I decided to give it my business. On
Orchard Street—near the centre of town, according to the clerk.
No more than a five-minute drive if you caught all the lights.

I bought cigarettes and came out into the white heat and
threw the toothpick away and got in behind the wheel. My
rear-view mirror showed an empty parking space directly in back
of me, and behind that a Pontiac hardtop in two tones of blue,
with a dent in one of the headlights. In the driver's seat a pair
of hands held up a newspaper, the crown of a man's brown hat
visible above the pages. It seemed a nice car for reading in.

I pulled out from the kerb, drove to the next corner, made a
left turn there and stopped for a red light a block farther along.
Next to me was a green Buick driven by a woman with a grim
expression and too many junk bracelets. Waiting behind me
was a blue Pontiac with a dented headlamp.

Another left turn, another four blocks. The Pontiac was still
there, a car-length back and in the next lane. I said, "How
quaint," under my breath and turned right at the next street.

So did the Pontiac.

I was on one of the main arteries, heading west. The Pontiac
hung on, dropping well back when traffic thinned out, closing
the gap when it thickened again. Any lingering doubt was gone.
I had a plaster.

My foot slowly grew heavy on the accelerator. The needle

climbed to sixty, then hung there quivering. A thirty-five mile zone according to the road markers. They didn't say what the limit was in case you were tailed.

Hardly any more store fronts this far out. More trees, more vacant lots. Bushes and hedges with big homes crouching behind them. Low hills to the west beginning to creep towards me. The air whipping in at the windows was hot and harsh.

Time to make my play. I kept an eye on the mirror until two or three cars were between me and my new friend, then I jerked the wheel sharply right and shot into a residential side-street, slowed at the first intersection until I saw the blue Pontiac poke a cautious nose around the corner behind me.

I slammed down on the accelerator, swung right again, travelled a hundred feet, touched the brake and rolled smoothly into an empty driveway bordering a two-story red-brick Colonial drowsing under mammoth elms in the baking sun.

Nobody around but the birds and the bees. I let the motor idle, set the gear shift at reverse and waited. Twenty seconds later tyres squealed and the hardtop flashed by. I backed out quickly and lit out after it.

Another three blocks, with the guy ahead swivelling his neck at every crossing, before he caught on to what had happened. I caught a glimpse of a white face and an open mouth, then the Pontiac leaped forward, took a corner like a scorched antelope and was up to fifty by the time I had it in sight again.

He was a good man with a wheel, but so was I. We slashed through the quiet sunflooded streets, whipping around corners like drunken stunt men, pouring on the power on straightaway runs. Mostly it was a clear track, with an occasional delivery truck and a few pop-eyed motorists, plus one Good Humour wagon that damned near jangled up a light pole giving us the street.

At the top of a slight rise the Pontiac disappeared around the far end of an eight-foot evergreen hedge. I came up fast, made the same turn—and hit my brake barely in time to keep from ploughing into a car drawn up sideways to block the street.

It was the hardtop. The driver was already out of the seat and moving along the pavement toward me, a hand in the right pocket of his light-grey jacket, his hat pushed back to show a face that had run into a lot of hard objects during its twenty-odd years.

I went on sitting, resting my fingers lightly on the wheel, waiting for him. He sidled up to the door and dropped his left hand delicately on the ledge of the open window and peered in at me. He looked hard and hungry and full of hate.

"Okay, handsome," he growled. "Let's pile outta there."

"Aw hell," I said. "I'm not either handsome."

His large and lumpy face darkened. "Wise guy, hunh? You comin' out or you wanta get yanked out?"

"You wouldn't really have a gun in that pocket," I said. "You just want to impress me."

His hand slid off the ledge, caught the outside handle and jerked the door open. His free hand was reaching for the front of my coat when I swung my legs around and put a foot in his belly and shoved. He back-pedalled furiously, managed to keep his balance, then danced lightly toward me on his toes, both hands now in sight and ready for use. I had an inch on him in height but he was heavier through the chest and longer in the arms.

There was no sense letting him catch me in cramped quarters. I slid out of the seat and shoved my hands deep in my pockets and leaned against the fender. He came up very close to me, his hands carried low and balled into craggy fists. His breath smelled of stale smoke and yesterday's beer. His scowl was a thing of awesome ferocity. Or so he was trying to make it.

I grinned pleasantly at him. "Relax," I said. "We don't have to fight."

Even with the scowl it was an empty face. A small white scar puckered the skin above one of his bushy brows and both ears were faintly cauliflowered. "I don't take that," he announced, "I don't take that from you nor nobody else."

"Take what?" I said.

"Like kickin' me like that. I know guys lost their teeth for less."

"Oh, that," I said. "Why the tail job? You got nothing better to do?"

"I could take you," he said dispassionately. "I could take you easy. Just like nothin' at all I could take you."

"You could be wrong about that," I said. "But I wouldn't argue with you. Let's talk about something else."

His mouth hung open a little. There were tiny white welts on the inner surface of his lower lip. He went on scowling but now it was a puzzled scowl. "We got nothin' to talk about," he grumbled.

"Sure we have. Like your tailing me, for instance. The Colonel put you up to it?"

He took time out to think that one over. Thinking wasn't his strong point. "What Colonel?"

"I thought there was only one," I said. "In Olympic Heights, anyway."

"Try talkin' some sense, hunh? I don't know no Colonel."

"Then who had you follow me?"

His small blue eyes got crafty. "Who says I was followin' you?"

"Nuts," I said. "Don't turn simple on me, friend. You were holding tight to my coat-tails until I decided to ride yours for a change."

He gave me a long level stare, then brought up his left hand half closed and brushed it lightly across my chest. "I can take you," he said musingly. "Just the old one-two and you're in dreamland."

"We could make a deal," I said. "Twenty bucks for the guy's name."

His eyes brightened. "What guy?"

"The guy," I said patiently, "who wanted me tailed."

"Hah!" he said. "Listen to you!"

He snapped his left lightly at my chin. Instinct brought my hands up to block it. He chuckled and threw his right. It went through my guard like a brick through a Japanese lantern, nailing me on the side of the jaw. I crashed against the Plymouth and saw the empty street turn on its axis and go slowly out of focus. I sat down hard on the pavement and rested my cheek against a fender.

"Pushover," a voice sneered. Another chuckle, then the sound of feet receding along the concrete. A car door slammed, a motor purred, raced, dwindled into the distance.

My head gradually cleared. The sun bathed my face. I ran my sleeve across my forehead and clawed myself up the side of the fender and stood there rubbing my jaw where the knuckles had landed. Something clattered behind a row of bushes across the street and a woman screeched. *"Andrew!* You stop that this minute!"

It meant nothing to me. My name wasn't Andrew. I crawled in behind the wheel and looked at my jaw in the mirror. It seemed slightly swollen but the colour was right. Later on it wouldn't be.

He'd taken me, all right. This time he had taken me.

CHAPTER FOURTEEN

THE Olympic Heights *Daily Telegram* took up all three floors
and the basement of a narrow brick building at Orchard and
Vine, across from Neuberger's Department Store. This was
Dollar Week at Neuberger's and heat or no heat the housewives were attending in droves.

According to the gold-leaf legend on the solid copper-and-
glass street doors, the *Telegram* subscribed to leading wire services
and maintained offices in New York, London and San Francisco.
That made it definitely the paper to read. Inside were counters
where you could place a classified ad, or get a helping of public
service, presided over by slender young virgins with cool eyes and
acres of teeth.

I told one of them what I was after and she pointed out a
doorway. Beyond it was a wide flight of steps going up. I climbed
them and came out into the city room. There were desks with
men in shirtsleeves behind them pecking at typewriters or drinking coffee out of cardboard containers or just sitting. Along
one wall was a row of glassed-in cubbyholes, most of them
occupied.

A crew-cut office boy looked up from a desk marked "Information". He was holding a comic book and seeing it reminded me
sharply of Deborah Ellen Frances Thronetree. . . .

"Yes sir?"

I said, "I want to look up an item in your file copies."

"What date?"

"I don't know that. A man named Edwin Delastone was found
dead a while back. Rather recent, I think."

"June second," he said without hesitation. He jerked a thumb
at a long counter against a side wall. Huge leather-bound
volumes were scattered across it, with more of them, many more,
stacked flat on shelves underneath. "Help yourself."

I thanked him and went over there. Nobody watched me.
Phones jangled and typewriters rattled and from the bowels of
the basement came the distant throb of presses. I found the
binder for the current month and flipped through it to the edition
datelined June 2nd.

The front page said the U.N. was expected to press for free
elections in Korea, a fire had caused minor damage at the

Cleequist Furniture Company, the senior senator from Illinois was to make a speech at the Civic Centre on the subject "The Threat to Democracy is Real". The Yankees had taken Baltimore 6 to 2 and the Dodgers led the Cubs 4 to 0 at the end of the seventh. The weatherman predicted higher temperatures for the next day, with probable showers by nightfall.

And nothing at all about Edwin Delastone.

I scratched an ear and turned the page. More items, mostly of local interest. Farther back was a rousing editorial about the need for a Youth Centre in Hamilton Park, next to a cartoon showing a teenager heaving a rock through a schoolhouse window. The caption said, "Give Him a Baseball Instead!". I couldn't see what difference it would make to the window.

Altogether fourteen pages, and at the foot of page eleven, next to an ad. for a guaranteed plant spray, was what I was after. The heading read: FOUND DEAD IN CAR.

I read the item. All of it. It was brief and to the point.

> Edwin Delastone, 31, 25 New Cambridge Road, was found dead early today in the front seat of a car registered in his name and parked at the end of Culver Street. According to the coroner's office, death had taken place four or five hours prior to discovery of the body by a resident of the area.
>
> Mr. Delastone was the only son of Colonel and Mrs. Quentin K. Delastone of the same address. Colonel Delastone is a member of the local Board of Commissioners and was at one time mayor of this city. Funeral arrangements are not yet completed.

Nothing at all on how it happened. You could think Edwin was driving along, felt a heart attack coming on, pulled the car over, cut the motor and lights, carefully set the handbrake, knocked off a fast prayer and died gracefully and without dramatics. It happens every day. To better men than Edwin Delastone.

Only it didn't happen like that at all. Edwin Delastone had died violently in the night. Suicide according to his sister Karen; something far worse judging from the Colonel's agitation. But either way you needed influence to arrange this kind of news coverage—the City Hall type of influence.

I spent a minute or two looking thoughtfully out the window at the crowd in front of Neuberger's, then closed the book and went back to where the office boy was on page twelve of his comic book. "You got a morgue here?" I asked. "The newspaper kind, I mean."

He tilted a casual hand toward one of the cubbyholes. "See Mr. Klingschmidt."

I walked over and rapped on the glass. A man with a great deal of naked scalp glanced up absently and took a pipe out of his mouth and said, "Yeah?"

"How's chances of getting a peek at the morgue file on some-body?" I said.

"Depends. Who're you?"

I took out a business card and laid it on the desk in front of him. He squinted at it, not touching it, grunted and lifted his eyes to me again. "Private boy, hunh? Whose folder?"

"Edwin Delastone's."

"You don't say!" I had his full attention now. His eyes crawled carefully over my face and he put the pipe slowly back in the hole under his nose. "What's your interest in him?"

"I hardly know myself, Mr. Klingschmidt."

He believed me like he believed in purple leprechauns. "Not that it makes any difference," he said. "No folder on him."

"You mean you don't have one?"

"I mean we don't have one."

"He must have led a dull life."

"It's a dull town, mister. Thanks for stopping by."

"How about the file on Harriet Beecher Stowe?"

He brought a hand up and ran it over the top of his head. All it smoothed down was skin. "You trying to kid me, fella?" he drawled.

"I just wanted to hear you say no again."

He put his nose back in his work and I walked out. Halfway down the stairs I heard feet behind me. They belonged to a man I recognized—a tall thin man with a narrow sallow-skinned face and sardonic brown eyes under drooping lids. We nodded to each other and I waited for him and we walked out to the street.

"Howdy, Pine," he said, his grin showing strong teeth. "I been hearing about you."

Ira Groat—the reporter called in by Lieutenant Fontaine two nights ago and told, along with me, that Sam Jellco's death was to be officially listed as suicide.

"Small world," I said. We shook hands. "How's your friend the lieutenant?"

"Hell, don't ask me. Far as I'm concerned he's only a news source. You are about to buy me a drink."

"Why would I do that?"

"So you can ask me questions. And maybe a little vice versa."

"Okay," I said. "Where do people go to buy you drinks so they can ask you questions?"

"Around the corner."

We went around the corner. It was a narrow place, cool and deep, with a darkwood bar down one side and a row of wooden booths on the other. A beefy man in a white apron was trying to strain the ball game out of a radio full of static. He nodded to us, made Groat a whisky sour, a gin and tonic for me. At the far end of the bar a TV set had an "Out of Order" card hanging from one of the knobs.

At Groat's suggestion we carried our glasses over to a booth and sat down across from each other. He pushed a bowl of potato chips out of the way, sipped some of his drink and winked at me.

"First one today with this hand," he said.

"Go on," I said. "You swiped that line out of a Donald Henderson Clarke novel."

He seemed honestly surprised. "No fooling? I've been saying it for years. Thought I made it up."

We drank. He didn't have that seedy look today. His lightweight suit was hand tailored and neatly pressed, his soft blue shirt right off the ironing board, a fresh four-in-hand snug and smooth between the points of his collar. Even his hat was a big improvement: a twenty-dollar summer felt pushed back on his narrow skull.

"Like I was saying," he said, his eyes on his glass, "there's talk around town about you and none of it happy. Especially over at the Hall. Hardly anybody there that wouldn't give their seniority for a legitimate chance to put the muscle on you. It could even get to where they forget the legitimate part. What's the matter, don't you like to be liked?"

"I'm not running for Miss Rheingold," I said. "When mud settles to the bottom you've got to stir the water to bring it up again. I'm in the water-stirring business. Is that all right with you?"

He shrugged hugely. "Me, I'm easy to please. What kind of mud you after?"

"Sam Jellco's killer."

"Uh-hunh. That's how I heard it. Nothing down that alley, neighbour. The boys say Jellco did the Dutch, the D.A. says so, two juries say so. What makes you so hard to convince?"

The Cubs came to bat, only they would have to wait until the beer commercial was over. The commercial came in nice and clear. For some reason they always do.

"A lot of things show it wasn't suicide," I said. "Little and big things. He was reasonably young, he was healthy, he had no money problems, his marriage was better than most. And if a guy's going to shoot himself why travel forty miles first? I could see it if he went four hundred or I could see him doing the job in his own bathroom. Those are some of the little things I mentioned. The very big one is that the cops tried too hard, going so far as to plant the gun under him instead of leaving it where I saw it, which was too far from the body. That makes it more than murder; that makes it a murder the cops were ordered to cover up on."

He formed a pair of wet circles on the wood with the bottom of his glass. "First I've heard of this business with the gun. There'd have to be a reason. Jellco'd have to be stepping on some mighty important toes in this town for the kind of fix you're talking about."

"Would the Delastones," I said, "be important enough?"

He stared silently at me out of sleepy eyes. His hand was motionless on the glass. And then he nodded once, a slow nod. "There's hardly anybody in Olympic Heights more important, neighbour. Only . . . why pick on them?"

"Mrs. Delastone used Jellco's services twice in the past few weeks. As recently as June sixth."

His chest rose and fell under even breathing. Nothing showed in his face. "A week ago, eh? To do what?"

I moved a shoulder and looked blank.

"Man, you interest me," he said quietly. "You really do. It means Serena Delastone hired your friend the day after her son was buried. And that could mean she called him in to investigate her son's death. How does that sound to you?"

"It's one of the reasons I was digging through back files of the *Telegram*," I said. "I found the item about him. He could have got more space by winning second prize at cooking school."

He grinned crookedly and finished his drink while somebody hit a double to right field, driving in two runs. Groat put down his empty glass and rapped loudly against the table top. The apron brought over fresh drinks and rounded up the empties. He said, "The Cubs hadda put in a new pitcher."

"What's news about that?" Groat said.

The apron nodded glumly. "You're so right," he said and went back behind the bar.

I finished lighting a cigarette. "How did it happen? To Edwin, I mean."

"I was off that night," Groat said, "and came damn near missing out on the fun. Along about eleven I drifted down to Headquarters and sat in on a little stud poker. The call came in around five-thirty, six o'clock. From some citizen out walking the dog. I rode out with the boys."

He smiled faintly for some reason. "He was in his car. A pearl grey Olds convertible with the top up. Out at the foot of Culver Street, clear across town from where he lived. He was in the front seat, his head on the wheel, a hole from a .32 under his chin and another hole, where the slug went out, high up on the opposite side of his head. The gun was on the floorboards between his feet. He didn't bleed much."

"Not another suicide?" I groaned. "This must be a tough town to be happy in."

Groat swallowed some of his drink. "It was his gun. Look up the death certificate and you'll see they wrote down heart failure where it says cause of death. It failed, all right."

"What makes you think it wasn't suicide?"

"I didn't say it wasn't. What I do say is he wasn't dressed for suicide. Not where they found him anyway."

"That's quite a remark. Just how *was* he dressed?"

"Pyjamas."

"What?"

"You heard me, neighbour. Pyjamas. Bright yellow babies with pearl buttons and an elastic belt. He was dressed over them but they were there just the same."

"Any blood on his clothing?"

He gave me a darting glance. "Yeah. Where it couldn't of soaked through."

"How did the cops explain that?"

"Officially it wasn't even mentioned. But deep back under the rose is a theory—a theory based on the kind of bastard Edwin Delastone really was."

"Tell me about him. As long as we're just sitting around drinking."

"Why not?" He licked at his glass, leaving very little of the contents by the time he set it down again. "You wouldn't of liked Edwin Delastone, Pine. In fact he'd make you want to puke

—and that's a compliment to you. A real Krafft-Ebing boy. Peeping Tom, child molester, two attempted rapes, dope pusher, shop-lifter, petty thief, and at least one try at blackmail. Not to mention a couple of hit-and-run charges and one bad smashup that left the girl with him still in a wheelchair. It's a record that goes back to his grade-school days, and he spent a few years during his teens in and out of Ridge Manor just outside Wilmette. You know Ridge Manor?"

"I know of it," I said. "A high-toned reform school where the rich put their problem children for so much per semester."

"That's the outfit. A dean that used to be a Commando and a collection of ex-pugs they call tutors."

We stopped talking and lifted our glasses. His hooded eyes held a remoteness that mystified me. He was off somewhere, maybe in the past, thinking his own thoughts, seeing what I couldn't see, maybe remembering what was better forgotten. Or it could be nothing more than my imagination at work again.

I rubbed out my cigarette and sniffed at a mixture of smells made up of alcohol and malt and sweeping compound. The ball game droned on and feet shuffled past in the street beyond the screen door. A hot day, a sticky day, a day for sitting in the shadows of old-fashioned barrooms and soaking up gin.

I said, "This theory the law has. About Edwin being decked out in pyjamas. Could I hear it?"

He sighed. "No reason why not. Theories are cheap. Say he was shacked up with some married dame that night. Say hubby came home unexpectedly from West Weehawken—or wherever husbands come home from—and found them in bed. Say Edwin pulled a gun to save his skin. Say the other guy tried to take it away from him and in the fight the gun went off, as guns will do, and Edwin fell down dead. Say the guy dressed Edwin as best he could and drove him over to Culver Street and left him there. Okay?"

"Isn't that kind of reaching?"

He laughed shortly. "Not if you knew Edwin, neighbour. Believe it or not, there were women who went for that creep. Even so-called nice women who could keep the fact they were tramps buried out of sight under soft skins and soulful brown eyes." He laughed again. Harshly. "Don't mind me, pal. In my business I see too much of the wrong kind of people. The kind that makes the news."

I said, "Anyway it beats living in the Jurassic age, I guess." I finished my drink and sat staring at the ice cubes. "The name Pod Hamp mean anything to you?"

He hesitated briefly, then shook his head. "Sounds like a character out of *Tobacco Road*. He fit into your plans?"

"I haven't got any plans," I said. "How about April Day?"

He grinned his crooked grin. "Hunh-uh. Cute name. Who's she supposed to be?"

"A name I heard. I think she knew Jellco, although maybe not in an important way."

He signalled the man at the bar and two new drinks appeared. The ball game was held up while the announcer spoke with passion about a beer that would make you rich, brilliant and thin.

Groat glanced briefly at the watch on his wrist and picked up his glass. "I'll keep an ear open," he said, "in case either of the names you mentioned floats by. Suppose I should want to reach you?"

"I'm in the Chicago book. Although I may be putting up at the Olympia House for tonight. I might find one of the help over there whose memory and powers of observance are better than most I've been running into. Outside of yours, that is."

"I like to talk," Groat said, showing his teeth. "I suppose I ought to tell you the Delastones own the Olympia."

"That should help," I said. "The way a broken leg helps."

He nodded lazily. "I'm ready to bet you won't get far. Since the city says your friend killed himself, that's the way it'll stay. Unless you can talk Dave Walgreen into some action."

"Dave Walgreen?"

"The local State's Attorney. A weak vessel but he doesn't admire the Colonel much. Not that he can do anything about it. The Delastone tribe runs this town, neighbour."

"I'm finding that out," I said.

"A couple of 'em I can stand. The old lady's tough as a railroad spike and she can handle the Colonel when it counts . . . . seeing as how she has all the money. Martha you met: the old-maid type who goes in for good works and getting out the vote. I never heard nothing against her. There was another —name of Evelyn as I recall. Married to a Ralph Thronetree until they both died in a plane crash three, four years back. Left a kid the old lady took over. That leaves Karen, the family beauty. A little on the wild side, spoiled as all hell, but a pretty square shooter from all accounts. Gambles like crazy and spends too much time with Arnie Algebra for her own good. Although she could do worse than Arnie."

One thing about Ira Groat: he would talk to you. "Tell me about Arnie Algebra."

"Runs a private club out on Clayfield Road. A plush joint backed, so the story goes, by a couple of big Chicago business men living here in town. Roulette, craps, poker upstairs; food, drinks and a floor show downstairs. Called the CCC Club for some reason and gets a heavy play from the local élite. Arnie stays satisfied with the percentages and keeps the games honest. Not that the local authorities take to the idea but they haven't hit on a way to stop it. A membership-only setup is tough to crack."

"Algebra," I said. "That couldn't be his real name."

"Algebretti. Used to fight back East years ago."

I touched the small discoloured area on the left side of my jaw and winced a little. "You wouldn't know a sandy-haired pug about twenty-five, around a hundred and eighty, lumpy face and a pair of twisted ears, would you?"

He seemed mildly intrigued. "That would fit Lyle Spence like a snapshot. Gets on a lot of small-town cards between here and Canada. Matter of fact he fought a prelim at the Chicago Stadium last winter. Not bright but handy with his mitts. Funny you bringing him up right after we spoke about Arnie. Lyle's kind of protégé of Algebra's."

I put away what was left in my glass and stood up. "Back to the trenches," I said. "I'm much obliged to you for the information, Mr. Groat. Maybe I can buy you another drink one of these bright afternoons. Before you take the pledge."

"That'll be the day," Groat said. "Good luck to you, shamus. Give my love to the Colonel the next time you tangle with him. Tell him I hope he comes down with hardening of the urine."

"Maybe I'd better not," I said. "Maybe he might pressure your boss into getting a new reporter."

He hiccupped softly. "Now why the hell didn't I think of that? Seeing as the Delastones own the paper, too. Guess maybe I forgot to mention it before."

I left him with his nose in the glass. The apron took my money and carefully counted out the change. "Them Cubs," he said bitterly. "They couldn't hit Shirley Temple if she was throwin' underhand."

CHAPTER FIFTEEN

THEY had a red and white muslin banner with WELCOME MID-
WESTERN DAIRY ASSOCIATION on it across the marquee of the
Olympia House. Just inside the doors a big display board held
a poster with the same message, plus some wit's quick pencil
sketch of a cow's udder in one corner.

The room clerk waited while a tall man in a five-gallon Stetson
signed in, then banged a bell and said, "Front," crisply. A bellboy came out from behind something. "907 for Mr. Ambrose,"
the clerk said. He made it sound as though 907 was equivalent
to four floors at the Roney-Plaza.

With Mr. Ambrose out of the way the clerk dropped the
registry card into a box on the back ledge and turned around to
welcome the next customer. Me.

"Good afternoon, sir," he said with a detached smile. He was
a smooth young man in faultless grey. A small white oblong
card under plastic was pinned to one of his lapels, notifying anybody with eyes that this was Mr. Cunningham. "You wish to
register?"

"Not at the moment," I said. "Later perhaps. I wonder if I
might have a word with your house detective."

Mr. Cunningham flinched a little. "Mr. Jennings is our security
officer, sir. Is something wrong?"

"Nope," I told him. "Just a friendly call."

"I see." He sounded doubtful and he looked doubtful. "I
wonder if you'd mind waiting. It may take a moment or two to
locate Mr. Jennings."

I said I'd rest myself in one of those nice easy chairs and to
take his time, no hurry, and wasn't it hot today.

I was in one of the chairs, smoking a cigarette and being careful to keep any ashes off the nice maroon carpet, when a stocky
number with a square solemn face sat down next to me. He took
off his hat and smoothed down a brown cowlick and gave me
the once-over, stem to stern, out of eyes that would miss anything
smaller that the nucleus of a hydrogen atom.

"The name's Jennings," he said finally in a soft rumble. "I
got word you was asking for me."

"You the house dick?"

"Lay off the house dick stuff," he said earnestly. "Around here it's security officer. Mister Davidson insists on it. Mister Davidson used to manage a six-hundred-room house in Boston and he knows the hotel business, Mister Davidson does, and he'll tell you so. Any old time at all, night or day, rain or shine, he'll tell you."

"Do we have to talk about Mr. Davidson?" I said. "What's six hundred rooms? The Hilton in Chicago's got three thousand."

"Yeah? Well, Mister Davidson would tell 'em how to run it. He'd have old man Hilton counting towels. What's on your mind?"

"It's about this unpleasantness you had here a night or two ago," I said. "Man named Jellco."

He eyed me out of a face filled with nothing at all. "You a lawyer?"

I took out a card and handed it to him. He read what was on it, wrinkled his forehead at me, read the card again and handed it back. "They write books about guys in your line," he said. "Always making time with the pretty girls."

"This trip I haven't even patted a dimpled knee," I said. "Let's talk about Jellco."

"The guy pushed hisself off," he said. "Up in 304. Some joker finds him cold and tips off the johns. They ease in real quiet and do their job without a word to nobody. First we know what's going on is when the dead wagon shows up to cart away the stiff. I wanta tell you Mister Davidson was mighty upset."

"Let's keep Mr. Davidson out of this," I said. "Were you on duty at the time?"

"That's a laugh," he said, not laughing. "This lousy job, you're on duty when you're sleeping even. I got woke up in time to see the remains carried out."

"You see anything that didn't fit a suicide picture? Such as the position of the gun, for instance."

He looked at me almost pityingly. "You got some idea they invited me in? All I did was run them down in the service car and unbar the alley door. Listen, I ain't at all sure I should even be chinning with you."

"Why not? Everything's all clear and aboveboard, isn't it?"

He flicked some imaginary dust from the crown of his hat, started to put it on, decided not to and held it in both hands instead. "Mister Davidson gave strict orders about discussing a guest's suicide. Gives the place a bad name, like having loose women sitting around the lobby showing travelling men the warm eye. You oughta know that much."

"This is just between you and me," I said.

"We had us a jumper last year," Jennings said. "Ninth floor that time. 916 as I recollect. Turned out his wife was running around with a cut-rate druggist. Bothered the poor guy so much he lifted the sash and dived. Lit on his head on the Locust Avenue side, damn near hitting a priest. Mister Davidson was upset over that one too, and when Mister Davidson gets upset hell wouldn't have him."

"You find anything unusual in the room after they took the body away?"

He rolled his eyes at me. "Just blood on the rug, brother. Just blood on the rug."

"Tough," I said. "Anybody ask for Jellco at the desk that night?"

"Not that I heard of. Don't mean nobody asked, though."

"Maybe room service sent up something," I suggested. "Maybe in that case the waiter could describe his visitor. If he had a visitor."

"Something else I don't know about. But it could of happened."

"Maybe you could find out for me," I said.

"All I have to do," he said thinly, "is start asking them kinda questions. Mister Davidson would call me into his nice sound-proof office and tell me about them six hundred rooms in Boston and then fire me for being unloyal to the home team. We're a team here y'see—all pulling together for the common good. Mister Davidson has a speech about that which I've heard seven-teen times now. Or is it eighteen? Hearing it again would be kinda hard on me."

I slid my wallet out, hiding it with my hat, and took out a ten-spot surreptitiously while watching his face. He saw the ten but nothing happened to his expression. After a moment I worked loose another ten and put it with the first and folded them small, cupping them in a palm while I slipped the wallet back where it came from.

"The name of the waiter," I said. "If there was a waiter. The name of the bellhop who brought up the ice-water, or whatever. A description of whoever called on him, if anybody did call on him. Such as a woman. If there was a woman."

I didn't tell him about the rouge-stained cigarette butts I'd seen in Jellco's ashtray. It would only have confused the issue.

Jennings stared at my closed hand without seeming to stare at it. "The night-shift comes on at nine," he said. "I'll do what I can do. Twenty bucks don't grow on no lilac trees. Not around Mister Davidson they don't."

I let my hand with the money in it droop carelessly over the arm of his chair. The folded bills fell soundlessly between his right leg and the upholstered arm. A minute passed, then his fist inched over and closed around them and they were gone like snow under a tropical sun.

"I'll take a room for the night," I said. "All I need is the names of the help involved. Of course you could just as easy tell me nothing was sent up to his room and no record of visitors. I would believe you."

"No reason for you not to," he said with quiet dignity. "You're a working man same as me. Why should I want to pick your pocket?"

"I beg your pardon," I said.

He put his hat on, said, "See you," and got out of the chair and walked away. He walked as if his feet hurt him.

The clerk pushed a registration card on a small oblong clipboard over for me to sign. I said no, I didn't have any luggage with me and that a nice room on the third floor, say, would be about right. In case the elevators blew a fuse I wouldn't have so far to climb. He seemed to find that mildly amusing. Not so amusing, however, that he failed to collect five-fifty in advance.

CHAPTER SIXTEEN

WITH the bellhop fifty cents richer and out of the way, I stripped and went into the bathroom to stand under the shower. While drying myself I looked in the mirror at the faintly purple area on my jaw where Lyle Spence's knuckles had landed. Spence was Arnie Algebra's protégé and Algebra was Karen Delastone's something or other. I thought that was interesting. It might even be important.

Back in the bedroom, wearing only a towel, I sat at the phone and looked in the directory for the number of the Delastone residence.

The elderly number with the bifocals answered. She agreed to find out if Mrs. Delastone would talk to me. She sounded dubious about it, but she would sound dubious about practically anything.

I waited, lighting a cigarette and looking through the open window at a sign across a storefront that said SHERWIN PAINTS "Save the Surface and You Save All"—and then a voice I recognized, clear and firm as all get-out, gouged my ear.

It belonged to Karen Delastone. "Is this *Paul* Pine?"

"Yeah," I told her. "Paul the purse-snatcher. I trust you got rid of that jemmy."

She wasn't in the mood for small talk. "Why are you calling here? What do you want with Mother?"

"Calm down," I said. "I'm not going to snitch on you. How's Deborah Ellen?"

A longish pause during which I could hear my strapwatch ticking away. ". . . What's that supposed to mean?" she demanded in a voice as tight as a toreador's pants.

"What it sounded like." I was getting fed up with her. "Look, Miss Delastone, I'm waiting to talk to your mother. Do you put her on or do I come out there and kick in the door? And don't think I'm kidding."

"That's just fine!" she almost snarled. "Now I'll tell you something: keep on meddling in what's none of your business and you'll get what's coming to you. And *I'm* not kidding either!"

"That's me you hear ringing the doorbell," I said.

It sounded as though she had thrown the receiver on the floor. At least she hadn't hung up. I waited and then there was a small click and Serena Delastone's hard baritone marched across the distance. "What is it, Mr. Pine?"

I listened, didn't hear what I wanted to hear, and said, "There seems to be an extension open, Mrs. Delastone." Then I heard another click and Serena's voice was clearer, saying dryly, "I scarcely expected to be hearing from you again, young man. After the way you behaved three days ago."

"Me neither, Mrs. Delastone. I guess you never know. Have you disposed of Pod Hamp?"

"Dis*posed* of him?"

"I mean is he still a problem? Has he been paid off and the goods delivered to you, or are you still dickering?"

She said stiffly, "I fail to see what possible interest that could have for you."

"I might be able to work on it for you. If your offer's still open."

"May I ask the reason behind this rather remarkable change of heart?"

I was sweating. I bent down and used a corner of the towel I was wearing to mop my forehead. I said, "Sam Jellco, the man you hired first, has been murdered. Maybe you already knew that. It's possible he was killed by Hamp or by somebody connected with Hamp. I thought you and I might work together."

"Exactly what is it you want, Mr. Pine?" If I was softening her up any you'd never know it by her tone.

"Well, right off, the phone number Hamp gave you where he could be reached. Jellco didn't seem to have it written down anywhere, so the assumption is that he was carrying it in his head. We could start with the number."

"I'm not at all interested," she said incisively. "To be quite frank with you, I have had no further word from this Hamp person since his initial call. Which leaves me to believe he had nothing detrimental to Karen to begin with. As far as I'm concerned the subject is closed."

"You're forgetting something," I said. "Sam Jellco saw the stuff. Otherwise he wouldn't have recommended that Hamp be paid off. This way, Mrs. Delastone, it's a ticking bomb. Wishful thinking won't turn it into a dud."

"You have my answer, Mr. Pine. Nor do I intend to be swayed by melodramatic figures of speech."

I kept my temper. It was easy—like keeping a tiger in my shirt pocket. "How about letting me have the number anyway?" I said hopefully. "For my own use, leaving you out entirely."

"Please don't take me for a fool, young man."

"A man's been murdered, Mrs. Delastone. That has to mean something to you. You could help."

"I'm sure I can't bring him back," she said tartly. "And you're quite mistaken about it being murder. The papers clearly stated that he took his own life."

"The way your son took his life, Mrs. Delastone?"

It was a crude remark and it got me hung up on. The hell with her. I could always join the Foreign Legion. I tried the directory again.

The CCC Club was on Clayfield Road, wherever that would be. I got an answer on the seventh ring. A tough voice said, "Yeah?" making it sound like a man who had to get out of the tub. I asked for Mr. Algebra.

"You nuts?" the voice yelped. "It ain't even five bells yet."

"Ten after," I said, just to be contrary. "Where do I reach him?"

"How should *I* know? He don't ever show up before nine. Get lost, willya, Mac? I'm busy."

"Watch your manners," I told him. "For all you know I could be Mr. Algebra's chiropractor."

"I don't give a good sweet damn if you're Jesus E. Christ!" the voice shouted, and for the second time in three minutes a receiver was banged in my ear.

Nobody named Algebra in the book. I pinched out what was left of my cigarette and walked over to look out of the window. It seemed hotter than before, if that was possible, and the thin green-and-grey drapes hung still as death in the humid air. The streets were a little less crowded; in another hour or so the shops would start closing up and the people would go home and kick off their shoes and drink lemonade or a Martini over the evening paper and eat a light dinner of cold cuts and salad and talk about taking in an air-cooled movie. To them murder was something put together by writers and directors, with perfectly timed close-ups of a gun and the feet of a corpse paid the union scale. Left out would be the loneliness of hotel rooms and the grey emptiness of mean streets and the weariness that comes from leg-work without results. They don't make entertainment out of such things, any more than they make party dresses out of gunny sacks.

I left the window and came back and sat on the bed and put through another call. After a while the ringing stopped and the quiet voice of Linda Jellco reached out to me.

"Paul Pine," I said. "How's it going?"

"Oh. Hello. All right, I suppose. I was just sitting here holding a drink. Where are you?"

"In Olympic Heights—at the hotel. You sound fine. Would you hang up on me if I ventured a small suggestion?"

"Of course not."

"Get into something shimmery and call up a friend and go out to dinner. Where's there's music and a laugh or two within easy reach. Or should I try minding my own business?"

"I think that's very thoughtful of you, Paul." The last word came out easily, without a trace of self consciousness. "As a matter of fact Ted Mather and his wife—they have the apartment down the hall from us . . . from me are picking me up in an hour for just that kind of evening."

"Good for you. That's one reason I called. The other was to make my report."

". . . You've found out something?"

"I don't know. It's a little too early to be sure. I've talked to the police and so on. Not that any of them was caught being co-operative."

"I'm not at all surprised." The grim note edged back into her voice. "Every time I think of that man Brill I can't help grinding my teeth."

"He's quite a boy. Did you manage to locate those phone numbers we talked about?"

"Only one of them. The one Sam left me the trip before last. Hold on a minute."

I waited with the receiver to my ear, hearing the small sounds of rustling paper at the other end. One of the hotel guests went past my room whistling tunelessly.

"Here it is," Linda Jellco's firm voice said in my ear. "Mulberry 3-1008. An Olympic Heights number. I checked."

I wrote it out on a sheet of hotel stationery. "It may help, Mrs. Jellco. I'll keep in touch. For the moment I guess there's not much else."

She said nothing, and then she said, "You might want to know that the—funeral is tomorrow, at ten. I mean—well, you knew Sam, and I was thinking. . . ."

And for a little while nothing was said. It was suddenly as though she sat opposite me, watching me from the unwavering depths of blue-green eyes below the fine curve of dark brows. A beautiful woman, but then there are too many beautiful women —an intelligent woman, and there are those too, although not enough of them to glut the market. Linda Jellco. Velvet and steel and good red meat. Sensitive, and yet with a fierce kind of pride. Some day the fog would lift and the pain would be gone and the world would open wide for her again and the right man would be there. And since he was the right man he would be a good man.

I said, "Where will the funeral be held?"

"At the Wagner Chapel. On East 79th, near Stony Island."

"Thanks. I'll be there if I can."

She thanked me and the wire went dead. I hung up and rubbed my face hard with the heel of my hand. I wanted a drink, several drinks, tall and cold and with authority. After that it would be time for food.

I dressed quickly and went out to the door.

CHAPTER SEVENTEEN

THE restaurant radio said a cool mass of air was on its way out of the northwest, with showers and a drop in temperature expected by midnight. When I got back to the hotel room shortly before eight, the window drapes were already stirring sluggishly and there was a smell of dust in the air.

I had stopped off to pick up a new shirt at the hotel haber-dashery and a cheap razor and assorted toiletries from the corner drugstore. After laying them out on the dresser, I took my shoes and shirt off and sat in front of the window, smoking a cigarette and watching a blue dusk come creeping into the almost empty streets. Neon began to burn against the gloom and a pair of night-blooming barflies came out of a pub next door to the paint shop and peered doubtfully at the darkening sky. A yellow convertible with the top down turned a corner too fast, the seats loaded with kids in bathing suits. At the end of the block a theatre marquee blossomed suddenly. Tonight was Spencer Tracy and Donald Duck.

At ten after nine the phone rang. It was Jennings, the security officer. "Guy on his way up. Waiter from Room Service. He brought some drinks up to Jellco's room that night. Says there was a visitor. Woman."

"Nice going," I said.

"Mister Davidson wouldn't think so," he said and hung up. I replaced the receiver, grinning. Jennings would have to watch it or he'd be ending up on a psychiatrist's couch getting rid of a complex named Davidson.

Five minutes later a subdued knock at the door. I opened up, letting in a small brown man with sad eyes. He was wearing a tux that needed pressing and his shirt front wasn't what you'd call immaculate. He moved past me with a sidewise crawl like a crab with a sore toe and put down a tray with a sandwich, an empty glass and a bottle of beer on it. He ducked his head in what he would call a bow and brought out an opener and pried the cap off the bottle and filled the glass.

I signed the charge slip and gave him a dollar and said, "Who told you I was hungry?"

"Mist' Jennin'," he murmured. "He say take you up this. Only way for me to leave kitchen. You know?"

"Uh-hunh. What's your name?"

"Infanté Nohahré," he said. Or so it sounded. He smiled shyly and ducked his head again. "In kitchen is Pete No-hurry. Joke."

I felt like patting him on the head. "Have a chair, Pete."

He shot a worried glance at the closed door. "Only one little while," he said. "Raise hell I stay away too much." He did the sidewise crawl again, this time to the desk chair, and perched on the edge.

I took out a cigarette and turned it in my fingers and said, "I hear you brought drinks up to 304 two nights ago. For a man named Jellco. There was a woman in his room at the time. You remember all this?"

"Sí," he said and flashed his teeth. "I remember good. Ver' pretty girl."

"You hear him call her by name?"

"No, sair. He don't talk while I am in room. Not to girl."

"She say anything? Anything at all?"

"No, sair. Jus' to look mad. Face all red."

"Can you furnish a description of the lady?"

He blinked. Too many syllables for him. I tried again. "How did the girl look? How big? What colour eyes and hair?"

He thought about it, grimacing. "I see many girls, sair. This one . . . she have kinda fur on shoulders. Not coat." He made motions with his hands to indicate what must have been a stole. "Ver' pretty soft fur. Kinda green dress with big hole for neck. Way down. Show lotsa skin." He giggled obscenely.

"Tell me about her face and her hair and her eyes. And how tall."

He spread his hands. "More tall as me. Brown hair. Ver' nice hair, with—with . . ."

He made curving motions with his hands and I said, "Curls?" and he nodded violently and looked anxiously at the door.

"Her face and eyes," I said.

"Is late," he muttered.

"Is early," I said. "Make it quick, Pete."

He wound his brown fingers together and unwound them and fidgeted with his shirt front. "Eyes brown like hair. Kinda funny eyes. Little like Chinaman eyes." He put up the forefinger of each hand and pushed at the outer corners of his eyes, slanting them. "Ver' nice," he said and brought down his hands and giggled again.

"I'll be darned," I said. Nohahré was no more than five-three.

Karen Delastone was at least four inches beyond that. Her hair was brown and had a wave in it. Her eyes were brown, too, and I was thinking of how they had that oriental cast.

"What time was this?" I asked.

He shrugged as only a man with a name like his could shrug. "Nine of the clock, I think. Maybe little more after. This I do not be sure."

"You would know this girl if you saw her again?"

"Sí." He flashed his teeth brilliantly. "Ver' pretty. Ver' saxy."

"Shame on you." I gave him another bill—this time a five—and he ducked his head and scuttled out, leaving the tray. I took the top off the sandwich. Ham. With a gob of mayonnaise in the centre of each of the two sections. I made a face and pushed the plate away and tried the beer. It was one of those thin brews fit for slopping the hogs, but it was cold enough to keep the tab I had signed from being a total loss.

So Karen Delastone had called on Sam Jellco the same night he was killed. This proved she had known I wasn't Jellco when I walked into his office and found her hiding in a copy of *Life*. It also proved she either knew or had a large idea why Jellco had been out to see Serena earlier. So she had gone to his hotel room and tried to pump him, wanting to make sure his visit to the old homestead involved her and whatever tomfoolery she had been up to that made her vulnerable for blackmail. Only Jellco wouldn't be easy to drain and she would end up frustrated and angry. Angry enough to pick up his gun and shoot him?

Quien sabé?

The sheet of hotel stationery with the number Linda Jellco had given me over the phone still lay on the writing desk. Mulberry 3-1008. A number left by a dead man and already a week old. The chances were heavy it would be the hall phone in a cheap rooming house of a booth in a bar. Who? Mr. Jellco? Nobody here by that name, buddy. You musta got the wrong number, hunh?

So I called it.

It rang for a long time. Not long enough to get an answer. I hung up and lighted the cigarette I'd been playing with and walked once around the room and came back and called Information. She was as polite as an Olympic Heights cop. Sorry, sir, but we do not locate by telephone number. That seemed to mean you weren't entitled to know the address where a phone was located just because you had the number. The supervisor said the same thing. The business office wouldn't be open until nine the next morning. Besides, I'd get the same answer there.

I scratched under an arm and called the *Telegram*. Ira Groat wasn't in and they weren't sure when he would be. His hours seemed elastic. They gave me his home phone. A throaty voice, female, answered and said he wasn't there either but I might catch him at Remotti's Bar & Grill. She furnished the number, evidently from memory, and I called it.

Not in. Any message? No message.

Three numbers on the paper now in my neat handwriting. I left it on the desk and went into the bathroom for some water to take the beer taste out of my mouth. I came out and prowled the room and looked at my strapwatch. 9:35. An hour yet before I could get back to work. I drank the rest of the beer and put on my stale shirt and my shoes and rode down to the lobby and bought an evening paper. The Olympia Room had Milo Mills and his orchestra, featuring the singing of lovely Connie Adair, whoever she was. A sign to that effect stood outside the glass doors to the room. The lobby wasn't crowded. Evidently the milkmen hadn't arrived in town yet. No sign of Jennings, and I didn't see anybody who resembled what I thought Mr. Davidson looked like.

I rode back up to the third floor and took off the shirt and shoes again and folded back the bedspread and pushed up the pillows. I was just stretching out with the paper when somebody knocked at the door.

CHAPTER EIGHTEEN

I slipped my shirt on, leaving it hanging, and opened up. It didn't surprise me that it was Martha Delastone. Nothing could surprise me in Olympic Heights.

She looked blank-faced at my unbuttoned shirt and shoeless feet. "I do hope you weren't getting ready for bed."

"Just lounging, Miss Delastone. Come on in."

"Thank you. I won't keep you long."

She marched stiffly to the centre of the room and stood there. Under a light-weight white three-quarter coat she wore a black-and-grey spun cotton something that did nothing at all for her skin. There were pearls at her throat and pearls at her ears. They didn't help either.

By the time I was through hanging her coat in the closet, she was in the lounge chair, not crossing her legs. Not that I minded: her ankles were thick and the calves had the wrong shape.

"I heard you were registered here," she said evenly. "I had to talk to you."

I nodded and sat on the edge of the bed. She had brought along a fairly large white faille bag that didn't appear to have a gun in it. Her shoes were the kind they call "sensible" which is another word for unattractive. She wore hardly any lipstick and what there was was the wrong shade. Her nose was shiny and her hair just untidy enough to be called untidy.

"You mustn't blame the Colonel for the way he acted today," she said. "He's terribly afraid you've come here to stir things up again."

"You mean by my yapping about Sam Jellco? I'll admit I've tried hard to get things moving, but so far I don't see a ripple on the pond."

She shook her head. "That's not what I'm referring to, Mr. Pine. The Colonel's convinced you've been hired to investigate my brother's death."

"Does it need investigating? The way the papers had it he could have died of indigestion."

"He was murdered," she said as calmly as anyone could say anything. "He was shot with his own gun, in his own car. I'm sure you knew that."

"How would I, Miss Delastone?"

"I think Mother told you. You saw her three days ago. At her request. Or do you intend telling me she brought you out from Chicago for another reason entirely?"

"Why not ask her?" I suggested.

"In other words you don't intend to tell me. May I have a cigarette?"

I got up to give her one and to hold the match. She tilted her thick unlovely neck and blew out a cloud of uninhaled smoke and coughed a little. She was no addict; the cigarette was just something to lean on.

"You see," she went on in her placid way, "I learned that Mother engaged this man Jellco four days after Edwin died—obviously to find out who had killed him, since the Colonel clearly had no intention of doing anything along those lines. Then a few days later she called you in—I assume for the same

purpose. Either Mr. Jellco had failed or Mother decided to put
two men on the case."

"The fog," I said, "begins to lift. No wonder the Colonel read
me the riot act this morning."

"Can you blame him?"

I grunted sourly. "Don't tempt me, lady. I'd enjoy blaming
him for most anything. Why doesn't he come right out and ask
Serena what she's up to? Or aren't they on speaking terms?"

Her face was a brittle mask. "My mother doesn't make explanations. Least of all to her own family. She's proud, inflexible,
dictatorial. She was left a great deal of money by her father,
which she uses to keep us utterly dependent on her."

"Including the Colonel? The job he's got with the City?"

"His salary is almost nothing. Being a commissioner is largely
a matter of prestige and power."

"Hell, he should be able to build up quite a bankroll. With
the advance information he gets on city projects and such."

I saw her teeth then in what wasn't a smile and what wasn't
intended as one. Her thick-fingered hands were very still on the
white faille bag. "Not my father. Money isn't that important to
him. He loves Olympic Heights, Mr. Pine. All he wants, everything he does, is to make it a better place to live."

"Covering up murders won't improve it much," I said.

"He's deathly afraid of another scandal. It could ruin him
politically. I think that would literally kill him."

"What do you want me to do about it, Miss Delastone?"

She leaned forward and for the first time there was animation
in her face. "Give up prying into this man Jellco's death. All
that's necessary is to tell his wife it *was* suicide. And—and I'll
pay you. Much more than you would get from her."

"Ten thousand," I said airily.

It rocked her but that was all it did. "Very well. If that's your
price. I'll bring you the money tomorrow."

"No fooling?" I said. "And all along you've been telling me
how you and the Colonel were strictly poorhouse bait. Who's
putting up the dough? Not Serena?"

"Does it matter?" she said impatiently. "You'll get your money.
Isn't that what you want?"

"Nope. What I want is to find out *why* you'll pay. Is it simply
because you're afraid finding Jellco's killer will blow the lid off
the story behind Edwin's murder? Is that what's giving the
Colonel and you the trots?"

She got red in the face and prim around the mouth. "Must you say things like that?"

"Like what?"

"Like . . . that. Vulgar things."

"It snuck out," I said. "The hell with it. I asked you if the reason I'm being blocked off on the Jellco thing is because you're afraid the truth will come out about Edwin."

Some ash fell on her lap from the cigarette she was holding and not smoking. She never even noticed. "After all, Mother hired Mr. Jellco to find out about Edwin's death. If you solve one killing you solve them both."

"What of it? The town's not going to lynch your old man just because he nabs a killer."

"The reason for the killings could do the harm, Mr. Pine."

I blew out my breath. "We're going around in circles, Miss Delastone. Nothing's changed. I'm in this to stay. Sorry and all that. Let's just put it down that I'm the bullheaded type. I'll get your coat."

She didn't move. "May I ask you something?"

"Anybody can ask me anything."

"Mother *did* hire you to find out about my brother?"

"Talk to her about it," I growled. "She might tear your leg off for asking, but then again she might tell you. Which is more than I'll do."

I stood up. "Are you angry with me?" she asked in a small voice.

I looked at her with my mouth open. I didn't laugh. I was too stunned to laugh. "Why should I be sore at you? All you did was to try to buy me off. It happens every day. You've got ashes on your dress."

She looked blank for a moment, then stood up and shook her skirt. She put the bag on the writing desk and took a long time to fish out a handkerchief. While that was going on I went to the closet to get her coat.

She brushed past me on the way to the bathroom. I heard water running, then silence and then she came out again. Her hair was now neat but still not attractive. There was fresh lipstick on her shapeless mouth and too much powder on her nose.

I went over to open the hall door for her. Before I could turn the knob she put a hand on my arm, stopping me. Her face was close to mine.

"There's something about you," she murmured.

I probably looked silly. I felt silly.

"You're very attractive," she almost whispered. "You must be quite strong . . . physically."

Before I could dig up an answer to that one, she slid the hand slowly up my arm and put it against the side of my neck and pulled my head down and kissed me hard on the mouth. Her tongue hit my lips, flicked lightly along them, and her body pushed tightly against me. Her breath was as hot as a blowlamp.

Then she drew abruptly away, the door opened and closed and she was gone.

CHAPTER NINETEEN

THERE was thunder now. Far off to the north, spaced far apart and just loud enough to be heard when you listened for it. The drapes moved under fitful gusts of air, were still, moved again, like an old woman working up enough nerve to cross the street. Along the walks people kept stopping to look up at the sky.

I took another shower and sprinkled talcum and brushed my teeth. Traces of Martha Delastone's lipstick were still visible, looking almost as bad on me as it had on her. I scrubbed it off. The face in the mirror didn't appear capable of arousing uncontrollable passion among the sensible-shoe set, but I knew different.

I tried to remember the number, couldn't, and had to look it up again. This time I got a woman with a voice as soft and creamy as peanut butter.

"Mr. Algebra? I'll inquire. Who is this calling, please?"

I told her my name.

"Mr. *Pine?* I see. May I ask what it was you wanted to speak with Mr. Algebra about?"

"About a minute," I said. "After that it'll be up to him."

"I'm afraid——"

"Don't be. He wouldn't fire you for a little thing like that. Just march right in and say, 'Guy named Pine wants to talk to you, boss. Won't give me a straight answer but he might you.' And I'll bet a pretty it works."

I liked her laugh, what there was of it. She said, "Hold on while I find out," and then there was the total absence of sound that comes when they close a key on you.

I waited. Time passed. It seemed she had a long way to go to get him. Maybe he was holding a king-high spade flush and couldn't be bothered. I practised balancing an unlighted cigarette on the point of my chin. It's hard to do, even when you don't have a receiver glued to your ear.

And then a man's voice, deep and vibrant as the purr of a panther, saying, "I'm Algebra. They tell me your name's Pine. What of it?"

"I'd like to come out and see you, Mr. Algebra. Tonight, if that's convenient for you."

"Do I know you, Pine?" His tone told me how little the answer would matter.

"Not personally, Mr. Algebra. Only my name and my business and my description and the licence number of my car."

"Really?" He sounded mildly amused. "Give me a reason for seeing you and I might try to arrange it."

"We know some of the same people," I said. "Karen Delastone, for one. We could kind of talk about her."

"Are you a friend of Miss Delastone's?"

"We've met. I wouldn't go so far as to say we're what you'd call friends."

"Come ahead," he said carelessly. "I'll get word to the gate. Are you bringing along a bodyguard?"

"I hadn't thought about it, Mr. Algebra. Will I need one?"

"Better bring two," he said and hung up.

It had been more than something tossed off to be funny. Not so much a threat as a warning. A warning as thinly veiled as a blonde at a lodge smoker. I put the phone down gently and stood there looking out at the night, seeing the rooftops and chimneys stark and black under the uneasy flicker of heat lightning, listening to the march of thunder down the sky. The room was suddenly chill and empty and without walls. I had no business being there. Even my coming to Olympic Heights had been a mistake. This was a job for a man who was naïve and inexperienced and even a little stupid. I was none of those things, yet in a way I was all of them and I knew it and didn't like knowing it. Only there was nothing to be done about it now. Not any more there wasn't.

By the time I had the pins out of the new shirt and was dressed, it was nearly ten-thirty. The paper with the phone numbers collected during the evening still lay on the writing desk. I folded it small and tucked it away in my wallet and reached for my hat.

Leaving the room was easy. Coming back to it would be the

hard part. Maybe I'd be lucky. Maybe Mr. Algebra would talk me out of coming back at all.

The CCC Club was out at the north end of town, a big sprawling frame building of two floors that had the look of an old mansion gone to seed. It was raining fairly heavily by the time I got out there and turned in at a wide driveway blocked off by the closed gate in a ten-foot cyclone fence. A man in slicker and rain-hat came out of a sentry box and put a light in my face through the Plymouth window. I told him my name and he nodded and went over to throw an electric switch that rolled back the gate. I drove in and parked among a cluster of cars under a pair of flood-lamps. A hatless youth appeared with an oversized umbrella and escorted me along a winding path between giant cottonwoods and elms and up the steps to a porch and the front door.

Inside was a big hushed foyer, all long-fringed oriental rugs and walnut panelling and polished brass under indirect lighting, with the muted sounds of music and voices from behind tall double doors at the far end. Back there, too, was a darkwood staircase curving in a majestic sweep to the upper floor, and coming down the steps towards me a middle-aged man in a dark suit.

I checked my hat while I waited for him. He was small and slim-waisted and looked to be fast on his feet if it should come to that. His hair was a smooth white at the temples, blending beautifully into iron-grey on top. He had an economical smile and emotionless grey eyes and a soft unhurried voice.

"Mr. Pine? Good evening, sir. The man at the gate said you were here. Come with me, please."

We went up the steps single-file and took the left corridor. Very wide, very elegant, very quiet. Along it were tall recessed doors, all of them tightly closed. Thick carpeting muffled our steps, and the lighting was as soft and subdued as a caliph's concubine.

And then we were stopping outside a door that looked no different from the others along the corridor and the grey-haired man was opening it and stepping aside, and I started in.

I caught a glimpse of panelled walls and a man in a chair and another man rising from behind a desk . . . then everything blew up in a soundless explosion of white fire laced with flashes of vivid orange. Pain blossomed across the back of my head and spread to the horizons. My knees melted. On the way down I grabbed for a chair. I missed it by nine miles. A section of plum-coloured broadloom floated up and smacked me alongside the face.

I didn't black out. It had been a hard blow but not that hard. No sound except a laboured breathing. Mine. Nausea burned in my throat. I gritted my teeth and lifted my face off the rug and shook it a little. I was panting like a dog in the sun. Anger fought panic for the upper hand. I got a knee under me. It was like picking up an anvil with my teeth. I said, "Son of a bitch," in a voice that whined, and brought up the other knee, bracing myself on the palms of my hands. Across a wavering distance I could make out the legs of a chair. It was one of those twisted metal and foam rubber things, as comfortable for sitting as a coal scuttle.

I began to crawl toward it. The floor was all uphill. Somebody chuckled. Somebody had a great sense of humour. I went on crawling. I reached the chair and took hold of it firmly. It was light and it wobbled. That was unfortunate. That was just too goddamned bad. See the complaint department. Talk to the manager. He might even give you your money back.

I climbed the chair, breathing hard, sweating, my legs like rubber bands. And after what seemed forever, I was up on my feet, holding tight to the chair to stay that way, blinking until the man behind the desk swam slowly into focus.

This would be Arnie Algebra. He half-sat on a corner of the desk, idly swinging a small narrow foot and watching me. He was smoking a brown-paper cigarette with the unobtrusive grace of a Spaniard. He had a beautiful mouth under a thin lip-hugging moustache in a lean dark face that looked dangerous. The whites of his eyes were almost too white, the brown of the irises almost black. His thick black hair looked as though the barber had just delivered it, combed with a side part and showing exactly the right amount of repressed wave.

A familiar face. A face I'd seen before. In a picture—a snapshot carried in the wallet of a young female burglar named Karen Delastone.

He stared back at me, his face dark and cold and indifferent. I licked my lips They had a hot puffy feel to my tongue. Anger was strong in me, bitter as bile. "Nice going," I said. "A belt in the head from behind. I hope I didn't hurt your rug."

"Now you know where you stand with me," Algebra said in a voice spun from steel wool. He put the cigarette aside and strolled over to stand in front of me, his left hand in the pocket of his beautifully fitted dinner jacket. "Tell me you don't like it."

"I don't like it," I said.

He folded his right hand and swung it in a short tight arc, getting his shoulder behind it. I tried to jerk my head out of its path but I was too slow. Far too slow. The punch nailed me under the left ear and I went down, taking the chair with me this time. I lay there gasping, not moving, gathering my strength like an old man gathering firewood. And after a while I rolled over and got shakily back on my feet.

From the depths of a big leather chair across the room the battered face of Lyle Spence grinned loosely up at me. He was wearing the same light-grey jacket and, from the looks of it, the same shirt. Only the Pontiac was missing. The slender grey-haired man who had brought me here just stood inside the closed door, his expression mildly troubled. The black-leather sap dangling from one of his hands didn't look at all troubled. Just efficient and with no blood on it.

Algebra hadn't moved. His eyes glistened in his dark face. "Tell me you don't like it," he said again.

"Hunh-uh," I said. "This time it's a secret." My jaw hurt saying it.

The stiff front of his dress shirt rose and fell under his quiet breathing. His hands hung at his sides, the long slim fingers curling in a little. "The big-city private eye," he said past a bent lip. "Large and tough and full of wind. Out here to put Arnie Algebra through the wringer and maybe show him a big black scowl if he's slow with the answers. Is that the way you figured it, hard boy?"

I put a hand up and felt below my left ear and bit down hard on my teeth and failed to answer him. Not with three of them waiting for any excuse at all.

Algebra turned on his heel and marched back to pick up his cigarette. "See what he's carrying, Otto."

The grey-haired man approached me briskly, the blackjack no longer visible but probably still handy. He said, "If you'll excuse me, sir," and got behind me and patted me firmly under the arms and around the waistline. Then he dipped expertly into my pockets and took out what was there and made a neat pile of everything on the desk.

Algebra laughed a short sour laugh. "I thought you guys always packed at least one gun. Where's the trusty .45?"

"Maybe next time," I said.

He didn't even look at me. I was the forgotten man. He put out a contemptuous forefinger and stirred my property around, finally weeding out the wallet. He went through the compartments and identification panels, taking his time, unfolding everything that was folded, reading everything that was written.

I stood there and watched him invade my privacy, while the tide of my anger rose like the water around a black rock. My mouth was dry and my eyes burned and the back of my skull was where the railroad had pushed a long winding tunnel. And nobody cared but me.

Presently Algebra refilled the wallet and tossed it down and reached for what was left of his cigarette. "You punk," he said in a voice tight with fury. "You stupid punk. Stupid for calling me in the first place, even stupider for coming out here at all. Why I even waste my time with you I don't know. Don't think you're the first small-change grifter I've had to step on. Punks who get the silly idea that all it takes to make me reach for my cheque book is to hint about having something hot on me or my friends. Well, now you know different."

He turned to bend gracefully and grind out his cigarette with hard quick stabs of his hand. Then he straightened and moved around behind the desk and into the chair. Then he leaned back and gave me another helping of his cold stare. "Okay, punk. You said you wanted to see me. You're seeing me. If you've got a piece to speak, speak it. Otherwise walk on out."

I walked up to the desk instead. He didn't do anything to stop me. I took what belonged to me off the glass and dropped it back in my pockets. I held out the cigarettes. They were only Camels, the plain old-fashioned kind, nothing exotic like Arnie Algebra's brown-paper imports, but they were kind to my throat and what I could afford. I shook one loose and lighted up and bent the matchstick and dropped it in the tray in front of him.

"The trouble with guys like you," I said, "is you're so busy proving how tough you are that you forget how to listen. Not that it matters. Listening is for people who want to learn. You already know it all. Like a couple of murders your high-society girl-friend is mixed up in. You know her brother was murdered and you know why he was murdered. You know she was in Sam Jellco's hotel room the night *he* was killed. You know she showed up at Jellco's office bright and early the very next morning, a jimmy in her bag and larceny in her heart. I think she was there to look up Jellco's file on Edwin's death, in case there is such a file and it implicates her. And maybe you. I could be wrong about that last part, since I don't know everything the way you do."

I stopped there to pick tobacco off my lower lip and to give him a chance to get back in the act.

His chair creaked faintly as he moved in it. He went on looking at me in the same chill way as always. Only there was the ghost of indecision in his dark eyes now, and behind the indecision a dim formless alarm that might not be alarm at all but only something I wanted to be alarm. In the silence a gust of wind whipped rain against the window behind him and there was a growl of thunder like lions beyond a campfire.

"Anything more, Pine?" he said in a grey voice.

"Yeah," I said. "Somehow I had the ridiculous notion that you and Karen Delastone weren't really mixed up in Jellco's death at all, that your interest came from thinking he knew something about Edwin's murder. So I rang you up and asked to see you. I should have known better. All you're interested in is proving how tough you are. You're not tough, Mr. Algebra. You're all mouth and borrowed muscle and as vacuum-headed as most men in your line. So I'm saying goodbye to you and I'm saying it now. Goodbye to you."

I turned and went towards the door. At my back Algebra said, "Hold it!" in a voice you could bend a crowbar on. He was standing now, a pinched look around his mouth, colour burning in his cheeks.

"Listen to me good, Pine," he said, picking his words with care. "If you ever go near Karen Delastone again, if I ever find out you've been asking questions about her or in any way try to drag her into whatever you're investigating—I'll break you in half. Now you can leave."

"Yeah," I said. "Now I can leave. And while we're at it, keep that punch-drunk clown of yours off my tail from now on unless you want a Plymouth bounced off him."

Lyle Spence said, "Hey!" in a wounded bellow and lunged to his feet, his mouth open in shocked disbelief. "Listen, Mr. Algebra, do I hafta take a crack like that from this schmeklehead?"

Algebra shrugged and said nothing. It was the green light. Spence said, "This I'm gonna like!" and came shuffling towards me, hands loosely clenched and held at eye level, weaving and bobbing from a fighter's crouch.

I waited until he was close enough, then kicked him in the shin.

He howled like an elephant in labour and threw a left at my head. Pain from the damaged shin spoiled his timing and I let the punch go over my shoulder and chopped down on the side of his neck with the edge of my hand. It dropped him to his knees hard enough to shake the room. He shook his head and tried to get up. I put my knee in his face to help him. He went over backwards and clapped both hands across his nose. His legs jerked like the legs of an overturned turtle. Bright blood spurted from between his fingers, staining the nice clean carpeting.

Feet whispered behind me and I whirled in time to duck under the path of Otto's swinging blackjack. While he was still off balance I hit him in the throat. He wasn't very robust. The sap flew out of his hand and he clawed at his throat and said "uh-uh-uh" and fell across the arm of a chair. I was bending to pick up the blackjack when Algebra's toneless voice said, "Let it lay, Pine."

Pointing at me from his right hand was a medium-sized black automatic pistol. I straightened gingerly and showed him my empty hands and said, "Now it's guns. Okay. Just keep your Pomeranians on a leash."

Lyle Spence was climbing to his feet the way a man climbs out of a well. His face was a crimson smear. He swung his head in a slow half-circle, said a strangled word and charged me.

It was a charge in slow motion. "Lyle!" Algebra said sharply. "That's enough!"

A thrown paper clip would have had the same effect. He kept on coming, seeing me only dimly, staggering as he came, his fists pawing the air. I stepped aside and put a foot out, tripping him up. He fell in sections, like a factory smokestack. The desklamp jiggled against the glass and one of the pictures on a side wall slid askew. He tried to rise, but it wasn't much more than his reflexes at work and he settled back again at full length. This time he stayed down.

Then the door opened into the room and Karen Delastone was standing there.

CHAPTER TWENTY

THIS time she wore something in pale blue, nothing to speak of upstairs and yards of the stuff below standing out over at least one stiff petticoat. Her cheeks had the flushed look and her eyes the bright shine that come with the fourth Martini of the evening.

She gave the man on the floor a startled look. "Well! Am I interrupting something or do I just yell *olé* and throw a rose?"

Then she saw me. Her teeth clicked shut and anger poured into her face. But before she could let loose at me, Algebra said, "Come on in, Karen, and shut the door."

She did both. Then she circled around Lyle Spence and stopped squarely in front of me. Her eyes blazed. "I might've known it. What did you do—hit him when his back was turned?"

"Good evening, Miss Delastone. I kicked him in the belly while he was sleeping."

She hauled off and slapped me across the face. She did it very quick. It made a sharp clean sound and stung like hell. I put my hand up slowly and rubbed my cheek and said, "Don't try it again, precious."

She turned her back on me. "What's he doing here, Arnie?"

Algebra looked at his watch, turning his wrist gracefully. "It's not important, darling. Mr. Pine was just leaving."

"You're going to let him walk out of here? After what he's done to Lyle?"

"To hell with Lyle, darling."

Spence stirred, groaned, and tried to sit up. The slender grey-haired man left off massaging his throat and got off the chair and went over to lend a hand. He seemed older than when we first met downstairs and not nearly so unruffled.

Algebra gave me a distant nod. "It would seem we've nothing more to discuss, Pine. Just keep in mind what I said about annoying my friends. Or me. Good night."

I looked away from him to the smeared features of Lyle Spence, from them to the hot eyes of Karen Delastone. As an evening's work it had been a complete washout. A sore head and some skinned knuckles and a great deal of windy anger. All of it useless, nothing solved.

I shrugged and went quietly to the door and out.

Downstairs the front door was standing open and a knot of early birds hanging around waiting for the rain to let up. Instead of waiting with them, I hunted up the bar.

It was all heavy beams and darkwood walls and wrought iron, fitted out to resemble a Dakota dirt-farmer's idea of an English pub. Behind a semi-circular sweep of mahogany bar were prints of red-coated aristocrats, riding through Sherwood Forest behind a pack of baying hounds or having kippers and tea on the manor terrace. The place was jammed with the carriage trade, foggy with tobacco smoke, jumping with the high-pitched voices and shrill laughter of women in their cups.

At the far end of the bar I found a vacant stool next to a small shapely young woman wearing a party frock and harlequin glasses with jewelled frames. Except for a Bacardi cocktail and a cigarette in a long jet holder, she was alone. She sat with both elbows resting on the wood, staring down into the pink depths of her glass, her pointed face solemn as a church wedding. She didn't even twitch an eyebrow when I climbed up next to her.

An elderly barkeep, very correct in white coat and dark trousers, asked my pleasure and went away to hunt up the right bottle of brandy. I lighted a cigarette and closed my ears to the noise. And presently I thought of Linda Jellco.

. . . Right now you are out for the evening, and it is the right and sensible thing for you to do. You are out with the couple down the hall. Fred Mather and his wife. (Or is it Ted?) There is dinner and a few drinks at that nice restaurant and afterwards the long cool drive to a roadhouse on the South Side. (Or West, or North; it doesn't matter.) So you dance a little and drink more than is par for you, and a time or two there you laugh out loud at something Ted (Fred?) says.

Only it's a mistake to laugh, because then is when the black thoughts come. They are always the same, those thoughts. Your man is lying in a polished box with a satin pillow under his head and his hands folded across his chest, waiting for the hole to be dug and the words to be said before they put him down in the dark and cover him up and it will be as though he never lived. Oh, they'll tell you that he is not dead, that he is waiting Up There or on the Other Shore, and that he would be happy if you did not grieve for him. Only nobody really believes that any more.

Tomorrow will be the hard day to get through, and the thought that you may not be able to manage it without cracking up completely really scares you. So you shove your thoughts aside, only it's like shoving four mountains, and you pick up your glass and listen to the pretty music and the sounds made by happy people, and for a little while the pain is gone. Only it's not gone at all. It is still there, a micro-inch under the surface, stabbing you with a familiar chord from a clarinet, the echo of a word, the edge of a laugh. Then the ache comes back, not blunted at all, and the thought of tomorrow. . . .

"Your Delamain, sir," the barkeep said.

I gulped half of it, instead of sipping it the way they tell you, and shivered a little. Beyond the leaded glass of casement windows rain made a sound like a drunken waterfall.

"Men," the girl on the next stool said in a high clear voice, "are bedbugs. In the full, unexpurgated, unabridged sense of the word. Bedbugs. Little crawly filthy bedbugs."

I looked at her. She hadn't moved. Her elbows were still planted on the bar and she was still staring into her glass, the liquid in it still at the same level. The cigarette in the jet holder had built a long grey ash due to let go any second.

"I'm a man," I said. "So kind of watch it, see?"

She lifted her chin slowly until it pointed straight ahead. Then she turned it as slowly in my direction. She did it the way the robots do it in the science-fiction movies. You could almost hear the gears mesh.

Behind the harlequin frames her eyes were dark and round and glazed. She was as full of alcohol as a preserved kidney. "They are bedbugs," she said, "because all they want to do is crawl in bed with you. That is all they want to do. All they want to do is crawl——"

"You said that," I said.

"All men are bedbugs," she said.

"You said that too," I said.

"Go to hell," she said.

"Could I wait till it stops raining?"

She moved her head vaguely. "You try to be intelligent," she said. "You read books and keep up with current events and the changes in the tax laws and who's the best hitter in the American League. Just so you can talk to them. Only they don't really listen. They just sit around and nod at you and all the time they're thinking about getting into bed with you."

"Sometimes they think about eating," I said. "Or shooting a little snooker. Or sometimes they just don't give a darn. Like right now."

"Are you a poet?" she said.

"Yeah," I said. "I'm a poet."

"Poets," she said. "They're the ones. Poets." The ash fell, narrowly missing her drink. "All they want to do is crawl in bed with you."

"Not me," I said. "I'm different. All I want to do is write poetry."

She moved a hand up aimlessly and pushed at her dark hair. Then she took her glasses off. She was almost lovely in a strictly off-centre way. She put the glasses carefully down on the bar and leaned over until her face was very close to mine. "You've got nice eyes," she said.

"You mustn't excite me," I said.

"You may kiss me," she breathed.

"Couldn't we just sit here and talk about Mickey Mantle?"

"You bastard," she said, and swung at me. Everybody was swinging at me tonight. I caught her before she reached the floor and propped her up on the stool again. She picked up her glass and threw it at nothing. It hit a cash register instead.

The barkeep came over fast. He seemed pained. "I'm very sorry, sir, but I'm afraid you'd better take her out."

"Don't look at me," I said. "I'm engaged to a blonde."

The girl put her head down on the bar and went to sleep. I paid for the brandy and got up to go.

The barkeep pointed a clean thumb at the dark head on the wood. "What about the lady, sir?"

"What about the lady?"

"I assumed you were a friend. She was speaking with you."

"She's a screwball," I said. "I attract screwballs. It seems there's something about me."

He was concerned in a nice gentlemanly way. "Perhaps I should call one of the powder-room matrons."

"Just so you don't call a poet," I said. "She's hell on poets."

By the time I came out of the men's room the rain had slacked off considerably and the crowd around the club entrance was down to a few faint hearts. I bought my hat back at the check-stand and turned the collar of my coat up and went out into the damp, ducking between the trees until I reached the Plymouth. I was under the wheel with the door shut before I found out I wasn't alone.

A girl sat huddled in the next seat, all the way over near the door. A girl with dark hair and a velvet stole and a white face watching me out of the night.

It was Karen Delastone.

CHAPTER TWENTY-ONE

"You injured him quite badly," she said dispassionately. "In fact it seems you broke his nose in two places. I thought you might want to know."

"Not especially. It was his idea. You mean you came all the way out here in the rain to tell me that?"

She drew the stole closer about her bare shoulders and went on watching me. Not enough light reached her face for me to make out her expression.

"Partly that," she said, answering my question. "And I was hoping you'd take me home. It seems Mr. Algebra is too busy at the moment."

A kind of weary impatience stirred in me. "Nothing doing. I've had about all the Delastones I can take for one day. I've been lied to and charmed and wheedled and threatened by them for something like twelve straight hours, not to mention being tailed and yelled at and punched around by their friends. So go find yourself another chauffeur."

"You can be pretty damned coldblooded, can't you, Pine?"

"Since when does saying no to you make me coldblooded?"

She crossed her knees and smoothed her skirt. "You know, you actually frightened me upstairs. When I slapped you. You should have seen your eyes."

"Uh-hunh."

"Oh, start the car, for God's sake. Let's get away from here."

I leaned down and turned the key. The motor purred quietly in the wet air. I snapped the headlights on and backed out of the slot and nosed up to the wire gate as it rolled back to let us through.

For the first mile or so neither of us had anything to say. I drove at a lawful speed along the sleeping streets, under the dripping trees, listening to the swish of tyres and the *snap-ah, snap-ah* of the windshield wipers. The rain was light but steady, with once in a while a breeze whipping spray in against my face. Lightning continued to flicker, but the big crackling bolts were gone now and the thunder distant and subdued to the south. I wondered if the hotel maid had remembered to close my apartment windows.

She stirred a little, drawing her legs up under her the way

they do, and then she sighed. She looked at me, then away, then back again. A lot I cared. She was trouble. I had all the trouble I could use for one day. Tomorrow would be time enough for another helping. Tomorrow we could be at each other's throats—she and the Colonel and Serena and Martha. Delastones all, and the hell with them and their loud voices and finishing school accents and sensible shoes and petty vices.

Karen Delastone put her open-toed shoes back on the floorboards and snapped open a small envelope bag that glittered and took out cigarettes. She bent forward to press in the dashboard lighter, then switched on the radio. A professional voice said, "—ain tonight and tomorrow, clearing by late evening, with temperatures in the low seventies. Light variable winds, mostly from the northwest. . . . And now here's Stan Davis and his boys with the Decca platter of 'The Lady's in Love'. Little Lila Lewis does the vocal—and nobody, but nobody, can do it better. Take it, Stan."

She cut the volume as a trumpet tore a hole in the night. She straightened slowly and leaned back and worked a pair of cigarettes from the pack, lighted them both and held one out to me with a hand that wasn't shaking.

"So very tough, aren't you?" she said evenly. "Tough and masculine and insufferably smug."

I took the cigarette. "If you're going to pump me," I said, "that's no way to go at it. You're supposed to bat your big brown eyes at me and get a pleading note in your voice and maybe rub a silken knee against my leg. Everybody knows that."

"There you go—being smug again! What makes you so sure I want to pump you—as you call it?"

"Why else would you be here, Miss Delastone? And don't try telling me it's for the ride."

". . . What is it you want out here anyway?"

"You mean here in Olympic Heights? To prove Sam Jellco didn't kill himself—as the authorities in this tight little town would like people to think. I told you that this morning. At least I think I told you."

"All I can say is you're certainly going about it in a funny way!"

"What's funny about it?"

"You know very well. Annoying my family and snarling at the police and badgering my friends. I suppose it makes some sense that you'd quarrel with the police over it, but there's certainly no excuse for the rest of your actions."

"I've got all the reasons anybody could want," I said. "For one thing it would have to be damn near impossible to cover up a murder in this town without the Colonel being a party to it. Another, you were in Jellco's hotel room the night he died there, and in his office hunting for something this morning. Also, your boy friend Arnie Algebra stuck a tail on me the minute I blew into town. On top of all that your sister tried buying me off tonight. Now you know what I mean by reasons."

She wasn't leaning back any more. She sat tall and tense, trying to read my face through the dark. "My *sister*? Martha? Why?"

"She seemed positive my real interest was in learning who killed your brother."

"Was she right?"

I didn't answer her.

"You love this, don't you?" she said hotly. "You really like prying into people's privacy. And if it wrecks a few lives, that's just fine with you! Does it pay well?"

"Fifty a day, when I'm lucky. I've been known to take less."

"Maybe I could buy you off. Maybe Martha didn't offer you enough. Is money all it takes?"

"What else is there?"

She leaned towards me. Her breath touched my cheek. "How would I do?" she whispered. "I'm told I've a beautiful body. Would you like to see it?"

"Sure."

She hung there, waiting, not moving. I could smell her a little: a faint heady smell that might be nothing more mysterious than bath powder. Her face was a pale oval marked by parted lips and the eyes large and dark. I didn't move. A long moment passed while the tyres sang against the wet street.

And then she drew back quickly and her laugh was harsh and unnatural. "Liar! I said you were coldblooded!" She glanced out the open window next to her. "Where are we, Pine? Can't you coax a little speed out of this relic?"

"I wouldn't want to break any Olympic Heights laws, Miss Delastonê. And it's not that I don't think you've got a fine body. They probably don't come any finer. Only you weren't really offering it to me at all."

"How gallant of you to say so," she said coolly. "Next you'll be telling me I couldn't murder anyone."

"I didn't say you had."

"What's the matter? You're not backing down, are you?"

"Go ahead," I said. "Go ahead and enjoy yourself if it makes you feel better. You're not the first one that's started out by handing me the big razoo. Only most of them end up with me wiping their runny noses for them."

"Don't count on adding me to the list."

"You're in this maze up to your diamond necklace, lady. You could use some help, if you'd only get down off your throne long enough to ask for it."

"The sympathetic approach? How nice!" The sneer in her voice was as wide as a boulevard. "Is this how you go about grilling suspects?"

"How's Deborah Ellen?"

In the glow of the cigarette her face held a frozen look. The glow died and the darkness took over again, with her voice coming through it. "Debbie told me about that. The idea—trying to question a child. Your kind certainly goes to any length."

"Nuts." I turned a corner. "You don't question a child. You just listen. I heard you've been up in an airplane and cry in your room with the door locked and smuggle in comic books to compete with the Bible. I found out that Uncle Edwin went to Heaven and that Debbie has nightmares you're trying to talk her out of and that I'm an old policeman."

We covered another block before she spoke. "Debbie's not a happy child. She shouldn't even be living in that house. Nobody in it knows how to talk to anybody under thirty. Serena dresses her out of the Middle Ages and of course none of the other children in the neighbourhood will have anything to do with her. No wonder she has nightmares."

"Somehow I got the idea they were kind of recent. The nightmares. What are they like?"

Silence. Not the light easy kind of silence. Then she said, "There's no point in talking about it. You turn left at the next corner."

"I'll turn it. There's what you might call a coincidence involved here, Miss Delastone. Uncle Edwin dies of a bullet and his niece starts having bad dreams. A thing like that gets you thinking."

"Damn you!" she whispered. "God damn you!"

The tyres squealed a little on the turn. Hardly any traffic in sight. Still raining, but down now to not much more than a drizzle.

"It was those yellow pyjamas," I said. "There's a theory around that a cuckolded husband squeezed the trigger, then tried a cover-up by dressing the body and driving it far from the scene. That seems kind of cumbersome to me. I'd like it better having him shot in his own bed—or anyway in his own bedroom. And I don't mean suicide, either. Guys like Edwin aren't the type. No matter how deep the water, they always expect a last-minute miracle to pull them out."

Not a sound out of her. I drew in some smoke and threw the cigarette away. The air coming in at the side window smelled pleasantly of wet earth and growing things. Getting on toward midnight, if that mattered.

"What if," I said, "an argument took place in Edwin's room that night? An argument loud enough to wake Deborah Ellen. She sees her uncle killed, or maybe just the body being carried out—something that gives her an awful jolt. It means she's got to be sold a quick bill of goods that it didn't really happen at all, that it was no more than a bad dream. It can be done when they're that age and when they trust you—and it had to be done, not only to spare her but to protect whoever fired the gun."

The way she shook her head was more nearly a shudder. Yet her voice came out calm enough. "You don't really believe that. You couldn't."

"Why couldn't I believe it? Sure, it's a theory. But it's a theory with hair on the chest. Show me it isn't."

"Then why not take it all the way?" she suggested bitterly. "You claim I'm the one who convinced Debbie she had a nightmare. Why not come right out and accuse me of killing my own brother? Or would you rather make it the Colonel, or Serena, or Martha?"

"Or Arnie Algebra," I said.

"Oh, stop it!"

"There's a theory for that, too, Miss Delastone. Based on the kind of unmentionable Edwin was. Something simple, like blackmail, say, would've been right down his alley. Even if it involved one of his own clan. Just to be talking, let's assume he got hold of something poisonous on you and tried to fashion it into an income. You run to Arnie and he drops in on Edwin late one night. One word leads to another and Arnie tries roughing him up and he pulls a gun. In the excitement the gun goes off and Edwin is dead. It's Arnie who drives the body to a lonely place for the cops to find and puzzle over. Only it turns out there isn't any puzzle. The fix goes in at the top and Edwin's unlamented passing gets no publicity and is tucked deep in the closed file down at City Hall and your sigh of relief rattles the windows."

I slowed the car to read a street sign. Myrtle Avenue. I remembered it from the day I called on Serena. The ride was almost over.

Karen Delastone bent to drop her cigarette into the tray. In the light from the dash her face had the white hard look of fine marble. "So now I'm somebody who can be blackmailed. You certainly have a high opinion of me."

"You're not one of the vestal virgins," I said. "All of us do things we can justify at the time, even though the rules say different."

"You're so understanding!" Still the big sneer. She looked away from me and fiddled with the stole again and appeared to be thinking. Nearly a minute passed before she had more to say.

"Why are you so interested in the Delastones and their problems, Mr. Pine? You made quite a point of telling me you were working on another case altogether."

"I don't have any choice," I said. "The two paths keep crossing. I'd be out of my head not to work both sides of the street."

"I can't see that."

"That there's a connection? You know better. The Colonel as much as told me Jellco was killed because somebody got the idea he was dabbling in your brother's death. He could've told me that just to scare me off. I wouldn't know if he's that devious. But there's this business of your being in Sam Jellco's hotel room the night he was killed. You wouldn't want to tell me what you were doing there, would you?"

"I . . . Who says I was in his room?"

"At least one witness, Miss Delastone. I could probably uncover more of them if you made me."

"Goodness, you're efficient! That waiter, I suppose."

"So why the big act this morning? At Jellco's office."

"Being cautious. You could have been the police."

"Lucky for you I wasn't. You knew he was dead?"

"It was in the local papers."

"That was the first you heard about it? From the papers?"

". . . Yes."

"So you hunted up his office and went down there and broke in to get something. What was it?"

"But I didn't break in," she said seriously. "All right, I intended to—I'll grant that. It seems somebody got there ahead of me. I don't know who—or why. The lock was forced and the files a mess."

"You didn't get what you were after?"

"You should know," she said acidly. "The way you went through my handbag."

"That isn't what I asked you."

Her shoulders jerked angrily. "No. I didn't get it."

"What were you hunting for?"

"None of your business!"

"Why did you call on Jellco at the hotel?"

"None of your business!"

"Where do I find Pod Hamp?"

". . . Who?"

"How about April Day?"

She yawned a small yawn. "Is that what's known as the third degree?"

"Cute," I said. "You're real cute. And clever. Here you're tied in two murders and possibly three, and all you want to do is sit there and crack wise. I don't know what they teach at finishing schools these days, but if it's how to use good sense you flunked four courses. It's fine with me, though. I'd like you to know that. You'll start yelling for help when they shove your neck in the noose. Only nobody will listen to you then. Least of all me."

She reached a languid hand out to take the glittery bag off the seat. "They won't do anything to me, Mr. Pine. They'd have no reason to. Nobody has."

I turned another corner, this time the last one, and drew up in front of 25 New Cambridge Drive. A faint yellow glimmer from the porch was the only light, and the only sound the rustle of oak leaves under the soft rain and a small breeze.

The engine idled quietly. Karen Delastone swung the door all the way back and gathered up the hem of her skirt in one hand and stepped out. She stood on the parkway crosswalk and closed the door and bent her head to look in at me.

"Thank you. For the lift."

"I was the one who took the ride," I said.

"Good night. You're a strange man."

"Good night," I said.

I watched her turn and run lightly across the walk and out of sight through the opening in the hedge. The radio played something from Cole Porter. I lighted a cigarette and went on sitting, waiting to hear the closing of a distant door. The air was cool and moist against my forehead.

No sound of a door closing. She would do it nice and easy at this hour. I was reaching for the shift lever when something moved in the deep shadows beyond the hedge and a man stepped out.

He was a big man, big in all directions, and his shaggy mane of hair was bared to the elements. He stood there for a long moment staring at the Plymouth, then with slow deliberate steps he came over to it and put a wide hand on the window ledge and leaned down. It was the Colonel. Colonel Quentin Delastone.

"Mr. Pine," he rumbled. "You brought my daughter home."

"So I did," I said.

"I believe, sir, that you owe me an explanation."

"I wouldn't know what to explain, Colonel."

"You were told to leave Olympic Heights. Hours ago."

I peered at him. "I won't try to tell you it's a free country, Colonel. Short of knocking me on the head and hauling me out by the heels, I don't know of any way to make me leave before I'm ready to go. And as I told you earlier, I won't be ready until I'm through with the business that brought me to your fair city."

The fingers of his hand closed down hard on the ledge. "Very well, young man. I have warned you. I shall not warn you again."

"You're getting rained on, Colonel."

He removed his hand. I didn't see any dents in the metal. He turned slowly without a word and stalked through the hedge, every inch the Indian chief on his way to round up the braves.

I made a U turn and set the nose of the Plymouth towards downtown Olympic Heights and drove off through the rain.

CHAPTER TWENTY-TWO

THE elderly attendant at the hotel parking lot allowed as how things had sure cooled off nice and a couple days' rain was just what the doctor ordered. I agreed with him. I was tired enough to agree with a Republican. There was a spongy feel to the back of my head where Otto's sap had landed, and while people generally had been too polite to mention the bruise left by Lyle Spence's right cross to my chin, it was there all right.

The room seemed cooler. The maid had been in to turn down the spread and hang my dirty shirt in the closet. If the Dela-stones had sneaked in and planted any bombs they would have to wait till morning. I shucked off my work clothes and took my third shower of the evening, then collected the newspaper and crawled under the sheet with it.

I burned a cigarette over the headlines and the editorials and the sports page. Jewel robberies and love nests and the cool war and pictures of pretty girls in bathing suits having fun at the beach. Everything had a familiar ring as though I had read it all last week and last year and the year before that.

And slowly the dull ache in my head went away. The muscles grew slack and the nerves no longer jumped. Rain beat softly at the window and a youthful breeze swaggered in and plucked at the corners of my newspaper. And I thought of Karen Delastone's sharp tongue and Arnie Algebra's chilled eyes, of Lyle Spence's broken nose, of the Colonel and his warnings, of the restful gloom of the bar where Ira Groat had sat across a table from me while filling in the picture of Olympic Heights and the people who ran it. And all of it seemed far away and long ago, along with the hard voices promising violence and the eyes bright with anger.

And presently I was thinking of Linda Jellco and the pale drawn look of her face, of her wheat-field hair and the even blue-green eyes under the bold brows, of the voice which was some-times soft and sometimes firm and sometimes small, but never shrill. . . .

I folded the paper neat and put it in the wastebasket and drank two glasses of water from the bathroom faucet. It was close to one A.M. when I turned the light out. I didn't fall asleep until my head hit the pillow.

I swam up slowly from the depths of nothing and opened my eyes to darkness . . . and felt a naked belly pressed into my back and a slender arm settle around my chest. A throaty voice said, "Move over, for Chrisake. Ya want the whole bed?"

I jerked out from under the arm and sat up quick and groped for the lamp on the nightstand. The light came on. It was a girl, and naked as your thumb. A girl in her twenties and a face in its forties—a hard-bitten, sharp-featured, blonde girl whose ribs showed, whose neck was long and stringy, whose teeth had the hungry shine of a ferret's, whose washed-out blue eyes had seen too many men with their clothes off to care about it any more. She lay there smirking up at me, as exclusive as a waste basket, as desirable as a case of cholera.

The hall door was closed and presumably locked. I could remember locking it. On the lounge chair was an untidy pile of feminine wear: a bargain-basement dress in pale blue, a wrinkled white slip, pink rayon panties, a pair of suntan nylons, and on the floor brown-and-white straw shoes with runover heels. No brassière in sight. I looked down at the girl on the bed. She could use a brassière all right, but not in her business.

She moved her hips and said coyly, "Aw, what'sa matter, honey? Din'cha ever see a girl before?"

It was probably too late, but I had to take a stab at it anyway. I swung off the bed and reached for my shorts and stepped into them. "On your feet, glue neck."

"Aw now, honey. You——"

I grabbed the nearest arm and yanked. She came out of the bed like a cork out of a champagne bottle. She spit out a word I seldom used myself and I put a hand in the small of her back and shoved.

She sailed across the room and only the quick use of her hands kept her face off the wall. She screamed. I scooped her clothes up and crossed over fast to where she was standing, shoved the stuff in her arms and reached for the door. She was going out in the hall and she was going out fast. She could dress out there. Or she could stay naked. It was all the same to me.

Knuckles hit the door on the hall side. The girl opened her mouth to yell. I showed her the flat of my hand and the yell was stillborn. I put my face close to her ear and said, "Get dressed. In fifteen seconds or you lose your teeth."

But there wasn't going to be any fifteen seconds. A key clicking into the lock said as much. The bolt turned and the door swung in and three men filed into the room.

"Well, well," Captain Benton Brill of the Olympic Heights police said cheerfully. "What have we here?"

One of the others was the same plain clothes officer who had escorted me to Chief Maller's office the day before. Andrews, as I remembered. Number three was a short plump bird with a round self-righteous face and a pair of pop eyes that kept sliding off the blonde. He was the one with the key and he had the look of a guy who could tell you the value of teamwork in running a six-hundred-room house in Boston.

I said, "I rented this room. I plunked down five and a half bucks in advance and got a receipt. Where do you get off barging in here without a warrant?"

Brill's smile was polite. "Were you thinking of filing a complaint, Mr. Pine?"

I turned my back on all of them and walked over and took a cigarette from the pack on the nightstand and lighted it. I sat on an arm of the lounge chair and watched them watch me. I said nothing.

Brill strolled over to the bathroom, snapped the light on in there, looked behind the door, snapped the light off, sauntered over to the closet, opened it and looked in, closed it again and came up to where I sat.

He was still wearing some of his smile. "A misdemeanour, sir. I can furnish statute and code number if you want to hear them. Get your clothes on."

"Then I'm under arrest, Captain?"

"You are. Yes, sir."

"On what charge?"

"Disturbing the peace. Conduct in a lewd and lascivious manner while consorting with a common prostitute. Engaging a hotel room for immoral purposes."

"You left out spitting on the sidewalk and second degree mopery."

"A little masculine fun is fine," Brill said. "Ordinarily we don't like to interfere with a man's pleasure. But this happens to be a respectable hotel—not one of your Chicago joints. The management keeps an eye open. I'm waiting for you to get dressed."

I shrugged and stood up to locate my trousers. Brill swung his eyes to where the blonde stood clutching her things. "You too, Gracie."

The short plump man must have been disappointed by the last order. He shifted his feet, gave me a disapproving glance and said, "I'm sure you won't be needing me any longer, Captain. We're very grateful for your help in curbing this sort of behaviour. I trust there will be no publicity."

"You run right along, Mr. Davidson," Brill said. "Sorry to drag you out of bed, but then this has to be done right."

The manager left. I finished dressing and tied my shoes and stood up. Brill took my coat off the back of the desk chair and tossed it to me. "I assume you're ready, Mr. Pine."

"Is this how you handle all your tourists? Or just the ones who won't bluff?"

He was adjusting the French cuffs of his white-on-white shirt. A lightweight dark grey suit this time, with a dark green bow tie and black loafers. "Only those who break our laws, sir."

"Uh-hunh. And if they don't break the law, you break it for them."

His jaw hardened. "If you expect to claim a frame-up, I'd advise you to forget it. You haven't a leg to stand on."

"Gracie'd better have a good memory," I said. "Especially under oath."

He stood very still and his eyes gleamed at me. "I'm waiting to hear the rest of it," he said softly.

"You'll hear it," I said. "You're going to be charged with criminal conspiracy, Captain. When this is over I'm going to the State's Attorney and swear out a complaint of my own. I want to find out if the cops in this town are as far above the law as they like to think."

"You do that, Mr. Pine," he said almost pleasantly. "You run right over and file your complaint—after you get past this little bump in the road."

"What about Gracie, here?" I asked. "Does she go to jail, or do you get really tough and make her sleep with a cop?"

He hit me in the mouth. I spun halfway around and crashed into the table beside the bed. The lamp tipped over and fell to the floor and rolled. The bulb didn't break. I straightened and wiped my hand against my lips, tasting blood and bile. I bent and picked the lamp up and set it back where it belonged and got my handkerchief out.

Captain Brill was examining the knuckles of his right hand. He appeared to be chagrined. "Resisting arrest," he said in a reproachful way. "I'm afraid you're acting very unwisely, sir. Our courts don't like for people to resist an officer in the line of duty."

"That's just too goddam bad," I croaked. "Maybe you could shoot me and get to be Inspector."

His face turned a dull red and some of his veneer blistered. "That will be enough of that, Pine. Let's get moving."

The blonde girl was dressed. Her face showed a sullen scowl. "Hey now, look, Captain," she mewed. "I ain't gonna——"

"Be quiet," he said, not looking at her.

We walked out of there, the four of us, and on down the hall.

There was nobody else around. At two-fifteen in the morning there wouldn't be. Not in a nice quiet respectable hotel like the Olympia House.

CHAPTER TWENTY-THREE

THEY brought us in out of the night, into the City Hall by a side door and on up in the night elevator to the second floor, through the same twin frosted-glass doors I had entered the day before on my way to have it out with the police department. A sergeant had replaced the young lieutenant at the uncluttered desk, and on the back wall Mr. Washington went on signing the same sheet of foolscap under the same crossed flags.

The sergeant turned out to be every bit as courteous as the rest of the force. Take away the uniform and give him a cutaway coat and a carnation and he could pass for a department-store floorwalker directing eager housewives to the perfume counter. He was smoking a curved pipe with a yellow bit. He put it aside politely while booking Gracie and me.

I gave up what I had in my pockets, except for my cigarettes and matches. They let me keep my tie, belt and shoelaces. It was nice to know I wasn't expected to hang myself. Then Andrews escorted me along an inner corridor to where a steel door, the upper half a heavy wire mesh, marked the cell block.

A placid-faced elderly turnkey crawled out from behind a desk and opened up. He said, "Morning, Frank," to Andrews and gave me a steady look. "What you been up to, friend?"

"A cop hit me," I said. "I suppose I'll get life."

"He goes up before Kellogg at nine o'clock," Andrews said. "Don't let him oversleep."

The elderly number picked a circle of keys off the desk and jerked his chin at me. He unlocked one of the cells and I went past him, into it. The door clanged shut and the key was turned. I did what they all do when that steel door closes on them: I took hold of two of the bars and shook them a little, not really testing them, just sort of proving that they were there and that they were real and that I was on the wrong side of them.

Andrews left. The turnkey locked up after him and shuffled back to my cell and peered in at me. His square face ran to a great many shallow wrinkles and his hair was bone-white and still plentiful. He had an inquisitive-looking nose, humorous eyes of a faded blue and a mouthful of teeth like those of an old horse.

"You all set in there, young feller?" he asked.

"Me? I'm fine."

"You want somethin', I'll be camped right down there at my desk. Keep it quiet, that's all. I might be catchin' a nap, this bein' a slow night an' all."

"Whatever you say," I said. "How are you on Shakespeare?"

He sniffed suspiciously. "What kinda talk's that? You ain't been drinkin', have you, friend?"

"Not lately," I said. "You don't sound like a college man to me."

He snorted. "You mean like them pretty boys they got stuck out in the front office? They think they're cops, them boys. Hell, I was poundin' a beat in this here town while they was still wettin' their didies."

He walked away. I let go of the bars and turned around. I had the cell all to myself. It was a nice clean cell with a nice clean smell. Not big, but big enough. Two bunks, one above the other, bolted to a side wall. In one corner a flush toilet next to a gleaming white porcelain sink. Paper towels in a wall container, liquid soap in a dispenser. The toilet paper didn't appear to be monogrammed. The floor was painted a blue-grey, the same shade of grey as the bars and walls. And everything clean—far, far cleaner than you expect any jail to be.

There were five other cells, three of them across the aisle from the three on my side. The three I could see into weren't occupied. A quiet night in Olympic Heights. No crime wave going on. Only one criminal to lock up and he didn't amount to much. One of these big-city private detectives out here annoying the landed gentry. Bat him around a little so he'll know who's boss, then stick him in pokey. He won't give you any trouble after that. Not if he knows what's good for him he won't.

I went over and put my face under the cold water faucet and gulped down some water. My mouth felt like an ulcerated tooth. Captain Brill had lost his temper a little stronger than I had anticipated.

I tried the lower bunk. The mattress was cotton, no springs, suspended on a grillwork of thin metal slats. Folded at the foot of it a rough blanket smelling of strong soap. No pillow; this wasn't the Olympia House.

Light came from a sunken bulb in the ceiling, protected by a wire netting so some prisoner who liked the lights out couldn't get at it with a shoe. It wasn't a very bright light.

I shed my shoes and took off my coat and rolled it into a pillow. I stretched out and loosened my tie and smoked a cigarette and listened to the silence.

Not at all hard to figure out why I was here. The Colonel's blunt Italian hand. I had had my warnings and I had ignored them. You don't kid around with the Colonel, brother. Tomorrow, or rather later this morning, I would be yanked up before a magistrate for a helping of justice, Olympic Heights style. Not that they could strap me in the fireless cooker over the kind of frame I was wearing, but they would do the most with what they had. And I could always hire a lawyer. He might get me off on a plea of temporary insanity by claiming that anybody who tried bucking Colonel Delastone was clearly a candidate for the cackle academy.

A harness cop came by for me at eight-thirty. I washed up and wished I had a razor and got into my coat. We stopped off at the outer desk and I turned in my property slip and signed the original and got back what had been taken from me the night before. I figured that was a good sign. They don't hand you back your stuff if the city expects to go on being your landlord.

Next a pushbutton elevator and a ride up to the fifth floor. I wasn't wearing handcuffs, probably because Captain Brill hadn't thought of it. We walked down a corridor past a handful of rubbernecks and then into a small anteroom. The cop and I had it all to ourselves. I sat on a bench across from him and smoked cigarettes and waited. I waited a long time.

At ten-twenty a bailiff opened another door and I went through it into a courtroom.

It was like any other courtroom. A little less dust, a little brighter at the windows, a little less of the musty smell the contractors seem to build into them all. Among the spectator seats was a scatter of citizens with the patiently solemn expressions of people waiting to pay traffic fines and answer summonses for failure to curb the dog.

There was the usual flag and the elevated bench, and behind the bench a small severe-looking bird with grey hair and a pair of steel-rimmed cheaters. No robe of office. You don't often get the black robes and the ribboned pince-nezes and the sonorous platitudes at the magistrate level. They deal justice off the arm, like a waitress in a fast-track beanery, no back-talk and no kidding around.

It was my turn. The cop stuck his uniform cap under an arm and brought a folded form out of an inner pocket and gave it to the court clerk. An entry was made in a ledger and the form passed up to the judge. He memorized it, then swung around and glinted his eye-glasses at me.

"Your name is Paul Pine?" he said crisply. "A private detective, residing in Chicago?"

"Yes, Your Honour."

"You are charged with disturbing the peace, consorting with a prostitute and resisting arrest. What have you got to say for yourself?"

"Are you asking how I plead?" I said.

He continued to stare at me. The fingers of one hand tapped the blotter gently. "Go right ahead, Mr. Pine."

"Make it nolo contendere," I said.

He looked surprised. The clerk looked surprised. The cop looked surprised. I probably looked surprised myself.

The man on the bench leaned forward and put an elbow on the desk and looked at me across the back of his hand. "Do you happen to be an attorney as well as a private detective, Mr. Pine?"

"Nope," I said.

"I beg your pardon?"

"No, Your Honour."

"You realize, of course, that a plea of nolo contendere is tantamount to an admission of guilt?"

"No, sir," I said. "It's not an admission of anything, even though I can be convicted on it. But in case the sentence is excessive or unjust, I am left free to deny the truth of the charges in a collateral proceeding."

His lips thinned down to almost no lips at all. "You feel this Court will show bias in sentencing you, sir?"

"I don't know," I said. "I haven't heard the sentence."

He picked up the form and skewered it harder than necessary on the point of a spindle file. "Very well, Mr. Pine. Fifty dollars and costs on each of the first two charges. On the third—resisting an officer—thirty days in the County Jail. Jail sentence to be suspended on condition that you are out of this town within the next two hours and that you stay out. We don't want your kind in Olympic Heights."

I didn't say anything.

"You may pay the clerk."

I paid the clerk. One hundred and twelve dollars and fifty cents. I got a receipt for it, too. It didn't leave much in the wallet, but what was left would get me to Chicago. According to the man on the bench, that was all that counted.

I left the courtroom through the big doors and went along the two-tone corridor and into an elevator run by the same gum-chewer I had given my business to on the day before. The doors were about to close when steps sounded quickly along the hallway and a voice said, "Hold her, neighbour," and Ira Groat got aboard.

He gave me a broad grin and an obscene wink as the car started down. "Hi, shamus. You dirty old man, you!"

"How'd she make out?" I said.

"Gracie? Kellogg gave her a suspended sentence at nine sharp. A matron had a bag packed for her and she caught the 9:32 for Chicago. By now she's on the way to Sioux City or Jackson Hole to spend a month or two with her grey-haired old mother."

"One thing you can say for the Captain," I said. "He's not a guy to leave any loose ends that might unravel on him."

The elevator stopped at the first floor and Groat and I walked towards the heavy bronze doors at the front of the building. The reporter said, "You don't pay the big money to a cop who leaves loose ends, Pine. Fifteen thousand a year, less withholding and social security."

I looked at him with my mouth open. "For being a police captain?"

"For being a police captain in Olympic Heights, neighbour. Out here a sergeant pulls down seventy-five hundred, a lieutenant up to ten. Chief Maller is good for thirty grand—five thousand more than they pay the mayor."

"No wonder everybody's so polite," I said. "At those prices they can afford to be."

"A town's as good as its police," Groat said quietly. "Olympic Heights happens to be a mighty fine little city. No organized crime, no big-city syndicates muscling in on the local merchants, no hotshot racketeers. They can't get a foothold, let alone operate, without police support. That much we owe to Colonel Delastone. His idea is to make being a cop in this town a respectable career instead of a quick opening to grab everything in sight before a reform administration comes along and puts in a new collection of thieves. It's no accident that every officer in plain clothes, along with a big percentage of the uniform police, is a college man. They've got a solid future and they're paid enough to hang on to their self-respect. They don't have to depend on being iced by some crumbum who runs a dozen handbooks or controls the floating crap games or operates a chain of girlie houses."

We were outside now. It was a grey day. Not a speck of blue showed overhead. A cool wind blew in from the lake, whipping the girls' dresses and flapping the awnings on the store fronts.

"You make a nice pitch," I said. "Only you'll excuse me if I restrain my admiration. It so happens these dream cops twisted a couple of murders into suicides. Maybe that leaves them aces with you, but for my money they're no different from the brand of flatfeet I've been rubbing tempers with for years. Maybe your boys don't split any infinitives or get gravy stains on their hand-made ties, but it ends right there. They take their orders from the guy upstairs—and if he happens to want the truth mangled for his own interests or protection, that's the way it's done."

His smile was almost sad. "You try too hard, Pine. Look, nobody's saying the department is a branch of the church. Sure, Edwin Delastone got himself murdered. He was born to it and it's too damned bad it didn't happen while he was still in the fourth grade. And this friend of yours: if you insist he died of murder, I wouldn't argue with you. Why would I? You're in the detective business and I assume you're good at it. But if there's some reason the Colonel wants either or both of those deaths buried, I'm willing to bet it's a good reason and that you won't get anywhere with trying to dig it up."

"Okay," I said. "You'll get no more sermons from me." I glanced at my strapwatch. "The man gave me two hours. It's now down to an hour and forty-four minutes. Nice meeting you, Groat. Turn down a glass for me the next time you visit that saloon."

We shook hands and I left him standing there in front of the City Hall. I walked the six blocks to the Olympia House, collected my few possessions, checked out under the disapproving eyes of the room clerk and went into the parking lot to get the Plymouth.

Nothing left for me now except to drive back to Chicago and hunt up Linda Jellco and let her know that I was stymied, that if she still wanted proof her husband hadn't shot himself, she would need a different man for the job. One who wouldn't be risking a month in stir just for crossing the line into Olympic Heights.

A police car, its motor idling, was standing at the kerb near the parking-lot exit. It started up as I made the turn into Locust Avenue. By the time I had gone two blocks it was practically in my trunk.

I didn't miss a traffic sign. Not one. I slowed when it said slow, went when it said go, held my speed two miles under the posted limits. The cops held tight to my tail. There were two of them and I had a closeup of the amused expressions while we waited out a stoplight bumper to bumper.

After a while I came to a monster billboard beside the highway that said: YOU ARE NOW LEAVING OLYMPIC HEIGHTS. WE TRUST YOUR STAY WITH US WAS PLEASANT AND THAT YOU WILL SOON RETURN. *Olympic Heights Chamber of Commerce.* I pulled up just short of the sign. My mirror showed the squad car rolling to a stop half a block behind me. I drew over to the kerb and killed the motor, set the handbrake and leaned back and lighted a cigarette.

Time passed. The boys in blue went on watching me. I got out and kicked a tyre and looked at my watch. 11.10. I got back behind the wheel and took my hat off and rested the back of my neck on the seat. The car behind me stayed where it was.

Twenty minutes marched by. A fine misting rain began to fall. The prowl car started up, made a sweeping U and went back the way it had come, trailing a blue exhaust. I watched it dwindle in the distance. I went on sitting.

At eleven-fifty-five it came roaring back and drew up alongside the Plymouth with a squeal of tyres. The man next to the driver put his head out and gave me the fishy eye. "What's the trouble, sir?"

"No trouble, officer."

"Waiting for someone?"

"Hunh-uh."

"Then what's the idea?"

"Of what?"

His face got very red. "Of being parked there. You're on a highway, mister. Not a parking lot."

"Am I breaking a law, officer?"

"Your name's Pine, isn't it?"

"Yeah."

"You were ordered out of town. You're still in town. So what're you waiting for?"

"My time limit was two hours," I said. "I figure I've got thirty-three minutes left."

"Get moving!"

I started the motor and rolled a foot or two beyond the City Limits marker. I stopped again and leaned out, looking back. "How's this, officer?"

The police car jerked around in a tight half circle that took an inch of rubber off the tyres. I waited until it was out of sight, then turned on the wipers to fight the rain and drove off.

They would be back. More than once, probably. Hoping to get their paws on the wise guy. Not finding me would ruin the day for them.

Twelve straight hours in Olympic Heights had earned me a lumpy head, a purple chin, a sore mouth, assorted threats, a night behind bars, a receipt for a hundred-dollar fine, a suspended jail sentence. For my client, nothing. Nothing except a few theories hardly worth the gasoline I had burned getting them.

Twelve hours. It didn't seem more than a month.

CHAPTER TWENTY-FOUR

JEFFERY AVENUE'S 7400 block, well out on Chicago's south-east side, was wearing a quiet, hunched-shoulders look under the rain. Young trees marked the bright green strips of parkway, and the buildings were mostly small modern apartment houses where a man could likely get by on six thousand a year if he had a tight-fisted wife, no more than two kids and only one Isotta-Fraschini.

What with the traffic and the rain, plus a brief stop-over at the apartment for a shave and a change of clothes, the trip had used up better than two hours. I left the car at the kerb directly across from 7498, a four-storeyed yellow-brick walkup, and ducked through the wet to where a dark green canvas canopy sheltered the entrance.

For a moment I stood there watching the rain and thinking of Linda Jellco and what I would say to her. Not that there was much worth saying, but what there was had to be said and I was all set to say it. Afraid I drew a blank, Mrs. Jellco. They went and stacked the deck on me, Mrs. Jellco. Like you said, everything's

been buried too deep. Why not take the insurance money—ten
thousand nice round dollars, wasn't it, Mrs. Jellco—and go off
somewhere and try to get your bearings? Sure, Sam was a great
guy. Only now he's dead and gone and you can't go around the
rest of your life with a corpse on your back. You ought to know
that. A nice intelligent attractive woman like you. I hope you
don't mind my calling you attractive. If you want the truth of it,
I happen to think that you're one hell of a lot more than just
another curved collection of sexual stimuli, if you'll pardon the
expression. No, ma'am. I hardly ever carry on this way. Especially
when it comes to clients. Gives the business a bad name.

I made a fist of my right hand and reached up and hit myself
lightly on the side of the jaw where it didn't hurt already and
walked into the lobby.

It wasn't a very large lobby, lined with what the management
fondly hoped would be mistaken for imported marble, and they
had a big rainy-day mat down for visitors to wipe their feet on
and not go around tracking up the carpets. Sunk flush into a
side wall was a row of brass mailboxes sporting black-and-gold
name plates, very flossy and high-toned, with one of the plates
reading: *Linda M. Jellco 2D.*

Nobody in sight and the only sound the distant rustle of rain.
I put a thumb briefly to the little black button under the Jellco
name. The silence continued. After a decent interval I tried again.

Nothing doing. Mrs. Jellco wasn't home. I remembered the
name of the people down the hall. *Theo R. Mather 2A.* I rang
their bell. No answer.

The funeral was at ten o'clock. More than four hours ago.
Either she had come home and gone out again or she hadn't
come home at all. It was that simple. And since this part of Jeffery
Avenue was a long way out from downtown, I would wait awhile.
I had the time. I had all the time anybody could waste.

I left the lobby and went back to the Plymouth and pushed in
behind the wheel. I opened the no-draught wing and lighted a
cigarette and turned on the radio. The air-waves were filled with
the throbbing voices of women who were due to be wheeled into
Surgery as soon as their husbands recovered from some rare disease
they had picked up while waiting to stand trial on trumped-up
charges of embezzlement. I shut the set off and sat back and
continued to keep the eagle eye on the entrance across the way.

At three-twelve a green Dodge sedan slashed through the
puddles and stopped in front of the canopy and Linda Jellco

got out. She had on a transparent raincoat over a tobacco-brown tailormade with severe lines that gave her an even taller and more slender look. She said something to the couple in the front seat and the sedan moved off.

I got over there in time to open the lobby door for her. She glanced up, startled, and for a long moment neither of us had anything to say. She was tired, very tired. It showed in the slope of her shoulders, the drawn look around the eyes, the almost imperceptible quiver of her lips. She was a woman home from burying her husband, and the day's wounds were still with her.

"I had hoped you'd be there," she said unevenly. "There weren't very many, you see. We don't have many friends."

"Sorry, Mrs. Jellco. I intended to make it. Only I was in the cooler."

She looked vaguely shocked. "The cooler? You mean, in *jail*? What in the world for?"

"They made up some charges. If you feel like it, let's go somewhere and talk sitting down. Over a drink, maybe."

She nodded slowly. "Of course." She opened her bag and took out a small folder of keys. "Come upstairs. We can talk there. And I would like a drink very much."

She unlocked the inner door and we climbed one flight and walked between cheerful pale yellow walls to a door marked 2D. She used the same key on it as on the one downstairs and I trailed her into a fair-sized living room dim in the grey light through a row of windows overlooking the street.

I helped her off with the transparent thing and shrugged out of my trenchcoat. Her face was pale and serious. "Thank you, Paul. There's the closet. If you don't mind I'm going to get into a dress."

"Fine."

She switched on a table lamp at the far end of a long straight-lined couch while I was putting away the coats and my hat. There was a portable bar in blond wood over near a fireplace with a gas log. "If you'd care to make the drinks I'll have Scotch and water. Not too strong, please. The kitchen's just off the dinette. Through there."

"I'll find everything. Not too strong you said."

She smiled a little and turned away and walked off down a hallway. I opened the bar and got out two tall glasses and a bottle of medium-priced Scotch. I unscrewed the top and poured what I hoped would be the right amount for her and a little more for me. I was on the point of going into the kitchen in search of ice, when her voice reached me from down the hall.

"Paul!"

The shocked surprise in her tone took me back there fast. Linda Jellco was standing in front of a long low blondwood dresser. A pair of small lamps with silk shades in an off-white burned at either end of the glass top. One of the drawers stood open and she was staring down into it.

Her eyes came up slowly and found mine reflected in the mirror above the dresser. "Someone's been here," she said quietly.

The contents of the drawer seemed orderly enough to me. "How do you know?"

"Well, for one thing my handkerchief box is closed. I remember distinctly leaving it open when I took a fresh one this morning. And those white gloves were on the left side of my black cotton ones; now they're on the right. Little things like that. Believe me, I know what I'm talking about."

"I'm not arguing with you. Anything missing?"

"I can certainly find out soon enough."

"Do that. I'll be taking a look around."

I went back to the living room and looked the hall door over. No signs of forcible entry. I went through the dinette and into a small sparkling clean kitchen. It had a back door leading on to a small porch with a flight of steps leading up to it at one end and another flight to the third floor at the other. The door was closed all right, only it wasn't locked. Not any more it wasn't. A glass cutter had removed a semi-circle from one of the four panes, leaving an opening large enough for a hand to reach through and turn the lock. The missing segment lay on the drainboard of the sink, traces of a black sticky substance still adhering to the curved edge where a strip of tyre tape was used to lift it away after the cutter had done its work. The mark of a professional. No point in dusting for prints, even if it had been my job to dust for them. Professionals don't leave prints.

I sniffed at the cool damp air coming in through the hole and went back to the bedroom. Linda Jellco was closing the bottom drawer of a highboy between the room's two windows.

"How bad is it?" I asked her.

"They didn't take anything, if that's what you mean." She flushed slightly. "I hope you're not thinking I imagined all this. I tell you somebody was in here going through my things while I was out. Was it you?"

I grinned at her. Her flush got a little deeper and her eyes wavered. "Well, after all you do have a key to the apartment and ... I'm sorry, Paul."

"You're sure nothing's gone? Jewellery, fur pieces, perfumes, pin money hidden under the nightgowns?"

"All accounted for. And I don't hide money under nightgowns."

"Some do." I looked across the brown corduroy spread on the double bed to where the door of a closet stood open with clothing neatly suspended from hangers along a metal rod. "What about mink coats, fancy gowns, things like that?"

"I have a fur coat," she said stiffly. "One—a beaver, three years old and at present in storage for the summer. I have two evening dresses, both of which I made myself and neither of them what you'd call fancy."

"You were burgled, all right," I said. "Forcible entry, through the kitchen door. Could be the work of one of those handy lads who make a career out of following the obit pages for addresses to break into while the family's at the funeral. Only I don't think so this time. Your luggage would be gone, stuffed with everything they could cram into it."

She sank slowly down on the foot of the bedspread and went on staring at me out of the depths of those direct blue-green eyes. "Then if it wasn't robbery—"

"It could tie in with your husband's death."

"How? I mean, why would ..."

"Sam's office was prowled and his files pawed through. I found that out yesterday morning. It's more than likely they didn't find what they went there to get. So they tried the house."

"For what?"

"I don't know that. Not for sure. Perhaps the duplicate of a report Sam made for his client in Olympic Heights. One they're afraid could fall into the wrong hands. He keep any of his papers here at the apartment?"

"No. Nothing like that."

"Then I expect they'll keep up the hunt. You understand that 'they' is just a word. It may be only one—man or woman. After a day and a half on this job I hardly know anything of what's actually going on. About that drink. You don't really have to change clothes, do you?"

Her smile seemed a little dazed. "I guess not." She got off the bed and we went back to the living room. I took the glasses into the kitchen and put ice cubes and tap water into both of them.

She was standing at the windows, her back to me, staring down into the wet street. A cigarette smouldered in the slender fingers of her left hand and lamplight made a smooth shining cap of her blonde hair. I gave her the correct glass and she thanked me gravely and we came back and sat down at opposite ends of the couch and lifted our glasses silently to each other and drank. And for a little while after that neither of us had anything to say.

Presently she sipped some more of the watered Scotch and set the glass on a corner of the lamp table. The curve of a breast and shoulder made a poetic line. She turned toward me and drew a silken leg up under her and looked at her cigarette and from it to me.

"I get the impression," she said in a businesslike tone, "that you haven't been able to find out very much. About what really happened that night."

"Practically nothing at all."

"Was it . . . very bad? I mean—well, you said something about being in jail, and there's a bruise on your chin . . ."

"There was some trouble," I said. "Nothing I wasn't able to limp away from."

"You still think Sam shot himself?"

"I never said I thought that." I lifted a hand to shut off what she was about to say. "I'll admit I wasn't eager to prove he hadn't, but that wasn't because I don't like to see justice done. I knew then that once any city hall wants a load of dirty laundry buried instead of washed there's almost nothing anybody can do about it. I learned that all over again in Olympic Heights—and it's about all I did learn."

She said stiffly, "I should think you'd have found out *some*thing else."

"Okay," I said. "Here they are and you're welcome to them. About three weeks ago an elderly number named Serena Delastone hired your husband to recover a stolen brooch. The thief was probably her own son—a thirty-year-old delinquent named Edwin —and Sam was able to get it back for her.

"A few days later Edwin Delastone was found shot to death— nobody seems to know exactly why—and his father, a local wheel, managed to get it hushed up as suicide, not wanting any more scandals than the family had been through already."

I stopped long enough to dampen my throat with Scotch. Linda Jellco drew deeply on her cigarette, her eyes never leaving my face, a small frown creasing her forehead.

"Things quieted down for a couple of weeks," I went on. "Then Serena Delastone found herself being blackmailed by a guy named Pod Hamp over some canoodling one of her daughters was involved in. So the old lady called in Sam to take over a second time.

"Somehow the idea got around that he was hired to find out who killed Edwin, and even though Serena fired him for talking back, he returned to Olympic Heights a day or so later. He was killed the same night."

She bit her lip and reached out blindly for the glass on the table, almost upsetting it. I watched her take a long shuddering pull at the contents before she put it down again and used a handkerchief to dry her fingers. I met her eyes, seeing the pain and bitterness in them. "But *why? Why* was he killed?"

"No answer, Mrs. Jellco. He might have kept after Pod Hamp, even though the client had bounced him off the case, and Hamp got nervous and plugged him. Or maybe whoever it was that fed Edwin a bullet figured Sam was after *him*. Or the Delastone girl may have thought Sam knew too much about her and talked the boy friend into doing the job. Even old man Delastone could have ordered up the artillery."

Not a sound out of her. I glanced at my strapwatch without seeing the time and finished what was in my glass and thought about a refill and went on sitting, holding the glass and listening to the rattle of the rain against the windows.

"This report you spoke of," Linda Jellco said suddenly in a voice that seemed unnaturally loud. "The one somebody is so anxious to find. Couldn't it give you the answer?"

I shrugged. "I was guessing. I don't even know for sure there *is* a report. It's the only reason I can think of for sifting Sam's office and this apartment. That doesn't mean it's the real reason."

I stood up and set the glass gently on the cocktail table and stared hard at the base of my thumb. "I haven't been what you'd call brilliant on this case. I expect it's just as well that I'm letting go of it."

When the silence began to get louder than the rain, I looked up. She was looking at me, and in her eyes was something I didn't like seeing. A spot of harsh colour burned in her cheeks.

"You mean you're quitting." She could barely get the words out. "Is that it?"

"Uh-hunh. I don't have any choice. Not any more I don't. The minute I—"

She wasn't listening. "Where does that leave me? What am I supposed to do now—pretend that Sam fell off a bridge or caught pneumonia? Or am I to spend the rest of my life knowing somebody deliberately murdered my husband and got away with it? Do you think I can do that?"

I didn't say anything. There was nothing I could say that she would hear.

She brought her arms up slowly and folded them and pressed them tightly against her breasts in a gesture of grief and hopelessness that would have shaken a cigar-store Indian. "Very well, then. I talked you into it the first time. It wasn't easy and I didn't enjoy it even a little bit. I'm not going to try again. Good-bye, Mr. Pine."

The silence came back. Neither of us made a move. Her face was ice, her eyes far colder, her breathing unhurried.

I said, "You're entitled to know why, Mrs. Jellco. If for no other reason than you paid me to work for you. The answer you want is in Olympic Heights. The minute I set foot in that town again they slap me in jail for thirty days. Legally. Like I told you before, this is a case of fighting the City Hall. Sometimes I think I'm a good man in my line, but I'm not that good. Nobody is, outside of books."

She turned her head away. I went quietly to the closet and took down my hat and trenchcoat and put them on, then looked back into the living room.

Linda Jellco hadn't moved. The lamplight was still beautiful against her bowed head. I closed the door softly behind me, hearing the latch click into place, and walked off down the hall.

CHAPTER TWENTY-FIVE

FIVE o'clock came in quiet and left the same way, with me behind the office desk and the backs of my non-skid heels on the blotter, thinking my grey thoughts and listening to the whine of the fat little dentist's drill from next door. Behind me the window was up, the rain falling and the sound of rush-hour traffic like the sodden thud of a dropped boot.

The mail has been picked off the floor, opened, read, read again in case you missed something unimportant the first time around, and laid to rest. In a little while it will be time for you

to put your feet back on the floor and stand up and walk across
the waiting-room and lock up and ride down and go out into the
wet and hunt up a restaurant filled with loud voices and grinding
molars. And you wait for a table or settle for a counter stool and
sit there and shovel down the same tasteless stuff they all throw
at you and charge too much for, getting it down quick because
some standee is breathing on your neck to remind you he's waiting
and don't go dawdling over a second cuppa java, buddy. It's not
that you're there because you happen to be hungry but because,
like everybody else, you were brought up to eat by the clock
instead of your stomach.

That leaves you the rest of the big beautiful evening all for
yourself. You can take in a movie in gorgeous glowing Technicolor
on a screen the size of Switzerland and look at powdered cleavages
and assembly-line legs and glistening teeth as big as the palace
portcullis. Or you find a bar and lean against the polished wood
and listen to the apron tell you all about the time he caught his
wife with the trap-drummer from the Hi-Hat Club. Or you can
leaf through the little black book and pick out a number and end
up in bed with a cute trick who cries a little afterward and
explains that all she really wants is somebody to love, along with
a ring for her naked finger, a few charge accounts and an eight-
room duplex overlooking Lincoln Park West.

I got off the chair and went over to the window and leaned
my forehead against its coolness and watched the blossoming
umbrellas and the cars slithering past with a hooded look. My
breath misted the glass and I wrote my name in the mist with
the end of a finger. It was fun but it didn't seem to help any.

Five-twenty. Too late in the day for the phone to ring with a
job waiting at the other end of the line. It might not ring tomorrow
either, or for a week. There were times like that. Maybe I had it
coming. The way I walked off jobs before they were finished. So
the going had got a little tough. That had happened before and it
would happen again. Only this time you had done more than just
walk out. You had left a woman haunted by the restless ghost of
her dead husband, and right or wrong she would stay haunted
until the one who killed him was laid by the heels. You could
do it, Pine. Sure you could.

I went back and sat down again and got out the inevitable
cigarette and listened to the scurry of my thoughts like mice
behind the baseboards. Out in Olympic Heights Colonel Delastone
and his daughter Martha would be getting home from the City

Hall along about now, and Deborah Ellen Frances Thronetree would be up in her room with her nose in a comic book or the Bible, depending on how close she was being watched. Karen Delastone would be on her third cocktail, her laughter as brittle as an icicle and with about as much warmth. Arnie Algebra might be with her or he might have got up late and bathed his knuckles and read the paper over fruit juice and coffee and one of his brown-paper cigarettes.

That was the Olympic Heights crowd, leaving out a few others such as Lieutenant Fontaine and Captain Benton Brill and Ira Groat and little naked Gracie and Lyle Spence and Mister Davidson and his hotel.

And Mrs. Serena Delastone. You couldn't very well overlook her. She was the one to give you your first glimpse at a family you weren't likely to forget for a while. She was also the one who could've put you in touch with a man named Pod Hamp—the now strangely silent blackmailer Sam Jellco had called on in the line of duty. . . .

I thought about that for a while and then I nodded and lighted my cigarette and nodded again and took the nice clean handkerchief from my breast pocket and put it on the desk in front of me. Then I looked up a number and found out it could be dialled direct. I dialled it and spread three thicknesses of the handkerchief over the mouthpiece the way the directions read in the paperback detective novels.

On the third ring a receiver was lifted and the same querulous whine I was getting to know told me I had the Delastone residence.

I pitched my voice to a low growl and explained through the handkerchief what I wanted.

"Who's this callin' her?"

"No names," I said. "Just tell her nice and private that I don't have all day."

I got back a throat noise that expressed an opinion of such goings-on and then there was a spell of quiet in which rain fell and cars tooted along Jackson Boulevard and a mop handle banged against a pail outside my office door. And finally the crisp tenor bite of Serena Delastone's voice identifying herself and demanding to know who this was.

"Pod Hamp, Mrs. Delastone. How much longer you think I'll wait?"

She didn't question the voice I was using, which had been my big worry. There was the briefest of pauses. "Mr. Hamp. I see. What is it that you want?"

"You know what I want, lady. But quick. I'm thinking of raising the ante to twenty-five."

Her voice was still the same unflinching voice, saying, "I shall need a day or so to—"

"Nothing doing. By two-thirty tomorrow or I find another customer. I mean business."

"How do I know that you actually have these . . . things?"

"Lay off," I said. "That private dick you sent around would've told you the score. Like I said, two-thirty tomorrow."

I hung up fast, feeling the muscles around my mouth knot into a grin that was no grin at all but a symptom of the same tension that comes when you draw to an open-end straight and raise the opener blind.

Ten minutes. It shouldn't take any more than that. In ten minutes you can buy a suit, change the water in the fish bowl, get a bill of divorcement, open a savings account. In ten minutes you could go down the hall and look in the mirror over the sink and watch your hair turn grey. That was silly. Only the passing years can grey your hair. Now and then you read in the papers about it happening overnight but that's only the sensational press at work. Guys have been known to lie for days in foxholes dug with fingernails and teeth and listen to the mortars hunting for them, and then come out with their hair mussed but still the same colour.

Besides, this wasn't that important. What if it didn't work out? You only met Linda Jellco a day or two ago and all she amounts to is just another client who paid you money for just another job. She had a husband shot out from under her, so to speak, and you don't see any signs of *her* hair turning—

The phone rang.

I didn't jump more than two feet. I dropped my cigarette and bent and picked it off the floor and laid it carefully in a corner of the dime-store ashtray and stood up to close the window and came back and raised the receiver in the middle of the third ring.

"Am I speaking to Mr. Pine?"

"Uh-hunh."

"Serena Delastone, Mr. Pine. Are you free at the moment?"

"Just finished locking up the safe."

"I see. It appears that I shall be able to use your services after all. How soon can you be here?"

"To do what, Mrs. Delastone?"

"It has to do with this man Hamp. He called again. About the matter I discussed with you earlier."

"Wants his money, hunh? Why me?"

Her voice, never soft, took on the old familiar edge. "You seemed anxious enough on the telephone last evening."

"That was last evening," I said. "There've been some changes since then."

"Are you refusing the assignment, young man? If you are, say so at once and stop wasting my time."

"I'd work for you if I could, Mrs. Delastone. Only the cops out there are laying for me. The minute I stick a toe over the Olympic Heights line I get clapped in jail for a month. Or maybe this isn't news to you."

' I can't say I'm surprised," she said acidly.

"Uh-hunh. You could check with the Colonel or with Judge Kellogg in case you're interested. The particulars may redden your ears some. On second thought they probably won't. But that's how it is."

"And this is the reason for your reluctance?"

"It's the big reason. I can't spare the thirty days. Besides I don't think I'd care for the food."

She wasted some of her valuable time thinking it over before she said, "Very well, Mr. Pine. Amos Kellogg is a man I can handle. You may come out. I'll see to it that you're not bothered."

"That's bully," I said. "Only it's not enough. What I'll need from his honour is a signed statement saying he's reviewed my case and has decided to vacate the part that says I serve the jail sentence for returning to Olympic Heights."

"I'm quite sure he'll refuse to sign any such statement."

"If you tell him to, Mrs. Delastone? He wouldn't dare."

She made a sound. From anybody else I'd have said it was a chuckle. "How soon can you be here, Mr. Pine?"

"It's a nasty night out and my bones are tired. And you'll need time to get that statement. Tomorrow morning will be fine. Say at eleven."

"I shall expect you to be prompt."

I was going to be polite and thank her for calling, but the line had gone dead. I really didn't mind a small-potatoes discourtesy like that. Not when I considered the fat ones she was capable of.

I dropped the receiver back between the prongs and got up and smoothed my hair and picked the cigarette out of the ashtray and blew a little smoke around. I said aloud:

"You played that one smart, baby. You really did."

The words seemed to float hollowly in the still air. The shadows of approaching night filled the corners of the room. Outside, the rain went on and on.

CHAPTER TWENTY-SIX

NOTHING had really changed. It was the same room and the same time of day and the same stone-faced woman propped up on the chintz-covered chaise over near the windows, wearing the blue-silk robe and with the afghan covering her legs, watching me steer a course through the shoals of bric-a-brac.

Even the obsidian stare was the same. "Good morning, Mr. Pine. I must say you are prompt. However, I'm quite sure you realize all this could have been avoided if you hadn't been so pig-headed the first time. Sit down."

I pulled the same chair up and sat in it, facing her. I dropped my hat on the same lamp table and crossed my legs and tried to appear rested and bright and eager. Yesterday's weather, according to the radio, was centred somewhere west of Harrisburg, Pennsylvania, and sunlight dappled the elm leaves outside the open window behind Serena Delastone.

"We might as well get right to it," she said abruptly. "This man Hamp has threat—"

"One minute," I said. "While we're still on speaking terms I'd better have that statement you got from Judge Kellogg. You did get it, Mrs. Delastone?"

"I managed to, yes," she growled. "Not that it was at all easy. Amos Kellogg explained the circumstances. I must say I was surprised at your disgraceful conduct."

"You weren't anything of the kind," I told her. "You must've known darn well that the Colonel had ordered me out of town, and I give you credit for being smart enough to figure out that he more than likely set the whole thing up through the local law when he discovered I was still around. Not that it matters. Right now I'll take that statement. If you don't mind."

She glared at me but there was nothing novel about that. Then one of her taloned hands slid under the checkered wool blanket covering her lap and came out with a sheet of white paper folded twice. I got up to take it from her and sat down again and opened it. The words were neatly typed and said what I wanted them to say. Down near the bottom, in ink, was the big scrawled signature of the right man.

While I was refolding the paper and tucking it away in the inner pocket of my jacket, Serena Delastone said, "Since we're on the subject of your activities of the past few days, just what was my daughter Martha doing in your room at the Olympia House two evenings ago?"

I gave her an admiring glance. "Not much you don't know what's going on! Well, there's no reason for me not to tell you. She came to ask if you had hired me to find out who killed your son."

Her face turned four colours and she began to swell up again. But her voice came out curiously soft—for her. "Nonsense. She knows perfectly well Edwin wasn't . . . that it was nothing of the kind. He took his own life, poor boy."

"You're about the only one," I said, "who thinks so. The Colonel and both your daughters have done their best to pressure me into admitting I'm working on it for you. When I tried to tell them the only killing I was interested in was Sam Jellco's, all I got back was the glassy eye and assorted threats and one nice fat offer of a payoff. If they're as sold on it being suicide as you seem to think, what's all the noise about?"

Her hands rested lightly and without motion on the afghan. Her pale eyes gleamed in the half light. "You're satisfied that my son was murdered, Mr. Pine?"

"I know damned well he was, Mrs. Delastone."

"Are you of the opinion that the same person killed this man Jellco?"

"It's possible. I don't know."

"Do you suspect a member of this family?"

We sat there in the heavy silence and stared at each other while the clock ticked off a full ten seconds before I said:

"I wouldn't lie to you. That's also possible."

"And your real reason for working for me is that there is no other way you can be free to operate here in Olympic Heights. Free, in short, to learn who killed your friend. Isn't that it, Mr. Pine?"

I said, "You're not a fool, Mrs. Delastone, and I never took you for one. You want whatever it is Pod Hamp is holding on

Karen and I aim to get it for you. But you're right: that's not all I'm after."

She nodded, stone-faced, and put her hand back under the wrap and brought out a slip of paper. I took it from her and read the pencilled notation. *Mulberry 3-2178. Ask for Pod Hamp.*

It was the information I wanted. I could have had it a long time before if I had been able to see into the future the way they do in *Amazing Stories.* I took out my wallet and removed the sheet of hotel stationery with the other phone numbers I had collected lately and used a pencil to add Hamp's number to the list.

I handed Mrs. Delastone's slip back to her. "You'll want to keep it," I explained. "In case I get run over by a scooter or something."

She put it back under the afghan. I thought she looked a little glum, but with her kind of face it was hard to tell. "You don't have much time. Hamp threatens to offer the evidence to someone else unless arrangements are made by two-thirty this afternoon. He also spoke of raising the price to twenty-five thousand."

"I was going to mention the money, Mrs. Delastone. You may have to pay him something."

The wrinkles moved in her throat. "Ten thousand is as high as I'll go. Not one cent more. And I'll pay you a bonus of a hundred dollars for every thousand under that figure."

"I'll do what I can." I put the wallet away and stood up to get my hat off the table. "You'll hear from me as soon as I have something to report. Very soon, I hope."

She nodded slowly. "You seem to be a competent man, Mr. Pine. In spite of your temper, I have a great deal of faith in you. I shan't rest until this threat to my daughter is removed."

The way she said the last part of it made me come close to liking her. So of course she had to go and spoil it: "But then I suppose she'll only go getting herself involved in some other sordid affair and disgrace us all."

"I met your daughter," I said. "Karen, that is. She's an attractive girl."

"Pretty is as pretty does, Mr. Pine."

I dug my fingers into my hat brim. "Uh-hunh. So I've heard. A lot of girls have been known to drink too much and run around with the wrong kind of men and come home at all hours. They've also been known to do much worse when they get nagged into it or spied on or yelled at."

"You're not trying to tell me how to raise my children, are you, Mr. Pine?" she said coldly.

"Not at this late date. And not even if I knew how—which I don't. All I know is human nature and there are times I get my head torn off on that."

She shrugged her big shoulders. "I'm not at all interested in this discussion, young man. Please go about doing what I'm paying you to do."

"Check," I said.

Downstairs, the elderly number with the bifocals was vacuuming the living-room carpet, the bright chrome trim of the sweeper out of place among the relics. I stepped over the cord and went past her to the heavy front door and opened it.

On the porch, sitting primly in one of the big wicker chairs and eyeing me blank-faced above the open pages of a comic book, was Deborah Ellen Frances Thronetree.

"Good morning," I said.

She sniffed. It seemed that was the only answer I was going to get. I dragged the door shut and crossed over and leaned against a pillar and speared a cigarette from behind my display handkerchief. Deborah Ellen's eyes followed every move.

The comic book cover had all the colours, including a left field shade of purple, and showed an underclad young woman diving into a river clogged with hungry crocodiles. It looked a good deal more interesting than the Epistles.

I screwed my head around to get a better view. "I guess I missed that one," I said.

Her nose climbed an inch. "I'm not supposed to talk to you."

"Who says?"

"Aunt Karen, that's who. She says you're just a nosy old snoop who goes around asking ever'body lots of questions that's none of your business."

"Fie on her," I said. "She ought to be ashamed, talking like that."

She looked as though she had just stepped out of the pages of a 1912 Sears catalogue. She was wearing a white dimity pinafore with starched ruffles at the shoulders and a matching bow in back. White ribbed stockings again and brown sandals. An eddying breeze stirred the straight strands of brown hair, bringing my way the barest suggestion of a bottled scent not designed for the seven-year-old trade.

"You've been at the perfume again," I said.

Her eyes flashed. "I have *not*! Aunt Karen squirted the teeniest tiny bit on my neck is all. And I didn't even ask her to, so there!"

"You smell fine," I said. "Just like Leslie Caron."

The shell began to crack. "Like who?"

"Leslie Caron. Don't you go to the movies?"

"Grandmother Se'en says I'm not old enough yet."

"I saw her in a picture once," I said. "She looks like you a little. She danced a lot and talked to some puppets in some kind of a circus. As I remember, it turned out to be a dream. In colour."

The corners of her mouth drew down suddenly and a shadow seemed to flicker in the blue eyes. "I don't like dreams. They're *scary*."

"Not all of them," I said.

"*This* one was." She leaned forward in the chair, toward me. Her eyes were very round. "There was this big black gun on the table by the lamp and he said something awful loud and then Aunt Ka—"

She stopped there abruptly and put the back of her hand hard against her lips and I could see the tears beginning to form. "It was a *dream*! I promised not to—"

And then the comic book went flying and she was running along the porch away from me, her head down, her heels thudding against the planks. I watched her turn the far corner and then there was nothing more to watch and nothing more to hear.

I bent down slowly and picked the comic book up and smoothed its pages. The crocodiles were still waiting for lunch. I dropped the book on the chair and lighted the cigarette I had been holding all along and stood there looking at the sunlight on the grass.

"It's a living," I explained to nobody. "God damn it, it's a living."

CHAPTER TWENTY-SEVEN

Two blocks north of the Risewood Terrace section was a small snooty-looking shopping district. I parked in front of a salon with nothing in the window except one pale pink shirt catty-cornered on a black velvet plaque, and walked on down to a fluorescent-and-blondwood drugstore at the corner. I closed myself in a booth and dropped a dime and dialled the Mulberry number Serena Delastone had been pried out of.

A man with a shirt-sleeved drawl answered. I asked for Pod

Hamp and the drawl told me to hold on and I heard feet fade into nothing.

Presently the feet came back. "Ain't in."

"When do you expect him?"

"Why would I bother?" the voice sneered. "Tell you the truth, I ain't seen the guy in three-four days. Don't mean he couldn't been in and out, though."

"I'm out at Baylor and Woodbine," I said. "How do I get to your place?"

"Nothin' to it, friend. Take Baylor all the way down till you hit Temple, turn right 'bout a mile to Bleecher, left on that two'n a half blocks. Number's 1134."

I hung up and smoothed the sheet of stationery again and wrote 1134 Bleecher under the phone number. There was another Mulberry number on the paper: 3-1008. The one Linda Jellco had given me over the phone at the hotel, the one her husband left with her on his next to last trip to Olympic Heights. According to Mrs. Jellco's story, it would be nearly three weeks old by this time and, as a lead, probably as cold as cafeteria gravy.

I pushed open the booth's fold-back door and filled my lungs with the aroma of hotwater bottles and melted cheese and hunted up another dime. No harm in giving it a try. As long as there was a telephone handy and since I was just resting at the moment anyway.

"Hello?" A woman's voice, light, hurried, hardly more than a taut whisper.

All I could do was play it by ear and hope for the best. "Let me talk to Sam," I said.

"*Sam?*" It came out as a shocked gasp that was almost a sob. "My God, are you kidding? Sam's—"

And then abruptly there was nothing except the rustle of uneven breathing.

"Sam's what?" I said.

"... Who is this?"

"Look, Miss Day," I said patiently. "I— This *is* April Day?" I waited for an answer, didn't get one and tried again. "Sam left your number just before I was called out of town last week. If something's gone wrong I'd better come over and talk to you. Give me that address again."

Not even ragged breathing now. Nothing except the hum of a dead wire. I rattled the hook a time or two, got more of the hum and put back the receiver.

No point in calling her back. Miss Day would just hang up on me again—if it was Miss Day and if she bothered to answer at all.

I ate a ham salad sandwich and drank a coke at the soda fountain. It was a good sandwich. At seventy-five cents it had better be good.

1134 Bleecher Street was a brown frame house, two floors, set back from the street in a bare patch of grey hard-packed earth that had about everything on it except grass. The breezes had deposited bits of paper here and there, along with a couple of empty whisky bottles, a rusted rake minus the handle, an ancient automobile tyre and a broken bushel basket that still showed a rain-streaked sticker reading, "Washington's Pride Choice Apples." A fly-haunted cardboard sign nailed to one of the porch posts said, "Rooms—Day or Week. Inquire Within."

It seemed Mr. Hamp could use twenty thousand dollars.

I went up the crippled steps and found a locked screen door. Beyond it was a dusty hall and a lot of gloom, with the outlines of the lower end of a flight of steps all the way back. I counted three doors off the hall, all of them closed.

Not finding a bell I pounded the heel of my hand against a side of the screen and presently one of the closed hall doors opened and a chunky man in a short-sleeved sweatshirt and wrinkled brown slacks came out and over. He put his face close to the screen and peered through it at me, looking annoyed. "Yeah? Whaddayuh want?"

"I called up a little while back," I said. "Come to see Mr. Pod Hamp."

"He still ain't around."

"Tough," I said.

His round rocky face was the hairiest I'd ever seen—and he was what he would call clean shaven. Clumps of hair stuck out of his nose, his ears, from under the grimy neckline of his shirt. His eyebrows looked a foot across, his forearms and the backs of his hands were a jungle.

"I could kind of come in and wait," I said brightly.

"Ha," he said. "Like where?"

"Maybe in the library," I suggested. "Over a volume of G. A. Henty and a beaker of brandy."

"Come back after a while," he said. "Like tomorrow. Or the year after."

"What's the matter with right in his room?" I said. "The stairs don't scare me."

"There's that long walk to the end of the hall too," he said with a sour smirk. "You think we let any old body go waltzing into the guests' rooms?"

"I could see where it would be a mistake," I said. "They might pry up the flooring and steal the family jewels."

"Wise guy," he said. He turned his back and walked away, through the door he had come out of. He banged it behind him.

I took out a folder of matches and opened it and bent the matches all the way back until I had a length of cardboard at least three inches long. I leaned against the screen, whistling lightly through my teeth, and worked the folder in under the hook and raised the hook nice and gentle out of the eye. To any one on the street who might bother to look up the porch steps to where I stood, I was just a man leaning against a screen door.

The matchbook came out of the crack, was refolded, went back into the pocket. I straightened up and opened the screen, listened and heard nothing and stepped into the hall. I let the door ease shut and took enough quick soundless steps along the naked wood floor to reach the staircase. I went up it quickly.

The upper hall smelled of insect powder and damp wood. It was no cleaner than the one downstairs and even more badly lighted. I tiptoed along it, past three or four closed doors, listening to the silence. At the end of the hall was a window, closed, with a fire extinguisher on a wall bracket next to it and a rusted fire escape outside. None of them appeared to be likely to stand in the way in case the owner wanted to collect on his insurance.

Two doors, one across from the other. No name on either to point the way. Each had a keyhole big enough to lose your hat in. I bent down and peered through the one on the right, seeing the foot of a bed with the empty folds of a flowered housecoat draped across it. It hardly seemed possible that Pod Hamp would wear flowered housecoats, so I tried the knob on the left.

Locked. I knocked lightly. No answer. The lock looked as uncomplicated as a stroll in the park. A bent hairpin could have taken it easy. I got out my keycase instead and unshipped a skeleton slug I seldom had the chance to use and tried it.

The lock snicked back. I returned the key to my pocket and pushed the door open and went in quiet, sniffing at the dead air.

Nobody yelled for the police or pulled any triggers. I closed the door as gently as I had opened it and stood there drinking in the view.

It wasn't anything they'd put on picture postcards. A bed that was just a mattress on legs and covered with a pale green blanket you could read the evening paper through. An ugly brown dresser below a mottled mirror. A narrow closet with four wire hangers, empty, spaced along the rod. A kitchen chair drawn up to a rickety table about the size of the ace of spades. And for those long dark nights a naked bulb overhead, the pull string grey from many hands.

I began to move around delicately, listening for sounds that could mean trouble. A smeared window overlooked a back yard even more cluttered than the one out front. No luggage in sight, or hidden, and the dresser drawers held only an empty iodine bottle with the stopper missing and layers of yellowing newspaper lining. A headline yelled: DEWEY SURE WINNER, POLLS SHOW.

It appeared that Mr. Hamp had moved on to greener meadows, in spite of the indication by the hairy hero downstairs that the rent was still being paid. Whatever the price, it was far, far too much.

I was reaching for the doorknob on my way out when I saw the slip of paper. It lay just within the room, where somebody had shoved it under the door. A hunk of brown wrapping paper, ragged along two edges, bearing a pencilled message dated four days earlier. It read: "Some woman called. Said you'd know who and call her back, important." The last word was underlined twice.

As a clue it amounted to zero. I let the paper float back to the floor and opened the door. The man with the hair was leaning against the wall. He let me see his teeth. "You should of hooked that screen back, fella. That way I wouldn't of knowed."

"He's not in," I said. "Hamp, that is. I guess I won't bother to wait after all."

"Maybe I should toss your ass down the stairs," he said smoothly. "Maybe I should kick out a tooth or three while I'm at it. You lousy sneak thief."

"You might want to chin yourself on a cloud too," I said. "It would be just as easy."

He thought about it while counting my shoulders and then he nodded. "Hell," he said, with an expansive gesture, "why would

I work up a sweat? What sense you being here if you was goniff? Go on, beat it."

"Let's go some place private and visit," I said.

His over-sized brows pulled sharply together. "Ha. Convince me I should."

"Would money help?" I asked.

His eyes snapped. "For what?"

"For a visit."

He explored my face and found nothing there he could do much with. He pawed absently at the hair at the base of his throat. "You a gumshoe?"

"You don't hear them called that much any more," I said. "I'm a man with some questions and some money to pay for the answers. Not much money, but some. Okay?"

"Could be." He turned around and went along the hall and clumped down the stairs. I followed a step behind, watching his broad back and the ragged hairline at the nape of his neck where no barber had worked for far too long.

He used the same door he had first popped out of and we entered a narrow kitchen with cracked tan linoleum along the floor. There was about what you would expect to find in an out-of-heels kitchen, plus a table with red-and-white-checked oilcloth tacked to the top, and a pair of peeling chairs related to the one in Hamp's room upstairs.

"Set," the hairy hero said, and I straddled one of the chairs and took my smokes out and lighted one, leaving the pack and the matches in the centre of the table.

He opened the door of an old-fashioned ice-box with streaks of brown showing under the white paint somebody had tried to dress it up with. He took out a bottle of beer, quart-size, and reached two genuine Anchor-Hocking jelly glasses off an open shelf and poured beer into them and plopped one down on my side of the oilcloth. He took the chair across from me and drank half of what was in his glass, filled it to the brim again and eyed me across it in a half-friendly, half-guarded way.

"About Pod Hamp," I said.

"You said a little something about dough," he said.

"The price goes with what I get. I wouldn't rob you."

He chewed that over along with another gulp of the beer. He seemed a little unhappy, but not unhappy enough to break into tears. Finally he nodded and reached for one of the cigarettes.

"Start anywhere," I said.

"Hell, Hamp's just another guy." He struck a match and used it. "Dresses better'n most of the crumbs you get in this part of town. Talks real soft and polite, minds his own business and keeps from falling down the stairs drunk. Paid a month ahead when he took the room, which for me makes him somebody to remember."

"He does what? For a living."

"We don't get no references, chum. So I wouldn't know."

"Who cleans his room, changes the linens, empties the waste-basket?"

"I do." A corner of a lip lifted. "When it gets done at all."

"You must've seen something around that told you something about him. A cheque book or a laundry slip or a letter from his broker. A sharp-eyed landlord like you."

He shook his head slowly and let smoke seep from his nose. "Not a thing—and I'm not saying I wouldn't of looked. Not even a dirty sock laying around. I guess you could call him neat."

"Or careful," I said and sampled the beer. It was dry the way the ads claimed it should be and as refreshing as a blotter. "How long has he been holed up here?"

"Well . . . a couple weeks. Closer to three, even."

"You know, of course, that he doesn't keep anything personal up there. Not so much as a shirt or a toothbrush or a few loose coins on the dresser top."

"You must of got restless waiting," he observed, grinning.

I picked the beer glass up again, looked at the bubbles and put it down unquaffed. A faucet dripped somewhere behind me. "What has he told you about himself?" I asked, just to stay on the subject.

"Not a goddam thing. And I don't ask. I thought we covered that."

"What about visitors?"

"Not that I ever seen."

"And you're a man who would see."

"Yeah," he said, and grinned again. It appeared I had paid him a compliment.

"Let's not overlook anything," I said. "How about phone calls?"

He knocked ash off the cigarette. It lit on the floor, where he had aimed it. "Once in a while. Not many. Some dame named Day called two-three times. She's the only one left a name."

"Day," I said. I looked at him stupidly and drank some of the beer before I realized I was drinking it. "What can you tell me about her?"

"A voice on the phone is all she was to me, chum." He was beginning to get bored and showed it.

"These other calls you mentioned," I said. "Also from women?"

"Well . . . no." His eyebrows moved under a scowl the way underbrush moves in a breeze. "Least I don't think. There was some guy called up a time or two for him. No name."

A dame named Day, he had said. It would have to be April Day. A girl whose phone number was likely right in my pocket. A girl who had known Sam Jellco, according to what his wife had told me. A girl who knew Pod Hamp, according to the man across the table. That made her a link between the two men. A link in what way? As a go-between on the Delastone blackmail attempt?

"A question," I said. "What kind of a looking man would you say Hamp is?"

"Le'see." He scratched his chin, then his chest, then drank his beer, draining the glass with three smooth ripples of his throat muscles. He wiped his mouth with the back of his hand and yawned hugely and reached for the bottle and filled the glass for the third time. "Maybe about your height," he said, squinting at me like a dowager at a Picasso. "A little bit heavier in the shoulders. Black hair, kind of light-coloured eyes, and his chin's got one of them parts in it like Robert Taylor in the movies. Scar across the back of his hand—right hand. Neat dresser, like I said, and kind of good-looking in an unflashy way."

I looked dazedly at the cigarette in my fingers. I pinched it out and got up the way an old man gets up and walked over and dropped the butt into an open pail under the sink. I came back and sat down again and said, "That Robert Taylor. Best thing he ever did was 'Waterloo Bridge'. He even looked good in the fog. He must be pushing fifty by now."

The man with the hair was staring at me strangely. "Skip it," I said wearily. "Anybody named Delastone ever call Hamp up?"

"Delastone?" He seemed to back away from me without actually moving. "Only Delastone I ever heard of's old Colonel Delastone, who just about owns this town. That who you mean?"

"Any Delastone will do." There was a brackish taste in my mouth that might have come from the beer. "The name Sam Jellco mean anything to you?"

He thought, then shook his head, no. I put my cigarettes back in the breast pocket of my pocket and took out my wallet and gave him ten dollars. He snapped the bill a time or two, folded it carefully and made it disappear. I gave him a business card.

"In case you think of something," I said.

"Sure."

We both stood up and he walked out to the front door with me. He said, "I guess I better put a bolt on this thing. Too easy to get past the way it is."

I walked down the steps and went back to the Plymouth. I was thinking—sharp, ugly thoughts that stuck in my craw and burned there. I was thinking of the description of Pod Hamp furnished by the hairy hero, remembering what he had said about the scarred hand and the cleft chin and the black hair and the height and the build. But most of all I was thinking of that scarred hand.

A great many men had black hair and were about my height. I could name a dozen inside of two minutes. But only one of them had a scarred hand.

A man named Sam Jellco.

CHAPTER TWENTY-EIGHT

You play them the way they come. Sometimes they come fast and true and your mind sees them in three dimensions, like things seen on a bright winter's day when the air is clear and images sharply defined, and they add up quickly to the answer, the whole answer, no fractions left over. And the answer is always the correct one and the client is grateful and a little staggered by your brilliance and he pays your modest fee and thanks you twice and goes away happy.

Sometimes it's not like that at all. Then you get the black days, the days when the puzzle makes advanced calculus simple by comparison, when nothing fits anything else, when everything is distorted and unreal. And so you grope around in the jungle of your mind, seeking to put your hand on something beside wet leaves, getting nowhere and learning nothing. And all the time this goes on you have the sneaking conviction that there's really nothing complicated about the case at all, it's just that you're astigmatic and slow-witted and fumbling and that you couldn't find a hearse in a thimble.

Like right now.

Five days had come and gone since the morning I first called on Mrs. Serena Delastone and got myself pitched into a case I didn't want and had tried four times to get out of. Five days of being yelled at and snooted and threatened and worked over with sundry hard hands and framed and jailed and fined and run the hell out of town. Such things happen, sure. They're part of the job and you can take them, although never gracefully, if along with them you pick up a fact here, a working assumption there.

I had picked up nothing. Certainly nothing to take me in the direction I had been hired to go. What I knew was interesting, but that was all it was: that Edwin Delastone was dead and deserved to be, that every member of his family was afraid to have his death investigated—although not necessarily for the same reasons, and that the police either knew who the killer was or could find out if free to do so. And I knew now that Sam Jellco had been no more than a cheap crook after all—an extortionist, a blackmailer of women. Not at all what his wife had tried to sell me on.

There was still a thread left to follow. As far as I knew it was the only thread. A girl. A girl so anxious to reach Sam Jellco the night he died that she had called his wife. A girl who more than once telephoned him while he was rooming under the name of Hamp at the Bleecher Street address.

A girl named April Day.

I didn't have her address, but if the phone number in my wallet belonged to her, the address could be had. Not from the close-mouthed phone company, of course, but I had a friend in the State Attorney's office in Chicago who would run it down for me. It might take an hour or two, what with coffee breaks and late lunches, but he would do it.

Only there might not be an hour or two. For all I could tell, April Day, jumpy from my phone call, was packing her bag to blow town, and with her would go the only lead I could put my hands on. What I needed, and needed quick, was a short cut to that address. That meant somebody who wasn't after my scalp and who knew the ropes.

That narrowed the field to one. Ira Groat.

One block over and four down was a green-fronted drugstore with a window display of abdominal supports and elastic stockings for varicose veins. A sign lettered in gold paint on the door glass said *Se Habla Espanol,* but the phones inside worked in English.

Groat's number was on the sheet of hotel stationery, next to the one for Remotti's Bar & Grill. I called his home and got the same throaty voice, female, I'd listened to briefly once before.

"Well, hello there!" she purred, after I'd spoken my piece. "I remember you, Mr. Pine. You called up here night before last and asked for Ira, didn't you? You have a very nice voice."

"I was the one," I said. "I wouldn't know about the voice, Mrs. Groat. This *is* Mrs. Groat?"

She laughed. It was one of those cosy, let's-pull-down-the-shades-and-disconnect-the-doorbell laughs, as intimate as a left-handed honeymoon. "Of course. But you must call me Valerie. Simply everybody does. . . . So you're Mr. Pine. The things I've been hearing about you! Ira told me how they arrest—" She stopped there and turned on the laugh again. "But then I don't suppose we should talk about *that!*"

"I guess not," I said. "Is he in?"

"Ira? I'm dreadfully sorry. Although he's sure to be along any minute now. Could I help?"

"I'll call back. Would twenty minutes be about right?"

"I should certainly think so. Better still, why don't you stop by and wait for him here? I'd love to offer you a drink."

"I wouldn't want to be any trouble, Mrs. Groat."

"Now isn't that silly! Of course you'll come. Frankly I'm dying to meet you, Mr. Pine. Where are you calling from?"

It turned out I was no more than fifteen minutes north of the apartment building where the Groats lived. I took down directions and the address and said, "If your husband shows up ahead of me, ask if he'd mind waiting. I won't keep him long."

"You're sure you know how to get here?"

"Uh-hunh. And thanks again, Mrs. Groat."

"It's Valerie, remember?" the voice throbbed. "You don't *have* to be so formal, do you?"

I said something or other and replaced the receiver and walked out into the bright warm air and climbed in behind the steering wheel and started up the motor.

Valerie Groat. A friendly woman with a friendly voice and a nice sense of hospitality. In this day of speed and bad manners a combination like that was rare.

In Olympic Heights it was damned near incredible.

CHAPTER TWENTY-NINE

SHE was wearing a bright yellow taffeta hostess gown with a tight bodice, a deep-slashed V neckline and a flaring skirt that narrowly missed the floor. Her face had that angular half-starved look found on models in the higher-priced fashion magazines and her ash-blonde hair was parted down the centre and drawn severely back, covering the upper half of her small tight-set ears. She resembled a small-town reporter's wife the way I resembled Anne of Green Gables.

"How nice!" she said throatily, pulling the door wide. "I see you had no trouble finding the way."

"Nothing to it. Ira hasn't shown up yet?"

"I'm afraid not. Perhaps he stopped off somewhere for a drink. He often does. We're what the neighbours call drinking people, Ira and I."

Her wide too-red mouth smiled saying it. The words floated gently towards me on a cloud of Scotch fumes. She was holding a tall glass that didn't have much in it except an ice cube or two. Not any more it didn't.

She took my hat and dropped it on the foyer bookcase, closed the door and brought me into a large square living room fitted out with darkwood period pieces that looked new and expensive. She waved a hand at the sofa and I took a corner of it and watched her drift with languid grace toward a portable bar in walnut, its double doors open for business.

"There's plenty of Scotch," she said across one of her thin shoulders. "And I think some bourbon. Or even gin if you like, although I don't see how anybody in his right mind can bear the stuff."

"Scotch is fine, Mrs. Groat."

She fetched a bottle, an ice bucket, water in a silver pitcher and a mate to her own glass, and plunked them down on the cocktail table in front of the couch. She needed two trips to do it. She sank down next to me with a rustling sound and bent forward and put together a pair of highballs, man-sized, with the nice economy of movement that comes with long practice. The neck of the gown gaped alarmingly while this was going on and what she was wearing underneath wouldn't have been five minutes' work for a very tired silkworm. The blood began to move around inside me.

We touched glasses and traded smiles. "*Tiers état*," she murmured.

"There is no god but Allah," I said.

We drank. Mine went down smooth and easy, all the way down, radiating a cheerful warmth, making the room brighter and the air clearer. I lowered the glass and saw with mild shock that half the contents were gone. It was that kind of Scotch.

Valerie Groat leaned back and crossed her legs, a little too carelessly. Her smile was as faint as a loser's cheers. "Ira tells me you're a private detective. I'll bet you're a good one."

"Not this trip," I said.

"Something about one of your friends being killed, isn't it? Does that happen often?"

"Only once," I said. "Then they bury you."

Her head went back and her laugh hit the ceiling. Her neck was a shade on the stringy side. "Serves me right!" she said, still laughing. "I did make that sound awfully damned patronizing, didn't I? But then I suspect to most people a private detective is something out of a rental library. I'm so sorry. Was he a friend of yours?"

"We'd met."

She stopped smiling suddenly. "Perhaps you'd rather not talk about it. Let me have your glass."

It wasn't empty, so I emptied it and handed it over. She made two more of the same, strong enough to build a garage on, then settled back and drew a foot up and sipped a time or two at the fresh supply. The housecoat had slipped open slightly, letting me see a length of sheer stocking and the inner curve of a freshly powdered thigh. Instead of chewing the rug, I drank from my glass.

"You remind me of a man I used to know," Mrs. Groat said conversationally. "This was back in New York; a newspaper photographer. Four wives in something like six years, every cent he made tied up in alimony, and hell-bent to make me number five. He was cynical and not much good, but he could charm the pants off you."

"My charm's a little rusty," I said.

"Something should be done about that," she said coolly.

We nodded to each other and tilted our glasses again. I passed around the cigarettes. She bent her head to take a light, letting her fingers rest lightly on the back of my hand. They were long tapering fingers, too red at the ends, cool and a little moist. With her face so close I could see a small hot flame flickering in the depths of soulful brown eyes. Soulful? My memory stirred vaguely. Why soulful?

The glasses were empty again. The stuff seemed to drink itself. This time I got to the bottle first and mixed two more of the same, nearly forgetting the water. I was getting that floating feeling, the one that assures you that whatever you do is timely and good and the mark of genius. Without it the distillers would be out of business.

"That where you met him?" I asked. "In New York?"

"Met—? Oh, you mean Ira? Yes, as a matter of fact. He was covering sports for one of the tabloids and proved to be the only man I ever met that I couldn't out-drink. What a thing to be boasting about! I was a model in those days."

"I can see why," I said, looking at her leg.

She drank some more. So did I. She gave me a lingering smile that shrank my shorts. "I hated the life. Glaring lights and big cameras and the boys with careless hands. Mink coats in the summer and bathing suits all winter I was forever taking off my clothes and putting them on again."

"You wouldn't happen to have a few in-between shots around, would you?"

She laughed. I drank. She drank. She lowered her glass and gave me another slow smile and put her hand well above my knee and squeezed. I didn't yell for help. I could walk away from this anytime.

Time for another round. The bottle was fading fast but plenty of others were waiting across the room. I gave her her glass and she dropped her cigarette into the tray and moved closer to me. The long length of her thigh was pressed tight against my leg. It felt as though somebody had built a fire there.

She went into her glass like a diver off the high board. When she surfaced again, better than three-quarters of the liquid was gone. After a jolt like that she should have fallen off the couch. But not her. Not Valerie Groat. To her bonded Scotch was just something wet. Her brown eyes, looking at my full glass, were as cool and clear as a Minnesota morning. "You're not drinking, Paul."

"Maybe not by your standards," I said. My voice sounded a little thick. "I want to be in shape to talk to your husband."

The pressure of her thigh was getting insistent. "Ira? The hell with him, darling. He won't be home for hours yet, if I know him."

"You said different. On the phone."

"Of course I did. From what he told me yesterday, I made up my mind that you were one of these virile men."

"I'm a cream-puff, lady."

"Not with that build, mister."

We drank. She drained what little was left in her glass and set it on the table and gave me a long level look that said more than an hour of oratory. Then she reached over and took the glass away from me and put it down. Then she turned toward me and slid a hand behind my head and yanked it down and slammed her mouth against mine. I gave as good as I got. Her lips seemed to dissolve and her tongue went crazy and then she was all over me.

Finally I drew my head back and gulped some air. She lay across my knees, not moving, smiling dreamily up at me, her breath even and unhurried. The housecoat was open and her skin glistened like pearls on a jeweller's pad.

"Kiss me," she breathed. "Kiss me, you handsome bastard."

I lifted her a little and bent my head and exercised what was left of my technique. She moaned a little and her breath scorched my cheek and her body began to move—small undulating movements that had an effect on me. I put a hand under the robe and almost lost my lower lip as a result. Her breathing was no longer even and no longer unhurried.

"The bedroom," she panted. "Carry me, Paul!"

I got an arm under her knees and the other around her back and managed to stand up. There were no thoughts in me; the liquor and the feel and the smell of Valerie Groat had taken over. I wavered across the rug and was almost to a closed door in the inner wall when a key turned in the hall door and feet came into the room.

I turned around slowly and lifted my head and looked across the room at Ira Groat. He was standing there watching us, the key still trailing from his hand, his face a mask without expression.

Valerie Groat stirred in my arms. She heard nothing, saw nothing. "Hurry," she mumbled. "Please, darling. Now!"

I set her on her feet. Hard. It jarred her eyes open and she looked at me, from me to where I was looking. Her eyes got very round and her smile was as brilliant as a desert sunrise. "Why, darling!" she said throatily. "You're early. How nice."

He said nothing. There was a dull flush to the sallow skin over his cheekbones. He dropped the key into a pocket of his coat and pushed his hat back with a thumb and walked toward us, not hurrying. My face was as stiff as Clancy, the night he fell off the streetcar.

"Let me make you a drink, sweetheart," Valerie Groat said.

He slapped her across the face. It was done very quick and very hard and it made a noise like a lath breaking. It spun her in a half circle and only an instinctive grab on my part kept her off the floor.

She put a hand up and touched her cheek gently where there were four white marks that were going to be very red very soon. "That hurt," she said in a child's voice.

There was some silence. Valerie Groat brought her hand down and drew the front of the yellow hostess gown together.

"I'm rather tired," she said very calmly. "I think I'll lie down for a while." She gave me an untroubled smile. "Goodbye, Mr. Pine. I enjoyed meeting you."

She turned and walked gracefully to the bedroom, into it. The door clicked shut behind her, leaving Ira Groat and me staring at each other.

"My turn?" I said, not smiling.

He balled a hand and brought it down hard against the side of his leg, then turned away without a word and crossed to the bar. He dumped Scotch into a wide-mouthed glass, a great deal of Scotch, and threw it down his throat. He thumped the glass against the bartop and turned around, facing me.

"You can come down off your toes, Pine," he said in a grey voice. "You're not the first one—or the fifth." He filled the glass again and stared at it with brooding eyes. "It just so happens my wife's a tramp. Maybe she's a tramp because she drinks so much. Or maybe she drinks so much because she's a tramp. But there it is."

He sipped from the glass, put it aside and lighted a cigarette. "I'm wondering why you're here. Suppose you tell me."

It was no time to say it but it had to be said. "Edwin Delastone was one of them, wasn't he? You came home one day and found him here. With her."

His thin face twisted sharply and it seemed a long time before he spoke. "I see. You heard that he made the grade and you figured if you could, that would be proof enough."

"No," I said. "I stopped by to ask a favour of you. I had no ideas about your wife and Edwin Delastone. Then a few items dropped into place. Like your telling me in that bar how even nice women went for Edwin—nice women who could hide what they really were under soft skins and soulful brown eyes. You sounded too bitter to be objective—and Mrs. Groat does have that kind of eyes and—ah—skin. And then you mentioned just now that there have been several men."

I stopped there, waiting. One corner of his mouth pulled up in a wry smirk. "Which proves what? That I killed him?"

"Only that you had a reason to kill him," I said.

He threw his hands wide, then grabbed the glass again. "Well, I didn't kill him—although I'd have been proud to. The time of death was between one and two in the morning. Look up the coroner's report some time."

"The one that says heart failure?" I said.

He eyed me steadily. "We're talking about *when* Edwin died, not how. At the time he was shot I was in the middle of losing seventeen bucks at draw poker. Check with the local law if you want proof."

"They'd co-operate with me," I said. "About the way they'd co-operate with diphtheria."

"Well, don't expect me to do it for you." He took off his hat and tossed it across the room to land on the couch. Then he swallowed some more of his drink and went on standing there, staring down into the glass.

"This business of looking for Jellco's killer," he said suddenly. "That's not really why you're out here, is it? It's whoever knocked off Edwin you're after. Jellco was hired by the old lady for the same job, and when he ended up dead, she called you in to pick up the torch. Only the Colonel doesn't want any investigation, which is why you were run out of town. The fact that you're back shows that the old woman is fronting for you. I say that because I give you credit for having sense enough not to come back without being damned sure of staying out of jail. Is that how it is?"

"I'm after Jellco's killer," I said. "I told you that. In fact there's hardly anybody in Olympic Heights I haven't told it to. If, as seems likely, the same person killed Edwin too—then all the loose ends get tied up."

He nodded slowly and went on looking at me from under the hooded lids of hard brown eyes. "You want to know how I feel about it, neighbour? Well, I hope to Christ you nor nobody else ever finds the guy. Tough about your friend; but on Edwin Delastone he did the town a favour—and I don't mean only because of my wife, either. So you run right along and earn your money, only don't think you're going to get any help from me."

"Okay."

"Anything else on your mind?"

"Nope."

"You haven't told me what brought you over here in the first place."

"I wanted a favour," I said. "A small one, like getting me an address from a phone number. I thought probably I could get it quicker through you."

"Whose address?"

"You wouldn't know her," I said. "You told me so earlier. And if you'll remember, I'm not to expect any help from you."

He shrugged and drank some of his whisky.

"Besides," I added, "I don't lift a guy's watch, then ask him for the time. If you know what I mean. So long, Mr. Groat."

I went into the foyer and took my hat off the bookshelf. Ira Groat stayed where he was, the glass tight in his hand, his eyes studying the carpet. The door to the bedroom was closed tight and no sound came through it. Maybe Valerie Groat had dropped off to sleep, her mind untroubled, her breath heavy with Scotch. I wished her nothing but the best.

Ira Groat didn't look up when I opened the door. There was no reason why he should.

It was nearly four o'clock when the information came through from Chicago on the phone number. The listing was for an Arline Dreyfoos, in the Mulberry Square section of Olympic Heights.

Not the name I had expected, but the initials were right. I figured that was good enough.

CHAPTER THIRTY

MULBERRY SQUARE was a triangular-shaped district south of the business section and cut in two by the North Shore Railway tracks. It was old town: crumbling brick paving along narrow streets lined with sagging frame buildings that housed grimy little stores, basement social clubs, pool rooms where you could even play pool, and a great many taverns with good homey names like Pete's Place and George's Grotto and Bob's Bar.

The address was on Salem Street, over a hardware store on the northwest corner of an intersection. I parked below a fire hydrant and took my time about getting out from behind the wheel. There was a good deal of foot traffic: women with children and women with shopping bags and women with nothing beyond a loose gait and looser eyes. A few of the wise boys lounged in front of shop windows and in hall doorways, holding cigarettes behind cupped hands and blowing smoke out of the holes in their faces, very tough and letting you know it.

I locked up and moved on down to the corner, around that and on down to the second-floor entrance to number 719. The heavy street door, divided into small smeared squares of glass, gave reluctantly. I pushed past it into the deceased air of a four-by-four hall, with no inner door between me and a flight of dusty green stair-carpeting rising up into dimness.

Three lumpy tin mail boxes along one wall. Around them a childish hand had scrawled words in white chalk. But not childish words. The name plate on the last box read: *A. Dreyfoos, 2C.*

It had been a long time coming but here it was. A. Dreyfoos. April Day sounded better. It was a nice name. The name for a girl young and slender, with budding breasts and a silvery laugh, wearing white organdie and with daisies in her golden hair.

I climbed the steps to a small square landing covered with patched linoleum. There was a door in each of the three walls. The paint was a blotchy green, blistered in spots, and the smell was of ancient cooking. Enough light came through a dusty skylight for me to make out names on small thumb-marked cards tacked to the doors.

Apartment 2C was farthest from the stairhead and facing it. No bell in sight, so I knocked. Briskly, to let Miss Day, or Dreyfoos, know this was business. I heard the sound of a vague movement from the other side, so faint and so brief that I might only have imagined hearing it. Then nothing.

I knocked again.

Close to the wood a woman's voice said, "What is it, please?" The voice sounded a little breathless.

I said, "Miss Dreyfoos?"

". . . Yes."

"Want to talk to you."

Another small pause filled with nothing except nothing. ". . . No. Not now. I—I'm not dressed. Come back later."

You can't let them stall you or the days would never be long enough. "Later," I said, "could be too late. Slip something on, lady. This won't take long."

"But I—I can't let you in now," the voice said hoarsely. "Come back in—in an hour. I'll talk to you then."

"That's all right," I said. "No hurry. I'll just wait out here in this nice comfortable hall. Take your time. I'll just lean up against one of these nice comfortable walls and sniff at the incense."

Thirty seconds went by. I heard nothing. Then a chain rattled and hit the door and the door swung cautiously back no more than a foot, shielding whoever was standing behind it. I made out a puff of fair hair and the shadowy outlines of a shoulder with an arm hanging down.

"Come in," the voice whispered. The door began another slow retreat and I started through.

In the faint light something flashed up and then down, coming at my head in a silvery blur. I jumped sideways and caught a raking blow along my back. I grabbed the wrist before it could lift again and twisted it sharply. The voice gave a painful gasp and something clattered against the floor.

"You're hurting me," the voice cried.

"Pardon me," I said, not letting go. I came all the way into the room, shoving the owner of the voice ahead of me, and closed the door with the heel of my shoe. All I was able to make out was that she was taller than average, with blonde hair and the right kind of figure. There was enough light for me to see her face, except that she was holding her head down and turned away. So I took hold of her chin with my free hand and brought it up and around.

We stood there that way, our faces inches apart, our breath mingled. Hers was a face I had called lovely before. Wide blue-green eyes stared dazedly at me from it. They got even wider as recognition dawned in them.

"Paul!"

"Yeah," I said. "I guess I slept through the second act, or something. What are you doing here, Mrs. Jellco?"

"My . . . arm."

I let go of her wrist. She stood there rubbing it absently, her expression a mixture of relief and anxiety. A strand of blonde hair had slipped down on her forehead, making her look very young and somehow helpless.

"I—I didn't know who it was," she stammered. "You sounded so coarse and—well, threatening. I was frightened."

"What of?"

"Of—" She brushed the wick of hair back with the side of her hand. "It was just that— Well, I didn't really—"

I stooped and picked up what she had taken a swipe at me with. A copper candlestick with a fluted base. I hefted it appraisingly. It weighed more than enough. "Lucky for both of us my reflexes were on the job," I said. "Otherwise you'd have had a body on your hands. The way you were swinging."

She shuddered and her knees began to give up. I put an arm around her to keep her off the floor. She made a small whimpering sound and leaned against me, still shaking. Her hair brushed my face, filling my nose with a scent too light to classify but nice to remember. "For God's sake, Paul," she said into my collar, "let's get away from this awful place."

All by itself my arm tightened around her slim waist, drawing her even closer. She didn't resist and she didn't melt. Slowly her head came up and we looked long into each other's eyes. She was beautiful and altogether desirable.

Her lips parted ever so slightly, light from the windows moving along them. She stood very still now, trembling a little, her eyes half-closed and bright as with unshed tears.

All I had to do was bend my head and put my mouth against hers. The way I felt about her I would be crazy not to. I said, "Why 'awful'?"

Linda Jellco stiffened and drew back against my arm and some of the previous terror came back into her expression. Then her eyes seemed to veil over and she looked away.

"I don't know what you mean," she said dully.

"I was quoting you. 'Let's get away from this awful place.' Why?"

". . . It's just that it's so—so depressing, I suppose. And kind of—cheap." She put a hand on my arm and pushed it firmly away from her. "Could we go now?" she asked in the manner and tone of a polite child.

"Where's April Day?"

She seemed honestly surprised at the question. "April Day? The woman who telephoned me the night Sam was killed? How in the world would I know where she is?"

"This is her apartment. You didn't know that?"

"I certainly did not! After you refused to work for me any longer, I had a friend of Sam's check on the same phone number I gave to you earlier—the only thing I really had to go on. It was listed in the name of Arline Dreyfoos, at this address. I came out here to find out if she couldn't give me some information—anything at all to go on."

"And could she?"

Her eyes slid away. "I—I didn't see her."

"How did you get in?"

Her chin came up, then, and anger began to edge into her voice. "If you must know, I found the door partly open, and when no one answered my knock, I walked in and called to her, thinking she might be asleep or—"

"With the door open?"

She flared up at that. I liked her for it. "You think I'm lying —is that it? Then why ask me these ridiculous questions?"

"Not ridiculous," I said. "Not when you were willing to stave in a skull just to get away from here unseen. I came to see the same person you did. As long as she's not home, let's you and me kind of look around."

She moistened her lips and drew back slightly. "I—what is it you expect to find?"

"Maybe only what's got you scared half to death. Come on."

She didn't move. Her beautiful face began to crumple. "She's . . . in there, Paul. On— She's dead."

I took hold of her arms, above the elbows, and shook her a little. "All right, she's dead. You've got no time to throw a wing-ding. Tell me about it and tell me quick."

"I—I—" She sunk her teeth in her lower lip and tried again. "It was like I said. Nobody answered and I walked in. She's on the floor in there—in the bedroom. With a h-hole in . . . where the bullet went. I saw the gun."

"You touch anything?"

"No, no."

"How long have you been here?"

"Only a few minutes. I saw her that way and was going to leave. And then you came."

"Did you kill her?"

I felt her stiffen but her voice didn't change. "No, Paul."

"You're not holding anything back? Give it to me straight, Mrs. Jellco, or they'll bury all of us."

"I've told you everything."

"Okay." I walked around in a tight circle, making up my mind. I stopped in front of her again and said, "How did you get here?"

"Why, I drove out. They turned Sam's car back to me day before yesterday, with the rest of his things."

"You're parked where?"

"Around the corner."

"All right," I said. "Go on down and get in it and drive back to Chicago. Watch the speedometer and the traffic signs. Stay near your phone until you hear from me."

"What are *you* going to do?"

I said, "In one little minute I'm calling Captain Benton Brill of the Olympic Heights police. He's going to love this and I'm going to let him."

Her eyes were troubled. "But—well, I mean—do you *have* to? Nobody knows we've been here. Nobody can connect either of us with this—girl. Can't we just—just leave? Both of us?"

I shook my head patiently. "The man who gave me this address is an Assistant State's Attorney and a friend of mine. But he's the kind of guy who puts duty ahead of friendship. Let them find April Day dead and me not around—and he'd blow the whistle on me fast."

"Will they arrest you?"

"Who knows? Goodbye, Mrs. Jellco. Try not to be noticed leaving the building. And I don't mean skulk. Just wait inside the street door until nobody is going by, then step out nice and easy, no hurry and no loitering, get into your car and drive away."

She looked at me steadily. "Was Sam mixed up with this woman, Paul?"

"I just got here," I said impatiently. "Like all of us in the business, we get tangled with all kinds. Is that what you mean?"

"You know what I mean," she said levelly.

"Sam was your husband, Mrs. Jellco. That makes your question one you'll have to answer."

Her eyes dug into my face and found nothing there except bruises. "Call me, Paul."

"Uh-hunh."

She slipped out and went softly down the stairs. I waited until I heard the outer door close, then I shut the apartment door and stood in the centre of the living room and gave it the once over.

It was a narrow room, nothing fancy, a pullman kitchen at one end, a gaslog fireplace at the other. In the fireplace wall was another door, closed. Sunlight struggled through a pair of sash windows with tartan drapes behind a studio couch in faded green. There was a walnut console television set across from the couch that looked new and costly, which was more than could be said for the rest of the stuff. Ashtrays overflowed, a fifth of Four Roses stood on an end table next to a pair of smeared highball glasses, and a rumpled newspaper was half on a coffee table, half on the floor. Three battered Matisse prints in a line on one wall looked even uglier than usual. And over everything the smell of dust and buried air and yesterday's fried potatoes.

I fumbled out a cigarette and lighted it and walked carefully down the room and opened the door next to the fireplace and found a short narrow hall. Halfway along it was a bathroom the size of a phone booth, and at the far end another closed door.

It's always easier when you know what to expect. I went in and closed the door gently and leaned against it.

It was the bedroom, all right. There was a bed in it, along with the other things found in bedrooms. On the floor near the window lay the body of a woman.

I stood there stiff-legged and stared at the body. A young woman, not yet thirty years and no more to come. Hair the colour of a thundercloud spilled to her shoulders. Round black eyes under thin high-arched brows stared wonderingly at the ceiling. She was flat on her back, the heels of her black-satin slippers close together and the toes turned out to form a wide V. She was wearing a white wraparound housedress, with one corner hiked high up on one side to expose a long length of shapely bare leg and thigh and the lacy edge of something made of black rayon.

There was a gout of red on the cloth covering her left breast. A rather large stain, still fresh enough to be shiny, with a black-edged hole slightly off the centre. Not a large hole but still large enough. The gun was there too, over in front of the dressing table where somebody had thrown or dropped it. A Banker's Special, .22 calibre. Just right for a humming-bird safari, unless you were very close and had all the time in the world.

She had stood there and looked down the muzzle of that gun. She had known she was going to die, and knowing it had frozen her tongue and tightened her muscles and widened her eyes and put a cold steel bar of fear below her ribs. And then a finger had moved, just a small flicker of motion that you wouldn't think could mean much. But the finger had been on the gun trigger and what followed was a hard quick sound. And that had been all for April.

I went slowly over and squatted down and put my fingers gently against the white flesh of the neck. She was an hour dead, I thought, no longer than an hour and possibly much less. Some ash from my cigarette fell on her upper lip. I winced for her and blew it away quickly. It left no mark. Her lipstick had the oily sheen of fresh blood. She lay there waiting for the meat wagon and the coroner's scalpel, her eyes bright and empty, still with the faintly astonished expression they would bury her with.

I straightened and turned away from her. The room seemed orderly enough. The yellow chenille bedspread was mussed and the mattress had slid a little to one side on the box springs, but that could happen to anyone. A blue linen handbag caught my eye from the dresser top and I pawed through it. Not much in the way of identification, but what there was gave the name of Arline Dreyfoos. Her age was twenty-six, she had been a dancer at an East St. Louis nightclub eight months before, she had worked as hostess for one of the better Chicago restaurants as recently as the previous March. What happened after that, job-wise, wasn't stated. Please Notify: Mrs. Alvinah Dreyfoos, Rt. 2, McCook, Nebraska. A second notice from the light company and, in the coin-purse, seventeen dollars in cash.

It wasn't until I was scooping the stuff back into the bag that I came across the snapshot. I took it over to the window for more light. It showed, in colour, a man and a girl holding on to each other and leaning against the front fender of a sporty looking pearl grey convertible while grinning into the camera. The girl was the girl on the floor; the guy a handsome hunk, mostly teeth and shoulders, radiating a lot of free charm that didn't look as though it would wear well. Not that anything definite can come from a snapshot, but at times you get an impression.

I turned it over. On the back some cramped pencil marks that deciphered out to: "Edwin and me and his new car. Wow is he a crazy driver ! ! !" Under that a date—a date not yet a month gone.

It would have to be Edwin Delastone. For it to be another Edwin would be more coincidence than even I could expect. I peered at his face some more but got nothing to add to my first reaction.

The snap went into the bag where it had come from. It was of no use to me, and having the cops find it in one of my pockets would only complicate matters. I put the bag back where it came from and tried the dresser drawers.

The first one looked as though a herd of elephants had passed through it on the way to the watering hole. A supply of too-frilly underthings was a tangle of disorder, a three-drawer hosiery box ripped apart, a leather jewel case dumped. The rest of the drawers were no better off. The same for the drawer in the vanity table, and what had been in the boxes on the single closet shelf was now mostly on the floor.

Somebody had wanted something in a hurry. Somebody with a reason for hurrying and no reason for being subtle. The man with the gun? Probably. If it was a man to begin with.

Only my thoughts were mostly on what I had found in a tangle in the bottom drawer of the dresser. Two pairs of men's pyjamas with the initials SJ worked into the pocket of each coat. A half-dozen men's handkerchiefs, same last initial. A pair of gold cuff links, same initials. I wondered what Linda Jellco's reaction would be once she learned about such items.

I wondered if she had already learned about them.

CHAPTER THIRTY-ONE

IT took some time to get through to her. I sat on the bed and ate cigarette smoke and kept my eyes away from the girl on the floor. Finally an extension went up and her solid voice came over the wire, chilly and hard, like always.

"This is Serena Delastone, Mr. Pine."

I waited until I heard the first receiver replaced, then I said, "Are you where you can talk to me, Mrs. Delastone? Without being overhead, I mean?"

She made a humph noise loud enough to knock any stray linesman off the telephone poles. "We can do nicely without the dramatics, I'm sure. What is it you have to tell me?"

I didn't drive a fist through the bedroom wall. "I asked a question," I said. "If I sounded dramatic it's because we've got a drama on our hands. There's been some trouble."

"Trouble? What kind of trouble?"

"The big kind, Mrs. Delastone. The kind that comes out of guns. Murder. Would that be dramatic enough for you?"

That stopped her—for all of five seconds. Then: "I find your impudence in very bad taste, Mr. Pine. Tell me at once who is dead."

"A girl," I said. "Name of Arline Dreyfoos—when it isn't April Day. Does either name mean anything to you?"

"Certainly not. Why are you telling me this?"

"For several reasons," I said. "It ties in directly with what I was hired to do. By you. It means I'm going to have to report finding the body to the cops. The cops out here aren't crazy about me,

Mrs. Delastone. Let them even get a hint that I'm not giving the whole story and they'll use more than a fraternity pin on me. I don't have to remind you that the whole story includes Hamp's attempt to blackmail you—something I'm sure you don't want aired. Which is why I figured you'd want to do something toward putting in the fix—ahead of time."

"I'll do nothing of the sort," she barked. "If you feel it necessary to call in the police, that's your affair. Just be sure you keep my name and our relationship out of it. Is that clear?"

"They're going to find out anyway," I said through my teeth. "Judge Kellogg can tell them; he signed that order at your request. You don't think they'll drag you in for questioning, do you? The minute they know for sure I'm working for you, it's all over. I'll be permitted to make a brief statement and walk out the front door, no fresh bruises and my kidneys still working."

"I'll not consent to having my name brought in, Mr. Pine. And don't concern yourself about Amos Kellogg. He knows when to keep his mouth shut and I shall expect you to do the same."

I yanked the phone away to keep from chewing the mouthpiece. I took a couple of slow breaths and put the phone back in front of my face and said, "It's like this, Mrs. Delastone. Without you, I'll have to tell them. Let a private operator hold out on the law when it comes to a major felony, and losing his licence is the least that can happen to him."

"I refuse to believe you haven't the right to protect a client."

I had to keep trying. "This is a matter of murder. At that level my rights aren't important. Like I said, let them suspect I'm playing it cute and I get tromped on. What makes you think I'm willing to take risks like that for you?"

It moved her the way a faint breeze moves the Black Hills. "I hired you, Mr. Pine. I trusted you. Obviously you think nothing of betraying a trust, no matter how trivial the reason."

"Hold the wire," I said. I put the receiver down and got off the bed and walked over to the window. It overlooked an alley. The garbage truck hadn't been around in days. A man came out of the back entrance of the hardware store and put a canvas bag of tools through the rear door of a panel truck and drove off. I lighted a cigarette and breathed smoke and held out my hand at eye level and stared hard at it. The fingers were not the steadiest fingers in the world. I turned and came back to the phone and picked it up and said into it:

"It probably won't take them long, but I'll carry you until they tear my arm off. And don't ask me why."

She started to say something but I banged the receiver up. If it broke one of her eardrums she could take it out of my salary. I picked a burning cigarette off the edge of the nightstand. It and the one I had just finished lighting at the window made two. For a guy about to have his licence torn up I was certainly extravagant.

I carried both cigarettes into the bathroom and threw them where they'd set no fires. Then I got the envelope out with the names and phone numbers I'd collected during the past few days, burned it, dropped the ashes in with the cigarettes and tripped the lever. I took a long drink from the cold tap, using the plastic glass next to the medicine chest. It tasted faintly of a pleasant brand of toothpaste.

My feet dragged going back to the telephone. Captain Brill was in. Without me around he probably had little to do. He said he would be right over and not to go away. He didn't even raise his voice saying it.

I continued to sit on the edge of the bed, watching the grey-blue shadows of late afternoon begin to creep along the baseboards and collect in the corners. The room was silent in the way rooms are silent when there is death in them. In a way, I was as dead as the girl on the floor.

CHAPTER THIRTY-TWO

THEY sat me on a plain wooden chair placed in a corner of a basement room at police headquarters. There were four of them, none more than a year or two past thirty, fitted out in conservatively cut tailormades, sober ties, shirts right off the ironing board. Their black shoes held a high gloss, in case you wanted to see your face while they kicked your teeth in. They drew chairs up to form a rude semi-circle around me. The light of a fading day came in through a barred window over my head.

"You feel like talking, Mr. Pine?" one of them asked politely.

"Oh, I don't know," I said.

"We could talk about the Dreyfoos girl," another one said. "While we're waiting for the captain."

"We've already talked about that," I said. "The captain and I. Out at her apartment and up in the captain's nice air-conditioned office, with a man taking it all down in a notebook. We kind of wore the subject out, the captain and I."

"You only think you wore it out," the first one said.

The third one said, "Captain Brill's not a man to monkey around with, Mr. Pine. I'd co-operate a little better with him if I were you."

"He seems a real gentleman," I said. "Like all you boys."

"I wouldn't rely too much on that," the fourth one said.

"Just a friendly tip," the second one said.

"We can trace that gun, you know," the first one said.

"I hope so," I said. "It looked pretty old to me."

"You shouldn't have handled it," the third one said.

"I didn't handle it," I said. "It just looked old."

"Your prints were on it," the first one said.

"Nuts to you," I said.

"That's not a nice way to talk," the fourth one said.

"I apologize," I said.

"When did you last fire a gun?" the first one said.

"Not since I shot a bishop," I said.

"We have a witness who saw you go in," the second one said.

"That certainly proves I was there," I said.

The door opened and Captain Benton Brill came in with some papers in one hand. A dead pipe jutted from the corner of his mouth. He moved an empty chair directly in front of me after the four cops shoved over, and sat down. His black hair didn't seem as crisp as usual and his blue eyes were filled with storm clouds. "You've given us a lot of trouble, Mr. Pine."

That didn't call for an answer, so I didn't make one.

"I've been reading over what you told me upstairs." He placed the papers on his knee and leaned toward me, over them. "To anyone who didn't know better, what you said up there would make sense. But I know better, so it doesn't."

I still didn't answer him. It was just warm-up talk.

"Which," he said, "is why we're going over it again, you and I. And this time don't hold out on me."

"I wouldn't think of it, Captain."

He had been speaking around the stem of the pipe. He took it out of his face, holding it by the carved bole. "Before we get into that, though, let's clear up this business of Judge Kellogg vacating that jail sentence. How did you work that?"

"Around here," I said, "my word's not too good. Why not check with the judge? You'd want to anyway."

"I'm asking you."

"I'm not at liberty to say."

His tight-set ears reddened. "This is murder, mister. I'm not going to fool around with you."

"My getting that sentence set aside isn't murder, Captain Brill. If you have to have an answer, I could tell you I called the judge up and talked him into writing it out. Or that I have a friend well up in State politics. You'd still have to check with Kellogg."

He let his eyes drift down to the top sheet of the papers in his lap. "What do you know about this Arline Dreyfoos?"

"Only what was on the stuff in her bag."

"What gave you the right to rifle her bag?"

"I didn't rifle it, Captain. I wanted to be in a position to tell the police her identity."

"That won't stand up, Pine. You already knew she was Arline Dreyfoos."

"I thought she was. It was her apartment. But I never saw her before and I didn't have her description."

His jaw was more like a cliff than ever. "You fancy yourself as a pretty slick number, don't you?" he said in a soft voice that wasn't soft at all.

"No, sir."

"We know how to handle the slick ones."

I nodded and looked at my thumb. In the silence Captain Brill turned the top sheet.

"You said you went up to call on her. No answer to your knock, so you opened the door and walked in."

"The door was already open a foot or so," I said.

"You walked back to the bedroom and found her dead on the floor. You went through her bag, touched nothing else, and immediately put through a call to us. Is that still your story?"

I had wiped clean everything I had touched. At least I thought I had. My prints were now on a card upstairs. For comparison purposes they had explained politely.

"I'm a bit vague about the first minute or two," I said. "Finding her dead was something of a shock, Captain."

"I'm asking if you are still sticking to your story?"

"Within reason, yes, sir."

"You called on her for what purpose?"

"It had to do with the Jellco case."

"In what way?"

"We've been all through this, Captain."

"Answer the question."

"Her phone number was in Sam Jellco's possession."

"Go on."

"I hoped she could throw some light on his murder."

"And could she?"

"She was dead, Captain."

"How well did she know Jellco?"

"I don't know."

"Maybe very well? Intimately, as they say?"

"I don't know."

"How well did *you* know Jellco?"

"As I told you, I met him only once. Alive."

"How well do you know Mrs. Jellco?"

"I'm working for her."

"That's as far as it goes?"

"That's as far as it goes."

"When did Jellco first meet Arline Dreyfoos?"

"I don't know."

He took another paper from the pile. "I have here a list of the items found in the dresser drawers in Arline Dreyfoos' bedroom. Shall I tell you what those items include?"

"You'll have to tell me, Captain. If you want me to know."

"A man's pyjamas," he said, reading from the paper. "Six men's handkerchiefs. A pair of cuff links. Two men's shirts. All bearing the initials S. J., except the shirts; on those the laundry marks were checked out as belonging to a Samuel Jellco, 719 Salem Street, Apartment 2C."

I made a throat noise and took out a cigarette and smoothed it between my fingers and said nothing. Brill was watching my face the way a cat watches a freshly gnawed mouse hole. The four other cops were motionless on their chairs, watching me in the same way.

"You know what I'm wondering?" Brill said finally. "I'm wondering if Mrs. Jellco knew about this."

"You haven't asked her?" I said, keeping my face blank.

"Not yet. There's plenty of time. Would you prefer that I didn't ask her?"

"Would it make a difference what I preferred, Captain?"

"Certainly be a terrible blow to her, wouldn't you say? The man she was so crazy about, keeping house with another woman. Wives have shot their husbands for less. Which brings us to an interesting theory."

A cold draught of air passed across the back of my neck. Only there was nothing to create a draught, just as there was no cold air this side of Wisconsin. Brill leaned back and got a pouch out and packed his pipe with roughcut and put a match to it. It had that cured-in-wine aroma. I knew that because the first puff went straight into my face.

"The theory being," he said, taking the pipe out of his mouth, "that Mrs. Jellco killed her husband *and* the Dreyfoos girl. . . . Any comment, sir?"

I stared hard at him. "You serious, Brill?"

"Never more so."

"Then I've got a comment. You and your whole City Hall couldn't make it stick in a hundred years. At the time Jellco was shot, his wife was forty-odd miles south of Olympic Heights. That alone is enough, but let's take it still further. She lacked motive— and don't give me that noise about a crime of passion. If she'd walked in and found her husband in bed with Arline Dreyfoos and yanked out a gun and plugged them both then and there, that would make sense. But she's not coldbloodedly going to take a forty-mile trip and drop in on him at a busy hotel to do it, then wait a week before calling on the woman involved and shooting her.

"That takes care of opportunity and motive. Try building a case without them and you won't even get past the preliminary hearing, let alone before the Grand Jury."

He put the pipe back between his teeth and dragged on it twice before removing it again. He was smiling a little, a calm and confident smile that bothered me far more than anything he had said. Somebody scraped a foot against the room's concrete floor and a throat was cleared.

"Opportunity and motive," Brill said. "Let's take them in that order." He located still another paper in the pile and placed it on top of the others. "I have here a composite report based on the statements Mrs. Jellco and you made the night Jellco was shot. In it she states that she telephoned her husband at the Olympia House at ten-thirty that evening from her apartment. He asked her to call back in twenty minutes. She did so at eleven, received no answer and requested the hotel to check his room. The hotel has no record of such a request, although a call slip shows she did telephone at that time. Three subsequent slips show she made calls at eleven-twenty, eleven-forty, and one-forty-four. Your statement says she telephoned you at eleven-forty or thereabouts, which she also told us. All these calls, she claims, were made from her own apartment, although she has no real proof to offer."

"They were toll calls," I said. "The phone company records will bear her out."

"Only the date they were made. Not the time. She could have put through three of those calls earlier in the day to get them on the records."

"I telephoned her myself at her apartment, Captain."

"So I see. At a quarter to one—an hour and forty-five minutes *after* Jellco died."

"Make your point, Brill."

"I'll make it," he said coldly. "Linda Jellco could have gone to that hotel room, shot her husband at ten-thirty and driven back to her apartment as fast as the law permitted. She stopped twice on the way to make additional phone calls to the hotel and to you. By the time you called her to say you'd go to Olympic Heights and find out what was wrong, she was safely home, her shoes kicked off and a cold drink to settle her nerves."

"Then why bother to call me? What could she expect to gain by chasing me out here?"

He nodded slowly. "There's an answer for that, too. She needed that alibi firmly set. Waiting for a hotel maid to stumble on the body twelve hours or so later might very well weaken her claim that she was home at the time Jellco died. This way she would have your testimony that her husband had been in some kind of trouble and that she was worried enough to send a man all the way out from Chicago to investigate."

"And all this," I said, "for what? Because she found out there was another woman in his life? A dame that, for all you know, she never even heard of? No sale, Captain. Not to me, and much more important, not to a jury. If it ever gets that far."

His pipe was out. He got it going again and looked at me over a layer of blue smoke. He had an ace in the hole and he was about to flip it over and reach for the pot. He said:

"The motive, Mr. Pine, was money—as it so often is. In this case, twenty thousand dollars. A ten-thousand-dollar insurance policy with a double-indemnity clause. How does that sound to you?"

It was coming back to me, slowly, slowly. Linda Jellco had mentioned that policy. At my apartment, the night she came there to hire me. The double-indemnity clause wasn't mentioned at the time. A policy, she said, taken out the year before. That made the policy eighteen months old. At the most, it was eighteen months. Less than two years. . . .

"We knew it wasn't suicide," Brill was saying quietly. "We knew that from the first. A man gets murdered, we check first on his wife —or on the husband when it's the other way around. Jellco was carrying an identification card issued by an insurance company, so we got a company official out of bed to check on it, and learned the date a policy was taken out, the name of the beneficiary and the amount involved."

I knew what was coming. Maybe he knew that I knew. I sat there with my hands weighing a ton and listened to him pour it on.

"From the holes in Mrs. Jellco's story," Brill continued, "we were convinced she was guilty as hell. If she sat tight, those holes weren't big enough for us to do much with. But if we could force her to move around, to start something, there was a chance we could nail her. The insurance-money angle was made to order for our purpose. That policy was in force only fifteen months. As I'm sure you know, a policy less than two years old doesn't pay off on suicide. So we set it up as suicide, got a coroner's jury to back us up on it innocently enough, then sat back to wait for the grief-stricken widow to make her move. She *had* to make a move, for unless that finding of suicide was reversed, there would be no twenty thousand dollars for her. Sure enough; not twenty-four hours later you were at my office, hired by Linda Jellco to get the goods on us for tampering with the evidence she'd left for us to find."

I said, "Because a woman refuses to believe her husband a suicide, that makes her guilty of killing him. Is that your argument?"

Light glinted on the dusting of grey at his temples as he shook his head. "Normally, no. But this time it indicated we were on the right track. All we did then was wait for the expected break—and today we got it."

"I'm not surprised," I said. "Cops like you always get the breaks —even if you have to manufacture them."

Nothing could ruffle him. Not now. "Somehow Arline Dreyfoos knew her boy-friend's wife had killed him. It might have been no more than guesswork—although it's entirely possible she had got hold of something much more substantial. Instead of coming to us with it, she tried blackmailing Linda Jellco—or at least make her suffer by threatening to expose her. Either way, Arline Dreyfoos was fooling with a buzz-saw. This afternoon somebody walked in on her and shot her dead."

"Meaning Linda Jellco?"

"Or you."

I just looked at him.

"The possibility remains, Mr. Pine," he said evenly, "that you and she were in together on this entire operation, once she discovered the twenty thousand wasn't going to drop into her lap after all. When she told you about Arline Dreyfoos, you came out here and handled the matter—permanently."

"And then picked up the phone and called you," I said. "That was certainly intelligent of me."

He nodded, straight-faced. "It would be the most intelligent thing you could have done. I would doubt that you came for the express intention of killing her. More likely it would be to reason with her or frighten her into silence. But she, let's say, was beyond reason or fear—so you shot her. You couldn't be sure you had walked in on her unobserved. You decided to call us and brazen it out."

I said, "You know where I made my mistake, Captain?"

"Well?"

"Not by underestimating you. My error was failing to overestimate you. You had no idea who killed Sam Jellco and you didn't give a damn. What you did want was to get his death hushed up fast and forever—because Colonel Delastone was positive it tied in with the death of his son. I don't know what made him so afraid to let the truth come out, and I doubt if he knows—not really. Possibly because he knew his son for what he was—and another scandal would be something he's too old and too tired to bear up under.

"But now there's another killing. Number three. This time a former girl-friend of Edwin—and calling it suicide, too, would start tongues wagging all over town. The Colonel shrugs wearily and tells you to do the best you can . . . and your best is a solid try at framing Linda Jellco for the death of her husband *and* his sweetie. Period. But let's leave out Edwin. His part in the puzzle won't even get honorable mention. Pretty, hunh?"

I stopped there and looked down. The unlighted cigarette I'd been fooling around with had come to pieces in my fingers. I let the wreckage fall to the floor and brought my eyes back up to Captain Benton Brill's stern and rockbound expression.

"It's not going to work," I said politely. "There's still a killer loose. He—or she—has knocked off Edwin Delastone and Sam Jellco and Arline Dreyfoos. There has to be a reason and I don't think that reason has been resolved—which means there will be more kill—"

The door opened and a uniformed cop stuck his head in "Phone for you, Captain. Urgent."

Brill stood up and knocked the ash out of his pipe. "While I'm busy, you gentlemen might want to talk with Mr. Pine. In case you think of a question or two I neglected to ask him."

He went out without looking back and the door was shut.

"You know what I think, Mr. Pine," the third one said. He left his chair and came up to stand over me. "I don't think you intended to kill the girl at all. You're a sex maniac, that's your trouble. Look at this business with that little whore Gracie, over at the hotel. You went up to see Arline Dreyfoos for the purpose of frightening her, like the skipper says. She was wearing this thin wraparound and she got a little careless and let you see her leg. That inflamed you and you jumped her. She put up a fight and grabbed a gun from somewhere and you took it away from her and let her have it. Come on, fellow, isn't that how it happened?"

"Wrong," I said. "She tried to tell me the cops in this town were a bunch of framing sons-of-bitches who thought a clean shirt and a jar of deodorant made them admirable. That got me mad, because I hate to hear anybody praised so highly when they don't deserve it."

One of them took a smooth leather sap out and rubbed it softly with a palm. "I don't believe I heard you correctly," he said. "Would you mind repeating that?"

"Repeat what?" I said.

"What you just said."

"I didn't say anything," I said. "It must have been your conscience talking."

The fourth one stood in front of me. "Why did you kill her?"

"She was a communist," I said.

"What?"

"The hell with you," I said.

A hand grabbed my hair and yanked my head back. "You killed her and we can prove it. Why did you do it?"

"I'll tell it in court," I said.

"You're not going to court for a while," the second one said. "You might fall down a flight of stairs and maybe get a mild concussion, if you're lucky. That means you'll have to stay in bed for a day or two. The steps we have around here are rather tricky."

"Spoken like a true cop," I said.

A fist swung and caught me behind the ear. My head rang like the Liberty Bell, crack and all. I shook my head. "Maybe you'd better tie me up and call four more cops in."

"We've got all we need," the third one said, "for a cheap punk like you."

"So you have," I said. "Four of this town's cops just about adds up to one cheap punk."

"Where did you get the gun you killed her with?"

"No comment," I said.

The leather sap was dangled in front of my eyes. "Make a comment," a voice said. "Make a comment and make it quick!"

"You need a fresh manicure," I said.

The sap jumped and hit me above the knee. My leg seemed to fall apart—and this was only the overture.

"Your prints were all over that gun," another voice said. "Tell us how they got there."

I ground my teeth and said nothing. A groan formed at the back of my throat.

The sap swam back in front of my eyes. "You can always turn State's evidence, Pine. Think about it."

"I want a lawyer," I said.

"He wants a lawyer," a voice said. "Imagine that."

"You don't need a lawyer to tell the truth," a voice said. "Be fair with us and we'll be fair with you. We know how these things are."

"I'll bet you do," I said.

The hand grabbed my hair again. Or it might have been a different hand. It yanked and the tears sprang to my eyes. "You're only making it difficult for yourself, mister. We don't like this any better than you do. Why not go along with us on this and avoid any unpleasantness?"

"I can't believe you'd actually be unpleasant," I said.

Then the door opened and Brill was back. The hand digging into my scalp fell away and the voices stopped. A small cold smile touched the captain's lips—a smile that said the grave was dug and the winding sheet ready.

"We can stop wondering about Linda Jellco, Mr. Pine," he said in a voice that matched the smile. "She was there this afternoon. At the Dreyfoos girl's apartment. We were able to locate a witness, fortunately."

"Only one?" I said. "Wouldn't five be better?"

"Seems she had trouble starting her car," he said. "One of the shopkeepers along there came over with an offer to help. The way a man will for a nice-looking woman. She tried to brush him off quick, keeping her head turned away like somebody with something to hide. That made him all the more curious and he took a good look at her—even to what she was wearing. A light blue dress, he said, with a short jacket of the same material. No hat. A blonde. To quote him, the kind of blonde you don't forget easy."

The description of the clothing was accurate. They had what they needed. Stick her in a line-up with twenty blondes and she'd still stand out like a good deed in a naughty world.

"He even remembered the time," Brill said dreamily. "That, I found particularly interesting. You see, it was *after* the time you reached the dead girl's apartment. In other words, you went there with Linda Jellco, or she was there when you showed up. Would you care to clarify that part?"

"Are you booking me, Captain?"

He appeared to hesitate. "I doubt if that's necessary. Not unless Mrs. Jellco implicates you. In that case we shouldn't have too much trouble picking you up again."

I stood up. My leg yelled with pain from where the sap had hit it. "Anytime you want me," I said.

The five of them watched me with mild interest. I put a hand down and rubbed my leg. There was a small hard knot there as full of agony as an over-ripe boil.

I said, "When are you taking Mrs. Jellco in, Captain? If you don't mind my asking."

He moved a shoulder. "There's no particular hurry. As soon as I do a little more checking, I suppose. I may run in tomorrow and talk it over with her."

"So that's why you're letting loose of me," I said. "So I can tip her off and she can make a run for it. You'd like that fine. Only the guilty flee where no man pursueth. Pardon my erudition."

I limped over to the door. It was only about fifteen feet away. It seemed that many miles.

CHAPTER THIRTY-THREE

IT wasn't the Olympia House, although it was in Olympic Heights. It was two floors of dirty brick a block down from the railway station and over a wholesale plumbing house. I was in one of the rooms, such as it was, lying on my back on a very narrow, very hard bed, lying in the dark with my mind a black river in which nothing lived, lying there with my eyes open, watching the reflection of headlights slide up the wall and on across the scaly ceiling and into nothing, lying there with only my coat and hat off, like an alcoholic waiting through election day for the polls to close and the bars to open.

I lay there, rubbing my hurt leg when the throbbing got too bad, thinking thoughts that were bitter and without form and which led to nothing. I thought of well-paid young police officers who dressed like account executives in high-budget pictures, and who said sir and please and thank you until you got a fingernail under the polish and discovered they were no different from the old-line cops who thought violence was justice if it was violent enough. I thought of a hard-faced old woman on a chaise-longue in a decaying mansion, growing wrinkled and tough on the hatred of her family, like a pickle soaking in brine. I thought of a dead man on the floor of a hotel room, with the ceiling light glinting on his half-open eyes and the scar on his hand, a man I had met and liked, a man who had turned out to be as crooked as they come.

I flopped over on my side and thought of Linda Jellco and the shine of her yellow hair, of the cool blue-green eyes and the right kind of voice and the fine firm lines of her face, and what she would be like once the wounds were healed. I thought of Arnie Algebra and his fury, of Karen Delastone and her arrogance, of Deborah Ellen Frances Thronetree and her nightmares, of Valerie Groat and her body, of Martha Delastone and her choice of lipstick.

I thought these thoughts and others as meaningless. I moved on the bed and massaged my leg and mumbled words that were only a mumble. I sat up and found the floor with my feet and snicked on the table lamp and stared at my watch.

After nine o'clock. Ten minutes after. Time for you to get started, Pine. Started on what? There's nothing for you to do, no place for you to go. Tomorrow you're likely to be in one Olympic Heights cell, Linda Jellco in another. You've got no strings left to pull, no leads left to follow. Pod Hamp was one of the leads, only his name wasn't Pod Hamp after all and he was dead before you started. It took you four days to find even that much out. That's a fine sharp mind you've got there.

April Day was another lead, but by the time you caught up to her she had become Arline Dreyfoos and also dead. Karen Delastone is a promising lead. It's a cinch Sam Jellco was blackmailing her; she had ransacked his office after his death, and she was in his hotel room the night he died. Except that she was with him an hour and a half *before* he died. You can't tell me she would stick around that long, then shoot him—especially when she knew the waiter could put the finger on her. Of course, you could hunt her up again and ask her some more questions. Only you'd have nothing to back them up with, and you'd get laughed at by her and pounded out of shape by Arnie Algebra's stable of experts.

I stood up and limped over to the door and opened it and looked both ways along the dimly lit hall. Nobody in sight. Why would there be? I closed the door and came back and dug in my coat for a cigarette and lighted it and sat on the bed again.

Let's start at the beginning.

Sam Jellco, while on a confidential job for Serena Delastone, gets hold of something hot on one of her daughters. He figures the old lady will shell out plenty for the stuff, and he comes up with the very smart idea of putting the bite on her as Pod Hamp, figuring Serena will hire him, as Jellco, to handle his own pay-off.

But the idea backfires when Serena balks at paying blackmail and fires Jellco as go-between. So he tries to pressure Karen into paying. She doesn't have that kind of money, and turns to Arnie Algebra for help. Arnie solves everything the way he solves anything: send around a man with a gun. Curtains for Jellco.

But then Jellco's girl-friend gets hold of the dirt on Karen and tries to cash in on it—and *she* ends up in the same morgue a few days later.

Is that how it goes? That's how it could go—if you're satisfied to leave Edwin Delastone's murder out of the picture entirely—plus the fact that you have about as much proof as an eel has feathers.

I shrugged a big shrug and rose up again and went over to stand in front of the smeared window. A nice night out—reasonably cool, a big moon riding high, a small breeze off the lake. People walking and cars rolling by. Under a street lamp a slim girl in a white coat stood at the kerb shaking her head to a chunky guy trying to talk her into the front seat of a flashy coupe. I placed a small bet with myself that he wasn't going to make it. Not this girl. You can always tell. She started to walk away. He caught her arm and went on pouring out the words. Her head continued to shake and she tried to pull away. He wasn't giving up. He gestured and argued. Her head-shaking began to slack off and the odds slipped. Suddenly she jerked her arm free and moved off. I doubled the bet. He called something to her and she stopped in her tracks and turned around. She walked back slowly and now she was laughing. He opened the door and she got in with him and the car moved off.

You can always tell.

I walked the floor. A drink would be fine. There was a saloon down the block. There's always a saloon down every block. They put them there for people who can't think without a glass to lean on. Or for people who have to lean on a glass to keep from thinking.

I walked the floor. I went on thinking. I thought of the people I had come up against in this peaceful little community, every last one of them, starting with Deborah Ellen Frances Thronetree sunning herself on the front steps one morning a hundred years ago, and ending with Captain Benton Brill and his eyes boring into my back as I closed the door to that basement room on my way out of Headquarters.

I thought of each of them, of their activities and their attitudes, of their warnings and their threats and their lies. I dredged up what they had said and their expressions while they were saying it.

It was hard work. It was like wading hip-deep in quicksand. It put sweat on my face and twisted my mouth into a crooked line. It took what seemed forever. And what finally came out of it was hardly more than a glimmering of grey not much more than the darkness itself.

The killer was hunting for something.

I sat down in the room's one chair and looked at my fingernails. There was some dirt under a couple of them. It was good honest dirt. Let it stay. You find so few honest things around these days.

I walked the floor.

Whatever it was, was worth killing for. Then what was it? The blackmail material, of course. The killer had originally traced it to Sam Jellco, then lost sight of it.

Proof? Jellco's office had been searched. His apartment had been combed the day of his funeral. The apartment of his girl-friend had been given a going-over, probably while she lay dead on the bedroom floor.

Who was so hot to get hold of the stuff? Karen Delastone? She was sure as hell implicated. Why else would she be in Jellco's hotel room that night? Why else would she go to his office within hours of his murder? And the clincher: Jellco, as Hamp, had told Serena Delastone that the dirt he was trying to peddle involved Karen.

Go to the police with the story? Fat chance. You'd need a ton of hard proof to support a charge against a Delastone. All right, then get the proof. You know what will prove it. The blackmail material.

Uh-hunh. You know *what* will prove it. Now let's see you do something easy. Let's see you find the proof.

I was back on the bed. How had that happened? I got up and found another cigarette and forgot to light it and went back to pounding the carpet.

Either the material is still around or it isn't. If the Dreyfoos girl died while trying her hand at blackmail, then the killer found it in the apartment and it's ashes by now and my chances along with it.

Unless she didn't have the stuff at all. Unless she tried running a bluff based entirely on what Jellco had spilled to her.

Let's go back to the evening Jellco was shot. He calls Karen Delastone, tells her what he's got on her and how much he wants for it. She comes to his room, gets nowhere without cash, leaves empty-handed and angry. Then Algebra calls Jellco, says he'll foot the bill for Karen, that he'll be right over to close the deal and kindly have the stuff ready.

Good enough—except that Sam Jellco wasn't hatched last week. He knows goddam well Arnie Algebra could just as easy knock him in the head and walk out with the papers *and* the dough.

So let's say he stashes the stuff in a safe place and sits down to wait. Pretty soon in walks one of Algebra's boys with orders to get the goods, no money down and no monthly payments. One word leads to another, Jellco pulls a gun, there's a fight, the gun goes bang, Jellco is dead. No real harm done, only the messenger can't find what he came for, or is afraid to take time to look.

Obviously Jellco left those things where he could get hold of them fast in case Algebra was willing to play it straight and make the pay-off. Fine—but where had he left them?

And then I knew.

CHAPTER THIRTY-FOUR

"THEY found out you were there this afternoon," I said. "They managed to come up with a witness. On top of that, they've got a theory that covers practically everything this side of Cripple Creek.

Unless we come up with the right answer before morning, you're going to be picked up for questioning."

"I'm not afraid, Paul. Why should I be? I've nothing to hide. You know perfectly well that I had—"

"What I know is what you told me. It's not enough, Mrs. Jellco. It's not enough for them and it's not enough for me. That's why I'm calling you. We need a miracle and it's possible you can furnish it."

"I don't think I un—"

"You told me earlier that the cops out here returned Sam's personal belongings to you. Where are they now?"

"Why, right here. In one of the bedroom closets."

"Nothing was held back that you know of?"

"Well, they gave me his wallet and keys—whatever he had in his pockets—the first morning I was out there. Everything else they put in his travelling bag and left in the car. I haven't even opened the bag."

"The suit he was wearing?"

"Yes. Th-that, too." Her voice started to skid and she yanked it firmly back into place. "I have it."

"Here's how it is." I shifted the receiver to the other ear and twisted around to rest my back against the headboard. It meant putting my shoes on the spread, but from the looks of it a lot of shoes had been there ahead of mine. "It's likely Sam left a package in a checkroom somewhere shortly before he died. I want the stub he got for it. You come across anything like that?"

"No."

"Then it means you'll have to go through everything they sent back. And I mean go through it. Turn out every pocket, including the watchpockets of his trousers. Look under the lapels of the coats, in his shoes, in the folds of unused handkerchiefs, shirts and underwear, under the sweatband of his hat. Everything. Be quick and be thorough. You understand all this?"

"What if the police found it and are holding it?"

"Anything's possible."

"All right. Where can I reach you?"

I told her. She said she'd call back. Inside half an hour.

I held the bar down long enough to break the connection, then called the Olympia House and asked for Jennings, the security officer. I was careful to say security officer. It took almost five minutes before the soft rumble of his voice reached me. He sounded cautious, in case it was Mister Davidson calling.

"The last time we visited," I said, "you picked up a fast twenty bucks. I thought you might like to know there's more where that came from."

That told him who I was. "Uh-hunh. You got me in a jam, you know that? Mister Davidson jumped on me for that girl being in your room."

"I got fifty bucks here," I said. "It could have your name on it easy as not."

"For what?" he said, after a pause.

"Anybody occupying 304 at the moment?"

"Right off-hand I couldn't tell you. Might not be. Kinda slow tonight."

"It's this way," I said. "Sam Jellco may have checked a package that night. If he did, the ticket is missing. There's a strong chance it's still in that room. Taped under a dresser drawer or behind the sink. I don't have to tell you the places they pick."

"You paying fifty for it?"

"Yeah."

"And if I can't turn it up?"

"Then you earn twenty just for getting a little dust on your sleeve."

"I guess you private boys make a lotta money," he sighed. "The way you throw it around."

"There's that," I said. "But then we don't have the opportunity of working for Mister Davidson."

"Ha," he said. "Gimme an hour."

I lay back on the bed and massaged my leg and waited. At five minutes past ten the phone rang. It was Linda Jellco.

"I'm sorry, Paul." She sounded very depressed. "There's no sign of a claim check."

"All right. There's still a good chance it'll turn up."

"Is it something important?"

"I think it is."

"You'll let me know. No matter how late?"

"I'll call you."

". . . Please don't hang up, Paul." It was a voice lost in a fog. "Not—not just yet. I know you're busy, but . . ."

"Sure."

"It's—well, it's just that talking to you I don't feel so . . . alone. Everything's so quiet and my thoughts keep churning around and there's nothing to do but go to bed, but I'd just lie there and think. All I do is keep remembering all the things—all the little things that aren't really important, only they're so terribly important and . . . I'm not making any sense, am I?"

"What about these friends down the hall?"

"No. Not tonight. I realize that doesn't sound very grateful, but they try so hard to talk of things that are . . . safe. Then some completely innocent remark is passed that could have two meanings, and they get red in the face and freeze up and I have to pretend not to notice—"

And then she was crying—harsh, tearing sobs that set my teeth on edge. "I miss him, Paul! My God, how I miss him! What am I going to *do*?"

It's a question that has no answer. Not at the time it's asked and not when it's asked that way. I held on to the phone and said nothing and waited. And presently the storm passed and I heard the politely subdued sound of a nose being blown, and then her voice, clear and reasonably steady, saying: "I suppose that was bound to happen sometime. I'm sorry. Please call me if you learn anything. Anything at all. Goodnight, Paul."

The clerk in the liquor store, two blocks from the hotel, wrapped a pint of bourbon for me. He was alone in the place and he seemed a little nervous, as though he expected me to lean a gun against his lip and clean out the till. I bought cigarettes from a machine near the door and limped back along the dimly lighted street to the hotel and climbed the sagging stairs to the second floor. A radio brayed from behind one of the doors, while behind another a woman was reading somebody the riot act in a voice like breaking crockery.

I tore the wrappings off the bottle and set it on the nightstand and went into the bathroom for a glass. I uncapped the pint and filled half the glass and sat on the edge of the bed, holding the glass between both palms and staring down into it. I wondered how many other men were alone in hotel rooms, sitting on beds and tilting bottles as an answer to their problems. Not that I had nothing else to think about. I sniffed at the glass and put it down untasted, next to the bottle and lay down on the bed.

The radio next door talked about shaving soap and the woman went on yelling. The walls were like paper. I kneaded my leg and counted the dragging minutes. An hour, Jennings had said. How many weeks in an hour?

At ten-forty I put through my call. Jennings was ready to talk to me.

"I just come down from there," he said in his slow earnest rumble. "Ain't nothing up there like what you're after. Not in 304 there ain't."

I felt nothing. The words were only words strung along a length of wire, bringing no sense of disappointment, fanning no anger. Another blind alley in a world of blind alleys. Except that this was the last one. This was the one that was blind at both ends.

"Even unscrewed the goddam shower head in there," Jennings was saying. "Not to mention tearing up the rug practically. No ticket. He didn't leave nothing in the hotel safe, neither. Or at the two checkrooms we got here."

"You did what you could," I said. "I owe you a little money. Not tonight, though. If it's all the same to you."

I hung up and took the glass off the night table and went into the bathroom with it and poured the whisky down the sink and ran water after it to kill the smell. I rinsed the glass out and put it back where it belonged and washed up and combed my hair. Office hours were over. No more brain-wracking tonight. Tomorrow the law would look me up and ask me questions and maybe get out the well-oiled blackjacks and swish them under my nose. And all I would have working for me was a pair of bent shoulders and a couple of empty hands.

A face looked at me out of the mirror. It was a face Olympic Heights hadn't been gentle with. The mouth was still faintly puffy where Captain Benton Brill's fist had stopped. I thought the chin looked a little better. Then I remembered Lyle Spence's busted nose, and thinking of that made the chin look even better.

Olympic Heights. I had called on its residents on both sides of the tracks, visited its City Hall, spent a night in its jail, walked its streets, eaten its food, drank its liquor, read its papers, quarrelled with its leading citizens.

Olympic Heights. It sounded like the tag end of a dirty joke. Somewhere in this shining little city were the papers and photographs Sam Jellco and Edwin Delastone and Arline Dreyfoos had died over. I saw Sam Jellco hang up the phone in his hotel room after talking to Arnie Algebra. I saw him take the neatly wrapped package off the desk and bounce it thoughtfully on his palm. I saw his eyes rove the room in search of a place to hide that package until the deal was closed. I saw him give up the idea, then get a new one. I saw him put his coat on and stick the package in one of the pockets and head for the door. He rides down to the first floor, on his way to leave the package where only he can get at it when the time is right. Not the hotel safe. Not the checkrooms.

Then where?

A dime-a-day locker? In that case there would be a key. The hotel cigar-stand? Too easy for the wrong . . .

A key.

My mouth was open. I had never looked more stupid. I began to go through my pockets. I took out the worn leather keycase Sam Jellco's widow had turned over to me three days before. I almost dropped it unsnapping the catch.

It was there. The short thin one. The one with the number stamped into its side. 707. And on the thumb piece, two letters I hadn't noticed the first time around. The letters: O. H. Olympia House.

I began to laugh. I doubled up and held on to the sides of the sink and went on laughing. I couldn't stop. I didn't want to stop. It was a nice night for laughing.

CHAPTER THIRTY-FIVE

THEY had a fraternity dance going at the Olympia House and the parking lot and the kerb slots along both sides of the street were full up. I left the Plymouth around a corner and walked back through the cool night air to the hotel entrance and on into the lobby.

The chairs and divans across from the desk were mostly taken up by a knot of pretty girls in summer formals and tall young men in white coats and black bow ties. The air bristled with college humour and flourished cigarettes and struck poses, and the laughter was self-conscious and too loud.

I found Jennings with a hip propped against a pillar and his hat on the back of his head, viewing the scenery. He lifted a calm eyebrow at me. "You, hunh? Think of something else?"

"Where's your pay lockers?"

"So that's the answer. You find a key?"

"I found a key."

"Well now, we got a bunch of 'em downstairs. Between the men's room and the barber shop. Then there's a row up on the mezzanine, across from the beauty parlour and the travel bureau. What number you after?"

"Seven-oh-seven."

"That'd be the mezzanine, as I recollect. Want some help?"

"No, sir. As of right now I'm fine." I took out two tens. "Twenty bucks," I said. "As agreed."

He swivelled his head to take a careful look around the lobby. Mister Davidson wasn't in sight. The bills disappeared. Houdini would have been interested in the way they disappeared. "A real pleasure doing business with you," Jennings rumbled. "Drop in any time."

The mezzanine was up a bending flight of steps with an ornamental iron hand rail. I climbed them and went past a double row of empty writing desks with soft amber lights burning under silken shades, past a corner where a couch held a young couple who had Found Each Other, through an archway and down two steps and into a long wide corridor lined on one side with shops.

That was where I found the lockers.

It was very quiet up there. The shops were closed for the night and my reflection moved in the dark glass of the windows. I listened to my feet echo along the stone flooring and it was like two people walking. I stopped short and looked quickly back over my shoulder. Nobody in sight. Nothing in sight except a stretch of empty hallway under the harsh glare of ceiling bulbs.

The bank of lockers was mounted six high, ten to a row. Keys protruded from most of them. Number 707 was part of the top row. I got Jellco's case out, separated the short thin key from the others and shoved it into the lock.

It went in about a quarter of an inch and stopped. I leaned against it, hard. Nothing doing. I maintained the pressure and twisted the key back and forth. Still nothing doing. I took the key out and looked at the number on it. 707. I looked at the number on the box. 707. I reversed the key and tried again.

This time it wouldn't go in at all.

I slapped a hand hard against the cold grey steel of the locker door. It made a noise like a dropped oil drum. The door leered blankly at me. I made a fist. The door said, "Go right ahead, chum. See what it gets you."

Or I might have been the one who said it. I put away the keycase and turned around and went back down to the lobby.

Jennings was nowhere in sight. I found a bellhop ten years past my age and showed him a dollar.

"Yessir?"

"Got a problem," I said.

"Glad to help, sir."

"The key won't work on one of your lockers."

"It has to work, sir."

"You want to tell the locker that?"

His ears turned pink. "May I see the key, sir?"

I detached it and handed it over. He squinted at it. "The number is seven-oh-seven, sir."

"No argument there," I said.

"Are you sure you tried the right locker?"

"Seven-oh-seven," I said. "You're still a long way from this dollar."

"I'm trying to help, sir," he said with dignity. "When was it you rented the locker?"

I counted back. "Four days ago."

His expression was patient. "Those happen to be twenty-four-hour lockers, sir. You see—"

I moved a hand in a weary gesture, stopping him. "You'll have to excuse me," I said. "My thinking hasn't been any too clear here of late. They changed the lock on me, hunh?"

His head bobbed. "Yessir. There's like a meter that registers when a dime goes in. If the checker should find the same number showing two days straight, he—"

"Where's the package now?"

"Should be in the baggage room, sir. I could get it for you. There'll be a thirty-cent—"

"Let's get it."

The baggage room was down a flight, next to the service elevator. The bellhop folded back a section of counter-top and disappeared behind a row of shelves. When he came back he was holding a small oblong package wrapped in pale green paper.

"That's thirty cents, sir. And you'll have to sign a receipt to show you—"

I gave him the dollar and another one to keep it company and took the thing away from him. While he filled out a form in triplicate, I stood there turning it in my hands, squeezing it a little, listening to the paper crackle. The paper was identical to the piece I had found in Jellco's wastebasket, with the words *Olympic Florists* worked into it. The ends were sealed tightly with Scotch tape. I resisted an impulse to tear it open and learn the name of whoever was going around pulling triggers because of it.

I wrote my name where the bellhop's finger indicated and

tucked the package under an arm and went up the stairs to the lobby, across that and on out into the busy street.

Ten minutes past midnight. Sunday morning in Olympic Heights. In a few hours the church bells would start and the sound would flow over the quiet streets and their green lawns and bright homes. It was the morning to sleep late and make love to the wife and eat an unhurried breakfast before washing the car and driving the family to services or over to the inlaws for dinner and a hand or two of pinochle.

I might even sleep a little late myself.

I drank some of the clean air and lighted a cigarette and walked on down to the corner, around that and along the quiet side street with its darkened shop fronts. Still a few cars at both kerbs. I reached the Plymouth and got the keys out and opened up.

I caught the slither of leather against concrete directly behind me. I turned fast—but not fast enough.

A man was standing there. The muzzle of a gun stared at me from his right hand.

"Let's use my car," Ira Groat said.

CHAPTER THIRTY-SIX

HE told me to take the wheel, then shoved in next to me and closed the door. He was sweating and his eyes jumped wildly and his breathing came fast and harsh. The breathing of a man on the run. The odour of Scotch filled the car, heavy and not at all pleasant.

The gun went on pointing at me as he put out the other hand, palm up. "Let's have what you got there," he said in a low-voiced growl.

My fingers clamped hard on the green-wrapped package. "This? Just the laundry," I whined. "You wouldn't look good in a sixteen collar."

"Don't horse with me, damn you!" He slashed the gun barrel across the back of my hand in a swift savage motion. I let go of the bundle and watched him scoop it up and place it on the seat between his legs. He settled back away from me and gestured with the gun.

"Start her up," he ordered.

The key was in the ignition. I leaned down and turned it and the motor hummed to life. The back of my hand throbbed dully and a trickle of wetness moved across it.

"On down to the corner," Groat said, "then left. And keep your paws high on that wheel where I can see 'em."

I did as I was told. I'd have been crazy not to. He was half-tanked and jumpy as hell and holding a gun—not a combination to argue with.

His orders took us south and west, away from the business district and toward the Mulberry Square section of town. We stuck to the main arteries and there was traffic all the way. Twice we waited out stop lights with cars bunched around us. I thought of sticking my head out of the window and yelling for help. It was a thought, just as swimming the Pacific is a thought.

Groat was restless. He squirmed on the seat and kept putting his empty hand down to touch the package. But the gun pointing my way never wavered.

"You missed your chance, Pine." The words seemed to jerk out of his throat. "When Brill ran you out of town, you should've stayed out. You try too hard, you know that?"

"Yeah."

"Good thing for me," he went on in the same way, "that you didn't quit. I could've spent months trying to find this stuff and still missed it. I wanted it and you wanted it. When I ran out of places to look, I figured keeping an eye on you might do the trick. That's how it's been ever since you walked out of Police Head-quarters this afternoon." He stroked the package with the tips of his fingers. "I started just in time, hunh?"

"Yeah."

"Jellco's hotel room and his office and his apartment—I tried 'em all and ended up with nothing. Real smart of him to check the stuff before I kept our appointment. Only he had no business pulling a gun on me. His own goddam fault he caught a bullet—the lousy blackmailer."

He had to talk, to let off steam, to break the silence. His nerves were pulled tight as fiddle strings He was all set to fly into a rage or into hysterical laughter or into tears. He might faint at the touch of a hand or shoot me if I sneezed.

"That Dreyfoos girl," he said after a brooding pause. "I came close to missing on that one, Pine. You had her phone number and so did I—but I didn't connect her with Jellco until you said too much at my place this afternoon. It seems Jellco had told her the whole story, and she figured I'd plugged him and walked out with the evidence. Not that she was going to do anything about it. She was satisfied that I didn't even know she existed, so I was no threat to her as long as she kept quiet. Maybe she would've gone on keeping quiet—but I couldn't afford to gamble. You know how it is."

"Yeah."

His mood shifted suddenly, as moods will do in a man in his condition. " 'Yeah, yeah, yeah'—is that all you got to say? You the big, brave, silent type—or just scared dumb?"

"You're doing the talking," I said. "You're the boy with the big mouth and the loaded gun and the evidence you killed three people to get. What else do you want—admiration?"

The hand holding the gun jerked. "Keep talking," he said softly. "I like hearing you talk that way. It could make things a lot easier for me."

"You're working hard," I said. "Straining to build up the old nerve. You've got a long line of bodies behind you and maybe one more coming up. But there's still plenty you can't be sure of, Groat. Still a lot of angles you haven't even thought of. Maybe you won't think of them at all—until the roof falls in."

I wasn't just talking to stir up a breeze. I had to make him hesitate, to reconsider, to doubt. If he could be made to panic even briefly, there could be a chance to get my hands on that gun. There couldn't be much time left. One chance was all I could hope for—if that.

"Hell," I plunged on, "you don't even know for sure what's in that package you're sitting on. It could be nothing more than a plant—bait to pull a killer out in the open. Without anyone left alive to finger you, knowing only that you were after something, that would be the way to do it."

I didn't have to see his sneer to know it was there. "And I suppose there's a carful of cops tailing us right now, just waiting to close in?"

"It's your question," I said. "You answer it. You don't think Brill would let me walk out of Headquarters without sticking a plaster on me, do you? The way he feels about me?"

For a second there I thought he was going to turn his head and look back. My right hand tensed on the wheel, ready to grab for the gun. Then the moment was gone and he settled back. "Shut up," he muttered. "Shut up and drive. I'm sick of your gabble."

I went on driving. There was moisture on my face and a throbbing ache along the back of my hand where the gun barrel had hit it. The streets slid smoothly by. It was a fine heavy car with an automatic shift and a motor as quiet as kittens sleeping.

The street lights were still doing business but the neighbourhood had gone steadily downhill. Coal-and-lumber yards, warehouses, factories and grain elevators began to loom up darkly around us. The wheels took the brick paving in stride. Hardly any traffic now, but still a few cars ahead of us and several more behind. The wanderlusting smell of soft-coal smoke swirled in at the open window next to me, and from close by an unseen switch engine whistled mournfully above the clatter of freight cars along a siding.

I chewed a corner of my lip and drove on. Ira Groat sat in his corner brooding at me from under the shadow of his hatbrim, his restless fingers petting the package that could have fried him.

He hiccupped gently and bent forward to peer through the windshield. "Make a right at the next corner and pull up."

I flipped the turn indicator, slowed, made the turn and set a foot against the brake. The train whistle sobbed again, a long trailing ribbon of sound. Groat put a hand behind his back, keeping his eyes and the gun on me, fumbled for the handle and swung the door wide. The dome light winked on.

"Kill the lights," he said thickly. "Then turn the motor off and drop the keys on the seat."

I followed instructions. The keys went into his pocket, the package under his gun arm, and a pencil flash appeared in his hand. He backed gingerly away, on to the kerb. "Slide out," he said. "On this side. And don't try anything cute."

He moved aside as I came through. The beam from the flash hit me high on the chest. We were standing in front of a two-storey sagging frame building, its empty windows like the eye-sockets of a corpse. Along one side ran the street we had just left, at the other stood a long high wooden fence plastered with circus posters.

Groat butted the car door shut with his knee. "Start walking, neighbour. The corner of the building nearest the fence."

I walked. The sound of my steps was loud in the night. The rays from the flash danced ahead of me along the cracked cement. Groat stayed close—but not close enough. He was a man who thought of everything.

We reached the corner of the building. Tight beside it a rusted iron railing guarded a short flight of stone steps going down. I went down them. It was what the man wanted and he had the gun.

The flashlight moved across a solid wood door, closed, at the foot of the steps.

"Open her up," Groat said.

I turned the knob and shoved. The door retreated reluctantly, creaking on elderly hinges. Nothing was ever blacker than the hole it uncovered.

"Basement steps dead ahead," the reporter said from behind me. "Just take it easy." His sudden giggle held a note as chilling as a winter's wind. "Can't have you breaking your neck!"

My groping fingers closed on a hand-rail and I started down. I took it easy all right. It was dark. It was like walking around in an elephant. I heard the door bang shut, then a switch clicked loudly and there was light, plenty of light, streaming from a big dusty bulb dangling from the ceiling of a basement.

The basement was as wide and as long as the building above it and no partitions chopping it up. It smelled of dampness and disuse and was empty of everything except an acre of dust and a battered raw-wood workbench against the near wall. Meters and fuse cabinets broke the naked expanse of grey concrete walls, and where a furnace had once been was a patch of broken floor and a cobweb of galvanized tin ducts fanning out across the ceiling.

Groat circled past me to lean his thin buttocks against the edge of the bench, leaving a good ten feet of space between us. He didn't look well. There was a smear of dust across one of his flushed cheeks, a wick of damp hair hung low on his forehead, and his hooded eyes were faintly bloodshot. He stood there blinking at me, the hand holding the gun hanging along his leg.

I said, "What happens now?"

The muscles moved in his throat. He glanced quickly down at the gun, then quickly up again. "You know goddam well what happens now. You're not stupid."

"It doesn't have to be this way," I said carefully. "My life's nothing to envy but it's all I've got. We could make a deal."

His eyes burned at me. "Deal, hell. I'm not stupid either."

I listened to the gritty sound of his voice saying it. I nodded and said, "I'm going to put a hand in my pocket and take out a cigarette. And matches. Will that be all right with you?"

He didn't answer me. He knew I had nothing of danger to him, since he had shaken me down expertly even before we entered his car. He watched me light up and blow a twisting cloud of smoke that fell apart in the damp still air.

He said, "I'm a busy man, Pine," in a curiously soft voice. The hand with the gun began to rise. It floated slowly up like a reluctant balloon, a thing apart, not attached to Groat at all.

I said, "Exactly what do you think's in that package, Groat?"

The gun stopped rising. Groat's eyes shifted to the bundle in his other hand, then quickly to me. "Stalling for time, is that it?"

I pulled hard on the cigarette, dragging the smoke to my toes, fighting the cold ball of fear below my ribs.

"Time for what?" I said. "If the cops were coming at all, they'd be here by now. I was just thinking, that's all. Of how your face would look when you finally get around to unwrapping your prize."

It was the long chance. There couldn't be a longer one. But if I could get him to try opening that package, his attention might waver just enough to give me a try at that gun.

Groat's lips pulled back in a smile like a scar. "Go ahead," he said. "Tell me what I'll find."

"I spotted you following me," I lied. "I had the bellhop at the hotel fix me up a packet to carry, hoping it would pull you out into the open. Like I was telling you in the car. I can't tell you what's under that green paper, but I can tell you it's not what you've been shooting up the town to get. You know what's going to happen, don't you, Groat? Some day somebody's going to trip over the missing stuff and that will be the end of you. It could happen tomorrow or it might take a year. But until it does happen you're going to have to live with it, brother. Like the guy who used to spend his time sitting under a sword that hung from a hair."

That got to him a little. He looked at me a long time with nothing showing on his face but the colour. And then he said, "Why tell me all this? Either way, you won't be around."

"I will be if you're smart. There's more to tell you, only you'll have to convince yourself I'm not lying about that package. There's one sure way to find out."

He nodded thoughtfully and then he smiled. It was not at all a pleasant smile. He turned his body slightly to one side and jammed the package between his hip and the edge of the bench and began to work the tape loose with the fingers of his left hand. It was a clumsy method at best and would take a long time. He turned another inch away from me and the muscles of my legs bunched for action.

He swung back and laid the bundle on the bench. "Turn around," he said.

"...Why?"

"You heard me. Turn around and put your hands against the wall even with your head and lean your weight on them."

There went my last chance. It was an old cop's trick, used to frisk the tough boys. By the time I could regain my balance from a position like that, whirl around and jump across the distance between us, he could shoot the lint out of my navel.

Groat's gun came up a little. His lips strained back from the even line of his teeth in a wolfish grimace. I could take orders or I could take a bullet then and there. It was all the same to him. I was through and I knew I was through and the knowledge was a knife twisting in the billows of my mind.

Above us, the basement door opened and closed. A pair of black flat-heeled shoes appeared on the stairs, followed by thick ankles and the hem of a black linen skirt, and Martha Delastone came into the room.

CHAPTER THIRTY-SEVEN

"You lied to me, Ira," she said with a kind of grotesque dignity. "You didn't find Mr. Jellco dead at all. You killed him. The way you killed Edwin and that girl."

Her face was as frozen and as white as a face can get and still have life. Against the whiteness her muddy brown eyes were very large, very dark, very still. Empty eyes, with no shine to them. The eyes of a sleepwalker, of a zombie.

Groat stood pinned to the workbench, his mouth a little open, his gun pointing vaguely at one of my shins. A slow scowl cut a vertical line between his eyes. "For Christ's sake, Martha. You should've had better sense than come here."

His words didn't reach her. She brought up the large white envelope bag she carried and pressed it hard against her stomach with both hands in a curiously awkward gesture.

"I had to find you," she said, the words marching stiffly past her lips. "The minute I heard the girl was dead I knew I had to find you. At the paper a man said he'd seen you in the hotel drugstore. And then I saw you driving away with Mr. Pine and I knew you meant to kill him too."

She took a deep breath and let it out, shuddering a little. "It's over, isn't it? All over. I wanted the money but I didn't want murder. I'm not strong enough for that. Perhaps I'm not even bad enough."

"Shut up!" Groat said wildly. "You went into this with your eyes open and whining isn't going to change it any." He jerked his chin toward the basement stairs. "Get out of here. I'll handle this."

She looked at him strangely, as though she had never seen him before. A muscle moved in her throat. It was the only thing about her that did move. She said nothing.

Groat's neck swelled with sudden, sharp fury. "I said get out!" he yelled. "Go on—beat it, you ugly bitch!"

I think she smiled then. Sometimes I wake up in the night and think back and try to remember if she smiled. I would like to believe that she did but I can never be sure.

Martha Delastone turned back the flap of her bag and took out a small black gun and shot him three times through the chest.

The bullets going in slammed him back hard against the edge of the bench. His face went slack and stupid with shock. He coughed once and blood, very dark under the harsh light, appeared at the corner of his mouth. He took a vague step going nowhere and his right leg buckled slowly under him and he sat down almost gently on the concrete floor.

He seemed to be staring at the gun still locked in his hand. He tried hard to lift it, but he was past lifting anything. His head dropped and he toppled sideways in slow motion and the breath went out of him and he was dead.

I tried to look at her then, but all I could see was the thin black automatic pistol dangling at the end of her hanging arm. I licked my lips and said, "I guess you ought to give me the gun now, Miss Delastone."

"I wanted the money very much," she said.

"Yes, ma'am," I said.

"I think my father will understand," she said.

"I'm sure he will," I said.

"Thank you," she said in a firm clear voice and brought the gun up and shot herself through the head.

CHAPTER THIRTY-EIGHT

THE sun in my face woke me up. I turned my head but the sun was still there, and presently I untangled my legs from the sheet and limped into the bathroom.

I came out and lay down on the bed again, this time where the sun couldn't get at me. Nine-thirty-five. Five hours since I sat in Colonel Quentin Delastone's office, across from him and Captain Brill.

The events of the night had shaken Brill. They had come close to breaking the Colonel entirely. His face was the colour of the Dead Sea scrolls and his once sagging features had fallen in on themselves. He sat at his desk and listened while staring at his hands. When he spoke at all, it was through a closed throat and he failed to finish most of his sentences.

Eventually they drained me dry. They had all I knew and most of what I surmised. What they didn't have was the green-wrapped package.

Not that they didn't try.

I was polite about it. I said of course I wanted to be co-operative. I said I agreed it was evidence and that it was my duty to my client as well. I said if they would just call up Serena Delastone and get her okay, I would hand over the package and walk out of there and go back to Chicago and stay there as far as Olympic Heights was concerned. I probably sounded a little shrill on that last point.

We talked about it some more but nobody reached for the phone. Serena would've said she didn't know what they were talking about, that I wasn't working for her and never had been—and that if anybody so much as laid a hangnail on the contents of that package, she personally would knit his entrails into a lampshade.

Finally Brill thanked me politely and said I was free to go. The Colonel didn't say anything. I lifted my hat off the leather couch where Martha Delastone had been reading a law book the first time I saw her, and tucked the package under an arm and went quickly out and away.

Now it was another day and the sun was high and I was lying naked on a crummy bed in a crummy hotel room, wanting to get up and not getting up, listening to a distant church bell and thinking of the dark blood at the corner of a dead man's mouth, of a small hole in one side of a woman's head where a bullet had gone in, of a larger hole on the opposite side where the bullet had come out. Not pleasant thoughts. If there were pleasant thoughts in Olympic Heights I would never get to know them.

When I woke up again it was close to noon. I showered and brushed my teeth with hotel soap and an index finger. Shaving would have to wait. I sat on the edge of the bed and took the package from under the other pillow and bounced it on the palm of one hand. One of the corners was loose where Ira Groat had started to work at it. A little extra urging and it would open the rest of the way. Certainly I had earned the right.

Except that I didn't want the right. Too many people had lied and cheated and bled over what that green paper covered. Let one of them peel back the wrapper and rake through the dirt underneath.

No need to look the number up. By now it was engraved on the memory cells. A voice I didn't recognize, male, answered and put me through without argument.

Her voice was just as steady, just as full of bite. If anything it was deeper. "Serena Delastone speaking. Who is this?"

I told her who it was.

"I haven't the time for you now," she said rigidly. "There's been a death in the family."

She made the suicide of a daughter sound on a par with the milkman's failure to leave that extra quart. From the way she said it, it would seem she hadn't been told of the part I played in Martha Delastone's death. It figured. This was a hard woman to tell anything to—especially the truth.

"I'm sorry to hear that, Mrs. Delastone. I called to let you know I have what you hired me to get for you. I can wait a few days if you like before turning it over to you."

"I see. And just how much did you agree to pay for its return?"

"Not a cent," I said, through my teeth. "This is your lucky day."

"Bring it here at once," she rasped. "And I might as well warn you, holding out any part of it to get money out of me later on will do you absolutely no good."

I said, "Half an hour, Mrs. Delastone," and hung up. The fingers that had held the receiver were bent into the shape of claws. I used my other hand to straighten them, one at a time, until they were back to being fingers again.

At twelve-forty I turned in at New Cambridge Drive and parked at the kerb in front of number 25. No other cars in sight and no one visible at the front of the house. I got out holding the package and went along the flagstones to the steps, up those and to the door and rang the bell. The elderly maid answered. Her eyes were red-rimmed and a corner of her apron looked as though she'd been wiping her nose with it. I liked her for it.

This time she showed me into the small sitting room off the parlour—the room where the Colonel had been sleeping it off on my first visit—and closed the door behind me.

She was in the barrel chair, sitting tall, her hands resting together in her lap. She looked a little pinched around the mouth, a little sharper in the chin. Her dress was black taffeta, with loose sleeves caught at the wrists and black lace at the neck. A thin gold chain held a gold filagree lavaliere set with a single amethyst.

"Give it to me," she said.

I crossed over and handed her the package, watching her thin strong fingers close around it. "You may sit down, Mr. Pine."

I sat across from her and waited while she examined the tape where the ends of the paper lapped.

I got a helping of glacial eye. "This appears to have been tampered with."

"Tampered with," I said. "But not opened."

She let the package come to rest on the black silk covering her thighs. "I assume you expect to be paid."

"One thousand dollars," I said.

Her eyes glinted at me frostily but I was long since used to that from her. "Why should I pay you any such ridiculous fee?"

"You'll pay it," I said. "A hundred bucks for every thousand under ten thousand. You set the price yourself."

She shrugged her solid shoulders. "Very well. I don't intend to haggle with you. You may send your bill."

"I'll send my bill," I said.

She looked away from me to the bundle in her lap. She put a hand down and pressed it lightly against the green paper. It crackled faintly in the room's brooding silence.

"I suppose you're wondering why I don't ask for the whole story," she said. "I don't want to hear it. All I can do is hope I won't have to put up with something like this from her again."

She glanced up in time to catch the blank expression I was wearing. "Do you find that so strange, Mr. Pine?" she said testily.

"I told you Karen is a wild, unprincipled girl. You don't expect she'll change overnight, do you?"

"I was right," I said. "They don't tell you a thing, do they?" I could feel my face getting hot. "Well, it's your own fault. You've got the Colonel so buffaloed he's afraid to give you the right time —and since he's the one who calls the signals at City Hall, everybody down there's trained to hold out on you, too."

"I think you'd better leave," she snapped.

I shook my head. "Hunh-unh. Not until you hear the truth, Mrs. Delastone. From me. Not because I want to tell it or because I'm that crazy about you. But you've got one daughter left. I'm not crazy about her either, but as far as I know she's never gone in for blackmail or murder."

She started to say something unpleasant, but I ploughed ahead without waiting to hear it.

"Whatever's in that package hasn't a thing to do with Karen. You wanted to think it did because she ran around with people you didn't approve of and took a drink now and then and was able to get hold of money you were too tight-fisted to give her. And I went along with you on it because I figured you knew your own children and because this blackmail evidence sounded like a volume of Kinsey in picture, song and story. Judging from your description of Martha I couldn't see her as much of a sexpot—so Karen was elected. That was my first mistake."

"You're making this up," she said harshly. "It had to be Karen. She has the cheap flashy prettiness that attracts the wrong kind of men."

"And Martha!" I said. "Martha couldn't even attract the wrong kind. Martha went in for getting out the vote and good works in the parish. It wasn't enough. She wanted to love and be loved, like the rest of us. She must have figured money—a great deal of money—was the only bait she could use to get a man.

"It was a cinch she'd never get it out of you. Nobody could. To you, money was what kept your husband in line, your son and daughters under your thumb, the tradespeople jumping when you snarled . . . and you didn't dare let any of it get away. So Martha, to get hold of the big money, went into partnership with a crook and a killer."

I got out my handkerchief and wiped my forehead. It wasn't a warm day, or at least not that warm, but I was sweating just the same.

This time I waited for her to say something. Her mouth hung

a little open, her breathing a whisper in the stillness. She was wounded and bleeding, but she still was a hell of a long way from the cemetery.

"Lies," she said. "All lies." Every word hurt her throat. "You can't prove anything."

I jerked a thumb wearily at the package on her knees. "It's all in there, Mrs. Delastone. It's true I don't know the form her crookedness took. She was on the inside at the City Hall. That could do it. If the city was going to build a new recreational centre, say, she could pass the word along to her partner ahead of time; he could pick up the land for next to nothing and stick the city plenty for it. The same goes for a new highway or a school—not to mention peddling information on bids for the construction jobs themselves. That's only a guess, of course, but like they say, an educated guess.

"Anyway, your son Edwin found out what was going on. There must have been notes and letters he got his paws on. He couldn't very well put the squeeze on his sister openly, so he hired a front man to do it for him. When your son died, the front man tried to go on on his own hook and was killed for his ambition. When I got into the picture, Martha came to the hotel where I was staying and tried to pump me. All she got was the telephone number of the blackmailer's girl friend—a number I was careless enough to leave lying around where she could see it. She passed it on to her partner. You see, the stuff in that package was missing and he was going nuts trying to find it. The girl friend was killed and her apartment searched. Three dead, Mrs. Delastone. Not that Martha expected things to go that far. If she hadn't baulked at murder, I wouldn't be here now. But that's not the point. The law says an accomplice is every bit as guilty as the one that pulls the trigger."

All of it added up to the rack and thumbscrews for Serena Delastone. But she didn't give an inch. "Are you quite finished, Mr. Pine?"

"I never wanted to start," I said. "But you wouldn't have it any other way. Try to get it through your head that Martha was the one caught in the wringer, that Karen had nothing to do with any of this. Not that you have to believe me. Open that package you're holding on to and see for yourself."

I watched her sit there like a boulder on a cliff for all of thirty seconds. I watched her rise deliberately from the chair. I watched her walk steadily across the room to the fireplace. I watched her push aside the firescreen and place the package between the andirons. I watched her straighten and take a kitchen match from a small ornamental box on the mantel and strike it against the bricks with a single firm movement of her hand and bend down again and set fire to the green paper at both ends. I watched the flames flicker and rise and burn fiercely, and the black flakes swirl up and away. And then there was only a small bed of glowing ashes, and then not even that as the glow faded and died and only ashes were left.

Not until then did she turn away. We looked at each other across the distance. Her expression was exactly the same as before, but in the grey light through the side window I thought I saw something glitter along her cheek.

Then she moved her head and the glitter was gone—if it had been there at all. "I'm very tired," she said quietly. "Please go away."

"I'm sorry," I said. I didn't know why I said it, but there it was. I stood up and shaped the crown of my hat carefully and walked over to the door and out.

The parlour was deserted. Everything in it seemed remote and not quite real. Halfway across it, I turned around and went back and gently drew the door shut.

It seemed the thing to do.

CHAPTER THIRTY-NINE

On my way along the flagstones I caught a flash of colour below the level of the hedge on the street side.

It was Deborah Ellen Frances Thronetree. She had the tricycle out for a spin before Sunday dinner, using the sidewalk for a roadway. She was bent over the handlebars, her legs pumping hard, her head bobbing, her hair flying. She made a sweeping U at the corner and came tearing back, saw me waiting, hooked a toe expertly under a pedal, stopped on a dime and sat there while she made up her mind how I was to be handled, if at all.

"Good afternoon," I said politely. "May I see your licence?"

She started to smile, decided against it and ended up looking noncommittal. There was some colour in her cheeks for a change and her dark eyes squinted a little against the sun.

"Are you talking to me today?" I said.

She thought about it, then nodded shyly.

"You first," I said.

That one got by her.

"You start it," I explained. "You say something and I'll say something. Ought to go fine after that."

She backed the tricycle up a foot or two, turned it slowly in a full circle and looked at me again. "Your whiskers look funny," she said.

"I have to agree with you," I said. "They look funny. But then one gets so few laughs these days."

She couldn't reach that one either. She bent down and scratched an ankle. By the time that was over with she had a new gambit ready.

"Aunt Martha went up to Heaven," she said.

I nodded and went on looking at her. "It's all right," I said "They were expecting her."

She turned her head, watching me from the corners of her very blue eyes. "Are you really truly a policeman?"

"No," I said. "I'm not a policeman. I'm just a tired old man who needs a shave." I stood there and bent my head a little and listened to the last piece of the puzzle click into place. "Goodbye, Deborah Ellen. You won't be seeing me again."

I went past her and on along the walk and across the strip of green parkway with its trees to where the car was waiting.

Karen Delastone was there, on the front seat.

I circled around and opened the door next to the wheel and slid in next to her. She didn't look quite so glamorous today. She was wearing grey shantung with a wide white collar and a line of small white cloth buttons from the neck to the waist. Her face seemed a little drawn, her expression distant and somehow subdued. She was holding a lighted cigarette.

"It's all over, isn't it?" she said quietly. "You've tied up all the loose ends, dropped the nice round pegs in the nice round holes, picked up your pay and walked away with only a minor bruise or two. Everything solved and out in the open for everybody to see."

"Not everything," I said just as quietly.

Her eyes widened, burlesquing surprise. But down deep in them was a sudden sick apprehension impossible to mistake. "Don't tell me there's something you've missed?" she sneered. "Not you!"

"Your brother, Miss Delastone. Edwin. His murder is still open on the books."

"That's not true," she said sharply. For the moment her voice sounded almost like her mother's. "Ira Groat killed him—just as he killed the others. You even told the police so."

I shook my head. "I was tired when I said it. Not thinking clear. I forgot he had an alibi covering the time Edwin got it. Not that I've checked. I don't need to check. He claimed to be in a card game with several cops at the time. A thing like that's far too easy to check for a guilty man to use."

Her eyes were nailed to my face. "Then you don't know?"

"For a time I thought you killed him," I said. "Or that you had a reason to and Arnie Algebra arranged it for you. But when it turned out Martha was the one involved, that let you off the hook."

"Then you don't know?" she said again, in exactly the same way.

"I know all right," I said heavily. "I know because it couldn't be any other way and make sense. The answer is in the kind of man your brother was. Groat told me about Edwin. He told me of some of the nasty things he'd pulled in his day. One of them was molesting children."

Her face was like scraped bone. Her hands shook in her lap. "Damn you," she whispered. "Damn you, damn you."

I looked past her to the sidewalk. Deborah Ellen Frances shot past, the tricycle spokes a silver blur in the sunlight.

"She must've got up in the night for some reason," I said. "I suppose he called her into his room. She knew what he did to her then was wrong. Maybe she knew about guns from the comic books. Maybe it was the Bible that told her the evil must perish. Edwin was evil and the gun was there somewhere handy and she shot him. Even the angle the bullet took bears out that she shot him."

She brought up the cigarette and dragged at it a time or two before throwing it out the window on to the grass. Her hands no longer shook. There was nothing left for them to shake about.

"Arnie brought me home that night," she said dully. "I had the door open when we heard the shot. When we got there he was on the floor and she was holding her wrist where the recoil had hurt it. She didn't know what had happened—not really. Arnie got rid of the body. I put her to bed and quieted her by explaining that it was only a bad dream and that she mustn't talk about it or even think about it ever again. In time I think she'll forget."

I got my keys out and put the right one in the ignition and

started the motor and waited for her to get out and go about her business.

She looked at me resignedly. "What are you going to do?"

"Me?" I said. "I'll tell you what I'm going to do. I'm getting the hell out of Olympic Heights—and now. I'm going home and take a shower and a shave and put on a shirt that doesn't smell like goats have been living in it. Then I'm going out to see a client who's waiting to be told about her dead husband. She wants to hear what a great guy he was, how he died a hero's death in line of duty and to keep up the payments on the TV set. Only he wasn't a great guy at all. He was a two-timing, blackmailing, crooked son of a bitch and the sooner she gets his ghost off her back, the quicker she can go back to living. You get the picture. Now how do you go about telling a woman that?"

She looked at me wonderingly. "You don't tell her," she almost whispered. "Nobody could."

I didn't say anything. She reached out and touched my hand and then turned quickly and got out on to the parkway.

"Goodbye," she said. "Goodbye—and thank you."

I nodded and she closed the door. She was still standing there when I made the turn at the corner.

CHAPTER FORTY

SHE hadn't slept well. It showed in her eyes and in the faint smudges of weariness under them. But her back was still straight and her chin still up and her smile still in place although a bit uncertain around the edges.

"I was thinking about you," she said. She drew the door all the way back. "When you didn't call me this morning I began to worry."

I followed her into the living room. She was wearing something dark and simple that flared a little below the waist. At the windows the blinds were raised and a bar of afternoon sun lay lightly along the carpet. Everything had a neat, newly dusted look and there was a freshly vacuumed smell to the air.

We sat on the couch. I bent to drop my hat on a corner of the cocktail table. When I straightened I saw her watching me intently, her lips a little apart, her dark brows pulled together questioningly.

"You're very quiet," she said after a moment.

"I've been talking for a week,' I said. "Without a let up. I suppose you could say the reaction has set in."

"Can I get you something? A drink perhaps?"

"I don't think so. Thanks all the same."

More silence. I got out the cigarettes for something else to do and offered her one. The rings on her left hand flashed taking it. Light moved along her hair as she bent to the match.

She leaned back and looked gravely at me through the smoke. "You said something last night about the police coming here. They haven't shown up."

"They're not going to," I said. "You're in the clear and so am I. It's over with, Mrs. Jellco. All of it."

"And Sam?" she said steadily. "What about Sam?"

"We both knew he didn't kill himself. Now the Olympic Heights cops know it. The official records out there will be corrected and you're free to file your claim for the insurance money."

Her eyebrows lifted very slightly. "You mean I couldn't file before this?"

"Not when it's suicide and the policy in effect less than two years. Didn't you know?"

"No. I hadn't examined the policy. I intended to turn it over to Ted Mather's attorney when he gets back to town next week."

"Anyway," I said, "you'll get the money. Double indemnity will run it up to twenty thousand."

"I see." Her eyes watched my face, very calm, very still. "You haven't told me why Sam was killed."

I took a slow deep breath and let it out as slowly. And in the time that that took I had made up my mind.

"He tried to blackmail a man," I said. "The man killed him."

She put her head down quickly and a sound like a moan was torn from her throat. That was all. I don't know how much time passed before she moved again. There's no way to measure that kind of time.

She stood up suddenly and walked over to the windows and stood there stiffly, her back to me. When she spoke again the words seemed to come from a long way off.

"And Arline Dreyfoos?" she said. "What did she have to do with—with it?"

"She was just a girl who got in the way, Mrs. Jellco. She took up with the wrong kind of men and one of them killed her."

"The wrong kind of men," she repeated. "I suppose you mean men like my husband."

I didn't say anything. She turned quickly and came a few steps toward me. "Go ahead, say it. That's what you meant, isn't it?"

I shrugged. "He was one of them."

"He was living with her?"

"He was living with her. I don't know for how long and I don't think she was important to him. But that's how it was."

She said bitterly, "Did you have to tell me all this?"

I continued to look at her. "I wasn't going to tell you. It would have been a lot easier to tell you he was the kind of guy we both took him to be. But I'm paying you the compliment of thinking you'd hate to be lied to—that you've got something more than meringue for a backbone."

I ground out my cigarette and stood up. "I told you once I make a lot of mistakes. Maybe levelling with you adds one more to the list. I don't know that and you don't know—not yet. Goodbye, Mrs. Jellco."

She didn't move. She didn't speak. All she did was look at me—and that didn't tell me anything. I picked up my hat and walked out.

It wasn't more than a month after that when I got a call from a man in Olympic Heights. Seemed his only daughter was in too deep with an ex-wrestler and he thought maybe I could break it up. All it did was make me think of a woman with blue-green eyes and a mouth I'd never kissed. I didn't take the job and I never saw Linda Jellco again.

S.759.1R.Q.L.

MADE AND PRINTED IN

GREAT BRITAIN BY ODHAMS (WATFORD) LTD.

WATFORD, HERTS